For my grandmother, Camilla,
who crossed mountains and seas,
and whose own remarkable story is my favorite epic of all

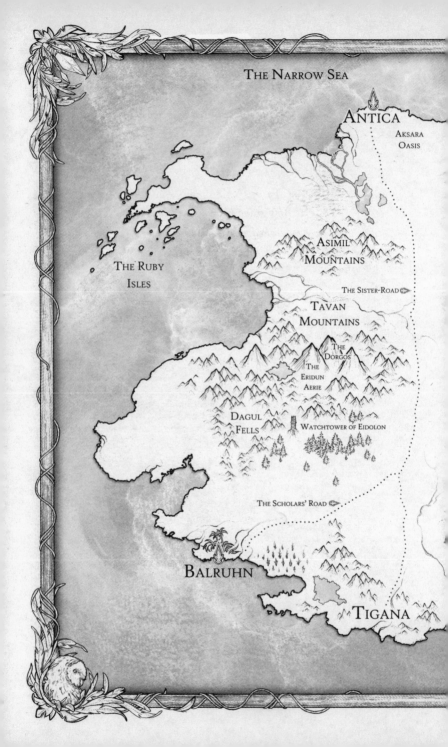

TOWER
of
DAWN

SARAH J. MAAS

BLOOMSBURY
LONDON OXFORD NEW YORK NEW DELHI SYDNEY

Bloomsbury Publishing, London, Oxford, New York, New Delhi and Sydney

First published in Great Britain in September 2017 by
Bloomsbury Publishing Plc
50 Bedford Square, London WC1B 3DP

First published in the USA in September 2017 by
Bloomsbury Children's Books
1385 Broadway, New York, New York 10018

www.sarahjmaas.com
www.bloomsbury.com

BLOOMSBURY is a registered trademark of Bloomsbury Publishing Plc

Text copyright © Sarah J. Maas 2017
Map copyright © Charlie Bowater 2017
Exclusive edition artwork © Merwild/Coralie Jubénot

The moral rights of the author and illustrators have been asserted

A CIP catalogue record for this book is available from the British Library

ISBN 978 1 4088 8797 4

MIX
Paper from
responsible sources
FSC® C020471

Printed and bound in Great Britain by CPI Group (UK) Ltd, Croydon CR0 4YY

1 3 5 7 9 10 8 6 4 2

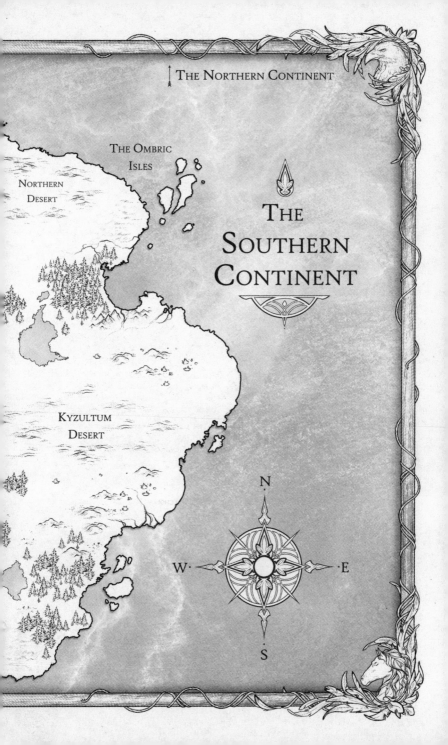

PART ONE

THE GOD-CITY

Chaol Westfall, former Captain of the Royal Guard and now Hand to the newly crowned King of Adarlan, had discovered that he hated one sound above all others.

Wheels.

Specifically, their clattering along the planks of the ship on which he'd spent the past three weeks sailing through storm-tossed waters. And now their rattle and thunk over the shining green marble floors and intricate mosaics throughout the Khagan of the Southern Continent's shining palace in Antica.

With nothing to do beyond sit in the wheeled chair that he'd deemed had become both his prison and his only path to seeing the world, Chaol took in the details of the sprawling palace perched atop one of the capital city's countless hills. Every bit of material had been taken from and built in honor of some portion of the khagan's mighty empire:

Those polished green floors his chair now clattered over were hewn from quarries in the southwest of the continent. The red pillars fashioned like mighty trees, their uppermost branches stretching across the domed ceilings high above—all part of one endless receiving hall—had been hauled in from the northeastern, sand-blasted deserts.

The mosaics that interrupted the green marble had been assembled by craftsmen from Tigana, another of the khagan's prized cities at the mountainous southern end of the continent. Each portrayed a scene from the khaganate's rich, brutal, glorious past: the centuries spent as a nomadic horse-people in the grassy steppes of the continent's eastern lands; the emergence of the first khagan, a warlord who unified the scattered tribes into a conquering force that took the continent piece by piece, wielding cunning and strategic brilliance to forge a sweeping empire; and then depictions of the three centuries since—the various khagans who had expanded the empire, distributing the wealth from a hundred territories across the lands, building countless bridges and roads to connect them all, ruling over the vast continent with precision and clarity.

Perhaps the mosaics provided a vision of what Adarlan might have been, Chaol mused as the murmurings of the gathered court flitted between the carved pillars and gilded domes ahead. That is, if Adarlan hadn't been ruled by a man controlled by a demon king hell-bent on turning this world into a feast for his hordes.

Chaol twisted his head to peer up at Nesryn, stone-faced behind him as she pushed his chair. Only her dark eyes, darting over every passing face and window and column, revealed any sort of interest in the khagan's sprawling home.

They'd saved their finest set of clothes for today, and the newly appointed Captain of the Guard was indeed resplendent in her crimson-and-gold uniform. Where Dorian had dug up one of the uniforms Chaol had once worn with such pride, he had no idea.

He'd initially wanted to wear black, simply because color . . . He'd never felt comfortable with colors, save the red and gold of his kingdom. But black had become the color of Erawan's Valg-infested guards. They had worn those black-on-black uniforms as they'd terrorized Rifthold. As they'd rounded up, tortured, and then butchered his men.

Then strung them along the palace gates to swing in the wind.

He'd barely been able to look at the Antican guards they'd passed on their way here, both in the streets and in this very palace—standing proud and alert, swords at their backs and knives at their sides. Even now, he resisted the urge to glance to where he knew they'd be stationed in the hall, exactly where he would have positioned his own men. Where he himself would undoubtedly have been standing, monitoring all, while emissaries from a foreign kingdom arrived.

Nesryn met his stare, those ebony eyes cool and unblinking, her shoulder-length black hair swaying with each step. Not a trace of nerves flickered across her lovely, solemn face. No inkling that they were about to meet one of the most powerful men in the world—a man who could alter the fate of their own continent in the war surely now breaking out across Adarlan and Terrasen.

Chaol faced forward without saying a word. The walls and pillars and arched doorways had ears and eyes and mouths, she'd warned him.

It was that thought alone that kept Chaol from fiddling with the clothes he'd finally decided upon: light brown pants, knee-high chestnut-colored boots, a white shirt of finest silk, mostly concealed by a dark teal jacket. The jacket was simple enough, the cost of it only revealed by the fine brass buckles down the front and the glimmer of delicate golden thread skimming the high collar and edges. No sword hung from his leather belt—the absence of that comforting weight like some phantom limb.

Or legs.

Two tasks. He had two tasks while here, and he still was not certain which one would prove the more impossible:

Convincing the khagan and his six would-be heirs to lend their considerable armies to the war against Erawan . . .

Or finding a healer in the Torre Cesme who could discover some way to get him walking again.

To—he thought with no small ripple of disgust—fix him.

He hated that word. Almost as much as the clattering of the wheels. *Fix*. Even if that's what he was beseeching the legendary healers to do for him, the word still grated, made his gut churn.

He shoved the word and the thought from his mind as Nesryn followed the near-silent flock of servants who had led them from the docks, through the winding and dusty cobblestoned streets of Antica, all the way up the sloped avenue to the domes and thirty-six minarets of the palace itself.

Strips of white cloth—from silk to felt to linen—had been hanging from countless windows and lanterns and doorways. Likely because of some official or distant royal relation dying recently, Nesryn had murmured. Death rituals were varied and often a blend from the countless kingdoms and territories now governed by the khaganate, but the white cloth was an ancient holdover from the centuries when the khagan's people had roamed the steppes and laid their dead to rest under the watchful, open sky.

The city had been hardly gloomy, though, as they traveled through it. People still hurried about in clothes of various makes, vendors still called out their wares, acolytes in temples of wood or stone—every god had a home in Antica, Nesryn supplied—still beckoned to those on the street. All of it, even the palace, watched over by the shining, pale-stoned tower atop one of its southern hills.

The Torre. The tower that housed the finest mortal healers in the world. Chaol had tried not to look too long at it through the carriage windows, even if the massive tower could be seen from nearly every street and angle of Antica. None of the servants had mentioned it, or pointed out the dominant presence that seemed to rival even the khagan's palace.

No, the servants hadn't said much at all on the trek here, even regarding the mourning-banners flapping in the dry wind. Each of them remained silent, men and women alike, their dark hair shining and

6

straight, and each wore loose pants and flowing jackets of cobalt and bloodred edged with pale gold. Paid servants—but descendants of the slaves who had once been owned by the khagan's bloodline. Until the previous khagan, a visionary and firebrand, had outlawed slavery a generation ago as one of her countless improvements to the empire. The khagan had freed her slaves but kept them on as paid servants—along with their children. And now their children's children.

Not a single one of them appeared underfed or undercompensated, and none had shown even a flicker of fear as they'd escorted Chaol and Nesryn from the ship to the palace. The current khagan, it seemed, treated his servants well. Hopefully his yet-undecided Heir would as well.

Unlike Adarlan or Terrasen, inheritance of the empire was decided by the khagan—not by birth order or gender. Having as many children as possible to provide him or her with a wide pool to choose from made that choice only somewhat easier. And rivalry amongst the royal children . . . It was practically a blood sport. All designed to prove to their parent who was the strongest, the wisest, the most suited to rule.

The khagan was required by law to have a sealed document locked away in an unmarked, hidden trove—a document that listed his or her Heir, should death sweep upon them before it could be formally announced. It could be altered at any time, but it was designed to avoid the one thing the khaganate had lived in fear of since that first khagan had patched together the kingdoms and territories of this continent: collapse. Not from outside forces, but from war within.

That long-ago first khagan had been wise. Not once during the three hundred years of the khaganate had a civil war occurred.

And as Nesryn pushed him past the graceful bowing of the servants now paused between two enormous pillars, as the lush, ornate throne room spread before them with its dozens of people gathered around the golden dais glittering in the midday sun, Chaol wondered which of the five figures standing before the enthroned man would one day be chosen to rule this empire.

7

The only sounds came from the rustling clothing of the four dozen people—he counted in the span of a few casual blinks—gathered along either side of that glinting dais, forming a wall of silk and flesh and jewels, a veritable avenue through which Nesryn wheeled him.

Rustling clothing—and the clatter and squeak of the wheels. She'd oiled them this morning, but weeks at sea had worn on the metal. Every scrape and shriek was like nails on stone.

But he kept his head high. Shoulders back.

Nesryn paused a healthy distance from the dais—from the wall of five royal children, all in their prime, male and female, standing between them and their father.

Defense of their emperor: a prince or princess's first duty. The easiest way to prove their loyalty, to angle for being tapped Heir. And the five before them . . .

Chaol schooled his face into neutrality as he counted again. Only five. Not the six Nesryn had described.

But he didn't scan the hall for the missing royal sibling as he bowed at the waist. He'd practiced the movement over and over this final week at sea, as the weather had turned hotter, the air becoming dry and sunbaked. Doing it in the chair still felt unnatural, but Chaol bowed low—until he was staring at his unresponsive legs, at his spotless brown boots and the feet he could not feel, could not move.

From the whisper of clothing to his left, he knew Nesryn had come to his side and was bowing deeply as well.

They held it for the three breaths Nesryn claimed were required.

Chaol used those three breaths to settle himself, to shut out the weight of what was upon them both.

He had once been skilled at maintaining an unfaltering composure. He'd served Dorian's father for years, had taken orders without so much as blinking. And before that, he'd endured his own father, whose words had been as cutting as his fists. The true and current Lord of Anielle.

The *Lord* now in front of Chaol's name was a mockery. A mockery and a lie that Dorian had refused to abandon despite Chaol's protests.

Lord Chaol Westfall, Hand of the King.

He hated it. More than the sound of wheels. More than the body he now could not feel beneath his hips, the body whose stillness still surprised him, even all these weeks later.

He was Lord of Nothing. Lord of Oath-Breakers. Lord of Liars.

And as Chaol lifted his torso and met the upswept eyes of the white-haired man on that throne, as the khagan's weathered brown skin crinkled in a small, cunning smile . . . Chaol wondered if the khagan knew it as well.

⇥ 2 ⇤

There were two parts of her, Nesryn supposed.

The part that was now Captain of Adarlan's Royal Guard, who had made a vow to her king to see that the man in the wheeled chair beside her was healed—and to muster an army from the man enthroned before her. That part of Nesryn kept her head high, her shoulders back, her hands within a nonthreatening distance of the ornate sword at her hip.

Then there was the other part.

The part that had glimpsed the spires and minarets and domes of the god-city breaking over the horizon as they'd sailed in, the shining pillar of the Torre standing proud over it all, and had to swallow back tears. The part that had scented the smoky paprika and crisp tang of ginger and beckoning sweetness of cumin as soon as she had cleared the docks and knew, deep in her bones, that she was *home*. That, yes, she lived and served and would die for Adarlan, for the family still there, but this place, where her father had once lived and where even her Adarlan-born mother had felt more at ease . . . These were her people.

The skin in varying shades of brown and tan. The abundance of that shining black hair—*her* hair. The eyes that ranged from uptilted to wide and round to slender, in hues of ebony and chestnut and even the rare hazel and green. Her people. A blend of kingdoms and territories, yes, but . . . Here there were no slurs hissed in the streets. Here there would be no rocks thrown by children. Here her sister's children would not feel different. Unwanted.

And that part of her . . . Despite her thrown-back shoulders and raised chin, her knees indeed quaked at who—at *what*—stood before her.

Nesryn had not dared tell her father where and what she was leaving to do. Only that she was off on an errand of the King of Adarlan and would not be back for some time.

Her father wouldn't have believed it. Nesryn didn't quite believe it herself.

The khagan had been a story whispered before their hearth on winter nights, his offspring legends told while kneading endless loaves of bread for their bakery. Their ancestors' bedside tales to either lull her into sweet sleep or keep her up all night in bone-deep terror.

The khagan was a living myth. As much of a deity as the thirty-six gods who ruled over this city and empire.

There were as many temples to those gods in Antica as there were tributes to the various khagans. *More.*

They called it the god-city for them—and for the living god seated on the ivory throne atop that golden dais.

It was indeed pure gold, just as her father's whispered legends claimed.

And the khagan's six children . . . Nesryn could name them all without introduction.

After the meticulous research Chaol had done while on their ship, she had no doubt he could as well.

But that was not how this meeting was to go.

For as much as *she* had taught the former captain about her homeland these weeks, he'd instructed her on court protocol. He had rarely been so directly involved, yes, but he had witnessed enough of it while serving the king.

An observer of the game who was now to be a prime player. With the stakes unbearably high.

They waited in silence for the khagan to speak.

She'd tried not to gawk while walking through the palace. She had never set foot inside it during her few visits to Antica over the years. Neither had her father, or his father, or any of her ancestors. In a city of gods, this was the holiest of temples. And deadliest of labyrinths.

The khagan did not move from his ivory throne.

A newer, wider throne, dating from a hundred years ago—when the seventh khagan had chucked out the old one because his large frame didn't fit in it. He'd eaten and drunk himself to death, history claimed, but at least had the good sense to name his Heir before he clutched his chest one day and slumped dead . . . right in that throne.

Urus, the current khagan, was no more than sixty, and seemed in far better condition. Though his dark hair had long since gone as white as his carved throne, though scars peppered his wrinkled skin as a reminder to all that *he* had fought for this throne in the final days of his mother's life . . . His onyx eyes, slender and uptilted, were bright as stars. Aware and all-seeing.

Atop his snowy head sat no crown. For gods among mortals did not need markers of their divine rule.

Behind him, strips of white silk tied to the open windows fluttered in the hot breeze. Sending the thoughts of the khagan and his family to where the soul of the deceased—whoever they might be, someone important, no doubt—had now rejoined the Eternal Blue Sky and Slumbering Earth that the khagan and all his ancestors still honored in lieu of the pantheon of thirty-six gods their citizens remained free to worship.

Or any other gods outside of it, should their territories be new enough to not yet have had their gods incorporated into the fold. There had to be several of those, since during his three decades of rule, the man seated before them had added a handful of overseas kingdoms to their borders.

A kingdom for every ring adorning his scar-flecked fingers, precious stones glinting among them.

A warrior bedecked in finery. Those hands slid from the arms of his ivory throne—assembled from the hewn tusks of the mighty beasts that roamed the central grasslands—and settled in his lap, hidden beneath swaths of gold-trimmed blue silk. Indigo dye from the steamy, lush lands in the west. From Balruhn, where Nesryn's own people had originally hailed, before curiosity and ambition drove her great-grandfather to drag his family over mountains and grasslands and deserts to the god-city in the arid north.

The Faliqs had long been tradesmen, and not of anything particularly fine. Just simple, good cloth and household spices. Her uncle still traded such things and, through various lucrative investments, had become a moderately wealthy man, his family now dwelling in a beautiful home within this very city. A definitive step up from a baker—the path her father had chosen upon leaving these shores.

"It is not every day that a new king sends someone so important to our shores," the khagan said at last, using their own tongue and not Halha, the language of the southern continent. "I suppose we should deem it an honor."

His accent was so like her father's—but the tone lacked the warmth, the humor. A man who had been obeyed his entire life, and fought to earn his crown. And executed two of the siblings who proved to be sore losers. The surviving three . . . one had gone into exile, and the other two had sworn fealty to their brother. By having the healers of the Torre render them infertile.

Chaol inclined his head. "The honor is mine, Great Khagan."

Not *Majesty*—that was for kings or queens. There was no term high or grand enough for this man before them. Only the title that the first of his ancestors had borne: Great Khagan.

13

"Yours," the khagan mused, those dark eyes now sliding to Nesryn. "And what of your companion?"

Nesryn fought the urge to bow again. Dorian Havilliard was the opposite of this man, she realized. Aelin Galathynius, however . . . Nesryn wondered if the young queen might have more in common with the khagan than she did with the Havilliard king. Or would, if Aelin survived long enough. If she reached her throne.

Nesryn shoved those thoughts down as Chaol peered at her, his shoulders tightening. Not at the words, not at the company, but simply because she knew that the mere act of having to look *up*, facing this mighty warrior-king in that chair . . . Today would be a hard one for him.

Nesryn inclined her head slightly. "I am Nesryn Faliq, Captain of the Royal Guard of Adarlan. As Lord Westfall once was before King Dorian appointed him as his Hand earlier this summer." She was grateful that years spent living in Rifthold had taught her not to smile, not to cringe or show fear—grateful that she'd learned to keep her voice cool and steady even while her knees quaked.

Nesryn continued, "My family hails from here, Great Khagan. Antica still owns a piece of my soul." She placed a hand over her heart, the fine threads of her gold-and-crimson uniform, the colors of the empire that had made her family often feel hunted and unwanted, scraping against her calluses. "The honor of being in your palace is the greatest of my life."

It was, perhaps, true.

If she found time to visit her family in the quiet, garden-filled Runni Quarter—home mostly to merchants and tradesmen like her uncle—they would certainly consider it so.

The khagan only smiled a bit. "Then allow me to welcome you to your true home, Captain."

Nesryn felt, more than saw, Chaol's flicker of annoyance. She wasn't entirely certain what had triggered it: the claim on her homeland, or the official title that had now passed to her.

But Nesryn bowed her head again in thanks.

The khagan said to Chaol, "I will assume you are here to woo me into joining this war of yours."

Chaol countered a shade tersely, "We're here at the behest of my king." A note of pride at that word. "To begin what we hope will be a new era of prosperous trade and peace."

One of the khagan's offspring—a young woman with hair like flowing night and eyes like dark fire—exchanged a wry look with the sibling to her left, a man perhaps three years her elder.

Hasar and Sartaq, then. Third and secondborn, respectively. Each wore similar loose pants and embroidered tunics, with fine leather boots rising to their knees. Hasar was no beauty, but those eyes . . . The flame dancing in them as she glanced to her elder brother made up for it.

And Sartaq—commander of his father's ruk riders. The rukhin.

The northern aerial cavalry of his people had long dwelled in the towering Tavan Mountains with their ruks: enormous birds, eagle-like in shape, large enough to carry off cattle and horses. Without the sheer bulk and destructive weight of the Ironteeth witches' wyverns, but swift and nimble and clever as foxes. The perfect mounts for the legendary archers who flew them into battle.

Sartaq's face was solemn, his broad shoulders thrown back. A man perhaps as ill at ease in his fine clothes as Chaol. She wondered if his ruk, Kadara, was perched on one of the palace's thirty-six minarets, eyeing the cowering servants and guards, waiting impatiently for her master's return.

That Sartaq was here . . . They had to have known, then. Well in advance. That she and Chaol were coming.

The knowing glance that passed between Sartaq and Hasar told Nesryn enough: they, at least, had discussed the possibilities of this visit.

Sartaq's gaze slid from his sister to Nesryn.

She yielded a blink. His brown skin was darker than the others'— perhaps from all that time in the skies and sunlight—his eyes a solid ebony. Depthless and unreadable. His black hair remained unbound save for a small braid that curved over the arch of his ear. The rest of his hair fell to just past his muscled chest, and swayed slightly as he gave what Nesryn could have sworn was a mocking incline of his head.

A ragtag, humbled pair, Adarlan had sent. The injured former captain, and the common-bred current one. Perhaps the khagan's initial words about *honor* had been a veiled mention of what he perceived as an insult.

Nesryn dragged her attention away from the prince, even as she felt Sartaq's keen stare lingering like some phantom touch.

"We arrive bearing gifts from His Majesty, the King of Adarlan," Chaol was saying, and twisted in his chair to motion the servants behind them to come forward.

Queen Georgina and her court had practically raided the royal coffers before they'd fled to their mountain estates this spring. And the former king had smuggled out much of what was left during those final few months. But before they'd sailed here, Dorian had ventured into the many vaults beneath the castle. Nesryn still could hear his echoed curse, filthier than she'd ever heard him speak, as he found little more than gold marks within.

Aelin, as usual, had a plan.

Nesryn had been standing beside her new king when Aelin had flipped open two trunks in her chambers. Jewelry fit for a queen—for a Queen of Assassins—had sparkled within.

I've enough funds for now, Aelin had only said to Dorian when he began to object. *Give the khagan some of Adarlan's finest.*

In the weeks since, Nesryn had wondered if Aelin had been glad to be rid of what she'd purchased with her blood money. The jewels of Adarlan, it seemed, would not travel to Terrasen.

And now, as the servants laid out the four smaller trunks—divided from the original two to make it seem like *more*, Aelin had suggested—as they flipped open the lids, the still-silent court pressed in to see.

A murmur went through them at the glistening gems and gold and silver.

"A gift," Chaol declared as even the khagan himself leaned forward to examine the trove. "From King Dorian Havilliard of Adarlan, and Aelin Galathynius, Queen of Terrasen."

Princess Hasar's eyes snapped to Chaol at the second name.

Prince Sartaq only glanced back at his father. The eldest son, Arghun, frowned at the jewels.

Arghun—the politician amongst them, beloved by the merchants and power brokers of the continent. Slender and tall, he was a scholar who traded not in coin and finery but in knowledge.

Prince of Spies, they called Arghun. While his two brothers had become the finest of warriors, Arghun had honed his mind, and now oversaw his father's thirty-six viziers. So that frown at the treasure . . .

Necklaces of diamond and ruby. Bracelets of gold and emerald. Earrings—veritable small chandeliers—of sapphire and amethyst. Exquisitely wrought rings, some crowned with jewels as large as a swallow's egg. Combs and pins and brooches. Blood-gained, blood-bought.

The youngest of the assembled royal children, a fine-boned, comely woman, leaned the closest. Duva. A thick silver ring with a sapphire of near-obscene size adorned her slender hand, pressed delicately against the considerable swell of her belly.

Perhaps six months along, though the flowing clothes—she favored purple and rose—and her slight build could distort that. Certainly her first child, the result of her arranged marriage to a prince hailing from an overseas territory to the far east, a southern neighbor of Doranelle that had noted the rumblings of its Fae Queen and wanted to secure the protection of the southern empire across the ocean. Perhaps the first attempt, Nesryn and others had wondered, of the khaganate greatly expanding its own considerable continent.

Nesryn didn't let herself look too long at the life growing beneath that bejeweled hand.

For if one of Duva's siblings were crowned khagan, the first task of the new ruler—after his or her sufficient offspring were produced—would be to eliminate any other challenges to the throne. Starting with the off-spring of his or her siblings, if they challenged their right to rule.

She wondered how Duva was able to endure it. If she had come to love the babe growing in her womb, or if she was wise enough to not allow such a feeling. If the father of that babe would do everything he could to get that child to safety should it come to that.

The khagan at last leaned back in his throne. His children had straightened again, Duva's hand falling back at her side.

"Jewels," Chaol explained, "set by the finest of Adarlanian craftsmen."

The khagan toyed with a citrine ring on his own hand. "If they came from Aelin Galathynius's trove, I have no doubt that they are."

A beat of silence between Nesryn and Chaol. They had known—anticipated—that the khagan had spies in every land, on every sea. That Aelin's past might be just a tad difficult to work around.

"For you are not only Adarlan's Hand," the khagan went on, "but also the Ambassador of Terrasen, are you not?"

"Indeed I am," Chaol said simply.

The khagan rose with only the slightest stiffness, his children immediately stepping aside to clear a path for him to step off the golden dais.

The tallest of them—strapping and perhaps more unchecked than Sartaq's quiet intensity—eyed up the crowd as if assessing any threats within. Kashin. Fourthborn.

If Sartaq commanded the ruks in the northern and central skies, then Kashin controlled the armies on land. Foot soldiers and the horse-lords, mostly. Arghun held sway over the viziers, and Hasar, rumor claimed, had the armadas bowing to her. Yet there remained something less polished about Kashin, his dark hair braided back from his broad-planed face. Handsome, yes—but it was as if life amongst his troops had rubbed off on him, and not necessarily in a bad way.

The khagan descended the dais, his cobalt robes whispering along the floor. And with every step over the green marble, Nesryn realized that this man had indeed once commanded not just the ruks in the skies, but also the horse-lords, *and* swayed the armadas to join him. And then Urus and his elder brother had gone hand-to-hand in combat at the behest of their mother while she lay dying from a wasting sickness that even the Torre could not heal. The son who walked off the sand would be khagan.

The former khagan had a penchant for spectacle. And for this final fight between her two selected offspring, she had placed them in the great amphitheater in the heart of the city, the doors open to any who could claw inside to find a seat. People had sat upon the archways and steps, with thousands cramming the streets that flowed to the white-stoned building. Ruks and their riders had perched on the pillars crowning the uppermost level, more rukhin circling in the skies above.

The two would-be Heirs had fought for six hours.

Not just against each other, but also against the horrors their mother unleashed to test them: great cats sprang from hidden cages beneath the sandy floor; iron-spiked chariots with spear-throwers had charged from the gloom of the tunnel entrances to run them down.

Nesryn's father had been amongst the frenzied mob in the streets, listening to the shouted reports from those dangling off the columns.

The final blow hadn't been an act of brutality or hate.

The now-khagan's elder brother, Orda, had taken a spear to the side thanks to one of those charioteers. After six hours of bloody battle and survival, the blow had kept him down.

And Urus had set aside his sword. Absolute silence had fallen in the arena. Silence as Urus had extended a bloodied hand to his fallen brother—to help him.

Orda had sent a hidden dagger shooting for Urus's heart.

It had missed by two inches.

And Urus had ripped that dagger free, screaming, and plunged it right back into his brother.

Urus did not miss as his brother had.

Nesryn wondered if a scar still marred the khagan's chest as he now strode toward her and Chaol and the jewels displayed. If that long-dead khagan had wept for her fallen son in private, slain by the one who would take her crown in a matter of days. Or if she had never allowed herself to love her children, knowing what must befall them.

Urus, Khagan of the Southern Continent, stopped before Nesryn and Chaol. He towered over Nesryn by a good half foot, his shoulders still broad, spine still straight.

He bent with only a touch of age-granted strain to pluck up a necklace of diamond and sapphire from the chest. It glittered like a living river in his scar-flecked, bejeweled hands.

"My eldest, Arghun," said the khagan, jerking his chin toward the narrow-faced prince monitoring all, "recently informed me of some fascinating information regarding Queen Aelin Ashryver Galathynius."

Nesryn waited for the blow. Chaol just held Urus's gaze.

But the khagan's dark eyes—Sartaq's eyes, she realized—danced as he said to Chaol, "A queen at nineteen would make many uneasy. Dorian Havilliard, at least, has been trained since birth to take up his crown, to control a court and kingdom. But Aelin Galathynius . . ."

The khagan chucked the necklace into the chest. Its thunk was as loud as steel on stone.

"I suppose some would call ten years as a trained assassin to be experience."

Murmurs again rippled through the throne room. Hasar's fire-bright eyes practically glowed. Sartaq's face did not shift at all. Perhaps a skill learned from his eldest brother—whose spies had to be skilled indeed if they'd learned of Aelin's past. Even though Arghun himself seemed to be struggling to keep a smug smile from his lips.

"We may be separated by the Narrow Sea," the khagan said to Chaol, whose features did not so much as alter, "but even we have heard of Celaena Sardothien. You bring me jewels, no doubt from her own collection. Yet they are jewels for *me*, when my daughter Duva"—a glance toward his pregnant, pretty daughter standing closely beside Hasar—"has yet to receive any sort of wedding gift from either your new king or returned queen, while every other ruler sent theirs nearly half a year ago."

Nesryn hid her wince. An oversight that could be explained by so many truths—but not ones that they dared voice, not here. Chaol didn't offer any of them as he remained silent.

"But," the khagan went on, "regardless of the jewels you've now dumped at my feet like sacks of grain, I would still rather have the truth. Especially after Aelin Galathynius shattered your own glass castle, murdered your former king, and seized your capital city."

"If Prince Arghun has the information," Chaol said at last with unfaltering coolness, "perhaps you do not need it from me."

Nesryn stifled her cringe at the defiance, the tone—

"Perhaps not," the khagan said, even as Arghun's eyes narrowed slightly. "But I think *you* should like some truth from me."

Chaol didn't ask for it. Didn't look remotely interested beyond his, "Oh?"

Kashin stiffened. His father's fiercest defender, then. Arghun only exchanged glances with a vizier and smiled toward Chaol like an adder ready to strike.

"Here is why I think you have come, Lord Westfall, Hand to the King."

Only the gulls wheeling high above the dome of the throne room dared make any noise.

The khagan shut lid after lid on the trunks.

"I think you have come to convince me to join your war. Adarlan is cleaved, Terrasen is destitute, and will no doubt have some issue convincing her surviving lords to fight for an untried queen who spent ten years indulging herself in Rifthold, purchasing these jewels with blood money. Your list of allies is short and brittle. Duke Perrington's forces are anything but. The other kingdoms on your continent are shattered and separated from your northern territories by Perrington's armies. So you have arrived here, fast as the eight winds can carry you, to beg me to send my armies to your shores. To convince me to spill our blood on a lost cause."

"Some might consider it a noble cause," Chaol countered.

"I am not done yet," the khagan said, lifting a hand.

Chaol bristled but did not speak out of turn again. Nesryn's heart thundered.

"Many would argue," the khagan said, waving that upraised hand toward a few viziers, toward Arghun and Hasar, "that we remain out of it. Or better yet, ally with the force sure to win, whose trade has been profitable for us these ten years."

A wave of that hand toward some other men and women in the gold robes of viziers. Toward Sartaq and Kashin and Duva. "Some would say that we risk allying with Perrington only to potentially face his armies in our harbors one day. That the shattered kingdoms of Eyllwe and Fenharrow might again become wealthy under new rule, and fill our coffers with good trade. I have no doubt you will promise me that it shall be so. You will offer me exclusive trading deals, likely to your own disadvantage. But you are desperate, and there is nothing you possess that I do not already own. That I cannot take if I wish."

Chaol kept his mouth shut, thankfully. Even as his brown eyes simmered at the quiet threat.

The khagan peered into the fourth and final trunk. Jeweled combs and brushes, ornate perfume bottles made by Adarlan's finest glassblowers. The same who had built the castle Aelin had shattered. "So, you have come to convince me to join your cause. And I shall consider it while you stay here. Since you have undoubtedly come for another purpose, too."

A flick of that scarred, jeweled hand toward the chair. Color stained Chaol's tan cheeks, but he did not flinch, did not cower. Nesryn forced herself to do the same.

"Arghun informed me your injuries are new—that they happened when the glass castle exploded. It seems the Queen of Terrasen was not quite so careful about shielding her allies."

A muscle feathered in Chaol's jaw as everyone, from prince to servant, looked to his legs.

"Because your relations with Doranelle are now strained, also thanks to Aelin Galathynius, I assume the only path toward healing that remains open to you is here. At the Torre Cesme."

The khagan shrugged, the only reveal of the irreverent warrior-youth he'd once been. "My beloved wife will be deeply upset if I were to deny an injured man a chance at healing"—the empress was nowhere to be seen in this room, Nesryn realized with a start—"so I, of course, shall grant you permission to enter the Torre. Whether its healers will agree to work upon you shall be up to them. Even I do not control the will of the Torre."

The Torre—the Tower. It dominated the southern edge of Antica, nestled atop its highest hill to overlook the city that sloped down toward the green sea. Domain of its famed healers, and tribute to Silba, the healer-goddess who blessed them. Of the thirty-six gods this empire had welcomed into the fold over the centuries, from religions near and far, in this city of gods . . . Silba reigned unchallenged.

Chaol looked like he was swallowing hot coals, but he mercifully managed to bow his head. "I thank you for your generosity, Great Khagan."

"Rest tonight—I will inform them that you shall be ready tomorrow morning. Since you cannot go to them, one will be sent to you. If they agree."

Chaol's fingers shifted in his lap, but he did not clench them. Nesryn still held her breath.

"I am at their disposal," Chaol said tightly.

The khagan shut the final trunk of jewels. "You may keep your presents, Hand of the King, Ambassador to Aelin Galathynius. I have no use for them—and no interest."

Chaol's head snapped up, as if something in the khagan's tone had snared him. "Why."

Nesryn barely hid her cringe. More of a demand than anyone ever dared make of the man, judging by the surprised anger in the khagan's eyes, in the glances exchanged between his children.

But Nesryn caught the flicker of something else within the khagan's eyes. A weariness.

Something oily slid into her gut as she noted the white banners streaming from the windows, all over the city. As she looked to the six heirs and counted again.

Not six.

Five. Only five were here.

Death-banners at the royal household. All over the city.

They were not a mourning people—not in the way they could be in Adarlan, dressing all in black and moping for months. Even amongst the khagan's royal family, life picked up and went on, their dead not stuffed in stone catacombs or coffins, but shrouded in white and laid beneath the open skies of their sealed-off, sacred reserve on the distant steppes.

Nesryn glanced down the line of five heirs, counting. The eldest five were present. And just as she realized that Tumelun, the youngest—barely seventeen—was not there, the khagan said to Chaol, "Your spies are indeed useless if you have not heard."

With that, he strode for his throne, leaving Sartaq to step forward, the second-eldest prince's depthless eyes veiled with sorrow. Sartaq gave Nesryn a silent nod. Yes. Yes, her suspicions were right—

Sartaq's solid, pleasant voice filled the chamber. "Our beloved sister, Tumelun, died unexpectedly three weeks ago."

Oh, gods. So many words and rituals had been passed over; merely coming here to demand their aid in war was uncouth, untoward—

Chaol said into the fraught silence, meeting the stares of each taut-faced prince and princess, then finally the weary-eyed khagan himself, "You have my deepest condolences."

Nesryn breathed, "May the northern wind carry her to fairer plains."

Only Sartaq bothered to nod his thanks, while the others now turned cold and stiff.

Nesryn shot Chaol a silent, warning look not to ask about the death. He read the expression on her face and nodded.

The khagan scratched at a fleck on his ivory throne, the silence as

24

heavy as one of the coats the horse-lords still wore against that bitter northern wind on the steppes and their unforgiving wooden saddles.

"We've been at sea for three weeks," Chaol tried to offer, his voice softer now.

The khagan did not bother to appear understanding. "That would also explain why you are so unaware of the other bit of news, and why these cold jewels might be of more use for *you*." The khagan's lips curled in a mirthless smile. "Arghun's contacts also brought word from a ship this morning. Your royal coffers in Rifthold are no longer accessible. Duke Perrington and his host of flying terrors have sacked Rifthold."

Silence, pulsing and hollow, swept through Nesryn. She wasn't sure if Chaol was breathing.

"We do not have word on King Dorian's location, but he yielded Rifthold to them. Fled into the night, if rumor is to be believed. The city has fallen. Everything to the south of Rifthold belongs to Perrington and his witches now."

Nesryn saw the faces of her nieces and nephews first.

Then the face of her sister. Then her father. Saw their kitchen, the bakery. The pear tarts cooling on the long, wooden table.

Dorian had left them. Left them all to . . . to do what? Find help? Survive? Run to Aelin?

Had the royal guard remained to fight? Had anyone fought to save the innocents in the city?

Her hands were shaking. She didn't care. Didn't care if these people clad in riches sneered.

Her sister's children, the great joy in her life . . .

Chaol was staring up at her. Nothing on his face. No devastation, no shock.

That crimson-and-gold uniform became stifling. Strangling.

Witches and wyverns. In her city. With those iron teeth and nails. Shredding and bleeding and tormenting. Her family—her *family*—

"Father."

Sartaq had stepped forward once more. Those onyx eyes slid between Nesryn and the khagan. "It has been a long journey for our guests. Politics aside," he said, giving a disapproving glance at Arghun, who seemed amused—*amused* at this news he'd brought, that had set the green marble floors roiling beneath her boots—"we are still a nation of hospitality. Let them rest for a few hours. And then join us for dinner."

Hasar came to Sartaq's side, frowning at Arghun while she did. Perhaps not from reprimand like her brother, but simply for Arghun not telling *her* of this news first. "Let no guest pass through our home and find its comforts lacking." Even though the words were welcoming, Hasar's tone was anything but.

Their father gave them a bemused glance. "Indeed." Urus waved a hand toward the servants by the far pillars. "Escort them to their rooms. And dispatch a message to the Torre to send their finest—Hafiza, if she'll come down from that tower."

Nesryn scarcely heard the rest. If the witches held the city, then the Valg who had infested it earlier this summer . . . There would be no one to fight them. No one to shield her family.

If they had survived.

She couldn't breathe. Couldn't think.

She should not have left. Should not have taken this position.

They could be dead, or suffering. Dead. Dead.

She did not notice the female servant who came to push Chaol's chair. Barely noticed the hand Chaol reached out to twine through her own.

Nesryn didn't so much as bow to the khagan as they left.

She could not stop seeing their faces.

The children. Her sister's smiling, round-bellied children.

She should not have come.

⇥ 3 ⇤

Nesryn had gone into shock.

And Chaol could not go to her, could not scoop her into his arms and hold her close.

Not when she had walked, silent and drifting like a wraith, right into a bedroom of the lavish suite they'd been appointed on the first floor of the palace, and shut the door behind her. As if she had forgotten anyone else in the world existed.

He didn't blame her.

Chaol let the servant, a fine-boned young woman with chestnut hair that fell in heavy curls to her narrow waist, wheel him into the second bedroom. The suite overlooked a garden of fruit trees and burbling fountains, cascades of pink and purple blossoms hanging from potted plants anchored into the balcony above. They provided living curtains before his towering bedroom windows—doors, he realized.

The servant mumbled something about drawing a bath, her use of his language unwieldy compared to the skill of the khagan and his children.

Not that he was in any position to judge: he was barely fluent in any of the other languages within his own continent.

She slipped behind a carved wooden screen that no doubt led into his bathing chamber, and Chaol peered through his still-open bedroom door, across the pale marble foyer, to the shut doors of Nesryn's bedroom.

They should not have left.

He couldn't have done anything, but . . . He knew what the not-knowing would do to Nesryn. What it was already doing to him.

Dorian was not dead, he told himself. He had gotten out. Fled. If he were in Perrington's grip—Erawan's grip—they would have known. Prince Arghun would have known.

His city, sacked by the witches. He wondered if Manon Blackbeak had led the attack.

Chaol tried and failed to recount where the debts were stacked between them. Aelin had spared Manon's life at Temis's temple, but Manon had given them vital information about Dorian under the Valg thrall. Did it make them even? Or tentative allies?

It was a waste to hope that Manon would turn against Morath. But he sent up a silent prayer to whatever god might be listening to protect Dorian, to guide his king to friendlier harbors.

Dorian would make it. He was too clever, too gifted, not to. There was no other alternative—none—that Chaol would accept. Dorian was alive, and safe. Or on his way to safety. And when Chaol got a moment, he was going to squeeze the information out of the eldest prince. Mourning or no. Everything Arghun knew, *he* would know. And then he'd ask that servant girl to comb every merchant ship for information about the attack.

No word—there had been no word about Aelin. Where she was now, what she'd been doing. Aelin, who might very well be the thing that cost him this alliance.

He ground his teeth, and was still grinding them as the suite doors opened and a tall, broad-shouldered man strode in as if he owned the place.

Chaol supposed he did. Prince Kashin was alone and unarmed, though he moved with the ease of a person confident in his body's unfailing strength.

How, Chaol supposed, he himself had once walked about the palace in Rifthold.

Chaol lowered his head in greeting as the prince shut the hall door and surveyed him. It was a warrior's assessment, frank and thorough. When his brown eyes at last met Chaol's, the prince said in Adarlan's tongue, "Injuries like yours are not uncommon here, and I have seen many of them—especially among the horse-tribes. My family's people."

Chaol didn't particularly feel like discussing his injuries with the prince, with anyone, so he only nodded. "I'm sure you have."

Kashin cocked his head, scanning Chaol again, his dark braid slipping over his muscled shoulder. Reading, perhaps, Chaol's desire not to start down this particular road. "My father indeed wishes you both to join us at dinner. And more than that, to join us every night afterward while you are here. And sit at the high table."

It wasn't a strange request of a visiting dignitary, and it was certainly an honor to sit at the khagan's own table, but to send his son to do it . . . Chaol considered his next words carefully, then simply chose the most obvious one. "Why?"

Surely the family wished to keep close to one another after losing their youngest member. Inviting strangers to join them—

The prince's jaw tightened. Not a man used to veiling his emotions, as his three elder siblings were. "Arghun reports our palace is safe of spies from Duke Perrington's forces, that his agents have not yet come. I am not of that belief. And Sartaq—" The prince caught himself, as if not wanting to bring in his brother—or potential ally. Kashin grimaced. "There was a reason I chose to live amongst soldiers. The double-talk of this court . . ."

Chaol was tempted to say he understood. Had felt that way for most of his life. But he asked, "You think Perrington's forces have infiltrated this court?"

How much did Kashin, or Arghun, know of Perrington's forces—know the truth of the Valg king who wore Perrington's skin? Or the armies he commanded, worse than any their imaginations might conjure? But that information . . . He'd keep that to himself. See if it could somehow be used, if Arghun and the khagan did not know of it.

Kashin rubbed at his neck. "I do not know if it is Perrington, or someone from Terrasen, or Melisande, or Wendlyn. All I know is that my sister is now dead."

Chaol's heart stumbled a beat. But he dared ask, "How did it come about?"

Grief flickered in Kashin's eyes. "Tumelun was always a bit wild, reckless. Prone to moods. One day, happy and laughing; the next, withdrawn and hopeless. They . . ." His throat bobbed. "They say she leaped from her balcony because of it. Duva and her husband found her later that night."

Any death in a family was devastating, but a suicide . . . "I'm sorry," Chaol offered quietly.

Kashin shook his head, sunlight from the garden dancing on his black hair. "I do not believe it. My Tumelun would not have jumped."

My Tumelun. The words told enough about the prince's closeness to his younger sister.

"You suspect foul play?"

"All I know is that no matter Tumelun's moods . . . I knew her. As I know my own heart." He put a hand over it. "She would not have jumped."

Chaol considered his words carefully once again. "As sorry as I am for your loss, do you have any reason to suspect why a foreign kingdom might have engineered it?"

Kashin paced a few steps. "No one within *our* lands would be stupid enough."

"Well, no one within Terrasen or Adarlan would ever do such a thing—even to manipulate you into this war."

Kashin studied him for a heartbeat. "Even a queen who was once an assassin herself?"

Chaol didn't let one flicker of emotion show. "Assassin she might have

30

been, but Aelin had hard lines that she did not cross. Killing or harming children was one of them."

Kashin paused before the dresser against the garden wall, adjusting a gilded box on its polished dark surface. "I know. I read that in my brother's reports, too. Details of her kills." Chaol could have sworn the prince shuddered before he added, "I believe you."

No doubt why the prince was even having this conversation with him.

Kashin went on, "Which leaves not many other foreign powers who might do it—and Perrington at the top of that short list."

"But why target your sister?"

"I do not know." Kashin paced another few steps. "She was young, guileless—she rode with me amongst the Darghan, our mother-clans. Had no *sulde* of her own yet."

At Chaol's narrowed brows, the prince clarified, "It is a spear all Darghan warriors carry. We bind strands of our favored horse's hair to the shaft, beneath the blade. Our ancestors believed that where those hairs waved in the wind, there our destinies waited. Some of us still believe in such things, but even those who think it mere tradition . . . we bring them everywhere. There is a courtyard in this palace where my *sulde* and those of my siblings are planted to feel the wind while we remain at our father's palace, right beside his own. But in death . . ." Again, that shadow of grief. "In death, they are the only object that we keep. They bear the soul of a Darghan warrior for eternity, and are left planted atop a steppe in our sacred realm." The prince closed his eyes. "Now her soul will roam with the wind."

Nesryn had said as much earlier. Chaol only repeated, "I'm sorry."

Kashin opened his eyes. "Some of my siblings do not believe me about Tumelun. Some do. Our father . . . he remains undecided. Our mother will not even leave her room thanks to her grief, and mentioning my suspicions might—I cannot bring myself to mention them to her." He rubbed his strong jaw. "So I have convinced my father to have you join us at dinner every night, as a gesture of diplomacy. But I should like you to watch

31

with an outsider's eyes. To report on anything amiss. Perhaps you will see something we don't."

Help them . . . and perhaps receive help in return. Chaol said baldly, "If you trust me enough to have me do that, to tell me all this, then why not agree to join with us in this war?"

"It is not my place to say or guess." A trained soldier. Kashin examined the suite as if assessing any potential enemies lying in wait. "I march only when my father gives the order."

If Perrington's forces were already here, if Morath was indeed behind the princess's murder . . . It'd be too easy. Too easy to sway the khagan into siding with Dorian and Aelin. Perrington—Erawan was far smarter than that.

But if Chaol himself were to win over the commander of the khagan's terrestrial armies to their cause—

"I do not play those games, Lord Westfall," said Kashin, reading whatever sparked in Chaol's eyes. "My other siblings are the ones you will wish to convince."

Chaol tapped a finger on the arm of his chair. "Any advice on that front?"

Kashin snorted, smiling faintly. "Others have come before you—from kingdoms far richer than your own. Some succeeded, some didn't." A glance at Chaol's legs, a flicker of pity entering the prince's eyes. Chaol clenched the arms of the chair at that pity, from a man who recognized a fellow warrior. "Wishes for good luck are all I can offer you."

Then the prince was striding for the doors, his long legs eating up the distance.

"If Perrington has an agent here," Chaol said as Kashin reached the suite doors, "then you've already seen that everyone in this palace is in grave danger. You must take action."

Kashin paused with his hand on the carved doorknob, glancing over his shoulder. "Why do you think I've asked a foreign lord for assistance?"

Then the prince was gone, his words hanging in the sweet-scented air. The tone wasn't cruel, wasn't insulting, but the warrior's frankness of it . . .

Chaol struggled to master his breathing, even as the thoughts swirled. He'd seen no black rings or collars, but then he hadn't been looking for them. Had not even considered that the shadow of Morath might have already stretched this far.

Chaol rubbed at his chest. Careful. He'd have to be careful in this court. With what he said publicly—with what he said in this room, too.

Chaol was still staring at the shut door, mulling over all Kashin had implied, when the servant emerged, her tunic and pants replaced by a tied robe of thinnest, sheerest silk. It left nothing to the imagination.

He clamped down on the urge to shout for Nesryn to assist him instead. "Only wash me," he said, as clearly and firmly as he could.

She showed no nerves, no tremor of hesitation. And he knew she had done this before, countless times, as she only asked, "Am I not to your liking?"

It was a stark, honest question. She was paid well for her services—all the servants were. She chose to be here, and another could easily be found at no risk to her status.

"You are," Chaol said, only half lying, refusing to let his gaze drop below her eyes. "Very pleasing," he clarified. "But I only want a bath." He added, just to be sure, "Nothing else from you."

He'd expected her gratitude, but the servant only nodded, unruffled. Even with her, he'd have to be careful with what he said. What he and Nesryn might discuss in these rooms.

There hadn't been a sound or flicker of movement behind Nesryn's closed bedroom doors. And there certainly wasn't now.

So he motioned to let the servant push his chair into the bathing chamber, veils of steam rippling through the white-and-blue-tiled room.

The chair glided over carpet and tile, curving around the furniture with little effort. Nesryn herself had found the chair in the now-vacant healers' catacombs of Rifthold's castle, right before they'd sailed here. One of the few items the fleeing healers had left behind, it seemed.

Lighter and sleeker than what he'd expected, the large wheels flanking the seat rotated easily, even when he used the slender metal hand rim to guide them himself. Unlike the stiff bulk of others he'd seen, this chair came equipped with two small front wheels, just on either side of the wooden footrests, each capable of swiveling in any direction he chose. And now they smoothly turned into the wafting steam of the bathing chamber.

A large sunken pool filled most of it, oils gleaming on the surface, interrupted only by scattered, drifting petals. A small window high in the far wall peeked into the greenery of the garden, and candles gilded the billowing steam.

Luxury. Utter luxury while his city suffered. While they pleaded for help that had not come. Dorian would have wanted to stay. Only absolute defeat, no chance of survival, would have prompted him to leave. Chaol wondered if his magic had played any part. Helped any of them.

Dorian would find his way to safety, to allies. He knew it in his bones, though his stomach continued to roil. There was nothing he could do to help his king from here—save for forging this alliance. Even if every instinct screamed at him to return to Adarlan, to find Dorian, he'd stay the course.

Chaol barely noticed the servant removing his boots in efficient tugs. And though he could have done it himself, he barely remarked on her removing his teal jacket, then the shirt beneath. But he dragged himself from his thoughts at last when she began to remove his pants—when he leaned in to help, gritting his teeth as they worked together in stilted silence. It was only when she reached to remove his undershorts that he gripped her wrist.

He and Nesryn still hadn't touched each other. Beyond an ill-fated bout on the ship three days ago, he hadn't conveyed any sort of desire to take that step once again. He'd wanted to, though. Woke up most mornings aching to, especially when they'd shared that bed in their stateroom. But the thought of being so prone, of not being able to take her the way he'd once done . . . It had curdled any brimming lust. Even while grateful that certain parts of him still undoubtedly worked.

"I can get in on my own," Chaol said, and before the servant could move, he gathered the strength in his arms, his back, and began easing

34

himself from the chair. It was an unceremonious process, one he'd figured out during the long days at sea.

First he flicked the locking mechanism on the wheels, the click echoing off the stone and water. With a few motions, he maneuvered himself to the edge of the chair, then removed his feet from the wooden plates and onto the floor, angling his legs to his left as he did so. With his right hand, he gripped the edge of the seat by his knees, while he curled the left into a fist as he bent over to brace it on the cool, steam-slick tiles. Slippery—

The servant only padded over, laid a thick white cloth before him, and backed away. He gave her a grateful, close-lipped smile as he braced his left fist again on the floor, atop the plush cloth, distributing his weight throughout the arm. With an inhaled breath, his right hand still gripping the edge of his chair, he carefully lowered himself to the ground, swinging his rear away from the chair as his knees bent unbidden.

He landed with a thud, but he was on the floor, at least—hadn't toppled over, as he had the first half-dozen times he'd tried it on the ship.

Carefully, he scooted to the edge of the pool stairs, until he could set his feet into the warm water, right atop the second step. The servant strode into the water a heartbeat later, graceful as an egret, her gossamer robe turning as insubstantial as dew while water crept up its length. Her hands were gentle but steady while she gripped him under the arm and helped him hoist himself the last bit into the pool, setting himself down on the top step. Then she guided him down another and another, until he was sitting up to his shoulders. Eye-level with her full, peaked breasts.

She didn't seem to notice. And he immediately averted his gaze toward the window as she reached for the small tray of supplies she'd left near the lip of the pool. Oils and brushes and soft-looking cloths. Chaol slid his undershorts off while she turned, setting them with a loud, wet smack upon the edge of the pool.

Nesryn still didn't emerge from her room.

So Chaol closed his eyes, submitting himself to the servant's ministrations, and wondered what the hell he was going to do.

⊰ 4 ⊱

Of all the rooms in the Torre Cesme, Yrene Towers loved this one best.

Perhaps it was because the room, located at the very pinnacle of the pale-stoned tower and its sprawling complex below, had unparalleled views of the sunset over Antica.

Perhaps it was because this was the place where she'd felt the first shred of safety in nearly ten years. The place she had first looked upon the ancient woman now sitting across the paper- and book-strewn desk, and heard the words that changed everything: *You are welcome here, Yrene Towers.*

It had been over two years since then.

Two years of working here, living here, in this tower and in this city of so many peoples, so many foods and caches of knowledge.

It had been all she'd dreamed it would be—and she had seized every opportunity, every challenge, with both hands. Had studied and listened and practiced and saved lives, changed them, until she had climbed to the very top of her class. Until an unknown healer's daughter from Fenharrow was approached by healers old and young, who had trained their entire lives, for her advice and assistance.

The magic helped. Glorious, lovely magic that could make her breathless or so tired she couldn't get out of bed for days. Magic demanded a cost—to both healer and patient. But Yrene was willing to pay it. She had never minded the aftermath of a brutal healing.

If it meant saving a life . . . Silba had granted her a gift—and a young stranger had given her another gift, that final night in Innish two years ago. Yrene had no plans to waste either.

She waited in silence as the slender woman across from her finished reading through some message on her chronically messy desk. Despite the servants' best efforts, the ancient rosewood desk was always chaotic, covered with formulas or spells or vials and jars brewing some tonic.

There were two such vials on the desk now, clear orbs atop silver feet fashioned after ibis legs. Being purified by the endless sunshine within the tower.

Hafiza, Healer on High of the Torre Cesme, plucked up one of the vials, swirled its pale blue contents, frowned, and set it down. "The damned thing always takes twice as long as I anticipate." She asked casually, using Yrene's own language, "Why do you think that is?"

Yrene leaned forward in the worn, tufted armchair on her side of the desk to study the tonic. Every meeting, every encounter with Hafiza, was a lesson—a chance to learn. To be challenged. Yrene lifted the vial from its stand, holding it to the golden light of sunset as she examined the thick azure liquid within. "Use?"

"Ten-year-old girl developed a dry cough six weeks ago. Saw the physicians, who advised honey tea, rest, and fresh air. Got better for a time, but returned a week ago with a vengeance."

The physicians of the Torre Cesme were the finest in the world, distinguished only from the Torre's healers by the fact that they did not possess magic. They were the first line of inspection for the healers in the tower, their quarters occupying the sprawling complex around its base.

Magic was precious, its demands costly enough that some Healer on High centuries ago had decreed that if they were to see a patient, a physician must first inspect the person. Perhaps it had been a political maneuver—a bone tossed to the physicians so often passed over by a people clamoring for the cure-all remedies of magic.

Yet magic could not cure all things. Could not halt death, or bring someone back from it. She'd learned it again and again these past two years, and earlier. And even with the protocols with the physicians, Yrene still—as she had always done—found herself walking toward the sound of coughing in the narrow, sloped streets of Antica.

Yrene tilted the vial this way and that. "The tonic might be reacting to the heat. It's been unseasonably warm, even for us."

With the end of summer finally near, even after two years, Yrene was still not entirely accustomed to the unrelenting, dry heat of the god-city. Mercifully, some long-ago mastermind had invented the *bidgier*, wind-catching towers set atop buildings to draw in fresh air to the rooms below, some even working in tandem with the few underground canals winding beneath Antica to transform hot wind into cool breezes. The city was peppered with the small towers, like a thousand spears jutting toward the sky, ranging from the small houses made of earthen bricks to the great, domed residences full of shaded courtyards and clear pools.

Unfortunately, the Torre had predated that stroke of brilliance, and though the upper levels possessed some cunning ventilation that cooled the chambers far below, there were plenty of days when Yrene wished some clever architect would take it upon themselves to outfit the Torre with the latest advances. Indeed, with the rising heat and the various fires burning throughout the tower, Hafiza's room was near-sweltering. Which led Yrene to add, "You could put it in a lower chamber—where it's cooler."

"But the sunlight needed?"

Yrene considered. "Bring in mirrors. Catch the sunlight through the window, and focus it upon the vial. Adjust it a few times a day to match the path of the sun. The cooler temperature and more concentrated sunlight might have the tonic ready sooner."

A little, pleased nod. Yrene had come to cherish those nods, the light in those brown eyes. "Quick wits save lives more often than magic," was Hafiza's only reply.

She'd said it a thousand times before, usually where Yrene was involved—to her eternal pride—but Yrene bowed her head in thanks and set the vial back upon its stand.

"So," Hafiza said, folding her hands atop each other on the near-glowing rosewood desk, "Eretia informs me that she believes you are ready to leave us."

Yrene straightened in her seat, the very same chair she'd sat in that first day she'd climbed the thousand steps to the top of the tower and begged for admittance. The begging had been the least of her humiliations that meeting, the crowning moment being when she dumped the bag of gold on Hafiza's desk, blurting that she didn't care what the cost was and to take it all.

Not realizing that Hafiza did not take money from students. No, they paid for their education in other ways. Yrene had suffered through endless indignities and degradations during her year working at the backwater White Pig Inn, but she had never been more mortified than the moment Hafiza ordered her to put the money back in that brown pouch. Scraping the gold off the desk like some cardplayer scrambling to collect his winnings, Yrene had debated leaping right out the arc of windows towering behind Hafiza's desk.

Much had changed since then. Gone was the homespun dress, the too-slim body. Though Yrene supposed the endless stairs of the Torre had kept in check the weight she'd gained from steady, healthy eating, thanks to the Torre's enormous kitchens, the countless markets teeming with food stalls, and the dine-in shops along every bustling street and winding alley.

Yrene swallowed once, trying and failing to glean the Healer on High's face. Hafiza had been the one person here whom Yrene could never read, never anticipate. She'd never once shown a display of temper—something that couldn't be said of many of the instructors here, Eretia especially—and had never raised her voice. Hafiza had only three expressions: pleased, neutral, and disappointed. Yrene lived in terror of the latter two.

Not for any punishment. There was no such thing here. No rations held, no pain threatened. Not like at the White Pig, where Nolan had docked her pay if she stepped out of line or was overgenerous with a customer, or if he caught her leaving out nightly scraps for the half-feral urchins who had prowled the filthy streets of Innish.

She'd arrived here thinking it would be the same: people who took her money, who made it harder and harder to leave. She'd spent a year working at the White Pig due to Nolan's increases in her rent, decreases in her pay, his cut of her meager tips, and knowledge that most women in Innish worked the streets, and his place, disgusting as it had been, was a far better alternative.

She'd told herself never again—until she'd arrived here. Until she'd dumped that gold on Hafiza's desk and had been ready to do it all over, indebt and sell herself, just for a chance to learn.

Hafiza did not even consider such things. Her work was in direct opposition to the people who did, the people like Nolan. Yrene still remembered the first time she'd heard Hafiza say in that thick, lovely accent of hers, nearly the same words that Yrene's mother had told her, over and over: they did not charge, students or patients, for what Silba, Goddess of Healing, gifted them for free.

In a land of so many gods that Yrene was still struggling to keep them all straight, at least Silba remained the same.

Yet another clever thing the khaganate had done upon patching together the kingdoms and territories during their years of conquest: keep and adapt the gods of *everyone*. Including Silba, whose dominance over the healers had been established in these lands long ago. History was written by the victors, apparently. Or so Eretia, Yrene's direct tutor, had once told her. Even the gods seemed no more immune to it than mere mortals.

But it didn't stop Yrene from offering up a prayer to Silba and whatever gods might be listening as she said at last, "I am ready, yes."

"To leave us." Such simple words, offered with that neutral face—calm and patient. "Or have you considered the other option I presented to you?"

Yrene had. She'd thought about it endlessly in the two weeks since Hafiza had summoned her to this office and spoke the one word that had clenched a fist around her heart: *Stay.*

Stay, and learn more—stay, and see what this fledgling life she'd built here might grow into.

Yrene rubbed at her chest as if she could still feel that viselike grip. "War is coming to my home again—the northern continent." So they called it here. Yrene swallowed. "I want to be there to help those fighting against the empire's control."

At last, after so many years, a force was rallying. Adarlan itself had been sundered, if rumors were to be believed, by Dorian Havilliard in the north, and the dead king's Second, Duke Perrington, in the south. Dorian was backed by Aelin Galathynius, the long-lost queen now ripe with power and ravenous for vengeance, judging by what she'd done to the glass castle and its king. And Perrington, rumor also claimed, was aided by horrors birthed from some dark nightmare.

But if this was the only chance at freedom for Fenharrow . . .

Yrene would be there to help, in whatever way she could. She still smelled smoke, late at night or when she was drained after a hard healing. Smoke from that fire those Adarlanian soldiers had built—and burned her mother upon. She still heard her mother's screaming and felt the wood of that tree trunk dig beneath her nails as she'd hidden at the edge of Oakwald. As she watched them burn her mother alive. After her mother had killed that soldier to buy Yrene time to run.

It had been ten years since then. Nearly eleven. And though she had crossed mountains and oceans . . . there were some days when Yrene felt as if she were still standing in Fenharrow, smelling that fire, splinters slicing under her nails, watching as the soldiers took their torches and burned her cottage, too.

The cottage that had housed generations of Towers healers.

Yrene supposed it was fitting, somehow, she'd wound up *in* a tower herself. With only the ring on her left hand as proof that once, for hundreds of years, there had existed a line of prodigally gifted female healers in the south of Fenharrow. A ring she now toyed with, that last shred of proof that her mother and mother's mother and all the mothers before them had once lived and healed in peace. It was the first of only two objects Yrene would not sell—even before selling herself.

Hafiza had not replied, and so Yrene went on, the sun sinking farther toward the jade waters of the harbor across the city, "Even with magic now returned to the northern continent, many of the healers might not have the training, if any survived at all. I could save many lives."

"War could also claim *your* life."

She knew this. Yrene lifted her chin. "I am aware of the risks."

Hafiza's dark eyes softened. "Yes, yes, you are."

It had come out during that first, mortifying meeting with the Healer on High.

Yrene had not cried for years—since that day her mother had become ash on the wind—and yet the moment Hafiza had asked about Yrene's parents . . . she had buried her face in her hands and wept. Hafiza had come from around that desk and held her, rubbing her back in soothing circles.

Hafiza often did that. Not just to Yrene, but to all her healers, when the hours were long and their backs had cramped and the magic had taken *everything* and it was still not enough. A quiet, steady presence who steeled them, soothed them.

Hafiza was as close to a mother as Yrene had found since she was eleven. And now weeks away from twenty-two, she doubted she'd ever find another like her.

"I have taken the examinations," Yrene said, even though Hafiza knew that already. She'd given them to Yrene herself, overseeing the grueling week of tests on knowledge, skill, and actual human practice. Yrene had made sure she received the highest marks of her class. As near to a perfect score as anyone had ever been given here. "I'm ready."

"Indeed you are. And yet I still wonder how much you might learn in five years, ten years, if you have already learned so much in two."

Yrene had been too skilled to begin with the acolytes in the lower levels of the Torre.

She'd shadowed her mother since she was old enough to walk and talk, learning slowly, over the years, as all the healers in her family had done. At eleven, Yrene had learned more than most would in another decade. And even during the six years that had followed, where she'd pretended to be an ordinary girl while working on her mother's cousin's farm—the family unsure what to really do with her, unwilling to get to know her when war and Adarlan might destroy them all—she'd quietly practiced.

But not too much, not too noticeably. During those years, neighbor had sold out neighbor for even the whisper of magic. And even though magic had vanished, taking Silba's gift with it, Yrene had been careful never to appear more than a simple farmer's relative, whose grandmother had perhaps taught her a few natural remedies for fevers or birthing pain or sprained and broken limbs.

In Innish, she'd been able to do more, using her sparse pocket money to purchase herbs, salves. But she didn't often dare, not with Nolan and Jessa, his favored barmaid, watching her day and night. So these past two years, she'd *wanted* to learn as much as she could. But it had also been an unleashing. Of years of stifling, of lying and hiding.

And that day she'd walked off the boat and *felt* her magic stir, felt it reach for a man limping down the street . . . She had fallen into a state of shock that had not ended until she wound up weeping in this very chair three hours later.

Yrene sighed through her nose. "I could return here one day to continue my studies. But—with all due respect, I *am* a full healer now." And she could venture wherever her gift called her.

Hafiza's white brows rose, stark against her brown skin. "And what of Prince Kashin?"

Yrene shifted in her seat. "What of him?"

"You were once good friends. He remains fond of you, and that is no small thing to ignore."

Yrene leveled a look few dared to direct toward the Healer on High. "Will he interfere with my plans to leave?"

"He is a prince, and has been denied nothing, save the crown he covets. He may find that your leaving is not something he will tolerate."

Dread sluiced through her, starting at her spine and ending curled deep in her gut. "I've given him no encouragement. I made my thoughts on that matter perfectly clear last year."

It had been a disaster. She'd gone over it again and again, the things she'd said, the moments between them—everything that had led up to that awful conversation in that large Darghan tent atop the windswept steppes.

It had started a few months after she'd arrived in Antica, when one of Kashin's favored servants had fallen ill. To her surprise, the prince himself had been at the man's bedside, and during the long hours Yrene worked, the conversation had flowed, and she'd found herself . . . smiling. She'd cured the servant, and upon leaving that night, she'd been escorted by Kashin himself to the gates of the Torre. And in the months that followed, friendship had sprung up between them.

Perhaps freer, lighter than the friendship she also wound up forming with Hasar, who had taken a liking to Yrene after requiring some healing of her own. And while Yrene had struggled to find companions within the Torre thanks to her and her fellow students' conflicting hours, the prince and princess had become friends indeed. As had Hasar's lover, the sweet-faced Renia—who was as lovely inside as she was out.

44

A strange group they made, but . . . Yrene had enjoyed their company, the dinners Kashin and Hasar invited her to, when Yrene knew she had no reason to really be there. Kashin often managed to find a way to sit next to her, or near enough to engage her in conversation. For months, things had been fine—better than fine. And then Hafiza had brought Yrene out to the steppes, the native home of the khagan's family, to oversee a grueling healing. With Kashin as their escort and guide.

The Healer on High now examined Yrene, frowning slightly. "Perhaps your lack of encouragement has made him more eager."

Yrene rubbed her eyebrows with her thumb and forefinger. "We've barely spoken since then." It was true. Though mostly due to Yrene avoiding him at the dinners to which Hasar and Renia still invited her.

"The prince does not seem like a man easily deterred—certainly not in matters of the heart."

She knew that. She'd liked that about Kashin. Until he'd wanted something she couldn't give him. Yrene groaned a bit. "Will I have to leave like a thief in the night, then?" Hasar would never forgive her, though she had no doubt Renia would try to soothe and rationalize it to the princess. If Hasar was pure flame, then Renia was flowing water.

"Should you decide to remain, you will not have to worry about such things at all."

Yrene straightened. "You would really use Kashin as a way to keep me here?"

Hafiza laughed, a crow of warmth. "No. But forgive an old woman for trying to use any avenue necessary to convince you."

Pride and guilt eddied in her chest. But Yrene said nothing—had no answer.

Returning to the northern continent . . . She knew there was no one and nothing left there for her. Nothing but unforgiving war, and those who would need her help.

She did not even know where to *go*—where to sail, how to find those armies and their wounded. She'd traveled far and wide before, had evaded

enemies bent on slaughtering her, and the thought of doing it all again . . .
She knew some would think her mad. Ungrateful for the offer Hafiza
had laid before her. She'd thought those things of herself for a long while
now.

Yet not a single day passed without Yrene gazing toward the sea at the
foot of the city—gazing northward.

Yrene's attention indeed slid from the Healer on High to the windows
behind her, to the distant, darkening horizon, as if it were a lodestone.

Hafiza said, a shade more gently, "There is no rush to decide. Wars
take a long time."

"But I will need—"

"There is a task I would first have you do, Yrene."

Yrene stilled at that tone, the hint of command in it.

She glanced to the letter Hafiza had been reading when she'd entered.
"What is it?"

"There is a guest at the palace—a special guest of the khagan. I would
ask you to treat him. Before you decide whether now is the right time to
leave these shores, or if it is better to remain."

Yrene angled her head. Rare—very rare for Hafiza to pass off a task
from the khagan to someone else. "What is his ailment?" Common, standard words for healers receiving cases.

"He is a young man, age twenty-three. Healthy in every regard, in fit
condition. But he suffered a grave injury to his spine earlier this summer
that left him paralyzed from the hips downward. He cannot feel or move
his legs, and has been in a wheeled chair since. I am bypassing the initial
physicians' examination to appeal directly to you."

Yrene's mind churned. A complex, long process to heal that manner of
injury. Spines were nearly as difficult as brains. Connected to them quite
closely. With that sort of healing, it wasn't a matter of letting her magic
wash over them—that wasn't how it worked.

It was finding the right places and channels, in finding the correct
amount of magic to wield. It was getting the brain to again send signals

to the spine, down those broken pathways; it was replacing the damaged, smallest kernels of life within the body with new, fresh ones. And on top of it . . . learning to walk again. Weeks. *Months*, perhaps.

"He is an active young man," Hafiza said. "The injury is akin to the warrior you aided last winter on the steppes."

She'd guessed as much already—it was likely why she'd been asked. Two months spent healing the horse-lord who'd taken a bad fall off his mount and injured his spine. It was not an uncommon injury among the Darghan, some of whom rode horses and some of whom soared on ruks, and they had long relied on the Torre's healers. Working on the warrior had been her first time putting her lessons on the subject into effect, precisely why Hafiza had accompanied her to the steppes. Yrene was fairly confident she could do another healing on her own this time, but it was the way Hafiza glanced down at the letter—just once—that made Yrene pause. Made her ask, "Who is he?"

"Lord Chaol Westfall." Not a name from the khaganate. Hafiza added, holding Yrene's gaze, "He was the former Captain of the Guard and is now Hand to the new King of Adarlan."

Silence.

Yrene was silent, in her head, her heart. Only the crying of the gulls sailing above the Torre and the shouts of vendors going home for the night in the streets beyond the compound's high walls filled the tower room.

"No."

The word pushed out of Yrene on a breath.

Hafiza's slim mouth tightened.

"No," Yrene said again. "I will not heal him."

There was no softness, nothing motherly in Hafiza's face, as she said, "You took an oath upon entering these halls."

"No." It was all she could think to say.

"I am well aware how difficult it may be for you—"

Her hands started shaking. "No."

"Why?"

47

"You know why." The words were a strangled whisper. "Y-y-you know."

"If you see Adarlanian soldiers suffering on those battlefields, will you stomp right over them?"

It was the cruelest Hafiza had ever been to her.

Yrene rubbed the ring on her finger. "If he was Captain of the Guard for the last king, he—he worked for the man who—" The words spilled and stumbled out. "He took *orders* from him."

"And now works for Dorian Havilliard."

"Who indulged in his father's riches—the riches of *my* people. Even if Dorian Havilliard did not participate, the fact that he stood *back* while it happened . . ." The pale stone walls pressed in, even the solid tower beneath them feeling unwieldy. "Do you know what the king's men *did* these years? What his armies, his soldiers, his guards *did*? And you ask me to heal a man who commanded them?"

"It is a reality of who you are—who *we* are. A choice all healers must make."

"And you have made it so often? In your peaceful kingdom?"

Hafiza's face darkened. Not with ire, but memory. "I was once asked to heal a man who was injured while evading capture. After he had committed a crime so unspeakable . . . The guards told me what he'd done before I walked into his cell. They wanted him patched up so he could live to be put on trial. He'd undoubtedly be executed—they had victims willing to testify and proof aplenty. Eretia herself saw the latest victim. His last one. Gathered all the evidence she needed and stood in that court and condemned him with what she had seen." Hafiza's throat bobbed. "They chained him down in that cell, and he was hurt enough that I knew . . . I knew I could use my magic to make the internal bleeding worse. They'd never know. He'd be dead by morning, and no one would dare question me." She studied the vial of blue tonic. "It was the closest I have ever come to killing. I *wanted* to kill him for what he had done. The world would be better for it. I had my hands on his chest—I was ready to do it. But I remembered. I remembered that oath I had taken, and

48

remembered that they had asked me to heal him so that he would live—so that justice might be found for his victims. And their families." She met Yrene's eyes. "It was not my death to dole out."

"What happened?" The words were a wobble.

"He tried to plead innocent. Even with what Eretia presented, with what that victim was willing to talk about. He was a monster through and through. They convicted him, and he was executed at sunrise the next day."

"Did you watch it?"

"I did not. I came back up here. But Eretia did. She stood at the front of the crowd and stayed until they hauled his corpse into a cart. She stayed for the victims who could not bear to watch. Then she returned here, and we both cried for a long, long while."

Yrene was quiet for a few breaths, enough that her hands steadied. "So I am to heal this man—so he may find justice elsewhere?"

"You do not know his story, Yrene. I suggest listening to it before contemplating such things."

Yrene shook her head. "There will be no justice for him—not if he served the old and new king. Not if he's cunning enough to remain in power. I know how Adarlan works."

Hafiza watched her for a long moment. "The day you walked into this room, so terribly thin and covered with the dust of a hundred roads . . . I had never sensed such a gift. I looked into those beautiful eyes of yours, and I nearly gasped at the uncut power in you."

Disappointment. It was disappointment on the Healer on High's face, in her voice.

"I thought to myself," Hafiza went on, *"Where has this young woman been hiding? What god reared you, guided you to my doorstep?* Your dress was in tatters around your ankles, and yet you walked in, straight-backed as any noble lady. As if you were the heir to Kamala herself."

Until Yrene had dumped the money on the desk and fallen apart moments later. She doubted the very first Healer on High had ever done such a thing.

"Even your family name: *Towers*. A hint at your foremothers' long-ago association with the Torre, perhaps. I wondered in that moment if I had at last found *my* heir—my replacement."

Yrene felt the words like a blow to the gut. Hafiza had never so much as hinted . . .

Stay, the Healer on High had offered. To not only continue the training, but to also take up the mantle now laid before her.

But it had not been Yrene's own ambition, to one day claim this room as her own. Not when her sights had always been set across the Narrow Sea. And even now . . . it was an honor beyond words, yes. But one that rang hollow.

"I asked what you wanted to do with the knowledge I would give you," Hafiza went on. "Do you remember what you said to me?"

Yrene did. She had not forgotten it for a moment. "I said I wanted to use it to do some good for the world. To do something with my useless, wasted life."

The words had guided her these years—along with the note she carried every day, moving it from pocket to pocket, dress to dress. Words from a mysterious stranger, perhaps a god who had worn the skin of a battered young woman, whose gift of gold had gotten her here. Saved her.

"And so you shall, Yrene," Hafiza said. "You shall one day return home, and you shall do good, you shall do *wonders*. But before you do, I would ask this of you. Help that young man. You have done the healing before—you can do it again now."

"Why can't you?"

She'd never sounded so sullen, so . . . ungrateful.

Hafiza gave her a small, sad smile. "It is not my own healing that is needed."

Yrene knew the Healer on High did not mean the man's healing, either. She swallowed against the thickness in her throat.

"It is a soul-wound, Yrene. And letting it fester these years . . . I cannot blame you. But I will hold you accountable if you let it turn into something worse. And I will mourn you for it."

Yrene's lips wobbled, but she pressed them together, blinking back the burning in her eyes.

"You passed the tests, better than anyone who has ever climbed into this tower," Hafiza said softly. "But let this be my personal test for you. The final one. So that when you decide to go, I may bid you farewell, send you off to war, and know . . ." Hafiza put a hand on her chest. "Know that wherever the road takes you, however dark, you will be all right."

Yrene swallowed the small sound that tried to come out of her and instead looked toward the city, its pale stones resplendent in the last light of the setting sun. Through the open windows behind the Healer on High, a night breeze laced with lavender and cloves flitted in, cooling her face and ruffling Hafiza's cloud of white hair.

Yrene slid a hand into the pocket of her pale blue dress, her fingers wrapping around the familiar smoothness of the folded piece of parchment. She clutched it, as she had often done on the sailing over here, during those initial few weeks of uncertainty even after Hafiza had admitted her, during the long hours and hard days and moments that had nearly broken her while she trained.

A note, written by a stranger who had saved her life and granted her freedom in a matter of hours. Yrene had never learned her name, that young woman who had worn her scars like some ladies wore their finest jewelry. The young woman who was a trained killer, but had purchased a healer's education.

So many things, so many good things, had come from that night. Yrene sometimes wondered if it had actually happened—might have believed she'd dreamed it if not for the note in her pocket, and the second object Yrene had never sold, even when the gold had thinned.

The ornate gold-and-ruby brooch, worth more than entire blocks of Antica.

Adarlan's colors. Yrene had never learned where the young woman had come from, who had bestowed the beating that had left lingering bruises on her pretty face, but she had spoken of Adarlan as Yrene did. As all the children who had lost everything to Adarlan did—those children with their kingdoms left in ash and blood and ruin.

Yrene ran a thumb over the note, the words inked there:

For wherever you need to go—and then some. The world needs more healers.

Yrene breathed in that first night breeze, the spices and brine it ushered into the Torre.

She looked back to Hafiza at last, the Healer on High's face calm. Patient.

Yrene would regret it, if she refused. Hafiza would yield, but Yrene knew that whether she left here, whether she somehow decided to remain, she would . . . regret. Think back on this. Wonder if she had repaid the extraordinary kindness she'd been given rather poorly. Wonder what her mother would have thought of it.

And even if this man hailed from Adarlan, even if he'd done the bidding of that butcher . . .

"I will meet with him. Assess him," Yrene conceded. Her voice only wobbled slightly. She clutched that piece of paper in her pocket. "And then decide if I will heal him."

Hafiza considered. "Fair enough, girl," she said quietly. "Fair enough."

Yrene blew out a shaking breath. "When do I see him?"

"Tomorrow," Hafiza said, and Yrene winced. "The khagan has asked you to come to Lord Westfall's chambers tomorrow."

⇥ 5 ⇤

Chaol had barely slept. Partially due to the unrelenting heat, partially due to the fact that they were in a tentative ally's fraught household, full of potential spies and unknown dangers—perhaps even from Morath itself—and partially due to what had befallen Rifthold and all he held dear.

And partially due to the meeting that he was now minutes away from having.

Nesryn paced with uncharacteristic nerves through the sitting room that was to be his sickroom. Low-lying couches and clusters of cushions filled the space, the shining floors interrupted only by rugs of thickest and finest weaving—from the skilled hands of craftswomen in the west, Nesryn told him. Art and treasures from across the khagan's empire adorned the space, interspersed with potted palms sagging in the heat and sunlight trickling through the garden windows and doors.

Ten in the morning, the khagan's eldest daughter had declared to him at dinner last night. Princess Hasar—plain and yet fierce-eyed. A lovely young woman had sat at her side, the only person at whom Hasar smiled. Her lover or wife, judging by the frequent touching and long looks.

There had been enough of an edge to Hasar's wicked grin as she told Chaol when the healer would arrive that he'd been left to wonder who, precisely, they were sending.

He still did not know what to make of these people, this place. This city of high learning, this blend of so many cultures and history, peacefully dwelling together . . . Not at all like the raging and broken spirits dwelling in Adarlan's shadow, living in terror, distrusting one another, enduring its worst crimes.

They'd asked him about the butchering of the slaves in Calaculla and Endovier at dinner.

Or the oily one, Arghun, did. Had the prince been among Chaol's new recruits to the royal guard, he would have easily gotten him to fall in line thanks to a few well-timed shows of skill and sheer dominance. But here, he had no authority to bring the conniving, haughty prince to heel.

Not even when Arghun wanted to know why the former King of Adarlan had deemed it necessary to enslave his people. And then put them down like animals. Why the man had not looked to the southern continent for education on the horrors and stain of slavery—and avoided instituting it.

Chaol had offered curt answers that verged on impolite. Sartaq, the only one of them beyond Kashin whom Chaol was inclined to like, had finally tired of his elder brother's questioning and steered the conversation away. To what, Chaol had no idea. He'd been too busy fighting against the roaring in his ears over Arghun's razor-sharp inquiries. And then too busy monitoring every face—royal, vizier, or servant—who made an appearance in the khagan's great hall. No signs of black rings or collars; no strange behavior to remark on.

He'd given Kashin a subtle shake of his head at one point to tell him as much. The prince had pretended not to see, but the warning flared in his eyes: *Keep looking*.

So Chaol had, half paying attention to the meal unfolding before him, half monitoring every word and glance and breath of those around him.

Despite their youngest sister's death, the heirs made the meal lively, conversation flowing, mostly in languages Chaol did not know or recognize. Such a wealth of kingdoms in that hall, represented by viziers and servants and companions—the now-youngest princess, Duva, herself wedded to a dark-haired, sad-eyed prince from a faraway land who kept close to his pregnant wife and spoke little to anyone around him. But whenever Duva smiled softly at him . . . Chaol did not think the light that filled the prince's face was feigned. And wondered if the man's silence was not from reticence but perhaps not yet knowing enough of his wife's language to keep up.

Nesryn, however, had no such excuse. She'd been silent and haunted at dinner. He'd only learned that she'd bathed before it thanks to the shout and slamming door in her chambers, followed by a huffy-looking male servant scrambling out of her rooms. The man did not come back again, nor did a replacement arrive.

Kadja, the servant assigned to Chaol, had helped him dress for dinner, then undress for bed, and had brought breakfast this morning immediately upon his awakening.

The khagan certainly knew how to eat well.

Exquisitely spiced and simmered meats, so tender they fell right off the bone; herbed rice of various colors; flatbreads coated in butter and garlic; rich wines and liquors from the vineyards and distilleries across his empire. Chaol had passed on the latter, accepting only the ceremonial glass offered before the khagan made a half-hearted toast to his new guests. For a grieving father, it was a warmer welcome than Chaol had expected.

Yet Nesryn had a sip of her drink, barely a bite of her meal, and waited a scant minute until the feast was cleared before asking to return to their suite. He'd agreed—of course he'd agreed, but when they'd closed the suite doors and he'd asked if she wanted to talk, she had said no. She wanted to sleep and would see him in the morning.

He'd had the nerve to ask Nesryn if she wanted to share his room or hers. The shutting of her door was emphasis enough.

So Kadja had helped him into bed, and he had tossed and turned, sweating and wishing he could kick off the sheets instead of having to throw them back. Even the cool breeze that drifted in through the cleverly crafted ventilation system—the air hauled from wind-snaring towers amid the domes and spires to be cooled by canals beneath the palace, then scattered amongst the rooms and halls—had not offered any reprieve.

He and Nesryn had never been good at talking. They'd tried, usually with disastrous results.

They'd done everything out of order, and he'd cursed himself again and again for not making it right with her. Not trying to *be* better.

She'd barely looked at him these past ten minutes they'd been waiting for the healer to arrive. Her face was haggard, her shoulder-length hair limp. She hadn't put on her captain's uniform, but rather returned to her usual midnight-blue tunic and black pants. As if she couldn't stand to be in Adarlan's colors.

Kadja had dressed him again in his teal jacket, even going so far as to polish the buckles down the front. There was a quiet pride to her work, not at all like the timidity and fear of so many of the castle servants in Rifthold.

"She's late," Nesryn murmured. Indeed, the ornate wooden clock in the corner announced the healer was ten minutes late. "Should we call for someone to find out if she's coming?"

"Give her time."

Nesryn paused before him, frowning deeply. "We need to begin immediately. There is no time to waste."

Chaol took a breath. "I understand that you want to return home to your family—"

"I will not rush you. But even a day makes a difference."

56

He noted the lines of strain bracketing her mouth. He had no doubt twin ones marked his own. Forcing himself to stop contemplating and dreading where Dorian might now be had been an effort of pure will this morning. "Once the healer arrives, why don't you go track down your kin in the city? Perhaps they've heard from your family in Rifthold."

A slicing wave of her slender hand. "I can wait until you're done."

Chaol lifted his brows. "And pace the entire time?"

Nesryn sank onto the nearest sofa, the gold silk sighing beneath her slight weight. "I came here to help you—with this, and with our cause. I won't run off for my own needs."

"What if I give you an order?"

She only shook her head, her dark curtain of hair swaying with the movement.

And before he could give that exact order, a brisk knock thudded on the heavy wood door.

Nesryn shouted a word that he assumed meant *enter* in Halha, and he listened to the footsteps as they approached. One set—quiet and light.

The door to the sitting room drifted open beneath the press of a honey-colored hand.

It was her eyes that Chaol noticed first.

She likely stopped people dead in the street with those eyes, a vibrant golden brown that seemed lit from within. Her hair was a heavy fall of rich browns amid flashes of dark gold, curling slightly at the ends that brushed her narrow waist.

She moved with a nimble grace, her feet—clad in practical black slippers—swift and unfaltering as she crossed the room, either not noticing or caring about the ornate furnishings.

Young, perhaps a year or two older than twenty.

But those eyes . . . they were far older than that.

She paused at the carved wooden chair across from the golden couch, Nesryn shooting to her feet. The healer—for there was no one else she could be, with that calm grace, those clear eyes, and that simple, pale blue muslin

57

dress—glanced between them. She was a few inches shorter than Nesryn, built with similar delicacy, yet despite her slender frame . . . He didn't look long at the other features the healer had been generously blessed with.

"Are you from the Torre Cesme?" Nesryn asked in Chaol's own tongue.

The healer only stared at him. Something like surprise and anger lighting those remarkable eyes.

She slid a hand into the pocket of her gown, and he waited for her to withdraw something, but it remained there. As if she was grasping an object within.

Not a doe ready to bolt, but a stag, weighing the options of fighting or fleeing, of standing its ground, lowering its head, and charging.

Chaol held her gaze, cool and steady. He'd taken on plenty of young bucks during the years of being captain—had gotten them all to heel.

Nesryn asked something in Halha, no doubt a repeat of her question.

A thin scar sliced across the healer's throat. Perhaps three inches long.

He knew what sort of weapon had given that scar. All the possibilities that burst into his head for why it might have happened were not pleasant ones.

Nesryn fell silent, watching them.

The healer only turned on her heel, walked to the desk near the windows, took a seat, and pulled a piece of parchment toward her from the neat stack in the corner.

Whoever these healers were, the khagan was right: they certainly did not answer to his throne. Or find it in themselves to be impressed with any manner of nobility and power.

She opened a drawer, found a glass pen, and held it poised over the paper.

"Name."

She did not have an accent—or, rather, the accent of these lands.

"Chaol Westfall."

"Age."

The accent. It was from—

58

"Fenharrow."

Her pen stalled. "Age."

"You're from Fenharrow?"

What are you doing here, so far from home?

She leveled a cool, unimpressed stare at him.

He swallowed and said, "Twenty-three."

She scribbled something down. "Describe where the injury begins."

Each word was clipped, her voice low.

Had it been an insult to be assigned his case? Had she other things to do when she was summoned here? He thought again of Hasar's wicked smile the night before. Perhaps the princess knew that this woman was not praised for her bedside manner.

"What is your name?"

The question came from Nesryn, whose face was beginning to tighten.

The healer stilled as she took in Nesryn, blinking like she had not really noticed her. "You—are from here?"

"My father was," Nesryn said. "He moved to Adarlan, wed my mother, and I now have family there—and here." She impressively hid any trace of dread at the mention of them as she added coaxingly, "My name is Nesryn Faliq. I am the Captain of the Royal Guard of Adarlan."

That surprise in the healer's eyes turned wary. But she again gazed at him.

She knew who he was. The look conveyed it—the analysis. She knew he'd once held that title, and now was something else. So the name, the age . . . the questions were bullshit. Or some bureaucratic nonsense. He doubted it was the latter.

A woman from Fenharrow, meeting with two members from Adarlan's court . . .

It didn't take much to read her. What she saw. Where that mark on her throat might have come from.

"If you don't want to be here," Chaol said roughly, "then send someone else."

Nesryn whirled on him.

The healer only held his stare. "There is no one else to do this." The unspoken words said the rest: *They sent their best.*

With that steady, self-assured posture, he didn't doubt it. She angled her pen again. "Describe where the injury begins."

A sharp knock on the sitting room door cut through the silence. He started, cursing himself for not having heard the approach.

But it was Princess Hasar, clad in green and gold and smirking like a cat. "Good morning, Lord Westfall. Captain Faliq." Her braided hair swaying with each swaggering step, Hasar strolled over to the healer, who looked up at her with an expression Chaol dared call exasperation, and leaned down to kiss her on either cheek. "You're not usually so grumpy, Yrene."

There—a name.

"I forgot my *kahve* this morning." The thick, spiced, bitter drink Chaol had choked down with his breakfast. An acquired taste, Nesryn had said when he'd asked about it later.

The princess took up a perch along the edge of the desk. "You didn't come to dinner last night. Kashin was sulking about it."

Yrene's shoulders tightened. "I had to prepare."

"Yrene Towers locking herself in the Torre to work? I might die of shock."

From the princess's tone, he filled in enough. The best healer in the Torre Cesme had become so thanks to that grueling work ethic.

Hasar looked him over. "Still in the chair?"

"Healing takes time," Yrene said mildly to the princess. Not an ounce of subservience or respect to the tone. "We were just beginning."

"So you agreed to do it, then?"

Yrene cut the princess a sharp glare. "We were assessing the lord's needs." She jerked her chin toward the doors. "Shall I find you when I'm done?"

Nesryn gave Chaol an impressed, wary glance. A healer dismissing a princess of the most powerful empire in the world.

Hasar leaned forward to ruffle Yrene's gold-brown hair. "If you weren't gods-blessed, I'd carve out your tongue myself." The words were honeyed venom. Yrene only offered a faint, bemused smile before Hasar hopped off the desk and gave him a mocking incline of the head. "Don't worry, Lord Westfall. Yrene has healed injuries similar and far worse than your own. She'll have you back on your feet and able to do your master's bidding again in no time." With that lovely parting shot, which left Nesryn cold-eyed, the princess vanished.

They waited a good few moments to make sure they heard the outer door shut.

"Yrene Towers," was all Chaol said.

"What of it."

Gone was the faint amusement. Fine.

"The lack of feeling and movement begins at my hips."

Yrene's eyes shot right to them, dancing over him. "Are you capable of using your manhood?"

He tried not to flinch. Even Nesryn blinked at the frank question.

"Yes," he said tightly, fighting the heat rising in his cheeks.

She looked between them, assessing. "Have you used it to completion?"

He clenched his jaw. "How is that relevant?" And how had she gleaned what was between them?

Yrene only wrote something down.

"What are you writing?" he demanded, cursing the damned chair for keeping him from storming to rip the paper out of her hands.

"I'm writing a giant *no*."

Which she then underlined.

He growled, "I suppose you'll ask about my bathroom habits now?"

"It was next on my list."

"They are unchanged," he bit out. "Unless you need Nesryn to confirm."

Yrene merely turned to Nesryn, unruffled. "Have you seen him struggle with it?"

"Do *not* answer that," he snarled at Nesryn.

Nesryn had the good wits to sink into a chair and remain quiet.

Yrene rose, setting down the pen, and came around the desk. The morning sunlight caught in her hair, bouncing off her head in a corona.

She knelt at his feet. "Shall you remove your boots or shall I?"

"I'll do it."

She sat back on her heels and watched him move. Another test. To discern how mobile and agile he was. The weight of his legs, having to constantly adjust their position . . . Chaol gritted his teeth as he gripped his knee, lifting his foot off the wooden slat, and bent to remove his boot in a few sharp tugs. When he finished with the other one, he asked, "Pants, too?"

Chaol knew he should be kind, should beseech her to help him, and yet—

"After a drink or two, I think," Yrene only said. Then looked over her shoulder to a bemused Nesryn. "Sorry," she added—and sounded only slightly less sharp-tongued.

"Why are you apologizing to her?"

"I assume she has the misfortune of sharing your bed these days."

It took his self-restraint to keep from going for her shoulders and shaking her soundly. "Have I *done* something to you?"

That seemed to give her pause. Yrene only yanked off his socks, throwing them atop where he'd discarded his boots. "No."

A lie. He scented and tasted it.

But it focused her, and Chaol watched as Yrene picked up his foot in her slim hands. Watched, since he didn't feel it—beyond the shift in his abdominal muscles. He couldn't tell if she was squeezing or holding lightly, if her nails were digging in; not without looking. So he did.

A ring adorned her fourth finger—a wedding band. "Is your husband from here?" Or wife, he supposed.

"I'm not—" She blinked, frowning at the ring. She didn't finish the sentence.

Not married, then. The silver ring was simple, the garnet no more than a droplet. Likely worn to keep men from bothering her, as he'd seen many women do in the streets of Rifthold.

"Can you feel this?" Yrene asked. She was touching each toe.

"No."

She did it on the other foot. "And this?"

"No."

He'd been through such examinations before—at the castle, and with Rowan.

"His initial injury," Nesryn cut in, as if remembering the prince as well, "was to the entire spine. A friend had some knowledge of healing and patched him up as best he could. He regained movement in his upper body, but not below the hips."

"How was it attained—the injury?"

Her hands were moving over his foot and ankle, tapping and testing. As if she'd indeed done this before, as Princess Hasar had claimed.

Chaol didn't immediately reply, sorting through those moments of terror and pain and rage.

Nesryn opened her mouth, but he cut her off. "Fighting. I received a blow to my back while fighting. A magical one."

Yrene's fingers were inching up his legs, patting and squeezing. He felt none of it. Her brows bunched in concentration. "Your friend must have been a gifted healer if you regained so much motion."

"He did what he could. Then told me to come here."

Her hands pushed and pressed on his thighs, and he watched with no small amount of growing horror as she slid them higher and higher. He was about to demand if she planned to ascertain for herself about the life in his *manhood*, but Yrene lifted her head and met his stare.

This close, her eyes were a golden flame. Not like the cold metal of Manon Blackbeak's, not laced with a century of violence and predator's instincts, but . . . like a long-burning flame on a winter's night. "I need to see your back," was all Yrene said. Then she peeled away. "Lie down on the nearest bed."

Before Chaol could remind her that it wasn't quite so easy to do that, Nesryn was instantly in motion, wheeling him into his room. Kadja had already made his bed, and left a bouquet of orange lilies on the table beside it. Yrene sniffed at the scent—as if it was unpleasant. He refrained from asking.

He waved off Nesryn when she tried to help him onto the bed. It was low enough that he could manage.

Yrene lingered in the doorway, observing while he braced one hand on the mattress, one on the arm of the chair, and in a powerful push, heaved himself into a sitting position on the bed. He unbuckled each of those newly polished buttons on his jacket, then peeled it off. Along with the white shirt beneath.

"Facedown, I assume?"

Yrene gave him a curt nod.

Gripping his knees, abdomen clenching, he pulled his legs onto the mattress as he lay flat on his back.

For a few heartbeats, spasms shook his legs. Not real, controlled motion, he'd realized after the first time it had happened weeks ago. He could still feel that crushing weight in his chest after he'd understood it was some effect of the injury—that it usually happened if he moved himself about a great deal.

"Spasms in the legs are common with such an injury," Yrene supplied, observing them fade away into stillness once again. "These may calm with time." She waved a hand to him in silent reminder to turn over onto his belly.

Chaol said nothing as he sat up to fold one ankle over the other, lay down again on his back, and then twisted over, his legs following suit.

Whether she was impressed that he'd picked up on the maneuverings so quickly, she didn't let on. Didn't even lift a brow.

Folding his hands under his chin, he peered over his shoulder and watched her approach, watched her motion Nesryn to sit when the woman began pacing again.

He scanned Yrene for any sort of flickering magic. What it'd look like,

64

he had not the faintest inkling. Dorian's had been ice and wind and flashing light; Aelin's had been raging, singing flame, but healing magic . . . Was it something external, something tangible? Or something only his bones and blood might witness?

He'd once balked at those sorts of questions—might once have even balked at the idea of letting magic touch him. But the man who had done those things, feared those things . . . He was glad to leave him in the shattered ruin of the glass castle.

Yrene stood over him for a moment, surveying his back.

Her hands were as warm as the morning sun when she laid them palm-down on the skin between his shoulder blades. "You were hit here," she observed quietly.

There was a mark. A faint, splattering paleness to his skin where the king's blow had hit. Dorian had shown him using a trick with two hand-mirrors before he'd left.

"Yes."

Her hands trailed along the groove of his spine. "It rippled down here, shredding and severing." The words were not for him—but as if she were speaking to herself, lost in some trance.

He fought against the memory of that pain, the numbness and oblivion it summoned.

"You can—tell that?" Nesryn asked.

"My gift tells me." Yrene's hand stalled along the middle of his back, pushing and prodding. "It was terrible power—what struck you."

"Yes," was all he said.

Her hands went lower, lower, until they shoved down the waist of his pants a few inches. He hissed through his teeth and glared over his bare shoulder. "A little warning."

Yrene ignored him and touched the lowest part of his back. He did not feel it.

She spider-walked her fingers up his spine as if counting the vertebrae. "Here?"

"I can feel you."

She backtracked one step. "Here?"

"Nothing."

Her face bunched, as if making a mental note of the location. She began on the outer edges of his back, creeping up, asking where he stopped feeling it. She took his neck and head in her hands, turning it this way and that, testing and assessing.

Finally, she ordered him to move. Not to rise, but to turn over again.

Chaol stared up at the arched, painted ceiling as Yrene poked and prodded his pectorals, the muscles of his abdomen, those along his ribs. She reached the vee of muscles leading beneath his pants, kept moving lower, and he demanded, "Really?"

Yrene shot him an incredulous look. "Is there something you're particularly embarrassed for me to see?"

Oh, she certainly had some fight in her, this Yrene Towers from Fenharrow. Chaol held her stare, the challenge in it.

Yrene only snorted. "I had forgotten that men from the northern continent are so proper and guarded."

"And here they are not?"

"No. Bodies are celebrated, not shamed into hiding. Men and women both."

That would explain the servant who had no qualms about such things.

"They seemed plenty dressed at dinner."

"Wait until the parties," Yrene countered coolly. But she lifted her hands from the already-low waist of his pants. "If you have not noticed any problems externally or internally with your manhood, then I don't need to look."

He shoved against the feeling that he was again thirteen years old and trying to talk to a pretty girl for the first time and ground out, "Fine."

Yrene withdrew a step and handed him his shirt. He sat up, arms and abdominal muscles straining, and slid it on.

"Well?" Nesryn asked, stalking close.

Yrene toyed with a heavy, loose curl. "I need to think. Talk to my superior."

"I thought you were the best," Nesryn said carefully.

"I am one of many who are skilled," Yrene admitted. "But the Healer on High assigned me to this. I should like to speak to her first."

"Is it bad?" Nesryn demanded. He was grateful she did—he didn't have the nerve to.

Yrene only looked to him, her gaze frank and unafraid. "You know it is bad."

"But can you help him?" Nesryn pushed, sharper this time.

"I have healed such injuries before. But this . . . it remains to be seen," Yrene said, meeting her gaze now.

"When—when will you know?"

"When I have had time to think."

To decide, Chaol realized. She wanted to *decide* whether to help him.

He held Yrene's stare again, letting her see that he, at least, understood. He was glad Nesryn had not entertained the idea. He had a feeling Yrene would be face-first against the wall if she did.

But for Nesryn . . . the healers were beyond reproach. Holy as one of the gods here. Their ethic unquestionable.

"When will you return?" Nesryn asked.

Never, he almost answered.

Yrene slid her hands into her pockets. "I'll send word," was all she said, and left.

Nesryn stared after her, then rubbed her face.

Chaol said nothing.

But Nesryn straightened, then dashed out—to the sitting room. Rustling paper, and then—

Nesryn halted in the doorway to his room, brows crossed, Yrene's paper in her hands.

She handed it to him. "What does this even mean?"

There were four names written on the paper, her handwriting messy.

Olgnia.

Marte.

Rosana.

Josefin.

It was the final name that had been written down several times.

The final name that had been underlined, over and over.

Josefin. Josefin. Josefin.

"Perhaps they're other healers in the Torre who could help," he lied. "Perhaps she feared spies overhearing her suggest someone else."

Nesryn's mouth quirked to the side. "Let's see what she says—when she returns. At least we know Hasar can track her down if need be." Or Kashin, whose very name had set the healer on edge. Not that he'd force Yrene to work on him, but . . . it was useful information.

Chaol studied the paper again. The fervent underlining of that final name.

As if Yrene had needed to remind herself while here. In his presence. As if she needed whoever they were to know that she remembered them.

He had met another talented young healer from Fenharrow. His king had loved her enough to consider fleeing with her, to seek a better life for them. Chaol knew what had gone on in Fenharrow during their youth. Knew what Sorscha had endured there—and what she'd endured in Rifthold.

He'd ridden through Fenharrow's scarred grasslands over the years. Had seen the burned or abandoned stone cottages, their thatched roofs long since gone. Owners either enslaved, dead, or fled elsewhere. Far, far away.

No, Chaol realized as he held that piece of paper, Yrene Towers would not be returning.

⊱ 6 ⊰

She'd known his age, but Yrene had still not expected the former captain to look so . . . young.

She hadn't done the math until she'd walked into that room and seen his handsome face, a mix of caution and hope written across the hardened, broad features.

It was that hope that had made her see red. Had made her ache to give him a matching scar to the slender one slicing across his cheek.

She'd been unprofessional in the most horrific sense. Never—*never* had she been so rude and unkind toward any of her patients.

Mercifully, Hasar had arrived, cooling her head slightly. But touching the man, thinking of ways to *help* him . . .

She had not meant to write the list of the last four generations of Towers women. Had not meant to write her mother's name over and over while pretending to record his information. It had not helped with the overwhelming roaring in her head.

Sweating and dusty, Yrene burst into Hafiza's office nearly an hour later, the trek from the palace through the clogged, narrow streets, then the endless steps up here, taking an eternity.

She'd been late—that had been her first truly unprofessional moment. She'd never been late to an appointment. Yet right at ten, she'd found herself in an alcove of the hallway outside his bedroom, hands over her face, struggling to breathe.

He hadn't been the brute she'd expected.

He'd spoken well, more lord than soldier. Though his body had most certainly belonged to the latter. She had patched up and healed enough of the khagan's favored warriors to know the feel of muscle beneath her fingers. The scars covering Lord Westfall's tan skin spoke volumes about how the muscles had been earned the hard way. And now aided him in maneuvering through the world with the chair.

And the injury to his spine . . .

As Yrene halted at the threshold of the Healer on High's office, Hafiza looked up from where she sat beside a sniffling acolyte.

"I need a word," Yrene said tightly, one hand gripping the doorjamb.

"You shall have one when we are done," Hafiza simply replied, handing a handkerchief to the weepy girl.

Some male healers existed, but the majority of those who received Silba's gift were female. And this girl, likely no more than fourteen . . . Yrene had been laboring on her cousin's farm at that age. *Dreaming* of being here. Certainly not crying to anyone about her sorry lot in life.

But Yrene walked out, shutting the door behind her, and waited against the wall on the narrow landing.

There were two other doors up here: one locked that led into Hafiza's personal workshop, and a door that led into the Healer on High's bedroom; the former carved with an owl taking flight, the latter with an owl at rest. Silba's symbol. It was everywhere in the tower—owls carved and embossed in the stone and wood, sometimes in unexpected places and with silly little expressions, as if some long-ago acolyte had etched them as a secret joke. But the owl on the Healer on High's private workshop . . .

Even though it perched atop a gnarled branch of iron that flowed across the door itself, wings flared wide as it prepared to leap into the skies, it seemed . . . alert. Aware of all who passed that door, who perhaps gazed too long in the direction of the workshop. None but Hafiza possessed the key to it, handed down by her predecessor. Ancient, half-forgotten knowledge and devices lay within, the acolytes whispered—unnatural things that were better locked up than set loose in the world.

Yrene always laughed at their hushed words, but didn't tell them she and a few select others had been granted the pleasure of joining Hafiza in that workshop, which, save for the sheer *age* of some of the tools and furniture, held nothing worth gossiping about. But the mystery of the Healer on High's workshop persisted, as it had likely done for centuries—yet another well-loved myth of the Torre, passed on from acolyte to acolyte.

Yrene fanned her face, still out of breath from the climb and the heat. She leaned her head back against the cool stone, and again felt for the scrap of paper in her pocket. She wondered if the lord had noticed how often she'd grabbed that stranger's note. If he'd thought she was reaching for a weapon. He'd seen everything, been aware of her every breath.

A man trained for it. He had to be, if he'd served the dead king. Just as Nesryn Faliq, a child of this continent, now served the king of a territory that had not treated outsiders very well at all.

Yrene could not make sense of it. There was some romantic bond, she knew from both the tension and comfort between them. But to what degree . . . It didn't matter. Save for the emotional healing the lord would need as well. A man not used to voicing his feelings, his fears and hopes and hurts—that much was obvious.

The door to Hafiza's office opened at last, and the acolyte emerged, smiling apologetically at Yrene, red-nosed and glassy-eyed.

Yrene sighed through her nose and offered a smile back. She was not the person who had just barged into the office. No, even busy as she was, Yrene had always taken time for the acolytes, the homesick ones especially.

71

No one had sat beside her in the mess hall below during those initial days.

Yrene still remembered those lonely meals. Remembered that she'd broken after two days and began taking her food to the vast healers' library belowground, hiding from the stiff-backed librarians who forbade such things, with only the occasional mercurial Baast Cat and carved owl for company.

Yrene had returned to the mess hall once her lessons had garnered enough acquaintances to make the prospect of finding a place to sit less daunting, spotting familiar and smiling faces giving her enough courage to leave the library and its enigmatic cats behind for anything but research.

Yrene touched the acolyte on the shoulder and whispered, "Cook made almond cookies this morning. I smelled them on the way out. Tell her I want six, but take four of those for yourself." She winked at the girl. "Leave the other two for me at my room."

The girl beamed, nodding. Cook was perhaps Yrene's first friend in the Torre. She'd spied Yrene eating alone and began sneaking extra treats onto her tray. Leaving them in her room. Even in her favorite secret spot in the library. Yrene had repaid Cook last year by saving her granddaughter from an insidious lung sickness that had crept up on her. Cook still got weepy whenever they ran into each other, and Yrene had made it a point to stop by the girl's house once a month to check on her.

When she left, she'd have to ask someone to look after the girl. Cleaving herself from this life she'd built . . . It would be no easy task. And come with no small amount of guilt.

Yrene watched the still-sniffling acolyte hop down the wide spiral stairs, then took a deep breath and strode into Hafiza's office.

"Will the young lord walk again?" Hafiza asked by way of greeting, white brows high on her forehead.

Yrene slid into her usual chair, the seat still warm from the girl who'd just vacated it.

"He will. The injury is nearly twin to the one I healed last winter. But it will be tricky."

"In regard to the healing, or you?"

Yrene blushed. "I behaved . . . poorly."

"That was to be expected."

Yrene wiped the sweat from her brow. "I'm embarrassed to tell you how badly."

"Then don't. Do better the next time, and we'll consider this another lesson."

Yrene sagged in her chair, stretching her aching legs on the worn carpet. No matter how Hafiza's servants begged, she refused to change the red-and-green rug. It had been good enough for the last five of her predecessors, and it was good enough for her.

Yrene leaned her head against the soft back of the chair, staring at the cloudless day beyond the open windows. "I think I can heal him," she said, more to herself than Hafiza. "If he cooperates, I could get him walking again."

"And will he cooperate?"

"I was not the only one who behaved poorly," she said. "Though he's from Adarlan—it could be his nature."

Hafiza huffed a laugh. "When do you return to him?"

Yrene hesitated.

"You *will* return, won't you?" Hafiza pushed.

Yrene picked at the sun-blanched threads of the chair's arm. "It was hard—hard to look at him, hear his accent, and . . ." She stilled her hand. "But you are right. I shall . . . try. If only so Adarlan may never hold it against me."

"Do you expect them to?"

"He has powerful friends who might remember. His companion is the *new* Captain of the Guard. Her family hails from here, yet she serves them."

"And what does that tell you?"

Always a lesson, always a test. "It tells me . . ." Yrene blew out a breath. "It tells me I don't know as much as I assumed." She straightened. "But it also doesn't forgive them of any sins."

Yet she had met plenty of bad people in her life. Lived among them, served them, in Innish. She had taken one look at Lord Westfall's brown eyes and had known, deep down, he was not one of them. Neither was his companion.

And with his age . . . He had been a boy when so many of those atrocities had been committed. He still could have played some part, and plenty more had been done in recent years—enough to make her ill at the thought—but . . .

"The injury to his spine," Yrene said. "He claims some foul magic did it."

Her magic had recoiled against the splattered mark. Curved away.

"Oh?"

She shivered. "I've never . . . I've never felt *anything* like that. As if it was rotted, yet empty. Cold as the longest winter night."

"I shall have to take your word on that one."

Yrene snorted, grateful for the dry humor. Indeed, Hafiza had never so much as seen snow. With Antica's year-round warm climate, the closest they'd gotten to winter these two years was perhaps a crust of frost sparkling over the lavender and lemon trees one morning.

"It was . . ." Yrene brushed off the memory of the echo still held within that scar. "It was not any magic-wound I had encountered before."

"Will it impact the healing of his spine?"

"I don't know. I haven't tried to probe with my power yet, but . . . I'll let you know."

"I'm at your disposal."

"Even if this is my final test?"

"A good healer," Hafiza said with a smile, "knows when to ask for help."

Yrene nodded absently. And when she sailed back home, to war and bloodshed, who would she turn to then?

"I'll go back," Yrene said at last. "Tomorrow. I want to look into spinal injuries and paralysis in the library tonight."

"I'll let Cook know where to find you."

Yrene gave Hafiza a wry grin. "Nothing escapes you, does it?"

Hafiza's knowing look wasn't comforting.

The healer didn't return that day. Nesryn waited for another hour, then two, Chaol filling his time with reading in the sitting room, before she finally declared she was going to see her family.

It had been years since she'd seen her aunt and uncle and their children. She prayed they were still in the house where she'd last visited.

She'd barely slept. Had barely been able to think or feel things like hunger or exhaustion thanks to the thoughts wreaking havoc within her.

The healer with her lack of answers hadn't soothed her.

And with no formal meeting scheduled with the khagan or his children today . . .

"I can entertain myself, you know," Chaol said, setting his book on his lap as Nesryn again looked to the foyer door. "I'd join you, if I could."

"You soon will be able to," she promised. The healer had seemed skilled enough, despite her refusal to even give them a shred of hope.

If the woman couldn't help them, then Nesryn would find another. And another. Even if she had to beg the Healer on High to help.

"Go, Nesryn," Chaol ordered. "You'll get no peace until you do."

She rubbed her neck, then rose from her spot on the golden couch and strode over to him. Braced her hands on either arm of his chair, currently positioned by the open garden doors. She brought her face close to his, closer than it'd been in days. His own eyes seemed . . . brighter, somehow. A smidge better than yesterday. "I'll come back as soon as I can."

He gave her a quiet smile. "Take your time. See your family." He had not seen his mother or brother in years, he'd told her. His father . . . Chaol did not talk about his father.

75

"Perhaps," she said quietly, "we could get an answer for the healer."

He blinked at her.

She murmured, "About the completion."

That fast, the light winked out from his eyes.

She withdrew quickly. He'd stopped her on the boat, when she'd practically leaped atop him. And seeing him without his shirt earlier, those muscles rippling along his back, his stomach . . . She'd almost begged the healer to let *her* do the inspecting.

Pathetic. Though she'd never been particularly good at avoiding her *cravings*. She'd started sleeping with him that summer because she didn't see the point in resisting where her interest tugged her. Even if she hadn't cared for him, not as she did now.

Nesryn slid a hand through her hair. "I'll be back by dinner."

Chaol waved her off, and was already reading his book again when she left the room.

They had made no promises, she reminded herself. She knew his tendencies drove him to want to do right by her, to honor her, and this summer, when that castle had collapsed and she'd thought him dead . . . She had never known such fear. She had never prayed as she had in those moments—until Aelin's flame spared her from death, and Nesryn had prayed that she had spared him, too.

Nesryn shut out the thoughts of those days as she strode through the palace halls, vaguely remembering where to find the gates to the city proper. What she'd thought she wanted, what was most important—or had been. Until the khagan had uttered the news.

She had left her family. She should have been there. To protect the children, protect her aging father, her fierce and laughing sister.

"Captain Faliq."

Nesryn halted at the pleasant voice, at the title she was still barely accustomed to answering. She was standing at one of the palace crossroads, the path ahead to take her to the front gates if she kept going straight. She had marked every exit they'd passed on the way in.

And at the end of the hallway that bisected hers was Sartaq.

Gone were the fine clothes of yesterday. The prince now wore close-fitting leathers, the shoulders capped with simple yet sturdy armor, reinforced at the wrists, knees, and shins. No breastplate. His long black hair had been braided back, a thin strap of leather tying it off.

She bowed deeply. Lower than she would have for the other children of the khagan. But for a rumored Heir apparent, who might one day be Adarlan's ally—

If they survived.

"You were in a hurry," Sartaq said, noting the hall she'd been striding down.

"I—I have family in the city. I was going to see them." She added halfheartedly, "Unless Your Highness has need of me."

A wry smile graced his face. And she realized she'd replied in her own tongue. *Their* tongue. "I'm headed for a ride on Kadara. My ruk," he clarified, falling into his language as well.

"I know," she said. "I've heard the stories."

"Even in Adarlan?" He lifted a brow. A warrior and a charmer. A dangerous combination, though she could not recall any mention of a spouse. Indeed, no ring marked his finger.

"Even in Adarlan," Nesryn said, though she did not mention that the average person on the street might not know such tales. But in her household . . . Oh, yes. The Winged Prince, they called him.

"May I escort you? The streets are a maze, even to me."

It was a generous offer, an honor. "I would not keep you from the skies." If only because she did not know how to talk to such men—born and bred to power, used to fine ladies and scheming politicians. Though his ruk riders, legend claimed, could come from anywhere.

"Kadara is accustomed to waiting," Sartaq said. "At least let me lead you to the gates. There is a new guard out today, and I will tell them to mark your face so you may be let back in."

Because with her clothes, her unadorned hair . . . Indeed, the guards might not permit her past. Which would have been . . . mortifying. "Thank you," she said, and fell into step beside him.

They were silent as they passed white banners streaming from one of the open windows. Chaol had told her yesterday of Kashin's worry that their youngest sister's death had been through foul play—that one of Perrington's agents might be responsible. It was enough to plant a seed of dread in her. To make her mark each face she encountered, peer into every shadow.

Keeping a smooth pace beside him, Nesryn glanced at Sartaq as those banners flitted by. The prince, however, nodded to a few bowing men and women in the gold robes of viziers.

Nesryn found herself asking, "Are there truly thirty-six of them?"

"We have a fascination with the number, so yes." He snorted, the sound most un-princely. "My father debated halving them, but feared the gods' wrath more than political repercussions."

It felt like a breath of crisp autumn air, to hear and speak her own tongue. To have it be the norm and not be gawked at. She'd always felt so when coming here.

"Did Lord Westfall meet with the healer?"

There was no harm in the truth, she decided, so Nesryn said, "Yes. Yrene Towers."

"Ah. The famed Golden Lady."

"Oh?"

"She is striking, no?"

Nesryn smiled slightly. "You favor her, I see."

Sartaq chuckled. "Oh, I wouldn't dare. My brother Kashin would not be pleased."

"They have an attachment?" Hasar had hinted at as much.

"They are friends—or were. I haven't seen them talk in months, but who knows what happened? Though I suppose I'm no better than the court gossips for telling you."

"It's still useful to know, if we are working with her."

78

"Was her assessment of Lord Westfall a positive one?"

Nesryn shrugged. "She was hesitant to confirm."

"Many healers will do that. They don't like to give hope and take it away." He flicked his braid over a shoulder. "Though I will also tell you that Yrene herself healed one of Kashin's Darghan riders last winter of a very similar injury. And the healers have long repaired such wounds amongst our people's horse-tribes and my own rukhin. They will know what to do."

Nesryn swallowed the hope that blossomed as brightness flared ahead— the open doors to the main courtyard and palace gates. "How long have you been a ruk rider, Prince?"

"I thought you'd heard the stories." Humor danced in his face.

"Only gossip. I prefer the truth."

Sartaq's dark eyes settled on her, their unwavering focus enough to make her glad not to be on the receiving end of it too often. Not for fear, but . . . it was unsettling, to have the weight of that gaze wholly upon you. It was an eagle's gaze—a ruk's gaze. Keen and piercing.

"I was twelve when my father brought us all to the mountain aerie. And when I snuck away and climbed onto the captain's own ruk, soaring into the skies and requiring them to chase me down . . . My father told me that if I had splattered on the rocks, I would have deserved to die for my stupidity. As punishment, he ordered me to live amongst the rukhin until I could prove I wasn't a complete fool—a lifetime, he suggested."

Nesryn quietly laughed, and blinked against the sunshine as they emerged into the grand courtyard. Ornate arches and pillars had been carved with flora and fauna, the palace rising up behind them like a leviathan.

"Thankfully, I did not die of stupidity, and instead came to love the riding, their lifestyle. They gave me hell because I was a prince, but I proved my mettle soon enough. Kadara hatched when I was fifteen, and I raised her myself. I have had no other mount since." Pride and affection brightened those onyx eyes.

And yet Nesryn and Chaol would ask him, beg him, to take that beloved mount into battle against wyverns many times the weight and with infinitely more brute strength. With venom in their tails. Her stomach roiled.

They reached the towering main gates, a small door cut into the enormous slabs of studded bronze, left open to allow access to pedestrians scurrying on errands to and from the palace. Nesryn remained still while Sartaq introduced her to the heavily armed guards on duty, ordering them to grant her unrestricted access. The sun glinted on the hilts of the swords crossed over their backs as the guards bowed their acquiescence, each with a fist over his heart.

She'd seen how Chaol could barely look at them—the palace guards and those at the docks.

Sartaq led her through the small door, the bronze of the gate nearly a foot thick, and onto the broad, cobblestoned avenue that sloped into the labyrinth of city streets. Fine houses and more guards lined the surrounding streets, residences of the wealthy who wished to dwell in the palace's shadow. But the street itself was crammed with people about their business or leisure, even some travelers who climbed all the way up here to gawk at the palace, and now tried to peer through the small door through which Nesryn and Sartaq had walked for a glimpse to the courtyard beyond. None seemed to recognize the prince beside her—though she knew the guards on the street and stationed at the gates monitored every breath and word.

One glance at Sartaq, and she had no doubt the prince was also well aware of his surroundings while he stood beyond the gates, as if he were an ordinary man. She studied the crowded streets ahead, listening to the clamor. It would take an hour on foot to reach her family's house across the city, but even longer in a carriage or on horseback thanks to the clogged traffic.

"Are you sure you don't need an escort?"

A half smile tugged on Nesryn's mouth as she found him watching her sidelong. "I can handle myself, Prince, but I thank you for the honor."

Sartaq looked her over, a quick warrior's assessment. Indeed, he was a man who had little to fear when stepping beyond the palace walls. "If you ever have the time or interest, you should come for a ride. The air up there is open—not like the dust and brine down here."

Open enough where listening ears might not hear them.

Nesryn bowed deeply. "I should like that very much."

She felt the prince still watching while she strode down the sunny avenue, dodging carts and conveyances fighting for passage. But she didn't dare look back. She wasn't entirely sure why.

$\preceq$ 7 $\succeq$

Chaol waited until Nesryn had been gone for a good thirty minutes before he summoned Kadja. She'd been waiting in the exterior hallway and slipped inside his suite mere moments after he'd called her name. Lingering in the foyer, he watched the serving girl approach, her steps light and swift, her eyes downcast as she awaited his order.

"I have a favor to ask you," he said slowly and clearly, cursing himself for not learning Halha during the years Dorian had studied it.

A dip of the chin was her only answer.

"I need you to go down to the docks, to wherever information comes in, to see if there's any news about the attack on Rifthold." Kadja had been in the throne room yesterday—she'd undoubtedly heard about it. And he'd debated asking Nesryn to do some searching while she was out, but if the news was grim . . . he didn't want her learning it alone. Bearing it alone, all the way back up to the palace. "Do you think you could do that?"

Kadja lifted her eyes at last, though she kept her head low. "Yes," she said simply.

He knew she was likely answering to one of the royals or viziers in this palace. But his asking for more information, while certainly a detail to mark, wasn't any threat to his cause. And if they deemed it weak or stupid to be concerned for his country, they could go to hell.

"Good," Chaol said, the chair beneath him groaning as he wheeled it forward a foot and tried not to scowl at the sound, at his silent body. "And there is another favor I would ask of you."

Just because Nesryn was occupied with her family didn't mean he had to be idle.

But as Kadja deposited him in Arghun's chambers, he wondered if he should have waited for Nesryn's return to have this meeting.

The eldest prince's entry room was as large as Chaol's entire suite. It was a long, oval space, the far end opening into a courtyard adorned with a sparkling fountain and patrolled by a pair of white peacocks. He watched them sweep by, the mass of their snowy feathers trailing over the slate tiles, their delicate crowns bobbing with each step.

"They are beautiful, are they not?"

A sealed set of carved doors to the left had opened, revealing the slim-faced, cold-eyed prince, his attention on the birds.

"Stunning," Chaol admitted, hating the way he had to angle his head upward to look the man in the eye. Had he been standing, he'd be a good four inches taller, able to use his size to his advantage during this meeting. Had he been standing—

He didn't let himself continue down that path. Not now.

"They are my prized pair," Arghun said, his use of Chaol's home tongue utterly fluent. "My country home is full of their offspring."

Chaol searched for an answer, something Dorian or Aelin might have easily supplied, but found nothing. Absolutely *nothing* that didn't sound inane and insincere. So he said, "I'm sure it's beautiful."

Arghun's mouth tugged upward. "If you ignore their screaming at certain points of the year."

Chaol clenched his jaw. His people were *dying* in Rifthold, if not already dead, and yet bandying words about screeching, preening birds . . . *this* was what he was to do?

He debated it, whether to parry more or get to the point, but Arghun said, "I suppose you are here to ask what I know regarding your city." The prince's cool glance finally landed on him, and Chaol held the look. This—the staring contest—was something he could do. He'd had plenty, with unruly guard and courtier alike.

"You supplied your father with the information. I want to know who gave you the details of the attack."

Amusement lit up the prince's dark brown eyes. "A blunt man."

"My people are suffering. I would like to know as much as I can."

"Well," Arghun said, picking at a piece of lint clinging to the golden embroidery along his emerald tunic, "in the spirit of honesty, I can tell you absolutely nothing."

Chaol blinked—once, and slowly.

Arghun went on, extending a hand toward the outer doors, "There are far too many eyes watching, Lord Westfall, and my being seen with you sends a message, for better or worse, regardless of what we discuss. So while I appreciate your visit, I will ask you to leave." The servants waiting at the door came forward, presumably to wheel him away.

And the sight of one of them reaching their hands toward the back of his chair . . .

Chaol bared his teeth at the servant, stopping him dead. "Don't."

Whether the man spoke his language, he clearly understood the expression on his face.

Chaol twisted back to the prince. "You really want to play this game?"

"It is no game," Arghun said simply, striding toward the office where

84

he'd been ensconced. "The information is correct. My spies do not invent stories to entertain. Good day to you."

And then the double doors to the prince's office were sealed.

Chaol debated banging on those doors until Arghun started talking, perhaps pounding his fist into the prince's face, too, but . . . the two servants behind him were waiting. Watching.

He'd met enough courtiers in Rifthold to sense when someone was lying. Even if those senses had failed him so spectacularly these past few months. With Aelin. With the others. With . . . everything.

But he didn't think Arghun was lying. About any of it.

Rifthold had been sacked. Dorian remained missing. His people's fate unknown.

He didn't fight the servant again when the man stepped up to escort him back to his room. And that might have enraged him more than anything.

⁓

Nesryn did not return for dinner.

Chaol did not let the khagan, his children, or the thirty-six hawk-eyed viziers get a whiff of the worry that wracked him with every passing minute that she did not emerge from one of the hallways to join them in the great hall. She had been gone hours with no word.

Even Kadja had returned, an hour before dinner, and one look at her carefully calm face told him everything: she'd learned nothing new at the docks about the attack on Rifthold, either. She only confirmed what Arghun claimed: the captains and merchants had spoken to credible sources who'd either sailed past Rifthold or barely escaped. The attack had indeed happened, with no accurate number on the lives lost or the status of the city. All trade from the southern continent was halted—at least to Rifthold and anywhere north of it that required passing near the city. No word had come at all of Dorian's fate.

It pressed on him, weighing him further, but that soon became secondary, once he'd finished dressing for dinner and found Nesryn had not

85

arrived. He eventually yielded and let Kadja bring him to the banquet in the khagan's great hall, but when long minutes passed and Nesryn still did not return, it was an effort to remain unaffected.

Anything could have happened to her. Anything. Especially if Kashin's theory regarding his late sister was correct. If Morath's agents were already here, he had little doubt that as soon as they learned of his and Nesryn's arrival, they'd begun hunting them.

He should have considered it before she'd gone out today. Should have thought beyond his own damn problems. But demanding a guard be sent out to search for her would only tell any potential enemies what he valued most. Where to strike.

So Chaol fought to get his food down, barely able to focus on conversation with the people beside him. On his right: Duva, pregnant and serene, asking about the music and dancing now favored in his lands; on his left: Arghun, who didn't mention his visit that afternoon, and instead prodded him about trade routes old and proposed. Chaol made up half the answers, and the prince smiled—as if well aware of it.

Still, Nesryn didn't appear.

Though Yrene did.

Halfway through the meal, she entered, in a slightly finer yet still simple gown of amethyst that set her golden-brown skin glowing. Hasar and her lover rose to greet the healer, clasping Yrene's hands and kissing her cheeks, and the princess kicked out the vizier seated on her left to make room for her.

Yrene bowed to the khagan, who waved her off without more than a glance, then to the royalty assembled. Arghun did not bother to acknowledge her existence; Duva beamed at Yrene, her quiet husband offering a more subdued smile. Only Sartaq bowed his head, while the final sibling, Kashin, offered her a close-lipped smile that didn't meet his eyes.

But Kashin's gaze lingered long enough while Yrene took her seat beside Hasar that Chaol remembered what the princess had teased Yrene about earlier that day.

But Yrene did not return the prince's smile, only offering a distant nod in return, and claimed the seat Hasar had conquered for her. She fell into conversation with Hasar and Renia, accepting the meat Renia piled on her plate, the princess's lover fussing that Yrene looked too tired, too skinny, too pale. Yrene accepted every morsel offered with a bemused smile and nod of thanks. Deliberately not looking anywhere near Kashin. Or Chaol, for that matter.

"I heard," a male voice to Chaol's right said in his own language, "that Yrene has been assigned to you, Lord Westfall."

He was not at all surprised to find that Kashin had leaned forward to speak to him.

And not at all surprised to see the thinly veiled warning in the male's gaze. Chaol had seen it often enough: *Territory claimed.*

Whether Yrene welcomed it or not.

Chaol supposed it was a mark in her favor that she did not seem to pay the prince much heed. Though he could only wonder why. Kashin was the handsomest of the siblings, and Chaol had witnessed women literally falling over themselves for Dorian's attention during those years in the castle. Kashin had a self-satisfied look to him that he'd often glimpsed on Dorian's face.

Once—long ago. A different lifetime ago. Before an assassin and a collar and everything.

The guards stationed throughout the great hall somehow turned looming, as if they were kindled flames that now tugged at his gaze. He refused to even glance toward the nearest one, which he'd marked out of habit, standing twenty feet to the side of the high table. Right where he'd once stood, before another king, another court.

"She has," was all Chaol could manage to say.

"Yrene is our most skilled healer—save for the Healer on High," Kashin went on, glancing at the woman who still paid him no heed and indeed seemed to fall deeper into conversation with Renia as if to emphasize it.

"So I have heard." *Certainly the sharpest-tongued.*

"She received the highest marks anyone has ever attained on her formal examinations," Kashin continued while Yrene ignored him, something like hurt flickering across the prince's face.

"See how he trips over himself," Arghun muttered over Duva, her husband, *and* Chaol to say to Sartaq. Duva swatted at Arghun's arm, snapping at him for interrupting her fork's path to her mouth.

Kashin did not appear to hear or care for his elder brother's disapproval. And to his credit, Sartaq didn't, either, choosing instead to turn to a golden-robed vizier while Kashin said to Chaol, "Unheard of marks for anyone, let alone a healer who has been here for just over two years."

Another seedling of information. Yrene had not spent long in Antica, then.

Chaol found Yrene watching him beneath lowered brows. A warning not to drag her into the conversation.

He weighed the merits of either option: the petty revenge for her taunting earlier, or . . .

She was helping him. Or was debating it, at least. He'd be stupid to alienate her further.

So he said to Kashin, "I hear you usually dwell down in Balruhn and look after the terrestrial armies."

Kashin straightened. "I do. For most of the year, I make my home there and oversee the training of our troops. If I'm not there, then I'm out on the steppes with our mother-people—the horse-lords."

"Thank the gods," Hasar muttered from across the table, earning a warning look from Sartaq. Hasar only rolled her eyes and whispered something in her lover's ear that made Renia laugh, a bright, silvery sound.

Yrene was still watching him, though, an ember of what he could have sworn was annoyance in her face—as if Chaol's mere presence at this table was enough to set her clenching her jaw—while Kashin began explaining his various routines in his city on the southwestern coast, and the contrasting life amongst the horse-tribes on the steppes.

Chaol shot Yrene back an equally displeased look the moment Kashin paused to sip his wine, and then launched question after question to the prince regarding his life. Helpful information, he realized, about their army.

He was not the only one who realized it. Arghun cut in while his brother was midsentence about the forges they had constructed near their northern climes, "Let us not discuss business at dinner, brother."

Kashin shut his mouth, ever the trained soldier.

And somehow Chaol knew—that fast—that Kashin was not being considered for the throne. Not when he obeyed his eldest brother like any common warrior. He seemed decent, though. A better alternative than the sneering, aloof Arghun, or the wolflike Hasar.

It did not entirely explain Yrene's utter need to distance herself from Kashin. Not that it was any of his business, or of any interest to him. Certainly not when Yrene's mouth tightened if she so much as turned her head in Chaol's direction.

He might have called her out on it, might have demanded if this meant she'd decided *not* to treat him. But if Kashin favored her, Yrene's subtle rejections or not, it surely wouldn't be a wise move to get into it with her at this table.

Footsteps sounded from behind, but it was only a vizier's husband, come to murmur something in her ear before vanishing.

Not Nesryn.

Chaol studied the dishes strewn over the table, calculating the remaining courses. With the feasting, last night's meal had gone on for ages. Not one dessert delicacy had been brought out yet.

He looked again to the exits, skipping over the guards stationed there, searching for her.

Facing the table again, Chaol found Yrene observing him. Wariness, displeasure still darkened those golden eyes, but . . . warning, too.

She knew who he looked for. Whose absence gnawed at him.

To his shock, she subtly shook her head. *Don't reveal it*, she seemed to say. *Don't ask them to look for her.*

He knew it already but gave Yrene a terse nod back and continued on.

Kashin attempted to engage Yrene in conversation, but each time he was promptly and politely shut down with simple answers.

Perhaps the healer's disdain toward Chaol that morning was simply her nature, rather than hatred born of Adarlan's conquest. Or perhaps she just hated men. It was hard not to look toward the faint scar across her throat.

Chaol managed to wait until dessert arrived before feigning exhaustion and leaving the table. Kadja was already there, waiting by the farthest pillars of the hall with the other servants, and said nothing as she wheeled that chair away, every rattle making him grate his teeth.

Yrene didn't say a word of parting, or offer a promise of returning the next day. She didn't so much as look in his direction.

But Nesryn was not in the room when he returned. And if he searched for her, if he drew attention to the threat, to their closeness and how any enemy might wield it against them . . .

So he waited. Listened to the garden fountain, the singing of the nightingale perched in a fig tree within it, listened to the steady count of the clock on the sitting room mantel.

Eleven. Twelve. He told Kadja to go to sleep—that he'd care for himself and get himself in bed. She did not leave, only took up a place against the painted foyer wall to wait.

It was nearly one when the door opened.

Nesryn slipped in. He knew it, simply because he'd learned her sounds of moving.

She saw the candles in the sitting room and strode in.

Not a mark on her. Only—light. Her cheeks were flushed, her eyes brighter than they'd been this morning. "I'm sorry I missed dinner," was all she said.

His reply was low, guttural. "Do you have any idea how worried I've been?"

She halted, hair swaying with the movement. "I was not aware I had to send word of my comings and goings. You told me to go."

"You went into a foreign city and did not come back when you said you would." Every word was biting, slicing.

"It is not a foreign city—not to me."

He slammed his palm onto the arm of the chair. "One of the princesses was murdered a few weeks ago. A *princess*. In her own palace—the seat of the most powerful empire in the world."

She crossed her arms. "We don't know if it was murder. Kashin seems to be the only one who thinks so."

It was utterly beside the point. Even if he'd barely remembered to study his dinner companions tonight for any sign of the Valg's presence. He said too quietly, "I couldn't even go looking for you. I didn't *dare* tell them that you were missing."

She blinked, slow and long. "My family was glad to see me, in case you were wondering. And they received a brief letter from my father yesterday. They got out." She began unbuttoning her jacket. "They could be anywhere."

"I'm glad to hear it," Chaol said through his teeth. Though he knew that *not* knowing where her family was would eat at her as much as the terror of the past day of not knowing whether they lived. He said as calmly as he could, "This thing between us doesn't work if you don't tell me where you are, or if your plans change."

"I was at their house, eating dinner. I lost track of time. They begged me to stay with them."

"You know better than to not send word. Not after the shit we've been through."

"I have nothing to fear in this city—this place."

She said it with enough bite that he knew she meant that in Rifthold . . . in Rifthold she did.

He hated that she felt that way. Hated it and yet: "Isn't that what we are fighting for? So that our own lands might be so safe one day?"

Her face shuttered. "Yes."

She finished unbuttoning her jacket, peeling it off to reveal the shirt beneath, and slung it over a shoulder. "I'm going to bed. I'll see you in the morning."

She didn't wait for his farewell before she strode into her room and shut the door.

Chaol sat for long minutes in the sitting room, waiting for her to emerge. And when he finally let Kadja bring him into his room and help change him into his bedclothes, after she blew out the candles and left on silent feet, he waited for his door to open.

But Nesryn did not come in. And he could not go to her—not without dragging poor Kadja from wherever she slept, listening for any sound that she might be needed.

He was still waiting for Nesryn when sleep claimed him.

❧ 8 ❧

Yrene made sure to be on time the next morning. She hadn't sent word ahead, but she was willing to gamble that Lord Westfall and the new captain would be waiting at ten. Though from the glares he threw her way last night, she wondered if he doubted she'd return at all.

Let him think what he wanted.

She debated waiting until eleven, since Hasar and Renia had dragged her out drinking—or rather, Yrene had watched them drink, sipping at her own glass of wine—and she hadn't crawled into her room in the Torre until nearly two. Hasar had offered her a suite at the palace for the night, but given the fact that they'd narrowly escaped Kashin joining them at the quiet, elegant taproom in the bustling Rose Quarter, Yrene was not inclined to risk running into him again.

Honestly, whenever the khagan ordered his children back to their various outposts, it would not be soon enough. They'd lingered after Tumelun's death—which Hasar had still refused to even mention. Yrene had barely known the youngest princess, the girl having spent most of her time with Kashin among the Darghan on the steppes and the walled cities scattered around them. But in those initial days after Tumelun's body had been found, after Hafiza herself had confirmed that the girl had jumped from the balcony, Yrene had the urge to seek out Kashin. To offer her sympathies, yes, but also to just see how he was doing.

Yrene knew him well enough to understand that despite the easy, unruffled manner he presented to the world, the disciplined soldier who obeyed his father's every order and fearlessly commanded his terrestrial armies . . . beneath that smiling face lay a churning sea of grief. Wondering what he could have done differently.

Things had indeed turned awkward and awful between Yrene and Kashin, but . . . she still cared. Yet she had not reached out to him. Had not wanted to open that door she'd spent months trying to shut.

She'd hated herself for it, thought about it at least once a day. Especially when she spied the white banners flapping throughout the city, the palace. At dinner last night, she'd done her best not to crumple up with shame as she ignored him, suffered through his praise, the pride still in his words when he spoke of her.

Fool, Eretia had called her more than once, after Yrene had confessed during a particularly grueling healing what had occurred on the steppes last winter. Yrene knew it was true—but she . . . well, she had other plans for herself. Dreams she would not, could not, defer or yield entirely. So once Kashin, once the other royals, returned to their ruling posts . . . it would be easier again. Better.

She only wished Lord Westfall's own return to his hateful kingdom didn't rely so heavily upon her assistance.

Biting back a scowl, Yrene squared her shoulders and knocked on the suite doors, the lovely-faced servant answering before the sound had even finished echoing in the hall.

There were so many of them in the palace that Yrene had learned the names of just a few, but she'd seen this one before, had marked her beauty. Enough that Yrene nodded in recognition and strode in.

Servants were paid handsomely, and treated well enough that competition was fierce to land a spot in the palace—especially when positions tended to remain within families, and any openings went to those within them. The khagan and his court treated their servants as people, with rights and laws to protect them.

Unlike Adarlan, where so many lived and died in shackles. Unlike the enslaved in Calaculla and Endovier, never allowed to see the sun or breathe fresh air, entire families torn asunder.

She had heard of the massacres in the mines this spring. The butchering. It was enough that any neutral expression vanished from her face by the time she reached the lavish sitting room. She didn't know what their business was with the khagan, but he certainly looked after his guests.

Lord Westfall and the young captain were sitting precisely where they'd been the previous morning. Neither looked happy.

Indeed, neither was really glancing at the other.

Well, at least none of them would bother to pretend to be pleasant today.

The lord was already sizing Yrene up, no doubt marking the blue dress she'd worn yesterday, the same shoes.

Yrene owned four dresses, the purple one she'd worn to dinner last night being the finest. Hasar had always promised to procure finer clothes for her to wear, but the princess never remembered the next day. Not that Yrene particularly cared. If she received the clothes, she'd feel obligated to visit the palace more than she already did, and . . . Yes, there were some lonely nights when she wondered what the hell she was thinking by pushing away Kashin, when she reminded herself that most girls in the world would kill and claw their way to an open palace invitation, but she would not stay here for much longer. There was no point.

"Good morning," said the new captain—Nesryn Faliq.

The woman seemed more focused. Settled. And yet this new tension between her and Lord Westfall . . .

Not her business. Only if it interfered with her healing.

"I spoke to my superior." A lie, though she technically *had* spoken to Hafiza.

"And?"

Not one word from the lord so far. Shadows were smudged beneath his brown eyes, his tan skin paler than yesterday. If he was surprised she'd returned, he revealed nothing.

Yrene scooped the upper portions of her hair and tied it back with a small wooden comb, leaving the bottom half down. Her preferred style for working. "And I should like to get you walking again, Lord Westfall."

No emotion flickered in the lord's eyes. Nesryn, however, loosed a shuddering breath and leaned back against the deep cushions of the golden sofa. "How likely is it that you will succeed?"

"I have healed spinal injuries before. Though it was a rider who took a bad fall off his horse—not a wound in battle. Certainly not one from magic. I shall do my best, but I make no guarantees."

Lord Westfall said nothing, didn't so much as shift in his chair.

Say something, she demanded, meeting his cold and weary stare.

His eyes slid to her throat, to the scar she had not let Eretia heal when she'd offered last year.

"Will it be hours every day that you work on him?" Nesryn's words were steady, almost flat, and yet . . . The woman was not a creature who took well to a cage. Even a gilded one such as this.

"I would recommend," Yrene said to Nesryn over a shoulder, "that if you have other duties or tasks to attend to, Captain, these hours would be a good time for that. I shall send word if you are needed."

"What about moving him around?"

The lord's eyes flashed at that.

And though Yrene was predisposed to chuck them both to the ruks, she noted the lord's simmering outrage and self-loathing at the words and found herself saying, "I can handle most of it, but I believe Lord Westfall is more than capable of transporting himself."

Something like wary gratitude shot across his face. But he just said to Nesryn, "And I can ask my own damn questions."

Guilt flashed across Nesryn's face, even as she stiffened. But she nodded, biting her lip, before she murmured to Chaol, "I had some invitations yesterday." Understanding lit his eyes. "I plan to see about them."

Smart—not to speak too clearly of her movements.

Chaol nodded gravely. "Send a message this time."

Yrene had noted his worry at dinner last night when the captain had not appeared. A man unused to having the people he cared for out of his sight, and now limited in how he might look for them himself. She tucked away the information for later.

Nesryn bid her farewells, perhaps more tersely to the lord, and then was gone.

Yrene waited until she heard the door shut. "She was wise to not speak aloud of her plans."

"Why."

His first words to Yrene so far.

She jerked her chin toward the open doors to the foyer. "The walls have ears and mouths. And all the servants are paid by the khagan's children. Or viziers."

"I thought the khagan paid them all."

"Oh, he does," Yrene said, going to the small satchel she'd left by the door. "But his children and viziers buy the servants' loyalty through other means. Favors and comforts and status in exchange for information. I'd be careful with whoever was assigned to you."

Docile as the servant girl who'd let Yrene in might seem, she knew even the smallest snakes could contain the most lethal venom.

"Do you know who . . . owns them?" He said that word—*owns*—as if it tasted foul.

Yrene said simply, "No." She rooted through the satchel, pulling out twin vials of amber liquid, a stub of white chalk, and some towels. He followed every movement. "Do you own any slaves in Adarlan?" She kept the question mild, uninterested. Idle chatter while she readied.

"No. Never."

She set a black leather journal upon the table before lifting a brow. "Not one?"

"I believe in paying people for their work, as you do here. And I believe in a human being's intrinsic right to freedom."

"I'm surprised your king let you live if that is how you feel."

"I kept such opinions to myself."

"A wiser move. Better to save your hide through silence than speaking for the thousands enslaved."

He went still at that. "The labor camps and slave trade have been shut down. It was one of the first decrees that my king made. I was there with him when he drafted the document."

"New decrees for a new era, I suppose?" The words were sharper than the set of knives she carried with her—for surgery, for scraping away rotting flesh.

He held her gaze unflinchingly. "Dorian Havilliard is not his father. It was him I served these years."

"And yet you were the former king's honored Captain of the Guard. I'm surprised the khagan's children aren't clamoring to hear your secrets about how you played both so well."

His hands clenched on the arms of the chair. "There are choices in my past," he said tightly, "that I have come to regret. But I can only move on—and attempt to fix them. Fight to make sure they do not occur again." He jerked his chin toward the supplies she'd set down. "Which I cannot do while in this chair."

"You certainly could do such things from that chair," she said tartly, and meant it. He didn't respond. Fine. If he did not wish to talk about this . . . she certainly didn't wish to, either. Yrene jerked *her* chin toward the long, deep golden sofa. "Get on that. Shirt off and facedown."

"Why not the bed?"

"Captain Faliq was here yesterday. I would not enter your bedroom without her present."

"She is not my . . ." He trailed off. "It would not be an issue."

"And yet you saw last night how it might present an issue for me."

"With—"

"Yes." She cut him off with a sharp look toward the door. "The couch will do."

She had seen the look Kashin had given the captain at dinner. She'd wanted to slide off her chair and hide beneath the table.

"You have no interest where that is concerned?" he said, wheeling himself the few feet to the couch, then unbuttoning his jacket.

"I have no plans to seek such a life for myself." Not when the risks were so high.

Execution of herself, her husband, and their children if Kashin should challenge the new khagan, if he should stake a claim on the throne. Being rendered infertile by Hafiza at best—once the new khagan had produced enough heirs to ensure the continuation of the bloodline.

Kashin had waved away those concerns that night on the steppes, had refused to understand the insurmountable wall they would always present.

But Chaol nodded, likely well aware of the costs of wedding into the bloodline if your spouse was not the Heir selected. As Kashin would never be—not with Sartaq, Arghun, or Hasar likely to be chosen.

Yrene added before Chaol could inquire further, "And it is none of your concern."

He looked her over slowly. Not in the way that men sometimes did, that Kashin did, but . . . as if he was sizing up an opponent.

Yrene crossed her arms, distributing her weight evenly between her feet, just as she had been taught and now instructed others to do. A steady, defensive stance. Ready to take on anyone.

Even lords from Adarlan. He seemed to note that stance, and his jaw clenched.

"Shirt," she repeated.

With a simmering glare, he reached over his head and shucked off his shirt, setting it neatly atop where he'd folded his jacket over the rolled arm of the sofa. Then he removed his boots and socks with swift, brutal tugs.

"Pants this time," she told him. "Leave the undershorts."

His hands went to his belt, and hesitated.

He could not remove the pants without some degree of help—at least in the chair.

She didn't let a flicker of pity show in her face as she waved a hand toward the couch. "Get on, and I'll unclothe you myself."

He hesitated again. Yrene put her hands on her hips. "While I wish I could say you were my sole patient today," she lied, "I *do* have other appointments to keep. The couch, if you will."

A muscle beat in his jaw, but he braced one hand on the couch, another on the edge of the chair, and lifted himself.

The strength in the movement alone was worthy of some admiration.

So easily, the muscles in his arms and back and chest hoisted him upward and over. As if he'd been doing it his entire life.

"You've kept up your exercising since . . . how long has it been since the injury?"

"It happened on Midsummer." His voice was flat—hollow as he lifted his legs up onto the couch with him, grunting at the weight. "And yes. I was not idle before it happened, and I don't see the point of being so now."

This man was stone—rock. The injury had cracked him a bit, but not sundered him. She wondered if he knew it.

"Good," she simply said. "Exercising—both your upper body *and* your legs—will be a vital part of this."

He peered at his legs as those faint spasms rocked them. "Exercising my legs?"

"I will explain in a moment," she said, motioning him to turn over.

He obeyed with another reproachful glare, but set himself facedown.

Yrene took a few breaths to survey the length of him. He was large

100

enough that he nearly took up the entire couch. Well over six feet. If he stood again, he'd tower over her.

She strode to his feet and tugged his pants down in short, perfunctory bursts. His undershorts hid enough, though she could certainly see the shape of his firm backside through the thin material. But his thighs . . . She'd felt the muscle still in them yesterday, but studying them now . . .

They were starting to atrophy. They already lacked the healthy vitality of the rest of him, the rippling muscle beneath that tan skin seeming looser—thinner.

She laid a hand on the back of one thigh, feeling the muscle beneath the crisp hairs.

Her magic seeped from her skin into his, searching and sweeping through blood and bone.

Yes—the disuse was beginning to wear on him.

Yrene withdrew her hand and found him watching, hand angled on the throw pillow he'd dragged beneath his chin. "They're breaking down, aren't they?"

She kept her face set in a mask of stone. "Atrophied limbs may regain their full strength. But yes. We shall have to focus on ways to keep them as strong as we can, to exercise them throughout this process, so that when you stand"—she made sure he heard the slight emphasis on *when*—"you will have as much support as possible in your legs."

"So it will not just be healing, but training as well."

"You said you liked to be kept active. There are many exercises we can do with a spinal injury that will get blood and strength flowing to your legs, which will aid in the healing process. I will oversee you."

She avoided the alternative words—*help you*.

Lord Chaol Westfall was not a man who desired *help* from people. From anyone.

She took a few steps up the length of his body, to peer at his spine. At that pale, strange mark just beneath his nape. At that first prominent knob of his spine.

101

Even now, the invisible power that swirled along her palms seemed to recoil into her.

"What manner of magic gave that to you?"

"Does it matter?"

Yrene hovered her hand over it, but did not let her magic brush it. She ground her teeth. "It would help me to know what havoc it might have wreaked upon your nerves and bones."

He didn't answer. Typical Adarlanian bullishness.

Yrene pushed, "Was it fire—"

"Not fire."

A magic-given injury. It had to have happened . . . Midsummer, he'd said. The day rumors claimed that magic had returned to the northern continent. That it had been freed by Aelin Galathynius.

"Were you fighting against the magic-wielders who returned that day?"

"I was not." Clipped, sharp words.

And she looked into his eyes—his hard stare. Really looked.

Whatever had occurred, it had been horrible. Enough to leave such shadows and reticence.

She had healed people who'd endured horrors. Who could not reply to the questions she asked. And he might have served that butcher, but . . . Yrene tried not to grimace as she realized what lay ahead, what Hafiza had likely guessed at before assigning her to him: healers often did not just repair wounds, but also the trauma that went along with them. Not through magic, but . . . talking. Walking alongside the patient as they traveled those hard, dark paths.

And to do so with *him* . . . Yrene shoved the thought aside. Later. She'd think of it later.

Closing her eyes, Yrene unspooled her magic into a gentle, probing thread, and laid a palm on that splattered star atop his spine.

The cold slammed into her, spikes of it firing through her blood and bones.

Yrene reeled back as if she'd been given a physical blow.

Cold and dark and anger and agony—

She clenched her jaw, fighting past this echo in the bone, sending that thread-thin probe of power a little farther into the dark.

The pain would have been unbearable when it hit him.

Yrene pushed back against the cold—the cold and the lack and the oily, unworldly *wrongness* of it.

No magic of this world, some part of her whispered. Nothing that was natural or good. Nothing she knew, nothing she had ever dealt with.

Her magic screamed to draw back that probe, move away—

"Yrene." His words were far away while the wind and blackness and *emptiness* of it roared around her—

And then that echo of nothingness . . . it seemed to awaken.

Cold filled her, burned along her limbs, creeping wider, encircling.

Yrene flung out her magic in a blind flare, the light pure as sea-foam.

The blackness retreated, a spider scuttling into a shadowed corner. Just enough—just enough that she yanked back her hand, yanked back *herself,* and found Chaol gaping at her.

Her hands trembled as she gazed down at them. As she gazed at that splotch of paleness on his tan skin. That *presence* . . . She coiled her magic deep within herself, willing it to warm her own bones and blood, to steady herself. Even as she steadied it, too—some internal, invisible hand stroking her power, soothing it.

Yrene rasped, "Tell me what that is." For she had seen or felt or learned *nothing* like that.

"Is it inside me?" That was fear—genuine fear in his eyes.

Oh, he knew. Knew what manner of power had dealt this wound, what might be lurking within it. Knew enough about it to be afraid. If such a power existed in Adarlan . . .

Yrene swallowed. "I think . . . I think it's only—only the echo of something bigger. Like a tattoo or a brand. It is not living, and yet . . ." She flexed her fingers. If a mere probing of the darkness with her magic had triggered such a response, then a full-on onslaught . . . "Tell me what that

103

is. If I am going to be dealing with . . . with *that*, I need to know. Everything you can tell me."

"I can't."

Yrene opened her mouth. But the lord flicked his gaze toward the open door. Her warning to him silently echoed. "Then we shall try to work around it," she declared. "Sit up. I want to inspect your neck."

He obeyed, and she observed him while his heavily muscled abdomen eased him upright, then he carefully swung his feet and legs to the floor. Good. That he had not just this much mobility, but the steady, calm patience to work with his body . . . Good.

Yrene kept that to herself while she strode on still-wobbly knees to the desk where she'd left the vials of amber fluid—massage oils pressed from rosemary and lavender from estates just beyond Antica's walls, and eucalyptus from the far south.

She selected the eucalyptus, the crisp, smothering scent coiling around her as she pried off the stopper from the vial and took up a place beside him on the couch. Soothing, that scent. For both of them.

Seated together on that couch, he indeed towered over her—the muscled mass of him enough to make her understand why he'd been so adept at his position. Being perched beside him was different, somehow, than standing above him, touching him. Sitting beside a Lord of Adarlan . . .

Yrene didn't let the thought settle as she pooled a small amount of the oil into her palm and rubbed her hands together to warm it. He inhaled deeply, as if taking the scent into his lungs, and Yrene didn't bother to speak as she laid her hands upon his nape.

Broad, sweeping strokes around and down the broad column of his neck. Over his shoulders.

He let out a deep groan as she passed over a knot between his neck and shoulder, the sound of it reverberating into her palms, then stiffened. "Sorry."

She ignored the apology, digging her thumbs into the area. Another noise rumbled out of him. Perhaps it made her cruel not to comment on his slight embarrassment, not to dismiss it. But Yrene just leaned in, sliding her palms down his back, giving a wide berth to that horrid mark.

She reined her magic in tightly, not letting her power brush up against it again.

"Tell me what you know," she murmured in his ear, her cheek close enough to scrape the faint stubble coating his jaw. "Now."

He waited a moment, listening for anyone nearby. And as Yrene's hands stroked over his neck, kneading muscles that were knotted enough to make her cringe, Lord Westfall began whispering.

To Yrene Towers's credit, her hands did not falter once while Chaol murmured in her ear about horrors even a dark god could not conjure.

Wyrdgates and Wyrdstone and Wyrdhounds. The Valg and Erawan and his princes and collars. Even to him, it sounded no more than a bedtime story, something his mother might have once whispered during those long winter nights in Anielle, the wild winds howling around the stone keep.

He did not tell her of the keys. Of the king who had been enslaved for two decades. Of Dorian's own enslavement. He did not tell her who had attacked him, or Perrington's true identity. Only the power the Valg wielded, the threat they posed. That they sided with Perrington.

"So this—agent of these . . . demons. It was his power that hit you here," Yrene mused in a near-whisper, hand hovering over the spot on his spine. She didn't dare touch it, had avoided that area completely while she'd massaged him, as if dreading contact with that dark echo again. She indeed now moved her hand over to his left shoulder and resumed her glorious kneading. He barely kept in his groan at the tension she eased from his aching back and shoulders, his upper arms, his neck and lower head.

He hadn't known how knotted they were—how hard he'd worked himself in training.

"Yes," he said at last, his voice still low. "It meant to kill me, but . . . I was spared."

"By what?" The fear had long faded from her voice; no tremor lingered in her hands. But little warmth had replaced them, either.

Chaol angled his head, letting her work a muscle so tight it had him grinding his teeth. "A talisman that guarded me against such evil—and a stroke of luck." Of mercy, from a king who had tried to pull that final punch. Not just as a kindness to him, but to Dorian.

Yrene's miraculous hands stilled. She pulled back, searching his face. "Aelin Galathynius destroyed the glass castle. That was why she did it— why she took Rifthold, too. To defeat them?"

And where were you? was her unspoken demand.

"Yes." And he found himself adding into her ear, his words little more than a rumble, "She, Nesryn, and I worked together. With many others."

Who he had not heard from, had no idea where they were. Off fighting, scrambling to save their lands, their future, while he was here. Unable to so much as even get a private audience with a prince, let alone the khagan.

Yrene considered. "Those are the horrors allying with Perrington," she said softly. "What the armies will be fighting."

Fear returned to blanch her face, but he offered what truth he could. "Yes."

"And you—you will be fighting them?"

He gave her a bitter smile. "If you and I can figure this out." *If you can do the impossible.*

But she did not return the amusement. Yrene only scooted back on the sofa, assessing him, wary and distant. For a moment, he thought she'd say something, ask him something, but she only shook her head. "I have much to look into. Before I dare go any further." She gestured to his back, and he realized that he was still sitting in his undershorts.

He bit down on the urge to reach for his clothes. "Is there a risk—to you?" If there was—

"I don't know. I . . . I truly have never encountered anything like this before. I should like to look into it, before I begin treating you and compose an exercise regimen. I need to do some research in the Torre library tonight."

"Of course." If this damned injury got them both hurt in the process, he'd refuse. He didn't know what the hell he'd do, but he'd refuse to let her touch him. And for the risk, the effort . . . "You never mentioned your fee. For your help."

It had to be exorbitant. If they'd sent their best, if she had such skill—

Yrene's brows furrowed. "If you are so inclined, any donation may be made to help the upkeep of the Torre and its staff, but there is no price, no expectation."

"Why?"

Her hand slid into her pocket as she rose. "I was given this gift by Silba. It is not right to charge for what was granted for free."

Silba—Goddess of Healing.

He had known one other young woman who was gods-blessed. No wonder they both possessed such unbanked fire in their eyes.

Yrene took her vial of that lovely-smelling oil and began packing up her bag.

"Why did you decide to come back to help me?"

Yrene paused, her slim body going rigid. Then she turned to him.

A wind drifted in from the garden, blowing the strands of her hair, still half-up, over her chest and shoulder. "I thought you and Captain Faliq would use my refusal against me one day."

"We don't plan to live here forever." No matter what else she'd implied.

Yrene shrugged. "Neither do I."

She packed up the rest of her bag and headed for the door.

He stopped her with his next question. "You plan to return?" *To Fenharrow? To hell?*

Yrene looked to the door, to the servants listening, waiting, in the foyer beyond. "Yes."

She wished not just to return to Fenharrow, but also to help in the *war*. For in this war healers would be needed. Desperately. No wonder she had paled at the horrors he had whispered into her ear. Not only for what they would face, but what might come to kill her, too.

And though her face remained wan, as she noted his raised brows, she added, "It is the right thing to do. With all I have been granted—all the kindness thrown my way."

He debated warning her to stay, to remain here, safe and protected. But he noted the wariness in her eyes as she awaited his answer. Others, he realized, had likely already cautioned against her leaving. Perhaps made her doubt herself, just a bit.

So Chaol instead said, "Captain Faliq and I are not the sort of people who would hold a grudge against you—try to punish you for it."

"You served a man who did such things." *And likely acted on his behalf.*

"Would you believe me if I told you that he left his dirty work to others beyond my command, and I was often not told?"

Her expression told him enough. She reached for the doorknob.

"I knew," he said quietly. "That he had done and was doing unspeakable things. I knew that forces had tried to fight against him when I was a boy, and he had smashed them to bits. I—to become captain, I had to yield certain . . . privileges. Assets. I did so willingly, because my focus was on protecting the future. On Dorian. Even as boys, I knew he was not his father's son. I knew a better future lay with him, if I could make sure Dorian lived long enough. If he not only lived, but also survived—emotionally. If he had an ally, a true friend, in that court of vipers. Neither of us was old enough, strong enough to challenge his father. We saw what happened to those who whispered of rebellion. I knew that if I, if *he* set one foot out of line, his father would kill him, heir or no. So I craved the stability, the safety of the status quo."

Yrene's face had not altered, not softened or hardened. "What happened?"

He reached for his shirt at last. Fitting, he thought, that he'd laid

108

some part of himself bare while sitting here mostly naked. "We met someone. Who set us all down a path I fought against until it cost me and others much. Too much. So you may look at me with resentment, Yrene Towers, and I will not blame you for it. But believe me when I say that there is no one in Erilea who loathes me more than I do myself."

"For the path you found yourself forced down?"

He slung his shirt over his head and reached for his pants. "For fighting that path to begin with—for the mistakes I made in doing so."

"And what path do you walk now? How shall the Hand of Adarlan shape its future?"

No one had asked him. Not even Dorian.

"I am still learning—still . . . deciding," he admitted. "But it begins with wiping Perrington and the Valg from our homeland."

She caught the word—*our*. She chewed on her lip, as if tasting it in her mouth. "What happened on Midsummer, exactly?" He'd been vague. Had not told her of the attack, the days and months leading to it, the aftermath.

That chamber flashed in his mind—a head rolling across the marble, Dorian screaming. Blending with another moment, of Dorian standing beside his father, face cold as death and crueler than any level of Hellas's realm. "I told you what happened," he simply said.

Yrene studied him, toying with the strap of her heavy leather satchel. "Facing the emotional consequences of your injury will be a part of this process."

"I don't need to face anything. I know what happened before, during, and after."

Yrene stood perfectly still, those too-old eyes utterly unfazed. "We'll see about that."

The challenge hanging in the air between them, dread pooling in his stomach, the words curdled in Chaol's mouth as she turned on her heel and left.

⇥ 9 ⇤

Two hours later, her head leaning against the lip of the tub carved into the stone floor of the enormous cavern beneath the Torre, Yrene stared into the darkness lurking high above.

The Womb was nearly empty in the midafternoon. Her only company was the trickle of the natural hot spring waters flowing through the dozen tubs built into the cave floor, and the drip of water from jagged stalactites landing upon the countless bells strung on chains between the pillars of pale stone that rose up from the ancient rock.

Candles had been tucked into natural alcoves, or had been clumped at either end of each sunken tub, gilding the sulfurous steam and setting the owls carved into every wall and slick pillar in flickering relief.

A plush cloth cushioning her head against the unforgiving stone lip of the tub, Yrene breathed in the Womb's thick air, watching it rise and vanish into the clear, crisp darkness squatting far overhead. All around her echoed high-pitched, sweet ringing, occasionally interrupted by solitary clear notes.

No one in the Torre knew who had first brought the various bells of silver and glass and bronze down to the open chamber of Silba's Womb. Some bells had been there so long they were crusted with mineral deposits, their ringing as water dropped from the stalactites now no more than a faint *plunk*. But it was tradition—one Yrene herself had participated in—for each new acolyte to bring a bell of her choosing. To have her name and date of entry into the Torre engraved on it, and to then find a place for it, before she first immersed herself in the bubbling waters of the Womb floor. The bell to hang for eternity, offering music and guidance to all healers who came afterward; the voices of their beloved sisters forever singing to them.

And considering how many healers had passed through the Torre halls, considering the number of bells, large and small, that now hung throughout the space . . . The entire chamber, nearly the size of the khagan's great hall, was full of the echoing, layered ringing. A steady hum that filled Yrene's head, her bones, as she soaked in the delicious heat.

Some ancient architect had discovered the hot springs far beneath the Torre and constructed a network of tubs built into the floor so that the water flowed between them, a constant stream of warmth and movement. Yrene held her hand against one of the vents in the side of the tub, letting the water ripple through her fingers on its way to the vent on the other end, to pass back into the stream itself—and into the slumbering heart of the earth.

Yrene took another deep breath, brushing back the damp hair clinging to her brow. She'd washed before entering the tub, as all were required to do in one of the small antechambers outside the Womb, to clean away the dust and blood and stains of the world above. An acolyte had been waiting with a lightweight robe of lavender—Silba's color—for Yrene to wear into the Womb proper, where she'd discarded it beside the pool and stepped in, naked save for her mother's ring.

In the curling steam, Yrene lifted her hand before her and studied the ring, the way the light bent along the gold and smoldered in the garnet.

All around, bells rang and hummed and sang, blending with the trickling water until she was adrift in a stream of living sound.

Water—Silba's element. To bathe in the sacred waters here, untouched by the world above, was to enter Silba's very lifeblood. Yrene knew she was not the only healer who had taken the waters and felt as if she were indeed nestled in the warmth of Silba's womb. As if this space had been made for them alone.

And the darkness above her . . . it was different from what she had spied in Lord Westfall's body. The opposite of that blackness. The darkness above her was that of creation, of rest, of unformed thought.

Yrene stared into it, into the womb of Silba herself. And could have sworn she felt something staring back. Listening, while she thought through all Lord Westfall had told her.

Things out of ancient nightmares. Things from another realm. Demons. Dark magics. Poised to unleash themselves upon her homeland. Even in the soothing, warm waters, Yrene's blood chilled.

On those northern, far-off battlefields, she had expected to treat stab wounds and arrows and shattered bones. Expected to treat any of the diseases that ran rampant in army camps, especially during the colder months.

Not wounds from creatures that destroyed soul as well as body. That used talons and teeth and poison. The maleficent power coiled around the injury to his spine . . . It was not some fractured bone or tangled-up nerves. Well, it technically *was*, but that fell magic was tied to it. Bound to it.

She still could not shake the oily feel, the sense that something inside it had stirred. Awoken.

The ringing of the bells flowed and ebbed, lulling her mind to rest, to open.

She'd go to the library tonight. See if there was any information regarding all the lord had claimed, if perhaps someone before her had any thoughts on magically granted injuries.

Yet it would not be an injury that solely relied upon her to heal.

She'd suggested as much before leaving. But to battle that thing within him . . . *How?*

Yrene mouthed the word into the steam and dark, into the ringing, bubbling quiet.

She could still see her probe of magic recoiling, still feel its repulsion from that demon-born power. The opposite of what she was, what her magic was. In the darkness hovering overhead, she could see it all. In the darkness far above, tucked into Silba's earthly womb . . . it beckoned.

As if to say, *You must enter where you fear to tread.*

Yrene swallowed. To delve into that festering pit of power that had latched itself onto the lord's back . . .

You must enter, the sweet darkness whispered, the water singing along with it while it flowed around and past her. As if she were swimming in Silba's veins.

You must enter, it murmured again, the darkness above seeming to spread, to inch closer.

Yrene let it. And let herself stare deeper, move deeper, into that dark.

To fight that festering force within the lord, to risk it for some test of Hafiza's, to risk it for a son of Adarlan when her own people were being attacked or battling in that distant war and every day delayed her . . . *I can't.*

You won't, the lovely darkness challenged.

Yrene balked. She had promised Hafiza to remain, to heal him, but what she'd felt today . . . It could take an untold amount of time. If she could even find a way to help him. She'd promised to heal him, and though some injuries required the healer to walk the road with their patient, *this* injury of his—

The darkness seemed to recede.

I can't, Yrene insisted.

It did not answer again. Distantly, as if she were now far away, a bell rang, clear and pure.

Yrene blinked at the sound, the world tumbling into focus. Her limbs and breath returning, as if she'd drifted above them.

113

She peered at the darkness—finding only smooth, veiling black. Hollow and empty, as if it had been vacated. There, and gone. As if she had repelled it, disappointed it.

Yrene's head spun slightly as she sat up, stretching limbs that had gone a bit stiff, even in the mineral-rich water. How long had she soaked?

She rubbed at her slick arms, heart thundering as she scanned the darkness, as if it might still have another answer for what she must do, what lay before her. An alternative.

None came.

A sound shuffled through the cavern, distinctly not ringing or trickling or lapping. A quiet, shuddering intake of breath.

Yrene turned, water dripping off the errant strands of hair that had escaped the knot atop her head, and found another healer had entered the Womb at some point, claiming a tub on the opposite end of the parallel rows flanking either side of the chamber. With the drifting veils of steam, it was nearly impossible to identify her, though Yrene certainly didn't know the name of every healer in the Torre.

The sound rasped through the Womb again, and Yrene sat up farther, hands bracing on the cool, dark floor as she stood from the water. Steam curled off her skin as she reached for the thin robe and tied it around her, the fabric clinging to her soaked body.

The Womb's protocol was well established. It was a place for solitude, for silence. Healers entered the waters to reconnect with Silba, to center themselves. Some sought guidance; some sought absolution; some sought to release a hard day's worth of emotions they could not show before patients, perhaps could not show before anyone.

And though Yrene knew the healer across the Womb was entitled to her space, though she was prepared to leave and grant the healer privacy to weep . . .

The woman's shoulders shook. Another muffled sob.

On near-silent feet, Yrene approached the healer in the tub. Saw the

114

rivulets down her young face—her light brown skin and gold-kissed umber hair nearly identical to Yrene's own. Saw the bleakness in the woman's tawny eyes as she gazed at the darkness high above, tears dripping off her slender jaw and into the rippling water.

There were some wounds that could not be healed. Some illnesses that even the healers' power could not stop, if rooted too deeply. If they had come too late. If they did not mark the right signs.

The healer did not look at her as Yrene silently sat beside her tub, curling her knees to her chest before she picked up the healer's hand and interlaced their fingers.

So Yrene sat there, holding the healer's hand while she silently wept, the drifting steam full of the clear, sweet ringing of those bells.

After untold minutes, the woman in the tub murmured, "She was three years old."

Yrene squeezed the healer's damp hand. There were no words to comfort, to soothe.

"I wish . . ." The woman's voice broke, her entire body shaking, candlelight jumping along her beige skin. "Sometimes I wish this gift had never been given to me."

Yrene stilled at the words.

The woman at last turned her head, scanning Yrene's face, a flicker of recognition in her eyes. "Do you ever feel that way?" A raw, unguarded question.

No. She hadn't. Not once. Not even when the smoke of her mother's immolation had stung her eyes and she knew she could do nothing to save her. She had never once hated the gift she'd been given, because in all those years, she had never been alone thanks to it. Even with magic gone in her homeland, Yrene had still felt it, like a warm hand clasping her shoulder. A reminder of who she was, where she had come from, a living tether to countless generations of Towers women who had walked this path before her.

The healer searched Yrene's eyes for the answer she wanted. The answer Yrene could not give. So Yrene just squeezed the woman's hand again and stared into the darkness.

You must enter where you fear to tread.

Yrene knew what she had to do. And wished she didn't.

~

"Well? Has Yrene healed you yet?"

Seated at the high table in the khagan's great hall, Chaol turned to where Princess Hasar sat several seats down. A cooling breeze that smelled of oncoming rain flowed through the open windows to rustle the white death-banners hanging from their upper frames.

Kashin and Sartaq glanced their way—the latter giving his sister a disapproving frown.

"Talented as Yrene may be," Chaol said carefully, aware that many listened even without acknowledging them, "we are only in the initial stages of what will likely be a long process. She left this afternoon to do some research at the Torre library."

Hasar's lips curled into a poisoned smile. "How fortunate for you, that we shall have the pleasure of your company for a while yet."

As if he'd willingly stay here for a moment longer.

But Nesryn answered, still glowing from hours again spent with her family that afternoon, "Any chance for our two lands to build bonds is a fortunate one."

"Indeed," was all Hasar said, and went back to picking at the chilled tomato-and-okra dish on her plate. Her lover was nowhere to be seen— but neither was Yrene. The healer's fear earlier . . . he'd been able to almost taste it in the air. But sheer will had steadied her—will and temper, Chaol supposed. He wondered which would win out in the end.

Indeed, some small part of him hoped Yrene would stay away, if only to avoid what she so heavily implied they'd also be doing: *talking*. Discussing things. Himself.

116

He'd make it clear to her tomorrow that he could heal just fine without it.

For long minutes, Chaol remained in silence, marking those at the table, the servants flitting by. The guards at the windows and archways.

The minced lamb turned leaden in his stomach at the sight of their uniforms, at how they stood so tall and proud. How many meals had he himself been positioned by the doors, or out in the courtyard, monitoring his king? How many times had he laid into his men for slouching, for chattering amongst themselves, and reassigned them to lesser watches?

One of the khagan's guards noticed his stare and gave a curt nod.

Chaol looked away quickly, his palms clammy. But he forced himself to keep observing the faces around him, what they wore and how they moved and smiled.

No sign—none—of any wicked force, whether dispatched from Morath or elsewhere. No sign beyond those white banners to honor their fallen princess.

Aelin had claimed the Valg had a reek to them, and he'd seen their blood run black from mortal veins more times than he cared to count, but short of demanding everyone in this hall cut open their hands . . .

It actually wasn't a bad idea—if he could get an audience with the khagan to convince him to order it. To mark whoever fled, or made excuses.

An audience with the khagan to convince him of the danger, and perhaps make *some* progress with this alliance. So that the princes and princesses sitting around him might never wear a Valg collar. Their loved ones never know what it was to look into their faces and see nothing but ancient cruelty smirking back.

Chaol took a steadying breath and leaned forward, to where the khagan dined a few seats down, immersed in conversation with a vizier and Princess Duva.

The khagan's now-youngest seemed to watch more than participate, and though her pretty face was softened with a sweet smile, her eyes missed nothing. It was only when the vizier paused for a sip of wine and Duva turned toward her quiet husband on her left that Chaol cleared his throat and said to the khagan, "I would thank you again, Great Khagan, for offering the services of your healers."

The khagan slid weary, hard eyes toward him. "They are no more my healers than they are yours, Lord Westfall." He returned to the vizier, who frowned at Chaol for interrupting.

But Chaol said, "I was hoping to perhaps be granted the honor of a meeting with you in private."

Nesryn dug her elbow into his in warning as silence rippled down the table. Chaol refused to take his stare from anywhere but the man before him.

The khagan only said, "You may discuss such things with my Chief Vizier, who maintains my daily schedule." A jerk of the chin toward a shrewd-eyed man monitoring from down the table. One glance at the Chief Vizier's thin smile told Chaol the meeting wasn't going to happen. "My focus remains on assisting my wife through her mourning." The gleam of sorrow in the khagan's eyes wasn't feigned. Indeed, there was no sign of the khagan's wife at the table, not even a place left out for her.

Distant thunder grumbled in the thick silence that followed. Not the time or the place to insist. A man grieving for a lost child . . . He'd be a fool to push. And coarse beyond measure.

Chaol dipped his chin. "Forgive me for intruding in this difficult time." He ignored the smirk twisting Arghun's face while the prince observed from his father's side. Duva, at least, offered him a sympathetic smile-wince, as if to say, *You are not the first to be shut down. Give him time*.

Chaol gave the princess a shallow nod before returning to his own plate. If the khagan was set on ignoring him, grief or no . . . perhaps there were other avenues to convey information.

Other ways to gain support.

He glanced to Nesryn. She'd informed him when she'd returned before dinner that she'd had no luck seeking out Sartaq this morning.

118

And now, with the prince seated across from them, sipping from his wine, Chaol found himself casually asking, "I heard that your legendary ruk, Kadara, is here, Prince."

"Ghastly beast," Hasar muttered halfheartedly into her okra, earning a half smile from Sartaq.

"Hasar is still sore that Kadara tried to eat her when they first met," Sartaq confided.

Hasar rolled her eyes, though a glimmer of amusement shone there.

Kashin supplied from a few seats down, "You could hear her screeching from the harbor."

To Chaol's surprise, Nesryn asked, "The princess or the ruk?"

Sartaq laughed, a startled, bright sound, his cool eyes lighting. Hasar only gave Nesryn a warning look before turning to the vizier beside her.

Kashin grinned at Nesryn and whispered, "Both."

A chuckle escaped Chaol's throat, though he reined it in at Hasar's glare. Nesryn smiled, inclining her head in good-willed apology to the princess.

Yet Sartaq watched them closely over the rim of his golden goblet. Chaol asked, "Are you able to fly Kadara much while you're here?"

Sartaq didn't miss a beat as he nodded. "As often as I can, usually near dawn. I was in the skies right after breakfast today, and returned just in time for dinner, thankfully."

Hasar muttered to Nesryn without breaking from the vizier commanding her attention, "He's never missed a meal in his life."

Kashin barked a laugh that had even the khagan down the table glancing their way, Arghun scowling with disapproval. When had the royals last laughed since their sister's passing? From the khagan's tight face, perhaps a while.

But Sartaq tossed his long braid over a shoulder before patting the flat, firm stomach beneath his fine clothes. "Why do you think I come home so often, sister, if not for the good food?"

"To plot and scheme?" Hasar asked sweetly.

Sartaq's smile turned subdued. "If only I had time for such things."

A shadow seemed to pass over Sartaq's face—and Chaol marked where the prince's gaze drifted. The white banners still streamed from the windows set high in the walls of the hall, now caught in what was surely the heralding wind of a thunderstorm. A man who perhaps wished he'd possessed extra time for more vital parts of his life.

Nesryn asked a touch softly, "You fly every day, then, Prince?"

Sartaq dragged his stare from his youngest sister's death-banners to assess Nesryn. More warrior than courtier, yet he nodded—in answer to an unspoken request. "I do, Captain."

When Sartaq turned to respond to a question from Duva, Chaol exchanged a glance with Nesryn—all he needed to convey his order.

Be in the aerie at dawn. Find out where he stands in this war.

⊰ 10 ⊱

A summer storm galloped in off the Narrow Sea just before midnight.

Even tucked into the sprawling library at the base of the Torre, Yrene felt every shudder of thunder. Occasional flashes of lightning sliced down the narrow corridors of the stacks and halls, chased by wind that crept through the cracks in the pale stone, guttering the candles in its wake. Most were shielded within glass lanterns, the books and scrolls too precious to risk open flame. But the wind found them in there, too— and set the glass lanterns hanging from the arched ceilings swinging and groaning.

Seated at an oak desk built into an alcove far from the brighter lights and busier areas of the library, Yrene watched the metal lantern dangling from the arch above her sway in that storm wind. Stars and crescent moons had been cut from its sides and filled with colored glass that cast splotches of blue and red and green on the stone wall before her. The splotches bobbed and dipped, a living sea of color.

Thunder cracked, so loud she flinched, the ancient chair beneath her creaking in objection.

A few feminine yelps answered it, then giggles.

Acolytes—studying late for their examinations next week.

Yrene huffed a laugh, mostly at herself, and shook her head as she focused again upon the texts Nousha had dug up for her hours ago.

Yrene and the Head Librarian had never been close, and Yrene was certainly not inclined to seek out the woman if she spotted her in the mess hall, but . . . Nousha was fluent in fifteen languages, some of them dead, and had trained at the famed Parvani Library on the western coast, nestled amid the lush and spice-rich lands outside Balruhn.

The City of Libraries, they called Balruhn. If the Torre Cesme was the domain of healers, the Parvani was the domain of knowledge. Even the great road that linked Balruhn to the mighty Sister-Road, the main artery through the continent that flowed from Antica all the way to Tigana, had been named for it: the Scholars' Road.

Yrene didn't know what had brought Nousha here all those decades ago, or what the Torre had offered her to stay, but she was an invaluable resource. And for all of her unsmiling nature, Nousha had always found Yrene the information she needed, no matter how outlandish the request.

Tonight, the woman had not looked pleased when Yrene had approached her in the mess hall, apologies falling from her lips for interrupting the librarian's meal. Yrene might have waited until the morning, but she had lessons tomorrow, and Lord Westfall after that.

Nousha had met Yrene here after finishing her meal, and had listened, long fingers folded in front of her flowing gray robes, to Yrene's story—and needs:

Information. Any she could find.

Wounds from demons. Wounds from dark magic. Wounds from unnatural sources. Wounds that left echoes but did not appear to continue to wreak havoc upon the victim. Wounds that left marks but no scar tissue.

Nousha had found them. Stack after stack of books and bundles of scrolls. She'd piled them on the desk in silence. Some were in Halha. Some in Yrene's own tongue. Some in Eyllwe. Some were . . .

Yrene scratched her head at the scroll she'd weighted with the smooth onyx stones from the jar set on each library desk.

Even Nousha had admitted she did not recognize the strange markings—runes of some sort. From where, she had no inkling, either, only that the scrolls had been wedged beside the Eyllwe tomes in a level of the library so deep beneath the ground that Yrene had never ventured there.

Yrene ran a finger over the marking before her, tracing its straight lines and curving arcs.

The parchment was old enough that Nousha had threatened to flay Yrene alive if she got any food, water, or drink on it. When Yrene had asked just how old, Nousha had shook her head.

A hundred years? Yrene had asked.

Nousha had shrugged and said that judging by the location, the type of parchment, and ink pigment, it was over ten times that.

Yrene cringed at the paper she was so flagrantly touching, and eased the weighting stones off the corners. None of the books in her own language had yielded anything valuable—more old wives' warnings about ill-wishers and spirits of air and rot.

Nothing like what Lord Westfall had described.

A faint, distant *click* echoed from the gloom to her right, and Yrene lifted her head, scanning the darkness, ready to leap onto her chair at the first sign of a scurrying mouse.

It seemed even the library's beloved Baast Cats—thirty-six females, no more, no less—could not keep out all vermin, despite their warrior-goddess namesake.

Yrene again scanned the gloom to her right, cringing, wishing she could summon one of the beryl-eyed cats to go hunting.

But no one summoned a Baast Cat. No one. They appeared when and where they willed, and not a moment before.

The Baast Cats had dwelled in the Torre library for as long as it had existed, yet none knew where they had come from, or how they were replaced when age claimed them. Each was as individual as any human, save for those beryl-colored eyes they each bore, and the fact that all were just as prone to curl up in a lap as they were to shun company altogether. Some of the healers, old and young alike, swore the cats could step through pools of shadow to appear on another level of the library; some swore the cats had been caught pawing through the pages of open books—*reading*.

Well, it'd certainly be helpful if they bothered to read less and hunt *more*. But the cats answered to no one and nothing, except, perhaps, their namesake, or whatever god had found a quiet home in the library, within Silba's shadow. To offend one Baast Cat was to insult them all, and even though Yrene loved most animals—with the exception of some insects—she had been sure to treat the cats kindly, occasionally leaving morsels of food, or providing a belly rub or ear scratch whenever they deigned to command them.

But there was no sign of those green eyes glinting in the dark, or of a scurrying mouse fleeing their path, so Yrene loosed a breath and set aside the ancient scroll, carefully placing it at the edge of the desk before pulling an Eyllwe tome toward her.

The book was bound in black leather, heavy as a doorstop. She knew a little of the Eyllwe language thanks to living so close to its border with a mother who spoke it fluently—certainly not from the father who had hailed from there.

None of the Towers women had ever married, preferring either lovers who left them with a present that arrived nine months later or who perhaps stayed a year or two before moving on. Yrene had never known her father, never learned anything about who he was other than a traveler who had stopped at her mother's cottage for the night, seeking shelter from a wild storm that swept over the grassy plain.

Yrene traced her fingers over the gilt title, sounding out the words in the language she had not spoken or heard in years.

"The . . . The . . ." She tapped her finger on the title. She should have asked Nousha. The librarian had already promised to translate some other texts that had caught her eye, but . . . Yrene sighed again. "The . . ." Poem. Ode. Lyric—"*Song*," she breathed. "*The Song of* . . ." Start. Onset—"*Beginning*."

The Song of Beginning.

The demons—the Valg—were ancient, Lord Westfall had said. They had waited an eternity to strike. Part of near-forgotten myths; little more than bedside stories.

Yrene flipped open the cover, and cringed at the unfamiliar tangle of writing within the table of contents. The type itself was old, the book not even printed on a press. Handwritten. With some word variations that had long since died out.

Lightning flashed again, and Yrene rubbed at her temple as she leafed through the musty, yellow-lined pages.

A history book. That's all it was.

Her eye snagged on a page, and she paused, backtracking until the illustration reappeared.

It had been done in sparing colors: blacks, whites, reds, and the occasional yellow.

All painted by a master's hand, no doubt an illustration of whatever was written beneath it.

The illustration revealed a barren crag, an army of soldiers in dark armor kneeling before it.

Kneeling before what was *atop* the crag.

A towering gate. No wall flanking it, no keep behind it. As if someone had built the gateway of black stone out of thin air.

There were no doors within the archway. Only swirling black *nothing*. Beams of it shot from the void, some foul corruption of the sun, falling upon the soldiers kneeling before it.

She squinted at the figures in the foreground. Their bodies were human, but the hands clutching their swords . . . Clawed. Twisted.

"Valg," Yrene whispered.

Thunder cracked in answer.

Yrene scowled at the swaying lantern as the reverberations from the thunderhead rumbled beneath her feet, up her legs.

She flipped through the pages until the next illustration appeared. Three figures stood before the same gate, the drawing too distant to make out any features beyond their male bodies, tall and powerful.

She ran a finger over the caption below and translated:

Orcus. Mantyx. Erawan.

Three Valg Kings.

Wielders of the Keys.

Yrene chewed on her bottom lip. Lord Westfall had not mentioned such things.

But if there was a gate . . . then it would need a key to open. Or several.

If the book was correct.

Midnight chimed in the great clock of the library's main atrium.

Yrene riffled through the pages, to another illustration. It was divided into three panels.

Everything the lord had said—she had believed him, of course, but . . . it was true. If the wound wasn't proof enough, these texts offered no other alternative.

For there in the first panel, tied down upon an altar of dark stone . . . a desperate young man strained to free himself from the approach of a crowned dark figure. Something swirled around the figure's hand—some asp of black mist and wicked thought. No real creature.

The second panel . . . Yrene cringed from it.

For there was that young man, eyes wide in supplication and terror, mouth forced open as that creature of black mist slithered down his throat.

But it was the last panel that made her blood chill.

Lightning flashed again, illumining the final illustration.

The young man's face had gone still. Unfeeling. His eyes . . . Yrene glanced between the previous drawing and the final one. His eyes had been silver in the first two.

In the final one . . . they had gone black. Passable as human eyes, but the silver had been wiped away by unholy obsidian.

Not dead. For they had shown him rising, chains removed. Not a threat. No—whatever they had put inside him . . .

Thunder groaned again, and more shrieks and giggles followed. Along with the slam and clatter of the acolytes leaving for the night.

Yrene surveyed the book before her, the other stacks Nousha had laid out.

Lord Westfall had described collars and rings to hold the Valg demons within a human host. But even after they were removed, he'd said, they could linger. They were merely implantation devices, and if they remained on too long, feeding off their host . . .

Yrene shook her head. The man in the drawing had not been enslaved—he'd been infested. The magic had come from someone *with* that sort of power. Power from the demon host within.

A clash of lightning, then thunder immediately on its heels.

And then another *click* sounded—faint and hollow—from the dim stacks to her right. Closer now than that earlier one had been.

Yrene glanced again toward the gloom, the hair on her arms rising.

Not a movement of a mouse. Or even the scrape of feline claws on stone or bookshelf.

She had never once feared for her safety, not from the moment she had set foot within these walls, but Yrene found herself going still as she stared into that gloom to her right. Then slowly looked over her shoulder.

The shelf-lined corridor was a straight shot toward a larger hallway, which would, in three minutes' walk, take her back to the bright, constantly monitored main atrium. Five minutes at most.

Only shadows and leather and dust surrounded her, the light bobbing and tilting with the swaying lanterns.

Healing magic offered no defenses. She'd discovered such things the hard way.

But during that year at the White Pig Inn, she'd learned to listen. Learned to read a room, to *sense* when the air had shifted. Men could unleash storms, too.

The grumbling echo of the thunder faded, and only silence remained in its wake.

Silence, and the creaking of the ancient lanterns in the wind. No other click issued.

Foolish—foolish to read such things so late. And during a storm.

Yrene swallowed. Librarians preferred the books remain within the library proper, but . . .

She slammed shut *The Song of Beginning*, shoving it into her bag. Most of the books she'd already deemed useless, but there were perhaps six more, a mixture of Eyllwe and other tongues. Yrene shoved those into her bag, too. And gently placed the scrolls into the pockets of her cloak, tucked out of view.

All while keeping one eye over her shoulder—on the hall behind her, the stacks to her right.

You wouldn't owe me anything if you'd used some common sense. The young stranger had snapped that at her that fateful night—after she'd saved Yrene's life. The words had lingered, biting deep. As had the other lessons she'd been taught by that girl.

And though Yrene knew she'd laugh at herself in the morning, though maybe it *was* one of the Baast Cats stalking something in the shadows, Yrene decided to listen to that tug of fear, that trickle down her spine.

Though she could have cut down dark stacks to reach the main hallway faster, she kept to the lights, her shoulders back and head high. Just as the girl had told her. *Look like you'd put up a fight—be more trouble than you're worth.*

Her heart pounded so wildly she could feel it in her arms, her throat.

128

But Yrene made her mouth a hard line, her eyes bright and cold. Looking as furious as she'd ever been, her pace clipped and swift. As if she had forgotten something or someone had failed to retrieve a book for her.

Closer and closer, she neared the intersection of that broad, main hallway. To where the acolytes would be trudging up to bed in their cozy dormitory.

She cleared her throat, readying to scream.

Not rape, not theft—not something that cowards would rather hide from. Yell fire, the stranger had instructed her. *A threat to all. If you are attacked, yell about a fire.*

Yrene had repeated the instructions so many times these past two and a half years. To so many women. Just as the stranger had ordered her to. Yrene had not thought she'd ever again need to recite them for herself.

Yrene hurried her steps, jaw angled. She had no weapons save for a small knife she used for cleaning out wounds or cutting bandages—currently in the bottom of her bag.

But that satchel, laden with books . . . She wrapped the leather straps around her wrist, getting a good grip on it.

A well-placed swing would knock someone to the ground.

Closer and closer to the safety of that hallway—

From the corner of her eye, she saw it. Sensed it.

Someone in the next stack over. Walking parallel to her.

She didn't dare look. Acknowledge it.

Yrene's eyes burned, even as she fought the terror that clawed its way up her body.

Glimpses of shadows and darkness. Stalking her. Hunting her.

Quickening its pace to grab her—cut her off at that hallway and snatch her into the dark.

Common sense. Common sense.

Running—it would know. It would know she was aware. It might strike. Whoever it was.

Common sense.

A hundred feet left until the hallway, shadows pooling between the dim lanterns, the lights now precious islands in a sea of darkness.

She could have sworn fingers lightly thudded as they trailed over the books on the other side of the shelf.

So Yrene lifted her chin further and smiled, laughing brightly as she looked ahead to the hallway. "Maddya! What are you doing here so late?"

She hurried her pace, especially as whoever it was slowed in surprise. Hesitation.

Yrene's foot slammed into something soft—soft and yet hard—and she bit down her yelp—

She hadn't seen the healer curled on her side in the shadows along the shelf.

Yrene bent, hands grappling for the woman's thin arms, her build slender enough that when she turned her over—

The footsteps began once more just as she turned the healer over. As she swallowed the scream that tried to shatter out of her.

Light brown cheeks turned to hollowed husks, eyes stained purple beneath, lips pale and cracked. A simple healer's gown that had likely fit her that morning now hung loose, her slim form now emaciated, as if something had sucked the life from her—

She knew that face, gaunt as it was. Knew the golden-brown hair, nearly the twin to her own. The healer from the Womb, the very one she'd comforted only hours earlier—

Yrene's fingers shook as she fumbled for a pulse, the skin leathery and dry.

Nothing. And her magic . . . There was no life for it to swirl toward. No life at all.

The footsteps on the other side of the stack neared. Yrene stood on trembling knees, taking a steadying breath as she forced herself to walk again. Forced herself to leave that dead healer in the dark. Forced herself to lift her bag as if nothing had happened, as if showing the satchel to someone ahead.

But with the angle of the stacks—the person didn't know that.

"Just finishing up my reading for the night," she called to her invisible salvation ahead. She sent up a silent prayer of thanks to Silba that her voice held steady and merry. "Cook is expecting me for a last cup of tea. Want to join?"

Making it seem like someone was expecting her: another trick she'd picked up.

Yrene cleared five more steps before she realized whoever it was had again halted.

Buying her ruse.

Yrene dashed the last few feet to the hallway, spotted a cluster of acolytes just emerging from another haze of stacks, and hurtled flat out toward them.

Their eyes widened at Yrene's approach, and all she whispered was, "*Go.*"

The three girls, barely more than fourteen, caught the tears of terror in her eyes, the sure whiteness of her face, and did not look behind Yrene. They did not disobey.

They were in her class. She'd trained them for months now.

They saw the straps of her satchel wrapped around her fist and closed ranks around her. Smiled broadly, nothing at all wrong. "Come to Cook's to get tea," Yrene told them, fighting to keep her scream from shattering out of her. Dead. A healer was *dead*—"She is expecting me."

And will raise the alarm if I do not arrive.

To their credit, those girls did not tremble, did not show one lick of dread as they walked down the main hall. As they neared the atrium, with its roaring fire and thirty-six chandeliers and thirty-six couches and chairs.

A sleek black Baast Cat was lounging in one of those embroidered chairs by the fire. And as they neared, she leaped up, hissing as fiercely as her feline-headed namesake. Not at Yrene or the girls . . . No, those beryl-colored eyes were narrowed at the library *behind* them.

One of the girls tightened her grip on Yrene's arm. But not one of them left Yrene's side as she approached the massive desk of the Head

Librarian and her Heir. Behind them, the Baast Cat held her ground—held the line—as the Heir Librarian, on duty for the night, looked up from her book at the commotion.

Yrene murmured to the middle-aged woman in gray robes, "A healer has been gravely attacked in the stacks off the main hall. Get everyone out and call for the royal guard. *Now*."

The woman did not ask questions. Did not falter or shake. She only nodded before she reached for the bell bolted onto the desk's edge.

The librarian rang it thrice. To an outsider, it was no more than a final call.

But to those who lived here, who knew the library was open day and night . . .

First ring: Listen.

Second: Listen *now*.

The Heir Librarian rang it a third time, loud and clear, the pealing echoing down into the library, into every dark corner and hallway.

Third ring: *Get out*.

Yrene had once asked, when Eretia had explained the warning bell her first day here, after she had taken a vow never to repeat its meaning to an outsider. They all had. And Yrene had asked why it was needed, who had installed it.

Long ago, before the khaganate had conquered Antica, this city had passed from hand to hand, victim to a dozen conquests and rulers. Some invading armies had been kind. A few had not.

Tunnels still existed beneath the library that they had used to evade them—long since boarded up.

But the warning bell to those within remained. And for a thousand years, the Torre had kept it. Occasionally had drills with it. Just in case. If it should ever happen.

The third ring echoed off stone and leather and wood. And Yrene could have sworn she heard the sound of countless heads popping up from

132

where they bent over desks. Heard the sound of chairs shoved back and books dropped.

Run, she begged. *Keep to the lights.*

But Yrene and the others lingered in silence, counting the seconds. The minutes. The Baast Cat quieted her hissing and monitored the hall beyond the atrium, black tail slashing over the chair cushion. One of the girls beside Yrene sprinted off to the guards by the Torre gates. Who had likely heard that bell pealing and were already running toward them.

Yrene was shaking by the time quick steps and rustling clothing drew near. She and the Heir Librarian marked each face that emerged—each wide-eyed face that hurried out of the library.

Acolytes, healers, librarians. No one out of place. The Baast Cat seemed to be checking them all, too—those beryl eyes seeing things perhaps beyond Yrene's comprehension.

Armor and stomping steps, and Yrene clamped down on the weeping relief at the approach of half a dozen Torre guards now stalking through the open library doors, the acolyte at their heels.

The acolyte and her two companions remained with Yrene while she explained. While the guards called for reinforcements, while the Heir Librarian summoned Nousha, Eretia, and Hafiza. The three girls remained, two holding Yrene's trembling hands.

They did not let go.

❈ 11 ❧

Yrene was late.

Chaol had come to expect her at ten, though she had given no indication of when she might arrive. Nesryn had left well before he'd awoken to seek out Sartaq and his ruk, leaving him here to bathe and . . . wait.

And wait.

An hour in, Chaol began going through what exercises he could manage on his own, unable to stand the silence, the heavy heat, the endless trickle of water from the fountain outside. The thoughts that kept sliding back to Dorian, wondering where his king was now headed.

She'd mentioned exercises—some involving his legs, however she'd manage to accomplish that—but if Yrene didn't bother to arrive on time, then he certainly wouldn't bother to wait for her.

His arms were trembling by the time the clock on the sideboard chimed noon, little silver bells atop the carved wood piece filling the space with clear, bright ringing. Sweat slid down his chest, his spine, his face as he managed to haul himself into his chair, arms trembling with the effort. He was about to call for Kadja to bring him a jug of water and a cool cloth when Yrene appeared.

In the sitting room, he listened as she entered the main door, then halted.

She said to Kadja, waiting in the foyer, "I have a matter of discretion that I need you to personally oversee."

Obedient silence.

"Lord Westfall requires a tonic for a rash developing on his legs. Likely from some oil you dumped into his bath." The words were calm, yet edged. He frowned down at his legs. He'd seen no such thing this morning, but he certainly couldn't sense an itch or burning. "I need willow bark, honey, and mint. The kitchens will have them. Tell no one why. I don't want word getting around."

Silence again—then a door closing.

He watched the open doors to the sitting room, listening to *her* listen to Kadja leaving. Then her heavy sigh. Yrene emerged a moment later.

She looked like hell.

"What's wrong?"

The words were out before he could consider the fact that he had no right to ask such things.

But Yrene's golden-brown face was ashen, her eyes smudged with purple, her hair limp.

She only said, "You exercised."

Chaol glanced down at his sweat-soaked shirt. "It seemed as good a way to pass the time as anything else." Each of her steps toward the desk was slow—heavy. He repeated, "What's wrong?"

But she reached the desk and kept her back to him. He ground his teeth, debating wheeling the chair over just so he could see her face, as he might have once stormed over to see—to push into her space until she told him what the hell had happened.

Yrene just set her satchel on the desk with a thud. "If you wish to exercise, perhaps a better place for it would be the barracks." A wry look at the carpet. "Rather than sweating all over the khagan's priceless rugs."

His hands clenched at his sides. "No," was all he said. All he *could* say.

She lifted a brow. "You were Captain of the Guard, weren't you? Perhaps training with the palace guard will be beneficial to—"

"No."

She peered over her shoulder, those golden eyes sizing him up. He didn't balk, even as the still-shredded thing in his chest seemed to twist and rend itself further.

He had no doubt she marked it, no doubt she'd tucked away that bit of information. Some small part of him hated her for it, hated himself for revealing that wound through his obstinance, but Yrene only turned from the desk and strode toward him, face unreadable.

"I apologize if rumor now gets out that you have an unfortunate rash on your legs." That usual, sure-footed grace had been replaced by trudging feet. "If Kadja is as smart as I think she is, she'll worry that the rash being a result of *her* ministrations would get her in trouble and not tell anyone. Or at least realize that if word gets out, we'll know *she* was the only one told of it."

Fine. She still didn't want to answer his question. So he instead asked, "Why did you want Kadja gone?"

Yrene slumped onto the golden sofa and rubbed her temples. "Because someone killed a healer in the library last night—and then hunted me, too."

Chaol went still. "What?"

He glanced to the windows, the open garden doors, the exits. Nothing but heat and gurgling water and birdsong.

"I was reading—about what you told me," Yrene said, the freckles on her face so stark against her wan skin. "And I felt someone approaching."

"Who?"

"I don't know. I didn't see them. The healer . . . I found her as I fled." Her throat bobbed. "We cleared the library from top to bottom once she was . . . retrieved, but found no one." She shook her head, jaw tight.

136

"I'm sorry," he said, and meant it. Not just for the loss of life, but also for what seemed like the loss of a long-held peace and serenity. But he asked, because he could no more stop himself from getting answers, from assessing the risks, than he could halt his own breathing, "What manner of injuries?" Half of him didn't want to know.

Yrene leaned back against the sofa cushions, the down stuffing sighing as she stared at the gilded ceiling. "I'd seen her before in passing. She was young, a little older than me. And when I found her on the floor, she looked like a long-desiccated corpse. No blood, no sign of injury. Just . . . drained."

His heart stumbled at the too-familiar description. Valg. He'd bet all he had left, he'd bet everything on it. "And whoever did this just left her body there?"

A nod. Her hands shook as she dragged them through her hair, closing her eyes. "I think they realized they'd attacked the wrong person— and moved away quickly."

"Why?"

She turned her head, opening her eyes. Exhaustion lay there. And utter fear. "She looks—*looked* like me," Yrene rasped. "Our builds, our coloring. Whoever it was . . . I think they were looking for *me*."

"Why?" he asked again, scrambling to sort through all she'd said.

"Because what I was reading last night, about the potential source of the power that injured you . . . I left some books about it on the table. And when the guards searched the area, the books were gone." She swallowed again. "Who knew you were coming here?"

Chaol's blood chilled despite the heat.

"We did not make it a secret." It was instinct to rest his hand on a sword that was not there—a sword he had chucked in the Avery months ago. "It wasn't announced, but anyone could have learned. Long before we set foot here."

It was happening again. Here. A Valg demon had come to Antica— an underling at best, a prince at worst. It could be either.

The attack Yrene had described fit Aelin's account of the remains she and Rowan had found from the Valg prince's victims in Wendlyn. People teeming with life turned to husks as if the Valg drank their very souls.

He found himself saying quietly, "Prince Kashin suspects Tumelun was killed."

Yrene sat up, any lingering color draining from her face. "Tumelun's body was not drained. Hafiza—the Healer on High herself declared it was a suicide."

There was, of course, a chance the two deaths weren't connected, a chance that Kashin was wrong about Tumelun. Part of Chaol prayed it was so. But even if they were unrelated, what had happened last night—

"You need to warn the khagan," Yrene said, seeming to read his mind.

He nodded. "Of course. Of course I will." Damned as the entire situation was . . . Perhaps it was the in he'd been waiting for with the khagan. But he studied her haggard face, the fear there. "I'm sorry—to have brought you into this. Has security been increased around the Torre?"

"Yes." A breathy push of sound. She scrubbed at her face.

"And you? Did you come here under guard?"

She threw him a frown. "In plain daylight? In the middle of the city?"

Chaol crossed his arms. "I would put nothing past the Valg."

She waved a hand. "I won't be heading alone into any dark corridors anytime soon. None of us in the Torre will. Guards have been called in— stationed down every hall, in every few feet of the library. I don't even know where Hafiza summoned them from."

Valg underlings could take bodies of anyone they wished, but their princes were vain enough that Chaol doubted they'd bother to take the form of a lowly guard. Not when they preferred beautiful young men.

A collar and a dead, cold smile flashed before his eyes.

Chaol blew out a breath. "I am truly sorry—about that healer." Especially if his being here had somehow triggered this attack, if they pursued

138

Yrene only because of her helping him. He added, "You should be on your guard. Constantly."

She ignored the warning and scanned the room, the carpets, and the lush palms. "The girls—the young acolytes . . . They're frightened."

And you?

Before, he would have volunteered to stand watch, to guard her door, to organize the soldiers because he *knew* how these things operated. But he was no captain, and he doubted the khagan or his men would be inclined to listen to a foreign lord, anyway.

But he couldn't stop himself, that part of him, as he asked, "What can I do to help?"

Yrene's eyes shifted toward him, assessing. Weighing. Not him, but he had the feeling it was something inside herself. So he kept still, kept his gaze steady, while she looked inward. While she at last took a breath and said, "I teach a class. Once a week. After last night, they were all too tired, so I let them sleep instead. Tonight, we have a vigil for the healer who—who died. But tomorrow . . ." She chewed on her lip, again debating for a heartbeat before she added, "I should like you to come."

"What sort of class?"

Yrene toyed with a heavy curl. "There is no tuition for students here— but we pay our way in other forms. Some help with the cooking, the laundry, the cleaning. But when I came, Hafiza . . . I told her I was good at all those things. I'd done them for—a while. She asked me what else I knew beyond healing, and I told her . . ." She bit her lip. "Someone once taught me self-defense. What to do against attackers. Usually the male kind."

It was an effort not to look at the scar across her throat. Not to wonder if she had learned it after—or if even that had not been enough.

Yrene sighed through her nose. "I told Hafiza that I knew a little about it, and that . . . I had made a promise to someone, to the person who taught *me*, to show and teach it to as many women as possible. So I have. Once a week, I teach the acolytes, along with any older students, healers, servants, or librarians who would like to know."

This delicate, gentle-handed woman . . . He supposed he'd learned that strength could be hidden beneath the most unlikely faces.

"The girls are deeply shaken. There hasn't been an intruder in the Torre for a great while. I think it would go a long way if you were to join me tomorrow—to teach what you know."

For a long moment, he stared at her. Blinked.

"You realize I'm in this chair."

"And? Your mouth still works." Tart, crisp words.

He blinked again. "They might not find me the most reassuring instructor—"

"No, they'll likely be swooning and sighing over you so much they'll *forget* to be afraid."

His third and final blink made her smile slightly. Grimly. He wondered what that smile would look like if she ever was truly amused—happy.

"The scar adds a touch of mystery," she said, cutting him off before he could remember the slice down his cheek.

He studied her as she rose from the sofa to stride back to the desk and unpack her bag. "You would truly like me to be there tomorrow?"

"We'll have to figure out how to *get* you there, but it should not be so difficult."

"Stuffing me into a carriage will be fine."

She stiffened, glancing over her shoulder. "Save that anger for *our* training, Lord Westfall." She fished out a vial of oil and set it on the table. "And you will not be taking a carriage."

"A litter carried by servants, then?" He'd sooner crawl.

"A horse. Ever heard of one?"

He clenched the arms of his chair. "You need legs to ride."

"So it's a good thing you still have both of them." She went back to studying whatever vials were in that bag. "I spoke to my superior this morning. She has seen similarly injured people ride until they could meet with us—with special straps and braces. They are fashioning them for you in the workshops as we speak."

He let those words sink in. "So you assumed I would come with you tomorrow."

Yrene turned at last, satchel in her hand now. "I assumed you would wish to ride regardless."

He could only stare while she approached, vial in hand. Only a prim sort of irritation on her face. Better than the stark fear. He asked, voice a bit raw, "You think such a thing is possible?"

"I do. I'll arrive at dawn, so we have enough time to figure it out. The lesson begins at nine."

To ride—even if he could not walk, *riding* . . . "Please do not give me this hope and let it crumble," he said hoarsely.

Yrene set the satchel and vial down on the low-lying table before the sofa and motioned him to move closer. "Good healers don't do such things, Lord Westfall."

He hadn't bothered with a jacket today, and had left his belt in the bedroom. Sliding his sweat-soaked shirt over his head, he made quick work of unbuttoning the tops of his pants. "It's Chaol," he said after a moment. "My name—it's Chaol. Not Lord Westfall." He grunted as he hoisted himself from the chair onto the sofa. "Lord Westfall is my father."

"Well, you're a lord, too."

"Just Chaol."

"Lord Chaol."

He shot her a look as he positioned his legs. She did not reach to help, to adjust. "Here I was, thinking you still resented me."

"If you help my girls tomorrow, I'll reconsider."

From the gleam in those golden eyes, he very much doubted that, but a half smile tugged on his mouth. "Another massage today?" *Please*, he nearly added. His muscles already ached from his exercising, and moving so much between bed and sofa and chair and bath—

"No." Yrene gestured for him to lie facedown on the sofa. "I'm going to begin today."

"You found information on it?"

141

"No," she repeated, tugging off his pants with that cool, swift efficiency. "But after last night . . . I do not want to delay."

"I will—I can . . ." He ground his teeth. "We'll find a way to protect you while you research." He hated the words, felt them curl like rancid milk on his tongue, along his throat.

"I think they know that," she said quietly, and dabbed spots of oil along his spine. "I'm not sure if it's the information, though. That they want to keep me from finding."

His gut tightened, even as she ran soothing hands down his back. They lingered near that splotch at its apex. "What do you think they want, then?"

He already suspected, but he wanted to hear her say it—wanted to know if she thought the same, understood the risks as much as he did.

"I wonder," she said at last, "if it was not just what I was researching, but also that I'm healing *you*."

He craned his head to look at her as the words settled between them. She only stared at that mark on his spine, her tired face drawn. He doubted she'd slept. "If you're too tired—"

"I am not."

He clenched his jaw. "You can nap here. I'll look after you." Useless as it would be. "Then work on me later—"

"I will work on you now. I am not going to let them scare me away."

Her voice did not tremble or waver.

She added, more quietly but no less fiercely, "I once lived in fear of other people. I let other people walk all over me just because I was too afraid of the consequences for refusing. I did not know *how* to refuse." Her hand pushed down on his spine in a silent order to rest his head again. "The day I reached these shores, I cast aside that girl. And I will be damned if I let her reemerge. Or let someone tell *me* what to do with my life, my choices again."

The hair on his arms rose at the simmering wrath in her voice. A woman made of steel and crackling embers. Heat indeed flared beneath

142

her palm as she slid it up the column of his spine, toward that splotch of white.

"Let's see if it enjoys being pushed around for a change," she breathed.

Yrene laid her hand directly atop the scar. Chaol opened his mouth to speak—

But a scream came out instead.

⇥ 12 ⇤

Burning, razor-sharp pain sliced down his back in brutal claws.

Chaol arched, bellowing in agony.

Yrene's hand was instantly gone, and a crashing sounded.

Chaol panted, gasping, as he pushed up onto his elbows to find Yrene sitting on the low-lying table, her vial of oil overturned and leaking across the wood. She gaped at his back, at where her hand had been.

He had no words—none beyond the echoing pain.

Yrene lifted her hands before her face as if she had never seen them before.

She turned them this way and that.

"It doesn't just dislike my magic," she breathed.

His arms buckled, so he lay down again on the cushions, holding her stare as Yrene declared, "It *hates* my magic."

"You said it was an echo—not connected to the injury."

"Maybe I was wrong."

"Rowan healed me with none of those problems."

Her brows knotted at the name, and he silently cursed himself for revealing that piece of his history in this palace of ears and mouths. "Were you conscious?"

He considered. "No. I was—nearly dead."

She noticed the spilled oil then and cursed softly—mildly, compared to some other filthy mouths he'd had the distinct pleasure of being around.

Yrene lunged for her satchel, but he moved faster, grabbing his sweat-damp shirt from where he'd laid it on the sofa arm and chucking it over the spreading puddle before it could drip onto the surely priceless rug.

Yrene studied the shirt, then his outstretched arm, now nearly across her lap. "Either your lack of consciousness during that initial healing kept you from feeling this sort of pain, or perhaps whatever this is had not . . . settled."

His throat clogged. "You think I'm possessed?" By that *thing* that had dwelled inside the king, that had done such unspeakable things—

"No. But pain can feel *alive*. Maybe this is no different. And maybe it does not want to let go."

"Is my spine even injured?" He barely managed to ask the question.

"It is," she said, and some part of his chest caved in. "I sensed the broken bits—the tangled and severed nerves. But to heal those things, to get them communicating with your brain again . . . I need to get past that echo. Or beat it into submission enough to have space to work on you." Her lips pressed into a grim line. "This shadow, this thing that haunts you—your body. It will fight me every step of the way, fight to convince *you* to tell me to stop. Through pain." Her eyes were clear—stark. "Do you understand what I am telling you?"

His voice was low, rough. "That if you are to succeed, I will have to endure that sort of pain. Repeatedly."

"I have herbs that can make you sleep, but with an injury like this . . . I think I won't be the only one who has to fight back against it. And if you

145

are unconscious . . . I fear what it might try to do to you if you're trapped there. In your dreamscape—your psyche." Her face seemed to pale further.

Chaol slid his hand from where it still rested atop his shirt-turned-mop and squeezed her hand. "Do what you have to."

"It will hurt. Like that. Constantly. Worse, likely. I will have to work my way down, vertebra by vertebra, before I even reach the base of your spine. Fighting it and healing you at the same time."

His hand tightened on hers, so small compared to his. "Do what you have to," he repeated.

"And you," she said quietly. "You will have to fight it as well."

He stilled at that.

Yrene went on, "If these things feed upon us by nature . . . If they feed, and yet you are healthy . . ." She gestured to his body. "Then it must be feeding upon something else. Something within you."

"I sense nothing."

She studied their joined hands—then slid her fingers away. Not as violent as dropping his hand, but the withdrawal was pointed enough. "Perhaps we should discuss it."

"Discuss what."

She brushed her hair over a shoulder. "What happened—whatever it is that you feed this thing."

Sweat coated his palms. "There is nothing to discuss."

Yrene stared at him for a long moment. It was all he could do not to shrink from that frank gaze. "From what I've gleaned, there is quite a bit to discuss regarding the past few months. It seems as if it's been a . . . tumultuous time for you recently. You yourself said yesterday that there is no one who loathes you more than yourself."

To say the least. "And you're suddenly so eager to hear about it?"

She didn't so much as flinch. "If that is what is required for you to heal and be gone."

His brows rose. "Well, then. It finally comes out."

Yrene's face was an unreadable mask that could have given Dorian a run for his money. "I assume you do not wish to be here forever, what with war breaking loose in *our* homeland, as you called it."

"Is it not our homeland?"

Silently, Yrene rose to grab her satchel. "I have no interest in sharing anything with Adarlan."

He understood. He really did. Perhaps it was why he still had not told her who, exactly, that lingering darkness belonged to.

"And you," Yrene went on, "are avoiding the topic at hand." She rooted through her satchel. "You'll have to talk about what happened sooner or later."

"With all due respect, it's none of your business."

Her eyes flicked to him at that. "You would be surprised by how closely the healing of physical wounds is tied to the healing of emotional ones."

"I've faced what happened."

"Then what is that thing in your spine feeding on?"

"I don't know." He didn't care.

She fished something out of the satchel at last, and when she strode back toward him, his stomach tightened at what she held.

A bit. Crafted from dark, fresh leather. Unused.

She offered it to him without hesitation. How many times had she handed one over to patients, to heal injuries far worse than his?

"Now would be the time to tell me to stop," Yrene said, face grim. "In case you'd rather discuss what happened these past few months."

Chaol only lay on his stomach and slid the bit into his mouth.

~

Nesryn had watched the sunrise from the skies.

She'd found Prince Sartaq waiting in his aerie in the hour before dawn. The minaret was open to the elements at its uppermost level, and behind the leather-clad prince . . . Nesryn had braced a hand on the archway to the stairwell, still breathless from the climb.

Kadara was beautiful.

Each of the ruk's golden feathers shone like burnished metal, the white of her breast bright as fresh snow. And her gold eyes had sized Nesryn up immediately. Before Sartaq even turned from where he'd been buckling on the saddle across her broad back.

"Captain Faliq," the prince had said by way of greeting. "You're up early."

Casual words for any listening ears.

"The storm last night kept me from sleep. I hope I am not disturbing you."

"On the contrary." In the dim light, his mouth quirked in a smile. "I was about to go for a ride—to let this fat hog hunt for her breakfast for once."

Kadara puffed her feathers in indignation, clicking her enormous beak—fully capable of taking a man's head off in one snip. No wonder Princess Hasar remained wary of the bird.

Sartaq chuckled, patting her feathers. "Care to join?"

With the words, Nesryn suddenly had a sense of how very, very high the minaret was. And how Kadara would likely fly above it. With nothing to keep her from death but the rider and saddle now set in place.

But to ride a ruk . . .

Even better, to ride a ruk with a prince who might have information for them . . .

"I am not particularly skilled with heights, but it would be my honor, Prince."

It had been a matter of a few minutes. Sartaq had ordered her to switch from her midnight-blue jacket to the spare leather one folded in a chest of drawers shoved against the far wall. He'd politely turned his back when she changed pants as well. Since her hair fell only to her shoulders, she had difficulty braiding it back, but the prince had fished into his own pockets and supplied her with a leather thong to pull it back into a knot.

Always carry a spare, he told her. Or else she'd be combing her hair for weeks.

He'd mounted the keen-eyed ruk first, Kadara lowering herself like some oversized hen to the floor. He climbed her side in two fluid movements, then reached down a hand for Nesryn. She gingerly laid her palm against Kadara's ribs, marveling at the cool feathers smooth as finest silk.

Nesryn waited for the ruk to shift about and glare while Sartaq hauled her into the saddle in front of him, but the prince's mount remained docile. Patient.

Sartaq had buckled and harnessed them both into the saddle, triple-checking the leather straps. Then he clicked his tongue once, and—

Nesryn knew it wasn't polite to squeeze a prince's arms so hard the bone was likely to break. But she did so anyway as Kadara spread her shining golden wings and leaped out.

Leaped *down*.

Her stomach shot straight up her throat. Her eyes watered and blurred.

Wind tore at her, trying to rip her from that saddle, and she clenched with her thighs so tightly they ached, while she gripped Sartaq's arms, holding the reins, so hard he chuckled in her ear.

But the pale buildings of Antica loomed up, near-blue in the early dawn, rushing to meet them as Kadara dove and dove, a star falling from the heavens—

Then flared those wings wide and shot upward.

Nesryn was glad she had forgone breakfast. For surely it would have come spewing out of her mouth at what the motion did to her stomach.

Within the span of a few beats, Kadara banked right—toward the horizon just turning pink.

The sprawl of Antica spread before them, smaller and smaller as they rose into the skies. Until it was no more than a cobblestoned road beneath them, spreading into every direction. Until she could spy the olive groves and wheat fields just outside the city. The country estates and small towns speckled about. The rippling dunes of the northern desert to her left. The sparkling, snaking band of rivers turning golden in the rising sun that crested over the mountains to her right.

Sartaq did not speak. Did not point out landmarks. Not even the pale line of the Sister-Road that ran toward the southern horizon.

No, in the rising light, he let Kadara have her head. The ruk took them floating higher still, the air turning crisp—the awakening blue sky brightening with each mighty flap of her wings.

Open. So open.

Not at all like the endless sea, the tedious waves and cramped ship.

This was . . . this was *breath*. This was . . .

She could not look fast enough, drink it all in. How small everything was, how lovely and pristine. A land claimed by a conquering nation, yet loved and nurtured.

Her land. Her home.

The sun and the scrub and the undulating grasslands that beckoned in the distance. The lush jungles and rice fields to the west; the pale sand dunes of the desert to the northeast. More than she could see in a lifetime— farther than Kadara could fly in a single day. An entire world, this land. The entire world contained here.

She could not understand why her father had left.

Why he had stayed, when such darkness had crept into Adarlan. Why he had kept them in that festering city where she so rarely looked up at the sky, or felt a breeze that did not reek of the briny Avery or the rubbish rotting in the streets.

"You are quiet," the prince said, and it was more question than statement.

Nesryn admitted in Halha, "I don't have words to describe it."

She felt Sartaq smile near her shoulder. "That was what I felt—that first ride. And every ride since."

"I understand why you stayed at the camp those years ago. Why you are eager to return."

A beat of quiet. "Am I so easy to read?"

"How could you *not* wish to return?"

"Some consider my father's palace to be the finest in the world."

"It is."

His silence was question enough.

"Rifthold's palace was nothing so fine—so lovely and a part of the land."

Sartaq hummed, the sound reverberating into her back. Then he said quietly, "The death of my sister has been hard upon my mother. It is for her that I remain."

Nesryn winced a bit. "I'm so very sorry."

Only the rushing wind spoke for a time.

Then Sartaq said, "You said *was*. Regarding Rifthold's royal palace. Why?"

"You heard what befell it—the glass portions."

"Ah." Another beat of quiet. "Shattered by the Queen of Terrasen. Your . . . ally."

"My friend."

He craned his body around hers to peer at her face. "Is she truly?"

"She is a good woman," Nesryn said, and meant it. "Difficult, yes, but . . . some might say the same of any royalty."

"Apparently, she found the former King of Adarlan so difficult that she killed him."

Careful words.

"The man was a monster—and a threat to all. His Second, Perrington, remains that way. She did Erilea a favor."

Sartaq angled the reins as Kadara began a slow, steady descent toward a sparkling river valley. "She is truly that powerful?"

Nesryn debated the merits of the truth or downplaying Aelin's might. "She and Dorian both possess considerable magic. But I would say it is their intelligence that is the stronger weapon. Brute power is useless without it."

"It's dangerous without it."

"Yes," Nesryn agreed, swallowing. "Are . . ." She had not been trained in the mazelike way of speaking at court. "Is there such a threat within your court that warranted us needing to speak in the skies?"

He could very well be the threat posed, she reminded herself.

"You have dined with my siblings. You see how they are. If I were to arrange a meeting with you, it would send a message to them. That I am willing to hear your suit—perhaps press it to our father. They would consider the risks and benefits of undermining me. Or whether it would make them look better to try to join . . . my side."

"And are you? Willing to hear us out?"

Sartaq didn't answer for a long moment, only the screaming wind filling the quiet.

"I would listen. To you and Lord Westfall. I would hear what you know, what has happened to you both. I do not hold as much sway with my father as others, but he knows the ruk riders are loyal to me."

"I thought—"

"That I was his favorite?" A low, bitter laugh. "I perhaps stand a chance at being named Heir, but the khagan does not select his Heir based on whom he loves best. Even so, that particular honor goes to Duva and Kashin."

Sweet-faced Duva, she could understand, but—"Kashin?"

"He is loyal to my father to a fault. He has never schemed, never back-stabbed. I've done it—plotted and maneuvered against them all to get what I want. But Kashin . . . He may command the land armies and the horse-lords, he may be brutal when required, but with my father, he is guileless. There has never been a more loving or loyal son. When our father dies . . . I worry. What the others will do to Kashin if he does not submit, or worse: what his death will do to Kashin himself."

She dared ask, "What would you do to him?" *Destroy him, if he will not swear fealty?*

"It remains to be seen what sort of threat or alliance he could pose. Only Duva and Arghun are married, and Arghun has yet to sire offspring.

Though Kashin, if he has his way, would likely sweep that young healer off her feet."

Yrene. "Strange that she has no interest in him."

"A mark in her favor. It is not easy to love a khagan's offspring."

The green grasses, still dewy beneath the fresh sun, rippled as Kadara swept toward a swift-moving river. With those enormous talons of hers, she could easily snatch up fistfuls of fish.

But it was not the prey Kadara sought as she flew over the river, seeking something—

"Someone broke into the Torre's library last night," Sartaq said as he monitored the ruk's hunt over the dark blue waters. Mist off the surface kissed Nesryn's face, but the chill at his words went far deeper. "They killed a healer—through some vile power that rendered her into a husk. We have never seen its like in Antica."

Nesryn's stomach turned over. With that description—"Who? Why?"

"Yrene Towers sounded the alarm. We searched for hours and found no trace, beyond missing books from where she had been studying, and where it stalked her. Yrene was rattled, but fine."

Researching—Chaol had informed her last night that Yrene had planned to do some research regarding wounds from magic, from demons.

Sartaq asked casually, "Do you know what Yrene might have been looking into that posed such dark interest and theft of her books?"

Nesryn considered. It could be a trick—his revealing something personal from his family, his life, to lull her into telling him secrets. Nesryn and Chaol had not yielded any information of the keys, the Valg, or Erawan to the khagan or his children. They had been waiting to do so— to assess whom to trust. For if their enemies heard that they were hunting for the keys to seal the Wyrdgate . . .

"No," she lied. "But perhaps they are unannounced enemies of ours who wish to scare her and the other healers out of helping the captain. I mean—Lord Westfall."

Silence. She thought he'd push her on it, waited for it as Kadara skimmed closer to the river's surface, as if closing in on some prey. "It must be strange, to bear a new title, with the former owner right beside you."

"I was only captain for a few weeks before we left. I suppose I shall have to learn when I return."

"If Yrene is successful. Among other possible victories."

Like bringing that army with them.

"Yes," was all she managed to say.

Kadara dove, a sharp, swift motion that had Sartaq tightening his arms around her, bracing her thighs with his own.

She let him guide her, keeping them upright in the saddle as Kadara dipped into the water, thrashed, and sent something hurling onto the riverbank. A heartbeat later, she was upon it, talons and beak spearing and slashing. The thing beneath her fought, twisting and whipping—

A crunch. Then silence.

The ruk calmed, feathers puffing, then smoothing against the blood now splattered along her breast and neck. Some had splashed onto Nesryn's boots as well.

"Be careful, Captain Faliq," Sartaq said as Nesryn got a good look at the creature the ruk now feasted upon.

It was enormous, nearly fifteen feet, covered in scales thick as armor. Like the marsh beasts of Eyllwe, but bulkier—fatter from the cattle it no doubt dragged into the water along these rivers.

"There is beauty in my father's lands," the prince went on while Kadara ripped into that monstrous carcass, "but there is much lurking beneath the surface, too."

⇥ 13 ⇤

Yrene panted, her legs sprawled before her on the rug, her back resting against the couch on which Lord Chaol now gasped for breath as well.

Her mouth was dry as sand, her limbs trembling so violently that she could barely keep her hands limp in her lap.

A spitting sound and a little thump told her he'd removed the bit.

He'd roared around it. His bellowing had been almost as bad as the magic itself.

It was a void. It was a new, dark hell.

Her magic had been a pulsing star that flared against the wall that the darkness had crafted between the top of his spine and the rest of it. She knew—knew without testing—that if she bypassed it, jumped right to the base of his spine . . . it would find her there, too.

But she had pushed. Pushed and pushed, until she was sobbing for breath.

Still, that wall did not move.

It only seemed to laugh, quietly and sibilantly, the sound laced with ancient ice and malice.

She'd hurled her magic against the wall, letting its swarm of burning white lights attack in wave after wave, but—nothing.

And only at the end, when her magic could find no crack, no crevice to slide into . . . Only when she made to pull back did that dark wall seem to transform.

To morph into something . . . Other.

Yrene's magic had turned brittle before it. Any spark of defiance in the wake of that healer's death had cooled. And she could not see, did not dare to look at what she felt gathering there, what filled the dark with voices, as if they were echoing down a long hall.

But it had loomed, and she had slid a glance over her shoulder.

The dark wall was alive. Swimming with images, one after another. As if she were looking through someone's eyes. She knew on instinct they did not belong to Lord Chaol.

A fortress of dark stone jutted up amid ash-colored, barren mountains, its towers sharp as lances, its edges and parapets hard and slicing. Beyond it, coating the vales and plains amid the mountains, an army rippled away into the distance, more campfires than she could count.

And she knew the name for this place, the assembled host. Heard the name thunder through her mind as if it were the beat of a hammer on anvil.

Morath.

She'd pulled out. Had yanked herself back to the light and heavy heat.

Morath—whether it was some true memory, left by whatever power had struck him; whether it was something the darkness conjured from her own darkest terrors . . .

Not real. At least not in this room, with its streaming sunlight and chattering fountain in the garden beyond. But if it was indeed a true portrayal of the armies that Lord Chaol had mentioned yesterday . . .

156

That was what she would face. The victims of that host, possibly even the soldiers within it, should things go very wrong.

That was what awaited her back home.

Not now—she would not think about this now, with him here. Fretting about it, reminding him of what he must face, what might be sweeping down upon his friends as they sat here . . . Not helpful. To either of them.

So Yrene sat there on the rug, forcing her trembling to abate with each deep breath she inhaled through her nose and out her mouth, letting her magic settle and refill within her as she calmed her mind. Letting Lord Chaol pant on the couch behind her, neither of them saying a word.

No, this would not be a usual healing.

But perhaps delaying her return, remaining here to heal him for however long it took . . . There might be others like him on those battlefields—suffering from similar injuries. Learning to face this now, however harrowing . . . Yes, this delay might turn fruitful. If she could stomach, if she could endure, that darkness again. Find some way to shatter it.

Go where you fear to tread.

Indeed.

Her eyes drifted closed. At some point, the servant girl had come back with the ingredients Yrene had invented. Had taken one look at them and vanished.

It had been hours ago. Days ago.

Hunger was a tight knot in her belly—a strangely mortal feeling compared to the hours spent attacking that blackness, only half aware of the hand she'd placed on his back, of the screaming that came from him every time her magic shoved against that wall.

He had not once asked her to stop. Had not begged for reprieve.

Shaking fingers brushed her shoulder. "Are . . . you . . ." Each of his words was a burnt rasp. She'd have to get him peppermint tea with honey.

157

She should call to the servant—if she could remember to speak. Muster the voice herself. ". . . all right?"

Yrene cracked her eyelids open as his hand settled on her shoulder. Not from any affection or concern, but because she had a feeling that the exhaustion lay so heavily upon him that he couldn't move it again.

And she was drained enough that she couldn't muster the strength to brush off that touch, as she'd done earlier. "I should ask *you* if you're all right," she managed to say, voice raw. "Anything?"

"No." The sheer lack of emotion behind the word told her enough of his thoughts, his disappointment. He paused for a few heartbeats before he repeated, "No."

She closed her eyes again. This could take weeks. Months. Especially if she did not find some way to shove back that wall of darkness.

She tried and failed to move her legs. "I should get you—"

"Rest."

The hand tightened on her shoulder.

"Rest," he said again.

"You're done for the day," she said. "No additional exercise—"

"I mean—you. *Rest*." Each word was labored.

Yrene dragged her stare toward the large clock in the corner. Blinked once. Twice.

Five.

They had been here for *five* hours—

He had endured it all that time. Five *hours* of this agony—

The thought alone had her drawing up her legs. Groaning as she braced a hand on the low-lying table and rallied her strength, pushing up, up, until she was standing. Weaving on her feet, but—standing.

His arms slid beneath him, the muscles of his bare back rippling as he tried to push himself up. "Don't," she said.

He did so anyway. The considerable muscles in his arms and chest did not fail him as he shoved upward, until he was sitting. Staring at her, glassy-eyed.

Yrene rasped, "You need—tea."

"Kadja."

The name was little more than a push of breath.

The servant immediately appeared. Too quickly.

Yrene studied her closely as the girl slipped in. She'd been listening. Waiting.

Yrene did not bother to smile as she said, "Peppermint tea. Lots of honey."

Chaol added, "Two of them."

Yrene gave him a look, but sank onto the couch beside him. The cushions were slightly damp—with his sweat, she realized as she saw it gleaming on the contours of his bronzed chest.

She shut her eyes—just for a moment.

She didn't realize it was far longer than that until Kadja was setting two delicate teacups before them, a small iron kettle steaming in the center of the table. The woman poured generous amounts of honey into both, and Yrene's mouth was too dry, tongue too heavy, to bother telling her to stop or she'd make them ill from the sweetness.

The servant stirred both in silence, then handed the first cup to Chaol.

He merely passed it to Yrene.

She was too tired to object as she wrapped her hands around it, trying to rally the strength to raise it to her lips.

He seemed to sense it.

He told Kadja to leave his cup on the table. Told her to go.

Yrene watched as through a distant window while Chaol took her cup and lifted it to her lips.

She debated shoving his hand out of her face.

Yes, she'd work with him; no, he was not the monster she'd initially suspected he'd be, not in the way she'd seen men be; but letting him this close, letting him *tend* to her like this . . .

"You can either drink it," he said, his voice a low growl, "or we can sit like this for the next few hours."

She slid her eyes to him. Found his stare to be level—clear, despite the exhaustion.

She said nothing.

"So, that's the line," Chaol murmured, more to himself than her. "You can stomach helping me, but I can't return the favor. Or can't do anything that steps beyond your idea of what—who I am."

He was more astute than most people likely gave him credit for.

She had a feeling the hardness in his rich brown eyes was mirrored in her own.

"Drink." Pure command laced his voice—a man used to being obeyed, to giving orders. "Resent me all you want, but drink the damn thing."

And it was the faint kernel of worry in his eyes . . .

A man used to being obeyed, yes, but a man also inclined to care for others. Look after them. Driven to do it by a compulsion he couldn't leash, couldn't train out of him. Couldn't have broken out of him.

Yrene parted her lips, a silent yielding.

Gently, he set the porcelain teacup against her mouth and tipped it for her.

She sipped once. He murmured in encouragement. She did so again.

So tired. She had never been so tired in her *life*—

Chaol pushed the cup against her mouth a third time, and she drank a full gulp.

Enough. He needed it more than she did—

He sensed she was likely to bark at him, withdrew the cup from her mouth, and merely sipped it. One gulp. Two.

He drained it and grabbed the other one, offering her the first sips again before he took the dregs.

Insufferable man.

Yrene must have said as much, because a half smile kicked up on one side of his face. "You're not the first to call me that," he said, his voice smoother. Less hoarse.

"I won't be the last, I'm sure," she muttered.

Chaol simply gave her that half smile again and stretched to refill both cups. He added the honey himself—less than Kadja had. The right amount. He stirred them, his hands steady.

"I can do it," Yrene tried to say.

"So can I," was all he said.

She managed to hold the cup this time. He made sure she was well onto drinking hers before he lifted his own to his lips.

"I should go." The thought of getting out of the palace, let alone the trek to the Torre, then the walk up the stairs to her rooms . . .

"Rest. Eat—you must be starving."

She eyed him. "You're not?" He'd exercised heavily before she'd arrived; he had to be famished from that alone.

"I am. But I don't think I can wait for dinner." He added, "You could join me."

It was one thing to heal him, work with him, let him serve her tea. But to dine with him, the man who had served that butcher, the man who had worked for him while that dark army was amassed down in Morath . . . There it was. That smoke in her nose, the crackle of flame and screaming.

Yrene leaned forward to set her cup on the table. Then stood. Every movement was stiff, sore. "I need to return to the Torre," she said, knees wobbling. "The vigil is at sundown." Still a good hour from now, thankfully.

He noted her swaying and reached for her, but she stepped out of his range. "I'll leave the supplies." Because the thought of lugging that heavy bag back . . .

"Let me arrange a carriage for you."

"I can ask at the front gate," she said. If someone was hunting her, she'd opt for the safety of a carriage.

She had to grip the furniture as she passed to keep upright. The distance to the door seemed eternal.

"Yrene."

She could barely stand at the door, but she paused to look back.

"The lesson tomorrow." The focus had already returned to those brown eyes. "Where do you want me to meet you?"

She debated calling it off. Wondered what she'd been thinking, asking him of all people to come.

But . . . five hours. Five hours of agony, and he had not broken.

Perhaps it was for that alone that she had declined dinner. If he had not broken, then she would not break—not in seeing him as anything but what he was. What he'd served.

"I'll meet you in the main courtyard at sunrise."

Mustering the strength to walk was an effort, but she did it. Put one foot in front of the other.

Left him alone in that room, still staring after her.

Five hours of agony, and she'd known it had not all been physical.

She had sensed, shoving against that wall, that the darkness had also showed him things on the other side of it.

Glimmers had sometimes shivered past her. Nothing she could make out, but they felt . . . they had *felt* like memories. Nightmares. Perhaps both.

Yet he had not asked her to stop.

And part of Yrene wondered, as she trudged through the palace, if Lord Chaol had not asked her to stop not just because he'd learned how to manage pain, but also because he somehow felt he deserved it.

⁓

Everything hurt.

Chaol did not let himself think about what he had seen. What had flashed through his mind as that pain had wracked him, burned and flayed and shattered him. What—and who he'd seen. The body on the bed. The collar on a throat. The head that had rolled.

He could not escape them. Not while Yrene had worked.

So the pain had ripped through him, so he had seen it, over and over.

So he had roared and screamed and bellowed.

She'd stopped only when she'd slid to the floor.

He'd been left hollow. Void.

She still had not wanted to spend more than a moment necessary with him.

He didn't blame her.

Not that it mattered. Though he reminded himself that she'd asked him to help tomorrow.

In whatever way he could.

Chaol ate his meal where Yrene had left him, still in his undershorts. Kadja didn't seem to notice or care, and he was too aching and tired to bother with modesty.

Aelin would likely have laughed to see him now. The man who had stumbled out of her room after she'd declared that her cycle had arrived. Now sitting in this fine room, mostly naked and not giving a shit about it.

Nesryn returned before sundown, her face flushed and hair wind-blown. One look at her tentative smile told him enough. At least she'd been somewhat successful with Sartaq. Perhaps she'd manage to do what it seemed he himself was failing to: raising a host to bring back home.

He'd meant to speak to the khagan today—about the threat last night's attack had posed. Meant to, and yet it was now late enough to prevent arranging such a meeting.

He barely heard Nesryn as she whispered about Sartaq's possible sympathy. Her ride on his magnificent ruk. Exhaustion weighed on him so heavily he could hardly keep his eyes open, even while he pictured those ruks squaring off against Ironteeth witches and wyverns, even while he debated who might survive such battles.

But he managed to give the order that curdled on his tongue: *Go hunting, Nesryn.*

If one of Erawan's Valg minions had indeed come to Antica, time was not on their side. Every step, every request might be reported back to

Erawan. And if they were pursuing Yrene, either for reading up on the Valg or for healing the Hand of the King of Adarlan . . . He didn't trust anyone here enough to ask them to do this. Anyone other than Nesryn.

Nesryn had nodded at his request. Had understood why he'd nearly spat it out. To let her go into danger, to *hunt* that sort of danger . . .

But she'd done it before in Rifthold. She reminded him of that— gently. Sleep beckoned, turning his body foreign and heavy, but he managed to make his final request: *Be careful.*

Chaol didn't resist when she helped him into the chair, then wheeled him into his room. He tried and failed to lift himself into bed, and was only vaguely aware of her and Kadja hauling him onto it like a slab of meat.

Yrene—she never did such things. Never wheeled him when he could do so himself. Constantly told him to move himself instead.

He wondered why. Was too damn tired to wonder why.

Nesryn said she would make his apologies at dinner, and went to change. He wondered if the servants heard the whine of the whetstone against her blades from her bedroom door.

He was asleep before she left, the clock in the sitting room distantly chiming seven.

No one paid Nesryn much heed at dinner that night. And no one paid her any heed later, when she donned her fighting knives, sword, and bow and quiver, and slipped into the city streets.

Not even the khagan's wife.

As Nesryn stalked by a large stone garden on her way out of the palace, a glimmer of white caught her eye—and sent her ducking behind one of the pillars flanking the courtyard.

Within a heartbeat, she removed her hand from the long knife at her side.

Clad in white silk, her long curtain of dark hair unbound, the Grand

Empress strolled, silent and grave as a wraith, down a walkway wending through the rock formations of the garden. Only moonlight filled the space—moonlight and shadow, as the empress strode alone and unnoticed, her simple gown flowing behind her as if on a phantom wind.

White for grief—for death.

The Grand Empress's face was unadorned, her coloring far paler than that of her children. No joy limned her features; no life. No interest in either.

Nesryn lingered in the shadows of the pillar, watching the woman drift farther away, as if she were wandering the paths of some dreamscape. Or perhaps some empty, barren hell.

Nesryn wondered if it was at all similar to the ones she herself had walked during those initial months after her mother's passing. Wondered if the days also bled together for the Grand Empress, if food was ash on her tongue and sleep was both craved and elusive.

Only when the khagan's wife strode behind a large boulder, vanishing from sight, did Nesryn continue on, her steps a little heavier.

Antica under the full moon was a wash of blues and silvers, interrupted by the golden glow of lanterns hanging from public dining rooms and the carts of vendors selling *kahve* and treats. A few performers plucked out melodies on lutes and drums, a few gifted enough to make Nesryn wish she could pause, but stealth and speed were her allies tonight.

She stalked through the shadows, sorting through the sounds of the city.

Various temples were interspersed amongst the main thoroughfares: some crafted of marble pillars, some beneath peaked wooden roofs and painted columns, some mere courtyards filled with pools or rock gardens or sleeping animals. Thirty-six gods watched over this city—and there were thrice as many temples to them scattered throughout.

And with each one Nesryn passed, she wondered if those gods were peering out from the pillars or behind the carved rocks; if they watched from the eaves of that sloped roof, or from behind the spotted cat's eyes where it lay half awake on the temple steps.

She beseeched all of them to make her feet swift and silent, to guide her where she needed to go while she prowled the streets.

If a Valg agent had come to this continent—or worse, a possible Valg prince . . . Nesryn scanned the rooftops and the gargantuan pillar of the Torre. It gleamed bone white in the moonlight, a beacon watching over this city, the healers within.

Chaol and Yrene had made no progress today, but—it was fine. Nesryn reminded herself, again and again, that it was fine. These things took a while, even if Yrene . . . It was clear she had some personal reservations regarding Chaol's heritage. His former role in the empire.

Nesryn paused near an alley entrance while a band of young revelers staggered past, singing bawdy songs that would surely make her aunt scold them. And later hum along herself.

As she monitored the alley, the bordering, flat rooftops, Nesryn's attention snagged on a rough carving in the earthen brick wall. An owl at rest, its wings tucked in, those unearthly large eyes wide and eternally unblinking. Perhaps no more than vandalism, yet she brushed a gloved hand over it, tracing the lines etched into the building's side.

Antica's owls. They were everywhere in this city, tribute to the goddess worshipped perhaps more than any other of the thirty-six. No chief god ruled the southern continent, yet Silba . . . Nesryn again studied the mighty tower, shining brighter than the palace on the opposite end of the city. Silba reigned unchallenged here. For anyone to break into that Torre, to *kill* one of the healers, they had to be desperate. Or utterly insane.

Or a Valg demon, with no fear of the gods—only of their master's wrath if they should fail.

But if she were a Valg in this city, where to hide? Where to lurk?

Canals ran beneath some of the homes, but it was not like the vast sewer network of Rifthold. Yet perhaps if she studied the Torre's walls . . .

Nesryn aimed for the gleaming tower, the Torre looming with each nearing step. She paused in the shadows beside one of the homes across the street from the solid wall that enclosed the Torre's entire compound.

Torches flickered along brackets in the pale wall, guards stationed every few feet. And atop it. Royal guards, judging from their colors, and Torre guards in their cornflower blue and yellow—so many that none would get by without notice. Nesryn studied the iron gates, now sealed for the night.

"Were they open last night, is the answer no guard wants to yield."

Nesryn whirled, her knife angled low and up.

Prince Sartaq leaned against the building wall a few feet behind her, his gaze on the looming Torre. Twin swords peeked above his broad shoulders, and long knives hung from his belt. He'd changed from the finery of dinner back into his flying leathers—again reinforced with steel at the shoulders, silver gauntlets at his wrists, and a black scarf at his neck. No, not scarf—but a cloth to pull over his mouth and nose when the heavy hood of his cloak was on. To remain anonymous, unmarked.

She sheathed her knife. "Were you following me?"

The prince flicked his dark, calm eyes to her. "You didn't exactly try to be inconspicuous when you left through the front gate, armed to the teeth."

Nesryn turned toward the Torre walls. "I have no reason to hide what I'm doing."

"You think whoever attacked the healers is just going to be strolling around?" His boots were barely a scrape against the ancient stones as he approached her side.

"I thought to investigate how they might have gotten in. Get a better sense of the layout and where they'd likely find appealing to hide."

A pause. "You sound as if you know your prey intimately." *And didn't think to mention this to me during our ride this morning*, was the unspoken rest.

Nesryn glanced sidelong at Sartaq. "I wish I could say otherwise, but I do. If the attack was made by whom we suspect . . . I spent much of this spring and summer hunting their kind in Rifthold."

Sartaq watched the wall for a long minute. He said quietly, "How bad was it?"

Nesryn swallowed as the images flickered: the bodies and the sewers and the glass castle exploding, a wall of death flying for her—

"Captain Faliq."

A gentle prod. A softer tone than she'd expect from a warrior-prince.

"What did your spies tell you?"

Sartaq's jaw tightened, shadows crossing his face before he said, "They reported that Rifthold was full of terrors. People who were not *people*. Beasts from Vanth's darkest dreams."

Vanth—Goddess of the Dead. Her presence in this city predated even Silba's healers, her worshippers a secretive sect that even the khagan and his predecessors feared and respected, despite her rituals being wholly different from the Eternal Sky to which the khagan and the Darghan believed they returned. Nesryn had walked swiftly past Vanth's dark-stoned temple earlier, the entrance marked only by a set of onyx steps descending into a subterranean chamber lit with bone-white candles.

"I can see that none of this sounds outlandish to you," said Sartaq.

"A year ago, it might have."

Sartaq's gaze swept over her weapons. "So you truly faced such horrors, then."

"Yes," Nesryn admitted. "For whatever good it did, considering the city is now held by them." The words came out as bitterly as they felt.

Sartaq considered. "Most would have fled, rather than face them at all."

She didn't feel like confirming or denying such a statement, no doubt meant to console her. A kind effort from a man who did not need to do such things. She found herself saying, "I—I saw your mother earlier. Walking alone through a garden."

Sartaq's eyes shuttered. "Oh?"

A careful question.

Nesryn wondered if she perhaps should have held her tongue, but she continued, "I only mention it in case . . . in case it is something you might need, might want to know."

"Was there a guard? A handmaiden with her?"

"None that I saw."

That was indeed worry tightening his face as he leaned against the wall of the building. "Thank you for the report."

It was not her place to ask about it—not for anyone, and certainly not for the most powerful family in the world. But Nesryn said quietly, "My mother died when I was thirteen." She gazed up at the near-glowing Torre. "The old king . . . you know what he did to those with magic. To healers gifted with it. So there was no one who could save my mother from the wasting sickness that crept up on her. The healer we managed to find admitted to us that it was likely from a growth inside my mother's breast. That she might have been able to cure her before magic vanished. Before it was forbidden."

She had never told anyone outside of her family this story. Wasn't sure why she was really telling him now, but she went on, "My father wanted to get her on a boat to sail here. Was desperate to. But war had broken out up and down our lands. Ships were conscripted into Adarlan's service, and she was too sick to risk a land journey all the way down to Eyllwe to try to cross there. My father combed through every map, every trade route. By the time he found a merchant who would sail with them—just the two of them—to Antica . . . My mother was so sick she could not be moved. She would not have made it here, even if they'd gotten on the boat."

Sartaq watched her, face unreadable, while she spoke.

Nesryn slid her hands into her pockets. "So she stayed. And we were all there when she . . . when it was over." That old grief wrapped around her, burning her eyes. "It took me a few years to feel right again," she said after a moment. "Two years before I started noticing things like the sun on my face, or the taste of food—started enjoying them again. My father . . . he held us together. My sister and I. If he mourned, he did not let us see it. He filled our house with as much joy as he could."

She fell silent, unsure how to explain what she'd meant by starting down this road.

Sartaq said at last, "Where are they now? After the attack on Rifthold?"

"I don't know," she whispered, blowing out a breath. "They got out, but . . . I don't know where they fled, or if they will be able to make it here, with so many horrors filling the world."

Sartaq fell quiet for a long minute, and Nesryn spent every second of it wishing she'd just kept her mouth shut. Then the prince said, "I will send word—discreetly." He pushed off the wall. "For my spies to keep an eye out for the Faliq family, and to aid them, should they pass their way, in any form they can to safer harbors."

Her chest tightened to the point of pain, but she managed to say, "Thank you." It was a generous offer. More than generous.

Sartaq added, "I am sorry—for your loss. As long ago as it was. I . . . As a warrior, I grew up walking hand-in-hand with Death. And yet this one . . . It has been harder to endure than others. And my mother's grief perhaps even harder to face than my own." He shook his head, the moonlight dancing on his black hair, and said with forced lightness, "Why do you think I was so eager to run out after you into the night?"

Nesryn, despite herself, offered him a slight smile in return.

Sartaq lifted a brow. "Though it would help to know what, exactly, I'm supposed to be looking for."

Nesryn debated what to tell him—debated his very presence here.

He gave a low, soft laugh when her hesitation went on a moment too long. "You think I'm the one who attacked that healer? After I was the one who told you about it this morning?"

Nesryn bowed her head. "I mean no disrespect." Even if she'd seen another prince enslaved this spring—had fired an arrow at a queen to keep him alive. "Your spies were correct. Rifthold was . . . I would not wish to see Antica suffer through anything similar."

"And you're convinced the attack at the Torre was just the start?"

"I'm out here, aren't I?"

Silence.

Nesryn added, "If anyone, familiar or foreign, offers you a black ring or collars, if you see anyone with something like it . . . Do not hesitate. Not for a heartbeat. Strike fast, and true. Beheading is the only thing that keeps them down. The person within them is gone. Don't try to save them—or it will be you who winds up enslaved as well."

Sartaq's attention drifted to the sword at her side, the bow and quiver strapped to her back. He said quietly, "Tell me everything that you know."

"I can't."

The refusal alone could end her life, but Sartaq nodded thoughtfully. "Tell me what you can, then."

So she did. Standing in the shadows beyond the Torre walls, she explained everything she could, save for the keys and gates, and Dorian's enslavement, as well as that of the former king.

When she'd finished, Sartaq's face had not changed, though he rubbed at his jaw. "When did you plan to tell my father this?"

"As soon as he'd grant us a private meeting."

Sartaq swore, low and creative. "With my sister's death . . . It's been harder for him than he'll admit to return to our usual rhythms. He will not take my counsel. Or anyone else's."

It was the worry in the prince's tone—and sorrow—that made Nesryn say, "I'm sorry."

Sartaq shook his head. "I must think on what you told me. There are places within this continent, near my people's homeland . . ." He rubbed at his neck. "When I was a boy, they told stories at the aeries of similar horrors." He said, more to himself than her, "Perhaps it is time I paid my hearth-mother a visit. To hear her stories again. And how that ancient threat was dealt with, long ago. Especially if it is now stirring once more."

A record of the Valg . . . here? Her family had never told her any such tales, but then her own people had hailed from distant reaches of the continent. If the ruk riders had somehow either known of the Valg or even faced them . . .

Footsteps scuffed on the street beyond, and they pressed into the walls of the alley, hands on their sword hilts. But it was only a drunk stumbling home for the night, saluting the Torre guards along the wall as he passed, earning a few laughing grins in return.

"Are there canals beneath here—nearby sewers that might connect to the Torre?" Her question was little more than a push of air.

"I don't know," Sartaq admitted with equal quiet. He smiled grimly as he pointed toward an ancient grate in the sloped stones of the alley. "But it would be my honor to accompany you in discovering one."

⇥ 14 ⇤

Yrene didn't care if someone came to murder her in her sleep.

By the time the solemn, candlelit vigil in the Torre courtyard had finished, by the time Yrene crawled to her room near the top of the Torre, two acolytes propping her between them after she'd collapsed at the base of the stairs, she didn't care about anything.

Cook brought her dinner in bed. Yrene managed a bite before she passed out.

She awoke past midnight with her fork on her chest and spiced, slow-cooked chicken staining her favorite blue gown.

She groaned, but felt slightly more alive. Enough so that she sat up in the near-darkness of her tower room, and rose only to see to her needs and haul her tiny desk in front of the door. She stacked books and any spare objects she could find atop it, checked the locks twice, and stumbled back into bed, still fully clothed.

She awoke at sunrise.

Precisely when she said she'd meet Lord Chaol.

Cursing, Yrene hauled away the desk, the books, u   e locks, and flung herself down the tower stairs.

She'd ordered the brace for his horse to be brought directly to the castle courtyard, and she'd left her supplies at his room yesterday, so there was nothing for her to take beyond her own frantic self as she hurtled down the endless spiral of the Torre, scowling at the carved owls passing silent judgment while she flew by doors now beginning to open to reveal sleepy-faced healers and acolytes blinking blearily at her.

Yrene thanked Silba for the restorative powers of deep, dreamless sleep as she sprinted across the complex grounds, past the lavender-lined pathways, through the just-opened gates.

Antica was stirring, the streets mercifully quiet as she raced for the palace perched on its other side. She arrived in the courtyard thirty minutes late, gasping for breath, sweat pooling in every possible crevice of her body.

Lord Westfall had started without her.

Gulping down air, Yrene lingered by the towering bronze gates, the shadows still lying thick with the sun so low on the horizon, and watched the unfolding mounting.

As she'd specified, the patient-looking roan mare was on the shorter side—the perfect height for him to reach the saddle horn with an upraised hand. Which he was currently doing, Yrene noted with no small degree of satisfaction. But the rest . . .

Well, it seemed he'd decided *not* to use the wooden ramp that she'd also ordered crafted in lieu of a stepped mounting block. The mounting ramp now sat by the still-shadowed horse pens against the eastern wall of the courtyard—as if he'd outright refused to even go near it, and instead had them bring over the horse. To mount the mare on his own.

It didn't surprise her one bit.

Chaol did not look at any of the guards clustered around him—at least, more than was necessary. With their backs to her, she could only identify one or two by name, but—

One stepped in silently to let Chaol brace his other hand on his armor-clad shoulder as the lord pushed himself upright in a mighty heave. The mare stood patiently while his right hand gripped the saddle horn to balance himself—

She stepped forward just as Lord Westfall pushed off the guard's shoulder and into the saddle, the guard stepping in close as he did it. It left him sitting sidesaddle, but Chaol still did not give the guard much thanks beyond a tight nod.

Instead, he silently studied the saddle before him, assessing how he was to get one leg over the other side of the horse. Color stained his cheeks, his jaw a tight line. The guards lingered, and he stiffened, tighter and tighter—

But then he moved again, leaning back in the saddle and hauling his right leg over the horn. The guard who'd helped him lunged to support his back, another darting from the other side to keep him from tumbling off, but Chaol's torso remained solid. Unwavering.

His muscle control was extraordinary. A man who had trained that body to obey him no matter what, even now.

And—he was in the saddle.

Chaol murmured something to the guards that had them backing off as he leaned to either side to buckle the straps of the brace around his legs. It had been set into the saddle—the fit perfect based on the estimations she'd given the woman in the workshop—designed to stabilize his legs, replacing where his thighs would have clamped to keep him steady. Just until he became used to riding. He might very well not need them at all, but . . . it was better to be safe for this first ride.

Yrene wiped her sweaty forehead and approached, offering a word of thanks to the guards, who now filtered back to their posts. The one who'd directly helped Lord Westfall turned in her direction, and Yrene gave him a broad smile as she said in Halha, "Good morning, Shen."

The young guard returned her smile as he continued toward the small stables in the far shadows of the courtyard, winking at her as he passed by. "Morning, Yrene."

She found Chaol sitting upright in the saddle when she faced ahead once more—that stiff posture and clenched jaw gone as he watched her approach.

Yrene straightened her dress, realizing just as she reached him that she still wore yesterday's clothes. Now with a giant red splotch on her chest.

Chaol took in the stain, then her hair—oh, gods, her *hair*—and only said, "Good morning."

Yrene swallowed, still panting from her run. "I'm sorry I'm late." Up close, the brace indeed blended in enough for most people not to notice. Especially with the way he carried himself.

He sat tall and proud on that horse, shoulders squared, hair still wet from his morning bath. Yrene swallowed again and inclined her head toward the unused mounting ramp across the courtyard. "That was also meant for your use, you know."

He lifted his brows. "I doubt there will be one readily available on a battlefield," he said, mouth twisting to the side. "So I might as well learn to mount on my own."

Indeed. But even with the crisp golden dawn around them, what she'd glimpsed within his wound, the army they might both face, flashed before her, stretching the long shadows—

Motion caught her eye, snapping Yrene to alertness as Shen led a small white mare from those same shadows. Saddled and ready for her. She frowned at her dress.

"If I'm riding," Chaol said simply, "so are you." Perhaps *that* was what he'd muttered to the guards before they'd dispersed.

Yrene blurted, "I'm not—it's been a while since I rode one."

"If I can let four men help me onto this damned horse," he said simply, the color still blooming in his cheeks, "then you can get on one, too."

From the tone, she knew it must have been—embarrassing. She'd *seen* the expression on his face just now. But he'd done it. Gritted his teeth and done it.

And with the guards helping him . . . She knew there were multiple reasons why he could barely glance at them. That it was not just the lone reminder of what he'd once been that made him tense up in their presence, refuse to even consider training with them.

But that was not a conversation to be had now—not here, and not with the light starting to return to his eyes.

So Yrene hitched up her hem and let Shen help her onto the horse.

The skirts of her dress hiked up enough to reveal most of her legs, but she'd seen far more revealed here. In this very courtyard. Neither Shen nor any other guards so much as glanced her way. She turned to Chaol to order him to go ahead, but found his eyes on her.

On the leg exposed from ankle to midthigh, paler than most of her golden-brown skin. She darkened easily in the sun, but it had been months since she'd gone swimming and basked in any sunlight.

Chaol noticed her attention and snapped his eyes up to hers. "You have a good seat," he told her, as clinically as she often remarked on the status of her patients' bodies.

Yrene gave him an exasperated look before nodding her thanks to Shen and nudging her horse into a walk. Chaol snapped the reins and did the same.

She kept one eye on him as they rode toward the courtyard gates.

The brace held. The saddle held.

He was peering down at it—then at the gates, at the city awakening beyond them, the tower jutting high above it all as if it were a hand raised in bold welcome.

Sunlight broke through the open archway, gilding them both, but Yrene could have sworn it was far more than the dawn that shone in the captain's brown eyes as they rode into the city.

~

It was not walking again, but it was better than the chair.

Better than better.

The brace was cumbersome, going against all his instincts as a rider,

177

but . . . it held him firm. Allowed him to guide Yrene through the gates, the healer clutching at the pommel every now and then, forgetting the reins entirely.

Well, he'd found one thing she wasn't so self-assured at.

The thought brought a small smile to his lips. Especially as she kept adjusting her skirts. For all she'd chided him about his modesty, flashing her legs had given her pause.

Men in the streets—workers and peddlers and city guards—looked twice. Looked their fill.

Until they noticed his stare and averted their eyes.

And Chaol made sure they did.

Just as he'd made sure the guards in the courtyard had kept their attention polite the moment she'd run in, huffing and puffing, sun-kissed and flushed. Even with the stain on her clothes, even wearing yesterday's dress and coated in a faint sheen of sweat.

It had been mortifying to be helped into the saddle like unruly baggage after he'd refused the mounting ramp—mortifying to see those guards in their pristine uniforms, the armor on their shoulders and hilts of their swords glinting in the early morning sunlight, all watching him fumble about. But he'd dealt with it. And then he found himself forgetting that entirely at the appreciative glances the guards gave her. No lady, beautiful or plain, young or old, deserved to be gawked at. And Yrene . . .

Chaol kept his mare close beside hers. Met the stare of any man who glanced their way as they rode toward the towering spire of the Torre, the stones pale as cream in the morning light. Every single man swiftly found somewhere else to gape. Some even looked apologetic.

Whether Yrene noticed, he had no clue. She was too busy lunging for the saddle horn at any unexpected movements of the horse, too busy wincing as the mare increased her pace up a particularly steep street, causing her to sway and slide back in her saddle.

"Lean forward," he instructed her. "Balance your weight." He did the same—as much as the brace allowed.

Their horses slowly plowed up the streets, heads bobbing as they worked.

Yrene gave him a sharp glare. "I *do* know those things."

He lifted his brows in a look that said, *Could have fooled me.*

She scowled, but faced ahead. Leaned forward, as he'd instructed her.

He'd been sleeping like the dead when Nesryn returned late last night—but she'd roused him long enough to say she hadn't discovered anything in regard to potential Valg in the city. No sewers connected to the Torre, and with the heavy guard at the walls, no one was getting in that way. He'd managed to hold on to consciousness long enough to thank her, and hear her promise to keep hunting today.

But this cloudless, bright day . . . definitely not the Valg's preferred darkness. Aelin had told him how the Valg princes could summon darkness for themselves—darkness that struck down any living creature in its path, draining them dry. But even one Valg in this city, regardless of whether they were a prince or an ordinary grunt . . .

Chaol pushed the thought from his mind, frowning up at the mammoth structure that grew more imposing with each street they crossed.

"Towers," he mused, glancing toward Yrene. "Is it coincidence you bear that name, or did your ancestors once hail from the Torre?"

Her knuckles were white as she gripped the pommel, as if turning to look at him would send her toppling off. "I don't know," she admitted. "My—it was knowledge that I never learned."

He considered the words, the way she squinted at the bright pillar of the tower ahead rather than meet his stare. A child of Fenharrow. He didn't dare ask why she might not know the answer. Where her family was.

Instead, he jerked his chin to the ring on her finger. "Does the fake wedding band really work?"

She examined the ancient, scuffed ring. "I wish I could say otherwise, but it does."

"You encounter that behavior here?" *In this wondrous city?*

"Very, very rarely." She wriggled her fingers before settling them around the saddle's pommel again. "But it's an old habit from home."

For a heartbeat, he recalled an assassin in a bloody white gown, collapsing at the entrance to the barracks. Recalled the poisoned blade the man had sliced her with—and had used with countless others.

"I'm glad," he said after a moment. "That you don't need to fear such things here." Even the guards, for all their ogling, had been respectful. She'd even addressed one by name—and his returned warmth had been genuine.

Yrene clenched the saddle horn again. "The khagan holds all people accountable to the rule of the law, whether they're servants or princes."

It shouldn't have been such a novel concept, yet . . . Chaol blinked. "Truly?"

Yrene shrugged. "As far as I have heard and observed. Lords cannot buy their way out of crimes committed, nor rely on their family names to bail them out. And would-be criminals in the streets see the exacting hand of justice and rarely dare to tempt it." A pause. "Did you . . ."

He knew what she'd balked at asking. "I was ordered to release or look the other way for nobility who had committed crimes. At least, the ones who were of value in court and in the king's armies."

She studied the pommel before her. "And your new king?"

"He is different."

If he was alive. If he had made it out of Rifthold. Chaol forced himself to add, "Dorian has long studied and admired the khaganate. Perhaps he'll put some of its policies into effect."

A long, assessing glance now. "Do you think the khagan will ally with you?"

He hadn't told her that, but it was fairly obvious why he'd come, he supposed. "I can only hope."

"Would his forces make that much of a difference against . . . the powers you mentioned?"

Chaol repeated, "I can only hope." He couldn't bring himself to voice the truth—that their armies were few and scattered, if they existed at all. Compared to the gathering might of Morath . . .

"What happened these months?" A quiet, careful question.

"Trying to trick me into talking?"

"I want to know."

"It's nothing worth telling." His story wasn't worth telling at all. Not a single part of it.

She fell silent, the clopping of their horses' hooves the only sound for a block. Then, "You will need to talk about it. At some point. I . . . beheld glimpses of it within you yesterday."

"Isn't that enough?" The question was sharp as the knife at his side.

"Not if it is what the thing inside you feeds on. Not if claiming ownership of it might help."

"And you're so certain of this?" He should mind his tongue, he knew that, but—

Yrene straightened in her saddle. "The trauma of any injury requires some internal reflection during the healing and aftermath."

"I don't want it. Need it. I just want to stand—to walk again."

She shook her head.

He charged on, "And what about you, then? How about we make a deal: you tell me all your deep, dark secrets, Yrene Towers, and I'll tell you mine."

Indignation lit those remarkable eyes as she glared at him. He glared right back.

Finally, Yrene snorted, smiling faintly. "You're as stubborn as an ass."

"I've been called worse," he countered, the beginnings of a smile tugging on his mouth.

"I'm not surprised."

Chaol chuckled, catching the makings of a grin on her face before she ducked her head to hide it. As if sharing one with a son of Adarlan were such a crime.

Still, he eyed her for a long moment—the humor lingering on her

181

face, the heavy, softly curling hair that was occasionally caught in the morning breeze off the sea. And found himself still smiling as something coiled tight in his chest began to loosen.

They rode the rest of the way to the Torre in silence, and Chaol tipped his head back as they neared, walking down a broad, sunny avenue that sloped upward to the hilltop complex.

The Torre was even more dominating up close.

It was broad, more of a keep than anything, but still rounded. Buildings flanked its sides, connected on lower levels. All enclosed by towering white walls, the iron gates—fashioned to look like an owl spreading its wings—thrown wide to reveal lavender bushes and flower beds lining the sand-colored gravel walkways. Not flower beds. Herb beds.

The smells of them opening to the morning sun filled his nose: basil and mint and sage and more of that lavender. Even their horses, hooves crunching on the walkways, seemed to sigh as they approached.

Guards in what he assumed were Torre colors—cornflower blue and yellow—let them pass without question, and Yrene bowed her head in thanks. They did not look at her legs. Did not either dare or have the inclination to disrespect. Chaol glanced away from them before he could meet their questioning stares.

Yrene took the lead, guiding them through an archway and into the complex courtyard. Windows of the three-story building wrapped around the courtyard gleamed with the light of the rising sun, but inside the courtyard itself . . .

Beyond the murmur of awakening Antica outside the compound, beyond the hooves of their horses on the pale gravel, there was only the gurgle of twin fountains anchored against parallel walls of the courtyard—their spouts shaped like screeching owl beaks, spewing water into deep basins below. Pale pink and purple flowers lined the walls between lemon trees, the beds tidy but left to grow as the plants willed.

It was one of the more serene places he had ever laid eyes on. And watching them approach . . . Two dozen women in dresses of every color—though most of the simple make Yrene favored.

They stood in neat rows on the gravel, some barely more than children, some well into their prime. A few were elderly.

Including one woman, dark-skinned and white-haired, who strode from the front of the line and smiled broadly at Yrene. It was not a face that had ever held any beauty, but there was a light in the woman's eyes— a kindness and serenity that made Chaol blink in wonder.

All the others watched her, as if she were the axis around which they were ordered. Even Yrene, who smiled at the woman as she dismounted, looking grateful to be off the mare. One of the guards who had trailed them in came to retrieve the horse, but hesitated as Chaol remained astride.

Chaol ignored the man as Yrene finger-combed her tangled hair and spoke to the ancient woman in his tongue. "I take it the good crowd this morning is thanks to you?" Light words—perhaps an attempt at normalcy, considering what had happened in the library.

The old woman smiled—such warmth. She was brighter than the sun peeking above the compound walls. "The girls heard a rumor of a handsome lord coming to teach. I was practically trampled in the stampede down the stairs."

She cast a wry grin to three red-faced girls, no older than fifteen, who looked guiltily at their shoes. And then shot looks at him beneath their lashes that were anything but.

Chaol stifled a laugh.

Yrene turned to him, assessing the brace and the saddle as the crunch of approaching wheels on gravel filled the courtyard.

The amusement faded. Dismounting in front of these women . . .

Enough.

The word sounded through him.

If he could not endure it in front of a group of the world's best healers, then he would deserve to suffer. He had offered his help. He would give it.

For indeed, there were some younger girls in the back who were pale. Shifting on their feet. Nervous.

This sanctuary, this lovely place . . . A shadow had crept over it.

He would do what he could to push it back.

"Lord Chaol Westfall," Yrene said to him, gesturing to the ancient woman, "may I present Hafiza, Healer on High of the Torre Cesme."

One of the blushing girls sighed at the sound of his name.

Yrene's eyes danced. But Chaol inclined his head to the old woman as she extended her hands up to him. The skin was leathery—as warm as her smile. She squeezed his fingers tightly. "As handsome as Yrene said."

"I said no such thing," Yrene hissed.

One of the girls giggled.

Yrene cut her a warning look, and Chaol lifted his brows before saying to Hafiza, "It is an honor and a pleasure, my lady."

"So dashing," one of the girls murmured behind him.

Wait until you see my dismount, he almost said.

Hafiza squeezed his hands once more and dropped them. She faced Yrene. Waiting.

Yrene only clapped her hands together and said to the girls assembled, "Lord Westfall has suffered a severe injury to his lower spine and finds walking difficult. Yesterday, Sindra in the workshop crafted this brace for him, based upon the designs from the horse-tribes in the steppes, who have long dealt with such injuries for their riders." She waved a hand to indicate his legs, the brace.

With every word, his shoulders stiffened. More and more.

"If you are faced with a patient in a similar situation," Yrene went on, "the freedom of riding may be a pleasant alternative to a carriage or palanquin. Especially if they were used to a certain level of independence beforehand." She added upon consideration, "Or even if they have faced mobility difficulties their entire lives—it may provide a positive option while you heal them."

Little more than an experiment. Even the blushing girls had lost their smiles as they studied the brace. His legs.

Yrene asked them, "Who should like to assist Lord Westfall from his mount to his chair?"

A dozen hands shot up.

He tried to smile. Tried and failed.

Yrene pointed at a few, who rushed over. None looked up at him above the waist, or even bid him good morning.

Yrene lifted her voice as they crowded around her, making sure those assembled in the courtyard could also hear. "For patients completely immobilized, this may not be an option, but Lord Westfall retains the ability to move above his waist and can steer the horse with the reins. Balance and safety, of course, remain concerns, but another is that he retains use and sensation of his manhood—which also presents a few hiccups regarding the comfort of the brace itself."

One of the younger girls let out a giggle at that, but most only nodded, looking directly at the area indicated, as if he had no clothes on whatsoever. Face heating, Chaol restrained the urge to cover himself.

Two young healers began unstrapping the brace, some examining the buckles and rods. Still they did not look him in the eye. As if he were some new toy—new lesson. Some oddity.

Yrene merely went on, "Mind you don't jostle him too much when you—*careful*."

He fought to keep his features distant, found himself missing the guards from the palace. Yrene gave the girls firm, solid directions as they tugged him down from the saddle.

He didn't try to help the acolytes, or fight them, when they pulled at his arms, someone going to steady his waist, the world tilting as they hauled him downward. But the weight of his body was too great, and he felt himself slide farther from the saddle, the drop to the ground looming, the sun a brand on his skin.

The girls grunted, someone going to the other side to help move his leg up and over the horse—or he thought so. He only knew it because he saw her head of curls just peek over the horse's side. She pushed, jutting his leg upward, and he hung there, three girls gritting their teeth while they tried to lower him, the others watching in observational silence—

One of the girls let out an *oomph* and lost her grip on his shoulder. The world plunged—

Strong, unfaltering hands caught him, his nose barely half a foot from the pale gravel as the other girls shuffled and grunted, trying to heft him up again. He'd come free of the horse, but his legs were now sprawled beneath him, as distant from him as the very top of the Torre, high above.

Roaring filled his head.

A sort of nakedness crept over him. Worse than sitting in his undershorts for hours. Worse than the bath with the servant.

Yrene, gripping his shoulder from where she'd just barely caught him in time, said to the healers, "That could have been better, girls. A great deal better, for many reasons." A sigh. "We can discuss what went wrong later, but for now, move him to the chair."

He could barely stand to hear her, listen to her, as he hung between those girls, most of whom were half his weight. Yrene stepped aside to let the girl who'd dropped him back into place, whistling sharply.

Wheels hissed on gravel from nearby. He didn't bother to look at the wheeled chair that an acolyte pushed closer. Didn't bother to speak as they settled him in it, the chair shuddering beneath his weight.

"*Careful.*" Yrene warned again.

The girls lingered, the rest of the courtyard still watching. Had it been seconds or minutes since this ordeal had begun? He clenched the arms of the chair as Yrene rattled off some directions and observations. Clenched the arms harder as one of the girls stooped to touch his booted feet, to *arrange* them for him.

Words rose up his throat, and he knew they'd burst from him, knew

186

he could do little to stop his bellow to *back off* as that acolyte's fingers neared the dusty black leather—

Withered brown hands landed on the girl's wrist, halting her mere inches away.

Hafiza said calmly, "Let me."

The girls peeled back as Hafiza stooped to help him instead.

"Get the ladies ready, Yrene," Hafiza said over a slim shoulder, and Yrene obeyed, ushering them back into their lines.

The ancient woman's hands lingered on his boots—his feet, currently pointing in opposite directions. "Shall I do it, lord, or would you like to?"

Words failed him, and he wasn't certain he could use his hands without them shaking, so he gave the woman a nod of approval.

Hafiza straightened one foot, waiting until Yrene had walked a few steps away and begun giving stretching instructions to the ladies.

"This is a place for learning," Hafiza murmured. "Older students teach the younger." Even with her accent, he understood her perfectly. "It was Yrene's instinct, Lord Westfall, to show the girls what she did with the brace—to let them learn for themselves what it is to have a patient with similar difficulties. To receive this training, Yrene herself had to venture out onto the steppes. Many of these girls might not have that opportunity. At least not for several years."

Chaol met Hafiza's eyes at last, finding the understanding in them more damning than being hauled off a horse by a group of girls half his weight.

"She means well, my Yrene."

He didn't answer. He wasn't sure he had words.

Hafiza straightened his other foot. "There are many other scars, my lord. Beyond the one on her neck."

He wanted to tell the old woman that he knew that too damn well.

But he shoved down that bareness, that simmering roar in his head.

He had made these ladies a promise to teach them, to help them.

Hafiza seemed to read that—sense it. She only patted his shoulder before she rose to her full height, groaning a bit, and walked back to the place left for her in line.

Yrene had turned toward him, stretching done, and scanned him. As if Hafiza's lingering presence had indicated something she'd missed.

Her eyes settled on his, brows narrowing. *What's wrong?*

He ignored the question within her look—ignored the bit of worry. Shoved whatever he felt down deep and rolled his chair toward her. Inch by inch. The gravel was not ideal, but he gritted his teeth. He'd given these ladies his word. He would not back down from it.

"Where did we leave off the last lesson?" Yrene asked a girl in the front.

"Eye gouge," she said with a broad smile.

Chaol nearly choked.

"Right," Yrene said, rubbing her hands together. "Someone demonstrate for me."

He watched in silence as hands shot up, and Yrene selected one—a smaller-boned girl. Yrene took up the stance of attacker, grabbing the girl from the front with surprising intensity.

But the girl's slim hands went right to Yrene's face, thumbs to the corners of her eyes.

Chaol started from his chair—or would have, had the girl not pulled back.

"And next?" Yrene merely asked.

"Hook in my thumbs like this"—the girl made the motion in the air between them for all to see—"and *pop*."

Some of the girls laughed quietly at the accompanying *pop* the girl made with her mouth.

Aelin would have been beside herself with glee.

"Good," Yrene said, and the girl strode back to her place in line. Yrene turned to him, that worry again flashing as she beheld whatever was in his eyes, and said, "This is our third lesson of this quarter. We have covered front-based attacks only so far. I usually have the guards come in as willing victims"—some snickers at that—"but today I would like for you to tell us what *you* think ladies, young and old, strong and frail, could do against any sort of attack. Your list of top maneuvers and tips, if you'd be so kind."

He'd trained young men ready to shed blood—not heal people.

But defense was the first lesson he'd been taught, and had taught those young guards.

Before they'd wound up hanging from the castle gates.

Ress's battered, unseeing face flashed into his mind.

What good had it done any of them when it mattered?

Not one. Not one of that core group he'd trusted and trained, worked with for years . . . not one had survived. Brullo, his mentor and predecessor, had taught him all he knew—and what had it earned any of them? Anyone he'd encountered, he'd touched . . . they'd suffered. The lives he'd sworn to protect—

The sun turned bleaching, the gurgle of the twin fountains a distant melody.

What good had *any* of it done for his city, his people, when it was sacked?

He looked up to find the lines of women watching him, curiosity on their faces.

Waiting.

There had been a moment, when he had hurled his sword into the Avery. When he had been unable to bear its weight at his side, in his hand, and had chucked it and everything the Captain of the Guard had been, had meant, into the dark, eddying waters.

He'd been sinking and drowning since. Long before his spine.

He wasn't certain if he'd even tried to swim. Not since that sword had gone into the river. Not since he'd left Dorian in that room with his father and told his friend—his brother—that he loved him, and knew it was good-bye. He'd . . . left. In every sense of the word.

Chaol forced himself to take a breath. To try.

Yrene stepped up to his side as his silence stretched on, again looking so puzzled and concerned. As if she could not figure out why—*why* he might have been the least bit . . . He shoved the thought down. And the others.

Shoved them down to the silt-thick bottom of the Avery, where that eagle-pommeled sword now lay, forgotten and rusting.

Chaol lifted his chin, looking each girl and woman and crone in the face. Healers and servants and librarians and cooks, Yrene had said.

"When an attacker comes at you," he said at last, "they will likely try to move you somewhere else. *Never* let them do it. If you do, wherever they take you will be the last place you see." He'd gone to enough murder sites in Rifthold, read and looked into enough cases, to know the truth in that. "If they try to move you from your current location, you make that your battleground."

"We know that," one of the blushing girls said. "That was Yrene's first lesson."

Yrene nodded gravely at him. He again did not let himself look at her neck.

"Stomping on the instep?" He could barely manage a word to Yrene.

"First lesson also," the same girl replied instead of Yrene.

"What about how debilitating it is to receive a blow to the groin?"

Nods all around. Yrene certainly knew her fair share of maneuvers.

Chaol smiled grimly. "What about ways to get a man my size or larger flipped onto their backs in less than two moves?"

Some of the girls smiled as they shook their heads. It wasn't reassuring.

⊰ 15 ⊱

Yrene felt the anger simmering off Chaol as if it were heat rippling from a kettle.

Not at the girls and women. They adored him. Grinned and laughed, even as they concentrated on his thorough, precise lesson, even as the events in the library hung over them, the Torre, like a gray shroud. There had been many tears last night at the vigil—and a few red eyes still in the halls this morning as she'd hurtled past.

Mercifully, there had been no sign of either when Lord Chaol called in three guards to volunteer their bodies for the girls to flip into the gravel. Over and over.

The men agreed, perhaps because they knew that any injuries would be fussed over and patched up by the greatest healers outside Doranelle.

Chaol even returned their smiles, ladies and, to her shock, guards alike.

But Yrene . . . she received none of them. Not one.

Chaol's face only went hard, eyes glinting with frost, whenever she stepped in to ask a question or watch him walk an acolyte through the motions. He was commanding, his unrelenting focus missing nothing. If they had so much as one foot in the wrong position, he caught it before they moved an inch.

The hour-long lesson ended with each one of them flipping a guard onto his back. The poor men limped off, smiling broadly. Mostly because Hafiza promised them a cask of ale each—and her strongest healing tonic. Which was better than any alcohol.

The women dispersed as the bells chimed ten, some to lessons, some to chores, some to patients. A few of the sillier girls lingered, batting their eyelashes toward Lord Westfall, one even looking inclined to perch in his lap before Hafiza drily reminded her of a pile of laundry with her name on it.

Before the Healer on High hobbled after the acolyte, Hafiza merely gave Yrene what she could have sworn was a warning, knowing look.

"Well," Yrene said to Chaol when they were again alone—despite the gaggle of girls peering out one of the Torre windows. They noticed Yrene's stare and snapped their heads back in, slamming the window with riotous giggles.

Silba save her from teenage girls.

She'd never been one—not like that. Not so carefree. She hadn't even kissed a man until last autumn. Certainly had never giggled over one. She wished she had; wished for a lot of things that had ended with that pyre and those torches.

"That went better than expected," Yrene said to Chaol, who was frowning up at the looming Torre. "I'm sure they'll be begging me next week for you to return. If you're interested, I suppose."

He said nothing.

She swallowed. "I would like to try again today, if you're up for it. Would you prefer I find a room here, or shall we ride back to the palace?"

He met her stare then. His eyes were dark. "The palace."

Her stomach twisted at the icy tone. "All right," was all she managed to say, and walked off in search of the guards and their horses.

They rode back in silence. They'd been quiet during portions of the ride over, but this was . . . pointed. Heavy.

Yrene wracked her memory for what she might have said during the lesson—what she might have forgotten. Perhaps seeing the guards so active had reminded him of what he did not currently have. Perhaps just seeing the guards themselves had set him down this path.

She mused over it as they returned to the palace, while he was aided by Shen and another guard into the awaiting chair. He offered only a tight smile in thanks.

Lord Chaol looked up at her over a shoulder, the morning heat rising enough to make the courtyard stifling. "Are you going to push it, or shall I?"

Yrene blinked.

"You can move it yourself just fine," she said, her proverbial heels digging in at that tone.

"Perhaps you should ask one of your acolytes to do it. Or five of them. Or whatever number you deem fit to deal with an Adarlanian lord."

She blinked again. Slowly. And didn't give him any warning as she strode off at a clip. Not bothering to wait to see if he followed, or how fast he did.

The columns and halls and gardens of the palace passed in a blur. Yrene was so intent on reaching his rooms that she barely noticed someone had called her name.

It wasn't until it was repeated a second time that she recognized it—and cringed.

By the time she turned, Kashin—clad in armor and sweating enough to reveal he'd likely been exercising with the palace guards—had reached her side.

"I've been looking for you," he said, his brown eyes immediately going to her chest. No—to the stain still on her dress. Kashin's brows lifted. "If you want to send that to the laundry, I'm sure Hasar can lend you some clothes while it is cleaned."

She'd forgotten she was still in it—the stained, wrinkled dress. Hadn't really felt like she was quite as much of a mess until now. Hadn't felt like a barnyard animal.

"Thank you for the offer, but I'll manage."

She took a step away, but Kashin said, "I heard about the assailant in the library. I arranged for additional guards to arrive at the Torre after sundown every night and stay until dawn. No one will get in without our notice."

It was generous—kind. As he had always been with her. "Thank you."

His face remained grave as he swallowed. Yrene braced herself for the words he'd voice, but Kashin only said, "Please be careful. I know you made your thoughts clear, but—"

"Kashin."

"—it doesn't change the fact that we are, or were, friends, Yrene."

Yrene made herself meet his eyes. Made herself say, "Lord Westfall mentioned your . . . thoughts about Tumelun."

For a moment, Kashin glanced to the white banners streaming from the nearby window. She opened her mouth, perhaps to finally offer her condolences, to try to mend this thing that had fractured between them, but the prince said, "Then you understand how dire this threat may be."

She nodded. "I do. And I will be careful."

"Good," he said simply. His face shifted into an easy smile, and for a heartbeat, Yrene wished she'd been able to feel anything beyond mere friendship. But it had never been that way with him, at least on her part. "How is the healing of Lord Westfall? Have you made progress?"

"Some," she hedged. Insulting a prince, even one who was a former friend, by striding off was not wise, but the longer this conversation went on . . . She took a breath. "I would like to stay and talk—"

"Then stay." That smile broadened. Handsome—Kashin was truly a handsome man. If he had been anyone else, bore any other title—

She shook her head, offering a tight smile. "Lord Westfall is expecting me."

"I heard you rode with him this morning to the Torre. Did he not come back with you?"

She tried to keep the pleading expression off her face as she bobbed a curtsy. "I have to go. Thank you again for the concern—and the guards, Prince."

The title hung between them, pealing like a struck bell.

But Yrene walked on, feeling Kashin's stare until she rounded a corner.

She leaned against the wall, closing her eyes and exhaling deeply. Fool. So many others would call her a fool and yet—

"I almost feel bad for the man."

She opened her eyes to find Chaol, breathless and eyes still smoldering, wheeling himself around the corner.

"Of course," he went on, "I was far back enough that I couldn't hear you, but I certainly saw *his* face when he left."

"You don't know what you're talking about," Yrene said blandly, and resumed walking toward his suite. Slower.

"Don't check your pace on my account. You made impressive time."

She sliced him a glare. "Did I *do* something to offend you today?"

His level stare revealed nothing, but his powerful arms kept working the wheels of his chair as he pushed himself along.

"Well?"

"Why do you shove away the prince? It seems like you two were once close."

It was not the time or the place for this conversation. "That is none of your business."

"Indulge me."

"No."

He easily kept pace with her as she increased her own. All the way to the doors to his suite.

Kadja was standing outside, and Yrene gave her an inane order—"I need dried thyme, lemon, and garlic"—that might have very well been one of her mother's old recipes for fresh trout.

The servant vanished with a bow, and Yrene flung open the suite doors, holding one wide for him to pass.

"Just so you know," Yrene hissed as she shut the doors loudly behind him, "your piss-poor attitude helps no one and nothing."

Chaol slammed his chair to a halt in the middle of the foyer, and she winced at what it must have done to his hands. He opened his mouth, but shut it.

Right as the door to the other bedroom opened and Nesryn emerged, hair wet and gleaming.

"I was wondering where you went," she said to him, then gave Yrene a nod of greeting. "Early morning?"

It took Yrene a few heartbeats to reorder the room, the dynamic with Nesryn now in it. Yrene was not the primary . . . person. She was the help, the secondary . . . whatever.

Chaol shook out his hands—indeed red marks marred them—but said to Nesryn, "I went to the Torre to help the girls with a defense lesson."

Nesryn looked at the chair.

"On horseback," he said.

Nesryn's eyes now shot to Yrene, bright and wide. "You—how?"

"A brace," Yrene clarified. "We were just about to resume our second attempt at healing."

"And you could truly ride?"

Yrene felt Chaol's inward flinch—mostly because she flinched as well. At the disbelief.

"We didn't try out anything more than a fast walk, but yes," he said calmly. Evenly. Like he expected such questions from Nesryn. Had grown used to it. "Maybe tomorrow I'll try a trot."

Though without leverage from his legs, the bouncing . . . Yrene went through her mental archives on groin injuries. But she stayed quiet.

"I'll go with you," Nesryn said, dark eyes lighting. "I can show you the city—perhaps my uncle's home."

196

Chaol only replied, "I would like that," before Nesryn pressed a kiss to his cheek.

"I'm seeing them now for an hour or two," said Nesryn. "Then meeting with—you know. I'll be back this afternoon. And resume my . . . duties afterward."

Careful words. Yrene didn't blame her. Not with the weapons stacked on the desk in Nesryn's bedroom—barely visible through the ajar door. Knives, swords, multiple bows and quivers . . . The captain had a small armory in her chamber.

Chaol just grunted his approval, smiling slightly as Nesryn strode for the suite doors. The captain paused in the threshold, her grin broader than any Yrene had seen before.

Hope. Full of hope.

Nesryn shut the door with a click.

Alone in the silence again, still feeling very much the intruder, Yrene crossed her arms. "Can I get you anything before we begin?"

He just wheeled forward—into his bedroom.

"I'd prefer the sitting room," she said, snatching her supply bag from where Kadja had set it on the foyer table. And likely rifled through it.

"I'd prefer to be in bed while in agony." He added over his broad shoulder, "And hopefully you won't pass out on the floor this time."

He easily moved himself from the chair onto the bed, then began unbuckling his jacket.

"Tell me," Yrene said, lingering in the doorway. "Tell me what I did to upset you."

He peeled off his jacket. "You mean beyond displaying me like some broken doll in front of your acolytes and having them haul me off that horse like a limp fish?"

She stiffened, pulling out the bit before dumping the supply bag on the floor. "Plenty of people help you here in the palace."

"Not as many as you'd think."

"The Torre is a place of learning, and people with your injury do not

197

come often—not when we usually have to go to them. I was showing the acolytes things that might help with untold numbers of patients in the future."

"Yes, your prized, shattered horse. Look how well broken I am to you. How docile."

"I did not mean that, and you know it."

He ripped off his shirt, nearly tearing it at the seams as he hauled it over his head. "Was it some sort of punishment? For serving the king? For being from Adarlan?"

"*No.*" That he believed she could be that cruel, that unprofessional— "It was precisely what I just said: I wanted to *show* them."

"*I* didn't want you to show them!"

Yrene straightened.

Chaol panted through his gritted teeth. "*I* didn't want you to parade me around. To let them *handle* me." His chest heaved, the lungs beneath those muscles working like bellows. "Do you have *any* idea what it is like? To go from *that*"—he waved a hand toward her, her body, her legs, her spine—"to *this*?"

Yrene had the sense of the ground sliding from beneath her. "I know it is hard—"

"It is. But you made it *harder* today. You make me sit here mostly naked in this room, and yet I have *never* felt more bare than I did this morning." He blinked, as if surprised he'd vocalized it—surprised he'd admitted to it.

"I—I'm sorry." It was all she could think to say.

His throat bobbed. "Everything I thought, everything I had planned and wanted . . . It's gone. All I have left is my king, and this ridiculous, slim scrap of hope that we survive this war and I can find a way to *make* something of it."

"Of what?"

"Of *everything* that crumbled in my hands. *Everything.*"

His voice broke on the word.

198

Her eyes stung. Shame or sorrow, Yrene didn't know.

And she didn't want to know—what it was, or what had happened to him. What made that pain gutter in his eyes. She knew, she knew he had to face it, had to talk about it, but . . .

"I'm sorry," she repeated. She added stiffly, "I should have considered your feelings on the matter."

He watched her for a long moment, then removed the belt from his waist. Then took off his boots. Socks.

"You can leave the pants on, if—if you want."

He removed them. Then waited.

Still brimming with anger. Still gazing at her with such resentment in his eyes.

Yrene swallowed once. Twice. Perhaps she should have scrounged up breakfast.

But walking away, even for that . . . Yrene had a feeling, one she couldn't quite place, that if she walked away from him, if he saw her back turn . . .

Healers and their patients required trust. A bond.

If she turned her back on him and left, she didn't think that rift would be repaired.

So she motioned him to move to the center of the bed and turn onto his stomach while she took up a seat on the edge.

Yrene hovered a hand over his spine, the muscled groove cutting deep through it.

She hadn't considered—his feelings. That he might have them. The things haunting him . . .

His breathing was shallow, quick. Then he said, "Just to be clear: is your grudge against me, or Adarlan in general?"

He stared at the distant wall, the entrance to the bathing room blocked by that carved wood screen. Yrene held her hand steady, poised over his back, even as shame sluiced through her.

No, she had not been in her best form these past few days. Not even close.

That scar atop his spine was stark in the midmorning light, the shadow of her hand upon his skin like some sister-mark.

The thing that waited within that scar . . . Her magic again recoiled at its proximity. She'd been too tired last night and too busy this morning to even think about facing it again. To contemplate what she might see, might battle—what he might endure, too.

But he'd been good to his word, had instructed the girls despite her foolish, callous missteps. She supposed that she could only return the favor by doing as she'd promised as well.

Yrene took a steadying breath. There was no preparing for it, she knew. There was no bracing breath steeling enough to make this any less harrowing. For either of them.

Yrene silently offered Chaol the leather bit.

He slid it through his teeth and clamped down lightly.

She stared at him, his body braced for pain, face unreadable as he angled it toward the door.

Yrene said quietly, "Soldiers from Adarlan burned my mother alive when I was eleven."

And before Chaol could answer, she laid her hand on the mark atop his spine.

⇥ 16 ⇤

There was only darkness, and pain.

He roared against it, distantly aware of the bit in his mouth, the rawness of his throat.

Burned alive burned alive burned alive

The void showed him fire. A woman with golden-brown hair and matching skin screaming in agony toward the heavens.

It showed him a broken body on a bloody bed. A head rolling across a marble floor.

You did this you did this you did this

It showed a woman with eyes of blue flame and hair of pure gold poised above him, dagger raised and angling to plunge into his heart.

He wished. He sometimes wished that she hadn't been stopped.

The scar on his face—from the nails she'd gouged into it when she first struck him . . . It was that hateful wish he thought of when he looked in the mirror. The body on the bed and that cold room and that scream.

The collar on a tan throat and a smile that did not belong to a beloved face. The heart he'd offered and had been left to drop on the wooden planks of the river docks. An assassin who had sailed away and a queen who had returned. A row of fine men hanging from the castle gates.

All held within that slim scar. What he could not forgive or forget.

The void showed it to him, again and again.

It lashed his body with red-hot, pronged whips. And showed him those things, over and over.

It showed him his mother. And his brother. And his father.

Everything he had left. What he'd failed. What he'd hated and what he'd become.

The lines between the last two had blurred.

And he had tried. He had tried these weeks, these months.

The void did not want to hear of that.

Black fire raced down his blood, his veins, trying to drown out those thoughts.

The burning rose left on a nightstand. The final embrace of his king.

He had tried. Tried to *hope*, and yet—

Women little more than children hauling him off a horse. Poking and prodding at him.

Pain struck, low and deep in his spine, and he couldn't breathe around it, couldn't out-scream it—

White light flared.

A flutter. Far in the distance.

Not the gold or red or blue of flame. But white like sunlight, clear and clean.

A flicker through the dark, arcing like lightning riding through the night . . .

And then the pain converged again.

His father's eyes—his father's raging eyes when he announced he was leaving to join the guard. The fists. His mother's pleading. The anguish on her face the last time he'd seen her, as he'd ridden away from

Anielle. The last time he'd seen his city, his home. His brother, small and cowering in their father's long shadow.

A brother he had traded for another. A brother he had left behind.

The darkness squeezed, crushing his bones to dust.

It would kill him.

It would kill him, this pain, this . . . this endless, churning pit of *nothing*.

Perhaps it would be a mercy. He wasn't entirely certain his presence—his presence *beyond* made any sort of difference. Not enough to warrant trying. Coming back at all.

The darkness liked that. Seemed to thrive on that.

Even as it tightened the vise around his bones. Even as it boiled the blood in his veins and he bellowed and bellowed—

White light slammed into him. Blinding him.

Filling that void.

The darkness shrieked, surging back, then rising like a tidal wave around him—

Only to bounce off a shell of that white light, wrapped around him, a rock against which the blackness broke.

A light in the abyss.

It was warm, and quiet, and kind. It did not balk at the dark.

As if it had dwelled in such darkness for a long, long time—and understood how it worked.

Chaol opened his eyes.

Yrene's hand had slipped from his spine.

She was already twisting away from him, lunging for his discarded shirt on the bedroom carpet.

He saw the blood before she could hide it.

Spitting out the bit, he gripped her wrist, his panting loud to his ears. "You're hurt."

Yrene wiped at her nose, her mouth, and her chin before she faced him.

It didn't hide the stains down her chest, soaking into the neckline of her dress.

Chaol surged upright. "Holy gods, Yrene—"

"I'm fine."

The words were stuffy, warped with the blood still sliding from her nose.

"Is—is that common?" He filled his lungs with air to call for someone to fetch *another* healer—

"Yes."

"Liar." He heard the falsehood in her pause. Saw it in her refusal to meet his stare. Chaol opened his mouth, but she laid her hand on his arm, lowering the bloodied shirt.

"I'm fine. I just need—rest."

She appeared anything but, with blood staining and crusting her chin and mouth.

Yrene pressed his shirt again to her nose as a new trickle slid out. "At least," she said around the fabric and blood, "the stain from earlier now matches my dress."

A sorry attempt at humor, but he offered her a grim smile. "I thought it was part of the design."

She gave him an exhausted but bemused glance. "Give me five minutes and I can go back in and—"

"Lie down. Right now." He slid away a few feet on the mattress for emphasis.

Yrene surveyed the pillows, the bed large enough for four to sleep undisturbed beside one another. With a groan, she pressed the shirt to her face and slumped on the pillows, kicking off her slippers and curling her legs up. She tipped her head upward to stop the bleeding.

"What can I get you," he said, watching her stare blankly at the ceiling. She'd done this—done this while helping him, likely because of whatever shitty mood he'd been in before—

Yrene only shook her head.

In silence, he watched her press the shirt to her nose. Watched blood bloom across it again and again. Until it slowed at last. Until it stopped.

Her nose, mouth, and chin were ruddy with the remnants, her eyes fogged with either pain or exhaustion. Perhaps both.

So he found himself asking, "How?"

She knew what he meant. Yrene dabbed at the blood on her chest. "I went in there, to the site of the scar, and it was the same as before. A wall that no strike of my magic could crumble. I think it showed me . . ." Her fingers tightened on the shirt as she pressed it against the blood soaking her front.

"What?"

"Morath," she breathed, and he could have sworn even the birds' singing faltered in the garden. "It showed some memory, left behind in *you*. It showed me a great black fortress full of horrors. An army waiting in the mountains around it."

His blood iced over as he realized whose memory it might belong to. "Real or—was it some manipulation against you?" The way his own memories had been wielded.

"I don't know," Yrene admitted. "But then I heard your screaming. Not out here, but . . . in there." She wiped at her nose again. "And I realized that attacking that solid wall was . . . I think it was a distraction. A diversion. So I followed the sounds of your screaming. To you." To that place deep within him. "It was so focused upon ripping you apart that it did not see me coming." She shivered. "I don't know if it did anything, but . . . I couldn't stand it. To watch and listen. I startled it when I leaped in, but I don't know if it will be waiting the next time. If it will remember. There's a . . . sentience to it. Not a living thing, but as if a memory were set free in the world."

Chaol nodded, and silence fell between them. She wiped at her nose again, his shirt now coated in blood, then set the fabric on the table beside the bed.

For uncounted minutes, sunshine drifted across the floor, wind rustling the palms.

Then Chaol said, "I'm sorry—about your mother."

Thinking through the timeline . . . It had likely occurred within a few months of Aelin's own terror and loss.

So many of them—the children whom Adarlan had left such deep scars upon. If Adarlan had left them alive at all.

"She was everything good in the world," Yrene said, curling onto her side to gaze at the garden windows beyond the foot of the bed. "She . . . I made it out because she . . ." Yrene did not say the rest.

"She did what any mother would do," he finished for her.

A nod.

As healers, they had been some of the first victims. And continued to be executed long after magic had vanished. Adarlan had always ruthlessly hunted down the magically gifted healers. Their own townsfolk might have sold them out to Adarlan to make quick, cheap coin.

Chaol swallowed. After a heartbeat, he said, "I watched the King of Adarlan butcher the woman Dorian loved in front of me, and I could do nothing to stop it. To save her. And when the king went to kill me for planning to overthrow him . . . Dorian stepped in. He took on his father and bought me time to run. And I ran—I ran because . . . there was no one else to carry on the rebellion. To get word to the people who needed it. I let him take on his father and face the consequences, and I *fled*."

She watched him in silence. "He is fine now, though."

"I don't know. He is free—he is alive. But is he fine? He suffered. Greatly. In ways I can't begin to . . ." His throat tightened to the point of pain. "It should have been me. I had always planned for it to be me instead."

A tear slid over the bridge of her nose.

Chaol scooped it up with his finger before it could slide to the other side.

Yrene held his stare for a long moment, her tears turning those eyes near-radiant in the sun. He didn't know how long had passed. How long it had taken for her to even attempt to cleave that darkness—just a little.

The door to the suite opened and closed, silently enough that he knew it was Kadja. But it drew Yrene's stare away from him. Without it—there was a sense of cold. A quiet and a cold.

Chaol clenched his fist, that tear seeping into his skin, to keep from turning her face toward his again. To read her eyes.

But her head whipped upward so fast she nearly knocked his nose.

The gold in Yrene's eyes flared.

"Chaol," she breathed, and he thought it might have been the first time she'd called him such.

But she looked down, dragging his stare with her.

Down his bare torso, his bare legs.

To his toes.

To his toes, slowly curling and uncurling. As if trying to remember the movement.

⤝ 17 ⤞

Nesryn's cousins were off at school when she knocked on the outer door to her aunt and uncle's lovely home in the Runni Quarter. From the dusty street, all one could glimpse of the house beyond the high, thick walls was the carved oak gate, reinforced with scrolling iron.

But as it swung open under the hands of two guards who instantly beckoned her in, it revealed a shaded, broad courtyard of pale stone, flanked by pillars crawling with magenta bougainvillea, and a merry fountain inlaid with sea glass burbling in its center.

The house was typical of Antica—and of the Balruhni people from whom Nesryn and her family hailed. Long adjusted to desert climes, the entire building had been erected around sun and wind: outer windows never placed near the heat of the southern exposure, the breeze-catching narrow towers atop the building facing away from the sand-filled eastern wind to keep it from infiltrating the rooms it cooled. Her family was not fortunate enough to have a canal running beneath the house, as many of the wealthier in Antica did, but with the towering plants and carved wooden awnings, the shade kept the public lower levels around the court-yard cool enough during the day.

Indeed, Nesryn inhaled deeply as she strode through the pretty court-yard, her aunt greeting her halfway across with, "Have you eaten yet?"

She had, but Nesryn said, "I saved myself for your table, Aunt." It was a common Halha greeting amongst family—*no one* visited a house, espe-cially in the Faliq family, without eating. At least once.

Her aunt—still a full-figured beautiful woman whose four children had not slowed her down one bit—nodded in approval. "I told Brahim just this morning that our cook is better than the ones up at that palace."

A snort of amusement from a level up, from the wood-screened win-dow overlooking the courtyard. Her uncle's study. One of the few com-mon rooms on the usually private second level. "Careful, Zahida, or the khagan may hear you and haul dear old Cook to his palace."

Her aunt rolled her eyes at the figure just barely visible through the ornate wood screen and looped her arm through Nesryn's. "Snoop. Always eavesdropping on our conversations down here."

Her uncle chuckled but made no further comment.

Nesryn grinned, letting her aunt lead her toward the spacious interior of the home, past the curvy-bodied statue of Inna, Goddess of Peaceful Households and the Balruhni people, her arms upraised in welcome and defense. "Perhaps the palace's inferior cook is why the royals are so skinny."

Her aunt huffed, patting her belly. "And no doubt why I've added so much padding these years." She gave Nesryn a wink. "Perhaps I *should* get rid of old Cook, then."

Nesryn kissed her aunt's petal-soft cheek. "You are more beautiful now than you were when I was a child." She meant it.

Her aunt waved her off but still beamed as they entered the dim, cool interiors of the house proper. Pillars upheld the high ceilings of the long hallway, the wood beams and furniture carved and fashioned after the lush flora and fauna of their distant, long-ago homeland. Her aunt led her deeper into the house than most guests would ever see, right to the second, smaller courtyard at the back. The one just for family, most of it occupied by a long table and deep-seated chairs beneath the shade of an overhanging awning. At this hour, the sun was on the opposite side of the house—precisely why her aunt had chosen it.

Her aunt guided her into a seat adjacent to the head of the table, the place of honor, and hurried off to inform the cook to bring out refreshments.

In the silence, Nesryn listened to the wind sighing through the jasmine crawling up the wall to the balcony hanging above. As serene a home as she'd ever seen—especially compared to the chaos of her family's house in Rifthold.

An ache tightened her chest, and Nesryn rubbed at it. They were alive; they had gotten out.

But it did not answer where they now were. Or what they might face on that continent full of so many terrors.

"Your father gets that same look when he's thinking too hard," her uncle said from behind her.

Nesryn twisted in her chair, smiling faintly as Brahim Faliq entered the courtyard. Her uncle was shorter than her father, but slimmer— mostly thanks to *not* baking pastries for his livelihood. No, her uncle was still trim for a man of his age, his dark hair peppered with silver, both perhaps due to the merchant life that kept him so active.

But Brahim's face . . . it was Sayed Faliq's face. Her father's face. With less than two years separating them, some had thought them twins while growing up. And it was the sight of that kind, still-handsome face that made Nesryn's throat tighten. "One of the few traits I inherited from him, it seems."

Indeed, where Nesryn was quiet and prone to contemplation, her father's booming laugh had been as constant in their house as her sister's merry singing and giggling.

She felt her uncle studying her as he took the seat across from hers, leaving the head of the table for Zahida. Men and women governed the household together, their joint rule treated as law by their children. Nesryn had certainly fallen into line, though her sister . . . She could still hear the screeching fights between her sister and father as Delara had grown older and longed for independence.

"For the Captain of the Royal Guard," her uncle mused, "I am surprised you have the time to visit us so often."

Her aunt bustled in, bearing a tray of chilled mint tea and glasses. "Hush. Don't complain, Brahim, or she'll stop coming."

Nesryn smiled, glancing between them as her aunt gave them each a glass of the tea, set the tray on the table between them, and claimed the seat at the head of the table. "I thought to come by now—while the children are at school."

Another of the khaganate's many wonderful decrees: every child, no matter how poor or rich, had the right to attend school. Free of charge. As a result, nearly everyone in the empire was literate—far more than Nesryn could claim of Adarlan.

"And here I was," her uncle said, smiling wryly, "hoping you'd be back to sing more for us. Since you left the other day, the children have been yowling your songs like alley cats. I haven't the heart to tell them that their voices are not quite up to the same standard as their esteemed cousin's."

Nesryn chuckled, even as her face heated. She sang for very few—only her family. She'd never sung for Chaol or the others, or even mentioned that her voice was . . . better than good. It wasn't something that could easily be brought up in conversation, and the gods knew that the last several months had not been conducive to singing. But she'd found herself singing to her cousins the other night—one of the songs her father had taught her. A lullaby of Antica. By the end of it, her aunt and uncle had been gathered round, her aunt dabbing at her eyes, and . . . well, now there was no going back with it, was there?

She'd likely be teased about it until she never opened her mouth again.

But if only she had come here just for singing. She sighed a bit, steeling herself.

In the silence, her aunt and uncle exchanged looks. Her aunt asked quietly, "What is it?"

Nesryn sipped from her tea, considering her words. Her aunt and uncle, at least, gave her the gift of waiting for her to speak. Her sister would have been shaking her shoulders by now, demanding an answer. "There was an attack at the Torre the other night. A young healer was killed by an intruder. The murderer has not yet been found."

No matter how she and Sartaq had combed through the few sewers and canals beneath Antica last night, they had not found a single path toward the Torre; nor any sign of a Valg's nest. All they'd discovered were typical, awful city smells and rats scurrying underfoot.

Her uncle swore, earning a look from her aunt. But even her aunt rubbed at her chest before asking, "We'd heard the rumors, but . . . You have now come to warn us?"

Nesryn nodded. "The attack lines up with the techniques of enemies in Adarlan. If they are here, in this city, I fear it may be in connection to my arrival."

She had not dared tell her aunt and uncle too much. Not for lack of trust, but for fear of who might be listening. So they did not know of the Valg, or Erawan, or the keys.

They knew of her quest to raise an army, for that was no secret, but . . . She did not risk telling them of Sartaq. That he and his rukhin might be the path toward winning support from the khagan, that his people might know something about the Valg that even they had not discovered in dealing with them. She did not even risk telling them she'd been on the prince's ruk. Not that they'd really believe it. Well-off as her family might be, there was wealth, and then there was royalty.

Her uncle said, "Will they target our family—to get to you?"

Nesryn swallowed. "I don't believe so, but I would put nothing past them. I—it is still unknown if this attack *was* in relation to my arrival, or if we are jumping to conclusions, but on the chance that it is true . . . I came to warn you to hire more guards if you can." She looked between them, laying her hands palm-up on the table. "I am sorry to have brought this to your household."

Another glance between her aunt and uncle, then each took her by the hand. "There is nothing to be sorry for," her aunt said. Just as her uncle added, "Getting to see you so unexpectedly has been a blessing beyond measure."

Her throat closed up. This—this was what Erawan was poised to destroy.

She'd find a way to raise that army. Either to rescue her family from war, or keep it from reaching these shores.

Her aunt declared, "We will hire more guards, have an escort for the children to and from school." A nod to her husband. "And anywhere we go in this city."

Nesryn's uncle added, "And what of you? Traipsing about the city on your own." Nesryn waved a hand, though their concern warmed her. She refrained from telling them she'd hunted Valg in Rifthold's sewers for weeks, that she'd been stalking them through Antica's sewers last night. And most certainly refrained from telling them just how involved she'd been in the glass castle's demise. She had no wish to see her uncle keel over in his chair, or see her aunt's thick, beautiful hair go white. "I can handle myself."

Her aunt and uncle did not look so convinced, but they nodded all the same. Just as Cook emerged, smiling broadly at Nesryn, little dishes of chilled salads between her withered hands.

For long moments, Nesryn ate everything her aunt and uncle piled onto her plate, which was indeed as good as any food at the palace. By the time she was stuffed to the point of exploding, by the time she'd drained her tea to its dregs, her aunt said slyly to her, "I had hoped you'd be bringing a guest, you know."

Nesryn snorted, brushing the hair from her face. "Lord Westfall is quite busy, Aunt." But if Yrene had gotten him onto a horse this morning . . . perhaps she'd indeed get him here tomorrow. Introduce him to her family—to the four children who filled this house with chaos and joy.

Her aunt sipped daintily from her tea. "Oh, I didn't mean him." A wry grin between Zahida and Brahim. "I meant Prince Sartaq."

Nesryn was glad she'd finished her tea. "What of him?"

That sly smile didn't fade. "Rumor claims *someone*"—a pointed look at Nesryn—"was spotted riding with the prince at dawn yesterday. Atop his ruk."

Nesryn reined in her wince. "I . . . was." She prayed no one had seen her with him last night—that word would not reach the Valg agent's ears they were being hunted.

Her uncle chuckled. "And you planned to tell us when? The children were beside themselves with excitement that their beloved cousin had ridden on Kadara herself."

"I did not want to brag." A pathetic excuse.

"Hmmm," was all her uncle replied, mischief dancing in his gaze.

But Nesryn's aunt gave her a knowing look, steel in her brown eyes, as if she, too, did not forget for one moment the family who remained in Adarlan and perhaps now tried to flee to these shores. Her aunt simply said, "The ruks will not fear wyverns."

⇥ 18 ⇤

Yrene's heart thundered as she knelt beside Chaol on the bed and watched his toes shift.

"Can you—feel that?"

Chaol was still staring as if he didn't quite believe it.

"I . . ." The words stalled in his throat.

"Can you control the movement?"

He seemed to concentrate.

Then his toes stopped.

"Good," she said, sitting upright to watch more closely. "Now move them."

He again appeared to concentrate and concentrate, and then—

Two toes curled. Then three on the other foot.

Yrene smiled—broadly, widely. Remained smiling as she turned her head toward him.

He only stared at her. Her smile. A sort of focused intensity falling across his features that made her go a bit still.

"How?" he asked.

"The—maybe when I got to you, when my magic blasted back darkness a little . . ." It had been terrible. To find him inside all that dark. The void, the cold, the shrieking pain and horror.

She had refused to acknowledge what it tried to show her at that wall, again and again: that terrible fortress, the fate that awaited her when she returned. She had refused to acknowledge it as she had struck the wall, her magic begging her to stop, to pull away.

Until . . . until she'd heard *him*. Far off and deeper within.

She'd blindly lunged, a spear-throw toward that sound. And there he'd been—or whatever it was *of* him. As if *this* was the core of the tether between man and injury, not the wall against the nerves far, far above.

She'd wrapped herself around it, hugging tight even as the darkness pounded in again and again. And in answer, she'd sent her magic slashing into it, a scythe of light into the dark. A torch that burned just a fraction.

Just enough, it seemed.

"This is good," Yrene declared—perhaps uselessly. "This is wonderful."

Chaol was still staring at her as he said, "It is."

She became aware of the blood on her—the state of her.

"Let's start with this," she said. "Do a few exercises before we stop for the day."

What she had admitted about her mother . . . She had only told Hafiza upon entering the Torre. No one else. She had told no one else, not since she'd staggered onto her mother's cousin's farm and begged for sanctuary and shelter.

She wondered how long his own story had been locked in his chest.

"Let me order food first," Yrene decided. She glanced toward the wood screen shielding the bathing room from sight, then down at her blood-crusted chest and dress. "While we wait . . . I might beg to use your bath. And borrow a set of your clothes."

Chaol was still watching her with that focused, calm face. A different

216

one from any she'd seen on him before. As if in shaving off some of that darkness, it had revealed this facet beneath.

This man she had not yet met.

She wasn't sure what to do with it. With him.

"Take whatever you want," Chaol told her, his voice low—rough.

Yrene was light-headed when she crawled off the bed, taking his ruined shirt with her, and hurried for the bathing chamber. From the blood loss, she told herself.

Even as she smiled throughout her bath.

$\sim$

"I can't help but feel neglected, you know," Hasar drawled as she pored over maps Yrene didn't dare inquire about. From across the princess's lavish receiving room, she couldn't view them properly—and could only watch as Hasar moved several ivory figurines here and there, her dark brows scrunched in concentration.

"Renia, of course," Hasar went on, sliding a figure two inches to the right and frowning, "says I should not expect so much of your time, but perhaps I've grown spoiled these two years."

Yrene sipped her mint tea and did not comment one way or the other. Hasar had summoned her here upon learning that Yrene had been healing Lord Westfall all day, sending a servant to fetch her to the princess's rooms, with the promise of some much-needed refreshments. And indeed, the carob cookies and tea had pushed back the tide of her exhaustion just a fraction.

Her friendship with the princess had been purely accidental. In one of Yrene's first on-site lessons, Hafiza had brought her to tend to the princess, who had returned from her seaside palace in the northeast to be treated for an unrelenting stomach pain. They were both of similar age, and during the hours that Hafiza went about removing a truly horrific tapeworm from the princess's intestines, Hasar had ordered Yrene to talk.

So Yrene had, rambling about her lessons, occasionally mentioning

217

the more disgusting moments of her year working at the White Pig. The princess particularly enjoyed her tales of the rather messier bar fights. Her favorite story to hear, which she'd ordered Yrene to narrate thrice during the days Hafiza had extracted the magically slaughtered tapeworm through her mouth—one orifice or the other, the Healer on High had told the princess—was of the young stranger who had saved Yrene's life, taught her to defend herself, and left her a small fortune in gold and jewels.

Yrene had deemed it idle talk, not expecting the princess to remember her name once Hafiza had coaxed the last inches of the tapeworm from her body. But two days later, she'd been called to the princess's rooms, where Hasar was busy stuffing her face with all manner of delicacies to make up for the weight she'd lost.

Too thin, she'd told Yrene by way of greeting. She needed a fatter ass for her lover to grip at night.

Yrene had burst out laughing—the first bit of true laughter she'd had in a long, long time.

Hasar had only smirked, offered Yrene some smoked fish from the river-rich lowlands, and that had been that. Perhaps not a friendship of equals, but Hasar seemed to enjoy her company, and Yrene was in no position to deny her.

So the princess made a point to summon Yrene whenever she was in Antica—and had eventually brought Renia to the palace, both to meet her father and to meet Yrene. Renia, if Yrene was being honest, was far preferable to the demanding and sharp-tongued princess, but Hasar was prone to jealousy and territorialism, and often made sure Renia was kept well away from the court and would-be contenders for her affections.

Not that Renia had ever given cause for such a thing. No, the woman—older than Yrene by a month—only had eyes for the princess. Loved her with unflinching devotion.

Hasar called her a lady, had granted Renia lands within her own territory. Yet Yrene had heard some of the other healers whisper that when

Renia had first entered Hasar's orbit, Hafiza had been discreetly asked to heal her of . . . unpleasantries from her former life. Former profession, apparently. Yrene had never asked Hasar for the details, but given how loyal Renia was to the princess, she often wondered if the reason why Hasar so loved to hear Yrene's own story of her mysterious savior was because she, too, had once seen a woman suffering and reached out to help. And then to hold her.

"You're smiling more today, too," Hasar said, setting down her glass pen. "Despite those hideous clothes."

"Mine were sacrificed to the cause of healing Lord Westfall," Yrene said, rubbing at the dull throbbing in her temple that even the tea and carob cookies couldn't chase away. "He was kind enough to lend me some of his own."

Hasar smirked. "Some might see you and assume you lost your clothes for a far more pleasurable reason."

Yrene's face heated. "I'd hope they'd remember that I am a professional healer at the Torre."

"It'd make it even more valuable gossip."

"I'd think they'd have better things to do than whisper about a nobody healer."

"You are Hafiza's unofficial heir. That makes you slightly interesting."

Yrene wasn't insulted by the frank words. She didn't explain to Hasar that she'd likely be leaving, and Hafiza would have to find someone else. She doubted the princess would approve—and wasn't entirely certain that Hasar would *let* her leave. She'd been worried about Kashin for so long, yet Hasar . . .

"Well, regardless, I have no designs on Lord Westfall."

"You should. He's divertingly handsome. Even *I'm* tempted."

"Really?"

Hasar laughed. "Not at all. But I could see why *you* might be."

"He and Captain Faliq are involved."

"And if they weren't?"

Yrene took a long sip from her tea. "He is my patient, and I am his healer. There are plenty of other handsome men."

"Like Kashin."

Yrene frowned at the princess over the black-and-gold rim of her teacup. "You keep pushing your brother on me. Are *you* encouraging him?"

Hasar put a hand on her chest, her manicured nails gleaming in the late afternoon sun. "Kashin had no trouble with women until you came along. You two were once such close friends. Why shouldn't I wish that my dear friend and brother form a deeper attachment?"

"Because if you are appointed khagan, you might kill us if he doesn't submit."

"Him, possibly, if he doesn't bow. And if you prove to not be carrying his offspring, I might let you take the cleansing once my own line is established and keep your wealth."

Such bald casual words. Of such horrible methods meant to keep this wondrous, sweeping empire from fracturing. She wished Kashin were here to listen, to understand.

Yrene asked, "And what would you do—for producing offspring?"

With Renia as the possible future Grand Empress, Hasar would need to find *some* way to produce a blood heir.

Hasar began pushing her figures around the map again. "I have already told my father, and it is no concern of yours."

Right. For if she had selected some male to do the job . . . dangerous knowledge. Her siblings might very well try to destroy someone whom Hasar and Renia trusted enough to assist in that way. Or would pay handsomely to know that Hasar and Renia were even *considering* offspring at this point.

But Hasar then said, "I heard that killer in the library hunted you." Unforgiving will filled her face. "Why did you not come to me first?"

Before Yrene could answer, Hasar mercifully went on, "They said it was some strange death—not a typical one at all."

Yrene tried and failed to block out the memory of the gaunt, leathery face. "It was."

Hasar sipped her tea. "I don't care if the attack was a deliberate move on your life or whether it was just piss-poor coincidence." She set down her cup with delicate precision. "When I find whoever it is, I'll behead them myself." The princess tapped a hand on the sheathed blade discarded along the edge of her oak desk.

Yrene didn't doubt her. But she said, "I've been told the danger is . . . considerable."

"I do not take lightly to my friends being hunted like beasts." Not the voice of a princess—but a warrior-queen. "And I do not take lightly to Torre healers being killed and terrorized."

Hasar was many things, but she was loyal. To her core. To the few, few people whom she favored. It had always warmed something in Yrene. To have someone who actually meant what they said. Hasar *would* behead the killer if they were unfortunate enough to encounter her. She would ask no questions, either.

Yrene considered all she knew about the potential murderer and struggled to refrain from telling the princess that beheading was, in fact, the proper way to deal with a Valg demon.

Unless you were facing the remnants of it within someone. In which case . . . As awful, as exhausting as today's session with Lord Westfall had been, she'd already cataloged and tucked away the small scraps of information she'd gleaned. Not just for his healing, but if she should ever face it again—on those battlefields. Even if the prospect of seeing those Valg demons in the flesh . . .

Taking a steadying drink of her tea, Yrene asked, "Are you not concerned that perhaps it is no coincidence war is upon the northern continent, and now we have enemies in our midst?" She didn't dare mention Tumelun's death.

"Perhaps Lord Westfall and Captain Faliq brought in their own spies to track you."

"That is not possible."

"Are you so certain? They are desperate. And desperation breeds people who are willing to do anything to get what they need."

"And what would they need from me beyond what I am already giving them?"

Hasar beckoned Yrene over with a flick of her fingers. Yrene set down her teacup and strode across the deep blue carpet to the desk before the windows. Hasar's rooms commanded a view of the teal bay—the ships and the gulls and the glittering sprawl of the Narrow Sea beyond.

Hasar gestured to the map in front of her. "What do you see here?"

Yrene's throat tightened as she recognized the landmass. The northern continent—her own home. And all the figures on it, in red and green and black . . .

"Are those—armies?"

"This is Duke Perrington's force," Hasar said, pointing to the line of black figures stretching like a wall across the middle of the continent. Other clusters lay to the south.

And to the north: one small green cluster. And a lone red figure just beyond the shores of Rifthold.

"What are the others?"

Hasar said, "There is a small army in Terrasen." She snickered at the green figures clustered around Orynth.

"And in Adarlan?"

Hasar picked up the red figurine, twirling it between two figures. "No army to speak of. Dorian Havilliard remains unaccounted for. Will he flee north or south? Or perhaps cut inland—though there is certainly nothing beyond the mountains save for half-feral tribes."

"What is that figure?" Yrene asked, noting the gold pawn Hasar had set off the map entirely.

Hasar picked it up, too. "It is Aelin Galathynius. *Also* unaccounted for."

"She is not in Terrasen? With her army?"

"No." Hasar patted the documents she'd been referencing as she'd adjusted her own maps. Reports, Yrene realized. "The latest news indicates the Queen of Terrasen is nowhere to be found in her own kingdom. Or in any other." A slight smile. "Perhaps you should ask your lord that."

"I doubt he'll tell me." She refrained from saying he wasn't her lord.

"Then perhaps you should make him."

Yrene carefully asked, "Why?"

"Because I would like to know."

Yrene read between the words. Hasar wanted the information—before her father or siblings.

"To what end?"

"When a power broker of the realms goes missing, it is not a cause for celebration. Especially one who destroys palaces and takes cities on a whim."

Fear. Well hidden, but Hasar was at least considering the possibility that Aelin Galathynius might set her sights beyond her own lands.

But to play spy for Hasar . . . "You think the library attack has something to do with this?"

"I think that perhaps Lord Westfall and Captain Faliq are aware of how to play the game. And if they make it appear as if a threat from Perrington is in our midst, why wouldn't we consider allying with them?"

Yrene didn't think they played those sorts of games at all. "You think they're doing this to help Aelin Galathynius? Or because she is missing and they're frightened of losing a powerful ally themselves?"

"That's what I would like to know. Along with the queen's location. Or their best guess."

Yrene made herself hold the princess's stare. "And why should I help you?"

A Baast Cat's smile. "Beyond the fact that we are dear friends? Is there nothing I could give you to sweeten the offer, lovely Yrene?"

"I have all I need."

"Yes, but you do remember that the armadas are mine. The Narrow Sea is mine. And crossing it may be very, very difficult to those who forget."

Yrene did not dare back down. Didn't dare break the princess's dark gaze.

Hasar knew. Knew, or guessed, that Yrene wanted to leave. And if she did not aid the princess . . . Yrene had no doubt that as fiercely as Hasar loved, so, too, could her need for retribution drive her. Enough to make sure Yrene never left these shores.

"I shall see what I can learn," Yrene said, refusing to soften her voice.

"Good," Hasar declared, and cleared the figurines off the map with a wipe of her hand, scattering them into a drawer and shutting them inside. "To begin, why don't you join me at Tehome's feast the night after tomorrow? I can keep Kashin occupied, if it will clear the way for you."

Her stomach turned over. She'd forgotten that the sea goddess's holiday was in two days. Frankly, there were holidays nearly every other week, and Yrene participated when she could, but this one . . . With her fleet, with the Narrow Sea and several others under her jurisdiction, Hasar would certainly be honoring Tehome. And the khaganate would certainly not fail to honor the Lady of the Great Deep, either—not when the oceans had been good to them these centuries.

So Yrene didn't dare object. Didn't let herself so much as hesitate before Hasar's piercing eyes. "As long as you don't mind me wearing the same dress from the other night," she said as casually as she could, plucking at her oversized shirt.

"No need," Hasar countered, smiling broadly. "I have something already selected."

⊰ 19 ⊱

Chaol kept moving his toes long after Yrene had left. He wriggled them inside his boots, not quite *feeling* them, but just enough to know they *were* moving.

However Yrene had done it . . .

He didn't tell Nesryn when she returned before dinner, no sign of the Valg to report. And he'd only quietly explained that he was making enough progress with Yrene that he'd like to put off tomorrow's visit to her family until another day.

She'd seemed a tad crestfallen, but had agreed, that cool mask slipping back over her face within a few blinks.

He kissed her when she'd walked by to dress for dinner.

He'd grabbed her by the wrist and tugged her down, and kissed her once. Brief—but thorough.

She'd been surprised enough that by the time he'd pulled away, she hadn't so much as laid a hand on him.

"Get ready," he told her, motioning to her room.

With a backward glance at him, a half smile on her mouth, Nesryn obeyed.

Chaol stared after her for a few minutes, shifting his toes in his boots. There had been no heat in it—the kiss. No real feeling.

He expected it. He'd practically shoved her away these weeks. He didn't blame her at all for the surprise.

He was still flexing his toes in his boots when they arrived at dinner. Tonight, he'd ask the khagan for an audience. Again. Mourning or no, protocol or no. And then he'd warn the man of what he knew.

He would request it before Yrene's usual arrival—in case they lost time. Which seemed to be an occurrence. It had been three hours today. Three.

His throat was still raw, despite the honeyed tea Yrene had made him drink until he was nearly sick. Then she'd made him exercise, many of the movements ones she had to assist him with: rotating his hips, rolling each leg from side to side, rotating his ankles and feet in circles. All designed to keep the blood flowing to the muscles beginning to atrophy, all designed to re-create the pathways between his spine and brain, she said.

She'd repeated the sets over and over, until an hour had passed. Until she was swaying again on her feet, and that glassy look had crept over her eyes.

Exhaustion. For while she'd been rotating his legs, ordering him to move his toes every now and then, she'd sent tingles of her magic through his legs, bypassing his spine entirely. Little pinpricks in his toes—like swarms of fireflies had landed on him. That was all he felt, even as she kept trying to patch up those pathways in his body. What little she could do now, with the small progress she'd made hours ago.

But all that magic . . . When Yrene had swayed after his last set, he'd called for Kadja. Ordered an armed carriage for the healer.

Yrene, to his surprise, didn't object. Though he supposed it was hard to, when the healer was nearly asleep on her feet by the time she left,

Kadja supporting her. Yrene only murmured something about being on his horse again after breakfast, and was gone.

But perhaps the luck he'd had that afternoon was the last of it.

Hours later, the khagan was not at dinner. He was dining in private with his beloved wife, they said. The unspoken rest of it lay beneath the words: mourning was taking its natural course, and politics would be set aside. Chaol had tried to look as understanding as possible.

At least Nesryn seemed to be making some headway with Sartaq, even if the other royals had already grown bored with their presence.

So he dined, so he kept wriggling his toes within his boots, and did not tell anyone, even Nesryn, long after they'd returned to their suite and he'd tumbled off to bed.

He awoke with the dawn, found himself . . . eager to wash and dress. Found himself eating breakfast as quickly as he could, while Nesryn only raised her brows.

But she, too, was off early to meet Sartaq atop one of the palace's thirty-six minarets.

There was some holiday tomorrow, to honor one of the thirty-six gods those minarets each represented. Their sea goddess, Tehome. There would be a ceremony at sunrise down by the docks, with all the royals, even the khagan, attending to lay wreaths into the water. Gifts for the Lady of the Great Deep, Nesryn had said. Then a grand feast at the palace come sundown.

He'd been indifferent about his own holidays back in Adarlan, found them outdated rites to honor forces and elements his ancestors could not explain, and yet the buzz of activity, the wreaths of flowers and seashells being raised within the palace to at last replace the white banners, the scent of shellfish simmering in butter and spices . . . It intrigued him. Made him see a bit clearer, brighter, as he wheeled through the busy palace toward the courtyard.

The courtyard itself was a melee of arriving and departing vendors, bearing food and decorations and what seemed to be performers. All to beseech their sea goddess for mercy as the late summer gave way to annual violent storms that could rip apart ships and entire towns on the coastline.

Chaol scanned the courtyard for Yrene, flexing his toes. He spotted his horse and her mare alongside it in the few pens by the east wall, but . . . no sign of her.

She'd been late yesterday, so he waited until a lull in the deliveries before he motioned the stable hands to help him mount. But it was the guard from yesterday—the one who'd aided him most—who came forward when the mare was brought over. Shen, Yrene had called him; she'd greeted the guard as if she knew him well.

Shen said nothing, though Chaol knew every guard in this palace spoke an assortment of languages beyond Halha, only offering a nod of greeting. Which Chaol found himself returning before he silently mounted, his arms straining with the effort to haul himself upward. But he made it, perhaps easier than yesterday, earning what he could have sworn was a wink of approval from Shen before the guard sauntered back to his post.

Shutting out what that did to his chest, Chaol buckled the straps on his brace and surveyed the chaotic courtyard and open gates beyond. The guards inspected every wagon, every piece of paper that confirmed a royal order had been placed for the goods they bore.

Good. Regardless of whether he'd spoken to the khagan personally, at least someone had warned the guard to be careful—perhaps Kashin.

The sun drifted higher, raising the heat with it. Still Yrene did not come.

A clock chimed deep in the palace. An hour late.

The mare turned skittish, impatient beneath him, and he patted her thick, sweaty neck, murmuring.

Another fifteen minutes passed. Chaol studied the gates, the street beyond.

No word of alarm had come from the Torre, but staying still, just waiting here . . .

He found himself snapping the reins, tapping the horse's flank to launch it into a walk.

He'd marked the path Yrene had taken yesterday. Perhaps he'd run into her on her way over here.

Antica was crawling with vendors and people setting up for tomorrow's holiday. And those already toasting to the Lady of the Great Deep, filling the taverns and eating rooms lining the streets, musicians playing at each one.

It took him nearly twice as long to get to the Torre's owl-adorned gates, though part of that slowness was due to his scanning for Yrene on every crammed street and passing alley. But he found no sign of the healer.

He and his horse were sweating when they rode through the Torre gates, the guards smiling at him—faces he'd marked from yesterday's lesson.

How many times had he seen such a greeting in Adarlan? Taken it for granted?

He'd always ridden through the black iron gates to the glass palace without hesitation, without really doing more than noting who was stationed there and who wasn't looking up to snuff. He'd trained with those men, learned about their families and lives.

His men. They had been *his* men.

So Chaol's own answering smile was tight, and he couldn't stand to meet their bright eyes for more than a passing glance as he rode into the Torre courtyard, the scent of lavender wrapping around him.

But he paused a few feet in, wheeled his mare around, and asked the guard closest, "Has Yrene Towers left today?"

Like those at the khagan's palace, each of the Torre's guards was fluent in at least three languages: Halha, the tongue of the northern continent, and the language of the lands to the east. With visitors from all over Erilea, those at the Torre gates *had* to be fluent in the three common tongues.

229

The guard before him shook his head, sweat sliding down his dark skin in the rippling heat. "Not yet, Lord Westfall."

Perhaps it was rude to seek her out when she was likely too busy with other things to immediately tend to him. She'd mentioned other patients, after all.

With a nod of thanks, he again turned the roan mare toward the Torre, and was about to aim for the courtyard to its left when an ancient voice said from below, "Lord Westfall. Good to see you out and about."

Hafiza. The Healer on High stood a few feet away, a basket draped over her thin arm and two middle-aged healers flanking her. The guards bowed, and Chaol inclined his head.

"I was looking for Yrene," he said by way of greeting.

Hafiza's white brows rose. "Did she not come to you this morning?"

Unease tightened his gut. "No, though perhaps I missed her—"

One of the healers at Hafiza's side stepped forward and murmured to the Healer on High, "She is abed, my lady."

Hafiza now raised her brows at the woman. "Still?"

A shake of the head. "Drained. Eretia checked on her an hour ago— she was asleep."

Hafiza's mouth tightened, though Chaol had a feeling he knew what she was about to say. Felt guilty enough before the crone spoke. "Our powers can do great things, Lord Westfall, but they also demand a great cost. Yrene was . . ." She sought the words, either from not using her native tongue or to spare him from further guilt. "She was asleep in the carriage when she arrived last night. She had to be carried to her room."

He cringed.

Hafiza patted his boot, and he could have sworn he felt it in his toes. "It is of no concern, my lord. A day of sleep, and she will be back at the palace tomorrow morning."

"If tomorrow is a holiday," he volunteered, "she can have the day off."

Hafiza chuckled. "You do not know Yrene very well at all if you think she considers these holidays to be *days off*." She pointed at him. "Though

230

if *you* want the day off, you should certainly tell her, because she'll likely be knocking at your door come sunrise."

Chaol smiled, even as he gazed at the tower looming overhead.

"It is a restorative sleep," Hafiza supplied. "Utterly natural. Do not let it burden you."

With a final look at the pale tower high above, he nodded and wheeled his horse back to the gates. "May I escort you anywhere?"

Hafiza's smile was bright as the midday sun. "You certainly may, Lord Westfall."

⌒

The Healer on High was stopped every block by those wishing to merely touch her hand, or have her touch *them*.

Sacred. Holy. Beloved.

It took them thirty minutes to get even half a dozen blocks from the Torre. And though he offered to wait while Hafiza and her companions entered the modest home on a quiet street, they waved him off.

The streets were clogged enough to deter him from exploring, so Chaol soon headed back toward the palace.

But even as he steered his horse through the crowds, he found himself glancing to that pale tower—a behemoth on the horizon. To the healer sleeping within.

⌒

Yrene slept for a day and a half.

She hadn't meant to. Had barely been able to rouse herself long enough to see to her needs and wave off Eretia when she'd come to prod her, to make sure she was still alive.

The healing yesterday—two days ago, she realized as she dressed in the gray light before dawn—had decimated her. That bit of progress, the nosebleed afterward, had taken its toll.

But his toes had moved. And the pathways she'd sent her magic floating along, dots of light darting through him . . . Damaged, yes, but if she could slowly start to replace those frayed, tiny communicators within him . . . It would be long, and hard, yet . . .

Yrene knew it was not guilt alone that had her rising so early on Tehome's Day.

He was from Adarlan—she doubted he'd care if he got the day off.

Dawn had barely broken by the time Yrene slipped into the Torre courtyard and paused.

The sun had crept over the compound walls, spearing a few shafts of golden light into the purplish shadows.

And in one of those shafts of sunlight, the faint strands of gold in his brown hair gleaming . . .

"She wakes," Lord Chaol said.

Yrene strode for him, gravel crunching loudly in the drowsy dawn. "You rode here?"

"All by myself."

She only arched a brow at the white mare beside his. "And you brought the other horse?"

"A gentleman through and through."

She crossed her arms, frowning up at where he sat mounted. "Any further movement?"

The morning sun lit his eyes, turning the brown into near-gold. "How are you feeling?"

"Answer my question, please."

"Answer mine."

She gaped at him a bit. Debated scowling. "I'm fine," she said, waving a hand. "But have you felt any further—"

"Did you get the rest you needed?"

Yrene gaped at him truly this time. "*Yes.*" She scowled now, too. "And it's none of your concern—"

"It certainly is."

He said it so *calmly.* With such *male* entitlement. "I know that in

232

Adarlan, women bow to whatever men say, but here, if I say it's none of your business, then *it isn't*."

Chaol gave her a half smile. "So we're back to the animosity today."

She reined in her rising shriek. "*We* are not back to anything. I'm your healer, and you are my patient, and I asked you about the status of your—"

"If you're not rested," he said, as if it were the most rational thing in the world, "then I'm not letting you near me."

Yrene opened and closed her mouth. "And *how* will you decide that?"

Slowly, his eyes swept over her. Every inch.

Her heart thundered at the long look. The relentless focus. "Good color," he said. "Good posture. Certainly good sass."

"I'm not some prize horse, as *you* said yesterday."

"Two days ago."

She braced her hands on her hips. "I'm fine. Now, how are *you*?" Each word was accentuated.

Chaol's eyes danced. "I'm feeling quite well, Yrene. Thank you for asking."

Yrene. If she wasn't inclined to leap onto his horse and strangle him, she might have contemplated how the way he said her name made her toes curl.

But she hissed, "Don't mistake my kindness for stupidity. If you have had any progress, or regressions, I *will* find them out."

"If this is your kindness, then I'd hate to see your bad side."

She knew he meant the words in jest, yet . . . Her back stiffened.

He seemed to realize it, and leaned down in his saddle. "It was a joke, Yrene. You have been more generous than . . . It was a joke."

She shrugged, heading for the white horse.

He said, perhaps an attempt to steer them back toward neutral ground, "How are the other healers faring—after the attack?"

A shiver crawled up her spine as she grabbed the mare's reins, but made no move to mount. Yrene had offered to help with the burial, but Hafiza had refused, telling her to save her strength for Lord

Westfall. But it hadn't stopped her from visiting the death chamber beneath the Torre two days ago—from seeing the desiccated body laid out on the stone slab in the center of the rock-hewn chamber, the leathery, drained face, the bones that jutted out from paper-thin skin. She'd offered up a prayer to Silba before she'd left, and had not been awake yesterday when they'd buried her in the catacombs far beneath the tower.

Yrene now frowned up at the tower looming overhead, its presence always such a comfort, and yet . . . Since that night in the library, despite Hafiza's and Eretia's best efforts, there had been a hush in the halls, the tower itself. As if the light that had filled this place had guttered.

"They fight to retain a sense of normalcy," Yrene said at last. "I think in defiance against . . . against whoever did it. Hafiza and Eretia have led by example, staying calm, focused—smiling when they can. I think it helps the other girls not to be so petrified."

"If you want me to help with another lesson," he offered, "my services are at your disposal."

She nodded absently, running her thumb over the bridle.

Silence fell for a long moment, filled with the scent of swaying lavender and the potted lemon trees. Then—"Were you really planning on barging into my room at dawn?"

Yrene turned from the patient white mare. "You don't seem the type to laze in bed." She raised her brows. "Though, if you and Captain Faliq are engaging in—"

"You can come at dawn, if you wish."

She nodded. Even though she usually *loved* sleeping. "I was going to check on a patient before I visited you. Since we tend to . . . lose time." He didn't reply, so she went on, "I can meet you back at the palace in two hours, if you—"

"I can go with you. I don't mind."

She dropped the reins. Surveyed him. His legs. "Before we go, I should like to do some exercises with you."

"On the horse?"

234

Yrene strode to him, gravel hissing beneath her shoes. "It's actually a successful form of treatment for many—not just those with spinal injuries. The movements of a horse during riding can improve sensory processing, among other benefits." She unbuckled the brace and slid his foot from the stirrup. "When I was on the steppes last winter, I healed a young warrior who had fallen from his horse on a grueling hunt—the wound was nearly the same as yours. His tribe devised the brace for him before I got there, since he was even less inclined to remain indoors than you."

Chaol snorted, running a hand through his hair.

Yrene lifted his foot and began to rotate it, mindful of the horse he sat atop. "Getting him to do any of the exercising—the therapy—was an ordeal. He hated being cooped up in his *gir* and wanted to feel the fresh air on his face. So, just to give myself a moment's peace, I let him get into the saddle, ride a bit, and then we'd do the exercises while he was astride. Only in exchange for later doing *more* comprehensive exercises in the tent. But he made such progress while astride that it became a main part of our treatment." Yrene gently bent and straightened his leg. "I know you can't feel much beyond your toes—"

"Nothing."

"—but I want you to focus on wriggling them. *As much as you can.* Along with the rest of your leg, but concentrate on your feet while I do this."

He fell silent, and she didn't bother to look up as she moved his leg, going through what exercises she could with the horse beneath him. The solid weight of his leg was enough to get her sweating, but she kept at it, stretching and bending, pivoting and rolling. And beneath his boots, the thick black leather shifting . . . his toes indeed wriggled and pushed.

"Good," Yrene told him. "Keep at it."

His toes strained against the leather again. "The steppes—that's where the khagan's people originally hailed from."

She went through another full set of the exercises, making sure his toes were moving the entire time, before she answered. Setting his leg back within the brace and stirrup, giving the horse plenty of space as she

235

went around its front and unbuckled his other leg, she said, "Yes. A beautiful, pristine land. The grassy hills roll on forever, interrupted only by sparse pine forests and a few bald mountains." Yrene grunted against the weight of his leg as she began the same set of exercises. "Did you know that the first khagan conquered the continent with only a hundred thousand men? And that he did it in four years?" She took in the awakening city around them, marveling. "I knew about his people's history, about the Darghan, but when I went to the steppes, Kashin told me—" She fell silent, wishing she could take back the last bit.

"The prince went with you?" A calm, casual question. She tapped his foot in silent order to keep wriggling his toes. Chaol obeyed with a huff of laughter.

"Kashin and Hafiza came with me. We were there over a month." Yrene flexed his foot, up and down, working through the repetitive motions with slow, deliberate care. Magic aided in the healing, yes, but the physical element of it played equally as important a role. "Are you moving your toes as much as you can?"

A snort. "Yes, mistress."

She hid her smile, stretching his leg as far as his hip would allow and rotating it in small circles.

"I assume that trip to the steppes was when Prince Kashin poured his heart out."

Yrene nearly dropped his leg, but instead glared up at him, finding those rich brown eyes full of dry humor. "It is none of your business."

"You do love to say that, for someone who seems so intent on demanding I tell her everything."

She rolled her eyes and went back to bending his leg at the knee, stretching and easing. "Kashin was one of the first friends I made here," she said after a long moment. "One of my first friends anywhere."

"Ah." A pause. "And when he wanted more than friendship . . ."

Yrene lowered Chaol's leg at last, buckling it back into the brace and wiping the dust from his boots off her hands. She set her hands on her hips as she peered at him, squinting against the rising light. "I didn't want more than that. I told him as much. And that is that."

Chaol's lips twitched toward a smile, and Yrene at last approached her waiting mare, hauling herself into the saddle. When she straightened, arranging the skirts of her dress over her legs, she said to him, "My aim is to return to Fenharrow, to help where I am needed most. I felt nothing strong enough for Kashin to warrant yielding that dream."

Understanding filled his eyes, and he opened his mouth—as if he might say something about it. But he just nodded, smiling again, and said, "I'm glad you didn't." She lifted a brow in question, and his smile grew. "Where would I be without you here to bark orders at me?"

Yrene scowled, scooping up the reins and steering the horse toward the gates as she said sharply, "Let me know if you start to feel any discomfort or tingling in that saddle—and try to keep your toes moving as often as you can."

To his credit, he didn't object. He only said with that half smile, "Lead the way, Yrene Towers."

And though she told herself not to . . . a little smile tugged on Yrene's mouth as they rode into the awakening city.

❧ 20 ❧

With most of the city down by the docks for the sunrise ceremony to honor Tehome, the streets were quiet. Chaol supposed only the sickest would be bedbound today, which was why, when they approached a slender house on a sunny, dusty street, he wasn't at all surprised to be greeted by violent coughing before they'd even reached the door.

Well, before Yrene had even reached the door. Without the chair, he'd remain atop the horse, but Yrene didn't so much as comment on it as she dismounted, tied her mare to the hitching post down the street, and strode for the house. He kept shifting his toes every so often—as much as he could manage within the boots. The movement alone, he knew, was a gift, but it required more concentration than he'd expected; more energy, too.

Chaol was still flexing them when an elderly woman opened the house door, sighing to see Yrene and speaking in very slow Halha. For Yrene to understand, apparently, because the healer replied in the language as she entered the house and left the door ajar, her use of the words tentative and unwieldy. Better than his own.

From the street, he could see through the house's open windows and door to the little bed tucked just under the painted sill—as if to keep the patient in the fresh air.

It was occupied by an old man—the source of that coughing.

Yrene spoke to the crone before striding to the old man, pulling up a squat, three-legged stool.

Chaol stroked his horse's neck, wriggling his toes again, while Yrene took the man's withered hand and pressed another to his brow.

Each movement was gentle, calm. And her face . . .

There was a soft smile on it. One he'd never seen before.

Yrene said something he couldn't hear to the old woman wringing her hands behind them, then rolled down the thin blanket covering the man.

Chaol cringed at the lesions crusting his chest and stomach. Even the old woman did.

But Yrene didn't so much as blink, her serene countenance never shifting as she lifted a hand before her. White light simmered along her fingers and palm.

The old man, though unconscious, sucked in a breath as she laid a hand on his chest. Right over the worst of those sores.

For long minutes, she only laid her hand there, brows scrunched, light flowing from her palm to the man's chest.

And when she lifted her hand . . . the old woman wept. Kissed Yrene's hands, one after the other. Yrene only smiled, kissing the woman's sagging cheek, and bade her farewell, giving what had to be firm instructions for the man's continued care.

It was only after Yrene shut the door behind her that the beautiful smile faded. That she studied the dusty cobblestones and her mouth tightened. As if she'd forgotten he was there.

His horse nickered, and her head snapped up.

"Are you all right?" he asked.

She only unhitched her horse and mounted, chewing on her lower lip as they started into a slow walk. "He has a disease that will not go gently.

239

We have been battling it for five months now. That it flared up so badly this time . . ." She shook her head—disappointed. With herself.

"It doesn't have a cure?"

"It has been defeated in other patients, but sometimes the host . . . He is very old. And even when I think I've purged it from him, it comes back." She blew out a breath. "At this point, I feel as if I'm just buying him time, not giving him a solution."

He studied the tightness in her jaw. Someone who demanded excellence from herself—while perhaps not expecting the same from others. Or even hoping for it.

Chaol found himself saying, "Are there any other patients you need to see to?"

She frowned toward his legs. Toward the big toe he pushed against the top of his boot, the leather shifting with the movement. "We can return to the palace—"

"I like to be outside," he blurted. "The streets are empty. Let me . . ." He couldn't finish.

Yrene seemed to get it, though. "There's a young mother across the city." A long, long ride away. "She's recovering from a hard labor two weeks ago. I'd like to visit her."

Chaol tried not to look too relieved. "Then let's go."

⁓

So they went. The streets remained empty, the ceremony, Yrene told him, lasting until midmorning. Even though the empire's gods had been cobbled together, most people participated in their holidays.

Religious tolerance, she'd said, was something the very first khagan had championed—and all who had come after him, too. Oppressing various beliefs only led to discord within his empire, so he'd absorbed them all. Some literally, twining multiple gods into one. But always allowing those who wished to practice the freedom to do so without fear.

Chaol, in turn, told Yrene about the other use he'd learned while reading up on the history of the khagan rule: in other kingdoms, where religious minorities were ill-treated, he found *many* willing spies.

She'd known that already—and had asked him if he'd ever used spies for his own . . . position.

He told her no. Though he didn't reveal that he'd once had men who worked covertly, but they weren't like the spies Aedion and Ren Allsbrook had employed. That he himself had worked within Rifthold this spring and summer. But talking about his former guards . . . He fell silent.

She'd remained quiet after that, as if sensing his silence was not from lack of conversation.

She brought him into a quarter of the city that was full of small gardens and parks, the houses modest yet well kept. Firmly middle-class. It reminded him a bit of Rifthold and yet . . . Cleaner. Brighter. Even with the streets so quiet this morning, it teemed with life.

Especially at the elegant little house they stopped before, where a merry-eyed young woman spotted them from the window a level above. She called out to Yrene in Halha, then vanished inside.

"Well, that answers *that* question," Yrene murmured, just as the front door opened and that woman appeared, a plump babe in her arms.

The mother paused upon seeing Chaol, but he offered a polite bob of his head.

The woman smiled prettily at him, but it turned outright devious as she faced Yrene and waggled her eyebrows.

Yrene laughed, and the sound . . . Beautiful as the sound was, it was nothing like the smile on her face. The delight.

He'd never seen a face so lovely.

Not as Yrene dismounted and took the chubby baby—the portrait of newborn health—from the mother's outstretched arms. "Oh, she's beautiful," she cooed, brushing a finger over a round cheek.

241

The mother beamed. "Fat as a dirt-grub." She spoke in Chaol's own tongue, either because Yrene used it with her, or from noticing his own features, so different from the various norms here in Antica. "Hungry as a pig, too."

Yrene bobbed and swayed with the baby, cooing at the girl. "The feeding is going well?"

"She'd be on my breast day and night if I let her," the mother groused, not at all embarrassed to be discussing such things with him present.

Yrene chuckled, her smile growing as she let a tiny hand wrap around her finger. "She looks healthy as can be," she observed. Then looked over the mother. "And you?"

"I've been following the regimen you gave me—the baths helped."

"No bleeding?"

A shake of the head. Then she seemed to notice him, because she said a bit more quietly, and Chaol suddenly found the buildings down the street *very* interesting, "How long until I can—you know? With my husband."

Yrene snorted. "Give it another seven weeks."

The woman let out a squawk of outrage. "But you *healed* me."

"And you nearly bled out before I could." Words that brooked no argument. "Give your body time to rest. Other healers would tell you eight more weeks at a minimum, but . . . try it at seven. If there is *any* discomfort—"

"I know, I know," the woman said, waving a hand. "It's just . . . been a while."

Yrene let out another laugh, and Chaol found himself gazing toward her as the healer said, "Well, you can wait a little longer at this point."

The woman gave Yrene a wry smile as she took back her burbling baby. "I certainly hope *you* enjoy yourself, since I can't."

Chaol caught her meaningful glance in his direction before Yrene did.

And he got no small amount of smug satisfaction from watching Yrene blink, then stiffen, then go red. "What—oh. Oh, *no.*"

The way she spat that *no* . . . He took no satisfaction in *that*.

The woman only laughed, hefting the baby a bit higher as she headed into her charming house. "I certainly would."

The door shut.

Still red, Yrene turned to him, distinctly not meeting his eyes. "She's opinionated."

Chaol chuckled. "I hadn't realized that I was a firm *no*."

She glared at him, hauling herself onto her mare. "I don't share a bed with patients. And you're with Captain Faliq," she added quickly. "*And* you're—"

"Not in fit form to pleasure a woman?"

He was shocked he said it. But again more than a tad smug to see her eyes flare.

"No," Yrene said, somehow going redder. "Certainly not that. But you're . . . you."

"I'm trying not to be insulted."

She waved a hand, looking everywhere but at him. "You know what I mean."

That he was a man from Adarlan, that he'd served the king? He certainly did. But he said, deciding to have mercy on her, "I was joking, Yrene. I . . . am with Nesryn."

She swallowed, still blushing like mad. "Where is she today?"

"She went to attend the ceremony with her family." Nesryn hadn't invited him, and he'd claimed he wanted to put off their own ride through the city. Yet here he now was.

Yrene nodded distantly. "Are you going to the party tonight—at the palace?"

"Yes. Are you?"

Another nod. Stilted silence. Then she said, "I'm afraid to work on you today—just in case we lose track of time again and miss the party."

"Would it be so bad if we did?"

243

She eyed him while they turned a corner. "It would offend some of them. If it didn't offend the Lady of the Great Deep herself. I'm not sure which scares me more." He chuckled again as Yrene went on, "Hasar lent me a dress, so I have to go. Or risk her wrath."

Some shadow passed over her face. And he was about to ask about it when she said, "Do you want to have a tour?"

He stared at her, at the offer she'd thrown his way.

"I'll admit I don't know *that* much about the history, but my work has taken me to every quarter, so I can at least keep us from getting lost—"

"Yes," he breathed. "Yes."

Yrene's smile was tentative. Quiet.

But she led him onward, the streets beginning to fill as the ceremonies ended and celebrating began. As laughing people streamed down the avenue and alleys, music pouring from everywhere, the smell of food and spices wrapping around him.

He forgot about the heat, the baking sun, forgot to keep moving his toes every now and then, as they rode through the winding quarters of the city, as he marveled at the domed temples and free libraries, as Yrene showed him the paper money they used—mulberry bark backed in silk—in lieu of unwieldy coins.

She bought him her favorite treats, a confection made from carob, and offered smiles to anyone who came her way. Rarely to him, though.

There was no street she balked at turning down, no neighborhood or alley she seemed to fear. A god-city, yes—and also a city of learning, of light and comfort and wealth.

When the sun reached its zenith, she led them into a lush public garden, its overhanging trees and vines blocking out the brutal rays. They rode down the labyrinth of walkways, the garden near-empty thanks to everyone now partaking in the midday meal.

Raised beds of flowers overflowed with blossoms, hanging ferns swayed in the cool breeze off the sea, birds called to one another from the cover of the drooping fronds overhead.

"Do you think . . . ," Yrene said after long minutes of quiet, "that one day . . ." She gnawed on her bottom lip. "That we could have a place like this?"

"In Adarlan?"

"In anywhere," she said. "But yes—in Adarlan, in Fenharrow. I heard Eyllwe's cities were once as fine as this, before . . ."

Before the shadow between them. Before the shadow in his heart.

"They were," Chaol said, sealing away the thought of the princess who'd lived in those cities, who'd loved them. Even as the scar on his face seemed to twinge. But he considered her question. And from those shadows of his memory, he heard Aedion Ashryver's voice.

What do you suppose the people on other continents, across all those seas, think of us? Do you think they hate us or pity us for what we do to each other? Perhaps it's just as bad there. Perhaps it's worse. But . . . I have to believe it's better. Somewhere, it's better than this.

He wondered if he'd ever get to tell Aedion that he'd found such a place. Perhaps he would tell Dorian what he'd seen here. Help rebuild the ruins of Rifthold, of his kingdom, into something like this.

He realized he hadn't finished. That Yrene was still waiting, as she brushed aside a trailing vine of small purple flowers. "Yes," he said at last, at the wariness hiding that tiny burning kernel of hope in her eyes. "I believe we can build this for ourselves one day." He added, "If we survive this war." If he could leave here with an army behind him to challenge Erawan.

Time pressed on him, smothering him. Faster. He had to move *faster* with everything—

Yrene scanned his face in the heavy heat of the garden. "You love your people very much."

Chaol nodded, unable to find the words.

She opened her mouth, as if she'd say something, but closed it. Then said, "Even the people of Fenharrow were not blameless with their actions this past decade."

Chaol tried not to look at the faint scar across her throat. Had it been one of her own countrymen who had—

She sighed, studying the rose garden wilting in the blistering heat. "We should head back. Before the crowds get impossible."

He wondered what she'd thought of saying a moment ago but decided against. What caused that shadow to lurk in her eyes.

But Chaol only followed her, all those words hanging between them.

⁓

They parted ways at the palace, the halls packed with servants readying for the evening's festivities. Yrene went right to find Hasar and the dress—and bath—she'd been promised, and Chaol returned to his own suite, to wash off the dust and sweat and find something suitable to wear.

No sign of Nesryn until she'd returned midway through his bath, shouted that she was taking one of her own, and closed the door to her suite.

He'd opted for his teal jacket, and waited in the hall for Nesryn to emerge. When she did, he blinked at the well-cut amethyst jacket and pants. He hadn't seen a sign of her captain's uniform for days. And wasn't about to ask as he said, "You look beautiful."

Nesryn smiled, her glossy hair still damp from the bath. "You don't look so bad yourself." She seemed to note the color on his face and asked, "You were in the sun today?" Her slight accent had deepened, adding more of a twirl to certain sounds.

"I helped Yrene with some patients around the city."

Nesryn smiled as they headed into the hallway. "I'm glad to hear it." Not a word about the ride and visit he'd delayed with her—he wondered if she had even remembered.

He still hadn't told her about his toes. But as they reached the great hall of the palace . . . Later. They'd discuss it all later.

The great hall of the palace was a wonder.

That was the only word for it.

The party was not as large as he would have assumed, only a few more people than the usual gathering of the viziers and royals, but no expense had been spared on the decorations. The feast.

He gaped a bit, Nesryn doing the same, as they were led to their spots at the high table—an honor he was still surprised they received. The khagan and his wife would not be joining them, he was told by Duva. Her mother had not been doing well these last few days and wished to celebrate with her husband in private.

No doubt seeing those mourning banners at last coming down had been difficult. And tonight likely wasn't the time to press the khagan about their alliance anyway.

A few more guests poured in, along with Hasar and Renia, arm in arm with Yrene.

When Yrene had left him at the crossroads of one of the palace's main halls, she'd been gleaming with sweat and dust, her cheeks rosy, her hair curling slightly around her ears. Her dress, too, had been wrinkled from a day of riding, the hem coated in dust.

Certainly not at all like what she wore now.

He felt the attention of half the men at the table slide toward Hasar—toward Yrene—as they entered, trailed by two of the princess's servant girls. Hasar was smirking, Renia utterly stunning in ruby red, but Yrene . . .

For a beautiful woman clad in the finest clothes and jewels an empire could purchase, there was something resigned about her. Yes, her shoulders were back, her spine straight, but the smile that had hit him in the gut earlier was long gone.

Hasar had dressed Yrene in cobalt that brought out the warmth of her skin and set her brown hair glimmering as if it had indeed been gilded. The princess had even dusted cosmetics along Yrene's face—or perhaps the hint of color on her freckled cheeks was from the fact that the gown was cut low enough to reveal the lushness of her figure. Cut low, and tight through the bodice.

Yrene's dresses certainly didn't hide her body, but the gown . . . He

247

hadn't quite realized how slim her waist was, how her hips flared beneath it. How her other assets swelled above.

He wasn't the only one taking a second glance. Sartaq and Arghun had leaned forward in their seats as their sister led Yrene to the high table.

Yrene's hair had been left mostly down, only the sides swept back and pinned with combs of gold and ruby. Matching earrings dangled to brush the slender column of her throat.

"She looks regal," Nesryn murmured to him.

Yrene indeed looked like a princess—albeit one heading to the gallows for how solemn her face was as they reached the table. Whatever contentment she'd possessed when they'd parted ways had since vanished upon the two hours she'd spent with Hasar.

The princes stood to greet Yrene this time, Kashin rising first.

The Healer on High's undeclared heir; a woman who would likely wield considerable power in this realm. They seemed to realize it, the depth of that implication. Arghun especially, from the shrewd look he gave Yrene. A woman of considerable power—and beauty.

He saw the word in Arghun's eyes: *prize.*

Chaol's jaw tightened. Yrene certainly didn't want the attentions of the handsomest of the princes—he couldn't imagine she'd be inclined to desire the affections of the other two.

Arghun opened his mouth to speak to Hasar, but the princess strode right to Chaol and Nesryn and murmured in Nesryn's ear, "Move."

⇥ 21 ⇤

Nesryn blinked at Hasar.

The princess smiled, cold as a snake, and clarified, "It is not polite to only sit with your companion. We should have separated you two before now."

Nesryn glanced to him. Everyone watched. Chaol had no idea—absolutely none—what to say. Yrene seemed inclined to melt into the green marble floor.

Sartaq cleared his throat. "Join me here, Captain Faliq."

Nesryn stood quickly, and Hasar beamed up at her. The princess patted the back of the seat Nesryn had vacated and crooned to Yrene, lingering a few feet away, "You sit here. In case you are needed."

Yrene shot Chaol a look that might have been considered pleading, but he kept his face neutral and offered a close-lipped smile.

Nesryn found her seat beside Sartaq, who had asked a vizier to move down the table, and Hasar, satisfied that the adjustments had been done to her liking, deemed that her own usual seats were not to her taste and kicked out two viziers down by Arghun. The second seat was for Renia, who gave her lover a mildly disapproving glance, but smiled to herself—as if it were typical.

The meal resumed, and Chaol slid his attention to Yrene. The vizier on her other side paid her no heed. Platters were passed around by servants, food and drink piled and poured. Chaol muttered under his breath, "Do I want to know?"

Yrene cut into the simmered lamb and saffron rice heaped on her golden plate. "No."

He was willing to bet whatever shadows had been in her eyes earlier today, the thing she'd halted herself from saying to him . . . It went hand in hand with whatever was unfolding here.

He peered down the table, to where Nesryn watched them, half listening to Sartaq as the prince spoke about something Chaol could not hear over the clatter of silverware and discussion.

He shot her an apologetic look.

Nesryn threw him a warning one in answer—directed toward Hasar. *Be careful.*

"How are your toes?" Yrene said, taking tiny bites of her food. He'd seen her devour the box of carob sweets she'd gotten for them atop their horses. The dainty eating here—for show.

"Active," he said with a half smile. No matter that it had only been two hours since they'd last seen each other.

"Sensation?"

"A tingle."

"Good." Her throat bobbed, that scar shifting with it.

He knew they were being watched. Listened to. She did as well.

Yrene's knuckles were white as she clenched her utensils, her back ramrod straight. No smile. Little light in her kohl-lined eyes.

Had the princess maneuvered them to sit together to talk, or to manipulate Kashin into some sort of action? The prince was indeed watching, even while he engaged two gold-robed viziers in conversation.

Chaol murmured to Yrene, "The role of pawn doesn't suit you."

Those gold-brown eyes flickered. "I don't know what you're talking about."

But she did. The words weren't meant for him.

He scrambled for topics to get them through the meal. "When do you meet with the ladies for their next lesson?"

Some of the tension drained from Yrene's shoulders as she said, "Two weeks. It would normally be next week, but many of them have their examinations then, and will be focused on studying."

"Some exercise and fresh air might be helpful."

"I'd say so, but to them, these tests are life and death. They certainly were to me."

"Do you have any more remaining?"

She shook her head, her jeweled earrings catching the light. "I completed my final one two weeks ago. I am an official healer of the Torre." A bit of a self-effacing humor danced in her eyes.

He lifted his goblet to her. "Congratulations."

A shrug, but she nodded in thanks. "Though Hafiza thinks to test me one last time."

Ah. "So I am indeed an experiment."

A piss-poor attempt at making light of their argument days ago, of that rawness that had ripped a hole through him.

"No," Yrene said quietly, quickly. "You have very little to do with it. This last, unofficial test . . . It is about me."

He wanted to ask, but there were too many eyes upon them. "Then I wish you luck," he said formally. So at odds with how they'd spoken while riding through the city.

The meal passed slowly and yet swiftly, their conversation stilted and infrequent.

It was only when the desserts and *kahve* were served that Arghun clapped his hands and called for entertainment.

"With our father in his chambers," Chaol heard Sartaq confide to Nesryn, "we tend to have more . . . informal celebrations."

Indeed, a troupe of musicians in finery, bearing instruments both familiar and foreign, emerged into the space between the pillars beyond the table. Rumbling drums and flutes and horns announced the arrival of the main event: dancers.

A circle of eight dancers, both male and female—a holy number, Sartaq explained to a tentatively smiling Nesryn—emerged from the curtains to the side of the pillars.

Chaol tried not to choke.

They had been painted in gold, bedecked with jewels and gauzy, belted robes of thinnest silk, but beneath that . . . nothing.

Their bodies were lithe and young, the peak of youth and virility. Hips rolled, backs arched, hands twined in the air above them as they began to weave around one another in circles and lines.

"I told you," was all Yrene muttered to him.

"I think Dorian would enjoy this," he muttered back, and was surprised to find the corners of his mouth tugging upward at the thought.

Yrene threw him a bemused look, some light back in her eyes. People had twisted in their seats to better watch the dancers, their sculpted bodies and nimble, bare feet.

Perfect, precise movements, their bodies merely instruments of the music. Beautiful—ethereal and yet . . . tangible. Aelin, he realized, would have enjoyed this, too. Greatly.

As the dancers performed, servants hauled over chairs and couches, arranging pillows and tables. Bowls of smoking herbs were laid atop them, the smell sweet and cloying.

"Don't get too close if you want your senses intact," Yrene warned as a male servant bore one of the smoking metal dishes toward a carved wood table. "It's a mild opiate."

"They really let their hair down when their parents are away."

Some of the viziers were leaving, but many left the table to take up cushioned seats, the entirety of the great hall remade in a matter of moments to accommodate lounging, and—

Servants emerged from the curtains, well groomed and dressed in gauzy, rich silk as well. Men and women, all beautiful, found their way to laps and armrests, some curling at the feet of viziers or nobility.

He'd seen fairly unleashed parties at the glass castle, but there had still been a stiffness. A formality and sense that such things were hidden behind closed doors. Dorian had certainly saved it for his own room. Or someone else's. Or he just dragged Chaol into Rifthold, or down to Bell-haven, where the nobility held parties far more uninhibited than those of Queen Georgina.

Sartaq remained at the table beside Nesryn, who watched the skilled dancers with wide-eyed admiration, but the other royal children . . . Duva, a hand on her belly, bid her farewells, her husband at her side, silent as always. The smoke was not good for the babe in her womb, Duva claimed, and Yrene nodded in approval, though no one looked her way.

Arghun claimed a couch for himself around the dancing, reclining and breathing in the smoke rippling off the embers in those small metal bowls beside them. Courtiers and viziers vied for the seats nearest the eldest prince.

Hasar and her lover took a small couch for themselves, the princess's hands soon tangling in her lover's thick black hair. Her mouth found a spot on the woman's neck a moment later. Renia's answering smile was slow and broad—her eyes fluttering closed as Hasar whispered something against her skin.

Kashin seemed to wait for minutes as Yrene and Chaol watched the unfolding decadence from the emptying banquet table.

Waiting for Yrene, no doubt, to rise.

Color had stained her cheeks as she kept her eyes firmly on her *kahve*, steam curling from the small cup.

"You've seen this before?" Chaol asked her.

"Give it an hour or two, and they'll all slip away to their rooms—not alone, of course."

Prince Kashin seemed to have dragged out his conversation with the vizier beside him for as long as he could stomach. He opened his mouth, looking right toward Yrene, and Chaol read the invitation in his eyes before the man could speak.

Chaol had perhaps a heartbeat to decide. To see that Sartaq had invited Nesryn to sit with him—not at the table, not on one of the couches, but at a pair of chairs to the far back of the room, where there was no smoke and the windows were open, and yet they could still watch. She gave Chaol a reassuring nod, her pace unhurried as she walked with the prince.

So as Kashin leaned forward to invite Yrene to join him at a couch, Chaol turned to the healer and said, "I would like to sit with you."

Her eyes were slightly wide. "Where."

Kashin shut his mouth, and Chaol had the sense that there was a target being drawn on his chest.

But he held Yrene's gaze and said, "Where it is quieter."

There were only a few couches left free—all close to the thickest smoke and dancing. But there was one half hidden in shadow near an alcove across the room, a small brazier of those herbs smoldering on the low-lying table before it. "If we are meant to be seen together tonight," he said so quietly only Yrene could hear, "then remaining here for a while would be better than leaving together." What a message *that* would send, given the shift in the party's atmosphere. "And I would not have you walk alone."

Yrene rose silently, smiling grimly. "Then let us relax, Lord Westfall." She gestured toward the shadowed couch beyond the edge of the light.

She let him wheel himself over. Kept her chin high, the skirts of her gown trailing behind her as she headed for that alcove. The back of the dress was mostly open—revealing smooth, unblemished skin and the fine groove of her spine. It dipped low enough for him to make out the twin indentations in her lower back, as if some god had pressed his thumbs there.

He felt too many eyes upon them as she settled herself on the couch, the skirts of her dress twisted along the floor past her ankles, her arms bare as she spread one along the back of the plush cushions.

Chaol held her low-lidded stare as he reached the couch, faster than the servants could approach, and eased himself from chair to cushions. A few movements had him angled toward her—and he nodded his thanks to the servant who moved his chair away. From this vantage, they had an unobstructed view of the dancers, the seating areas, the servants and nobility now starting to run hands and mouths over skin and fabric, even as they watched the unparalleled entertainment.

Something twisted—not unpleasantly—in his gut at the display.

"They do not force servants here," Yrene said quietly. "It was the first thing I asked during my initial time at these gatherings. The servants are eager to raise their positions, and the ones who are here know what privilege it might bring them if they leave here with someone tonight."

"But if they are paid," he countered, "if they worry for their positions should they decline, then how can this ever be true consent?"

"It isn't. Not when you put it that way. But the khaganate has made sure that other lines are maintained. Age restrictions. Vocal consent. Punishments for those—even royalty—who break those rules." She'd said as much days ago.

A young woman and man had positioned themselves on either side of Arghun, one nibbling at his neck while the other traced circles along the prince's thighs. All the while, the prince continued conversation with a vizier seated in a chair to his left, unfazed.

"I thought he had a wife," Chaol said.

Yrene followed his gaze. "He does. She stays at his country estate. And servants are not considered affairs. The needs they see to . . . It might

255

as well be giving a bath." Her eyes danced as she said, "I'm sure you discovered that your first day."

His face heated. "I was . . . surprised at the attention to detail. And
involvement."

"Kadja was likely selected to please you."

"I'm not inclined to stray. Even with a willing servant."

Yrene glanced toward Nesryn, deep in conversation with Sartaq. "She
is lucky to have such a loyal companion, then."

He waited for a tug of jealousy at seeing Nesryn's smile to the prince,
whose body was the pinnacle of relaxed, his arm draped along the back of
the couch behind her, an ankle crossed over a knee.

Perhaps he just trusted Nesryn, but nothing stirred in him at the sight.

Chaol found Yrene watching him, her eyes like topaz in the shadows
and smoke.

"I met with my friend the other evening," she said, her lashes fluttering. No more than a woman lulled by the smoldering opiates. Even his
own head was starting to feel fuzzy. His body warm. Cozy. "And again
this evening before dinner."

Hasar.

"And?" He found himself studying the slight curl to the ends of Yrene's
long hair. Found his fingers shifting, as if imagining the feel of it between
them.

Yrene waited until a servant bearing a tray of candied fruits walked
past. "She told me *your* friend is still unaccounted for. And a net has been
stretched across the center of the table."

He blinked, sorting through the smoke and the words.

Armies. Perrington's armies had been stretched across the continent.
No wonder she hadn't discussed it earlier in the streets; no wonder it had
brought such shadows to her eyes. "Where?"

"Mountains to—your usual haunt."

He recalled a mental map of the land. From the Ferian Gap to Rifthold.
Holy gods.

"You are sure of it?"

A nod.

He felt eyes sliding toward them now and then.

Yrene did, too. He tried not to start at the hand she laid on his arm. As she looked up at him beneath lowered lashes, eyes sleepy—inviting. "I was asked the other day, and again today, in a manner I cannot refuse."

She was threatened. He clenched his jaw.

"I need a place. A direction," she murmured. "For where your *other* friend might go."

Aelin. "She is . . . where is she?"

"They do not know."

Aelin was—missing. Unaccounted for by even the khaganate's spies.

"Not in her home?"

A shake of the head that made Chaol's heart begin to pound wildly. Aelin and Dorian—both unaccounted for. Missing. If Perrington were to strike . . ."I don't know where she would go. What she planned to do." He laid his hand over hers. Blocked out the softness of her skin. "Her plan was to return home. Rally a host."

"She has not. And I do not doubt the clarity of the *eyes* here. And there."

Hasar's spies. And others.

Aelin was not in Terrasen. Had never reached Orynth.

"Wipe that look off your face," Yrene purred, and though her hand brushed his arm, her eyes were hard.

He struggled to do so, but managed to give her a sleepy smile. "Does your friend think they have fallen into the hands of someone else?"

"She does not know." Yrene trailed fingers up his arm, light and unhurried. That simple ring still sat upon her hand. "She wants me to ask you. Pry it from you."

"Ah." Her slender, beautiful hand slid along his arm. "Hence the new seating arrangement." And why Yrene had so often seemed on the verge of speaking today and then opted for silence.

257

"She will make life very difficult if I do not appear to get you to warm to me."

He halted her hand at his bicep, finding her fingers shaking slightly. Perhaps it was the sweet, cloying smoke curling around them, perhaps it was the music and the dancers with their bare skin and jewels, but Chaol said, "I would think you'd already done that, Yrene Towers."

He watched the color bloom on her face. Watched how it made the gold in her eyes brighten.

Dangerous. Dangerous and stupid and—

He knew others were watching. Knew Nesryn sat with the prince.

She'd understand that it was for show. Nesryn's presence with Sartaq was merely another part of it. Another display.

He told himself that as he continued to hold Yrene's gaze, continued to press her hand against his upper arm. Continued to watch the color stain her cheeks. The tip of her tongue darted out to moisten her lips.

He watched that, too.

A heavy, calming warmth settled deep into him.

"I need a place. Any place."

It took him a few heartbeats to figure out what she was asking. The threat the princess implied for not getting information from him.

"Why lie at all? I would have told you the truth." His mouth felt far away.

"After the lesson with the girls," she murmured, "I owed you something."

And this reveal of Hasar's interests . . . "Will she be swayed to our cause?"

Yrene studied the room, and Chaol found his hand drifting from hers. Sliding up her bare shoulder, to rest along her neck.

Her skin was soft as sun-warmed velvet. His thumb stroked up the side of her throat, so near that slender scar, and she cut her eyes to him.

There was warning there—warning and yet . . . He knew the warning was not directed at him. But herself. Yrene breathed, "She . . ." He couldn't resist a second stroke of his thumb down the side of her neck. Her throat

258

brushed against his hand as she swallowed again. "She is concerned about the threat of fire."

And fear could be a motivation that either helped or destroyed any chance of alliance.

"She thinks . . . thinks you are potentially behind the library attack. As some manipulation."

He snorted, but his thumb stilled, right over her fluttering pulse. "She gives us more credit than we're due." But that was alarm now flaring to life in Yrene's eyes. "What do you believe, Yrene Towers?"

She laid her hand atop his own but made no move to remove his touch from her neck.

"I think your presence may have triggered other forces to act, but I do not believe you are the sort of man who plays games."

Even if their current position said otherwise.

"You go after what you want," Yrene continued, "and you pursue it directly. Honestly."

"I used to be that sort of man," Chaol countered. He could not look away from her.

"And now?" Her words were breathless, her pulse hammering beneath his palm.

"And now," Chaol said, bringing his head closer to hers, near enough that her breath brushed his mouth, "I wonder if I should have listened to my father when he tried to teach me."

Yrene's eyes dropped to his mouth, and every instinct, every bit of focus, narrowed on that movement. Every part of him came to aching attention.

And the sensation of it, as he casually adjusted his jacket over his lap, was better than an ice bath.

The smoke—the opiates. It was some sort of aphrodisiac, some lulling of common sense.

Yrene was still watching his mouth as if it were a piece of fruit, her uneven breath lifting those lush, high breasts within the confines of her gown.

He forced himself to remove his hand from her neck. Forced himself to lean back.

Nesryn had to be watching. Had to be wondering what the hell he was doing.

He owed her better than this. He owed Yrene better than whatever he had just done, whatever madness—

"Skull's Bay," he threw out. "Tell her fire can be found at Skull's Bay."

It was perhaps the one place Aelin would never go—down to the domain of the Pirate Lord. He'd heard her story, once, of her "misadventure" with Rolfe. As if destroying his city and wrecking his prized ships were just another bit of fun. Heading there would indeed be the last thing Aelin would do, with the Pirate Lord's promise to slaughter her on sight.

Yrene blinked, as if remembering herself, the situation that had brought them here, to this couch, to be knee-to-knee and nearly nose-to-nose.

"Yes," she said, pulling away, blinking furiously again. She frowned at the smoldering embers within their metal cage on the table. "That will do."

She waved away an unfurling talon of smoke that tried to wend between them. "I should go."

A wild, keen-edged panic glinted in her eyes. As if she, too, had realized, had *felt*—

She stood, straightening the skirts of her gown. Gone was the sultry, steady woman who had strutted over to this couch. Here—here was the girl of about two-and-twenty, alone in a foreign city, prey to the whims of its royal children. "I hope . . . ," she said, glancing toward Nesryn. Shame. It was—shame and guilt now weighing her shoulders. "I hope you never learn to play those sorts of games."

Nesryn remained deep in conversation with Sartaq, showing no sign of distress, of knowledge of . . . of whatever had happened here.

He was a bastard. A gods-damned bastard.

"I'll see you tomorrow," was all he could think to say to Yrene. But he blurted as she walked away, "Let me get you an escort."

Because Kashin was watching them from across the room, a servant girl in his lap, running a hand through his hair. And that was . . . oh, that was cold violence in Kashin's face as he noticed Chaol's attention.

The others might think what had just gone on between him and Yrene was an act, but Kashin . . . The man wasn't as stupidly loyal as the others thought. No, he was well aware of those around him. He could read men. Assess them.

And it had not been the arousal that had let the prince realize it was genuine. But the guilt Chaol realized too late he and Yrene had let show.

"I will ask Hasar," Yrene said, and headed toward where the princess and her lover sat on their couch, mouths roving over each other with an unhurried attention to detail.

He remained on the couch, monitoring as Yrene approached the women. Hasar blinked up blearily at her.

But the lust fogging the princess's face cleared at the curt nod Yrene gave. Mission accomplished. Yrene leaned down and whispered into Hasar's ear as she kissed her cheeks in farewell. Chaol read the movement of her lips even from across the room. *Skull's Bay*.

Hasar smiled slowly, then snapped her fingers to a waiting guard. The man immediately strode for them. He watched her order the man, watched her undoubtedly threaten him with death and worse if Yrene did not make it back to the Torre safely.

Yrene only gave the princess an exasperated smile before bidding her and Renia good night and following the guard out. She glanced back at the archway.

Even across the nearly hundred feet of polished marble and towering pillars, the space between them went taut.

As if that white light he'd glimpsed inside himself two days ago was a living rope. As if she'd somehow planted herself in him that afternoon.

Yrene did not so much as nod before she left, skirts swirling around her.

When Chaol looked to Nesryn again, he found her attention upon him.

Found her face blank—so carefully blank—as she gave him a little nod of what he assumed was understanding. The match was over for tonight. She was waiting to hear the final score.

The smoke was still clinging to Chaol's nostrils, his hair, his jacket as he and Nesryn entered their suite an hour later. He had joined her and Sartaq in their quiet little area, watching guests peel off to their own chambers—or someone else's. Yes, Dorian would certainly have loved this court.

Sartaq escorted them to their room and offered them a somewhat stiff good night. More restrained than his words and smiles of earlier. Chaol didn't blame him. There were likely eyes everywhere.

Even if the prince's own lingered mostly on Nesryn as she bid Sartaq farewell and she and Chaol slipped into their suite.

The suite was mostly dark, save for a colored glass lantern Kadja had left burning on the foyer table. Their bedroom doors loomed like cavern mouths.

The pause in the dim foyer went on for a heartbeat too long.

Nesryn silently stepped toward her room.

Chaol grabbed her hand before she could make it a foot.

Slowly, she looked back over her shoulder, her dark hair shifting like midnight silk.

Even in the dimness, he knew Nesryn read what lay in his eyes.

His skin tightened around his bones, his heart a thundering beat, but he waited.

She said at last, "I think I am needed elsewhere than this palace right now."

He maintained his grip on her hand. "We shouldn't discuss this in the hall."

Nesryn's throat bobbed, but she nodded once. She made to push his chair, but he moved before she could, steering himself into his bedroom. Letting her follow.

Letting her shut the door behind them.

Moonlight leaked in through the garden windows, spilling upon the bed.

Kadja had not lit the candles, either anticipating the use of this room after the party for purposes other than sleeping or that he might not return at all. But in the dark, in the humming from the cicadas in the garden trees . . .

"I need you here," Chaol said.

"Do you?" A stark, honest question.

He gave Nesryn the respect of considering her question. "I . . . We were supposed to do this together. Everything."

She shook her head, short hair shifting. "Paths change. You know that as much as anyone."

He did. He really damn did. But it still . . . "Where do you mean to go?"

"Sartaq mentioned that he wishes to seek out answers amongst his people, about whether the Valg made it to this continent before. I . . . I am tempted to go with him, if he will let me. To see if there are indeed answers to be found, and if I might convince him to perhaps go against his father's orders. Or at least speak on our behalf."

"To go with him to where, though? The ruk riders in the south?"

"Perhaps. He mentioned at the party that he'll leave in a few days. But you and I have a slim enough shot. Maybe I can better our odds with the prince, find information of value amongst the rukhin. If one of Erawan's agents is in Antica . . . I trust the khagan's guard to protect this palace and the Torre, but you and I, we must gather what forces we can before Erawan can send more against us." She paused. "And you . . . you are making good progress. I would not interfere with that."

Unspoken words ran beneath her offer.

Chaol scrubbed at his face. For her to leave, to simply accept it, this fork in the path before them . . . He blew out a breath. "Let's wait until morning before we decide anything. No good comes from choices made late at night."

Nesryn fell silent, and he hoisted himself onto the mattress before removing his jacket and boots. "Will you sit with me? Tell me about your family—about the celebration today with them." He had only received the barest of details, and perhaps it was guilt that now fueled him, but . . .

Their eyes met in the dark, a nightingale's hymn flitting through the closed doors. He could have sworn he saw understanding shine in her face, then settle, a rock dropped into a pool.

Nesryn approached the bed on silent feet, unbuttoning her jacket and slinging it over a chair before toeing off her boots. She climbed onto the mattress, a pillow sighing as she leaned against it.

I saw, he could have sworn he read flickering in her gaze. *I know.*

But Nesryn spoke of the dockside ceremony, how her four little cousins had chucked flower wreaths into the sea and then run shrieking from the gulls that swarmed them to steal the little almond cakes out of their hands. She told him of her uncle, Brahim, and her aunt, Zahida, and their beautiful house, with its multiple courtyards and crawling flowers and lattice screens.

With every glance, those unspoken words still echoed. *I know. I know.*

Chaol let Nesryn talk, listened until her voice lulled him to sleep, because he knew, too.

⇥ 22 ⇤

Yrene debated not showing up the next day.

What had happened on the couch last night . . .

She'd returned to her room overheated and frantic, unable to settle. Peeling off Hasar's gown and jewels, she'd folded them neatly on her chair with shaking hands. Then she'd pushed her trunk in front of the door, just in case that murdering demon had spied her inhaling ungodly amounts of that smoke and thought to catch her out of her wits.

Because she had been. Utterly out of her mind. All she had known was the heat and smell and comforting size of him—the scrape of his calluses against her skin and how she wanted to feel them elsewhere. How she had kept looking at his mouth and it was all she could do to keep from tracing it with her fingers. Her lips.

She hated those parties. The smoke that made one abandon any sort of common sense. Inhibitions. Precisely why the nobility and wealthy loved to bring it out, but . . .

Yrene had paced her tower room, running her hands over her face until she smudged the cosmetics Hasar had personally applied.

She'd washed her face thrice. Slipped into her lightest nightgown and then tossed and turned in bed, the fabric clinging and chafing against her sweaty, burning skin.

Counting down the hours, the minutes, until that smoke's grip loosened. Cleared away.

It didn't let go easily. And it was only during the quietest, blackest hours of the night that Yrene took matters into her own hands.

A stronger dose than usual had been put out tonight. It crawled all over her, running talons along her skin. And the face it summoned, the hands she imagined brushing over her skin—

Release left her hollow—unsatisfied.

Dawn broke, and Yrene scowled at her haggard reflection in the sliver of mirror above the washbasin.

The opiate's grip had vanished with the few hours of sleep she'd managed to steal, but . . . Something twisted low in her gut.

She washed and dressed and packed Hasar's finery and jewels in a spare satchel. It was best to get it over with. She'd return the princess's clothes and jewels after. Hasar had been smug as a Baast Cat at the information Yrene had given her, the lie Chaol had fed her to hand to the princess.

She had debated not telling him, but even before the smoke, before that madness . . . When he'd offered to sit with her to avoid refusing Kashin, after a day spent wandering the city in unhurried ease, she'd decided. To trust him. And then lost her mind entirely.

Yrene could barely look the guards, the servants, the viziers and nobility in the face as she entered the palace and made her way to Lord Westfall's rooms. There was no doubt some had spied her on the couch with him. Some hadn't—though they might have heard.

She'd never shown such behavior at the palace. She should tell

Hafiza. Let the Healer on High hear of her brazenness before it reached the Torre from other lips.

Not that Hafiza would scold her, but . . . Yrene could not escape the feeling that she needed to confess. To make it right.

She'd keep today's session brief. Or as brief as they could, when she lost all sense of time and place in that dark, raging hell of his wound.

Professional.

Yrene entered the suite, telling Kadja, "Ginger, turmeric, and lemon," before walking to Chaol's bedroom. Kadja seemed inclined to object, but Yrene ignored her and pushed open the bedroom door.

Yrene halted so fast she nearly stumbled.

It was the rumpled sheets and pillows she noticed first. Then his naked chest, his hips barely covered by a swath of white silk.

Then a dark head, facedown on the pillow beside his. Still sleeping. Exhausted.

Chaol's eyes instantly flew open, and all Yrene managed was a silent, "Oh."

Shock and—something else flared in his gaze, his mouth opening.

Nesryn stirred beside him, brows knotting, her shirt wrinkled.

Chaol grabbed fistfuls of the sheet, the muscles of his chest and abdomen shifting as he rose up on his elbows—

Yrene simply walked out.

She waited on the gold sofa in the sitting room, her knee bouncing as she watched the garden, the climbing flowers just beginning to open up along the pillars outside the glass doors.

Even with the burbling fountain, it didn't quite block out the sounds of Nesryn murmuring as she awoke—then the pad of soft feet from his bedroom to her own, followed by the shutting of her door.

A moment later, wheels groaned, and there he was. In his shirt and pants. Hair still disheveled. As if he'd run his hands through it. Or Nesryn had. Repeatedly.

Yrene wrapped her arms around herself, the room somehow so very large. The space between them too open. She should have eaten breakfast. Should have done something to keep from this lightness. This hollow pit in her stomach.

"I didn't realize you'd be here so early," he said softly. She could have sworn guilt laced his tone.

"You said I could come at dawn," she replied with equal quiet, but hated the note of accusation in her voice and quickly added, "I should have sent word."

"No. I—"

"I can come back later," she said, shooting to her feet. "Let you two eat breakfast."

Together. Alone.

"No," he said sharply, pausing his approach near their usual couch. "Now is fine."

She couldn't look at him. Couldn't meet his eyes. Or explain why.

"Yrene."

She ignored the command in her name and went to the desk, seating herself behind it, grateful for the wall of carved wood between them. The stability of it beneath her palm as she opened up her satchel from where she'd left it along the edge and began unpacking her things with careful precision. Vials of oils she did not need. Journals.

Books—the ones she'd taken from the library, *The Song of Beginning* with them. Along with those ancient, precious scrolls. She had not been able to think of a safer place for them beyond here. Beyond him.

Yrene said very quietly, "I can make up a tonic. For her. If such a thing is needed. Isn't wanted, I mean."

A child, she couldn't bring herself to say. Like the fat babe she'd spied him smiling so broadly at yesterday. As if it was a blessing, a joy he one day might desire—

"And I can make up a daily one for you," she added, every word stumbling and tripping out of her mouth.

268

"She's already taking one," he said. "Since she was fourteen."

Likely since she first started bleeding. For a woman in a city like Rifthold, it was wise. Especially if she planned to enjoy herself as well.

"Good," was all Yrene could think to say, still stacking her books. "Smart."

He approached the desk until his knees slid beneath the other end. "Yrene."

She thumped book after book on top of each other.

"Please."

The word had her lifting her gaze. Meeting his stare—the sunwarmed soil of his eyes.

And it was the formation of those two words that she beheld brewing in his gaze—*I'm sorry*—that had her shooting up from the desk again. Walking across the room. Flinging open the garden doors.

There was nothing to be sorry for. Nothing.

They were lovers, and she . . .

Yrene lingered at the garden doors until Nesryn's bedroom door opened and closed. Until she heard Nesryn poke her head into the sitting room, murmur a farewell to Chaol, and leave.

Yrene tried to bring herself to look over a shoulder at Captain Faliq, to offer a polite smile, but she pretended not to hear the brief encounter. Pretended to be too busy examining the pale purple flowers unfurling in the morning sunlight.

She shoved back against the hollowness. She had not felt so small, so . . . insignificant for a long, long time.

You are the heir apparent to Hafiza, Healer on High. You are nothing to this man and he is nothing to you. Stay the course. Remember Fenharrow—your home. Remember those who are there—who need your help.

Remember all that you promised to do. To be.

Her hand slid into her pocket, curling around the note there.

The world needs more healers.

"It's not what you think," Chaol said behind her.

Yrene closed her eyes for a heartbeat.

Fight—fight for your miserable, useless, wasted life.

She turned, forcing a polite smile to her face. "It is a natural thing. A healthy thing. I'm glad you're feeling . . . up to the task."

From the ire that rippled in his eyes, the tightness of his jaw, Chaol perhaps was not.

The world needs more healers. The world needs more healers. The world needs more healers.

Finish with him, heal him, and she could leave Hafiza, leave the Torre, with her head held high. She could return home, to war and bloodshed, and make good on her promise. Make good on that stranger's gift of freedom that night in Innish.

"Shall we begin?"

It would be in here today. Because the prospect of sitting on that rumpled bed that likely still smelled of them—

There was a tightness to her throat, her voice, that she could not shake, no matter how many breaths she took.

Chaol studied her. Weighing her tone. Her words. Her expression.

He saw it—heard it. That tightness, that brittleness.

I expected nothing, she wanted to say. *I—I am* nothing.

Please don't ask. Please don't push. Please.

Chaol seemed to read that, too. He said quietly, "I didn't take her to bed."

She refrained from mentioning that the evidence seemed stacked against him.

Chaol went on, "We spoke long into the night and fell asleep. Nothing happened."

Yrene ignored the way her chest both hollowed out and filled at the words. Didn't trust herself to speak as the information settled.

As if sensing her need for a breath, Chaol began to turn toward the couch, but his attention snagged on the books she'd stacked on the table. On the scrolls.

The color drained from his face.

"What is that," he growled.

Yrene strode to the desk, picking up the parchment and unrolling it carefully to display the strange symbols. "Nousha, the Head Librarian, found it for me that night when I asked her for information on . . . the things that hurt you. In all the—upheaval, I forgot it. It was shelved near the Eyllwe books, so she threw it in, just in case. I think it's old. Eight hundred years at least." She was babbling, but couldn't stop, grateful for any subject but the one he'd been so near to breaching. "I think they're runes, but I've seen none like it. Neither had Nousha."

"They are not runes," Chaol said hoarsely. "They're Wyrdmarks."

And from what he had told her, Yrene knew there was much more. So much more he had not divulged. She stroked a hand over the dark cover of *The Song of Beginning*. "This book . . . It mentioned a gate. And keys. And three kings to wield them."

She wasn't certain he was breathing. Then Chaol said, voice low, "You read that. In that book."

Yrene opened the pages, flipping to the illustration of the three figures before that otherworldly gate. Approaching, she held the book open for him to see. "I couldn't read much of it—it's in an ancient form of Eyllwe— but . . ." She flipped to the other illustration, of the young man being infested by that dark power on the altar. "Is that . . . is that what they truly do?"

His hands slackened at the sides of his chair as he stared and stared at the panel featuring the young man's cold, dark eyes. "Yes."

The word held more pain and fear than she'd expected.

She opened her mouth, but he sliced a warning glare at her, mastering himself. "Hide it, Yrene. Hide *all* of it. Now."

Her heart thundered in her chest, her limbs, but she snatched up the books. The scrolls. He watched the doors, the windows, while she set about placing them under cushions and inside some of the larger vases. But the scroll . . . it was too precious. Too ancient to treat so callously. Even flattening it out might harm the integrity of the paper, the ink.

He noticed her looking around helplessly, the scroll in her hands. "My boots, if you will, Yrene," he said casually. "I have a second pair that I'd rather wear today."

Right. Right.

Yrene hurried from the sitting room into his bedroom, wincing at the askew bed linens, at what she'd so stupidly assumed and seemed like such an enormous fool about—

She strode into the small dressing room, spotted his boots, and slid the parchment down the neck of one. Then took the pair and shoved it in a drawer, covering it with a stack of linen towels.

She reentered the sitting room a moment later. "I couldn't find them. Perhaps Kadja sent them out for cleaning."

"Too bad," he said casually, his own boots now removed. Along with his shirt.

Her heart still raged as he eased onto the gold sofa but did not lie down.

"Do you know how to read?" she asked, kneeling before him and taking his bare foot in her hands. *The Wyrdmarks?*

"No." His toes shifted as she began careful rotations of his ankle. "But I know someone who does it for me when it's important." Careful, veiled words for anyone listening.

Yrene went about exercising his legs, stretching and bending, the motions repeated over and over while he moved his toes as much as he could. "I should show you the library sometime," she offered. "You might find something that strikes your fancy—for your reader to narrate to you."

"Do you have many similarly interesting texts?"

She lowered his left leg and started on the other. "I could ask— Nousha knows everything."

"When we're done. After you rest. It's been a while since I had a book to . . . intrigue me."

"It'd be my honor to escort you, my lord." He grimaced at the formal title, but Yrene worked his right leg, going through the same motions, before she bade him to lie down on the couch. They worked in silence while she rotated his hips, urging him to try to move them on his own, while bending and stretching as much of his leg as she could.

She said after a moment, her voice barely audible, "You only talk of Erawan." His eyes flashed in warning at the name. "But what of Orcus and Mantyx?"

"Who?"

Yrene began another set of the exercises on his legs and hips and lower back. "The other two kings. They are named in that book."

Chaol stopped wriggling his toes; she flicked them in reminder. The air whooshed from him as he resumed. "They were defeated in the first war. Sent back to their realm or slain, I can't recall."

Yrene considered as she lowered his leg to the couch, nudging him to flip onto his stomach. "I'm sure you and your companions are adept at this whole saving-the-world thing," she mused, earning a snort from him, "but I would make sure you know for certain. Which one it is."

She took up a perch on the thin lip of golden sofa cushion that his body did not cover.

Chaol twisted his head toward her, the muscles in his back bunching. "Why?"

"Because if they were merely banished to their realm, who is to say they aren't still waiting to be let back into our world?"

⊰ 23 ⊱

Chaol's eyes went vacant as Yrene's question hung between them, the color again draining from his face. "Shit," he murmured. "*Shit.*"

"You can't remember what happened to the other two kings?"

"No—no, I'd assumed they were destroyed, but . . . why is there mention of them *here*, of all places?"

She shook her head. "We could see—look into it more."

A muscle feathered in his jaw, and he blew out a long breath. "Then we will."

He reached a hand toward her in silent demand. For the bit, she realized.

Yrene studied his jaw and cheek again, the brimming anger and fear. Not a good state to begin a healing session. So she tried, "Who gave you that scar?"

Wrong question.

His back stiffened, his fingers digging into the throw pillow beneath his chin. "Someone who deserved to give it to me."

Not an answer. "What happened?"

He just extended his hand again for the bit.

"I'm not giving it to you," she said, her face an immovable mask as he turned baleful eyes on her. "And I'm not starting this session with you in a rage."

"When I'm in a rage, Yrene, you'll know."

She rolled her eyes. "Tell me what's wrong."

"What's wrong is that I'm barely able to move my toes and I might not have one Valg king to face, but *three*. If we fail, if we can't—" He caught himself before he could voice the rest. The plan that Yrene had no doubt was so secret he barely dared think about it.

"They destroy everything—everyone—they encounter," Chaol finished, staring at the arm of the couch.

"Did they give you that scar?" She clenched her fingers into a fist to keep from touching it.

"No."

But she leaned forward, instead brushing a finger down a tiny scar just barely hidden by the hair at his temple. "And this? Who gave you that one?"

His face went hard and distant. But the rage, the impatient, frantic energy . . . it calmed. Went cold and aloof, but it centered him. Whatever that old anger was, it steadied him again.

"My father gave that scar to me," Chaol said quietly. "When I was a boy."

Horror sluiced through her, but it was an answer. It was an admission.

She didn't press further. Didn't demand more. No, Yrene just said, "When I go into the wound . . ." Her throat bobbed as she studied his back. "I will try to find you again. If it's waiting for me, I might have to find some other way to reach you." She considered. "And might have to find some other plan of attack than an ambush. But we shall see, I suppose." And even though the corner of her mouth tugged up in what he knew was meant to be a reassuring, healer's smile, she knew he noted the quickening of her breathing.

"Be careful," was all he said.

Yrene just offered him that bit at last, bringing it to his lips.

His mouth brushed her fingers as she slid it between his teeth.

For a few heartbeats, he scanned her face.

"Are you ready?" she breathed as the prospect of facing that insidious darkness again loomed.

He lifted his hand to squeeze her fingers in silent answer.

But Yrene removed her fingers from his, leaving his own to drop back to the cushions.

He was still studying her, the way she took a bracing breath, as she laid her hand over the mark on his back.

~

It had snowed the day he told his father he was to leave Anielle. That he was abdicating his title as heir and joining the castle guard in Rifthold.

His father had thrown him out.

Thrown him right down the front stairs of the keep.

He'd cracked his temple on the gray stone, his teeth going through his lip. His mother's pleading screams had echoed off the rock as he slid along the ice at the landing. He didn't feel the pain in his head. Only the razor-sharp slice of the ice against his bare palms, cutting through his pants and ripping his knees raw.

There was only her pleading with his father, and the shriek of the wind that never stopped, even in summer, around the mountaintop keep that overlooked the Silver Lake.

That wind now tore at him, tugging at his hair—longer than he had kept it since. It hurled stray snowflakes into his face from the gray sky above. Hurled them to the grim city below that flowed to the banks of the sprawling lake and curved around its shores. To the west, to the mighty falls. Or the ghost of them. The dam had long since silenced them, along with the river flowing right from the White Fangs, which ended at their doorstep.

It was always cold in Anielle. Even in summer.

Always cold in this keep built into the curving mountainside.

"Pathetic," his father had spat, none of the stone-faced guards daring to help him rise.

His head spun and spun, throbbing. Warm blood leaked and froze down his face.

"Find your own way to Rifthold, then."

"Please," his mother whispered. "*Please.*"

The last Chaol saw of her was his father's arm gripping her above the elbow and dragging her into the keep of painted wood and stone. Her face pale and anguished, her eyes—his eyes—lined with silver as bright as the lake far below.

His parents passed a small shadow lurking in the open doorway to the keep itself.

Terrin.

His younger brother braved a step toward him. To risk those dangerously icy stairs and help him.

A sharp, barked word from his father within the darkness of the hall halted Terrin.

Chaol wiped the blood from his mouth and silently shook his head at his brother.

And it was terror—undiluted terror—on Terrin's face as Chaol eased to his feet. Whether he knew that the title had just passed to him . . .

He couldn't bear it. That fear on Terrin's round, young face.

So Chaol turned, clenching his jaw against the pain in his knee, already swollen and stiff. Blood and ice merged, leaking from his palms.

He managed to limp across the landing. Down the stairs.

One of the guards at the bottom gave him his gray wool cloak. A sword and knife.

Another gave him a horse and a bearing.

A third gave him a supply pack that included food and a tent, bandages and salves.

They did not say a word. Did not halt him more than necessary.

He did not know their names. And he learned, years and years later, that his father had watched from one of the keep's three towers. Had seen them.

His father himself told Chaol all those years later what happened to those three men who had aided him.

They were let go. In the dead of winter. Banished into the Fangs with their families.

Three families sent into the wilds. Only two were still heard from in the summer.

Proof. It had been proof, he'd realized after he'd convinced himself not to murder his father. Proof that his kingdom was rife with corruption, with bad men punishing good people for common decency. Proof that he had been right to leave Anielle. To stick with Dorian—to keep Dorian safe.

To protect that promise of a better future.

He'd still sent out a messenger, his most discreet, to find those remaining families. He didn't care how many years had passed. He sent the man with gold.

The messenger never found them, and had returned to Rifthold, gold intact, months later.

He had chosen, and it had cost him. He had picked and he had endured the consequences.

A body on a bed. A dagger poised above his heart. A head rolling on stone. A collar around a neck. A sword sinking to the bottom of the Avery.

The pain in his body was secondary.

Worthless. Useless. Anyone he had tried to help . . . it had made it worse.

The body on the bed . . . Nehemia.

She had lost her life. And perhaps she had orchestrated it, but . . . He had not told Celaena—Aelin—to be alert. Had not warned Nehemia's guards of the king's attention. He had as good as killed her. Aelin might

278

have forgiven him, accepted that he was not to blame, but he knew. He could have done more. Been better. Seen better.

And when Nehemia had died, those slaves had risen up in defiance. A rallying cry as the Light of Eyllwe was extinguished.

The king had extinguished them as well.

Calaculla. Endovier. Women and men and children.

And when he had acted, when he had chosen his side . . .

Blood and black stone and screaming magic.

You knew you knew you knew

You will never be my friend my friend my friend

The darkness shoved itself down his throat, choking him, strangling him.

He let it.

Felt himself open his jaws wide to let it in farther.

Take it, he told the darkness.

Yes, it purred to him. *Yes.*

It showed him Morath in its unparalleled horrors; showed him that dungeon beneath the glass castle, where faces he knew pleaded for mercy that would never come; showed him the young golden hands that had bestowed those agonies, as if they had stood side by side to do it—

He knew. Had guessed who had been forced to torture his men, to kill them. They both knew.

He felt the darkness swell, readying to pounce. To make him truly scream.

But then it was gone.

Rippling golden fields stretched away under a cloudless blue sky. Little sparkling streams wended through it, curling around the occasional oak tree. Strays from the tangled, looming green of Oakwald Forest to his right.

Behind him, a thatched roof cottage, its gray stones crusted in green and orange lichen. An ancient well sat a few feet away, its bucket balanced precariously on the stone lip.

Beyond it, attached to the house itself, a small pen with wandering chickens, fat and focused on the dirt before them.

And past them . . .

A garden.

Not a formal, beautiful thing. But a garden behind a low stone wall, its wooden gate open.

Two figures were stooped amongst the carefully plotted rows of green. He drifted toward them.

He knew her by the golden-brown hair, so much lighter in the summer sun. Her skin had turned a lovely deep brown, and her eyes . . .

It was a child's face, lit with joy, that looked upon the woman kneeling in the dirt, pointing toward a pale green plant with slender purple cones of blossoms swaying in the warm breeze. The woman asked, "And that one?"

"Salvia," the child—no more than nine—answered.

"And what does it do?"

The girl beamed, chin rising as she recited, "Good for improving memory, alertness, mood. Also assists with fertility, digestion, and, in a salve, can help numb the skin."

"Excellent."

The girl's broad smile revealed three missing teeth.

The woman—her mother—took the girl's round face in her hands. Her skin was darker than her daughter's, her hair a thicker, bouncier curl. But their builds . . . It was the woman's build that the girl would grow into one day. The freckles that she'd inherit. The nose and mouth.

"You have been studying, my wise child."

The woman kissed her daughter on her sweaty brow.

He felt the kiss—the love in it—even as a ghost at the gate.

For it was love that shaded the entirety of the world here, gilded it. Love and joy.

Happiness.

The sort he had not known with his own family. Or anyone else.

The girl had been loved. Deeply. Unconditionally.

This was a happy memory—one of a few.

"And what is that bush, there by the wall?" the woman asked the girl.

Her brow scrunched in concentration. "Gooseberries?"

"Yes. And what do we do with gooseberries?"

The girl braced her hands on her hips, her simple dress blowing in the dry, warm breeze. "We . . ." She tapped her foot with impatience—at her own mind, for not recalling. The same irritation he'd seen outside that old man's house in Antica.

Her mother crept up behind her, sweeping the girl into her arms and kissing her cheek. "We make gooseberry pie."

The girl's squeal of delight echoed across the amber grasses and clear streams, even into the tangled, ancient heart of Oakwald.

Perhaps even to the White Fangs themselves, and the cold city nestled at their edge.

He opened his eyes.

And found his entire foot pressing into the couch cushions.

Felt the silk and embroidery scratching against the bare arch of his foot. His toes.

Felt.

He bolted upright, finding Yrene not at his side.

Nowhere near.

He gaped at his feet. Below the ankle . . . He shifted and rotated his foot. *Felt* the muscles.

Words stalled in his throat. His heart thundered. "Yrene," he rasped, scanning for her.

She wasn't in the suite, but—

Sunlight on brown-gold caught his eye. In the garden.

She was sitting out there. Alone. Quietly.

He didn't care that he was half dressed. Chaol heaved himself into the chair, marveling at the sensation of the smooth wood supports beneath his feet. He could have sworn even his legs . . . a phantom tingling.

He wheeled himself into the small, square garden, breathless and wide-eyed. She'd repaired another fraction, another—

She'd settled herself in an ornate little chair before the circular reflection pool, her head propped up by her fist.

At first, he thought she was sleeping in the sun.

But he inched closer and caught the gleam of light on her face. On the wetness there.

Not blood—but tears.

Streaming silently, unendingly, as she stared at that reflection pool, the pink lilies and emerald pads covering most of it.

She stared as if not seeing it. Not hearing him.

"Yrene."

Another tear rolled down her face, dripping onto her pale purple dress. Another.

"Are you hurt," Chaol said hoarsely, his chair crunching over the pale white gravel of the garden.

"I'd forgotten," she whispered, lips wobbling as she stared and stared at the pool and did not move her head. "What she looked like. Smelled like. I'd forgotten—her voice."

His chest strained as her face crumpled. He hauled his chair beside her own but did not touch her.

Yrene said quietly, "We make oaths—to never take a life. She broke that oath the day the soldiers came. She had hidden a dagger in her dress. She saw the soldier grab me, and she . . . she leaped on him." She closed her eyes. "She killed him. To buy me time to run. And I did. I left her. I ran, and I left her, and I watched . . . I watched from the forest as they built that fire. And I could hear her screaming and screaming—"

Her body shook.

"She was good," Yrene whispered. "She was good and she was kind and she loved me." She still did not wipe her tears. "And they took her away."

The man he had served . . . *he* had taken her away.

Chaol asked softly, "Where did you go after that?"

Her trembling lessened. She wiped at her nose. "My mother had a cousin in the north of Fenharrow. I ran there. It took me two weeks, but I made it."

At eleven. Fenharrow had been in the middle of conquest, and she'd made it—at *eleven*.

"They had a farm, and I worked there for six years. Pretended to be normal. Kept my head down. Healed with herbs when it wouldn't raise suspicions. But it wasn't enough. It . . . There was a hole. In me. I was unfinished."

"So you came here?"

"I left. I meant to come here. I walked through Fenharrow. Through Oakwald. Then over . . . over the mountains . . ." Her voice broke into a whisper. "It took me six months, but I made it—to the port of Innish."

He'd never heard of Innish. Likely in Melisande, if she'd crossed—

She'd crossed mountains.

This delicate woman beside him . . . She had crossed mountains to be here. Alone.

"I ran out of money for the crossing. So I stayed. I found work."

He avoided the urge to look at the scar on her throat. To ask what manner of work—

"Most girls were on the streets. Innish was—is not a good place. But I found an inn by the docks and the owner hired me. I worked as a barmaid and a servant and . . . I stayed. I meant to only work for a month, but I stayed for a year. Let him take my money, my tips. Increase my rent. Put me in a room under the stairs. I had no money for the crossing, and I thought . . . I thought I would have to pay for my education here. I didn't want to go without funds for tuition, so . . . I stayed."

He studied her hands, now clutching each other tightly in her lap.

Pictured them with a bucket and mop, with rags and dirty dishes. Pictured them raw and aching. Pictured the filthy inn and its inhabitants—what they must have seen and coveted when they beheld her.

"How did you make it here?"

Yrene's mouth tightened, her tears fading. She loosed a breath. "It is a long story."

"I have time to listen."

But she shook her head again and at last looked at him. There was a . . . clarity to her face. Those eyes. And it did not falter as she said, "I know who gave you that wound."

Chaol went wholly still.

The man who had taken away the mother she so deeply loved; the man who had sent her fleeing across the world.

He managed to nod.

"The old king," Yrene breathed, studying the pool again. "He was—he was possessed, too?"

The words were hardly more than a whisper, barely audible even to him.

"Yes," he managed to say. "For decades. I—I'm sorry I did not tell you. We've deemed that information . . . sensitive."

"For what it might mean about the suitability of your new king."

"Yes, and open the door to questions that are best kept unasked."

Yrene rubbed at her chest, her face haunted and bleak. "No wonder my magic recoils so."

"I'm sorry," he said again. It was all he could think to offer.

Those eyes slid to him, any lingering fog clouding them clearing away. "It gives me further reason to fight it. To wipe away that last stain of him—of *it* forever. Just now, it was waiting for me. Laughing at me again. I managed to get to you, but then the darkness around you was too thick. It had made a . . . shell. I could see it—everything it showed you. Your memories, and his." She rubbed her face. "I knew then. What it was—who gave you the wound. And I saw what it was doing to you, and all I could think to stop it, to blast it away . . ." She pursed her lips, as if they might start trembling again.

"A bit of goodness," he finished for her. "A memory of light and goodness." He didn't have the words to convey his gratitude for it, for what it must have been like to offer up that memory of her mother against the demon that had destroyed her.

Yrene seemed to read his thoughts, and said, "I am glad it was a memory of her that beat the darkness back a little further."

His throat tightened, and he swallowed hard.

"I saw your memory," Yrene said quietly. "The—man. Your father."

"He is a bastard of the finest caliber."

"It was not your fault. None of it."

He refrained from commenting otherwise.

"You were lucky that you did not fracture your skull," she said, scanning his brow. The scar just barely visible, covered by his hair.

"I'm sure my father considers it otherwise."

Darkness flashed in her eyes. Yrene only said, "You deserved better."

The words hit something sore and festering—something he had locked up and not examined for a long, long time. "Thank you," he managed to say.

They sat in silence for long minutes. "What time is it?" he asked after a while.

"Three," she said.

Chaol started.

But Yrene's eyes went right to his legs. His feet. How they had moved with him.

Her mouth opened silently.

"Another bit of progress," he said.

She smiled—subdued, but . . . it was real. Not like the one she'd plastered on her face hours and hours ago. When she'd walked into his bedroom and found him there with Nesryn, and he'd felt the world slipping out from under him at the expression on her face. And when she had refused to meet his stare, when she'd wrapped her arms around herself . . .

He wished he'd been able to walk. So she could see him crawl toward her.

He didn't know why. Why he felt like the lowest sort of low. Why he'd barely been able to look at Nesryn. Though he knew Nesryn was too observant not to be aware. It had been the unspoken agreement between them last night—silence on the subject. And that reason alone . . .

Yrene poked at his bare foot. "Do you feel this?"

Chaol curled his toes. "Yes."

She frowned. "Am I pushing hard or soft?"

She ground her finger in.

"Hard," he grunted.

Her finger lightened. "And now?"

"Soft."

She repeated the test on the other foot. Touched each of his toes.

"I think," she observed, "I've pushed it down—to somewhere in the middle of your back. The mark is still the same, but it *feels* like . . ." She shook her head. "I can't explain it."

"You don't need to."

It had been her joy—the undiluted joy of that memory—that had won him that bit of movement. What she'd opened up, given up, to push back the stain of that wound.

"I'm starving," Chaol said, nudging her with an elbow. "Will you eat with me?"

And to his surprise, she said yes.

⇥ 24 ⇤

Nesryn knew.

She knew it hadn't been mere interest that had prompted Chaol to ask her to talk to him last night, but guilt.

She was fine with it, she told herself. She had been a replacement for not one, but two of the women in his life. A third one . . . She was fine with it, she repeated as she returned from stalking through Antica's streets—not a whisper of Valg to be found—and entered the palace grounds.

Nesryn braced herself as she peered up at the palace, not quite ready to return to their suite to wait out the brutal late afternoon heat.

A massive figure atop a minaret caught her eye, and she smiled grimly.

She was out of breath when she reached the aerie, but mercifully, Kadara was the only one present to witness it.

The ruk clicked her beak at Nesryn in greeting and went back to ripping at what appeared to be an entire slab of beef. Ribs and all.

"I heard you were headed here," Sartaq said from the stairs behind her.

Nesryn whirled. "I—how?"

The prince gave her a knowing smile and stepped into the aerie. Kadara puffed her feathers with excitement and dug back into her meal, as if eager to finish and be in the skies. "This palace is crawling with spies. Some of them mine. Is there anything you wanted?"

He scanned her—seeing the face that yesterday her aunt and uncle had complained looked tired. Worn out. Unhappy. They'd crammed her with food, then insisted she take their four children back down to the docks to select fish for their evening meal, then shoved more food down her throat before she'd returned to the palace for the feast. *Still peaky*, Zahida clucked. *Your eyes are heavy.*

"I . . ." Nesryn surveyed the view beyond, the city simmering in the late afternoon heat. "I just wanted some quiet."

"Then I'll let you have it," Sartaq said, and turned to the open archway into the stairwell.

"No," she blurted, reaching toward him. She halted her hand, dropping it immediately as it came within skimming distance of his leather jacket. No one grabbed a prince. No one. "I didn't mean you had to leave. I . . . I don't mind your company." She added quickly, "Your Highness."

Sartaq's mouth quirked up. "It's a bit late to be throwing in my fancy title, isn't it?"

She gave him a pleading look. But she'd meant what she said.

Last night, talking with him at the party, even talking with him in the alley outside the Torre a few nights before that . . . She had not felt quiet or aloof or strange. She had not felt cold or distant. He'd done her an honor in giving her such attention, and in escorting her and Chaol back to their rooms. She did not mind company—quiet as she could be, she *enjoyed* being around others. But sometimes . . .

"I spent most of yesterday with my family. They can be . . . tiring. Demanding."

"I know how you feel," the prince said drily.

A smile tugged at her lips. "I suppose you do."

"You love them, though."

"And you do not?" A bold, brash question.

Sartaq shrugged. "Kadara is my family. The rukhin, they are my family. My bloodline, though . . . It's hard to love one another, when we will one day contend with each other. Love cannot exist without trust." He smiled at his ruk. "I trust Kadara with my life. I would die for her, and she for me. Can I say the same of my siblings? My own parents?"

"It's a shame," Nesryn admitted.

"At least I have her," he said of the ruk. "And my riders. Pity my siblings, who have none of those blessings."

He was a good man. The prince . . . he was a good man.

She strode for the open archways overlooking the deadly drop to the city far, far below.

"I am going to leave soon—for the mountains of the rukhin," Sartaq said softly. "To seek the answers you and I discussed the other night in the city."

Nesryn peered over her shoulder at him, trying to gather the right words, the nerve.

His face remained neutral, even as he added, "I'm sure your family will have my head for offering, but . . . would you like to accompany me?"

Yes, she wanted to breathe. But she made herself ask, "For how long?"

For time was not on her side. Their side. And to hunt for answers while so many threats gathered close . . .

"A few weeks. No more than three. I like to keep the riders in line, and if I go absent for too long, they pull at the leash. So the journey will serve two purposes, I suppose."

"I—I would need to discuss. With Lord Westfall." She'd promised him as much last night. That they'd consider this precise path, weighing the pitfalls and benefits. They were still a team in that regard, still served under the same banner.

Sartaq nodded solemnly, as if he could read everything on her face. "Of course. Though I leave soon."

She then heard it—the grunt of servants coming up the aerie stairs. Bringing supplies.

"You leave *now*," Nesryn clarified as she noted the spear leaning against the far wall near the supply racks. His *sulde*. The russet horsehair tied beneath the blade drifted in the wind weaving through the aerie, the dark wood shaft polished and smooth.

Sartaq's onyx eyes seemed to darken further as he strode to his *sulde*, weighing the spirit-banner in his hands before resting it beside him, the wood thunking on the stone floor. "I . . ." It was the first she'd seen him stumble for words.

"You weren't going to say good-bye?"

She had no right to make such demands, expect such things, tentative allies or no.

But Sartaq leaned his *sulde* against the wall again and began braiding back his black hair. "After last night's party, I had thought you would be . . . preoccupied."

With Chaol. Her brows rose. "All day?"

The prince gave her a roguish smile, finishing off his long braid and picking up his spear once more. "I certainly would take all day."

By some god's mercy, Nesryn was saved from replying by the servants who appeared, panting and red-faced with the packs between them. Weapons glinted from some of them, along with food and blankets.

"How far is it?"

"A few hours before nightfall, then all day tomorrow, then another half day of travel to reach the first of the aeries in the Tavan Mountains," Sartaq said as he handed his *sulde* to a passing servant, and Kadara patiently allowed them to load her with various packs.

"You don't fly at night?"

"I tire. Kadara doesn't. Foolish riders have made that mistake—and tumbled through the clouds in their dreams."

She bit her lip. "How long until you go?"

"An hour."

An hour to think . . .

She had not told Chaol. That she'd seen his toes move last night. She'd seen them curl and flex in his sleep.

She had cried, silent tears of joy sliding onto the pillow. She hadn't told him. And when he'd awoken . . .

Let's have an adventure, Nesryn Faliq, he'd promised her in Rifthold. She had cried then, too.

But perhaps . . . perhaps neither of them had seen. The path ahead. The forks in it.

She could see down one path clearly.

Honor and loyalty, still unbroken. Even if it stifled him. Stifled her. And she . . . she did not want to be a consolation prize. Be pitied or a distraction.

But this other path, the fork that had appeared, branching away across grasslands and jungles and rivers and mountains . . . This path toward answers that might help them, might mean nothing, might change the course of this war, all carried on a ruk's golden wings . . .

She would have an adventure. For herself. This one time. She would see her homeland, and smell it and breathe it in. See it from high above, see it racing as fast as the wind.

She owed herself that much. And owed it to Chaol as well.

Perhaps she and this dark-eyed prince might find some scrap of salvation against Morath. And perhaps she might bring an army back with her.

Sartaq was still watching, his face carefully neutral as the last of the servants bowed and vanished. His *sulde* had been strapped just below the saddle, within easy reach should the prince need it, its reddish horsehairs trailing in the wind. Trailing southward.

Toward that distant, wild land of the Tavan Mountains. Beckoning, as all spirit-banners did, toward an unknown horizon. Beckoning to claim whatever waited there.

Nesryn said quietly, "Yes."

The prince blinked.

"I will go with you," she clarified.

A small smile tugged on his mouth. "Good." Sartaq jerked his chin to the archway through which the servants had vanished down the minaret. "Pack lightly, though—Kadara is already near her limit."

Nesryn shook her head, noting the bow and quiver stocked with arrows already atop Kadara. "I have nothing to bring with me."

Sartaq watched her for a long moment. "Surely you would wish to say good-bye—"

"I have nothing," she repeated. His eyes flickered at that, but she added, "I—I'll leave a note."

The prince solemnly nodded. "I can outfit you with clothes when we arrive. There is paper and ink in the cabinet by the far wall. Leave the letter in the box by the stairs, and one of the messengers will come to check at nightfall."

Her hands shook slightly as she obeyed. Not with fear, but . . . freedom.

She wrote two notes. The first one, to her aunt and uncle, was full of love and warning and well-wishes. Her second note . . . it was quick, and to the point:

I have gone with Sartaq to see the rukhin. I shall be gone three weeks.
I hold you to no promises. And I will hold to none of my own.

Nesryn shut both notes in the box, undoubtedly checked often for any messages from the skies, and changed into the leathers she'd left from the last time she'd flown.

She found Sartaq atop Kadara, waiting for her.

The prince extended a callused hand to help her up into the saddle.

She didn't hesitate as she took his hand, his strong fingers wrapping around hers, and let him pull her into the saddle before him.

He strapped and buckled them in, checked all of it thrice. But he reined in Kadara when she would have soared out of the minaret.

Sartaq whispered in Nesryn's ear, "I was praying to the Eternal Sky and all thirty-six gods that you'd say yes."

She smiled, even if he couldn't see it.

"So was I," Nesryn breathed, and they leaped into the skies.

⊰ 25 ⊱

Yrene and Chaol hurried to the Torre library immediately after lunch. Chaol mounted his horse with relative ease, Shen giving him a hearty pat on the back in approval. Some small part of Yrene had wanted to beam when she noticed that Chaol met the man's eyes to offer a tight smile of thanks.

And when they passed through those white walls, as the mass of the Torre rose above them and the scent of lemon and lavender filled Yrene's nose . . . some part of her eased in its presence. Just how it had done from the first moment she'd spied the tower rising above the city while her ship at last neared the shore, as if it were a pale arm thrust toward the sky in greeting.

As if to proclaim to her, *Welcome, daughter. We have been waiting for you.*

The Torre's library was located in the lower levels, most of its halls ramped thanks to the rolling carts the librarians used to transport the books around and collect any tomes that careless acolytes had forgotten to return.

There were a few stairs where Yrene had been forced to grit her teeth and haul him up.

He'd stared at her when she'd done it. And when she asked why, he'd said it was the first time she'd touched his chair. Moved it.

She supposed it was. But she'd warned him not to get used to it, and let him propel himself through the brightly lit corridors of the Torre.

A few of the girls from her defense class spotted them and paused to fawn over the lord, who indulged them with a crooked smile that set them giggling as they walked away. Yrene herself smiled at them as they departed, shaking her head.

Or perhaps the good mood was from the fact that his entire foot from the ankle down was regaining feeling *and* movement. She'd forced him to endure another set of exercises before coming here, sprawling him on the carpet while she aided him in moving his foot around and around, in stretching it, rotating it. All designed to get the blood flowing, to hopefully awaken more of his legs.

The progress was enough to keep Yrene smiling until they reached Nousha's desk, where the librarian was currently shoving a few tomes into her heavy satchel. Packing up for the day.

Yrene glanced at the bell that had been rung only a few nights ago, but refused to blanch. Chaol had brought a sword and dagger, and she'd been mesmerized while he'd buckled them on with such efficiency. He had barely needed to look, his fingers guided by sheer muscle memory. She could picture it—every morning and night that he'd put on and removed that sword belt.

Yrene leaned over the desk and said to Nousha, who was sizing up Chaol while he also assessed her, "I would like to see where you found those texts from Eyllwe. And the scrolls."

Nousha's white brows crossed. "Will it bring trouble?" Her gaze slid to the sword Chaol had positioned across his lap to keep it from clacking against his chair.

"Not if I can help it," Yrene said quietly.

Behind them, curled on an armchair in the large sitting area before the crackling hearth, a snow-white Baast Cat half slumbered, her long tail swishing like a pendulum as it draped over the edge of the cushion. No doubt listening to every word—likely to report to her sisters.

Nousha sighed sharply in a way that Yrene had witnessed a hundred times, but waved them toward the main hallway. She barked an order in Halha to a nearby librarian to mind the desk and led the way.

As they followed, the white Baast Cat cracked open a green eye. Yrene made sure to give her a respectful bow of the head. The cat merely went back to sleep, satisfied.

For long minutes, Yrene watched Chaol take in the colored lanterns, the warm stone walls, and endless stacks. "This would give the royal library in Rifthold a run for its money," he observed.

"Is it that large?"

"Yes, but this might be larger. Older, definitely." His eyes danced with shadows—bits of memory that she wondered if she would glimpse the next time she worked on him.

Today's encounter . . . It had left her reeling and raw.

But the salt of her tears had been cleansing. In a way she had not known she needed.

Down and down they went, taking the main ramp that looped through the levels. They passed librarians shelving books, acolytes in solitary or group study around the tables, healers poring over musty tomes in doorless rooms, and the occasional Baast Cat sprawled over the top of the shelves, or padding into the shadows, or simply sitting at a crossroads—as if waiting.

Still they went deeper.

"How did you know they were down here?" Yrene asked Nousha's back.

"We keep good records," was all the Head Librarian said.

Chaol gave Yrene a look that said, *We have cranky librarians in Rifthold, too.*

Yrene bit her lip to keep from grinning. Nousha could sniff out laughter and amusement like a bloodhound on a scent. And shut it down as viciously, too.

At last, they reached a dark corridor that reeked of stone and dust.

"Second shelf down. Don't ruin anything," Nousha said by way of explanation and farewell, and left without a look back.

Chaol's brows lifted in bemusement, and Yrene swallowed her chuckle.

It stopped being an effort as they approached the shelf the librarian had indicated. Piles of scrolls lay tucked beneath books whose spines glittered with the Eyllwe language.

Chaol let out a low whistle through his teeth. "How old is the Torre, exactly?"

"Fifteen hundred years."

He went still.

"This library has been here that long?"

She nodded. "It was all built in one go. A gift from an ancient queen to the healer who saved her child's life. A place for the healer to study and live—close to the palace—and to invite others to study as well."

"So it predates the khaganate by a great deal."

"The khagans are the latest in a long line of conquerors since then. The most benevolent since that first queen, to be sure. Even her palace itself did not survive so well as the Torre. What you stay in now . . . they built it atop the rubble of the queen's castle. After the conquerors who came a generation before the khaganate razed it to the ground."

He swore, low and creatively.

"Healers," Yrene said, scanning the shelves, "are in high demand, whether you are the current ruler or the invading one. All other posts . . . perhaps unnecessary. But a tower full of women who can keep you from death, even if you are hanging by a thread . . ."

"More valuable than gold."

"It begs the question of why Adarlan's last king . . ." She almost said *your* king, but the word clanged strangely in her head now. "Why he felt the need to destroy those of us with the gift in his own continent." *Why the thing in him felt the need*, she didn't say.

Chaol didn't meet her eyes. And not from shame.

He knew something. Something else.

"What?" she asked.

He scanned the dim stacks, then listened for anyone nearby. "He was indeed . . . taken. Invaded."

It had been a shock to realize whose dark power she'd been fighting against within his wound—a shock, and yet a rallying cry to her magic. As if some fog had been cleared away, some veil of fear, and all that had been left beneath were her blinding rage and sorrow, unfaltering as she'd leaped upon the darkness. But . . . the king truly had been possessed, then. All this time.

Chaol pulled a book from the shelf and flipped through it, not really reading the pages. She was fairly certain he didn't know how to read Eyllwe. "He knew what was happening to him. The man within him fought against it as best he could. He knew that their kind . . ." The Valg. "They found people with *gifts* . . . enticing." Magic-wielders. "Knew their kind wanted to conquer the gifted ones. For their power."

Infest them, as the king had been. As that drawing in *The Song of Beginning* had depicted.

Yrene's gut roiled.

"So the man within wrested control long enough to give the order that the magic-wielders were to be put down. Executed, rather than used against him. Us."

Turned into hosts for those demons and made into weapons.

Yrene leaned against the stack behind them, a hand sliding up to her throat. Her pulse pounded beneath her fingers.

"It was a choice he hated himself for. But saw as a necessary decision to make. Along with a way to make sure those in control could not *use* magic. Or find those who had it. Not without lists of them. Or those willing to sell them out for coin—to the men he ordered to hunt them down."

Magic's vanishing had not been natural at all. "He—he found a way to banish—?"

A sharp nod. "It is a long story, but he halted it. Dammed it up. To keep those conquerors from having the hosts they wanted. And then hunted the rest of them down to make sure their numbers were fewer still."

The King of Adarlan had stopped magic, killed its bearers, had sent his forces to execute her mother and countless others . . . not just from blind hatred and ignorance, but some twisted way of trying to *save* their kind?

Her heart thundered through her body. "But healers—we have no power to use in battle. Nothing beyond what you see from me."

Chaol was utterly still as he stared at her. "I think you might have something they want very badly."

The hair along her arms rose.

"Or want to keep you from knowing too much about."

She swallowed, feeling the blood leave her face. "Like—your wound."

A nod.

She blew out a shaky breath, going to the stack before her. The scrolls.

His fingers grazed her own. "I will not let any harm come to you."

Yrene felt him waiting for her to tell him otherwise. But she believed him.

"And what I showed you earlier?" she said, inclining her head to the scrolls. The Wyrdmarks, he'd called them.

"Part of the same thing. An earlier and different sort of power. Outside of magic."

And he had a friend who could read them. Wield them.

"We'd better be quick," she said, still careful of any potential listeners. "I'm sure the volume I need for your chronic toe fungus is down here somewhere, and I'm growing hungry."

Chaol gave her an incredulous look. She offered him an apologetic wince in return.

But laughter danced in his eyes as he began pulling books into his lap.

⁓

Nesryn's face and ears were numb with cold by the time Kadara alighted on a rocky outcropping high atop a small mountain range of gray stone. Her limbs were hardly better, despite the leathers, and were sore enough that she winced as Sartaq helped her down.

The prince grimaced. "I forgot that you aren't used to riding for so long."

It wasn't the stiffness that really brutalized her, but her bladder—

Clenching her legs together, Nesryn surveyed the campsite the ruk had deemed suitable for her master. It was protected on three sides by boulders and pillars of gray rock, with a broad overhang against the elements, but no possibility of concealment. And asking a prince where to see to her needs—

Sartaq merely pointed to a cluster of boulders. "There's privacy that way, if you need it."

Face heating, Nesryn nodded, not quite able to meet him in the eye as she hurried to where he'd indicated, slipping between two boulders to find another little outcropping that opened onto a sheer drop to the unforgiving rocks and streams far, far below. She picked a small boulder that faced away from the wind and didn't waste any time unbuckling her pants.

When she emerged again, still wincing, Sartaq had removed most of the packs from Kadara, but had left her saddle. Nesryn approached the mighty bird, who eyed her closely, lifting a hand toward the first buckle—

"Don't," Sartaq said calmly from where he'd set the last of the packs under the overhang, his *sulde* tucked against the wall behind them. "We leave the saddles on while we travel."

Nesryn lowered her hand, examining the mighty bird. "Why?"

Sartaq removed two bedrolls and laid them out against the rocky wall, claiming one for himself. "If we're ambushed, if there is some danger, we need to be able to get into the skies."

Nesryn scanned the surrounding mountain range, the sky stained pink and orange as the sun set. The Asimil Mountains—a small, lonely range, if her memory of the land served her correctly. Still far, far north from the Tavan Mountains of the rukhin. They hadn't passed a village or sign of civilization in over an hour, and up amongst these desolate peaks: landslides, flash floods . . . She supposed there were dangers aplenty.

Supposed that the only ones who could reach them up here were other ruks. Or wyverns.

Sartaq pulled out tins of cured meats and fruit, along with two small loaves of bread. "Have you seen them—the mounts of Morath?" His question was nearly ripped away by the howl of the wind beyond the wall of rocks. How he'd known where her mind had drifted, she couldn't guess.

Kadara settled herself near one of the three faces, folding in her wings tightly. They'd stopped once earlier—to let Kadara feed and for them to see to their needs—so the ruk wouldn't have to seek out dinner in these barren mountains. Belly still full, Kadara now seemed content to doze.

"Yes," Nesryn admitted, tugging free the leather strap around the base of her short braid and finger-combing her hair. Tangles snared on her still-freezing fingers as she coaxed them away, grateful that the task kept her from shuddering at the memory of the witches and their mounts. "Kadara is probably two-thirds to half the size of a wyvern. Maybe. Is she large or small, for a ruk?"

"I thought you'd heard all the stories about me."

Nesryn snorted, shaking out her hair a final time as she approached the bedroll and food he'd laid out for her. "Do you know they call you the Winged Prince?"

A ghost of a smile. "Yes."

"Do you like the title?" She settled on the roll, crossing her legs beneath her.

Sartaq passed her the tin of fruits, beckoning her to eat. She didn't bother to wait for him before she dug in, the grapes cool thanks to the hours in the crisp air.

"Do I like the title?" he mused, tearing off a piece of bread and passing it to her. She took it with a nod of thanks. "It's strange, I suppose. To become a story while you are still alive." A sidelong glance at her while he ripped into his bread. "You yourself are surrounded by some living tales. How do *they* feel about it?"

"Aelin certainly enjoys it." She'd never met another person with so many names and titles—and who enjoyed bandying them about so much. "The others ... I don't suppose I know them well enough to guess. Though Aedion Ashryver ... he takes after Aelin." She popped another grape into her mouth, her hair swaying as she leaned forward to pluck a few more into her palm. "They're cousins, but act more like siblings."

A considering look. "The Wolf of the North."

"You've heard of him?"

Sartaq passed the tin of cured meats, letting her pick through which slices she wanted. "I told you, Captain Faliq, my spies do their jobs well."

A careful line—nudging him toward a potential alliance was a careful line to walk. Look too eager, praise her companions too much and she'd be transparent, but to do nothing ... It went against her very nature. Even as a city guard, her day off had usually sent her looking for *something* to do, whether it was a walk through Rifthold or helping her father and sister prepare the next day's goods.

Wind-seeker, her mother had once called her. *Unable to keep still, always wandering where the wind calls you. Where shall it beckon you to journey one day, my rose?*

How far the wind had now called her.

Nesryn said, "Then I hope your spies have told you that Aedion's Bane is a skilled legion."

A vague nod, and she knew Sartaq saw right through all her plans.

But he finished off his part of the bread and asked, "And what are the tales they tell about you, Nesryn Faliq?"

She chewed on the salted pork. "No one has any stories about me."

It didn't bother her. Fame, notoriety . . . She valued other things more, she supposed.

"Not even the story about the arrow that saved a shape-shifter's life? The impossible shot fired from a rooftop?"

She snapped her head toward him. Sartaq only swigged from his water with a look that said, *I told you my spies were good.*

"I thought Arghun was the one who dealt in covert information," Nesryn said carefully.

He passed the waterskin. "Arghun's the one who boasts about it. I'd hardly call it covert."

Nesryn drank a few mouthfuls of water and lifted a brow. "But this is?"

Sartaq chuckled. "I suppose you're right."

The shadows grew deeper, longer, the wind picking up. She studied the rock around them, the packs. "You won't risk a fire."

A shake of his head, his dark braid swaying. "It'd be a beacon." He frowned at her leathers, the packs lumped around them. "I have heavy blankets—somewhere in there."

They fell into silence, eating while the sun vanished and stars began to blink awake among the last, vibrant ribbon of blue. The moon herself appeared, bathing the campsite with enough light to see by as they finished up, the prince sealing the tins and tucking them back into the packs.

Across the space, Kadara began to snore, a deep wheeze that rumbled through the rock.

Sartaq chuckled. "Apologies if that keeps you awake."

Nesryn just shook her head. Sharing a campsite with a ruk, in the mountains high above the grassy plains below, the Winged Prince beside her . . . No, her family would not believe it.

They watched the stars quietly, neither making a move to sleep. One by one, the rest of the stars emerged, brighter and clearer than she'd seen since those weeks on the ship here. Different stars, she realized with a jolt, than those up north.

Different, and yet these stars had burned for countless centuries above her ancestors, above her father himself. Had it been strange for him to leave them behind? Had he missed them? He'd never spoken of it, what it was like to move to a land with foreign stars—if he'd felt adrift at night.

"Neith's Arrow," Sartaq said after uncounted minutes, leaning back against the rock.

Nesryn dragged her gaze from the stars to find his face limned in moonlight, silver dancing along the pure onyx of his braid.

He rested his forearms on his knees. "That's what my spies called you, what I called you until you arrived. Neith's Arrow." The Goddess of Archery—and the Hunt, originally hailing from an ancient sand-swept kingdom to the west, now enfolded into the khaganate's vast pantheon. A corner of his mouth tugged upward. "So don't be surprised if there's now a story or two about you already finding its way across the world."

Nesryn observed him for a long moment, the howling mountain wind blending with Kadara's snoring. She'd always excelled at archery, took pride in her unmatched aim, but she had not learned because she coveted renown. She'd done it because she enjoyed it, because it gave her a direction to aim that wind-seeking inclination. And yet . . .

Sartaq cleared away the last of the food and did a quick check that the campsite was secure before heading off between the boulders himself.

With only those foreign stars to witness, Nesryn smiled.

⇥ 26 ⇤

Chaol dined in the Torre kitchens, where a rail-thin woman called only Cook had stuffed him with pan-fried fish, crusty bread, roasted tomatoes with mild cheese and tarragon, and then managed to convince him to eat a light, flaky pastry dripping with honey and crusted in pistachios.

Yrene had sat beside him, hiding her smiles as Cook kept piling more and more food onto his plate until he literally *begged* her to stop.

He was full enough that the idea of moving seemed a monumental task, and even Yrene had pleaded with Cook to have mercy upon them.

The woman had relented, though she'd turned that focus upon the workers in her kitchen—presiding over the serving of the evening meal to the hall a level above with a general's command that Chaol found himself studying.

He and Yrene sat in companionable silence, watching the chaos unfold around them until the sun had long since set through the wide windows beyond the kitchen.

He'd uttered half a mention of getting his horse saddled when Yrene *and* Cook told him he was spending the night and to not bother arguing.

So he did. He sent a note back to the palace through a healer on her way there to oversee a patient in the servants' quarters, telling Nesryn where he was and not to wait up.

And when he and Yrene had finally managed to get their overstuffed stomachs to settle, he followed her to a room in the complex. The Torre was mostly stairs, she said with no pity whatsoever, and there were no guest rooms anyway. But the adjacent physicians' complex—she'd gestured to the building they'd passed through, all angles and squares where the Torre was round—always had a few rooms on the ground level available for the night, mostly for the loved ones of sick patients.

She opened the door to a room that overlooked a garden courtyard, the space small but clean, its pale walls inviting and warm from the day. A narrow bed lay against one wall, a chair and small table before the window. Just enough space for him to maneuver.

"Let me see again," Yrene said, pointing to his feet.

Chaol lifted his leg with his hands, stretching it out. Then rolled his ankles, grunting against the considerable weight of his legs.

She removed his boots and socks as she knelt before him. "Good. We'll need to keep that up."

He glanced to the satchel full of books and scrolls she'd pillaged from the library, discarded by the doorway. He didn't know what the hell any of it said, but they'd taken as many as they could. If whoever or whatever had been in that library had stolen some, and perhaps not gotten the chance to return for more . . . He wouldn't risk them eventually returning to claim the rest.

Yrene had thought the scroll she'd hidden in his rooms to be eight hundred years old. But that deep in the library, considering the age of the Torre . . .

He didn't tell her he thought it might be much, much older. Full of information that might not have even survived in their own lands.

"I can find you some clothes," Yrene said, scanning the small room.

"I'll be fine with what I have." Chaol added without looking at her, "I sleep—without them."

"Ah."

Silence fell, as she no doubt remembered how she'd found him that morning.

That morning. Had it truly been only hours ago? She had to be exhausted.

Yrene gestured to the candle burning on the table. "Do you need more light?"

"I'm fine."

"I can get you some water."

"I'm fine," he said, the corners of his mouth twitching upward.

She pointed to the porcelain pot in the corner. "Then at least let me bring you to the—"

"I can manage that, too. It's all about aim."

Color stained her cheeks. "Right." She chewed on her bottom lip. "Well . . . good night, then."

He could have sworn she was lingering. And he would have let her, except . . . "It's late," he told her. "You should go to your room while people are still about."

Because while Nesryn had found no trace of the Valg in Antica, while it had been days since that attack in the Torre library, he would take no risks.

"Yes," Yrene said, bracing a hand on the threshold. She reached for the handle to pull the door shut behind her.

"Yrene."

She paused, angling her head.

Chaol held her stare, a small smile curling his mouth. "Thank you." He swallowed. "For all of it."

She only nodded and backed out, shutting the door behind her. But as she did so, he caught a glimmer of the light that danced in her eyes.

The following morning, a stern-faced woman named Eretia appeared at his door to inform him Yrene had a meeting with Hafiza and would meet him at the palace by lunch.

So Yrene had asked Eretia to escort him back to the palace—a task Chaol could only wonder why she'd bestowed on the old woman, who tapped her foot as he gathered his weapons, the heavy bag of books, and clicked her tongue at every minor delay.

But the ride through the steep streets with Eretia wasn't awful; the woman was a surprisingly skilled rider who brooked no nonsense from her mount. Yet she offered no pleasantries and little more than a grunted farewell before she left him in the palace courtyard.

The guards were just changing their shift, the morning rotation lingering to chat amongst one another. He recognized enough of them by now to earn a few nods of greeting, and to manage to return them as his chair was brought over by one of the stable hands.

He'd no sooner removed his feet from the stirrups and prepared himself for the still-daunting process of dismounting when light footsteps jogged over to him. He looked over to find Shen approaching, a hand on his forearm—

Chaol blinked. And by the time Shen stopped before him, the guard had tugged the glove back on his hand.

Or what Chaol had assumed was his hand. Because what he'd glimpsed beneath the glove and the sleeve of Shen's uniform, going right up to the elbow . . . It was a masterwork—the metal forearm and hand.

And only now that he looked, looked long enough to actually observe anything . . . he could indeed see the raised lines by Shen's bicep of where the metal arm was strapped to him.

Shen noticed his stare. Noticed it right as Chaol hesitated at the arm and shoulder Shen offered to aid him in dismounting.

The guard said in Chaol's own tongue, "I helped you just fine before you knew, Lord Westfall."

Something like shame, perhaps something deeper, cracked through him.

Chaol made himself brace a hand on the man's shoulder—the same shoulder that housed the metal arm. Found the strength beneath to be unwavering as Shen assisted him into the awaiting chair.

And when Chaol was seated in it, staring at the guard as the stable hands led his horse away, Shen explained, "I lost it a year and a half ago. There was an attack on Prince Arghun's life when he visited a vizier's estate, a rogue band from a disgruntled kingdom. I lost it during the fight. Yrene worked on me when I returned—I was one of her first considerable healings. She managed to repair as much as she could from here upward." He pointed to right below his elbow, then up his shoulder.

Chaol studied the hand that was so lifelike within the glove he could not notice the difference, save for the fact that it did not move at all.

"Healers can do many wonders," Shen said, "but growing limbs from thin air . . ." A soft laugh. "That is beyond their skill—even one such as Yrene."

Chaol didn't know what to say. Apologies felt wrong, but . . .

Shen smiled down at him—with no trace of pity. "It has taken me a long time to get to this place," he said a bit quietly.

Chaol knew he didn't mean the skilled use of his artificial arm.

Shen added, "But know that I did not get here alone."

The unspoken offer shone in the guard's brown eyes. Unbroken, this man before him. No less of a man for his injury, for finding a new way to move through the world.

And—Shen had stayed on as a guard. As one of the most elite palace guards in the world. Not from any pity of the others, but through his own merit and will.

Chaol still couldn't find the right words to convey what coursed through him.

Shen nodded as if he understood that, too.

It was a long trip back to his suite. Chaol didn't mark the faces he passed, the sounds and smells and streams of wind wending through the halls.

He returned to the rooms to find his note to Nesryn sitting on the foyer table. Unread.

It was enough to chase any other thoughts from his mind.

Heart thundering, his fingers shook as he picked up his unread, unseen letter.

But then he spotted the letter beneath it. His name written in her handwriting.

He ripped it open, reading the few lines.

He read it twice. Thrice.

He set it down on the table and stared at her open bedroom door. The silence leaking from it.

He was a bastard.

He'd dragged her here. Had nearly gotten her killed in Rifthold so many times, had implied so much about the two of them, and yet—

He didn't let himself finish the thought. He should have been better. Treated her better. No wonder she'd flown off to the ruk aeries to help Sartaq find any sort of information on the Valg history in this land—or their own.

Shit. *Shit.*

She might not hold him to any promises, but *he* . . . He held himself to them.

And he had let this thing between them go on, had used her like some crutch—

Chaol blew out a breath, crumpling Nesryn's letter and his own in his fist.

Perhaps he had not slept well in that tiny room at the physicians' compound, accustomed to far larger and finer accommodations, Yrene told herself that afternoon. It would explain his few words. The lack of smiling.

She'd had one on her face when she'd entered Chaol's suite after lunch. She'd explained her progress to Hafiza, who had been very pleased indeed. Even giving Yrene a kiss on her brow before she left. Practically skipping here.

Until she entered and found it quiet.

Found him quiet.

"Are you feeling well?" Yrene asked casually as she hid the books he'd brought back with him that morning.

"Yes."

She leaned against the desk to study where Chaol sat on the gold couch.

"You have not exercised in a few days." She angled her head. "The rest of your body, I mean. We should do it now."

For people accustomed to physical activity every day, going without for so long could feel like ripping an addict off a drug. Disoriented, restless. He'd kept up the exercises for his legs, but the rest . . . perhaps it was what clawed at him.

"All right." His eyes were glazed, distant.

"Here, or one of the guards' training facilities?" She braced herself for the shutdown.

But Chaol just said flatly, "Here is fine."

She tried again. "Perhaps being around the other guards will be beneficial to—"

"Here is fine." Then he moved himself onto the floor, sliding his body away from the couch and low-lying table and to the open carpet. "I need you to brace my feet."

Yrene checked her irritation at the tone, the outright refusal. But she still said as she knelt before him, "Have we really gone back to that place?"

He ignored her question and launched into a series of upward curls, his powerful body surging up, then down. One, two, three . . . She lost count around sixty.

He didn't meet her stare each time he rose up over his bent knees.

It was natural, for the emotional healing to be as difficult as the physical. For there to be hard days—hard *weeks*, even. But he'd been smiling when she'd left him last night, and—

"Tell me what happened. Something happened today." Her tone was perhaps not *quite* as gentle as a healer's ought to be.

"Nothing happened." The words were a push of air as he kept moving, sweat sliding down the column of his neck and into the white shirt beneath.

Yrene clenched her jaw, counting quietly in her head. Snapping would do neither of them any good.

Chaol eventually turned onto his stomach and began another set that required her to hold his feet in a position that would keep him slightly aloft.

Up and down, down and up. The sleek muscles of his back and arms bunched and rippled.

He went through six other exercises, then started the entire set again.

Yrene supported and held and watched in simmering silence.

Let him have his space. Let him think through it, if that's what he wants.

Damn what he wants.

Chaol finished a set, his breathing ragged, chest heaving as he stared up at the ceiling.

Something sharp and driving flickered across his face, as if in silent answer to something. He lurched upward to begin the next set—

"That's enough."

His eyes flashed, meeting hers at last.

Yrene didn't bother looking pleasant or understanding. "You'll do yourself an injury."

He glared toward where she had stabilized his bent knees and curled upward again. "I know my limits."

"And so do I," she snapped, jerking her chin toward his legs. "You might hurt your back if you keep this up."

He bared his teeth—the temper vicious enough that she let go of his feet. His arms shot out to brace him as he slid backward, but she lunged, grabbing for his shoulders to keep him from slamming to the ground.

312

His sweat-drenched shirt soaked into her fingers, his breathing rasping in her ear as she confirmed he wasn't about to fall. "I've got it," he growled in her ear.

"Forgive me if I don't take your word for it," she snipped, assessing for herself that he indeed could support himself before she withdrew and settled herself a few feet away on the carpet.

In silence, they glared at each other. "Exercising your body is vital," Yrene said, her words clipped, "but you will do more harm than good if you push yourself too hard."

"I'm fine."

"You think I don't know what you're doing?"

Chaol's face was a hard mask, sweat sliding down his temple.

"This was your sanctuary," she said, gesturing to his honed body, the sweat on him. "When things got hard, when they went wrong, when you were upset or angry or sad, you would lose yourself in the training. In sweating until it burned your eyes, in practicing until your muscles were shaking and begging you to stop. And now you can't—not as you once did."

Ire boiled in his face at that.

She kept her own face cool and hard as she asked, "How does that make you feel?"

His nostrils flared. "Don't think you can provoke me into talking."

"How does it feel, *Lord* Westfall?"

"You know how it feels, *Yrene*."

"Tell me."

When he refused to answer, she hummed to herself. "Well, since you seem determined to get a complete exercise routine in, I might as well work your legs a bit."

His stare was a brand. She wondered if he could sense the tightness that now clamped down on her chest, the pit that opened in her stomach as he remained quiet.

But Yrene rose up on her knees and moved down his body, beginning the series of exercises designed to trigger pathways between his mind and spine. The ankle and foot rotations, he could do on his own, though he certainly gritted his teeth after the tenth set.

But Yrene pushed him through it. Ignored his bubbling anger, keeping a saccharine smile on her face while she coaxed his legs through the movements.

It was only when she reached for his upper thighs that Chaol halted her with a hand on her arm.

He met her stare—then looked away, jaw tight, as he said, "I'm tired. It's late. Let's meet tomorrow morning."

"I don't mind starting now with the healing." Perhaps with the exercising, those wrecked pathways might be firing up more than usual.

"I want some rest."

It was a lie. Despite his exercising, he had good color in his face, his eyes were still bright with anger.

She weighed his expression, the request. "Resting doesn't seem at all like your style."

His lips tightened. "Get out."

Yrene snorted at the order. "You may command men and servants, Lord Westfall, but I don't answer to you." Still, she uncoiled to her feet, having had quite enough of his attitude. Bracing her hands on her hips, she stared at where he remained sprawled on the carpet. "I'll have food sent in. Things to help pack on the muscle."

"I know what to eat."

Of course he did. He'd been honing that magnificent body for years now. But she only brushed out the skirts of her dress. "Yes, but I've actually studied the subject."

Chaol bristled but said nothing. Returned to staring at the swirls and flora woven into the carpet.

Yrene gave him another honey-sweet smile. "I'll see you bright and early tomorrow, Lord—"

"Don't *call* me that."

314

She shrugged. "I think I'll call you whatever I want."

His head snapped up, his face livid. She braced herself for the verbal attack, but he seemed to check himself, shoulders stiffening as he only said once more, "Get out."

He pointed to the door with a long arm as he said so.

"I should kick that gods-damned finger you're pointing," Yrene snapped, striding to the door. "But a broken hand would only keep you here longer."

Chaol again bared his teeth, ire pouring off him in waves now, that scar down his cheek stark against his flushed skin. *"Get out."*

Yrene just flashed another sickly sweet smile at him and shut the door behind her.

She strode through the palace at a clip, fingers curling at her sides, reining in her roar.

Patients had bad days. They were entitled to them. It was natural, and a part of the process.

But . . . they had worked through so much of that. He had started to tell her things, and she'd told *him* things so few knew, and she'd enjoyed herself yesterday—

She mulled over every word exchanged the night before. Perhaps he'd been angry at something Eretia had said on their ride here. The woman wasn't known for her bedside manner. Yrene was honestly surprised the woman tolerated anyone, let alone felt inclined to *help* human beings. She could have upset him. Insulted him.

Or maybe he'd come to depend on Yrene's constant presence, and the interruption of that routine had been disorienting. She'd heard of patients and their healers in such situations.

But he'd shown no traits of dependency. No, the opposite went through him, a streak of independence and pride that hurt as much as it helped him.

Breathing uneven, his behavior dragging claws down her temper, Yrene sought out Hasar.

The princess was just coming from swordplay lessons of her own.

Renia was out shopping in the city, Hasar said as she looped her sweat-damp arm through Yrene's and led her toward her chambers.

"Everyone is busy-busy-busy today," Hasar groused, flicking her sweaty braid over a shoulder. "Even Kashin is off with my father at some meeting about his troops."

"Is there any reason why?" A careful question.

Hasar shrugged. "He didn't tell me. Though he probably felt inclined to do it, since Sartaq showed us all up by flying off to his nest in the mountains for a few weeks."

"He left?"

"And he took Captain Faliq with him." A wry smile. "I'm surprised you aren't consoling Lord Westfall."

Oh. *Oh.* "When did they leave?"

"Yesterday afternoon. Apparently, she said no word about it. Didn't take her things. Just left a note and vanished into the sunset with him. I didn't think Sartaq had it in him to be such a charmer."

Yrene didn't return the smile. She'd bet good money that Chaol had returned this morning to find that note. To find Nesryn gone.

"How did you learn she'd left a note?"

"Oh, the messenger told everyone. Didn't know what was inside it, but a note with Lord Westfall's name on it, left at the aerie. Along with one to her family in the city. The only trace of her."

Yrene made a mental mark to never send correspondence to the palace again. At least not letters that mattered.

No wonder Chaol had been restless and angry, if Nesryn had vanished like that.

"Do you suspect foul play?"

"From *Sartaq*?" Hasar cackled. The question was answer enough.

They reached the princess's doors, servants silently opening them and stepping aside. Little more than shadows made flesh.

But Yrene paused in the doorway, digging in her heels as Hasar tried to lead her in. "I forgot to get him his tea," she lied, disentangling her arm from Hasar's.

The princess only gave her a knowing smile. "If you hear any interesting tidbits, you know where to find me."

Yrene managed a nod and turned on her heel.

She didn't go to his rooms. She doubted Chaol's mood had improved in the ten minutes she'd been storming through the palace halls. And if she saw him, she knew she wouldn't be able to refrain from asking about Nesryn. From pushing him until that control shattered. And she couldn't guess where that would leave them. Perhaps a place neither of them was ready for.

But she had a gift. And a relentless, driving *thrum* now roared in her blood thanks to him.

She could not sit still. Did not want to go back to the Torre to read or help any of the others with their work.

Yrene left the palace and headed down the dusty streets of Antica.

She knew the way. The slums never moved. Only grew or shrank, depending on the ruler.

In the bright sun, there was little to fear. They were not bad people. Only poor—some desperate. Many forgotten and disheartened.

So she did as she had always done, even in Innish.

Yrene followed the sound of coughing.

⊰ 27 ⊱

Yrene healed six people by the time the sun set, and only then did she leave the slums.

One woman had a dangerous growth on her lungs that would have killed her. She'd been too busy with work to see a healer or physician. Three children had been burning up with fever in a too-cramped house, their mother weeping with panic. And then with gratitude as Yrene's magic soothed and settled and purified. One man had broken his leg the week before and visited a piss-poor physician in the slums because he could not afford a carriage to carry him up to the Torre. And the sixth one . . .

The girl was no more than sixteen. Yrene had noticed her first because of the black eye. Then the cut lip.

Her magic had been wobbling, her knees with it, but Yrene had led the girl into a doorway and healed her eye. The lip. The cracked ribs. Healed the enormous handprint-shaped bruises on her forearm.

Yrene asked no questions. She read every answer in the girl's fearful eyes anyway. Saw the girl consider whether it would land her with worse injuries to return home healed.

So Yrene had left the coloring. Left the appearance of bruises but healed all beneath. Leaving only the upper layer of skin, perhaps a little tender, to conceal the repaired damage.

Yrene did not try to tell her to leave. Whether it was her family or a lover or something else entirely, Yrene knew that no one but the girl would decide whether to walk out that door. All she did was inform her that should she ever need it, the door to the Torre would always be open. No questions asked. No fee demanded. And they would make sure that no one was allowed to take her out again unless she wished it.

The girl had kissed Yrene's knuckles in thanks and scurried home in the falling dark.

Yrene herself had hurried, following the glimmering pillar of the Torre, her beacon home.

Her stomach was grumbling, her head throbbing with fatigue and hunger.

Drained. It felt good to be drained. To help.

And yet . . . That hounding, restless energy still thrummed. Still pushed. *More more more.*

She knew why. What was left unsettled. Still raging.

So she changed course, spearing for the glowing mass of the palace.

She paused at a favorite food stall, indulging in a meal of slow-roasted lamb that she devoured in a few minutes. It was rare that she got to eat beyond the confines of the palace or the Torre, thanks to her busy schedule, but when she did . . . Yrene was rubbing her satisfied belly as she made her way up to the palace. But then spotted an open *kahve* shop and managed to find room in her stomach for a cup of it. And a honey-dipped pastry.

Dawdling. Restless and angry and stupid.

Disgusted with herself, Yrene stomped up to the palace at last. With the summer sun setting so late, it was well past eleven by the time she headed through the dark halls.

Perhaps he'd be asleep. Maybe it would be a blessing. She didn't know why she'd bothered to come. Biting off his head could have waited until tomorrow.

He was likely asleep.

Hopefully asleep. It'd probably be better if his healer didn't barge into his room and shake him silly. It definitely wasn't behavior approved by the Torre. By Hafiza.

And yet she kept walking, her pace increasing, steps near-clomping on the marble floors. If he wanted to take a step back on their progress, that was just fine. But she certainly didn't have to let him do it—not without trying.

Yrene stormed down a long, dim corridor. She wasn't a coward; she wouldn't back down from this fight. She'd left that girl in that alley in Innish. And if he was inclined to sulk about Nesryn, then he was entitled to do so. But to call off their *session* because of it—

Unacceptable.

She'd simply tell him that and leave. Calmly. Rationally.

Yrene scowled with each step, muttering the word under her breath. *Unacceptable.*

And she had *let* him kick her out, no matter what she might have tried to tell herself.

That was even *more* unacceptable.

Stupid fool. She muttered that, too.

Loud enough that she nearly missed the sound.

The footstep—the scrape of shoes on stone—just behind her.

This late, servants were likely heading back to their masters' rooms, but—

There it was. That sense, pricking again.

Only shadows and shafts of moonlight filled the pillar-lined hallway.

Yrene hurried her pace.

She heard it again—the steps behind. A casual, stalking gait.

Her mouth went dry, her heart thundering. She had no satchel, not even her little knife. Nothing in her pockets beyond that note.

Hurry, a small, gentle voice murmured in her ear. In her *head*.

She had never heard that voice before, but she sometimes felt its warmth. Coursing through her as her magic flowed out. It was as familiar to her as her own voice, her own heartbeat.

Hurry, girl.

Urgency laced each word.

Yrene increased her pace, nearing a run.

There was a corner ahead—she need only round it, make it thirty feet down that hall, and she'd be at his suite.

Was there a lock on the door? Would it be locked against her—or be able to keep whoever it was out?

Run, Yrene!

And that voice . . .

It was her mother's voice that bellowed in her head, her heart.

She didn't stop to think. To wonder.

Yrene launched into a sprint.

Her shoes slipped along the marble, and the person, the *thing* behind her—those footsteps broke into a run, too.

Yrene turned the corner and slid, skidding into the opposite wall so hard her shoulder barked in pain. Feet scrambling, she fought to regain momentum, not daring to look back—

Faster!

Yrene could see his door. Could see the light leaking out from beneath it.

A sob broke from her throat.

Those rushing steps behind her closed in. She didn't dare risk her balance by looking.

Twenty feet. Ten. Five.

Yrene hurled for the handle, gripping it with all her strength to keep from sliding past as she shoved against it.

The door opened, and she whirled in, legs slipping beneath her as she slammed her entire body into the door and fumbled for the lock. There were two.

She finished the first when the person on the other side barreled into the door.

The entire thing shuddered.

Her fingers shook, her breath escaping in sharp sobs as she fought for the second, heavier lock.

She flipped it closed just as the door buckled again.

"What in *hell*—"

"Get inside your room," she breathed to Chaol, not daring to take her eyes off the door as it shuddered. As the handle rattled. "Get in—*now*."

Yrene looked then to find him in the threshold of his bedroom, sword in his hand. Eyes on the door.

"Who the hell is that."

"Get inside," she said, her voice breaking. "*Please.*"

He read the terror in her face. Read and understood.

He shoved back into the room, holding the door for her and then sealing it behind her.

The front door cracked. Chaol locked his bedroom door with a click. Only one lock.

"The chest," he said, his voice unfaltering. "Can you move it?"

Yrene whirled to the chest of drawers beside the door. She didn't reply as she threw herself against it, shoes again slipping on the polished marble—

She kicked off her shoes, bare skin finding better grip on the stone as she heaved and grunted and shoved—

The chest slid in front of the bedroom door.

"The garden doors," Chaol ordered, finishing locking them.

They were solid glass.

Dread and panic curled in her gut, ripping the breath from her throat.

"Yrene," Chaol said evenly. Calmly. He held her gaze. Steadying her. "How far is the nearest entrance to the garden from the outer hall?"

"A two-minute walk," she replied automatically. It was only accessible from the interior rooms, and as most of these were occupied . . . They'd have to take the hall to the very end. Or risk running through the bedrooms next door, which . . . "Or one."

"Make it count."

She scanned the bedroom for anything. There was an armoire beside the glass doors, towering high above. Too high, too enormously heavy—

But the movable screen to the bathroom . . .

Yrene hurtled across the room, Chaol lunging for a set of daggers on his nightstand.

She grabbed the heavy wooden screen and hauled and shoved it, cursing as it snagged on the rug. But it moved—it got there. She flung open the armoire doors and wedged the screen between it and the wall, shaking it a few times for good measure. It held.

She rushed to the desk, throwing books and vases off it. They shattered across the floor.

Stay calm; stay focused.

Yrene hauled the desk to the wood screen and flipped it onto its side with a clattering crash. She shoved it against the barricade she'd made.

But the window—

There was one across the room. High and small, but—

"Leave it," Chaol ordered, sliding into place in front of the glass doors. Sword angled and dagger in his other hand. "If they try that route, the small size will force them to be slow."

Long enough for him to kill it—whoever it was.

"Get over here," he said quietly.

She did so, eyes darting between the bedroom door and the garden doors.

"Deep breaths," he told her. "Center yourself. Fear will get you killed as easily as a weapon."

Yrene obeyed.

"Take the dagger on the bed."

Yrene balked at the weapon.

"Do it."

She grabbed the dagger, the metal cool and heavy in her hand. Unwieldy.

His breathing was steady. His focus unrelenting as he monitored both doors. The window.

"The bathroom," she whispered.

"The windows are too high and narrow."

"What if it's not in a human body?"

The words ripped from her in a hoarse whisper. The illustrations she'd seen in that book—

"Then I'll keep it occupied while you run."

With the furniture in front of the exits—

His words sank in.

"You will do no such—"

The bedroom door shuddered beneath a blow. Then another.

The handle shook and shook.

Oh, gods.

They hadn't bothered with the garden. They'd simply gotten in the front doors.

Another bang that had her flinching away. Another.

"Steady," Chaol murmured.

Yrene's dagger trembled as he angled himself to the bedroom door, his blades unwavering.

Another bang, furious and raging.

Then—a voice.

Soft and hissing, neither male nor female.

"Yrene," it whispered through the crack in the door. She could hear the smile in its voice. "Yrene."

Her blood went cold. It was not a human voice.

"What is it you want," Chaol said, his own voice like steel.

"Yrene."

Her knees buckled so wildly she could barely stand. Every moment of training she'd done slithered right out of her head.

"*Get out*," Chaol snarled toward the door. "Before you regret it."

"Yrene," it hissed, laughing a bit. "*Yrene.*"

Valg. One had indeed been hunting her that night, and had come for her again tonight—

Clapping her free hand over her mouth, Yrene sank onto the edge of the bed.

"Don't you waste one heartbeat being afraid of a coward who hunts women in the darkness," Chaol snapped at her.

The thing on the other side of the door growled. The doorknob rattled. "Yrene," it repeated.

Chaol only held her stare. "Your fear grants it power over you."

"*Yrene.*"

He approached her, lowering his dagger and sword into his lap. Yrene flinched, about to warn him not to lower his weapons. But Chaol stopped before her. Took her face in his hands, his back wholly to the door now. Even though she knew he monitored every sound and movement behind it. "I am not afraid," he said softly, but not weakly. "And neither should you be."

"*Yrene,*" the thing snapped on the other side of the door, slamming into it.

She cringed away, but Chaol held her face tightly. Did not break her gaze.

"We will face this," he said. "Together."

Together. Live or die here—together.

Her breathing calmed, their faces so close his own breath brushed her mouth.

Together.

She hadn't thought to use such a word, to *feel* what it meant . . . She hadn't felt it since—

Together.

Yrene nodded. Once. Twice.

Chaol searched her eyes, his breath fanning her mouth.

He lifted her hand, still clutched around the dagger, and adjusted her grip. "Angle it up, not straight in. You know where it is." He put a hand on his chest. Over his heart. "The other places."

Brain. Through the eye socket. Throat, slashing to unleash the life's blood. All the various arteries that could be struck to ensure a swift bleed-out.

Things she had learned to save. Not—end.

But this thing . . .

"Beheading works best, but try to get it down first. Long enough to sever the head."

He'd done this before, she realized. He'd killed these things. Triumphed against them. Had taken them on with no magic but his own indomitable will and courage.

And she . . . she had crossed mountains and seas. She had done it on her own.

Her hand stopped shaking. Her breathing evened out.

Chaol's fingers squeezed around her own, the hilt's fine metal pushing into the palm of her hand. "Together," he said one last time, and released her to pluck up his own weapons again.

To face the door.

There was only silence.

He waited, calculating. Sensing. A predator poised to strike.

Yrene's dagger held steady as she rose to her feet behind him.

A crash sounded through the foyer—followed by shouting.

She started, but Chaol loosed a breath. One of shuddering relief.

He recognized the sounds before she did.

The shouts of guards.

They spoke in Halha—cries through the bedroom door about their status. Safe? Hurt?

Yrene replied in her own shoddy use of the language that they were unharmed. The guards said the servant girl had seen the broken suite door and come running to fetch them.

There was no one else in the suite.

326

⇥ 28 ⇤

Prince Kashin arrived swiftly, summoned by the guards at Yrene's request—before she or Chaol even dared to remove the furniture barring the door. Any of the other royals required too much explaining, but Kashin . . . He understood the threat.

Chaol knew the prince's voice well enough by that point—Yrene knew it well herself—that as it filled the suite foyer, he gave her the nod to haul away the furniture blocking the door.

Chaol was grateful, just for a heartbeat, that he remained in this chair. Relief might have buckled his legs.

He hadn't been able to discern a viable path out of it. Not for her. In the chair, against a Valg minion, he was as good as carrion, though he'd calculated that a well-timed throw of his dagger and sword might save them. That had been his best option: *throwing*.

He hadn't cared—not really. Not about what it meant for him. But about how much time that throw might buy her.

Someone had *hunted* her. Meant to kill her. Terrorize and torment her. Perhaps worse, if it was indeed a Valg-infested agent of Morath. Which it had sure as hell sounded like.

He hadn't been able to make out the voice. Male or female. Just one of them, though.

Yrene remained calm as she opened the door at last to reveal a wild-eyed Kashin, panting heavily. The prince scanned her from head to toe, gave Chaol a brief glance, then returned his focus to the healer. "What happened?"

Yrene lingered behind Chaol's chair as she said with surprising calm, "I was walking back here to make sure Lord Westfall took a tonic."

Liar. Smooth, pretty liar. She'd likely been coming back to give him the second earful Chaol had been waiting for all evening.

Yrene came around the chair to stand beside him, close enough that the heat of her warmed his shoulder. "And I was nearly here when I sensed someone behind me." Yrene then explained the rest, observing the room every now and then, as if whoever it had been would leap out of the shadows. And when Kashin asked if she suspected why someone might do her harm, Yrene glanced at Chaol, a silent conversation passing between them: it had likely been to spook her from helping him, for whatever wicked purpose of Morath. But she'd only told the prince she didn't know.

Kashin's face tightened with fury as he studied the cracked door to Chaol's bedroom. He said over his shoulder to the guards combing through the suite, "I want four of you outside this suite. Another four at the end of the hall. A dozen of you in the garden. Six more at the various hall crossroads that lead here."

Yrene let out a breath of what might very well have been relief.

Kashin heard it, putting a hand on the hilt of his sword as he said, "The castle is already being searched. I plan to join them."

Chaol knew it wasn't for Yrene alone. Knew that the prince had good reason to join the hunt, that there was likely still a white banner hanging from his windows.

328

Gallant and dedicated. Perhaps how all princes should be. And perhaps a good friend for Dorian to have. If everything went in their favor.

Kashin seemed to take a bracing breath. Then he asked Yrene quietly, "Before I go . . . why don't I escort you back to the Torre? With an armed guard, of course."

There was enough concern and hope in the prince's eyes that Chaol made a point to busy himself by monitoring the guards still examining every inch of the rooms.

Yet Yrene wrapped her arms around herself and said, "I feel safer here."

Chaol tried not to blink at her. At the words.

With him. She felt safer here with *him*.

He avoided the urge to remind her that he was in this chair.

Kashin's gaze now shifted to him, as if remembering he was there. And it was disappointment that now hardened his gaze—disappointment and warning as he met Chaol's stare.

Chaol clamped down on *his* warning to Kashin to stop giving him that look and go search the palace.

He'd keep his hands to himself. He'd been unable to stop thinking about Nesryn's letter all day. When he wasn't mulling over all that Shen had shown him—what it had done to him to see what lay beneath that proud guard's sleeve.

But the prince just bowed his head, a hand on his chest. "Send word if you need anything."

Yrene barely managed a nod in Kashin's direction. It was dismissive enough that Chaol almost felt bad for the man.

The prince moved out with a lingering glance at Yrene, some guards trailing him, the others remaining behind. Chaol watched through the garden doors as they settled into place just outside.

"Nesryn's bedroom is empty," he said when they were alone in his chamber at last.

He waited for the question about why—but realized she hadn't so

329

much as mentioned Nesryn when she'd fled in here. Hadn't tried to rouse her. She'd gone right to him.

So it was no surprise when Yrene just said, "I know it is."

Palace spies or gossip, he didn't care. Not as Yrene said, "I—can I stay in here? I'll sleep on the floor—"

"You can sleep in the bed. I doubt I'll get any rest tonight."

Even with the guards outside . . . He'd seen what one Valg could do against multiple men. He'd seen Aelin move, one assassin through a field of men. And cut them down in heartbeats.

No, he would not be sleeping tonight.

"You can't sit in that chair all night—"

Chaol gave her a look that said otherwise.

Yrene swallowed and excused herself to the bathing room. As she quickly washed up, he assessed the guards outside, the integrity of the bedroom lock. She emerged still in her dress, neckline wet, face wan again. She hesitated before the bed.

"They changed the sheets," Chaol said softly.

She didn't look at him as she climbed in. Each movement smaller than usual—brittle.

Terror still gripped her. Though she'd done beautifully. He wasn't sure if *he* would have been able to move that chest of drawers, but pure terror had given her a dose of strength. He'd heard stories of mothers lifting entire wagons off their children crushed beneath.

Yrene slid beneath the covers, but made no move to nestle her head onto the pillow. "What is it like—to kill someone?"

Cain's face flashed in his mind.

"I—I'm new to it," Chaol admitted.

She angled her head.

"I took my first life . . . just after Yulemas last year."

Her brows narrowed. "But—you—"

"I trained for it. Had fought before. But never killed someone."

"You were the Captain of the Guard."

"I told you," he said with a bitter smile, "it was complicated."

Yrene nestled down at last. "But you have done it since."

"Yes. But not enough to grow used to it. Against the Valg, yes, but the humans they infest . . . Some are lost forever. Some are still there, beneath the demon. Figuring out who to kill, who can be spared—I still don't know where the bad choices lie. The dead do not speak."

Her head slid against the pillow. "I took an oath before my mother. When I was seven. Never to kill a human being. Some healings . . . she told me offering death could be a mercy. But that it was different from slaughter."

"It is."

"I think—I might have tried to kill whoever it was tonight. I was that . . ." He waited for her to say *frightened*. *Frightened, with my only defender in a chair.* "I was that decided against running. You told me you'd buy me time, but . . . I can't do it. Not again."

His chest tightened. "I understand."

"I'm glad I didn't do it. But—whoever it is got away. Perhaps I should not be so relieved."

"Kashin may be lucky in his search."

"I doubt it. They were gone before the guards arrived."

He fell quiet. After a moment, he said, "I hope you never have to use that dagger—or any other, Yrene. Even as a mercy."

The sorrow in her eyes was enough to knock the breath from him. "Thank you," she said softly. "For being willing to take that death upon yourself."

No one had ever said such a thing. Even Dorian. But it had been expected. Celaena—*Aelin* had been grateful when he'd killed Cain to save her, but she had expected him to one day make a kill.

Aelin had made more than he could count by that point, and his own lack of it had been . . . embarrassing. As if such a thing were possible.

He had killed plenty since then. In Rifthold. With those rebels against the Valg. But Yrene . . . she made that number smaller. He hadn't looked at it that way. With pride. Relief.

"I'm sorry Nesryn left," Yrene murmured into the dim light.

I hold you to no promises. And I will hold to none of my own.

"I promised her an adventure," Chaol admitted. "She deserved to go on one."

Yrene was quiet enough that he turned from the garden doors. She had snuggled deep into his bed, her attention fixed wholly on him. "What about you? What do you deserve?"

"Nothing. I deserve nothing."

Yrene studied him. "I don't agree at all," she murmured, eyelids drooping.

He monitored the exits again. After a few minutes, he said, "I was given enough and squandered it."

Chaol looked over at her, but Yrene's face was softened with sleep, her breathing steady.

He watched her for a long while.

⁓

Yrene was still sleeping when dawn broke.

Chaol had dozed for a few minutes at a time, as much as he'd allow himself.

But as the sun crept across the bedroom floor, he found himself washing his face. Scrubbing the sleep from his eyes.

Yrene didn't stir as he moved out of the suite and into the hall. The guards were precisely where Kashin had ordered them to remain. And they told him precisely where he needed to go when he met them each in the eye and asked for directions.

And then he informed them that if Yrene were harmed while he was gone, he'd shatter every bone in their bodies.

Minutes later, he found the training courtyard Yrene had mentioned yesterday.

It was already full of guards, some of whom eyed him and some of whom ignored him fully. Some of whom he recognized from Shen's shift, and gave him a nod.

One of the guards he did not know approached him, older and grayer than the rest.

Like Brullo, his former instructor and Weapons Master.

Dead—hanging from those gates.

Chaol pushed away the image. Replaced it with the healer still asleep in his bed. How she had looked when she'd declared to the prince, the world, that she felt safer there. With him.

He replaced the pain that rippled through him at the sight of the exercising guards, the sight of this private training space, so similar to the one in which he'd spent so many hours of his life, with the image of Shen's artificial arm, the unwavering, quiet strength he'd felt supporting him while he'd mounted his horse. No less a man without that arm—no less a guard.

"Lord Westfall," said the gray-haired guard, using his language. "What can I do for you at this hour?" The man seemed astute enough to know if there had been something related to the attack, this would not be the place to discuss it. No, the man knew Chaol had come here for a different reason, and read the tension in his body as not a source of alarm, but intrigue.

"I trained for years with men from my continent," Chaol said, lifting the sword and dagger he'd brought with him. "Learned as much as they know."

The older guard's brows flicked up.

Chaol held the man's stare. "I would like to learn what *you* know."

The aging guard—Hashim—worked him until Chaol could barely breathe. Even in the chair. And out of it.

Hashim, who was a rank below captain and oversaw the guards' training, found ways for Chaol to do their exercises either with someone bracing his feet or modified versions from the chair.

He had indeed worked with Shen a year ago—many of the guards had. They'd banded together, assisting Shen in any way they could with the reorienting of his body, his way of fighting, during those long months of recovery.

So not one of them stared or laughed. Not one of them whispered.

They were all too busy, too tired, to bother anyway.

The sun rose over the courtyard, and still they worked. Still Hashim showed him new ways to strike with a blade. How to disarm an opponent.

A different way of thinking, of killing. Of defending. A different language of death.

They broke at breakfast, all of them near-trembling with exhaustion.

Even winded, Chaol could have kept going. Not for any reserve of strength, but because he *wanted* to.

Yrene was waiting when he returned to the suite and bathed.

Six hours, they then spent lost in that darkness. At the end of it, the pain had wrecked him, Yrene was shaking with exhaustion, but a precise sort of awareness had awoken within his feet. Crept up past his ankles. As if the numbness were a receding tide.

Yrene returned to the Torre that night under heavy guard, and he fell into the deepest sleep of his life.

Chaol was waiting for Hashim in the training ring before dawn.

And the next dawn.

And the next.

PART TWO

MOUNTAINS AND SEAS

⤜ 29 ⤛

Storms waylaid Nesryn and Sartaq on their way out of the northern Asimil Mountains.

Upon awakening, the prince had taken one look at the bruised clouds and ordered Nesryn to secure everything she could on their rocky outcropping. Kadara shifted from clawed foot to clawed foot, rustling her wings as her golden eyes monitored the storm galloping in.

That high up, the crack of thunder echoed off every rock and crevice, and as Nesryn and Sartaq sat pressed against the stone wall beneath the overhang, winds lashing them, she could have sworn even the mountain beneath shuddered. But Kadara held fast against the storm, settling herself in front of them, a veritable wall of white and golden feathers.

Still the icy rain managed to find them, freezing Nesryn down to her bones even with the thick ruk leathers and heavy wool blanket Sartaq insisted she wrap around herself. Her teeth chattered violently enough to make her jaw hurt, and her hands were so numb and raw that she kept them tucked beneath her armpits just to savor any scrap of warmth.

Even before magic had vanished, Nesryn had never longed for magical gifts. And after magic had disappeared, after the decrees banning it and the terrible hunts for those who had once wielded it, Nesryn hadn't dared to even *think* about magic. She'd been content to practice her archery, to learn how to wield knives and swords, to master her body until it, too, was a weapon. Magic had failed, she'd told her father and sister whenever they asked. Good steel would not.

Yet sitting on that cliff, whipped by the wind and rain until she couldn't remember what warmth felt like, Nesryn found herself wishing for a spark of flame in her veins. Or at least for a certain Fire-Bringer to come swaggering around the corner of the cliff to warm them.

But Aelin was far away—unaccounted for, if Hasar's report was to be believed, which Nesryn did. The true question was whether Aelin and her court's vanishing were due to some awful play by Morath, or some scheme of the queen herself.

Having seen what Aelin was capable of in Rifthold, the plans she'd laid out and enacted without any of them knowing . . . Nesryn's money was on Aelin. The queen would show up when and where she wished—at precisely the moment she intended. Nesryn supposed that was why she liked the queen: there were plans so long in the making that for someone who let the world deem her unchecked and brash, Aelin showed a great deal of restraint in keeping it all hidden.

And as that storm raged around Nesryn and Sartaq, she wondered if Aelin Galathynius might yet have some card up her sleeve that even her court might not know about. She prayed Aelin did. For all their sakes.

But magic had failed before, Nesryn reminded herself as her teeth clacked against each other. And she'd do everything she could to find a way to fight Morath without it.

It was hours before the storm at last lumbered off to terrorize other parts of the world, Sartaq only easing to his feet when Kadara fanned her feathers, shaking off the rain. Spraying them in the process, but Nesryn was in no position to complain, when the ruk had taken the brunt of the storm's wrath for them.

Of course, it also left the saddle damp, which in turn led to a fairly uncomfortable ride as they soared down the brisk, clean winds from the mountains and into the sprawling grasslands below.

With the delay, they were forced to camp for another night, this time in a copse of trees, again with not so much as an ember to warm them. Nesryn kept her mouth shut about it—the cold that lingered along her bones, the roots that dug into her back through the bedroll, the empty pit in her stomach that fruit and dried meat and day-old bread couldn't fill.

Sartaq, to his credit, gave her his blankets and asked if she wanted a change of his clothes. But she barely knew him, she realized. This man she'd flown off with, this prince with his *sulde* and sharp-eyed ruk . . . . He was little more than a stranger.

Such things didn't usually bother her. Working for the city guard, she'd dealt with strangers every day, in various states of awfulness or panic. The pleasant encounters had been few and far between, particularly in the past six months, when darkness had crept over the city and hunted beneath it.

But with Sartaq . . . As Nesryn shivered all night long, she wondered if she'd perhaps been a tad hasty in coming here, possible alliance or no.

Her limbs ached and eyes burned when the gray light of dawn trickled through the slim pines. Kadara was already stirring, eager to be off, and Nesryn and Sartaq exchanged less than a half-dozen sentences before they were airborne for the last leg of their journey.

They'd been flying for two hours, the winds growing crisper the farther south they sailed, when Sartaq said in her ear, "That way." He pointed due east. "Fly half a day in that direction, and you will reach the northern edges of the steppes. The heartland of the Darghan."

"Do you visit often?"

A pause. He said over the wind, "Kashin holds their loyalty. And—Tumelun." The way he spoke his sister's name implied enough. "But the rukhin and the Darghan were once one and the same. We chased down the ruks atop our Muniqi horses, tracked them deep into the Tavan Mountains." He pointed to the southeast as Kadara shifted, aiming for the towering, jagged mountains that clawed at the sky. They were peppered with forests, some peaks capped in snow. "And when we tamed the ruks, some of the horse-lords chose not to return down to the steppes."

"Which is why so many of your traditions remain the same," Nesryn observed, glancing down at the *sulde* strapped to the saddle. The drop far, far below loomed, dried grasses swaying like a golden sea, carved by thin, twining rivers.

She quickly looked ahead toward the mountains. Though she'd grown mostly accustomed to the idea of how very little stood between her and death atop this ruk, reminding herself of it did nothing to settle her stomach.

"Yes," Sartaq said. "It is also why our riders often band with the Darghan in war. Our fighting techniques differ, but we mostly know how to work together."

"A cavalry below and aerial coverage above," Nesryn said, trying not to sound too interested. "Have you ever gone to war?"

The prince was quiet for a minute. Then he said, "Not on the scale of what is being unleashed in your land. Our father ensures that the territories within our empire are well aware that loyalty is rewarded. And resistance is answered with death."

Ice skittered down her spine.

Sartaq went on, "So I have been dispatched twice now to remind certain restless territories of that cold truth." A hot breath at her ear. "Then there are the clans within the rukhin themselves. Ancient rivalries that I have learned to navigate, and conflicts I have had to smooth over."

The hard way, he didn't add. He instead said, "As a city guard, you must have dealt with such things."

She snorted at the thought. "I was mostly on patrol—rarely promoted."

"Considering your skill with a bow, I would have thought you ran the entire place."

340

Nesryn smiled. Charmer. Beneath that unfailingly sure exterior, Sartaq was certainly a shameless flirt. But she considered his implied question, though she had known the answer for years. "Adarlan is not as . . . open as the khaganate when it comes to embracing the role of women in the ranks of its guards or armies," she admitted. "While I might be skilled, men usually were promoted. So I was left to rot on patrol duty at the walls or busy streets. Handling the underworld or nobility was left for more important guards. And ones whose families hailed from Adarlan."

Her sister had raged anytime it happened, but Nesryn had known that if she'd exploded to her superiors, if she'd challenged them . . . They were the sort of men who would tell her to be grateful to be admitted at all, then demand she turn in her sword and uniform. So she'd figured it was better to remain, to be passed over, not for mere pay, but for the fact that there were so few other guards like her, helping those who needed it most. It was for them she stayed on, kept her head down while lesser men were appointed.

"Ah." Another beat of quiet from the prince. "I've heard they were not so welcoming toward people from other lands."

"To say the least." The words were colder than she'd meant. And yet that was where her father had insisted they live, thinking it offered some sort of better life. Even when Adarlan had launched its wars to conquer the northern continent, he'd stayed—though her mother had tried to convince him to return to Antica, the city of her heart. Yet for whatever reason, perhaps stubbornness, perhaps defiance against the people who wanted to throw him out again, he'd stayed.

And Nesryn tried not to fault him for it, she really did. Her sister couldn't understand it—Nesryn's occasional, simmering anger on the topic. No, Delara had always loved Rifthold, loved the bustle of the city and thrived on winning over its hard-edged people. It had been no surprise that she'd married a man born and raised in the city itself. A true child of Adarlan—that's what her sister was. At least, of what Adarlan had once been and might one day again become.

Kadara caught a swift wind and coasted along it, the world below passing in a blur as those towering mountains grew closer and closer. Sartaq asked quietly, "Were you ever—"

"It's not worth talking about." Not when she could sometimes still feel that rock as it collided with her head, hear the taunts of those children. She swallowed and added, "Your Highness."

A low laugh. "So my title makes an appearance again." But he didn't press further. He only said, "I'm going to beg you not to call me Prince or Your Highness around the other riders."

"You're going to beg me, or you are?"

His arms tightened around her in mock warning. "It took me years to get them to stop asking if I needed my silk slippers or servants to brush my hair." Nesryn chuckled. "Amongst them, I am simply Sartaq." He added, "Or Captain."

"Captain?"

"Another thing you and I have in common, it seems."

Shameless flirt indeed. "But you rule all six ruk clans. They answer to you."

"They do, and when we all gather, I am Prince. But amongst my family's own clan, the Eridun, I captain their forces. And obey the word of my hearth-mother." He squeezed her again for emphasis. "Which I'd advise you doing as well, if you don't want to be stripped and tied to a cliff face in the middle of a storm."

"Holy gods."

"Indeed."

"Did she—"

"Yes. And as you said, it's not worth talking about."

But Nesryn chuckled again, surprised to find her face aching from smiling so often these past few minutes. "I appreciate the warning, Captain."

The Tavan Mountains turned mammoth, a wall of dark gray stone higher than any she'd ever beheld in her own lands. Not that she'd seen many mountains up close. Her family had rarely ventured inland into

Adarlan or its surrounding kingdoms—mostly because her father had been busy, but partially because the rural people in those areas did not take so well to outsiders. Even when their children had been born on Adarlanian soil, with an Adarlanian mother. Sometimes that latter fact had been more enraging to them.

Nesryn only prayed that the rukhin would be more welcoming.

In all her father's stories, the descriptions of the aeries of the rukhin somehow still did not convey the sheer impossibility of what had been built into the sides and atop three towering peaks clustered in the heart of the Tavan Mountains.

It was no assortment of *gir*—framed, wide tents—that the horse-clans moved about the steppes. No, the Eridun aerie had been hewn into the stone, houses and halls and chambers, many of them originally nests for the ruks themselves.

Some of those nests remained, usually near a ruk's rider and their family, so the birds could be summoned at a moment's notice. Either through a whistled command or by someone climbing the countless rope ladders anchored to the stone itself, allowing movement between various homes and caves—though internal stairwells had also been built within the peaks themselves, mostly for the elderly and children.

The homes themselves each came equipped with a broad cave mouth for the ruks to land, the living quarters hewn behind them. A few windows dotted the rock face here and there, markers of rooms hidden behind the stone, and drawing fresh air to the chambers within.

Not that they needed much more fresh air here. The wind was a river between the three close-knit peaks that housed Sartaq's hearth-clan, full of ruks of various sizes soaring or flapping or diving. Nesryn tried and failed to count the dwellings carved into the mountains. There had to be hundreds here. And perhaps more lay within the mountains themselves.

"This—this is only *one* clan?" Her first words in hours.

Kadara soared up the face of the centermost peak. Nesryn slid back in the saddle, Sartaq's body a warm wall behind her as he leaned forward, guiding her to do so as well. His thighs bracketed hers, the muscles shifting beneath as he kept their balance with the stirrups. "The Eridun is one of the largest—the oldest, if we're to be believed."

"You're not?" The aerie around them had indeed seemed to have existed for untold ages.

"Every clan claims it is the oldest and first among riders." A laugh that rumbled into her body. "When there is a Gathering, you should only hear the arguments about it. You're better off to insult a man about his wife than to tell him to his face that your clan is the eldest."

Nesryn smiled, even as she squeezed her eyes shut against the sheer drop behind her. Kadara aimed, swift and unfaltering, for the broadest of overhangs—a veranda, she realized as the ruk banked toward it. People were already standing just beneath the enormous arch of the cave mouth, arms raised in greeting.

She felt Sartaq's smile at her ear. "There lies the Mountain-Hall of Altun, the home of my hearth-mother and my family." Altun—*Windhaven*, was the rough translation. It was indeed larger than any other dwelling amid the three peaks: the Dorgos, or Three Singers, they were called— the cave itself at least forty feet tall and thrice as wide. Far within, she could just make out pillars and what indeed seemed to be a massive hall.

"The reception court—where we host our meetings and celebrations," Sartaq explained, his arms tightening around her just as Kadara back-flapped. Squeezing her eyes shut again in front of the awaiting people would certainly not win her any admiration, but—

Nesryn gripped the saddle horn with one hand, the other clenching Sartaq's knee, braced behind hers. Hard enough to bruise.

The prince only laughed quietly. "So the famed archer does have a weakness, then."

"I'll find out yours soon enough," Nesryn countered, earning another soft laugh in reply.

344

The ruk mercifully made a smooth landing on the polished dark stone of the almost-balcony, those waiting at the entrance bracing themselves against the wind off her wings.

Then they were still, and Nesryn quickly straightened, releasing her death-grip on both saddle and prince to behold a hall full of pillars of carved, painted wood. The braziers burning throughout cast the gold paint glinting amongst the green and red, and thick carpets in bold, striking patterns covered much of the stone floor, interrupted only by a round table and what seemed to be a small dais against one of the far walls. And beyond it, the gloom brightened by bracketed torches, a hallway flowed into the mountain itself. Lined with doors.

But in the very center of the Mountain-Hall of Altun: a fire.

The pit had been carved into the floor, so deep and wide that layers of broad steps led down to it. Like a small amphitheater—the main entertainment not a stage but the flame itself. The hearth.

It was indeed a domain fit for the Winged Prince.

Nesryn squared her shoulders as people young and old pressed forward, smiling broadly. Some were clad in familiar riding leathers, some wore beautifully colored, heavy wool coats that flowed to their knees. Most possessed Sartaq's silken onyx hair and wind-chapped, golden-brown skin.

"Well, well," drawled a young woman in a cobalt-and-ruby coat, tapping her booted foot on the smooth rock floor as she peered up at them. Nesryn forced herself to keep still, to endure that sweeping stare. The young woman's twin braids, tied with bands of red leather, fell well past her breasts, and she brushed one over a shoulder as she said, "Look who decided to give up his fur muff and oiled baths to join us once more."

Nesryn schooled her face into careful calm. But Sartaq just dropped Kadara's reins, the prince giving Nesryn a distinct *I told you so* look before he said down to the girl, "Don't pretend that you haven't been praying I bring back more of those pretty silk slippers for you, Borte."

Nesryn bit her lip to keep from smiling, though the others certainly showed no such restraint as their chuckles rumbled off the dark stones.

Borte crossed her arms. "I suppose you'd know where to buy them, since you're so fond of wearing them yourself."

Sartaq laughed, the sound rich and merry.

It was an effort not to gawk. He had not made such a laugh, not once, at the palace.

And when had she last made such a bright sound? Even with her aunt and uncle, her laughter had been restrained, as if some invisible damper lay over her. Perhaps long before that, stretching back to days when she was only a city guard with no idea what crawled through the sewers of Rifthold.

Sartaq smoothly dismounted Kadara and offered a hand to help Nesryn down.

It was the hand he lifted that made the dozen or so gathered notice her—study her. None more closely than Borte.

Another shrewd, weighing look. Seeing the leathers, but none of the features that marked her as one of them.

She'd dealt with the judgment of strangers long before now—this was nothing new. Even if she now stood in the gilded halls of Altun, amongst the rukhin.

Ignoring Sartaq's offered hand, Nesryn forced her stiff body to smoothly slide one leg over the saddle and dismounted herself. Her knees popped at the impact, but she managed to land lightly, and didn't let herself touch her hair—which she was certain was a rat's nest despite her short braid.

A faint gleam of approval entered Borte's dark eyes just before the girl jerked her chin toward Nesryn. "A Balruhni woman in the leathers of a rukhin. Now, there's a sight."

Sartaq didn't answer. He only glanced in Nesryn's direction. An invitation. And challenge.

So Nesryn slipped her hands into the pockets of her close-fitting pants and sauntered to the prince's side. "Will it be improved if I tell you I caught Sartaq filing his nails this morning?"

346

Borte stared at Nesryn, blinking once.

Then she tipped back her head and howled.

Sartaq threw an approving yet beleaguered glance in Nesryn's direction before saying, "Meet my hearth-sister, Borte. Granddaughter and heir of my hearth-mother, Houlun." He reached between them to tug one of Borte's braids. She batted his hand away. "Borte, meet Captain Nesryn Faliq." He paused for a breath, then added, "Of the Royal Guard of Adarlan."

Silence. Borte's arched dark brows rose.

An aging man in rukhin leathers pressed forward. "But what is more unusual: that a Balruhni woman is their captain, or that a captain of Adarlan has ventured so far?"

Borte waved the man off. "Always the idle chatter and questions with you," she scolded him. And to Nesryn's shock, the man winced and shut his mouth. "The real question is . . ." A sly grin at Sartaq. "Does she come as emissary or bride?"

Any attempt at a steady, cool, calm appearance vanished as Nesryn gaped at the girl. Right as Sartaq snapped, "*Borte.*"

Borte gave a downright wicked grin. "Sartaq never brings such pretty ladies home—from Adarlan *or* Antica. Be careful walking around the cliff edges, Captain Faliq, or some of the girls here might give you a shove."

"Will you be one of them?" Nesryn's voice remained unruffled, even if her face had heated.

Borte scowled. "I should think not." Some of the others laughed again.

"As my hearth-sister," Sartaq explained, leading Nesryn toward the cluster of low-backed chairs near the lip of the fire pit, "I consider Borte a blood relative. Like my own sister."

Borte's devilish grin faded as she fell into step alongside Sartaq. "How fares your family?"

Sartaq's face was unreadable, save for the faint flicker in those dark eyes. "Busy," was all he said. A nonanswer.

But Borte nodded, as if she knew his moods and inclinations well, and kept quiet while Sartaq escorted Nesryn into a carved and painted wooden chair. The heat from the blazing fire was delicious, and she nearly groaned as she stretched out her frozen feet toward it.

Borte hissed. "You couldn't get your sweetheart a proper pair of boots, Sartaq?"

Sartaq growled in warning, but Nesryn frowned at her supple leather boots. They'd been more expensive than any she'd ever dared purchase for herself, but Dorian Havilliard had insisted. Part of the uniform, he'd told her with a wink.

She wondered if he still smiled so freely, or spent as generously, wherever he was.

But she glanced toward Borte, whose boots were leather, yet thicker—lined with what seemed to be thickest sheepskin. Definitely better-equipped for the chilly altitudes.

"I'm sure you can dig up a pair somewhere," Sartaq said to his hearth-sister, and Nesryn twisted in her chair while the two of them drifted back toward where Kadara waited.

The people pressed in around Sartaq, murmuring too softly for Nesryn to hear from across the hall. But the prince spoke with easy smiles, talking while he unloaded their packs, handing them off to whoever was closest, and then unsaddled Kadara.

He gave the golden ruk a stroke down her neck, then a solid thump on her side—and then Kadara was gone, flapping into the open air beyond the cave mouth.

Nesryn debated going over to them, offering to help with the packs that were now being hauled through the chamber and into the hallway beyond, but the heat creeping up her body had sapped the strength from her legs.

Sartaq and Borte appeared, the others dispersing, just as Nesryn noticed the man sitting near a brazier across the hall. A cup curling with steam sat on the small, wooden table beside his chair, and though there seemed to be an open scroll in his lap, his eyes remained fixed on her.

She didn't know what to remark upon: that while his skin was tan, it was clear that he did not hail from the southern continent; that his short brown hair was far from the long, silken braids of the ruk riders; or that his clothes seemed more akin to Adarlan's jackets and pants.

Only a dagger hung at his side, and while he was broad-shouldered and fit, he didn't possess the self-assured swagger, the pitiless surety of a warrior. He was perhaps in his late forties, pale white lines etched at the corner of his eyes, where he'd squinted in the sun or wind.

Borte led Sartaq around the fire pit, past the various pillars, and right to the man, who got to his feet and bowed. He stood roughly at Sartaq's height, and even from across the hall, with the crackling fire and groaning wind, Nesryn could make out his shoddy Halha: "It is an honor, Prince."

Borte snorted.

Sartaq just gave a curt nod and replied in the northern language, "I'm told you have been a guest of our hearth-mother for the past few weeks."

"She was gracious enough to welcome me here, yes." The man sounded slightly relieved to be using his native tongue. A glance toward Nesryn. She didn't bother to pretend she wasn't listening. "I couldn't help but overhear what I thought was mention of a captain from Adarlan."

"Captain Faliq oversees the royal guard."

The man didn't take his eyes off Nesryn as he murmured, "Does she, now."

Nesryn only held his stare from across the room. *Go ahead. Gawk all you like.*

Sartaq asked sharply, "And your name?"

The man dragged his gaze back to the prince. "Falkan Ennar."

Borte said to Sartaq in Halha, "He is a merchant."

And if he'd come from the northern continent . . . Nesryn slid to her feet, her steps near-silent as she approached. She made sure they were, as Falkan watched her the entire way, running an eye over her from foot to head. Made sure he noted that the grace with which she moved was not some feminine gift, but from training that had taught her how to creep up on others undetected.

349

Falkan stiffened as if he finally realized it. And understood that the dagger at his side would be of little use against her, if he was stupid enough to pull something.

Good. It made him smarter than a great number of men in Rifthold. Stopping a casual distance away, Nesryn asked the merchant, "Have you any news?"

Up close, the eyes she'd mistaken for dark were a midnight sapphire. He'd likely been moderately handsome in his youth. "News of what?"

"Of Adarlan. Of . . . anything."

Falkan stood with remarkable stillness—a man perhaps used to holding his ground in a bargain. "I wish that I could offer you any, Captain, but I have been in the southern continent for over two years now. You probably have more news than I do." A subtle request.

And one that would go unanswered. She was not about to blab her kingdom's business for all to hear. So Nesryn just shrugged and turned back toward the fire pit across the hall.

"Before I left the northern continent," Falkan said as she strode away, "a young man named Westfall was the Captain of the Royal Guard. Are you his replacement?"

Careful. She indeed had to be so, so careful not to reveal too much. To him, to anyone. "Lord Westfall is now Hand to King Dorian Havilliard."

Shock slackened the merchant's face. She marked it—every tick and flicker. No joy or relief, but no anger, either. Just . . . surprise. Honest, bald surprise. "Dorian Havilliard is king?"

At Nesryn's raised brows, Falkan explained, "I have been in the deep wilds for months now. News does not come swiftly. Or often."

"An odd place to be selling your goods," Sartaq murmured. Nesryn was inclined to agree.

Falkan merely gave the prince a tight smile. A man with secrets of his own, then.

"It has been a long journey," Borte cut in, looping her arm through

Nesryn's and turning her toward the dim hallway beyond. "Captain Faliq needs refreshment. And a bath."

Nesryn wasn't certain whether to thank the young woman or begrudge her for interrupting, but . . . Her stomach was indeed an aching pit. And it had been a long while since she'd bathed.

Neither Sartaq nor Falkan stopped them, though their murmuring resumed as Borte escorted her into the hallway that shot straight into the mountain itself. Wooden doors lined it, some open to reveal small bed-chambers—even a little library.

"He is a strange man," Borte said in Halha. "My grandmother refuses to speak of why he came here—what he seeks."

Nesryn lifted a brow. "Trade, perhaps?"

Borte shook her head, opening a door halfway down the hall. The room was small, a narrow bed tucked against one wall, the other occupied by a trunk and a wooden chair. The far wall held a washbasin and ewer, along with a pile of soft-looking cloths. "We have no goods to sell. *We* are usually the merchants—ferrying goods across the continent. Our clan here, not so much, but some of the others . . . Their aeries are full of treasures from every territory." She toed the rickety bed and frowned. "Not this old junk."

Nesryn chuckled. "Perhaps he wishes to assist you in expanding, then."

Borte turned, braids swaying. "No. He doesn't meet with anyone, or seem *interested* in that." A shrug. "It matters little. Only that he is *here*."

Nesryn folded away the tidbits of information. He didn't seem like one of Morath's agents, but who knew how far the arm of Erawan now stretched? If it had reached Antica, then it was possible it had delved into the continent. She'd be on her guard—had no doubt Sartaq already was.

Borte twirled the end of a braid around a finger. "I saw the way you sized him up. You don't think he's here for business, either."

Nesryn weighed the merits of admitting the truth, and opted for, "These are strange days for all of us—I have learned not to take men on their word. Or appearance."

Borte dropped her braid. "No wonder Sartaq brought you home. You sound just like him."

Nesryn hid her smile, not bothering to say that she found such a thing to be a compliment.

Borte sniffed, waving to the room. "Not as fine as the khagan's palace, but better than sleeping on one of Sartaq's shitty bedrolls."

Nesryn smiled. "Any bed is better than that, I suppose."

Borte smirked. "I meant what I said. You need a bath. And a comb."

Nesryn at last raised a hand to her hair and winced. Tangles and knots and more tangles. Just getting it out of the braid would be a nightmare.

"Even Sartaq braids better than that," Borte teased.

Nesryn sighed. "Despite my sister's best efforts to teach me, I'm useless when it comes to such things." She offered the girl a wink. "Why do you think I keep my hair so short?"

Indeed, her sister had practically fainted when Nesryn had come home one afternoon at age fifteen with hair cut to her collarbone. She'd kept the hair that length ever since—in part to piss off Delara, who still pouted about it, and partially because it was *far* easier to deal with. Wielding blades and arrows was one thing, but styling hair . . . She was hopeless. And showing up at the guards' barracks with a pretty hairstyle would *not* have been well received.

Borte only gave Nesryn a curt nod—as if she seemed to realize that. "Before you fly the next time, I'll braid it properly for you." Then she pointed down the hall, to a set of narrow stairs that led into the gloom. "Baths are this way."

Nesryn sniffed herself and cringed. "Oh, that's awful."

Borte snickered as Nesryn entered the hall. "I'm surprised Sartaq's eyes weren't watering."

Nesryn chuckled as she followed her toward what she prayed was a boiling-hot bath. She again felt Borte's sharp, assessing gaze and asked, "What?"

"You grew up in Adarlan, didn't you?"

Nesryn considered the question, why it might be asked. "Yes. I was born and raised in Rifthold, though my father's family comes from Antica."

Borte was quiet for a few steps. But as they reached the narrow stairwell and stepped into the dim interior, Borte smiled over a shoulder at Nesryn. "Then welcome home."

Nesryn wondered if those words might be the most beautiful she'd ever heard.

⁓

The baths were ancient copper tubs that had to be filled kettle by kettle, but Nesryn didn't object as she finally slid into one.

An hour later, hair finally detangled and brushed out, she found herself seated at the massive round table in the great hall, shoveling roast rabbit into her mouth, nestled in thick, warm clothes that had been donated by Borte herself. The flashes of embroidered cobalt and daffodil on the sleeves snared Nesryn's attention as much as the platters of roast meats before her. Beautiful clothes—layered and toasty against the chill that permeated the hall, even with the fires. And her toes . . . Borte had indeed found a pair of those fleece-lined boots for her.

Sartaq sat beside Nesryn at the empty table, equally silent and eating with as much enthusiasm. He had yet to bathe, though his windblown hair had been rebraided, the long plait falling down the center of his muscled back.

As her belly began to fill and her fingers slowed their picking, Nesryn glanced toward the prince. She found him smiling faintly. "Better than grapes and salted pork?"

She jerked her chin toward the bones littering her plate in silent answer, then to the grease on her fingers. Would it be uncouth to lick it off? The seasonings had been exquisite.

353

"My hearth-mother," he said, that smile fading, "is not here."

Nesryn paused her eating. They'd come here to seek the counsel of this woman—

"According to Borte, she will be returning tomorrow or the day after."

She waited for more. Silence could be just as effective as spoken questions.

Sartaq pushed back his plate and braced his arms on the table. "I'm aware that you're pressed for time. If I could, I'd go look for her myself, but even Borte wasn't sure where she'd gone off to. Houlun is . . . adrift like that. Sees her *sulde* waving in the wind and takes her ruk out to chase it. And will whack us with it if we try to stop her." A gesture toward the rack of spears near the cave mouth, Sartaq's own *sulde* among them.

Nesryn smiled at that. "She sounds like an interesting woman."

"She is. In some ways, I'm closer to her than . . ." The words trailed off, and he shook his head. *Than his own mother.* Indeed, Nesryn hadn't witnessed him being nearly so open, so teasing with his own siblings, as he was with Borte.

"I can wait," Nesryn said at last, trying not to wince. "Lord Westfall still needs time to heal, and I told him I'd be gone three weeks. I can wait a day or two more." *And please, gods, not another moment after it.*

Sartaq nodded, tapping a finger on the ancient wood of the table. "Tonight, we will rest, but tomorrow . . ." A hint of a smile. "How would you like a tour tomorrow?"

"It would be an honor."

Sartaq's smile grew. "Perhaps we could also do a bit of archery practice." He looked her over with a frankness that made her shift in her seat. "I'm certainly keen to match myself against Neith's Arrow, and I'm sure the young warriors are, too."

Nesryn pushed back her own plate, brows lifting. "They've heard of me?"

Sartaq grinned. "I might have told a story or two the last time I came here. Why do you think there were so many people gathered when we arrived? They certainly don't usually bother to drag themselves here to see *me*."

"But Borte seemed like she'd never—"

"Does Borte seem like a person who gives *anyone* an easy time?"

Something deeper in her warmed. "No. But how could they have known I was coming?"

His answering grin was the portrait of princely arrogance. "Because I sent word a day before that you were likely to join me."

Nesryn gaped at him, unable to maintain that mask of calm.

Rising, Sartaq scooped up their plates. "I told you that I was praying you'd join me, Nesryn Faliq. If I'd shown up empty-handed, Borte would have never let me hear the end of it."

≒ 30 ≓

Within the interior chamber of the hall, Nesryn had no way of telling how long she'd slept or what hour of the morning it was. She'd dozed fitfully, awakening to comb through the sounds beyond her door, to detect if anyone was astir. She doubted Sartaq was the type to scold her for sleeping in, but if the rukhin indeed teased the prince about his courtly life, then lazing about all morning was perhaps not the best way to win them over.

So she'd tossed and turned, catching a few minutes of sleep here and there, and gave up entirely when she noticed shadows interrupting the light cracking beneath the door. Someone, at least, was awake in the Hall of Altun.

She'd dressed, pausing only to wash her face. The room was warm enough that the water in the ewer wasn't icy, though she certainly could have used a freezing splash on her gritty eyes.

Thirty minutes later, seated in the saddle before Sartaq, she regretted that wish.

He'd indeed been awake and saddling Kadara when she'd emerged into the still-quiet great hall. The fire pit burned brightly, as if someone tended to it all night, but save for the prince and his ruk, the pillar-filled hall was empty. It was still empty when he hauled her up into the saddle and Kadara leaped from the cave mouth.

Freezing air slammed into her face, whipping at her cheeks as they dove.

A few other ruks were aloft. Likely out for their breakfasts, Sartaq told her, his voice soft in the emerging dawn. And it was in pursuit of Kadara's own meal that they went, sailing out of the three peaks of the Eridun's aerie and deep into the fir-crusted mountains beyond.

It was only after Kadara had snatched half a dozen fat silver salmon from a rushing turquoise river, hurling them each in the air before swallowing them in a slicing bite, that Sartaq steered them toward a cluster of smaller peaks.

"The training run," he said, pointing. The rocks were smoother, the drops between peaks less sharp—more like smooth, rounded gullies. "Where the novices learn to ride."

Though less brutal than the three brother-peaks of the Dorgos, it didn't seem any safer. "You said you raised Kadara from a hatchling. Is that how it is done for all riders?"

"Not when we are first learning to ride. Children take out the seasoned, more docile ruks, ones too old to make long flights. We learn on them until we are thirteen, fourteen, and then find our hatchling to raise and train ourselves."

"Thirteen—"

"We take our first rides at four. Or the others do. I was, as you know, a few years late."

Nesryn pointed to the training run. "You let four-year-olds ride alone through *that*?"

"Family members or hearth-kin usually go on the first several rides."

Nesryn blinked at the little mountain range, trying and failing to imagine her various nieces and nephews, who were still prone to running naked and shrieking through the house at the mere whisper of the word *bath*, responsible for not only commanding one of the beasts beneath her, but staying *in* the saddle.

"The horse-clans on the steppes have the same training," Sartaq explained. "Most can stand atop the horses by six, and begin learning to wield bows and spears as soon as their feet can reach the stirrups. Aside from the standing"—a chuckle at the thought—"our children have an identical process." The sun peeked out, warming the skin she'd left exposed to the biting wind. "It was how the first khagan conquered the continent. Our people were already well trained as a cavalry, disciplined and used to carrying their own supplies. The other armies they faced . . . Those kingdoms did not anticipate foes who knew how to ride across thick winter ice they believed would guard their cities during the cold months. And they did not anticipate an army that traveled light, engineers amongst them to craft weapons from any materials they found when they reached their destinations. To this day, the Academy of Engineers in Balruhn remains the most prestigious in the khaganate."

Nesryn knew that—her father still mentioned the Academy every now and then. A distant cousin had attended and gone on to earn a small degree of fame for inventing some harvesting machine.

Sartaq steered Kadara southward, soaring high above the snowcapped peaks. "Those kingdoms also didn't anticipate an army that conquered from behind, by taking routes that few would risk." He pointed to the west, toward a pale band along the horizon. "The Kyzultum Desert lies that way. For centuries, it was a barrier between the steppes and the greener lands. To attempt to conquer the southern territories, everyone had always taken the long way around it, giving plenty of time for the defenders to rally a host. So when those kingdoms heard the khagan and his hundred thousand warriors were on the move, they positioned their armies to intercept them." Pride limned his every word. "Only to discover that the khagan and his armies had directly crossed the Kyzultum, befriending local nomads long sneered at by the southern kingdoms to guide them. Allowing the khagan to creep right behind them and sack their unguarded cities."

She felt his smile at her ear and found herself settling a little farther into him. "What happened then?" She'd only heard fragments of the stories—never such a sweeping account, and certainly not from the lips of one born to this glorious bloodline. "Was it open war?"

"No," Sartaq said. "He avoided outright combat whenever he could, actually. Made a brutal example of a few key leaders, so that terror would spread, and by the time he reached many of those cities or armies, most laid down their arms and accepted his terms of surrender in exchange for protection. He used fear as a weapon, just as much as he wielded his *sulde*."

"I heard he had two—*sulde*, I mean."

"He did. And my father still does. The Ebony and the Ivory, we call them. A *sulde* with white horsehair to carry in times of peace and one with black horsehair to wield in war."

"I assume he brought the Ebony with him on those campaigns."

"Oh, he certainly did. And by the time he'd crossed the Kyzultum and sacked that first city, word of what awaited resistance, word that he was indeed carrying the Ebony *sulde*, spread so quick and so far that when he arrived at the next kingdom, they didn't even bother to raise an army. They just surrendered. The khagan rewarded them handsomely for it— and made sure other territories heard of that, too." He was quiet for a moment. "Adarlan's king was not so clever or merciful, was he?"

"No," Nesryn said, swallowing. "He was not." The man had destroyed and pillaged and enslaved. Not the man—the demon within him.

She added, "The army that Erawan has rallied . . . He began amassing it long before Dorian and Aelin matured and claimed their birthrights. Chaol—Lord Westfall told me of tunnels and chambers beneath the palace in Rifthold that had been there for years. Places where human and Valg had been experimented upon. Right under the feet of mindless courtiers."

"Which raises the question of why," Sartaq mused. "If he'd conquered most of the northern continent, why gather such a force? He thought Aelin Galathynius was dead—I assume he did not anticipate that Dorian Havilliard would turn rebel, too."

She hadn't told him of the Wyrdkeys—and still couldn't bring herself to divulge them. "We've always believed that Erawan was hell-bent on conquering this world. It seemed motive enough."

"But you sound doubtful now."

Nesryn considered. "I just don't understand why. Why all this effort, why want to conquer *more* when he'd secretly controlled the northern continent anyway. Erawan got away with plenty of horrors. Is it only that he wishes to plunge our world into further darkness? Does he wish to call himself master of the earth?"

"Perhaps things like motives and reason are foreign to demons. Perhaps he only has the drive to destroy."

Nesryn shook her head, squinting against the sun as it rose higher, the light turning blinding.

Sartaq returned to the Eridun aerie, left Kadara in the great hall, and continued Nesryn's tour. He spared her the embarrassment of begging not to use the rope ladders along the cliff face and led her through the internal stairwells and passageways of the mountain. To get to the other two peaks, he claimed, they'd need to either fly across or take one of the two bridges strung between them. One glance at the rope and wood and Nesryn announced she could wait for another day to try.

Riding on Kadara was one thing. Nesryn trusted the bird, and trusted her rider. But the swaying bridge, however well built . . . She might need a drink or two before trying to cross.

But there was plenty to see within the mountain itself—Rokhal, the Whisperer, he was called. The other two brother-peaks that made up the Dorgos were Arik, the Lilter; and Torke, the Roarer—all three named for the way the wind itself sang as it passed over and around them.

Rokhal was the biggest of them, the most delved, his crown jewel being the Hall of Altun near the top. But even in the chambers below Altun, Nesryn hardly knew where to look as the prince showed her through the winding corridors and spaces.

The various kitchens and small gathering halls; the ruk riders' houses and workshops; the nests of various ruks, who ranged in color from Kadara's gold to dark brown; the smithies where armor was forged from ore mined within the mountain; the tanneries where the saddles were meticulously crafted; the trading posts where one might barter for household goods and small trinkets. And lastly, atop Rokhal himself, the training rings.

There was no wall or fence along the broad, flat-topped summit. Only the small, round building that provided a reprieve from the wind and cold, as well as access to the stairwell beneath.

Nesryn was out of breath by the time they opened the wooden door to the rasping wind—and the sight that stretched before her certainly snatched away any remaining air in her lungs.

Even flying above and amongst the mountains felt somehow different from this.

Snowcapped, dominating peaks surrounded them, ancient as the earth, untouched and slumbering. Nearby, a long lake sparkled between twin ridges, ruks mere shadows over the teal surface.

She'd never seen anything so great and unforgiving, so vast and beautiful. And even though she was as insignificant as a mayfly compared with the size of the mountains around them, some piece of her felt keenly a part of it, born from it.

Sartaq stood at her side, following where her attention drifted, as if their gazes were bound together. And when Nesryn's stare landed upon a lonely, broad mountain on the other end of the lake, he drew in a swift breath. No trees grew on its dark sides; only snow provided a cape over its uppermost crags and summit.

"That is Arundin," Sartaq said softly, as if fearful of even the wind hearing. "The fourth Singer amid these peaks." The wind indeed seemed to flow from the mountain, cold and swift. "The Silent One, we call him."

Indeed, a heavy sort of quiet seemed to ripple around that peak. In the turquoise waters of the lake at his feet lay a perfect mirror image, so clear that Nesryn wondered if one might dive beneath the surface and find another world, a shadow-world, beneath. "Why?"

Sartaq turned, as if the sight of Arundin was not one to be endured for long. "It is upon his slopes that the rukhin bury our dead. If we fly closer, you'll see *sulde* covering his sides—the only markers of the fallen."

It was an entirely inappropriate and morbid question, but Nesryn asked, "Will you one day be laid there, or out in the sacred land of the steppes with the rest of your family?"

Sartaq toed the smooth rock beneath them. "That choice remains before me. The two parts of my heart shall likely have a long war over it."

She certainly understood it—that tug between two places.

Shouts and clanging metal drew her attention from the beckoning, eternal silence of Arundin to the real purpose of the space atop Rokhal: the training rings.

Men and women in riding leathers stood at various circles and stations. Some fired arrows at targets with impressive accuracy, some hurled spears, some sparred sword to sword. Older riders barked orders or corrected aim and posture, stalking amongst the warriors.

A few turned in Sartaq's direction as he and Nesryn approached the training ring at the far end of the space. The archery circuit.

With the wind, the cold . . . Nesryn found herself calculating those factors. Admiring the archers' skill all the more. And she was somehow not surprised to find Borte among the three archers aiming at stuffed dummies, her long braids snapping in the wind.

"Here to have your ass handed to you again, brother?" Borte's smirk was full of that wicked delight.

Sartaq let out his rich, pleasant laugh again, taking up a longbow and shouldering a quiver from the stand nearby. He nudged his hearth-sister aside with a bump of the hip, nocking an arrow with ease. He aimed, fired, and Nesryn smiled as the arrow found its mark, right in the neck of the dummy.

"Impressive, for a princeling," Borte drawled. She turned to Nesryn, her dark brows high. "And you?"

Well, then. Swallowing her smile, Nesryn shrugged out of the heavier wool overcoat, gave Borte an incline of her head, and approached the rack of arrows and bows. The mountain wind was bracing with only her riding leathers for warmth, but she blocked out Rokhal's whispering as she ran her fingers down the carved wood. Yew, ash . . . She plucked up one of the yew bows, testing its weight, its flexibility and resistance. A solid, deadly weapon.

Yet familiar. As familiar as an old friend. She had not picked up a bow until her mother's death, and during those initial years of grief and numbness, the physical training, the concentration and strength required, had been a sanctuary, and a reprieve, and forge.

She wondered if any of her old tutors had survived the attack on Rifthold. If any of their arrows had brought down wyverns. Or slowed them enough to save lives.

Nesryn let the thought settle as she moved to the quivers, pulling out arrows. The metal tips were heavier than those she'd used in Adarlan, the shaft slightly thicker. Designed to cut through brutal winds at racing speeds. Perhaps, if they were lucky, take out a wyvern or two.

She selected arrows from various quivers, setting them into her own before she strapped it across her back and approached the line where Borte, Sartaq, and a few others were silently watching.

"Pick a mark," Nesryn told Borte.

The woman smirked. "Neck, heart, head." She pointed to each of the three dummies, a different mark for each one. Wind rattled them, the aim and strength needed to hit each utterly different. Borte knew it—all the warriors here did.

Nesryn lifted an arm behind her head, dragging her fingers along the fletching, the feathers rippling against her skin as she scanned the three targets. Listened to the murmur of the winds racing past Rokhal, that wild summons she heard echoed in her own heart. *Wind-seeker,* her mother had called her.

One after another, Nesryn withdrew an arrow and fired.

Again, and again, and again.

Again, and again, and again.

Again, and again, and again.

And when she finished, only the howling wind answered—the wind of Torke, the Roarer. Every training ring had stopped. Staring at what she'd done.

Instead of three arrows distributed amongst the three dummies, she'd fired nine.

Three rows of perfectly aligned shots on each: heart, neck, and head. Not an inch of difference. Even with the singing winds.

Sartaq was grinning when she turned to him, his long braid drifting behind him, as if it were a *sulde* itself.

But Borte elbowed past him, and breathed to Nesryn, "Show me."

~

For hours, Nesryn stood atop the Rokhal training ring and explained how she'd done it, how she calculated wind and weight and air. And as much as she showed the various rotations that came through, *they* also demonstrated their own techniques. The way they twisted in their saddles to fire backward, which bows they wielded for hunting or warfare.

Nesryn's cheeks were wind-chapped, her hands numb, but she was smiling—wide and unfailingly—when Sartaq was approached by a breath-less messenger who had burst from the stairwell entrance.

His hearth-mother had returned to the aerie at last.

Sartaq's face revealed nothing, though a nod from him had Borte ordering all the onlookers to go back to their various stations. They did so with a few grins of thanks and welcome to Nesryn, which she returned with an incline of her head.

Sartaq set his quiver and bow on the wooden rack, extending a hand for Nesryn's. She passed him both, flexing her fingers after hours of grip-ping bow and string.

"She'll be tired," Borte warned him, a short sword in her hand. Her training, apparently, was not over for the day. "Don't pester her too much."

Sartaq threw an incredulous look at Borte. "You think I want to get smacked with a spoon again?"

Nesryn choked at that, but shrugged into the embroidered cobalt-and-gold wool coat, belting it tightly. She trailed the prince as he headed into the warm interior, straightening her wind-tossed hair as they descended the dim stairwell.

"Even though Borte is to one day lead the Eridun, she trains with the others?"

"Yes," Sartaq said without glancing over his shoulder. "Hearth-mothers all know how to fight, how to attack and defend. But Borte's training includes other things."

"Like learning the different tongues of the world." Her use of the northern language was as impeccable as Sartaq's.

"Like that. And history, and . . . more. Things even I am not told of by either Borte or her grandmother."

The words echoed off the stones around them. Nesryn dared ask, "Where's Borte's mother?"

Sartaq's shoulders tensed. "Her *sulde* stands on Arundin's slopes."

Just the way he spoke it, the cold cut of his voice . . . "I'm sorry."

"So am I," was all Sartaq said.

"Her father?"

"A man her mother met in distant lands, and whom she did not care to hold on to for longer than a night."

Nesryn considered the fierce, wicked young woman who'd fought with no small skill in the training rings. "I'm glad she has you, then. And her grandmother."

Sartaq shrugged. Dangerous, strange territory—she'd somehow waded into a place where she had no right to pry.

But then Sartaq said, "You're a good teacher."

"Thank you." It was all she could think to say. He'd kept close to her side while she walked the others through her various positions and techniques, but had said little. A leader who did not need to constantly be filling the air with talking and boasting.

He blew out a breath, shoulders loosening. "And I'm relieved to see that the reality lives up to the legend."

Nesryn chuckled, grateful to be back on safer ground. "You had doubts?"

They reached the landing that would take them to the great hall. Sartaq let her fall into step beside him. "The reports left out some key information. It made me doubt their accuracy."

It was the sly gleam in his eye that made Nesryn angle her head. "What, exactly, did they fail to mention?"

They reached the great hall, empty save for a cloaked figure just barely visible on the other side of the fire pit—and someone sitting beside her.

But Sartaq turned to her, examining her from head to toe and back again. There was little that he missed. "They didn't mention that you're beautiful."

Nesryn opened and closed her mouth in what she was sure was an unflattering impression of a fish on dry land.

With a wink, Sartaq strode ahead, calling, "*Ej.*" The rukhin's term for *mother*, he'd told her this morning. Nesryn hurried after him. They rounded the massive fire pit, the figure sitting atop the uppermost stair pulling back her hood.

She'd expected an ancient crone, bent with age and toothless.

Instead, a straight-backed woman with braided, silver-streaked onyx hair smiled grimly at Sartaq. And though age had indeed touched her features . . . it was Borte's face. Or Borte's face in forty years.

The hearth-mother wore a rider's leathers, though her dark blue cloak— actually a jacket she'd left hanging over her shoulders—covered much of them.

But at her side . . . Falkan. His face equally grave, those dark sapphire eyes scanning them. Sartaq checked his pace at the sight of the merchant, either irritated that he hadn't been first to claim her attention or simply that the merchant was present for this reunion.

Manners or self-preserving instincts kicked in, and Sartaq continued his approach, hopping down onto the first ledge of the pit to stride the rest of the way.

Houlun rose when he was near, enfolding him in a swift, hard embrace. She cupped his shoulders when she was done, the woman nearly as tall as him, shoulders strong and thighs well muscled, and surveyed Sartaq with a shrewd eye.

"Sorrow weighs heavily on you still," she observed, running a scar-flecked hand over Sartaq's high cheekbone. "And worry."

Sartaq's eyes shuttered before he ducked his head. "I have missed you, *Ej*."

"Sweet-talker," Houlun chided, patting his cheek.

To Nesryn's delight, she could have sworn the prince blushed.

The firelight cast the few strands of silver in Houlun's hair with red and gold as she peered around Sartaq's broad shoulders to where Nesryn stood atop the lip of the pit. "And the archer from the north arrives at last." An incline of her head. "I am Houlun, daughter of Dochin, but you may call me *Ej*, as the others do."

One glance into the woman's brown eyes and Nesryn knew Houlun was not one who missed much. Nesryn bowed her head. "It is an honor."

The hearth-mother stared at her for a long moment. Nesryn met her gaze, remaining as still as she could. Letting the woman see what she wanted.

At last, Houlun's eyes slid toward Sartaq. "We have matters to discuss."

Absent that fierce gaze, Nesryn loosed a breath but kept her spine ramrod straight.

Sartaq nodded, something like relief on his face. But he glanced toward Falkan, watching all from his seat. "They are things that should be told privately, *Ej*."

Not rude, but certainly not warm. Nesryn refrained from echoing the prince's sentiment.

Houlun waved a hand. "Then they may wait." She pointed to the stone bench. "Sit."

"Ej—"

Falkan shifted, as if he'd do them all a favor and go.

But Houlun pointed to him in silent warning to remain. "I would have you all listen."

Sartaq dropped onto the bench, the only sign of his discontent being the foot he tapped on the floor. Nesryn sat beside him, the stern woman reclaiming her perch between them and Falkan.

"An ancient malice is stirring deep in these mountains," Houlun said. "It is why I have been gone these past few days—to seek it out."

"Ej." Warning and fear coated the prince's voice.

"I am not so old that I cannot wield my *sulde*, boy." She glowered at him. Indeed, nothing about this woman seemed old at all.

Sartaq asked, frowning, "What did you go in pursuit of?"

Houlun glanced around the hall for any stray ears. "Ruk nests have been pillaged. Eggs stolen in the night, hatchlings vanishing."

Sartaq swore, filthy and low. Nesryn blinked at it, even as her stomach tightened. "Poachers have not dared tread in these mountains for decades," the prince said. "But you should not have pursued them *alone, Ej.*"

"It was not poachers I sought. But something worse."

Shadows lined the woman's face, and Nesryn swallowed. If the Valg had come here—

"My own *ej* called them the *kharankui.*"

"It means shadow—darkness," Sartaq murmured to Nesryn, dread tightening his face.

Her heart thundered. Should the Valg be here already—

"But in your lands," Houlun went on, glancing between Nesryn and Falkan, "they call them something different, don't they?"

Nesryn sized up Falkan as he swallowed, wondering herself how to lie or deflect revealing anything about the Valg—

But Falkan nodded. And he replied, voice barely audible above the flame, "We call them the stygian spiders."

⇥ 31 ⇤

"The stygian spiders are little more than myths," Nesryn managed to say to Houlun. "Spidersilk is so rare some even doubt it exists. You might be chasing ghosts."

But it was Falkan who replied with a grim smile, "I would beg to differ, Captain Faliq." He reached into the breast of his jacket, and Nesryn tensed, hand shooting for the dagger at her waist—

It was no weapon he pulled out.

The white fabric glittered, the iridescence like starfire as Falkan shifted it in his hand. Even Sartaq whistled at the handkerchief-sized piece of cloth.

"Spidersilk," Falkan said, tucking the piece back into his jacket. "Straight from the source."

As Nesryn's mouth popped open, Sartaq said, "You have seen these terrors up close." Not quite a question.

"I bartered with their kin in the northern continent," Falkan corrected, that grim smile remaining. Along with shadows. So many shadows. "Nearly three years ago. Some might deem it a fool's bargain, but I walked away with a hundred yards of Spidersilk."

The handkerchief in his jacket alone could fetch a king's ransom. A hundred yards of it . . ."You must be wealthy as the khagan," she blurted.

A shrug. "I have learned that true wealth is not all glittering gold and jewels."

Sartaq asked quietly, "What was the cost, then?" For the stygian spiders traded not in material goods, but dreams and wishes and—

"Twenty years. Twenty years of my life. Taken not from the end, but the prime."

Nesryn scanned the man, his face just beginning to show the signs of age, the hair still without gray—

"I am twenty-seven," Falkan said to her. "And yet I now appear to be a man of nearly fifty."

Holy gods. "What are you doing at the aerie, then?" Nesryn demanded. "Do the spiders here produce the silk, too?"

"They are not so civilized as their sisters in the north," Houlun said, clicking her tongue. "The *kharankui* do not create—only destroy. Long have they dwelled in their caves and passes of the Dagul Fells, in the far south of these mountains. And long have we maintained a respectful distance."

"Why do you think they now come to steal our eggs?" Sartaq glanced to the few ruks lingering at the cave mouth, waiting for their riders. He leaned forward, bracing his forearms on his thighs.

"Who else?" the hearth-mother countered. "No poachers have been spotted. Who else might sneak upon a ruk's nest, so high in the world? I flew over their domain these past few days. The webs indeed have grown from the peaks and passes of the Fells down to the pine forests in the ravines, choking off all life." A glance toward Falkan. "I do not believe it mere coincidence that the *kharankui* have again begun preying upon the world at the same time a merchant seeks out our aerie for answers regarding their northern kin."

371

Falkan raised his hands at Sartaq's sharp look. "I have not sought them out nor provoked them. I heard whispers of your hearth-mother's trove of knowledge and thought to seek her counsel before I dared anything."

"What do you want with them?" Nesryn asked, angling her head.

Falkan examined his hands, flexing the fingers as if they were stiff. "I want my youth back."

Houlun said to Sartaq, "He sold his hundred yards but still thinks he can reclaim the time."

"I *can* reclaim it," Falkan insisted, earning a warning glare from Houlun at his tone. He checked himself, and clarified, "There are . . . things that I still have left to do. I should like to accomplish them before old age interferes. I was told that slaying the spider who ate my twenty years was the only way to return those lost years to me."

Nesryn's brows narrowed. "Why not go hunt that spider back home, then? Why come here?"

Falkan didn't answer.

Houlun said, "Because he was also told that only a great warrior can slay a *kharankui*. The greatest in the land. He heard of our close proximity to the terrors and thought to try his luck here first—to learn what we know about the spiders; perhaps how to kill them." A faintly bemused look. "Perhaps also to find some backdoor way of reclaiming his years, an alternate route *here*, to spare him the confrontation *there*."

A sound enough plan for a man insane enough to barter away his life in the first place.

"What does any of this have to do with the stolen eggs and hatchlings, *Ej*?" Sartaq, too, apparently possessed little sympathy for the merchant who'd traded his youth for kingly wealth. Falkan turned his face toward the fire, as if well aware of that.

"I want you to find them," Houlun said.

"They have likely already died, *Ej*."

"Those horrors can keep their prey alive long enough in their cocoons.

372

But you are right—they have likely already been consumed." Rage flickered in the woman's face, a vision of the warrior beneath; the warrior her granddaughter was becoming as well. "Which is why I want you to find them the next time it happens. And remind those unholy piles of filth that we do not take kindly to theft of our young." She jerked her chin to Falkan. "When they go, you will go, too. See if the answers you seek are there."

"Why not go now?" Nesryn asked. "Why not seek them out and punish them?"

"Because we have no proof still," Sartaq answered. "And if we attack unprovoked . . ."

"The *kharankui* have long been the enemies of the ruks," Houlun finished. "They warred once, long ago. Before the riders climbed up from the steppes." She shook her head, chasing away the shadow of memory, and declared to Sartaq, "Which is why we shall keep this quiet. The last thing we need is for riders and ruks to fly out there in a rage, or fill this place with panic. Tell them to be on their guard at the nests, but do not say why."

Sartaq nodded. "As you will it, *Ej*."

The hearth-mother turned to Falkan. "I would have a word with my captain."

Falkan understood the dismissal and rose. "I am at your disposal, Prince Sartaq." With a graceful bow, he strode off into the hall.

When Falkan's steps had faded, Houlun murmured, "It is starting anew, isn't it?" Those dark eyes slid to Nesryn, the fire gilding the whites. "The One Who Sleeps has awoken."

"Erawan," Nesryn breathed. She could have sworn the great fire banked in answer.

"You know of him, *Ej*?" Sartaq moved to sit on the woman's other side, allowing Nesryn to scoot closer down the stone bench.

But the hearth-mother swept her sharp stare over Nesryn. "You have faced them. His beasts of shadow."

373

Nesryn clamped down on the memories that surfaced. "I have. He's built an army of terrors on the northern continent. In Morath."

Houlun turned toward Sartaq. "Does your father know?"

"Bits and pieces. His grief . . ." Sartaq watched the fire. Houlun placed a hand on the prince's knee. "There was an attack in Antica. On a healer of the Torre."

Houlun swore, as filthily as her hearth-son.

"We think one of Erawan's agents might be behind it," Sartaq went on. "And rather than waste time convincing my father to listen to half-formed theories, I remembered your tales, *Ej*, and thought to see if you might know anything."

"And if I told you?" A searching, sharp look—fierce as a ruk's gaze. "If I told you what I know of the threat, would you empty every aerie and nest? Would you fly across the Narrow Sea to face them—to never return?"

Sartaq's throat bobbed. And Nesryn realized that he had not come here for answers.

Perhaps Sartaq already knew enough about the Valg to decide for himself about how to face the threat. He had come here to win over his people—this woman. He might command the ruks in the eyes of his father, the empire. But in these mountains, Houlun's word was law.

And in that fourth peak, on Arundin's silent slopes . . . Her daughter's *sulde* stood in the wind. A woman who understood the cost of life—deeply. Who might not be so eager to let her granddaughter ride with the legion. If she allowed the Eridun rukhin to leave at all.

"If the *kharankui* are stirring, if Erawan has risen in the north," Sartaq said carefully, "it is a threat for all to face." He bowed his head. "But I would hear what you know, *Ej*. What perhaps even the kingdoms in the north might have lost to time and destruction. Why it is that our people, tucked away in this land, know such stories when the ancient demon wars never reached these shores."

Houlun surveyed them, her long, thick braid swaying. Then she braced a hand on the stone and rose, groaning. "I must eat first, and rest awhile.

Then I shall tell you." She frowned toward the cave mouth, the silvery sheen of sunlight staining the walls. "A storm is coming. I outran it on the flight back. Tell the others to prepare."

With that, the hearth-mother strode from the warmth of the pit and into the hall beyond. Her steps were stiff, but her back was straight. A warrior's pace, clipped and unfaltering.

But instead of aiming for the round table or the kitchens, Houlun entered a door that Nesryn had marked as leading into the small library.

"She is our Story Keeper," Sartaq explained, following Nesryn's attention. "Being around the texts helps to tunnel into her memory."

Not just a hearth-mother who knew the rukhin's history, but a sacred Story Keeper—a rare gift for remembering and telling the legends and histories of the world.

Sartaq rose, groaning himself as he stretched. "She's never wrong about a storm. We should spread the word." He pointed to the hall behind them. "You take the interior. I'll go to the other peaks and let them know."

Before Nesryn could ask who, exactly, she should approach, the prince stalked for Kadara.

She frowned. Well, it would seem that she'd only have her own thoughts for company. A merchant hunting for spiders that might help him reclaim his youth, or at least learn how he might take it back from their northern kin. And the spiders themselves . . . Nesryn shuddered to think of those things crawling here, of all places, to feed on the most vulnerable. Monsters out of legend.

Perhaps Erawan was summoning all the dark, wicked things of this world to his banner.

Rubbing her hands as if she could implant the heat of the flame into her skin, Nesryn headed into the aerie proper.

A storm was coming, she was to tell any who crossed her path.

But she knew one was already here.

The storm struck just after nightfall. Great claws of lightning ripped at the sky, and thunder shuddered through every hall and floor.

Seated around the fire pit, Nesryn glanced to the distant cave mouth, where mighty curtains had been drawn across the space. They billowed and puffed in the wind, but remained anchored to the floor, parting only slightly to allow glimpses of the rain-lashed night.

Just inside them, three ruks sat curled in what seemed to be nests of straw and cloth: Kadara, a fierce brown ruk that Nesryn had been told belonged to Houlun, and a smaller ruk with a reddish-dun coloring. The tiniest ruk belonged to Borte—a veritable runt, the girl had called her at dinner, even as she'd beamed with pride.

Nesryn stretched out her aching legs, grateful for the heat of the fire and the blanket Sartaq had dropped in her lap. She'd spent hours going up and down the aerie stairs, telling whoever she encountered that Houlun had said a storm approached.

Some had given her thankful nods and hurried off; others had offered hot tea and small samplings of whatever they were cooking in their hearths. Some asked where Nesryn had come from, why she was here. And whenever she explained that she had come from Adarlan but that her people hailed from the southern continent, their replies were all the same: *Welcome home.*

The trek up and down the various stairs and sloped halls had taken its toll, along with the hours of training that morning. And by the time Houlun settled herself on the bench between Nesryn and Sartaq—Falkan and Borte having drifted off to their own rooms after dinner—Nesryn was near nodding off.

Lightning cracked outside, limning the hall with silver. For long minutes, as Houlun stared into the fire, there was only the grumble of thunder and the howl of the wind and the patter of the rain, only the crackle of the fire and rustling of ruk's wings.

"Stormy nights are the domain of Story Keepers," Houlun intoned in Halha. "We can hear one approaching from a hundred miles away, smell

376

the charge in the air like a hound on a scent. They tell us to prepare, to ready for them. To gather our kin close and listen carefully."

The hair on Nesryn's arms rose beneath the warmth of her wool coat.

"Long ago," Houlun continued, "before the khaganate, before the horse-lords on the steppes and the Torre by the sea, before any mortal ruled these lands . . . A rip appeared in the world. In these very mountains."

Sartaq's face was unreadable as his hearth-mother spoke, but Nesryn swallowed.

A rip in the world—an open Wyrdgate. Here.

"It opened and closed swiftly, no more than a flash of lightning."

As if in answer, veins of forked lightning lit the sky beyond.

"But that was all that was needed. For the horrors to enter. The *kharankui*, and other beasts of shadow."

The words echoed through Nesryn.

The *kharankui*—the stygian spiders . . . and other infiltrators. None of them ordinary beasts at all.

But Valg.

Nesryn was grateful she was already sitting. "The Valg were *here*?" Her voice was too loud, too ordinary in the storm-filled silence.

Sartaq gave Nesryn a warning look, but Houlun only nodded, a jab of the chin. "Most of the Valg left, summoned northward when more hordes appeared there. But this place . . . perhaps the Valg that arrived here were a vanguard, who assessed this land and did not find what they were seeking. So they moved out. But the *kharankui* remained in the mountain passes, servants to a dark crown. They did not leave. The spiders learned the tongues of men as they ate the fools stupid enough to venture into their barren realm. Some who made it out claimed they remained because the Fells reminded them of their own, blasted world. Others said the spiders lingered to guard the way back—to wait for that door to open up again. And to go home.

"War waged in the east, in the ancient Fae realms. Three demon kings against a Fae Queen and her armies. Demons that passed through a door between worlds to conquer our own."

377

And so she went on, describing the story Nesryn knew well. She let the hearth-mother narrate as her mind spun.

The stygian spiders—actually Valg hiding in plain sight all this time.

Houlun went on, and Nesryn reeled herself back together until, "And yet, even when the Valg were banished to their realm, even when the final remaining demon king slithered into the dark places of the world to hide, the Fae came here. To these mountains. They taught the ruks to fight the *kharankui*, taught the ruks the languages of Fae and men. They built watchtowers along these mountains, erected warning beacons throughout the land. Were they a distant guard against the *kharankui*? Or were the Fae, too, like the spiders, waiting for that rip in the world to open again? By the time anyone thought to ask why, they had left those watchtowers and faded into memory."

Houlun paused, and Sartaq asked, "Is there . . . is there anything on how the Valg might be defeated—beyond mere battle? Any power to help us fight these new hordes Erawan has built?"

Houlun slid her gaze to Nesryn. "Ask her," she said to the prince. "She already knows."

Sartaq barely hid his ripple of shock as he leaned forward.

Nesryn breathed, "I cannot tell you. Any of you. If Morath hears a whisper of it, the sliver of hope we have is gone." The Wyrdkeys . . . she couldn't risk saying it. Even to them.

"You brought me down here on a fool's errand, then." Sharp, cold words.

"No," Nesryn insisted. "There is much we still don't know. That these spiders hail from the Valg's world, that they were *part* of the Valg army and have an outpost here as well as in the Ruhnn Mountains in the northern continent . . . Perhaps it is tied, somehow. Perhaps there is something we have not yet learned, some weakness amongst the Valg we might exploit." She studied the hall, calming her thundering heart. Fear helped no one.

Houlun glanced between them. "Most of the Fae watchtowers are gone, but some still stand in partial ruin. The closest is perhaps half a day's flight from here. Begin there—see if anything remains. Perhaps you might find an answer or two, Nesryn Faliq."

"No one has ever looked?"

"The Fae set them with traps to keep the spiders at bay. When they abandoned the towers, they left them intact. Some tried to enter—to loot, to learn. None returned."

"Is it worth the risk?" A cool question from a captain to the hearth-mother of his aerie.

Houlun's jaw clenched. "I have told you what I can—and even this is mere scraps of knowledge that have passed beyond most memories in this land. But if the *kharankui* are stirring again . . . Someone *should* go to that watchtower. Maybe you will discover something of use. Learn how the Fae fought these terrors, how they kept them at bay." A long, assessing look at Nesryn as thunder rattled the caves again. "Perhaps it will make that sliver of hope just a bit larger."

"Or get us killed," Sartaq said, frowning toward the ruks half asleep in their nests.

"Nothing valuable comes without a cost, boy," Houlun countered. "But do not linger in the watchtower after dark."

⊰ 32 ⊱

"Good," said Yrene, the heavy, solid weight of Chaol's leg braced against her shoulder while she slowly rotated it.

Spread below her on the floor of the workroom in the physicians' compound of the Torre several days later, Chaol watched her in silence. The day was already burning enough that Yrene was drenched in sweat; or would have been, if the arid climate didn't dry up the sweat before it could really soak her clothes. She could feel it, though, on her face—see it gleaming on Chaol's own, his features tight with concentration while she knelt over him.

"Your legs are responding well to the training," she observed, fingers digging into the powerful muscle of his thighs.

Yrene hadn't asked what had changed. Why he'd started going to the guards' courtyard at the palace. He hadn't explained, either.

"They are," Chaol merely answered, scrubbing his jaw. He hadn't shaved that morning. When she'd entered his suite after he'd returned from this morning's practice with the guard, he'd said he wanted to go for a ride—and to get a change in scenery for the day.

That he was so eager, so willing to see the city, to adapt to his surroundings . . . Yrene hadn't been able to say no. So they'd come here, after a meandering ride through Antica, to work in one of the quiet rooms down this hall. The rooms were all the same, each occupied by a desk, cot, and wall of cabinets, and each adorned with a solitary window that overlooked the neat rows of the sprawling herb garden. Indeed, despite the heat, the scents of rosemary, mint, and sage filled the chamber.

Chaol grunted as Yrene lowered his left leg to the cool stone floor and started on his right. Her magic was a low thrum flowing through her and into him, careful to avoid the black stain that slowly—so, so slowly—receded down his spine.

They fought against it every day. The memories devoured him, fed on him, and Yrene shoved back against them, chipping away at the darkness that pushed in to torment him.

Sometimes, she glimpsed what he endured in that whirling black pit. The pain, the rage and guilt and sorrow. But only flickers, as if they were tendrils of smoke drifting past her. And though he did not discuss what he saw, Yrene managed to push back against that dark wave. So little at a time, mere chips of stone off a boulder, but . . . better than nothing.

Closing her eyes, Yrene let her power seep into his legs like a swarm of white fireflies, finding those damaged pathways and congregating, surrounding the frayed bits that went silent during these exercises, when they should have been lit up like the rest of him.

"I've been researching," she said, opening her eyes as she rotated his leg in his hip socket. "Things ancient healers did for people with spinal injuries. There was one woman, Linqin—she was able to make a magical brace for the entire body. An invisible sort of exoskeleton that allowed the person to walk, until they could reach a healer, or if the healing was somehow unsuccessful."

Chaol cocked a brow. "I'm assuming you don't have one?"

Yrene shook her head, lowering his leg and again picking up the other to begin the next set. "Linqin only made about ten, all connected to talismans that the user could wear. They've been lost to time, along with her method of creating them. And there was another healer, Saanvi, who legend says was able to bypass the healing entirely by planting some sort of tiny, magical shard of stone in the brain—"

He cringed.

"I wasn't suggesting I experiment on you," she said, slapping his thigh. "Or need to."

A half smile tugged on his mouth. "So how did this knowledge become lost? I thought the library here contained all your records."

Yrene frowned. "Both were healers working at outposts far from the Torre. There are four throughout the continent—small centers for Torre healers to live and work. To help the people who can't make the trip here. Linqin and Saanvi were so isolated that by the time anyone remembered to fetch their records, they'd been lost. All we have now is rumor and myth."

"Do *you* keep records? Of all this?" He gestured between them.

Yrene's face heated. "Parts of it. Not when you're acting like a stubborn ass."

Again, that smile tugged on his face, but Yrene set down his leg and pulled back, though she remained kneeling on the tiles. "My point," she said, steering conversation from the journals in her room levels and levels above, "is that it *has* been done. I know it's taking us a long while, and I know you're anxious to return—"

"I am. But I'm not rushing you, Yrene." He sat up in a smooth movement. On the floor like this, he towered over her, the sheer size of him nearly overwhelming. He rotated his foot slowly—fighting for each movement as the muscles in the rest of his legs objected.

Chaol lifted his head, meeting her stare. Reading it easily. "Whoever is hunting you won't get the chance to hurt you—whether you and I finish tomorrow, or in six months."

"I know," she breathed. Kashin and his guards hadn't caught or found traces of whoever had tried to attack her. And though it had been quiet these last few nights, she'd barely slept, even in the safety of the Torre. Only exhaustion from healing Chaol granted her any measure of reprieve.

She sighed. "I think we should see Nousha again. Take another visit to the library."

His gaze turned wary. "Why?"

Yrene frowned at the open window behind them, the bright gardens and lavender bushes swaying in the sea breeze, the bees bobbing amongst them all. No sign of anyone listening nearby. "Because we still haven't asked *how* those books and scrolls wound up here."

⁓

"There are no records for acquisitions dating that far back," Nousha said in Yrene and Chaol's own tongue, her mouth a tight line of disapproval as she gazed at them over her desk.

Around them, the library was a dim hive of activity, healers and assistants flowing in and out, some whispering hello to Yrene and Nousha as they passed. Today, an orange Baast Cat lounged by the massive hearth, her beryl eyes tracking them from her spot draped over the rolled arm of a sofa.

Yrene offered Nousha her best attempt at a smile. "But maybe there's some record of why those books were even *needed* here?"

Nousha braced her dark forearms on the desk. "Some people might be wary of what knowledge they're seeking if they're being hunted—which *started* around the time you began poking into the topic."

Chaol leaned forward in his chair, teeth flashing. "Is that a threat?"

Yrene waved him off. Overprotective man. "I *know* it is dangerous— and likely tied to it. But it is *because* of that, Nousha, that any additional information about the material here, where it came from, who acquired it . . . It could be vital."

"For getting him to walk again." A dry, disbelieving statement.

Yrene didn't dare glance at Chaol.

"You can see that our progress is slow," Chaol answered tightly. "Perhaps the ancients have some sort of advice for how to make it go faster."

Nousha gave them both a look that said she wasn't buying it for a minute, but sighed at the ceiling. "As I said, there are no records here dating that far back. *But*," she added when Chaol opened his mouth, "there are rumors that out in the desert, caves exist with such information—caves this information came from. Most have been lost, but there was one in the Aksara Oasis . . ." Nousha's look turned knowing as Yrene winced. "Perhaps you should start there."

Yrene chewed on her lip as they walked from the library, Chaol keeping pace beside her.

When they were close to the Torre's main hallway, to the courtyard and horse that would take him home for the evening, he asked, "Why are you cringing?"

Yrene crossed her arms, scanning the halls around them. Quiet at this time of day, right before the dinner rush. "That oasis, Aksara. It's not exactly . . . easy to get to."

"Far?"

"No, not that. It's owned by the royals. *No one* is allowed there. It's their private refuge."

"Ah." He scratched at the shadow of stubble on his jaw. "And asking to access it outright will lead to too many questions."

"Exactly."

He studied her, eyes narrowing.

"Don't you dare suggest I use Kashin," she hissed.

Chaol lifted his hands, eyes dancing. "I wouldn't dare. Though he certainly ran the moment you snapped your fingers the other night. He's a good man."

Yrene braced her hands on her hips. "Why don't *you* invite him to a romantic interlude in the desert, then."

Chaol chuckled, trailing her as she started for the courtyard again. "I'm not versed in court intrigue, but you *do* have another palace connection."

Yrene grimaced. "Hasar." She toyed with a curl at the end of her hair. "She hasn't asked me to play spy recently. I'm not sure if I want to . . . open that door again."

"Perhaps you could convince her that a trip to the desert—an outing— would be . . . fun?"

"You want me to manipulate her like that?"

His gaze was steady. "We can find another way, if you're uncomfortable."

"No—no, it might work. It's just Hasar was *born* into this sort of thing. She might see right through me. And she's powerful enough that . . . Is it worth risking her entanglement, her anger, if we're just going on a suggestion from Nousha?"

He considered her words. In a way that only Hafiza really did. "We'll think on it. With Hasar, we'll need to proceed carefully."

Yrene stepped into the courtyard, motioning to one of the awaiting Torre guards that the lord needed his horse brought around from the stables. "I'm not a very good accomplice in intrigue," she admitted to Chaol with an apologetic smile.

He only brushed his hand against hers. "I find it refreshing."

And from the look in his eyes . . . she believed him. Enough that her cheeks heated, just a bit.

Yrene turned toward the Torre looming over them, just to buy herself some breathing room. Looked up, up, up to where her own little window gazed toward the sea. Toward home.

She lowered her gaze from the Torre to find his face grim. "I'm sorry to have brought all this upon you—all of you," Chaol said quietly.

"Don't be. Perhaps that's what it wants. To use fear and guilt to end this—stop us." She studied him, the proud lift of his chin, the strength he radiated in every breath. "Though . . . I do worry that time is not on our side." Yrene amended, "Take all the time you need to heal. Yet . . ." She rubbed at her chest. "I have a feeling we have not seen the last of that hunter."

Chaol nodded, his jaw tight. "We'll deal with it."

And that was that. Together—they'd deal with it together.

Yrene smiled slightly at him as the light steps of his horse approached on the pale gravel.

And the thought of climbing back to her room, the thought of hours spent fretting . . .

Maybe it made her pathetic, but Yrene blurted, "Would you like to stay for dinner? Cook will mope that you didn't say hello."

She knew it was not mere fear that spurred her. Knew that she just wanted to spend a few more minutes with him. Talk to him in a way that she so rarely did with anyone else.

For a long moment, Chaol only watched her. As if she were the only person in the world. She braced herself for the refusal, the distance. Knew she should have just let him ride off into the night.

"What if we ventured out for dinner instead?"

"You mean—in the city?" She pointed toward the open gates.

"Unless you think the chair in the streets—"

"The walkways are even." Her heart hammered. "Do you have any preference for what to eat?"

A border—this was some strange border that they were crossing. To leave their neutral territories and emerge into the world beyond, not as healer and patient, but woman and man—

"I'll try anything," Chaol said, and she knew he meant it. And from the way he looked to the open gates of the Torre, to the city just starting to glow beyond . . . She knew he *wanted* to try anything; was as eager for a distraction from that shadow looming over them as she herself was.

So Yrene signaled to the guards that they didn't need his horse. Not for a while yet. "I know just the place."

⌒

Some people stared; some were too busy going about their business or journeys home to remark on Chaol as he wheeled his chair alongside Yrene.

She had to step in only a few times, to help him over the bump of a curve, or down one of the steep streets. She led him to a place five blocks away, the establishment like nothing he'd seen in Rifthold. He'd visited a few private dining rooms with Dorian, yes, but those had been for the elite, for members and their guests.

This place . . . it was akin to those private clubs, in that it was *only* for eating, full of tables and carved wooden chairs, but this was open to anyone, like the public rooms at an inn or tavern. The front of the pale-stoned building had several sets of doors that were open to the night, leading out onto a patio full of more tables and chairs under the stars, the space jutting into the street itself so that diners could watch the passing city bustle, even glimpse down the sloping street to the dark sea sparkling under the moonlight.

And the enticing smells coming from within: garlic, something tangy, something smoky . . .

Yrene murmured to the woman who came to greet them, which must have amounted to a table for two and without one chair, because within a moment, he was being led to the street-patio, where a servant discreetly removed one of the chairs at a small table for him to pull up to the edge.

Yrene claimed a seat opposite him, more than a few heads turning their way. Not to gawk at him, but her.

The Torre healer.

She didn't seem to notice. The servant returned to rattle off what had to be the menu, and Yrene ordered in her halting Halha.

She bit her lower lip, glancing to the table, the public dining room. "Is this all right?"

Chaol took in the open sky above them, the color bleeding to a sapphire blue, the stars beginning to blink awake. When had he last relaxed? Eaten a meal not to keep his body healthy and alive, but to *enjoy* it?

He grappled for the words. Grappled to settle into the ease. "I've never done anything like this," he at last admitted.

His birthday this past winter, in that greenhouse—even then, with Aelin, he'd been half there, half focused on the palace he'd left behind, on remembering who was in charge and where Dorian was supposed to be. But now . . .

"What—eaten a meal?"

"Had a meal when I wasn't . . . Had a meal when I was just . . . Chaol."

He wasn't sure if he'd explained it right, if he could articulate it—

Yrene angled her head, her mass of hair sliding over a shoulder. "Why?"

"Because I was either a lord's son and heir, or Captain of the Guard, or now Hand to the King." Her gaze was unflinching as he fumbled to explain. "No one recognizes me here. No one has ever even heard of Anielle. And it's . . ."

"Liberating?"

"Refreshing," he countered, giving Yrene a small smile at the echo to his earlier words.

She blushed prettily in the golden light from the lanterns within the dining room behind them. "Well . . . good."

"And you? Do you go out with friends often—leave the healer behind?"

Yrene watched the people streaming by. "I don't have many friends," she admitted. "Not because I don't want them," she blurted, and he smiled. "I just—at the Torre, we're all busy. Sometimes, a few of us will go for a meal or drink, but our schedules rarely align, and it's easier to eat at the mess hall, so . . . we're not really a lively bunch. Which was why

388

Kashin and Hasar became my friends—when they're in Antica. But I've never really had the chance to do much of this."

He almost asked, *Go out to dinner with men?* But said, "You had your focus elsewhere."

She nodded. "And maybe one day—maybe I'll have the time to go out and enjoy myself, but . . . there are people who need my help. It feels selfish to take time for myself, even now."

"You shouldn't feel that way."

"And you're any better?"

Chaol chuckled, leaning back as the servant came, bearing a pitcher of chilled mint tea. He waited until the man left before saying, "Maybe you and I will have to learn how to live—if we survive this war."

It was a sharp, cold knife between them. But Yrene straightened her shoulders, her smile small and yet defiant as she lifted her pewter glass of tea. "To living, Lord Chaol."

He clinked his glass against hers. "To being Chaol and Yrene—even just for a night."

Chaol ate until he could barely move, the spices like small revelations with every bite.

They talked as they dined, Yrene explaining her initial months at the Torre, and how demanding her training had been. Then she'd asked about his training as captain, and he'd balked—balked at talking of Brullo and the others, and yet . . . He couldn't refuse her joy, her curiosity.

And somehow, talking about Brullo, the man who had been a better father to him than his own . . . It did not hurt, not as much. A lower, quieter ache, but one he could withstand.

One he was glad to weather, if it meant honoring a good man's legacy by telling his story.

So they talked, and ate, and when they finished, he escorted her to the glowing white walls of the Torre. Yrene herself seemed glowing as she smiled when they stopped within the gates while his horse was readied.

"Thank you," she said, her cheeks flushed and gleaming. "For the meal—and company."

"It was my pleasure," Chaol said, and meant it.

"I'll see you tomorrow morning—at the palace?"

An unnecessary question, but he nodded.

Yrene shifted from one foot to another, still smiling, still shining. As if she were the last, vibrant ray of the sun, staining the sky long after it had vanished over the horizon.

"What?" she asked, and he realized he'd been staring.

"Thank you for tonight," Chaol said, stifling what tried to leap off his tongue: *I can't take my eyes off you.*

She bit her lip again, the crunch of hooves on gravel approaching. "Good night," she murmured, and took a step away.

Chaol reached out. Just to brush his fingers over hers.

Yrene paused, her fingers curling, as if they were the petals of some shy flower.

"Good night," he merely said.

And as Chaol rode back to the illuminated palace across the city, he could have sworn that some weight in his chest, on his shoulders, had vanished. As if he'd lived with it his entire life, unaware, and now, even with all that gathered around him, around Adarlan and those he cared for . . . How strange it felt.

That lightness.

⊰ 33 ⊱

The Watchtower of Eidolon jutted up from the mist-shrouded pines like the shard of a broken sword. It had been situated atop a low-lying peak that overlooked a solid wall of gargantuan mountains, and as Nesryn and Sartaq swept near the tower, sailing along the tree-crusted hills, she had the sense of racing toward a tidal wave of hard stone.

For a heartbeat, a wave of lethal glass swept for her instead. She blinked, and it was gone.

"There," Sartaq whispered, as if fearful that any might hear while he pointed toward the enormous mountains lurking beyond. "Over that lip, that is the start of *kharankui* territory, the Dagul Fells. Those in the watchtower would have been able to see anyone coming down from those mountains, especially with their Fae sight."

Fae sight or not, Nesryn scanned the barren slopes of the Fells—a wall of boulders and shards of rock. No trees, no streams. As if life had fled. "Houlun flew over *that*?"

"Believe me," Sartaq grumbled, "I am not pleased. Borte got an earful about it this morning."

"I'm surprised your kneecaps still function."

"Didn't you notice my limp earlier?"

Despite the nearing watchtower, despite the wall of mountain that rose up beyond it, Nesryn chuckled. She could have sworn Sartaq leaned closer, his broad chest pushing into the quiver and bow she had strapped across her back, along with the twin long knives courtesy of Borte.

They hadn't told anyone where they were going or what they sought, which had earned no shortage of glares from Borte over breakfast, and curious glances from Falkan across the round table. But they had agreed last night, when Sartaq left Nesryn at her bedroom door, that secrecy was vital—for now.

So they'd departed an hour after dawn, armed and bearing a few packs of supplies. Even though they planned to be headed home well before sunset, Nesryn had insisted on bringing their gear. Should the worst happen, should *anything* happen, it was better to be prepared.

Borte, despite her ire at being left in the dark, had braided Nesryn's hair after breakfast—a tight, elegant plait starting at the crown of her head and landing just where her cape fell to cover her flying leathers. The braid was tight enough that Nesryn had avoided the urge to loosen it these hours that they'd flown, but now that the tower was in sight and her hair had barely shifted, Nesryn supposed the braid could stay.

Kadara circled the watchtower twice, dropping lower with each pass.

"No signs of webs," Nesryn observed. The upper levels of the watchtower had been destroyed by weather or some long-ago passing army, leaving only two floors above the ground. Both were exposed to the elements, the winding stairwell in the center coated in pine needles and dirt. Broken beams and blocks of stone also littered it, but no indications of life. Or any sort of miraculously preserved library.

With Kadara's size, the ruk had to find a clearing nearby to land, since Sartaq didn't trust the watchtower walls to hold her. The bird leaped into the air as soon as they'd begun the climb up the small incline to the watchtower proper. She'd circle overhead until Sartaq whistled for her, apparently.

Another trick of the rukhin and the Darghan on the steppes: the whistling, along with their whistling arrows. They had long allowed both peoples to communicate in a way that few noticed or bothered to comprehend, passing messages through enemy territory or down army lines. The riders had trained the ruks to understand the whistles, too—to know a call for help from a warning to flee.

Nesryn prayed with each grueling step through the thick pine trees and granite boulders that they would only need the whistle to summon the bird. She was no great tracker, but Sartaq, it seemed, was deftly reading the signs around them.

A shake of the prince's head told Nesryn enough: no hint of a presence, arachnid or otherwise. She tried not to look too relieved. Despite the tall trees, the Fells were a solid, looming presence to her right, drawing the eye even as it repelled every instinct.

Blocks of stone greeted them first. Great, rectangular chunks, half buried in the pine needles and soil. The full weight of summer lay upon the land, yet the air was cool, the shade beneath the trees outright chilly.

"I don't blame them for abandoning it if it's this cold in the summer," Nesryn muttered. "Imagine it in winter."

Sartaq smiled but pressed a finger to his lips as they cleared the last of the trees. Blushing that he'd needed to remind her, Nesryn unslung her bow and nocked an arrow, letting it hang limply while they tipped back their heads to take in the tower.

It must have been enormous, thousands of years ago, if the ruins were enough to make her feel small. Any barracks or living quarters had long since tumbled away or rotted, but the stone archway into the tower itself remained intact, flanked by twin statues of some sort of weather-worn bird.

Sartaq approached, his long knife gleaming like quicksilver in the watery light as he studied the statues. "Ruks?" The question was a mere breath.

Nesryn squinted. "No—look at the face. The beak. They're . . . owls." Tall, slender owls, their wings tucked in tight. The symbol of Silba, of the Torre.

Sartaq's throat bobbed. "Let's be swift. I don't think it's wise to linger."

Nesryn nodded, one eye behind them as they slipped through the open archway. It was a familiar position, the rearguard—in Rifthold's sewers, she'd often let Chaol stalk ahead while she covered behind, arrow aimed into the darkness at their backs. So her body acted on pure muscle memory while Sartaq took the first steps through the archway and she twisted back, arrow aimed at the pine forest, scanning the trees.

Nothing. Not a bird or rustle of wind through the pines.

She turned a heartbeat later, assessing efficiently, as she had always done, even before her training: marking exits, pitfalls, possible sanctuaries. But there wasn't much to note in the ruin.

The tower floor was well lit thanks to the vanished ceiling above, the crumbling staircase leading into the gray sky. Slits in the stone revealed where archers might have once positioned themselves—or watched from within the warmth of a tower on a freezing day. "Nothing up," Nesryn observed perhaps a bit uselessly, facing Sartaq just as he took a step toward an open archway leading down into a dark stairwell. She grabbed his elbow. "Don't."

He gave her an incredulous look over his shoulder.

Nesryn kept her own face like stone. "Your *ej* said these towers were laid with traps. Just because we have yet to see one does not mean they are not still here." She pointed with her arrow toward the open archway to the levels belowground. "We keep quiet, tread carefully. I go first."

To hell with being the rearguard, if he was prone to plunging into danger.

The prince's eyes flared, but she didn't let him object. "I faced some of the horrors of Morath this spring and summer. I know how to mark them—and where to strike."

Sartaq looked her over again. "You really should have been promoted."

Nesryn smiled, releasing his muscled bicep. Wincing as she realized the liberties she'd taken by grabbing him, touching a prince without permission—

"Two captains, remember?" he said, noting the cringe she failed to hide.

Indeed. Nesryn inclined her head and stepped in front of him—and into the archway of the stairs leading below.

Her arm strained as she pulled the bowstring taut, scanning the darkness immediately beyond the stairwell entrance. When nothing leaped out, she slackened the bow, placed her arrow back in the quiver, and plucked up a handful of rocks from the ground, shards and chips from the felled blocks of stone around them.

A step behind, Sartaq did the same, filling his pockets with them.

Listening carefully, Nesryn rolled one of the rocks down the spiral stairs, letting it bounce and crack and—

A faint *click*, and Nesryn hurled herself back, slamming into Sartaq and sending them both sprawling to the ground. A thud sounded within the stairwell below, then another.

In the quiet that followed, her heavy breathing the only sound, she listened again. "Hidden bolts," she observed, wincing as she found Sartaq's face mere inches away. His eyes were upon the stairwell, even as he kept a hand on her back, the other angling his long knife toward the archway.

"Seems I owe you my life, Captain," Sartaq said, and Nesryn quickly peeled back, offering a hand to help him rise. He clasped it, his hand warm around hers as she hauled him to his feet.

"Don't worry," Nesryn said drily. "I won't tell Borte." She plucked up another handful of rocks and sent them rolling and scattering down the gloom of the stairs. A few more clicks and thumps—then silence.

"We go slow," she said, all amusement fading, and didn't wait for his nod as she prodded the first step down with the tip of her bow.

She tapped and pushed along the stair, watching the walls, the ceiling. Nothing. She did it to the second, third, and fourth steps—as far as her bow could reach. And only when she was satisfied that no surprises waited did she allow them to step onto the stairs.

Nesryn repeated it with the next four steps, finding nothing. But when they reached the first turn of the spiral stairs . . ."I *really* owe you my life," Sartaq breathed as they beheld what had been fired from a slit in the wall at the ninth step.

Barbed iron spikes. Designed to slam into flesh and stay there—unless the victim wanted to rip out more of their skin or organs on the curved, vicious hooks on the way out.

The spike had been fired so hard that it had sunk deep into the mortar between the stones. "Remember that these traps were not for human assailants," she breathed.

But for spiders as large as horses. Who could speak, and plan, and remember.

She tapped the steps ahead, the wood of her bow a hollow echo through the dark chamber, prodding the slit where the bolt had been fired. "The Fae must have memorized what stairs to avoid while living here," she observed as they cleared another few feet. "I don't think they were stupid enough to do an easy pattern, though."

Indeed, the next bolt had emerged three steps down. The one after that, five apart. But after that . . . Sartaq reached into his pocket and pulled out another handful of stones. They both squatted as he rolled a few down the stairs.

Click.

Nesryn was so focused on the wall ahead that she didn't consider where the click had come from. Not in front, but below.

One heartbeat, she was crouched on a step.

The next, it had slid away beneath her feet, a black pit yawning open beneath—

Strong hands wrapped around her shoulder, her collar, a blade clattering on stone—

Nesryn scrabbled for the lip of the nearest stair as Sartaq held her, grunting at her weight, his long knife tumbling into the blackness beneath.

Metal hit metal. Bounced off it again and again, the clanking filling the stairwell.

Spikes. Likely a field of metal spikes—

Sartaq hauled her up, and her nails cracked on stone as she grappled for purchase on the smooth step. But then she was up, half sprawled on the stairs between Sartaq's legs, both of them panting as they peered to the gap beyond.

"I think we're even," Nesryn said, fighting and failing to master her shaking.

The prince clasped her shoulder, while his other hand brushed down the back of her head. A comforting, casual touch. "Whoever built this place had no mercy for the *kharankui*."

It took her another minute to stop trembling. Sartaq patiently waited, stroking her hair, fingers rippling over the ridges of Borte's braid. She let him, leaned into the touch while she studied the gap they'd now have to jump, the stairs still beyond.

When she could at last stand without her knees clacking together, they carefully jumped the hole—and made it several more steps before another one appeared, this time accompanied by a bolt. But they kept going, the minutes dripping by, until they at last reached the level below.

Shafts of pale light shone from carefully hidden holes in the ground above, or perhaps through some mirror contraption in the passageways high above. She didn't care, so long as the light was bright enough to see by.

And see they did.

The bottom level was a dungeon.

Five cells lay open, the doors ripped off, prisoners and guards long gone. A rectangular stone table lay in the center.

"Anyone who thinks the Fae are prancing creatures given to poetry and singing needs a history lesson," Sartaq murmured as they lingered on the bottom step, not daring to touch the floor. "That stone table was not used for writing reports or dining."

Indeed, dark stains still marred the surface. But a worktable lay against the nearby wall, scattered with an assortment of weapons. Any papers had long ago melted away in the snow and rain, and any leather-bound books . . . also gone.

"Do we risk it, or leave?" Sartaq mused.

"We've come this far," Nesryn said. She squinted toward the far wall. "There—there is some writing there." Near the floor, in dark lettering—a tangle of script.

The prince just reached into his pockets, casting more stones throughout the space. No clicks or groans answered. He chucked a few at the ceiling, at the walls. Nothing.

"Good enough for me," Nesryn said.

Sartaq nodded, though they both tested each block of stone with the tip of the bow or his fine, thin sword. They made it past the stone table, and Nesryn did not bother to examine the various instruments that had been discarded.

She'd seen Chaol's men hanging from the castle gates. Had seen the marks on their bodies.

Sartaq paused at the worktable, sorting through the weapons there. "Some of these are still sharp," he observed, and Nesryn approached as he pulled a long dagger from its sheath. The watery sunlight caught in the blade, dancing along the markings carved down the center.

Nesryn reached for a short-sword, the leather scabbard nearly crumbling beneath her hand. She brushed away the ancient dirt from the hilt, revealing shining dark metal inlaid with swirls of gold, the cross-guard curving slightly at its ends.

The scabbard was indeed so old that it fell apart as she lifted the sword, its weight light despite its size, the balance perfect. More markings had been engraved down the fuller of the blade. A name or a prayer, perhaps.

"Only Fae blades could remain this sharp after a thousand years," said Sartaq, setting down the knife he'd been inspecting. "Likely forged by the Fae smiths in Asterion, to the east of Doranelle—perhaps even before the first of the demon wars."

A prince who had studied not only his own empire's history, but that of many others.

History was certainly not her strongest subject, so she asked, "Asterion—like the horses?"

"One and the same. Great smiths and horse-breeders. Or so it once was—before borders closed and the world darkened."

Nesryn studied the short-sword in her hand, the metal shining as if imbued with starlight, interrupted only by the carvings down the fuller. "I wonder what the markings say."

Sartaq examined another blade, shards of light bouncing over the planes of his handsome face. "Likely spells against enemies; perhaps even against the—" He halted at the word.

Nesryn nodded all the same. The Valg. "Half of me hopes we never have to find out." Leaving Sartaq to pick one for himself, she fastened the short-sword to her belt as she approached the far wall and the scribbled dark writing along the bottom.

She tested each block of stone on the floor, but found nothing.

At last, she peered at the script in flaking black letters. Not black, but—

"Blood," Sartaq said, coming up beside her, an Asterion knife now at his side.

No sign of a body, or any lingering effects of whoever had written it, perhaps while they lay dying.

"It's in the Fae tongue," Nesryn said. "I don't suppose your fancy tutors taught you the Old Language during your history lessons?"

A shake of the head.

She sighed. "We should find a way to write it down. Unless your memory is the sort that—"

"It's not." He swore, turning toward the stairs. "I have some paper and ink in Kadara's saddlebags. I could—"

It wasn't his cut-off words that made her whirl. But the way he went utterly still.

Nesryn slid that Fae blade free from where she'd tied it.

"There is no need to translate it," said a light female voice in Halha. "It says, *Look up*. Pity you didn't heed it."

Nesryn indeed looked up at what emerged from the stairwell, crawling along the ceiling toward them, and swallowed her scream.

❧ 34 ❧

It was worse than Nesryn had ever dreamed.

The *kharankui* that slid from the ceiling and onto the floor was so much worse.

Bigger than a horse. Her skin was black and gray, mottled with splotches of white, her multiple eyes depthless pools of obsidian. And despite her bulk, she was slender and sleek—more black widow than wolf spider.

"Those Fae morsels forgot to *look up* when they built this place," the spider said, her voice so lovely despite her utter monstrosity. Her long front legs clicked against the ancient stone. "To remember who they laid these traps for."

Nesryn sized up the stairwell behind the spider, the light shafts, for any exits. Found none.

And this watchtower had now become a veritable web. Fool; utter fool for lingering—

The claws at the tops of the spider's legs scraped over the rock.

Nesryn sheathed her sword again.

"Good," the spider purred. "Good that you know how useless that Fae rubbish will be."

Nesryn drew her bow, nocking an arrow.

The spider laughed. "If Fae archers did not halt me long ago, human, you will not now."

Beside her, Sartaq's sword lifted a fraction.

Dying here, now, had not occurred to her at breakfast while Borte braided her hair.

But there was nothing to do as the spider advanced, fangs slipping from her jaws.

"When I am done with you, rider, I shall make your bird scream." Drops of liquid plopped from those fangs. Venom.

Then the spider lunged.

Nesryn fired an arrow, another aimed before her first found its mark. But the spider moved so swiftly that the blow intended for an eye hit the hard shell of her abdomen, barely embedding. The spider slammed into the stone torture table, as if she'd leap off to pounce on them—

Sartaq struck, a brutal slash toward the nearest clawed leg.

The spider shrieked, black blood spurting, and they hurtled for that distant doorway—

The *kharankui* intercepted them first. Slammed her legs between the wall and the stone table, blocking their path. So close, the reek of death leaking from those fangs—

"Human filth," the spider spat, venom spraying onto the stones at their feet.

From the corner of her eye, Nesryn saw Sartaq fling an arm in her path, to shove her away, to leap in front of those deadly jaws—

She didn't know what happened at first.

What the blur of motion was, what made the *kharankui* scream.

One heartbeat, she'd been ready to fight past Sartaq's self-sacrificing idiocy, the next . . . the spider was crashing through the room, tumbling over and over.

Not Kadara, but something large, armed with claws and fangs—

A gray wolf. As large as a pony, and utterly ferocious.

Sartaq wasted no time, and neither did Nesryn. They sprinted for the archway and stairs beyond, not caring how many bolts or arrows shot from the walls as they outraced even the traps. Tearing up the stairs, leaping the gaps between them, they did not stop at the crashing and screeching below—

A canine yelp sounded, then silence.

Nesryn and Sartaq hit the top of the stairs, running for the trees beyond the open doorway. The prince had a hand on her back, shoving her along, both of them half turned toward the tower.

The spider exploded from the gloom, aiming not for the trees, but the upper stairs of the watchtower. As if she'd climb up to ambush the wolf when it chased after her.

And exactly as she'd planned, the wolf flew from the stairwell, heading for the open archway to the woods, not even looking behind.

The spider leaped. Gold flashed from the skies.

Kadara's war cry sent the pines trembling, her claws ripping right into the abdomen of the *kharankui* and sending her toppling off the stairs.

The wolf darted away as Sartaq's roar of warning to his ruk was swallowed by the screaming of bird and spider. The *kharankui* landed on her back, precisely where Kadara wanted her.

Leaving her underbelly exposed to the ruk's talons. And her blade-sharp beak.

A few vicious slashes, black blood spraying and sleek limbs flailing, and—silence.

Nesryn's bow dangled from her shaking hands as Kadara dismembered the twitching spider. She whirled to Sartaq, but his eyes were turned away. To the wolf.

She knew. Right as the wolf limped toward them, a deep gash in its side, and she beheld its dark sapphire eyes.

Knew what it was, *who* it was, as the edges of his gray coat shimmered, his entire body filling with light that shrank and flowed.

And when Falkan waved on his feet before them, a hand pressed to the bloody wound in his ribs, Nesryn breathed, "You're a shape-shifter."

⊰ 35 ⊱

Falkan dropped to his knees, pine needles scattering, blood dribbling between his tan fingers.

Nesryn made to rush to him, but Sartaq blocked her with an arm. "Don't," he warned.

Nesryn shoved his arm out of her way and ran to the injured man, kneeling before him. "You followed us here."

Falkan lifted his head, pain lining his eyes. "I listened last night. At your fire."

Sartaq snarled, "No doubt as some rat or insect."

Something like shame indeed filled Falkan's face. "I flew here as a falcon—saw you go in. Then saw *her* creep up the hill after you." He shuddered as he glanced to where Kadara had finished ripping apart the spider and now sat atop the tower, studying *him* as if he were her next meal.

Nesryn waved toward the bird to hop down with their saddlebags. Kadara pointedly ignored her. "He needs help," she hissed to Sartaq. "Bandages."

"Does my *ej* know?" was all the prince demanded.

Falkan tried and failed to remove his blood-soaked hand from his side, panting through his teeth. "Yes," he managed to say. "I told her everything."

"And what court paid you to come here?"

"*Sartaq.*" She'd never heard him speak that way, never seen him so *furious*. She grabbed the prince's arm. "He saved our lives. Now we return the favor." She pointed to the ruk. "Bandages."

Sartaq turned those livid eyes on her. "His kind are assassins and spies," he snarled. "Better to let him die."

"I am neither," Falkan panted. "I am what I said: a merchant. In Adarlan, growing up, I didn't even *know* I had the gift. It—it ran in my family, but by the time magic vanished, I'd assumed I hadn't gotten it. Was *glad* for it. But I must not have matured enough, because when I set foot in these lands as a man, as *this* . . ." A gesture to his body. To the twenty years he'd given up. He winced against what the movement did to his wound. "I could use it. I could change. Badly, and not often, but I can manage it, if I concentrate." He said to the prince, "It is nothing to me, this heritage. It was my brother's gift, my father's—I never wanted it. I still don't."

"Yet you can change from bird to wolf to man as easily as if you trained."

"Trust me, it's more than I've done in my—" Falkan groaned, swaying.

Nesryn caught him before he could eat dirt, and snapped at Sartaq, "If you don't get him bandages and supplies right now, I'll give you a wound to match."

The prince blinked at her, mouth falling open.

Then he whistled through his teeth, sharp and swift, while he strode for Kadara, his steps clipped.

The ruk hopped from the tower to land upon one of the owl statues anchored into the archway walls, stone cracking beneath her.

"I am no assassin," Falkan insisted, still shaking. "I've met a few, but I'm not one."

"I believe you," Nesryn said, and meant it. Sartaq hauled the packs off Kadara, searching through them. "*The left one*," she barked. The prince threw her another look over his shoulder, but obeyed.

"I wanted to kill her myself," Falkan panted, his eyes glazing, no doubt from blood loss. "To see if . . . that might return the years. Even . . . even if she is not the one who took my youth, I thought maybe there was some . . . joint system between them, even across oceans. A web, as it were, of all that their kind has taken." A bitter, strained laugh. "But it seems my death blow was taken, too."

"I think we can all forgive Kadara for doing it instead," Nesryn said, noting the black blood splattered over the ruk's beak and feathers.

Another pained laugh. "You are not scared—of what I am."

Sartaq strode over with the bandages and salve. And what seemed to be a jar of a honey-like substance, to likely seal the wound until they could reach a healer. Good.

"One of my friends is a shifter," Nesryn admitted—just as Falkan fainted in her arms.

⁓

They were airborne within minutes of Nesryn cleaning out the gash down Falkan's ribs and Sartaq indeed packing the wound with what seemed to be some sort of leaves and a coating of honey. To keep infection away and stave the blood loss as they swiftly soared back to the aerie.

She and the prince barely spoke, though with Falkan propped behind them, the ride didn't afford much opportunity. It was a tight, perilous flight, Falkan's dead weight occasionally listing far enough to the side that Sartaq had to grunt at holding him in the saddle. There were only two sets of buckles, he'd told Nesryn when they climbed onto the saddle. He wasn't wasting either of their lives on a shifter, life debt or no.

But they made it, just as the sun was setting and the three peaks of the Dorgos were aglow with countless fires, like the mountains were crusted in fireflies.

Kadara loosed a shrill scream as they neared the Mountain-Hall of Altun. Some sort of signal, apparently, because by the time they landed, Borte, Houlun, and countless others were gathered, armed with supplies.

No one asked what happened to Falkan. No one wondered how he'd gotten out there. Either under order from Houlun not to pester them or simply from the chaos of getting him off the ruk and into a healer's care. No one, except Borte.

Sartaq was still fuming enough that he led his *ej* to a corner of the hall to begin demanding answers about the shifter. Or that's what it seemed like, with his set jaw and crossed arms.

Houlun only squared off against him, feet braced on the floor, her jaw as tight as his.

Alone with Kadara, Nesryn set to unbuckling the packs while Borte observed from a few feet away, "That he has the balls to lecture *her* tells me something went *very* wrong. And that she is allowing him to do so tells me she feels just a smidge guilty."

Nesryn didn't answer, grunting as she hauled down a particularly heavy pack.

Borte strode around Kadara, looking the bird over. Carefully.

"Black blood on her talons, her beak, and chest. Lots of black blood."

Nesryn dumped the pack against the wall.

"And *your* back is crusted in red blood."

From where Falkan had leaned against her during the ride.

"And that is a new blade. A *Fae blade*," Borte breathed, stepping up to examine the naked blade dangling from her sword belt. Nesryn backed up a step.

Borte's mouth tightened. "Whatever you know, I want to know it."

"It's not my call."

They glanced toward Sartaq, who was still seething, Houlun simply letting him vent.

Borte began rattling off items on her fingers. "*Ej* sails off on her own for days. Then you go, returning with a man who did not leave with you and who took no ruk. And poor Kadara returns covered in this . . . foulness." A sniff toward the black blood. The ruk clicked her beak in answer.

"It's mud," Nesryn lied.

Borte laughed. "And I'm a Fae Princess. Either I can start asking around, or—"

Nesryn dragged her to the wall with the packs. "Even if I tell you, you are *not* to breathe a word of it to anyone. Or be involved in any way."

Borte put a hand on her heart. "I swear it."

Nesryn sighed toward the distant, rocky ceiling, Kadara giving her a warning look as if to ask her to reconsider her judgment. But Nesryn told Borte everything.

She should have listened to Kadara. Borte, to her credit, did not tell anyone else. Other than Sartaq, who at last stalked over from Houlun, only to receive an earful and a smack on the shoulder for not informing his hearth-sister where he was going. And worse, for not *inviting* her along.

Sartaq had glared at Nesryn when he realized who'd told Borte, but she was too tired to care. Instead she only strode for her room, weaving between the pillars. She knew Sartaq was on her heels thanks to Borte's shouted, "*You will bring me next time, you stubborn ass!*"

And just before Nesryn reached the door to her room, to the sanctuary of a soft bed, the prince gripped her elbow. "I would have words with you."

Nesryn just shoved into the room, Sartaq stalking in behind her. Shutting the door and leaning against it. He crossed his arms at the same moment she did.

"Borte threatened to ask pointed questions around the aerie if I didn't tell her."

"I don't care."

Nesryn blinked. "Then what—"

"Who has the Wyrdkeys?" The question echoed between them.

Nesryn swallowed. "What's a Wyrdkey?"

Sartaq pushed off the door. "Liar," he breathed. "While we were gone, my *ej* recalled some of the other stories, dragged them up from whatever collective memory she possesses as Story Keeper. Tales of a Wyrdgate that the Valg and their kings passed through—could open at will with three keys when wielded together. Remembered that those keys went *missing*, after Maeve herself stole them and used them to send the Valg back. Hidden, she says. Throughout the world."

Nesryn only lifted a brow. "And what of it?"

A cold snort. "It is how Erawan has raised an army so quickly, why even Aelin of the Wildfire cannot take him on without assistance. He must have at least one. Not all, or we'd be calling Erawan our master already. But at least one, maybe two. So where is the third?"

She honestly had not a clue. Whether Aelin and the others possessed an inkling, they'd never told her. Only that their ultimate path, beyond war and death, was to retrieve the ones Erawan held. But even telling him that . . .

"Perhaps now you understand," Nesryn said with equal cold, "why we are so desperate for your father's armies."

"To be slaughtered."

"When Erawan is done slaughtering us, he will come to your doorstep next."

Sartaq swore. "What I saw today, that *thing* . . ." He scrubbed his face with shaking hands. "The Valg once used those spiders as foot soldiers. Legions of them." He lowered his hands. "Houlun has learned of three other watchtowers in ruin—to the south. We'll fly to the first as soon as the shifter is healed."

"We're taking Falkan?"

Sartaq yanked open the door, hard enough that she was surprised he didn't rip it clean off its hinges. "As piss-poor of a shifter as he claims to be, a man who can change into a wolf that big is too good a weapon not to bring into danger." A sharp glare. "He rides with me."

"And where will I be?"

Sartaq gave her a humorless smile before entering the hall. "You'll be flying with Borte."

❧ 36 ❧

The atrophying in his legs . . . It was reversing.

Three weeks later, Yrene marveled at it. They'd regained movement up through his knee, but not higher. Chaol could bend his legs now, but couldn't move his thighs. Couldn't stand on them.

But the morning workouts with the guards, the afternoons spent healing, tangled in darkness and memory and pain . . .

That was muscle, packing back onto his legs. Filling out those already-broad shoulders and that impressive chest. Thanks to training in the morning sun, his tan had deepened to a rich brown, the color lying well over arms rippling with muscle.

They worked every day in easy rhythm, settling into a routine that became as much a part of Yrene as washing her face and cleaning her teeth and craving a cup of *kahve* when she woke.

He'd joined her again at the defense lessons, the youngest acolytes still hopelessly giggly around him, but at least they'd never once been late since he'd arrived. He'd even taught Yrene herself new maneuvers regarding taking on larger assailants. And while there were often smiles aplenty in the Torre courtyard, he and Yrene were grave as he walked her through those methods, as they considered when she might need them.

But there had been no whisper of whoever had attacked her—no confirmation that it was indeed one of the Valg. A small mercy, Yrene supposed.

But still she paid attention in his lessons, and still Chaol carefully trained her.

The royal siblings had come and gone and come back again, and she had seen nothing of Kashin beyond the dinner where she'd sought him out to thank him for his help and generosity the night of the attack. He'd said it was unnecessary, but she had touched his shoulder in thanks anyway. Before taking her seat at the safety of Chaol's side.

Chaol's own, separate cause with the khagan . . . Chaol and Yrene didn't risk talking about the war—the need for armies. And the Aksara Oasis and well of knowledge, which might be hidden away beneath the palms, regarding why this place *had* such information on the Valg . . . Neither of them had come up with a way to manipulate Hasar into bringing them without raising her suspicions. Without risking the princess becoming aware of those scrolls Yrene and Chaol still had hidden in his room.

But Yrene knew time pressed on him. Saw how his eyes sometimes turned distant, as if staring toward a far-off land. Remembering the friends who fought there. For their people. He'd always push himself harder after that—and each inch of movement gained in his legs was as much due to himself as it was to her own magic.

But Yrene pushed herself, too. Wondered if the battles had begun; wondered if she'd ever make it in time to even help. Wondered what might be left for her to return to.

The darkness they encountered when she did heal him, from the demon that had dwelled inside the man who had destroyed so much of the world . . . They worked through that, too. She had not been dragged

413

into his memories as she had before, had not been forced to witness the horrors of Morath or endure the attentions of the *thing* that lingered in him, but her magic still shoved against that wound, swarming it like a thousand dots of white light, eating and gobbling and clawing at it.

He endured the pain, wading through whatever that darkness showed him. Never recoiling from it, day after day. Only stopping when her own strength flagged and he insisted Yrene break for food or a nap on the gold couch or just some conversation over chilled tea.

Yrene supposed that their steady pace had to end at some point.

She thought it'd likely be due to an argument between them. Not news from afar.

The khagan returned to the nightly formal dinner, after two weeks away at a seaside estate to escape the summer heat, ensconced with his still-mourning wife. A merry gathering—or so it had seemed from afar. With no further attacks in the palace or Torre, the hushed watchfulness had lifted considerably these last few weeks.

But as Yrene and Chaol entered the great hall, as she read the simmering tension along those seated at the high table, she debated telling him to leave. Viziers shifted in their seats. Arghun, who had certainly *not* been missed while he'd joined his parents at the seaside, smirked.

Hasar smiled broadly at Yrene—knowingly. Not good.

They got perhaps fifteen minutes into dinner before the princess pounced. Hasar leaned forward and said to Chaol, "You must be pleased tonight, Lord Westfall."

Yrene kept perfectly straight in her chair, her fork unfaltering as she lifted a bite of lemon-kissed sea bass to her mouth and forced herself to swallow.

Chaol countered smoothly, drinking from his goblet of water, "And why might that be, Your Highness?"

Hasar's smiles could be awful. Deadly. And the one she wore when she spoke next made Yrene wonder why she had ever bothered to answer the princess's summons. "Well, if one does the calculations, Captain Faliq should be returning with my brother tomorrow."

Yrene's hand tightened around her fork as she tallied the days.

Three weeks. It had been three weeks since Nesryn and Sartaq had left for the Tavan Mountains.

Nesryn would return tomorrow. And though nothing—*nothing*—had happened between Yrene and Chaol . . .

Yrene could not stop the sensation of her chest caving in. Couldn't halt the sense that there was about to be a door very permanently slammed in her face.

They hadn't spoken of Nesryn. Of whatever was between them. And he'd never touched Yrene more than was necessary, never looked at her as he had that night of the party.

Because of course—of course he was waiting for Nesryn. The woman he . . . he was loyal to.

Yrene made herself eat another bite, even as the fish turned sour in her mouth.

Fool. She was a *fool*, and—

"Didn't you hear the news?" Chaol drawled, just as irreverently as the princess. He set down his goblet, his knuckles brushing Yrene's where she'd rested her hand on the table.

To any, it might have been an accidental brush, but with Chaol . . . His every movement was controlled. Focused. The brush of his skin against hers, a whisper of reassurance, as if he could sense that the walls were indeed closing in around her—

Hasar shot Yrene a displeased look. *Why did you not inform me of this?*

Yrene gave her an innocent wince back. *I did not know.* It was the truth.

"I suppose you shall tell us?" Hasar replied coolly to the lord.

Chaol shrugged. "I received word today—from Captain Faliq. She and your brother have decided to extend their trip by another three weeks. It turns out, her skill with a bow and arrow was in high demand amongst

415

his rukhin. They have begged to keep her for a while longer. She obliged them."

Yrene schooled her face into neutrality. Even as relief and shame washed through her.

A good woman—a brave woman. That was who she was so relieved to hear was *not* returning. Not . . . interrupting.

"Our brother is wise," Arghun said from down the table, "to keep such a skilled warrior for as long as possible."

The barb was there, buried deep.

Chaol again shrugged. "He is wise indeed, to know how special she is." The words were spoken with truth, yet . . .

She was inventing things. Reading into it, assuming his tone had no affection beyond pride.

Arghun leaned forward to say to Hasar, "Well, then there's the matter of the *other* news, sister. Which I assume Lord Westfall has also heard."

A few places down, the khagan's conversation with his closest viziers faltered.

"Oh, yes," Hasar said, swirling her wine as she sprawled in her chair. "I'd forgotten."

Yrene tried to catch Renia's eye, to get the princess's lover to reveal *something* about what she now felt building, the wave about to crash. The reason the room was so charged. But Renia only watched Hasar, a hand on her arm as if to say, *Caution.*

Not for what she was to reveal, but *how* Hasar was to reveal it.

Chaol glanced between Arghun and Hasar. From the prince and princess's smirking, it was clear enough they were aware he hadn't heard. But Chaol still seemed to be debating the merits of appearing knowledgeable, or admitting the truth—

Yrene spared him from the choice. "I have not heard it," she said. "What has happened?"

Under the table, Chaol's knee brushed hers in thanks. She told herself it was merely pleasure at the fact he *could* move that knee that coursed through her. Even as dread coiled in her gut.

"Well," Hasar began, the opening chords to a dance she and Arghun had coordinated before this meal, "there have been some . . . developments on the neighboring continent, it seems."

Yrene now pressed *her* knee into Chaol's, a silent solidarity. *Together*, she tried to say through touch alone.

Arghun said to Yrene, to Chaol, and then down to his father, "So many developments up north. Royals gone missing, now revealing themselves once more. Both Dorian Havilliard and the Terrasen Queen. The latter did it in such dramatic fashion, too."

"Where," Yrene whispered, because Chaol could not. Indeed, the breath had gone out of him at the mention of his own king.

Hasar smiled at Yrene—that pleased smile she'd given her upon arrival. "Skull's Bay."

The lie, the guess that Chaol had given her to feed to the princess . . . It had proved true.

She felt Chaol tense, though his face revealed nothing but bland interest. "A pirate port in the south, Great Khagan," Chaol explained to Urus, seated down the table, as if he were indeed aware of this news—and a part of this conversation. "In the middle of a large archipelago."

The khagan glanced to his visibly displeased viziers, and frowned with them. "And why would they appear in Skull's Bay?"

Chaol had no answer, but Arghun was more than happy to supply it. "Because Aelin Galathynius thought to go head-to-head against the army Perrington had camped at the edge of the archipelago."

Yrene slid her hand off the table—to grip Chaol's knee. Tension radiated through every hard line of his body.

Duva asked, a hand on her growing belly, "Was the win in her favor, or Perrington's?" As if it were a sporting match. Her husband was indeed peering down the table to see the heads swivel.

"Oh, in hers," Hasar said. "We had eyes in the town already, so they were able to dispatch a full report." That smug, secret smile again in Yrene's direction. Spies she had sent using Yrene's information. "Her power is considerable," she added to her father. "Our sources say it burned the sky itself. And then wiped out most of the fleet assembled against her. In a single blow."

Holy gods.

The viziers shifted, and the khagan's face hardened. "The rumors of the glass castle's destruction were not exaggerated, then."

"No," Arghun said mildly. "And her powers have grown since then. Along with her allies. Dorian Havilliard travels with her court. And Skull's Bay and its Pirate Lord now kneel before her."

Conqueror.

"They fight *with* her," Chaol cut in. "Against Perrington's forces."

"Do they?" Hasar took up the assault, parrying with ease. "For it is not Perrington who is now sailing down Eyllwe's coast, burning villages as he pleases."

"That is a lie," Chaol said too softly.

"Is it?" Arghun shrugged, then faced his father, the portrait of the concerned son. "No one has seen her, of course, but entire villages have been left in ash and ruin. They say she sails for Banjali, intent on strong-arming the Ytger family into mustering an army for her."

"That is a *lie*," Chaol snapped. His teeth flashed, viziers tittered and gasped, but he said to the khagan, "I know Aelin Galathynius, Great Khagan. It's not her style, not in her nature. The Ytger family . . ." He stalled.

Is important to her. Yrene felt the words on his tongue, as if they were on her own. The princess and Arghun leaned forward, waiting for confirmation. Proof of Aelin Galathynius's potential weakness.

Not in magic, but in who was vital to her. And Eyllwe, lying between Perrington's forces and the khaganate . . . She could see the wheels turning in their heads.

418

"The Ytger family would be better used as an ally from the south," Chaol corrected, shoulders stiff. "Aelin is clever enough to know this."

"And I'd suppose you know," Hasar said, "since you were her lover at some point. Or was that King Dorian? Or both? The spies were never accurate on who was in her bed and when."

Yrene swallowed her surprise. Chaol—and Aelin Galathynius?

"I know her well, yes," Chaol said tightly.

His knee pressed into her own, as if to say, *Later. I will explain later.*

"But this *is* war," Arghun countered. "War makes people do things they might not ordinarily consider."

The condescension and mockery were enough to make Yrene grind her teeth. This was a planned attack, a temporary alliance between two siblings.

Kashin cut in, "Does she set her sights on these shores?" It was a soldier's question. Meant to assess the threat to his land, his king.

Hasar picked at her nails. "Who knows? With such power . . . Perhaps we're all hers for the taking."

"Aelin has one war to fight already," Chaol ground out. "And she is no conqueror."

"Skull's Bay and Eyllwe would suggest otherwise."

A vizier whispered in the khagan's ear. Another leaned in to listen. Already calculating.

Chaol said to Urus, "Great Khagan, I know some might spin these tidings to appear to Aelin's disadvantage, but I swear to you the Queen of Terrasen means only to liberate our land. My king would not ally with her if it were otherwise."

"*Would* you swear it, though?" Hasar mused. "Swear on Yrene's life?"

Chaol blinked at the princess.

"From all you have seen," Hasar went on, "all you've witnessed of her character . . . would you swear it upon Yrene Towers's life that Aelin Galathynius might not use such tactics? Might not try to *take* armies, rather than raise them? Including our own?"

Say yes. Say yes.

Chaol didn't so much as look at Yrene as he stared down Hasar, then Arghun. The khagan and his viziers pulled apart.

Chaol said nothing. Swore nothing.

Hasar's small smile was nothing short of triumphant. "I thought so."

Yrene's stomach turned.

The khagan took Chaol's measure. "If Perrington and Aelin Galathynius are rallying armies, perhaps they'll destroy each other and spare me the trouble."

A muscle flickered in Chaol's jaw.

"Perhaps if she's so powerful," Arghun mused, "she can take on Perrington by herself."

"Don't forget King Dorian," Hasar chimed in. "Why, I'd bet the two of them could handle Perrington and whatever army he's built without much assistance. Better to let them deal with it, than waste our blood on foreign soil."

Yrene was shaking. Trembling with—with *rage* at the careful play of words, the game Hasar and her brother had constructed to keep from sailing to war.

"But," Kashin countered, seeming to note Yrene's expression, "it might also be said that if we *do* assist such powerful royals, the benefits in years of peace might be far worth the risks now." He twisted to the khagan. "If we go to their aid, Father, should we ever face such a threat, imagine that power turned against our enemies."

"Or turned against us, if she finds it easier to break her oaths," Arghun cut in.

The khagan studied Arghun, his eldest son now frowning with distaste at Kashin. Duva, a hand still on her pregnant belly, only watched. Unnoted and unasked for, even by her husband.

Arghun turned back to his father. "Our people's magic is minimal. The Eternal Sky and the thirty-six gods blessed our healers mostly." A frown at Yrene. "Against such power, what is steel and wood? Aelin

420

Galathynius took Rifthold, then took Skull's Bay, and now seems poised to take Eyllwe. A wise ruler would have gone north, fortified her kingdom, then pushed south from the borders. Yet she stretches her forces thin, dividing them between north and south. If she is not a fool, then her advisors are."

"They are well-trained warriors, who have seen more war and battle than you ever will," Chaol said coldly.

The eldest prince stiffened. Hasar laughed quietly.

The khagan again weighed the words around him. "This remains a matter to discuss in council rooms, not dinner tables," he said, though there was no reassurance in it. Not for Chaol, not for Yrene. "Though I am inclined to agree with what the bare facts offer."

To his credit, Chaol did not argue further. Did not flinch or scowl. He only nodded once. "I thank you for the honor of your continued consideration, Great Khagan."

Arghun and Hasar swapped sneering looks. But the khagan just returned to his meal.

Neither Yrene nor Chaol touched the rest of their food.

⁓

Bitch. The princess was a bitch, and Arghun was as fine a bastard as any Chaol had ever encountered.

There was some truth to their reluctance—their fear of Aelin's powers and the threat she might pose. But he read them. Knew Hasar simply did not *want* to leave the comforts of her home, her lover's arms, to sail to war. Did not want the messiness of it.

And Arghun . . . The man dealt in power, in knowledge. Chaol had no doubt Arghun's arguing against him was more to force Chaol into a spot where he'd be desperate.

Even more than he was. Willing to offer anything up for their aid.

Kashin would do whatever his father told him. And as for the khagan . . .

Hours later, Chaol was still grinding his teeth as he lay in bed and stared at the ceiling. Yrene had left him with a squeeze to his shoulder, promising to see him the next day.

Chaol had barely been able to reply.

He should have lied. Should have sworn he trusted Aelin with his life.

Because Hasar had known that if she asked him to swear upon Yrene's life . . .

Even if their thirty-six gods did not care about him, he couldn't risk it.

He had seen Aelin do terrible things.

He still dreamed of her gutting Archer Finn in cold blood. Still dreamed of what she'd left of Grave's body in that alley. Still dreamed of her butchering men like cattle, in Rifthold and in Endovier, and knew just how unfeeling and brutal she could turn. He had quarreled with her earlier this summer about it—the checks on her power. The lack of them.

Rowan was a good male. Utterly unafraid of Aelin, her magic. But would *she* listen to his counsel? Aedion and Aelin were as likely to come to blows as they were to agree, and Lysandra . . . Chaol didn't know the shifter well enough to judge whether she'd keep Aelin in line.

Aelin had indeed changed—grown into a queen. Was still growing into one.

But he knew that there were no restraints, no inner ones, on how far Aelin would go to protect those she loved. Protect her kingdom. And if someone stood in her way, barred her from protecting them . . . No lines existed to cross within Aelin in regard to that. No lines at all.

So he had not been able to swear it, on Yrene's life, that he believed Aelin might be above those sorts of methods. With her fraught history with Rolfe, she likely had used the might of her magic to intimidate him into joining their cause.

But with Eyllwe . . . Had they given some sign of resistance, to prompt her to terrorize them? He couldn't imagine it, that Aelin would *consider* hurting innocent people, let alone the people of her beloved friend. And yet she knew the risks that Perrington—Erawan posed. What he'd do to them all, if she did not band them together. By whatever means necessary.

Chaol rubbed his face. If Aelin had kept herself in check, if she'd played the part of distressed queen . . . It would have made his task far easier.

Perhaps Aelin had cost them this war. This one shot at a future.

At least Dorian was accounted for—undoubtedly as safe as could be expected with Aelin's court for companions.

Chaol sent a silent prayer of thanks into the night for that small mercy.

A soft knock had him shooting up. Not from the foyer, but the glass doors to the garden.

His legs twitched, bending slightly at the knee—more reaction than controlled movement. He and Yrene had been going through the grueling leg routines twice a day, the various therapies buying him movement inch by inch. Along with the magic she poured into his body while he endured the darkness's horde of memories. He never told her what he saw, what left him screaming.

There was no point. And telling Yrene how badly he'd failed, how wrongly he'd judged, it made him just as nauseated. But what stood in the night-veiled garden . . . Not a memory.

Chaol squinted into the dark at the tall male figure standing there, a hand raised in quiet greeting—Chaol's own hand drifting to the knife beneath his pillow. But the figure stepped closer to the lantern light, and Chaol blew out a breath and waved the prince in.

With a flick of a small knife, Kashin unlocked the garden door and slipped in.

"Lock-picking isn't a skill I'd expect a prince to possess," Chaol said by way of greeting.

Kashin lingered just inside the doorway, the lantern from outside illuminating enough of his face for Chaol to make out a half smile. "Learned more for sneaking in and out of ladies' bedrooms than stealing, I'm afraid."

"I thought your court was a bit more open in regard to that sort of thing than my own."

That smile grew. "Perhaps, but cranky old husbands remain the same on either continent."

Chaol chuckled, shaking his head. "What can I do for you, Prince?"

Kashin studied the door to the suite, Chaol doing the same—searching for any flickering shadows on the other side. When they both found none, Kashin said, "I assume you have discovered nothing within my court about who might be tormenting Yrene."

"I wish I could say otherwise." But with Nesryn gone, he'd had little chance to hunt through Antica for any signs of a would-be Valg agent. And things had indeed been quiet enough these three weeks that part of him had hoped they'd just . . . left. A considerably calmer atmosphere had settled over the palace and Torre since then, as if the shadows were indeed behind them all.

Kashin nodded. "I know Sartaq departed with your captain to seek answers regarding this threat."

Chaol didn't dare confirm or deny. He wasn't entirely certain where Sartaq had left things with his family, if he'd received his father's blessing to go.

Kashin went on, "That might just be why my siblings mounted such a unified front against you tonight. If Sartaq himself takes this threat seriously, they know they might have a limited window to convince our father not to join this cause."

"But if the threat is real," Chaol said, "if it might spill into these lands, why not fight? Why not stop it before it can reach these shores?"

"Because it is war," Kashin said, and the way he spoke, the way he stood, it somehow made Chaol feel young indeed. "And though the manner in which my siblings presented their argument was unpleasant, I suspect Arghun and Hasar are aware of the costs that joining your cause requires. Never before has the entire might of the khaganate's armies been sent to a foreign land. Oh, some legions, whether it be the rukhin or the armada or my own horse-lords. Sometimes united, but never all, never what you require. The cost of life, the sheer drain on our coffers . . . it will be great. Don't make the mistake of believing my siblings don't understand that very, very well."

"And their fear of Aelin?"

Kashin snorted. "I cannot speak to that. Perhaps it is well founded. Perhaps it is not."

"So you snuck into my room to tell me?" He should speak with more respect, but—

"I came to tell you one more piece of information, which Arghun chose not to mention."

Chaol waited, wishing he weren't sitting in bed, bare from the waist up.

Kashin said, "We received a report from our vizier of foreign trade that a large, lucrative order had been placed for a relatively new weapon."

Chaol's breathing snagged. If Morath had found some way—

"It is called a firelance," Kashin said. "Our finest engineers made it by combining various weapons from across our continent."

Oh, gods. If Morath had it in its arsenal—

"Captain Rolfe ordered them for his fleet. Months ago."

Rolfe—"And when news arrived of Skull's Bay falling to Aelin Galathynius, it also came with an order for even more firelances to be shipped northward."

Chaol sorted through the information. "Why wouldn't Arghun say this at dinner?"

"Because the firelances are very, very expensive."

"Surely that's good for your economy."

"It is." And *not* good for Arghun's attempt to avoid this war.

Chaol fell silent for a heartbeat. "And you, Prince? Do you wish to join this war?"

Kashin didn't answer immediately. He scanned the room, the ceiling, the bed, and finally Chaol himself. "This will be the great war of our time," Kashin said quietly. "When we are dead, when even our grandchildren's grandchildren are dead, they will still be talking about this war. They will whisper of it around fires, sing of it in the great halls. Who lived and died, who fought and who cowered." His throat bobbed. "My *sulde* blows northward—day and night, the horsehairs blow north. So perhaps I will find my destiny on the plains of Fenharrow. Or before the white walls of Orynth. But it is northward that I shall go—if my father will order me."

Chaol mulled it over. Looked to the trunks against the wall near the bathing chamber.

Kashin had turned to leave when Chaol asked, "When does your father next meet with his foreign trade vizier?"

⊰ 37 ⊱

Nesryn had run out of time.

Falkan required ten days to recover, which had left her and Sartaq with too little time to visit the other watchtower ruins to the south. She'd tried to convince the prince to go without the shape-shifter, but he'd refused. Even with Borte now intent on joining them, he was taking no risks.

But Sartaq found other ways to fill their time. He'd taken Nesryn to other aeries to the north and west, where he met with the reigning hearth-mothers and the captains, both male and female, who led their forces.

Some were welcoming, greeting Sartaq with feasts and revels that lasted long into the night.

Some, like the Berlad, were aloof, their hearth-mothers and other various leaders not inviting them to stay for longer than necessary. Certainly not bringing out jugs of the fermented goat's milk that they drank—and that was strong enough to put hair on Nesryn's chest, face, and teeth. She'd nearly choked to death the first time she'd tried it, earning hearty claps on the back and a toast in her honor.

It was the warm welcome that still surprised her. The smiles of the rukhin who asked, some shyly, some boldly, for demonstrations with her bow and arrow. But for all she showed them, she, too, learned. Went soaring with Sartaq through the mountain passes, the prince calling out targets and Nesryn striking them, learning how to fire into the wind, *as* the wind.

He even let her ride Kadara alone—just once, and enough for her to again wonder how they let four-year-olds do it, but . . . she'd never felt so unleashed.

So unburdened and unbridled and yet settled in herself.

So they went, clan to clan, hearth to hearth. Sartaq checking up on the riders and their training, stopping to visit new babes and ailing old folk. Nesryn remained his shadow—or tried to.

Anytime she lingered a step back, Sartaq nudged her forward. Anytime there was a task to be done with the others, he asked her to do it. The washing-up after a meal, the returning of arrows from target practice, the cleaning-out of the ruk droppings from halls and nests.

The last task, at least, the prince joined her in. No matter his rank, no matter his status as captain, he did every chore without a word of complaint. No one was above work, he told her when she'd asked one night.

And whether she was scraping crusted droppings from the ground or teaching young warriors how to string a bow, something restless in her had settled.

She could no longer picture it—the quiet meetings at the palace in Rifthold where she had given solemn guards their orders and then parted ways amongst marble floors and finery. Could not remember the city barracks, where she'd lurked in the back of a crowded room, gotten her orders, and then stood on a street corner for hours, watching people buy and eat and argue and walk about.

Another lifetime, another world.

Here in the deep mountains, breathing in the crisp air, seated around the fire pit to hear Houlun narrate tales of rukhin and the horse-lords, tales of the first khagan and his beloved wife, whom Borte had been named after . . . She could not remember that life before.

And did not want to go back to it.

It was at one such fire, Nesryn combing out the tight braid that Borte had taught her to plait, that she surprised even herself.

Houlun had settled in, a whetstone in hand as she honed a dagger, preparing to work while she talked to the small gathering—Sartaq, Borte, a gray-faced and limping Falkan, and six others who Nesryn had learned were Borte's cousins of sorts. The hearth-mother scanned their faces, golden and flickering with the flame, and asked, "What of a tale from Adarlan instead?"

All eyes had turned to Nesryn and Falkan.

The shape-shifter winced. "I'm afraid mine are rather dull." He considered. "I did have an interesting visit to the Red Desert once, but . . ." He gestured as much as he could to Nesryn. "I should like to hear one of your stories first, Captain."

Nesryn tried not to fidget under the weight of so many stares. "The stories I grew up with," she admitted, "were mostly of you all, of these lands." Broad smiles at that. Sartaq only winked. Nesryn ducked her head, face heating.

"Tell a story of the Fae, if you know them," Borte suggested. "Of the Fae Prince you met."

Nesryn shook her head. "I don't have any of those—and I do not know him that well." As Borte frowned, Nesryn added, "But I can sing for you."

Silence.

Houlun set down her whetstone. "A song would be appreciated." A scowl at Borte and Sartaq. "Since neither of my children can carry a tune to save their lives." Borte rolled her eyes at her hearth-mother, but Sartaq bowed his head in apology, a crooked grin now on his mouth.

Nesryn smiled, even as her heart pounded at her bold offer. She'd never really performed for anyone, but this . . . It was not performing, as much as it was sharing. She listened to the wind whispering outside the cave mouth for a long moment, the others falling quiet.

"This is a song of Adarlan," she said at last. "From the foothills north of Rifthold, where my mother was born." An old, familiar ache filled her chest. "She used to sing this to me—before she died."

A glimmer of sympathy in Houlun's steely gaze. But Nesryn glanced to Borte as she spoke, finding the young woman's face unusually soft—staring at Nesryn as if she had not seen her before. Nesryn gave her a small, subtle nod. *It is a weight we both bear.*

Borte offered a small, quiet smile in return.

Nesryn listened to the wind again. Let herself drift back to her pretty little bedroom in Rifthold, let herself feel her mother's silken hands stroking her face, her hair. She had been so taken with her father's stories of his far-off homeland, of the ruks and horse-lords, that she had rarely asked for anything about Adarlan itself, despite being a child of both lands.

And this song of her mother's . . . One of the few stories she had, in the form she loved best. Of her homeland in better days. And she wanted to share it with them—that glimpse into what her land might again become.

Nesryn cleared her throat. Took a bracing breath.

And then she opened her mouth and sang.

The crackle of the fire her only drum, Nesryn's voice filled the Mountain-Hall of Altun, wending through the ancient pillars, bouncing off the carved rock.

She had the sense of Sartaq going very still, had the sense that there was nothing hard or laughing on his face.

But she focused on the song, on those long-ago words, that story of distant winters and speckles of blood on snow; that story of mothers and their daughters, how they loved and fought and tended to each other.

Her voice soared and fell, bold and graceful as a ruk, and Nesryn could have sworn that even the howling winds paused to listen.

And when she finished, a gilded, high note of the spring sun breaking across cold lands, when silence and the crackling fire filled the world once more . . .

Borte was crying. Silent tears streaming down her pretty face. Houlun's hand was tightly wrapped around her granddaughter's, the whetstone set aside. A wound still healing—for both of them.

And perhaps Sartaq, too—for grief limned his face. Grief, and awe, and perhaps something infinitely more tender as he said, "Another tale to spread of Neith's Arrow."

She ducked her head again, accepting the praise of the others with a smile. Falkan clapped as best he could manage and called for another song.

Nesryn, to her surprise, obliged them. A merry, bright mountain song her father had taught her, of rushing streams amid blooming fields of wildflowers.

But even as the night moved on, as Nesryn sang in that beautiful mountain-hall, she felt Sartaq's stare. Different from any he'd given before.

And though she told herself she should, Nesryn did not look away.

A few days later, when Falkan had at last healed, they dared venture down to the three other watchtowers Houlun had discovered.

They found nothing at the first two, both far enough to require separate trips. Houlun had forbidden them from camping in the wilds—so rather than risk her wrath, they returned each night, then stayed a few days to let Kadara and Arcas, Borte's sweet ruk, rest from being pushed so hard.

Sartaq warmed only a fraction to the shape-shifter. He watched Falkan as carefully as Kadara did, but at least attempted to make conversation now and then.

Borte, on the other hand, peppered Falkan with an endless stream of questions while they combed through ruins that were little more than rubble. *What does it feel like to be a duck, paddling beneath water but gliding so smoothly over the surface?*

When you eat as an animal, does the meat all fit in your human stomach?

Do you have to wait between eating as an animal and shifting back into a human because of it?

Do you defecate as an animal?

The last one earned a sharp laugh from Sartaq at least. Even if Falkan had gone red and avoided answering the question.

But after visiting two watchtowers, they had found nothing on why they had been built and who those long-ago guardians had battled—or *how* they had defeated them.

And with one tower left . . . Nesryn had done a tally of the days and realized that the three weeks she had promised Chaol were over.

Sartaq had known, too. Had sought her out as she stood in one of the ruk nests, admiring the birds resting or preening or sailing out. She often came here during quieter afternoons, just to observe the birds: their sharp-eyed intelligence, their loving bonds.

She was leaning against the wall beside the door when he emerged. For several minutes, they stood watching a mated pair nuzzle each other before one hopped to the edge of the massive cave mouth and dropped into the void below.

"That one over there," the prince said at last, pointing to a reddish-brown ruk sitting by the opposite wall. She'd seen the ruk often—mostly noting that he was alone, never visited by a rider, unlike some of the others. "His rider died a few months back. Clutched at his chest in a meal and died. The rider was old, but the ruk . . ." Sartaq smiled sadly at the bird. "He's young—not yet four."

"What happens to the ones whose riders die?"

"We offer them freedom. Some fly off to the wilds. Some remain." Sartaq crossed his arms. "He remained."

"Do they ever get new riders?"

"Some do. If they accept them. It is the ruk's choice."

Nesryn heard the invitation in his voice. Read it in the prince's eyes.

Her throat tightened. "Our three weeks are up."

"Indeed they are."

She faced the prince fully, tilting her head back to see his face. "We need more time."

"So what did you say?"

A simple question.

But she'd taken hours to figure out how to word her letter to Chaol, then given it to Sartaq's fastest messenger. "I asked for another three weeks."

He angled his head, watching her with that unrelenting intensity. "A great deal can happen in three weeks."

Nesryn made herself keep her shoulders squared, chin high. "Even so, at the end of it, I must return to Antica."

Sartaq nodded, though something like disappointment guttered his eyes. "Then I suppose the ruk in the aerie will have to wait for another rider to come along."

That had been a day ago. The conversation that left her unable to look too long in the prince's direction.

And during the hours-long flight this morning, she'd snuck a glance or two over to where Kadara sailed, Sartaq and Falkan on her back.

Now Kadara swung wide, spying the final tower far below, located on a rare plain amid the hills and peaks of the Tavan Mountains. This late in the summer, it was awash with emerald grasses and sapphire streams— the ruin little more than a heap of stone.

Borte steered Arcas with a whistle through her teeth and a tug on the reins, the ruk banking left before leveling out. She was a skilled rider, bolder than Sartaq, mostly thanks to her ruk's smaller size and agility. She'd won the past three annual racing contests between all the clans— competitions of agility, speed, and quick thinking.

"Did you pick Arcas," Nesryn asked over the wind, "or did she pick you?"

Borte leaned forward to pat the ruk's neck. "It was mutual. I saw that fuzzy head pop out of the nest, and I was done. Everyone told me to pick a bigger chick; my mother herself scolded me." A sad smile at that. "But I knew Arcas was mine. I saw her, and I knew."

Nesryn fell silent while they aimed for the pretty plain and ruin, the sunlight dancing on Kadara's wings.

"You should take that ruk in the aerie for a flight sometime," Borte said, letting Arcas descend into a smooth landing. "Test him out."

"I'm leaving soon. It wouldn't be fair to either of us."

"I know. But perhaps you should, anyway."

Borte loved finding the traps hidden by the Fae.

Which was fine by Nesryn, since the girl was far better at sussing them out.

This tower, to Borte's disappointment, had suffered a collapse at some point, blocking the lower levels. And above them, only a chamber open to the sky remained.

Which was where Falkan came in.

As the shifter's form blended and shrank, Sartaq did not bother to hide his shudder. And he shuddered once more when the fallen block of stone Falkan had been sitting on now revealed a millipede. Who promptly stood up and waved to them with its countless little legs.

Nesryn cringed with distaste, even as Borte laughed and waved back.

But off Falkan went, slithering between the fallen stones, to glean what might remain below.

"I don't know why it bothers you so," Borte said to Sartaq, clicking her tongue. "I think it's delightful."

"It's not *what* he is," Sartaq admitted, watching the pile of rock for the millipede's return. "It's the idea of bone melting, flesh flowing like water . . ." He shivered and turned to Nesryn. "Your friend—the shifter. It never bothered you?"

434

"No," Nesryn answered plainly. "I didn't even see her shift until that day your scouts reported on."

"The Impossible Shot," Sartaq murmured. "So it truly was a shifter that you saved."

Nesryn nodded. "Her name is Lysandra."

Borte nudged Sartaq with an elbow. "Don't you wish to go north, brother? To meet all these people Nesryn talks of? Shifters and fire-breathing queens and Fae Princes . . ."

"I'm beginning to think your obsession with anything related to the Fae might be unhealthy," Sartaq grumbled.

"I only took a dagger or two," Borte insisted.

"You carried so many back from the last watchtower that poor Arcas could barely get off the ground."

"It's for my trading business," Borte huffed. "Whenever our people get their heads out of their asses and remember that we *can* have a profitable one."

"No wonder you've taken so much to Falkan," Nesryn said, earning a jab in the ribs from Borte. Nesryn batted her away, chuckling.

Borte put her hands on her hips. "I will have you both know—"

The words were cut off by a scream.

Not from Falkan below.

But from outside. From Kadara.

Nesryn had an arrow drawn and aimed before they rushed out onto the field.

Only to find it filled with ruks. And grim-faced riders.

Sartaq sighed, shoulders slumping. But Borte shoved past them, cursing filthily as she kept her sword out—indeed an Asterion-forged blade from the arsenal at the last watchtower.

A young man of around Nesryn's age had dismounted from his ruk, the bird a brown so dark it was nearly black, and he now swaggered toward them, a smirk on his handsome face. It was to him that Borte stormed, practically stomping through the high grasses.

The unit of rukhin looked on, imperious and cold. None bowed to Sartaq.

"What in *hell* are you doing here?" Borte demanded, a hand on her hip as she stopped a healthy distance from the young man.

He wore leathers like hers, but the colors of the band around his arm . . . The Berlad. The least welcoming of all the aeries they'd visited, and one of the more powerful. Its riders had been meticulously trained, their caves immaculately clean.

The young man ignored Borte and called to Sartaq, "We spotted your ruks while flying overhead. You are far from your aerie, Captain."

Careful questions.

Borte hissed, "Be gone, Yeran. No one invited you here."

Yeran lifted a cool brow. "Still yapping, I see."

Borte spat at his feet. The other riders tensed, but she glared at them. They all lowered their stares.

Behind them, stone crunched, and Yeran's eyes flared, his knees bending as if he'd lunge for Borte—to hurl her behind him as Falkan emerged from the ruin.

In wolf form.

But Borte stepped out of Yeran's reach and declared sweetly, "My new pet."

Yeran gaped between girl and wolf as Falkan sat beside Nesryn. She couldn't resist scratching his fuzzy ears.

To his credit, the shape-shifter let her, even turning his head into her palm.

"Strange company you keep these days, Captain," Yeran managed to say to Sartaq.

Borte snapped her fingers in his face. "You cannot address me?"

Yeran gave her a lazy smile. "Do you finally have something worth hearing?"

Borte bristled. But Sartaq, smiling faintly, strolled to his hearth-sister's side. "We have business in these parts and stopped for refreshment. What brings you so far south?"

Yeran wrapped a hand around the hilt of a long knife at his side. "Three hatchlings went missing. We thought to track them, but have found nothing."

Nesryn's stomach tightened, imagining those spiders scuttling through the aeries, between the ruks, to the fuzzy chicks so fiercely guarded. To the human families sleeping so close by.

"When were they taken?" Sartaq's face was hard as stone.

"Two nights ago." Yeran rubbed his jaw. "We suspected poachers, but there was no human scent, no tracks or camp."

Look up. The bloody warning at the Watchtower of Eidolon rang through her mind.

Through Sartaq's, if the tightening of his jaw was any indication.

"Go back to your aerie, Captain," Sartaq said to Yeran, pointing to the wall of mountains beyond the plain, the gray rock so bare compared to the life humming around them. Always—the Dagul Fells always seemed to be watching. Waiting. "Do not track any farther than here."

Wariness flooded Yeran's brown eyes as he glanced between Borte and Sartaq, then over to Nesryn and Falkan. "The *kharankui.*"

The riders stirred. Even the ruks rustled their wings at the name, as if they, too, knew it.

But Borte declared, loud for all to hear, "You heard my brother. Crawl back to your aerie."

Yeran gave her a mocking bow. "Go back to yours, and I will return to mine, Borte."

She bared her teeth at him.

But Yeran mounted his ruk with easy, powerful grace, the others flapping away at a jerk of his chin. He waited until they had all soared into the skies before saying to Sartaq, "If the *kharankui* have begun to stir, we need to muster a host to drive them back. Before it is too late."

A wind tugged at Sartaq's braid, blowing it toward those mountains. Nesryn wished she could see his face, what might be on it at the mention of a host.

"It will be dealt with," Sartaq said. "Be on your guard. Keep children and hatchlings close."

Yeran nodded gravely, a soldier receiving an order from a commander—a captain ordered by his prince. Then he looked over to Borte.

She gave him a vulgar gesture.

Yeran only winked at her before he whistled to his ruk and shot into the skies, leaving a mighty breeze behind that set Borte's braids swinging.

Borte watched Yeran until he was sailing toward the mass of the others, then spat on the ground where his ruk had stood. "Bastard," she hissed, and whirled, storming to Nesryn and Falkan.

The shifter changed, swaying as his human form returned. "Nothing down below worth seeing," he announced as Sartaq prowled over to where they had gathered.

Nesryn frowned at the Fells. "I think it's time we craft a different strategy anyway."

Sartaq followed her gaze, coming close enough to her side that the heat from his body leaked into hers. Together, they stared toward that wall of mountains. What waited beyond.

"That young captain, Yeran," Falkan said carefully to Borte. "You seem to know him well."

Borte scowled. "He's my betrothed."

⊰ 38 ⊱

Though Kashin might have been loath to push his father in public or private, he certainly was not without his resources. And as Chaol approached the sealed doors to the khagan's trade meeting, he hid his grin when he discovered Hashim, Shen, and two other guards he'd trained with stationed outside. Shen winked at him, his armor glinting in the watery morning sunlight, and swiftly knocked with his artificial hand before opening the door.

Chaol didn't dare give Shen, Hashim, or the other guards so much as a nod of gratitude or acknowledgment. Not as he wheeled his chair into the sun-drenched council room and found the khagan and three golden-robed viziers around a long table of black polished wood.

They all stared at him in silence. But Chaol kept approaching the table, his head high, face set in a pleasant, subdued smile. "I hope I'm not interrupting, but there is a matter I should like to discuss."

The khagan's lips pressed into a tight line. He wore a light green tunic and dark trousers, cut close enough to reveal the warrior's body still lurking beneath the aged exterior. "I have told you time and again, Lord Westfall, that you should speak to my Chief Vizier"—a nod to the sour-faced man across from him—"if you wish to arrange a meeting."

Chaol halted before the table, flexing and shifting his feet. He'd gone through as much of his leg exercises as he could this morning after his workout with the palace guard, and though he'd regained movement up to his knees, placing weight on them, *standing* . . .

He cast the thought from his mind. Standing or sitting had nothing to do with it—this moment.

He could still speak with dignity and command whether he stood on his feet or was laid flat on his back. The chair was no prison, nothing that made him lesser.

So Chaol bowed his head, smiling faintly. "With all due respect, Great Khagan, I am not here to meet with you."

Urus blinked, his only show of surprise as Chaol inclined his head to the man in sky-blue robes whom Kashin had described. "I am here to speak to your foreign trade vizier."

The vizier glanced between his khagan and Chaol, as if ready to pro-claim his innocence, even as interest gleamed in his brown eyes. But he did not dare speak.

Chaol held the khagan's stare for long seconds.

He didn't remind himself that he had interrupted a private meeting of perhaps the most powerful man in the world. Didn't remind himself that he was a guest in a foreign court and the fate of his friends and country-men depended on what he accomplished here. He just stared at the kha-gan, man to man, warrior to warrior.

He had fought a king before and lived to tell.

The khagan at last jerked his chin to an empty spot at the table. Not a ringing welcome, but better than nothing.

Chaol nodded his thanks and approached, keeping his breathing even while he looked all four men in the eye and said to the vizier of foreign trade, "I received word that two large orders of firelances have been placed by Captain Rolfe's armada, one prior to Aelin Galathynius's arrival in Skull's Bay, and an even larger one afterward."

The khagan's white brows flicked up. The foreign trade vizier shifted in his seat, but nodded. "Yes," he said in Chaol's tongue. "That is true."

"How much, exactly, would you say each firelance costs?"

The viziers glanced among one another, and it was another man, whom Chaol presumed to be the domestic trade vizier, that named the sum.

Chaol only waited. Kashin had told him the astronomical number last night. And, just as he'd gambled, the khagan whipped his head to the vizier at that cost.

Chaol asked, "And how many are now being sent to Rolfe—and thus to Terrasen?"

Another number. Chaol let the khagan do the math. Watched from the corner of his eye as the khagan's brows rose even higher.

The Chief Vizier braced his forearms on the table. "Are you trying to convince us of Aelin Galathynius's good or ill intentions, Lord Westfall?"

Chaol ignored the barb. He simply said to the foreign trade vizier, "I would like to place another order. I would like to double the Queen of Terrasen's order, actually."

Silence.

The foreign trade vizier looked like he'd flip over in his chair.

But the Chief Vizier sneered, "With what money?"

Chaol turned a lazy grin on the man. "I came here with four trunks of priceless treasure." A kingdom's ransom, as it were. "I think it should cover the cost."

Utter quiet once more.

Until the khagan asked his foreign trade vizier, "And will it cover the cost?"

"The treasure would have to be assessed and weighed—"

"It is already being done," Chaol said, leaning back in his chair. "You shall have the number by this afternoon."

Another beat of silence. Then the khagan murmured in Halha to the foreign trade vizier, who gathered up his papers and scurried out of the room with a wary glance at Chaol. A flat word from the khagan to his Chief Vizier and the domestic trade vizier, and both men also left, the former throwing another cold sneer Chaol's way before departing.

Alone with the khagan, Chaol waited in silence.

Urus rose from his chair, stalking to the wall of windows that overlooked a blooming, shaded garden. "I suppose you think you are very clever, to use this to get an audience with me."

"I spoke true," Chaol said. "I wished to discuss the deal with your foreign trade vizier. Even if your armies will not join us, I don't see how anyone can object to our purchase of your weapons."

"And no doubt, this was meant to make me realize how lucrative this war might be, if your side is willing to invest in our resources."

Chaol remained silent.

The khagan turned from the garden view, the sunlight making his white hair glow. "I do not appreciate being manipulated into this war, Lord Westfall."

Chaol held the man's stare, even as he gripped the arms of his chair.

The khagan asked quietly, "Do you even know what warfare *is*?"

Chaol clenched his jaw. "I suppose I'm about to find out, aren't I."

The khagan didn't so much as smile. "It is not mere battles and supplies and strategy. Warfare is the absolute dedication of one army against their enemies." A long, weighing look. "That is what you stand against—Morath's rallied, solid front. Their conviction in decimating you into dust."

"I know that well."

"Do you? Do you understand what Morath is doing to you already? They build and plan and strike, and you can barely keep up. You are playing by the rules Perrington sets—and you will lose because of it."

His breakfast turned over in his stomach. "We might still triumph."

The khagan shook his head once. "To do that, your triumph must be complete. Every last bit of resistance squashed."

His legs itched—and he shifted his feet just barely. *Stand*, he willed them. *Stand*.

He pushed his feet down, muscles barking in protest.

"Which is why," Chaol snarled as his legs refused to obey, "we need your armies to aid us."

The khagan glanced toward Chaol's straining feet, as if he could see the struggle waging in his body. "I do not appreciate being hunted like some prize stag in a wood. I told you to wait; I told you to grant me the respect of grieving for my daughter—"

"And what if I told you that your daughter might have been murdered?"

Silence, horrible and hollow, filled the space between them.

Chaol snapped, "What if I told you that agents of Perrington might be here, and might already be hunting *you*, manipulating *you* into or out of this?"

The khagan's face tightened. Chaol braced himself for the roaring, for Urus to perhaps draw the long, jeweled knife at his side and slam it into his chest. But the khagan only said quietly, "You are dismissed."

As if the guards had listened to every word, the doors cracked open, a grim-faced Hashim beckoning Chaol toward the wall.

Chaol didn't move. Footsteps approached from behind. To physically remove him.

He slammed his feet into the pedals of his chair, pushing and straining, gritting his teeth. Like hell they'd haul him out of here; like hell he'd let them drag him away—

"I came to not only save my people, but *all* peoples of this world," Chaol growled at the khagan.

Someone—Shen—gripped the handles of his chair and began to turn him.

Chaol twisted, teeth bared at the guard. "*Don't touch it.*"

But Shen didn't release the handles, even as apology shone in his eyes. He knew—Chaol realized the guard knew just how it felt to have the chair touched, moved, without being asked. Just as Chaol knew what defying the khagan's order to escort him from the room might mean for Shen.

So Chaol again fixed his stare on the khagan. "Your city is the greatest I have ever laid eyes upon, your empire the standard by which all others should be measured. When Morath comes to lay waste to it, who will stand with you if we are all carrion?"

The khagan's eyes burned like coals.

Shen kept pushing his chair toward that door.

Chaol's arms shook with the effort to keep from shoving the guard away, his legs trembling as he tried and tried to rise. Chaol looked over his shoulder and growled, "I stood on the wrong side of the line for too damn long, and it cost me *everything*. Do not make the same mistakes that I—"

"Do not presume to tell a khagan what he must do," Urus said, his eyes like chips of ice. He jerked his chin to the guards shifting on their feet at the door. "Escort Lord Westfall back to his rooms. Do not allow him into my meetings again."

The threat lay beneath the calm, cold words. Urus had no need to raise his voice, to roar to make his promise of punishment clear enough to the guards.

Chaol pushed and pushed against his chair, arms straining as he fought to stand, to even rise slightly.

But then Shen had his chair through the doors, and down the gleaming bright hallways.

Still his body did not obey. Did not answer.

The doors to the khagan's council chamber shut with a soft click that reverberated through Chaol's every bone and muscle, the sound more damning than any word the khagan had uttered.

~

Yrene had left Chaol to his thoughts the night before.

Left them as she stormed back to the Torre and decided that Hasar . . .

Oh, she did not mind manipulating the princess one bit. And realized precisely how she'd get the princess to invite her to that damned oasis.

But it seemed that even a morning in the training ring with the guards had not soothed the jagged edge in Chaol's own temper. The temper still simmering as he waited in the sitting room while Yrene sent Kadja off on another fool's errand—*twine, goat's milk, and vinegar*—and at last readied to work on him.

Summer was boiling toward a steamy close, the wild winds of autumn beginning to lash at the waters of the turquoise bay. It was always warm in Antica, but the Narrow Sea turned rough and unwieldy from Yulemas to Beltane. If an armada did not sail from the southern continent before then . . . Well, Yrene supposed that after last night, one wouldn't sail anyway.

Sitting near their usual gold couch, Chaol didn't greet her with more than a cursory glance. Not at all like his usual grim smile. And the shadows under his eyes . . . Any thought of rushing in here to tell him of her plan flowed out of Yrene's head as she asked, "Were you up all night?"

"For parts of it," he said, his voice low.

Yrene approached the couch but did not sit. Instead, she simply watched him, folding her arms across her abdomen. "Perhaps the khagan will consider. He's aware of how his children scheme. He's too smart not to have seen Arghun and Hasar working in tandem—for once—and to not be suspicious."

"And you know the khagan so well?" A cold, biting question.

"No, but I've certainly lived here a good deal longer than you have."

His brown eyes flashed. "I don't have two years to spare. To play their games."

And she did, apparently.

Yrene stifled her irritation. "Well, brooding about it won't fix anything."

His nostrils flared. "Indeed."

She hadn't seen him like this in weeks.

445

Had it been so long already? Her birthday was in a fortnight. Sooner than she'd realized.

It wasn't the time to mention it, or the plan she'd hatched. It was inconsequential, really, given everything swarming around them. The burdens he bore. The frustration and despair she now saw pushing on those shoulders.

"Tell me what happened." Something had—something had shifted since they'd parted ways last night.

A cutting glance her way. She braced herself for his refusal as his jaw tightened.

But then he said, "I went to see the khagan this morning."

"You got an audience?"

"Not quite." His lips thinned.

"What happened?" Yrene braced a hand on the arm of the sofa.

"He had me hauled out of the room." Cold, flat words. "I couldn't even try to get around the guards. Try to make him listen."

"If you'd been standing, they'd have hauled you away all the same." Likely hurt him in the process.

He glared. "I didn't want to fight them. I wanted to *beg* him. And I couldn't even get onto my knees to do it."

Her heart strained as he looked toward the garden window. Rage and sorrow and fear all crossed over his face. "You've made remarkable progress already."

"I want to be able to fight alongside my men again," Chaol said quietly. "To die beside them."

The words were an icy slice of fear through her, but Yrene said stiffly, "You can do that from a horse."

"I want to do it shoulder-to-shoulder," he snarled. "I want to fight in the mud, on a killing field."

"So you'd heal here only so you can go die somewhere else?" The words snapped from her.

"Yes."

A cold, hard answer. His face equally so.

This storm brewing in him . . . She wouldn't see their progress ruined by it.

And war was truly breaking across their home. Regardless of what he wished to do with himself, he did not—*they* did not have time. Her people in Fenharrow did not have time.

So Yrene stepped up to him, gripped him under a shoulder, and said, "Then get up."

Chaol was in a shit mood, and he knew it.

The more he'd thought about it, the more he realized how easily the prince and princess had played him, toyed with him last night . . . It didn't matter *what* move Aelin had made. Anything she had done, they would have turned against her. Against him. Had Aelin played the damsel, they would have called her a weak and uncertain ally. There was no way to win.

The meeting with the khagan had been folly. Perhaps Kashin had played him, too. For if the khagan had been willing to hear him out before, he certainly was not going to now. And even if Nesryn returned with Sartaq's rukhin in tow . . . Her note yesterday had been carefully worded.

The rukhin are deft archers. They find my own skills intriguing, too.
I should like to keep instructing. And learning. They fly free here.
I'll see you in three weeks.

He didn't know what to make of it. The penultimate line. Was it an insult to him, or a coded message that the rukhin and Sartaq might disobey the commands of their khagan if he refused to let them leave? Would Sartaq truly risk treason to aid them? Chaol didn't dare leave the message unburned.

Fly free. He had never known such a feeling. It would never be his to

447

discover. These weeks with Yrene, dining in the city under the stars, talking to her about everything and nothing . . . It had come close, perhaps. But it did not change what lay ahead.

No—they were still very much alone in this war. And the longer he lingered, with his friends now in combat, now on the move . . .

He was still here. In this chair. With no army, no allies.

"Get up."

He slowly faced Yrene as she repeated her command, a hand tightly gripped under his shoulder, her face full of fiery challenge.

Chaol blinked at her. "What." Not quite a question.

"Get. Up." Her mouth tightened. "You want to die in this war so badly, then *get up*."

She was in a mood, too. Good. He'd been aching for a fight—the clashes with the guards still unsatisfactory in this gods-damned chair. But Yrene . . .

He hadn't allowed himself to touch her these weeks. Had made himself keep a distance, despite her unintentional moments of contact, the times when her head dipped close to his and all he could do was watch her mouth.

Yet he'd seen the tension in her at dinner last night, when Hasar had taunted about Nesryn's return. The disappointment she'd tried so hard to keep hidden, then the relief when he'd revealed Nesryn's extended trip.

He was a champion bastard. Even if he'd managed to convince the khagan to save their asses in this war . . . He would leave here. Empty handed or with an army, he'd leave. And despite Yrene's plans to return to their continent, he wasn't certain when he'd see her again. If ever.

None of them might make it anyway.

And this one task, this one task that his friends had given him, that Dorian had given him . . .

He'd failed.

Even with all he'd endured, all he'd learned . . . It was not enough.

Chaol gave a pointed look to his legs. *"How?"* They'd made more progress than he could have dreamed, yet this—

Her grip tightened to the point of pain. "You said it yourself: you don't have two years. I've repaired enough now that you *should* be able to stand. So get up." She even went so far as to tug on him.

He stared at her beneath lowered brows, letting his temper slip its leash by a few notches. "Let go."

"Or *what?*" Oh, she was pissed.

"Who knows what the spies will feed to the royals?" Cold, hard words.

Yrene's mouth tightened. "I have nothing to fear from their reports."

"Don't you? You didn't seem to mind the privileges that came when you snapped your fingers and Kashin ran here. Perhaps he'll grow tired of you stringing him along."

"That is nonsense and you know it." She tugged on his arm. "Get up."

He did no such thing. "So a prince is not good enough for you, but the disowned son of a lord is?"

He'd never even voiced the thought. Even to himself.

"Just because you're pissed off that Hasar and Arghun outmaneuvered you, that the khagan still won't listen to you, doesn't give you the right to try to drag *me* into a fight." Her lips curled back from her teeth. "Now get up, since you're so eager to rush off into battle."

He yanked his shoulder out of her grip. "You didn't answer the question."

"I'm not going to answer the question." Yrene didn't grab his shoulder again, but slid her entire arm under him and grunted, as if she'd lift him herself, when he was nearly double her weight.

Chaol gritted his teeth, and just to avoid her injuring herself, he shook her off again and set his feet on the floor. Braced his hands on the arms of the chair and hauled himself forward as far as he could manage. "And?"

He could move his knees and below, and his thighs had been tingling this past week every now and then, yet . . .

"And you remember how to stand, don't you?"

He only shot back, "Why did you look so relieved when I said Nesryn would be delayed a few more weeks?"

Color bloomed on her freckled skin, but she reached for him again, looping her arms through his. "I didn't want it to distract you from our progress."

"Liar." Her scent wrapped around him as she tugged, the chair groaning as he began to push down on the arms.

And then Yrene parried and went on the offensive, sleek as a snake. "I think *you* were relieved," she seethed, her breath hot against his ear. "I think *you* were glad for her to remain away, so you can pretend that you are honor-bound to her and let that be a wall. So that when you are here, with me, you don't need to see her watching, don't need to *think* about what she is to you. With her away, she is a memory, a distant ideal, but when she is here, and you look at her, what do you *see*? What do you *feel*?"

"I had her in my bed, so I think that says enough about my feelings."

He hated the words, even as the temper, the sharpness . . . it was a relief, too.

Yrene sucked in a breath, but didn't back down. "Yes, you had her in your bed, but I think she was likely a distraction, and was sick of it. Perhaps sick of being a consolation prize."

His arms strained, the chair wobbling as he pushed and pushed upward, if only so he could stand long enough to glare into her face. "You don't know what you're talking about." She had not mentioned Aelin at all, hadn't asked after last night's dinner. Until—

"Did she pick Dorian, then? The queen. I'm surprised she could stomach either of you, given your history. What your kingdom did to hers."

Roaring filled his ears as he began shifting his weight onto his feet, willing his spine to hold while he spat at her, "You didn't seem to mind it one bit, that night at the party. I had you practically begging me." He didn't know what the hell was coming out of his mouth.

450

Her nails dug into his back. "You'd be surprised the people that opiate makes you consider. Who you'll find yourself willing to sully yourself with."

"Right. A son of Adarlan. An oath-breaking, faithless traitor. That's what I am, isn't it?"

"I wouldn't know—you rarely even attempt to talk about it."

"And you are so good at it, I suppose?"

"This is about you, not me."

"Yet you were assigned to me because your Healer on High saw otherwise. Saw that no matter how high you climbed in that tower, you're still that girl in Fenharrow." A laugh came out of him, icy and bitter. "I knew another woman who lost as much as you. And do you know what she did with it—that loss?" He could barely stop the words from pouring out, could barely think over the roar in his head. "She hunted down the people responsible for it and *obliterated* them. What the hell have *you* bothered to do these years?"

Chaol felt the words hit their mark.

Felt the stillness shudder through her body.

Right as he pushed up—right as his weight adjusted and knees bent, and he found himself standing.

Too far. He'd gone too far. He'd never once believed those things. Even thought them.

Not about Yrene.

Her chest rose in a jagged breath that brushed against his, and she blinked up at him, mouth closing. And with the movement, he could see a wall rising up. Sealing.

Never again. She'd never again forgive him, smile at him, for what he'd said.

Never forget it. Standing or no.

"Yrene," he rasped, but she slid her arms from him and backed away a step, shaking her head. Leaving him standing—alone. Alone and exposed as she retreated another step and the sunlight caught in the silver starting to line her eyes.

451

It ripped his chest wide open.

Chaol put a hand on it, as if he could feel the caving within, even as his legs wavered beneath him. "I am *no one* to even mention such things. I am *nothing*, and it was *myself* that I—"

"I might not have battled kings and shattered castles," she said coldly, voice shaking with anger as she continued her retreat, "but I am the heir apparent to the Healer on High. Through my own work and suffering and sacrifice. And you're standing right now because of that. People are *alive* because of that. So I may not be a warrior waving a sword about, may not be worthy of your glorious tales, but at least I *save* lives—not end them."

"I know," he said, fighting the urge to grip the arms of the chair now seeming so far below him as his balance wavered. "Yrene, *I know.*" Too far. He had gone too far, and he had never hated himself more, for wanting to pick a fight and being so gods-damned *stupid*, when he'd really been talking about himself—

Yrene backed away another step.

"Please," he said.

But she was heading for the door. And if she left . . .

He had let them all go. Had walked out himself, too, but with Aelin, with Dorian, with Nesryn, he had let them go, and he had not gone after them.

But that woman backing toward the door, trying to keep the tears from falling—tears from the hurt *he'd* caused her, tears of the anger he so rightfully deserved—

She reached the handle. Fumbled blindly for it.

And if she left, if he let her walk out . . .

Yrene pushed down on the handle.

And Chaol took a step toward her.

❧ 39 ❧

Chaol did not think.

He did not marvel at the sensation of being so high. At the weight of his body, the sway of it as he took that staggering step.

There was only Yrene, and her hand on the doorknob, and the tears in her furious, lovely eyes. The most beautiful he'd ever seen.

They widened as he took that step toward her.

As he lurched and swayed. But he managed another.

Yrene stumbled toward him, studying him from head to toe, a hand rising to cover her open mouth. She stopped a few feet away.

He hadn't realized how much smaller she was. How delicate.

How—how the world looked and seemed and *tasted* this way.

"Don't go," he breathed. "I'm sorry."

Yrene surveyed him again, from his feet to his face. Tears slipped down her cheeks as she tipped her head back.

"I'm sorry," Chaol said again.

Still she did not speak. Tears only rolled and rolled.

"I meant none of it," he rasped, his knees beginning to ache and buckle, his thighs trembling. "I was spoiling for a fight and—I meant none of it, Yrene. None of it. And I'm sorry."

"A kernel of it must have been in you, though," she whispered.

Chaol shook his head, the motion making him sway. He gripped the back of a stuffed armchair to stay upright. "I meant it about myself. What you have done, Yrene, what you are willing to still do . . . You did this—*all* this not for glory or ambition, but because you believe it is the right thing to do. Your bravery, your cleverness, your unfaltering will . . . I do not have words for it, Yrene."

Her face did not change.

"Please, Yrene."

He reached for her, risking a staggering, wobbling step.

She took a step back.

Chaol's hands curled around empty air.

He clenched his jaw as he fought to remain upright, his body swaying and strange.

"Perhaps it makes you feel better about yourself to associate with meek, pathetic little people like me."

"I *do not* . . ." He ground his teeth, and lurched another step toward her, needing to just touch her, to take her hand and squeeze it, to just *show* her he wasn't like that. Didn't think like that. He swayed left, throwing out a hand to balance him as he bit out, "You know I didn't mean it."

Yrene backed away, keeping out of reach. "Do I?"

He pushed forward another step. Another.

She dodged him each time.

"You know it, damn you," he growled. He forced his legs into another jerking step.

Yrene sidled out of the way.

He blinked, pausing.

Reading the light in her eyes. The tone.

The witch was tricking him into walking. Coaxing him to move. To follow.

She paused, meeting his stare, not a trace of that hurt in them, as if to say, *It took you long enough to figure it out*. A little smile bloomed on her mouth.

He was standing. He was . . . walking.

Walking. And this woman before him . . .

Chaol made it another step.

Yrene retreated.

Not a hunt, but a dance.

He did not remove his eyes from hers as he staggered another step, and another, his body aching, trembling. But he gritted through it. Fought for each inch toward her. Each step that had her backing up to the wall.

Her breath came in shallow pants, those golden eyes so wide as he tracked her across the room. As she led him one foot after another.

Until her back hit the wall, the sconce on it rattling. As if she'd lost track of where she was.

Chaol was instantly upon her.

He braced one hand upon the wall, the wallpaper smooth beneath his palm as he put his weight upon it. To keep his body upright as his thighs shook, back straining.

They were smaller, secondary concerns.

His other hand . . .

Yrene's eyes were still bright with those tears he'd caused.

One still clung to her cheek.

Chaol wiped it away. Another one he found down by her jaw.

He didn't understand—how she could be so delicate, so small, when she had overturned his life entirely. Worked miracles with those hands and that soul, this woman who had crossed mountains and seas.

She was trembling. Not with fear, not as she looked up at him.

And it was only when Yrene settled her hand on his chest, not to push him away but to feel the raging, thunderous heartbeat beneath, that Chaol lowered his head and kissed her.

455

He was standing. He was *walking*.

And he was kissing her.

Yrene could barely breathe, barely keep inside her skin, as Chaol's mouth settled over hers.

It was like waking up or being born or falling out of the sky. It was an answer and a song, and she could not think or feel fast enough.

Her hands curled into his shirt, fingers wrapping around fistfuls of fabric, tugging him closer.

His lips caressed hers in patient, unhurried movements, as if tracing the feel of her. And when his teeth grazed her lower lip . . . She opened her mouth to him.

He swept in, pressing her farther into the wall. She barely felt the molding digging into her spine, the sleekness of the wallpaper against her back as his tongue slid into her mouth.

Yrene moaned, not caring who heard, who might be listening. They could all go to hell for all she cared. She was burning, glowing—

Chaol laid a hand against her jaw, angling her face to better claim her mouth. She arched, silently begging him to *take*—

She knew he hadn't meant what he said, knew it had been himself he'd been raging at. She'd goaded him into that fight, and even if it had hurt . . . She'd known the moment he stood, when her heart had stopped dead, that he hadn't meant it.

That he would have crawled.

This man, this noble and selfless and remarkable man . . .

Yrene dragged her hands around his shoulders, fingers slipping into his silken brown hair. *More, more, more*—

But his kiss was thorough. As if he wanted to learn every taste, every angle of her.

She brushed her tongue against his, and his growl had her toes curling in her slippers—

She felt the tremor go through him before she registered what it was. The strain.

Still he kissed her, seemed intent to do so, even if it brought him crashing to the floor.

Small steps. Small measures.

Yrene broke away, putting a hand on his chest when he made to claim her mouth again. "You should sit."

His eyes were wholly black. "I—let me—*please*, Yrene."

Each word was a broken rasp. As if he'd freed some tether on himself.

She fought to keep her breathing steady. To gather her wits. Too long on his feet and he might strain his back. And before she could encourage the walking and—*more*, she needed to go into his wound to look around. Perhaps it had receded enough on its own.

Chaol brushed his mouth against hers, the silken heat of his lips enough to make her willing to ignore common sense.

But she shoved back against it. Gently slid out of his reach. "Now I'll have ways to reward you," she said, trying for humor.

He didn't smile back. Didn't do anything but watch her with near-predatory intent as she backed away a step and offered her arm to him. To walk back to the chair.

To *walk*.

He was *walking*—

He did so. Pushed off the wall, and swayed—

Yrene caught him, steadied him.

"I thought you never stepped in to help me," he said drily, raising a brow.

"In the chair, yes. You have much farther to fall now."

Chaol huffed a laugh, then leaned in to whisper in her ear, "Will it be the bed or the couch now, Yrene?"

She swallowed, daring a sidelong look up at him. His eyes were still dark, his face flushed and lips swollen. From her.

Yrene's blood heated, her core near-molten. How the hell would she have him nearly naked before her now?

"You are still my patient," she managed to say primly, and guided him into his chair. Nearly shoved him onto it—and nearly leaped atop him, too. "And while there is no official vow about such things, I plan to keep things professional."

Chaol's answering smile was anything but. So was the way he growled, "Come here."

Yrene's heartbeat pounded through every inch of her as she closed the foot of space between them. As she held his burning gaze and settled into his lap.

His hand slid beneath her hair to cup the back of her neck, drawing her face to his as he brushed a kiss over the corner of her mouth. Then the other. She gripped his shoulder, fingers digging into the hard muscle beneath, her breathing turning jagged as he nipped at her bottom lip, as his other hand began to explore up her torso—

A door opened in the hallway, and Yrene was instantly up, striding across the sitting room for the desk—to the vials of oil there. Just as Kadja slipped through the door, a tray in her hands.

The servant girl had found the "ingredients" Yrene needed. Twine, goat's milk, and vinegar.

Yrene could barely remember words to thank the servant as the girl set the tray on the desk.

Whether Kadja saw their faces, their hair and clothes, and could read the white-hot line of tension between them, she said nothing. Yrene had no doubt she might suspect, would no doubt report it to whoever held her leash, but . . . Yrene found herself not caring as she leaned against the desk, Kadja departing as silently as she had come.

Found Chaol still watching her, chest heaving.

"What do we do now?" Yrene asked quietly.

For she didn't know—how to go *back*—

Chaol didn't reply. He just stretched out one leg wholly in front of him. Then the other. Did it again, marveling.

"We don't look back," he said, meeting her stare. "It helps no one and nothing to look back." The way he said it . . . It seemed as if it meant something more. To him, at least.

But Chaol's smile grew, his eyes lighting as he added, "We can only go on."

Yrene went to him, unable to stop herself, as if that smile were a beacon in the dark.

And when Chaol wheeled himself to the couch and peeled off his shirt, when he lay down and she set her hands on his warm, strong back . . . Yrene smiled as well.

⊰ 40 ⊱

Standing and walking a few steps wasn't the same as being back to full capacity.

The next week proved it. Yrene still battled with whatever lurked in Chaol's spine, still clinging—down to the very base, she explained—and still keeping him from full motion. Running, most jumping, kicking: out of the question. But thanks to the sturdy wooden cane she procured for him, he could stand, and he could walk.

And it was a gods-damned miracle.

He brought the cane and the chair to his morning training with Hashim and the guards, for the moments when he pushed himself too hard and couldn't manage the return trip to his rooms. Yrene joined him during the early lessons, instructing Hashim on where to focus in his legs. To rebuild more muscle. To stabilize him further. She'd done the same for Shen, Hashim had confided one morning—had come to supervise most of his initial training sessions after his injury.

So Yrene had been there, watching from the sidelines, that first day Chaol had taken up a sword against Hashim and dueled. Or did it as best he could with the cane in one hand.

His balance was shit, his legs unreliable, but he managed to get in a few good hits against the man. And a cane . . . not a bad weapon, if the fight called for it.

Yrene's eyes had been wide as saucers when they stopped and Chaol approached her spot on the wall, leaning heavily on the cane as his body trembled.

The color on her face, he realized with no small amount of male satisfaction, was from far more than the heat. And when they'd eventually left, walking slowly into the cool shadows of the halls, Yrene had tugged him into a curtained-off alcove and kissed him.

Leaning against a supply shelf for support, his hands had roved all over her, the generous curves and small waist, tangling into her long, heavy hair. She'd kissed and kissed him, breathless and panting, and then licked—actually *licked* the sweat from his neck.

Chaol had groaned so loudly that it was no surprise a servant appeared a heartbeat later, ripping the curtain away, as if to chide two workers for shirking their duties.

Yrene had blanched as she'd righted herself and asked the bowing and scraping male servant not to say anything. He assured her that he wouldn't, but Yrene had been shaken. She'd kept her distance for the rest of the walk back.

And maintained it every day since. It was driving him mad.

But he understood. With her position, both in the Torre and within the palace, they should be smarter. More careful.

And with Kadja always in his rooms . . .

Chaol kept his hands to himself. Even when Yrene laid her own hands upon his back and healed him, pushed and pushed herself, to break through that final wall of darkness.

461

He wanted to tell her, debated telling her, that it was already enough. He would gladly live with the cane for the rest of his life. She had given him more than he could ever hope for.

For he saw the guards every morning. The weapons and shields.

And he thought of that war, unleashing itself at last upon his friends. His homeland.

Even if he did not bring an army with him when he returned, he'd find some way to stand on those battlefields. Riding, at least, was now a viable option while fighting alongside them.

Fighting for—her.

He was thinking of it as they walked to dinner one night, over a week later. With the cane, it took him longer than usual, but he did not mind any extra moment spent in her company.

She was wearing her purple gown—his favorite—her hair half up and curling softly from the unusually humid day. But she was jumpy, unsettled.

"What is it?"

The royals hadn't cared the first night he'd walked on his own two legs to dinner. Another everyday miracle of the Torre, though the khagan himself had commended Yrene. She'd beamed at the praise. Even as the khagan had ignored Chaol—as he had done since that ill-fated meeting.

Yrene rubbed at the scar on her neck as if it ached. He hadn't asked about it—didn't want to know. Only because if he did . . . Even with a war upon them, he might very well take the time to hunt down whoever had done it and bury them.

"I convinced Hasar to throw me a party," Yrene said quietly.

He waited until they'd passed a cluster of servants before asking, "For what reason?"

She blew out a breath. "It's my birthday. In three days."

"Your birthday?"

"You know, the celebration of the day of your birth—"

He nudged her with an elbow, though his spine slipped and shifted with the movement. The cane groaned as he pressed his weight upon it. "I had no idea that she-devils actually had them."

She stuck out her tongue. "Yes, even my kind has them."

Chaol grinned. "So you asked her to throw one for you?" Considering how the last *party* had gone . . . He might very well wind up one of those people slipping away into a darkened bedroom. Especially if Yrene wore that dress again.

"Not exactly," Yrene said wryly. "I mentioned that my birthday was coming up, and how dull *your* plans for it were . . ."

He chuckled. "Presumptuous of you."

She batted her eyelashes. "And I *might* have mentioned that in all my years here, I've never been to the desert and was debating a trip of my own, but that I'd be sad to not celebrate with her . . ."

"And I'm guessing that she suggested an oasis owned by her family instead?"

Yrene hummed. "A little overnight excursion to Aksara—half a day's ride to the east, to their permanent tented camp within the oasis."

So the healer could scheme after all. But—"It'll be boiling in this heat."

"The princess wants a party in the desert. So she shall have one." She chewed on her lip, those shadows dancing again. "I also managed to ask her about it—Aksara. The history." Chaol braced himself. "Hasar grew bored before she told me much, but she said that she'd once heard that the oasis grew atop a city of the dead. That the ruins now there were merely the gateway inside. They don't like to risk disturbing the dead, so they never leave the spring itself—to venture into the jungle around it."

No wonder she'd seemed concerned. "Not only caves to be found, then."

"Perhaps Nousha means something different; perhaps there are also caves there with information." She blew out a breath. "I suppose we'll see. I made sure to yawn while Hasar told me, enough that I doubt she'll wonder why I asked at all."

463

Chaol kissed her temple, a swift brush of his mouth that no one might see. "Clever, Yrene."

"I meant to tell you the other week, but then you stood, and I forgot. Some court schemer I am."

He caressed his free hand down the length of her spine. A bit lower. "We've been otherwise engaged." Her face flushed a beautiful shade of pink, but a thought settled into him. "What do *you* really want for your birthday? And which one is it?"

"Twenty-two. And I don't know. If it wasn't for this, I wouldn't have brought it up at all."

"You weren't going to tell me?"

She gave him a guilty frown. "I figured that with everything pressing on you, birthdays were inconsequential." Her hand slid into her pocket—to hold that thing he'd never inquired about.

They neared the clamor of dinner in the great hall. He brushed his fingers against hers. She halted at the silent request, the hall spreading away before them, servants and viziers striding past.

Chaol leaned on his cane while they rested, letting it stabilize his weight. "Am I invited to this desert party, at least?"

"Oh, yes. You, and all my other favorite people: Arghun, Kashin, and a handful of delightful viziers."

"I'm glad I made the cut, considering that Hasar hates me."

"No." Yrene's eyes darkened. "If Hasar hated you, I don't think you'd be alive right now."

Gods above. This was the woman she'd befriended.

Yrene went on, "At least Renia will be there, but Duva shouldn't be in the heat in her condition and her husband won't leave her side. I'm sure that once we get there, information or no, I'll probably wish I could have made a similar excuse."

"We've got a few days. We could, technically, make the same one if we need to leave."

464

The words settled in. The invitation and implication. Yrene's face went delightfully red, and she smacked his arm. "Rogue."

Chaol chuckled, and eyed the hallway for a shadowed corner. But Yrene breathed, "We can't."

Not about his sorry joke, but about the want she no doubt saw building in his eyes. The want he beheld simmering in hers.

He adjusted his jacket. "Well, I'll attempt to find you a suitable present that can compare to an entire desert *retreat*, but don't hold me to it."

Yrene looped her arm through Chaol's free one, no more than a healer escorting her patient to the table. "I have everything I need," was all she said.

⊰ 41 ⊱

It took over a week to plan it.

Over a week alone for Sartaq and Houlun to dig up ancient maps of the Dagul Fells.

Most were vague and useless. What riders had assessed from the air but not dared get too close to detail. The *kharankui*'s territory was small, but had grown larger, bolder these last few years.

And it was into the dark heart of their territory that they would go.

The hardest part was convincing Borte to remain behind.

But Nesryn and Sartaq left that up to Houlun. And one sharp word from the hearth-mother had the girl falling in line. Even as Borte's eyes simmered with outrage, she bowed to her grandmother's wishes. As heir, Houlun had snapped, Borte's first obligation was to their *people*. The bloodline ended with her. Should Borte head into the dim tangle of Dagul, she might as well spit upon where her mother's *sulde* stood on the slopes of Arundin.

Borte had insisted that if she, as Houlun's heir, was to stay, then Sartaq, as the khagan's potential successor, should remain as well.

To that, Sartaq had merely stalked off into the interior hallways of Altun, saying that if being his father's successor meant sitting idly by while others fought for him, then his siblings could have the damn crown.

So only the three of them would go, Nesryn and Sartaq flying on Kadara, Falkan tucked away as a field mouse in Nesryn's pocket.

There had been a final debate last night about bringing a legion. Borte had argued for it, Sartaq against it. They did not know how many *kharankui* dwelled in the barren peaks and forested vales between them. They could not risk needlessly losing many lives, and did not have the time to waste on thorough reconnaissance. Three could sneak in—but an army of ruks would be spotted long before they arrived.

The argument had raged over the fire pit, but Houlun had settled it: the small company would go. And if they did not return within four days, an army would follow. Half a day to fly down, a day to survey the area, a day to go in, and then return with the stolen hatchlings. Perhaps even learn what the Fae had feared from the spiders, how they'd fought them. If they were lucky.

They'd been flying for hours now, the high wall of the Fells growing closer with every flap of Kadara's wings. Soon, now, they'd cross that first ridge of the gray mountains and enter into the spiders' territory. Nesryn's breakfast sat heavy in her stomach with each mile closer, her mouth as dry as parchment.

Behind her, Sartaq had been silent for most of the ride. Falkan dozed in her breast pocket, emerging only now and then to poke out his whiskered snout, sniff at the air, and then duck back inside. Conserving his strength while he could.

The shifter was still sleeping when Nesryn said to Sartaq, "Did you mean what you said last night—about refusing the crown if it meant not fighting?"

Sartaq's body was a warm wall at her back. "My father has gone to war—all khagans have. He possesses the Ebony and Ivory *sulde* precisely for that. But if it somehow became the case that I would be denied such things in favor of the bloodline surviving . . . Yes. A life confined to that court is not what I want."

"And yet you are favored to become khagan one day."

"So the rumors say. But my father has never suggested or spoken of it. For all I know, he could crown Duva instead. The gods know she'd certainly be a kind ruler. And is the only one of us to have produced offspring."

Nesryn chewed her lip. "Why—why is it that you haven't married?" She'd never had the nerve to ask. Though she'd certainly found herself wondering it during these weeks.

Sartaq's hands flexed on the reins before he answered. "I've been too busy. And the women who have been presented as potential brides . . . They were not for me."

She had no right to pry, but she asked, "Why?"

"Because whenever I showed them Kadara, they either cowered, or pretended to be interested in her, or asked just how much time I'd be spending away."

"Hoping for frequent absences, or because they'd miss you?"

Sartaq chuckled. "I couldn't tell. The question itself felt like enough of a leash that I knew they were not for me."

"So your father allows you to wed where you will?" Dangerous, strange territory. She waited for him to tease her about it, but Sartaq fell quiet.

"Yes. Even Duva's arranged marriage . . . She was all for it. Said she didn't want to have to sort through a court of snakes to find one good man and still pray he hadn't deceived her. I wonder if there's something to be said for it. She lucked out, anyway—quiet as he is, her husband adores her. I saw his face the moment they met. Saw hers, too. Relief, and . . . something more."

And what would become of them—of their child—if another Heir

468

were chosen for the throne? Nesryn asked carefully, "Why not end this tradition of competing with each other?"

Sartaq was silent for a long minute. "Perhaps one day, whoever takes the throne will end it. Love their siblings more than they honor the tradition. I like to believe we have moved past who we were centuries ago— when the empire was still fledgling. But perhaps now, these years of relative peace, perhaps this is the dangerous time." He shrugged, his body shifting against hers. "Perhaps war will sort the matter of succession for us."

And maybe it was because they were so high above the world, because that dim land swept ever closer, but Nesryn asked, "There is nothing that would keep you from war if it called, then?"

"You sound as if you are reconsidering this goal of yours to drag us into the north."

She stiffened. "I will admit that these weeks here . . . It was easier before to ask for your aid. When the rukhin were a nameless, faceless legion. When I did not know their names, their families. When I did not know Houlun, or Borte. Or that Borte is *betrothed*."

A low laugh at that. Borte had refused—outright refused—to answer Nesryn's questions about Yeran. She said it wasn't even worth talking about.

"I'm sure Borte would be glad to go to war, if only to compete with Yeran for glory on the battlefield."

"A true love match, then."

Sartaq smiled at her ear. "You have no idea." He sighed. "It began three years ago—this competition between them. Right after her mother died."

His pause was heavy enough that Nesryn asked, "You knew her mother well?"

It took him a moment to answer. "I mentioned to you once that I've been sent to other kingdoms to sort out disputes or murmurings of malcontent. The last time my father sent me, I brought a small unit of rukhin along, Borte's mother with them."

Again, that heavy quiet. Nesryn slowly, carefully laid her hand on his forearm that encircled her. The strong muscles beneath the leather shifted—then settled.

"It is a long story, and a hard one, but there was violence between the rukhin and the group that sought to bring down our empire. Borte's mother . . . One of them got in a coward's shot from behind. A poisoned arrow through her neck, right when we were about to allow them to surrender." The wind howled around them. "I didn't let any of them walk away after that."

The hollow, cold words said enough.

"I carried her body back myself," Sartaq said, the words ripped away by the wind. "I can still hear Borte's screaming when I landed in Altun. Still see her kneeling alone on the slopes of Arundin after the burial, clinging to her mother's *sulde* where it had been planted in the ground."

Nesryn tightened her grip on his arm. Sartaq placed his own gloved hand upon hers and squeezed gently as he blew out a long breath.

"Six months later," he went on, "Borte competed in the Gathering— the annual three days of contests and races among all the clans. She was seventeen, and Yeran was twenty, and they were neck and neck for the final, great race. As they neared the finish, Yeran pulled a maneuver that *might* be considered cheating, but Borte saw it coming a mile off and beat him anyway. And then beat him soundly when they landed. Literally. He leaped off his ruk and she *tackled* him to the ground, pounding his face for the shit he'd pulled that nearly got Arcas killed." He laughed to himself. "I don't know the particulars of what went on later at the celebration, but I saw him attempt to talk to her at one point, and saw her laugh in his face before walking away. He scowled until they left the next morning, and as far as I know, they didn't see each other for a year. Until the next Gathering."

"Which Borte won again," Nesryn guessed.

"She did indeed. Barely. *She* pulled the questionable maneuver this time, getting herself banged up in the process, but she technically won. I think Yeran was secretly more terrified of how close she'd come to permanent injury or death, so he let her have the victory. She never told me the particulars of *that* celebration, but she was shaken for a few days after. We all assumed it was from her injuries, but such things had never bothered her before."

"And this year?"

"This year, a week before the Gathering, Yeran appeared at Altun. Didn't see Houlun, or me. Just went right to wherever Borte was in the hall. No one knows what happened, but he stayed for less than thirty minutes from landing to leaving. A week later, Borte won the race again. And when she was crowned victor, Yeran's father stepped up to declare her engagement to his son."

"A surprise?"

"Considering that whenever Borte and Yeran are together, they're at each other's throats, yes. But also a surprise to Borte. She played it off, but I saw them arguing in the hall later. Whether or not she even *knew* about it, or wanted it revealed that way, she still won't say. But she has not disputed the betrothal. Though she hasn't embraced it, either. No day has been claimed for the wedding, even though the union would certainly ease our . . . strained ties to the Berlad."

Nesryn smiled a bit. "I hope they sort it out."

"Perhaps this war will do that for them, too."

Kadara swept closer and closer to the wall of the Fells, the light turning thin and cold as clouds passed over the sun. They cleared the towering lip of the first peaks, soaring on an updraft high above as all of Dagul spread before them.

"Holy gods," Nesryn whispered.

⁓

Dark gray peaks of barren rock. Thin pine trees crusting the vales deep below. No lakes, no rivers save for the occasional trickling stream.

Barely visible through the shroud of webbing over all of it.

Some webs were thick and white, choking the life from trees. Some were sparkling nets between peaks, as if they sought to catch the wind itself.

No life. No hum of insect or cry of beast. No sighing leaves or fluttering wings.

Falkan poked his head out of her pocket as they surveyed the dead land below and let out a squeak. Nesryn nearly did the same.

"Houlun was not exaggerating," Sartaq murmured. "They have grown strong."

"Where do we even land?" Nesryn asked. "There's barely a safe spot to be seen. They could have taken the hatchlings and eggs anywhere."

She combed the peaks and valleys for any sign of movement, any flicker of those sleek black bodies scuttling about. But saw nothing.

"We'll make a pass around the territory," Sartaq said. "Get a sense of the layout. Perhaps figure out a thing or two regarding their feeding habits."

Gods above. "Keep Kadara high. Fly casual. If we look like we're hunting for something, they might emerge in force."

Sartaq whistled sharply to Kadara, who indeed soared higher, faster than her usual ascent. As if glad to rise a little farther from the shrouded territory below.

"Stay hidden, friend," Nesryn said to Falkan, her hands shaking as she patted her breast pocket. "If they watch us from below, we'd best keep you secret until they least expect it."

Falkan's tiny paws tapped in understanding, and he slid back into her pocket.

They flew in idle circles for a time, Kadara occasionally diving as if in pursuit of some eagle or falcon. On the hunt for lunch, perhaps.

"That cluster of peaks," Sartaq said after a while, pointing toward the highest point of the Fells. Like horns spearing toward the sky, two sister-peaks jutted up so close to each other they might have very well once been a single mountain. Between their clawed summits, a shale-filled pass wended away into a labyrinth of stone. "Kadara keeps looking toward it."

472

"Circle it, but keep your distance."

Before Sartaq could give the order, Kadara obeyed.

"Something is moving in the pass," Nesryn breathed, squinting.

Kadara flapped closer, nearer to the peaks than was wise. "Kadara," Sartaq warned.

But the ruk pumped her wings, frantic. Rushing.

Just as the thing in the pass became clear.

Racing over the shale, bobbing and flapping fuzz-lined wings . . .

A hatchling.

Sartaq swore. "Faster, Kadara. *Faster*." The ruk needed no encouragement.

The hatchling was squawking, those too-small wings flailing as it tried and failed to lift from the ground. It had broken from the pine trees that flowed right to the edge of the pass, and now aimed for the center of the maze of rock.

Nesryn unslung her bow and nocked an arrow into place, Sartaq doing the same behind her. "*Not a sound, Kadara,*" Sartaq warned, just as the ruk opened her beak. "You will alert them."

But the hatchling was screeching, its terror palpable even from the distance.

Kadara caught a wind and *flew*.

"Come on," Nesryn breathed, arrow aimed at the woods, at whatever horrors the hatchling had escaped, undoubtedly barreling after it.

The baby ruk neared the broadest part of the pass mouth, balking at the wall of stone ahead. As if it knew that more waited within.

Trapped.

"Sweep in, cut through the pass, and sail out," Sartaq ordered the ruk, who banked right, so steeply Nesryn's abdomen strained with the effort to keep in the saddle.

Kadara leveled out, dropping foot by foot toward the hatchling now twisting about, screaming toward the sky as it beheld the ruk rushing in.

"Steady," Sartaq commanded. "Steady, Kadara."

Nesryn kept her arrow trained on the labyrinth of rock ahead, Sartaq twisting to cover the forest behind. Kadara sailed closer and closer to the shale-coated pass, to the grayish fuzzy hatchling now holding so still, waiting for the salvation of the claws that Kadara unfurled.

Thirty feet. Twenty.

Nesryn's arm strained to keep the arrow drawn.

A wind shoved at Kadara, knocking her sideways, the world tilting, light shimmering.

Just as Kadara leveled out, just as her talons opened wide to scoop up the hatchling, Nesryn realized what the shimmering was. What the shift in angle revealed ahead.

"Look out!"

The scream shattered from her throat, but too late.

Kadara's talons closed around the hatchling, plucking it up from the ground right as she swept up through the pass peaks.

Right into the mammoth web woven between them.

⇥ 42 ⇤

The hatchling had been a trap.

It was the last thought Nesryn had as Kadara crashed into the web—the *net* woven between the two peaks. Built not to catch the wind, but *ruks*.

She only had the sense of Sartaq throwing his body into hers, anchoring her into the saddle and holding tight as Kadara screamed.

Snapping and shimmering and rock; shale and gray sky and golden feathers. Wind howling, the hatchling's piercing cry, and Sartaq's bellow.

Then twisting, slamming into stone so hard the impact sang through her teeth, her bones. Then falling, tumbling, Kadara's restrained body curving, curving as Sartaq was curled over Nesryn, shielding that hatchling in her talons from the final impact.

Then the *boom*. And the bounce—the bounce that snapped the leather straps on the saddle. Still tied to it, they were still tied together as they soared off Kadara's body, Nesryn's bow scattering from her hand, her fingers clasping on open air—

Sartaq pivoted them, his body a solid wall around hers as Nesryn realized where the sky was, where the pass floor was—

He roared as they struck the shale, as he kept her atop him, taking the full brunt of the impact.

For a heartbeat, there was only the skittering trickle of shifting shale and the thud of crumbling rock off the pass walls. For a heartbeat, she could not remember where her body was, her breath was—

Then a scrape of wing on shale.

Nesryn's eyes snapped open, and she was moving before she had the words to name her motions.

A cut slashed down her wrist, caked with small rocks and dust. She didn't feel it, barely noticed the blood as she blindly fumbled for the straps to the saddle, snapping them free, panting through her teeth as she managed to lift her head, to dare to look—

He was dazed. Blinking up at the gray sky. But alive, *breathing*, blood sliding down his temple, his cheek, his mouth . . .

She sobbed through her teeth, her legs at last coming free, allowing her to roll over to get to his own, to the tangled bits of leather shredded between them.

Sartaq was half buried in shale. His hands sliced up, but his legs—

"Not broken," he rasped. "Not broken." It was more to himself than her. But Nesryn managed to keep her fingers steady as she freed the buckles. The thick riding leathers had saved his life, saved his skin from being flayed off his bones. He'd taken the impact for her, moved her so that he'd hit it first—

She clawed at the shale covering his shoulders and his upper arms, sharp rock cutting into her fingers. The leather strap at the end of her braid had come free in the impact, and her hair now fell about her face, half blocking her view of the forest behind and rock around them. "Get up," she panted. "Get up."

He took a breath, blinking furiously. "*Get up*," she begged him.

Shale shifted ahead, and a low, pained cry echoed off the rock.

Sartaq snapped upright. "*Kadara*—"

Nesryn twisted on her knees, scanning for her bow even as she took in the ruk.

Lying thirty feet ahead, Kadara was coated in the near-invisible silk. A phantom net, her wings pinned, her head tucked in—

Sartaq scrambled upright, swaying, slipping on the loose shale as he drew his Asterion knife.

Nesryn managed to rise, her legs shaking, head spinning as she scanned and scanned the pass for her bow—

There. Near the pass wall. Intact.

She hurtled for it while Sartaq ran to the ruk, reaching her weapon just as he sliced the first of the webbing free.

"You'll be fine," he was saying to Kadara, blood coating his hands, his neck. "I'll get you out—"

Nesryn shouldered her bow, pressing a hand to her pocket. Falkan—

A little leg pushed against her in answer. *Alive.*

She wasted no time rushing to the ruk, drawing her own Fae blade from the sheath Borte had found for her and slicing at the thick strands. It clung to her fingers, ripping away skin, but she severed and sliced, working her way down the wing as Sartaq hacked his way down the other.

They reached Kadara's legs at the same time.

Saw that her talons were empty.

Nesryn's head snapped up, scanning the pass, the piles of disturbed shale—

The hatchling had been thrown during the collision. As if even Kadara's talons couldn't keep shut against the pain of impact. The baby ruk now lay on the ground near the lip of the pass, struggling to rise, low chirps of distress echoing off the rock.

"Up, Kadara," Sartaq commanded, his voice breaking. "*Get up.*"

Great wings shifted, shale clacking as the ruk tried to obey. Nesryn staggered toward the hatchling, blood unmistakable on its fluffy gray head, its large dark eyes wide with terror and pleading—

It happened so fast Nesryn didn't have time to shout.

One heartbeat, the hatchling had opened its beak to cry for help.

The next it screamed, eyes flaring as a long ebony leg emerged from behind a pillar of rock and slammed through its spine.

Bone crunched and blood sprayed. And Nesryn threw herself into a stop, swaying so hard she teetered backward onto her ass, a wordless cry on her lips as the hatchling was hauled around the rock, flailing and shrieking—

It went silent.

And she had seen horrific things, things that had made her sick and kept her from sleep, and yet that baby ruk, terrified and pleading, in pain and dragged away, going *silent*—

Nesryn whirled, feet slipping on the shale as she scrambled toward Kadara, toward Sartaq, who beheld the hatchling being snatched behind that rock and screamed at Kadara to fly—

The mighty ruk tried and failed to rise.

"*FLY*," Sartaq bellowed.

Slowly, so slowly the ruk lumbered to her legs, her scraped beak dragging through the loose rock.

She wasn't going to make it. Wasn't going to get airborne in time. For just beyond the web-shrouded tree line . . . Shadows writhed. Scuttled closer.

Nesryn sheathed her sword and drew her bow, arrow shaking as she aimed it toward the rock the hatchling had been hauled behind, then the trees a hundred yards off.

"*Go, Kadara*," Sartaq begged. "*Get up!*"

The bird was barely in shape to fly, let alone carry riders—

Rock clacked and skittered behind her. From the labyrinth of rock within the pass.

Trapped. They were trapped—

Falkan shifted in her pocket, trying to wriggle free. Nesryn covered him with her forearm, pressing hard. "Not yet," she breathed. "Not yet."

His powers were not Lysandra's. He had tried and failed to shift into a ruk this week. But the large wolf was as big as he could manage. Anything larger was beyond his magic.

"*Kadara*—"

The first of the spiders broke from the tree line. As black and sleek as her fallen sister.

Nesryn let her arrow fly.

The spider fell back, screaming—an unholy sound that shook the rocks as that arrow sank into an eye. Nesryn instantly had another arrow drawn, backing toward Kadara, who was just now beginning to flap her wings—

The ruk stumbled.

Sartaq screamed, "*FLY!*"

Wind stirred Nesryn's hair, sending shards of shale skittering. The ground rumbled behind, but Nesryn did not dare take her eyes off the second spider that emerged from the trees. She fired again, the song of her arrow drowned out by the flap of Kadara's wings. A heavy, pained beat, but it held steady—

Nesryn glanced behind for a breath. Just one, just to see Kadara bobbing and waving, fighting for every wing beat upward through the narrow pass, blood and shale dripping from her. Right as a *kharankui* emerged from one of the shadows of the rocks high up the peak, legs bending as if it would leap upon the ruk's back—

Nesryn fired, a second arrow on its tail. Sartaq's.

Both found their marks. One through an eye, the other through the open mouth of the spider.

It shrieked, tumbling down from its perch. Kadara swung wide to dodge it, narrowly avoiding the jagged face of the peak. The spider's splat thudded through the maze of rock ahead.

But then Kadara was up, into the gray sky, flapping like hell.

Sartaq whirled toward Nesryn just as she looked back at the pine forest.

To where half a dozen *kharankui* now emerged, hissing.

Blood coated the prince, his every breath ragged, but he managed to grab Nesryn's arm and breathe, "*Run.*"

So they did.

Not toward the pines behind.

But into the gloom of the winding pass ahead.

⇥ 43 ⇤

Without the brace, Chaol was given a black mare, Farasha, whose name was about as ill-fitting as they came. It meant *butterfly*, Yrene told him as they gathered in the palace courtyard three days later.

Farasha was anything but.

Yanking at the bit, stomping her hooves and tossing her head, Farasha savored testing his limits long before the desert-bound company finished gathering. Servants had gone ahead the day before to prepare the camp.

He'd known the royals would give him their fiercest horse. Not a stallion, but one close enough to match it in fury. Farasha had been born furious, he was willing to bet.

And he'd be damned if he let those royals make him ask for another horse. One that would not strain his back and legs so much.

Yrene was frowning at Farasha, at him, as she stroked a hand down her chestnut mare's night-black mane.

Both beautiful horses, though neither compared to the stunning Asterion stallion Dorian had gifted Chaol for his birthday last winter.

Another birthday celebration. Another time—another life.

He wondered what had happened to that beautiful horse, whom he had never named. As if he'd known, deep down, how fleeting those few happy weeks were. He wondered if it was still in the royal stables. Or if the witches had pillaged him—or let their horrible mounts use him to fill their bellies.

Perhaps that was why Farasha resented his very presence. Perhaps she sensed that he had forgotten that noble-hearted stallion in the north. And wanted to make him pay for it.

The breed was an offshoot of the Asterions, Hasar had tittered as she'd trotted past on her white stallion, circling him twice. The refined, wedge-shaped head and high tails were twin markers of their Fae ancestry. But these horses, the Muniqi, had been bred for the desert climes of this land. For the sands they were to cross today, and the steppes that had once been the khagan's homeland. The princess had even pointed to a slight bulge between the horses' eyes—the *jibbah*—the marker of the larger sinus capacity that allowed the Muniqi to thrive in the dry, unyielding deserts of this continent.

And then there was the Muniqi's speed. Not as fast, Hasar admitted, as an Asterion. But close.

Yrene had watched the princess's little *lesson*, face carefully neutral, using the time to adjust where she'd strapped Chaol's cane behind her saddle, then fiddle with the clothes she wore.

While Chaol was in his usual teal jacket and brown pants, Yrene had forgone a dress.

They'd swathed her in white and gold against the sun, her long tunic flowing to her knees to reveal loose, gauzy pants tucked into high brown boots. A belt cinched her slim waist, and a glinting bandolier of gold and silver beading sliced between her breasts. Her hair, she'd left in her usual half-up fashion, but someone had woven bits of gold thread through it.

Beautiful. As lovely as a sunrise.

There were perhaps thirty of them in total, none people Yrene really knew, as Hasar had not bothered to invite any of the healers from the Torre. Swift-legged hounds paced in the courtyard, weaving under the hooves of the dozen guards' horses. Definitely not Muniqi, those horses. Fine indeed for guards—his men had received beasts nowhere near their quality—but without that *awareness* the Muniqi possessed, as if they listened to every word spoken.

Hasar signaled to Shen, standing proud at the gate, who blew a horn—
And then they were off.

For a woman who commanded ships, Hasar seemed far more interested in the equine heritage of her family's people. And seemed more than eager to unleash her skills as a Darghan rider. The princess cursed and scowled as the city streets slowed them. Even with word given well in advance to clear the path out of Antica, the narrow and steep streets checked their speed considerably.

And then there was the brutal heat. Already sweating, Chaol rode beside Yrene, keeping a tight leash on Farasha, who tried to take a bite out of not one but two vendors gawking from the sidewalks. *Butterfly* indeed.

He kept one eye upon the mare and the other upon the city passing by. And as they rode for the eastern gates into the arid, scrub-covered hills beyond, Yrene pointed out landmarks and tidbits of information.

Water ran through aqueducts wending between the buildings, feeding the houses and public fountains and countless gardens and parks scattered throughout. A conqueror might have taken this city three centuries ago, but that same conqueror had loved it well. Treated it well and nourished it.

They cleared the eastern gate, then passed down a long, dusty road that cut through the sprawl beyond the city proper. Hasar didn't bother to wait, and launched her stallion into a gallop that left them waving away her dust.

Kashin, claiming he didn't want to eat her dust the entire way to the oasis, followed suit after giving a small smile toward Yrene and a whistled command to his horse. Then most of the nobles and viziers, apparently

483

having already taken bets, launched into various races at breakneck speed through towns cleared well in advance. As if this kingdom were their playground.

Birthday party indeed. The princess had likely been bored and didn't want to look too irresponsible to her father. Though he was surprised to find that Arghun had joined them. Surely with most of his siblings away, he would have seized the chance to hatch some plot. But there was Arghun, galloping close to Kashin as they blended into the horizon.

Some of the nobility remained back with Chaol and Yrene, letting the others put some miles between them. They cleared the last of the outlying towns, their horses sweat-soaked and panting as they ascended a large, rocky hill. The dunes began just on its other side, Yrene had told him. They would water the horses here—then make the last leg of the trek across the sands.

She was smiling faintly at him as they ascended the crag, taking a deer path through the scrub. Horses had trampled through here; bushes were broken and shattered under careless riders. A few bushes even bore speckles of blood, already dried in the brutal sun.

Someone should flay the rider who'd been so reckless with their mount.

Others had reached the top of the crag, watered their horses, and moved on. All he saw of them were bodies and horseflesh disappearing into the sky—as if they simply walked off the edge of the cliff and into thin air.

Farasha stomped and surged her way up the hill, and his back and thighs strained to keep seated without the brace to steady him. He didn't dare let her get a whiff of discomfort.

Yrene reached the summit first, her white clothes like a beacon in the cloudless blue day around them, her hair shining bright as dark gold. She waited for him, the chestnut mare beneath her panting heavily, its rich coat gleaming with hues of deepest ruby.

She dismounted as he urged Farasha up the last of the hill, and then—

It knocked the breath from him.

The desert.

It was a barren, hissing sea of golden sand. Hills and waves and ravines, rippling on forever, empty and yet humming. Not a tree or bush or gleam of water to be seen.

The unforgiving hand of a god had shaped this place. Still blew his breath across it, shifting the dunes grain by grain.

He had never seen such a sight. Such a wonder. It was a new world entirely.

Perhaps it was an unexpected boon that the information they sought dwelled out here.

Chaol dragged his attention to Yrene, who was reading his face. His reaction.

"Its beauty is not for everyone," she said. "But it sings to me, somehow."

This sea where no ships would ever sail, some men would look upon it and see only burning death. He saw only quiet—and clean. And slow, creeping life. Untamed, savage beauty.

"I know what you mean," he said, carefully dismounting from Farasha. Yrene monitored, yet did nothing but hold out the cane, letting him find the best way to swing his leg over, back groaning and wobbling, and then slide down to the sandy rock. The cane was instantly in his hand, though Yrene made no move to steady him while he finally released the saddle and reached for Farasha's reins.

The horse tensed, as if considering lunging for him, but he gave her a no-nonsense glare, the cane groaning as he dug it into the rock beneath him.

Farasha's dark eyes glowed as if she'd been forged in Hellas's burning realm, but Chaol stood tall—as tall as he could. Didn't break her stare.

Finally, the horse huffed, and deigned to let him haul her toward the sand-crusted trough that was half crumbling with age. The trough perhaps had been here for as long as the desert had existed, had watered the horses of a hundred conquerors.

Farasha seemed to grasp that they were to enter that ocean of sand and drank heartily. Yrene led her horse over, keeping the chestnut a healthy distance away from Farasha, and said, "How are you feeling?"

"Solid," he said, and meant it. "I'll be aching by the time we get there, but the strain isn't so bad." Without the cane, he didn't dare try to walk more than a few steps. Could barely manage it.

She still put a hand on his lower spine, then his thighs, letting her magic assess. Even with the clothes and the heat, the press of her hands left him aware of every inch of space between them.

But others gathered around the ancient, enormous trough, and so he pulled out of Yrene's assessing touch, leading Farasha a safe distance away. Mounting the mare again, though . . .

"Take your time," Yrene murmured, but remained a few steps away.

He'd had a block at the palace. Here, short of climbing onto the precarious lip of the trough . . . The distance between his foot and the stirrup had never seemed so long. Balancing on one foot while he lifted it, pushing down with the other to propel him up, swinging his leg around the saddle . . . Chaol went through the steps, feeling the motions he'd done a thousand times before. He'd learned to ride before he was six—had been on a horse nearly his entire life.

Of course he'd been given a devil of a horse to do this with.

But Farasha held still, staring toward the sifting sea of sand, to the path that had been trampled down the hill—their entry into the desert. Even with the shifting winds hauling the sands into new shapes and valleys, the tracks the others had left were clear enough. He could even spy some of them cresting hills and then flying down them, little more than specks of black and white.

And yet he remained here. Staring at the stirrups and saddle.

Yrene offered casually, "I can find a block or bucket—"

Chaol moved. Perhaps not as graceful as he'd like, perhaps more struggling than he'd intended, but he managed, the cane groaning as he used it to push upward, then clattering to the rock as he let go to grab

486

the pommel of the saddle, right as his foot slid—barely—into the stirrup. Farasha shifted at his weight while he hauled himself higher into the saddle, his back and thighs barking as he swung his leg over, but he was up.

Yrene strode to the fallen cane and dusted it off. "Not bad, Lord Westfall." She strapped the cane behind her saddle and mounted her mare. "Not bad at all."

He hid his smile, his face still over-warm, and nudged Farasha down the sandy hill at last.

They followed the tracks the others had left slowly, the heat rippling off the sands.

Up, and down, the only sounds the muffled thumping of their horses and the sighing sands. Their party meandered in a long, snaking line. Guards had been posted throughout, standing with towering poles topped with the khagan's flag and insignia of a dark running horse. Markers of the general direction toward the oasis. He pitied the poor men ordered to stand in the heat for a princess's whim, but said nothing.

The dunes evened out after a time, the horizon shifting to reveal a flat, sandy plain. And in the distance, waving and bobbing in the heat . . .

"There we make our camp," Yrene said, pointing toward a dense cluster of green. No sign of the ancient, buried city of the dead that Hasar claimed the oasis had grown over. Not that they expected to see much of anything from their vantage point.

From the distance, it might very well be another thirty minutes. Certainly at their pace.

Despite the sweat soaking through her white clothes, Yrene was smiling. Perhaps she, too, had needed a day away. To breathe the open air.

She noticed his attention and turned. The sun had brought out her freckles, darkening her skin to a glowing brown, and tendrils of hair curled about her smiling face.

Farasha tugged on the reins, her body quivering with impatience.

"I own an Asterion horse," he said, and her mouth curved in an impressed frown. Chaol shrugged. "I'd like to see how a Muniqi measures up."

Her brows narrowed. "You mean . . ." She noted the flat, smooth spread of land between them and the oasis. Perfect for running. "Oh, I can't—a gallop?"

He waited for the words about his spine, his legs. None came.

"Are you afraid?" he asked, arching a brow.

"Of these things? *Yes.*" She cringed at her mount, restless beneath her.

"She's as sweet as a dairy cow," he said of Yrene's chestnut mare.

Chaol leaned down to pat "Butterfly's" neck.

She tried to bite him. He yanked on the reins enough to tell her he was fully aware of her bullshit.

"I'll race you," he said.

Yrene's eyes sparkled. And to his shock she breathed, "The prize?"

He could not remember the last time. The last time he had felt so aware of every bit of breath and blood, simmering and thrumming, in his body.

"A kiss. When and where of my choosing."

"What do you mean *where.*"

Chaol only grinned. And let Farasha run free.

Yrene cursed, more viciously than he'd ever heard her, but he didn't dare look back—not as Farasha became a black storm upon the sand.

He'd never gotten to test out the Asterion. But if it was faster than *this*—

Flying over the sand, Farasha was a bolt of dark lightning spearing across the golden desert. It was all he could do to keep up, to grit his teeth against his barking muscles.

He forgot about them anyway at the blur of reddish brown and black that emerged in the corner of his eye—and the white rider atop it.

Yrene's hair rose and fell behind her in a golden-brown tangle of curls, lifting with each thunderous pound of her mare's legs on the hard sand. White clothes streaming in the wind, the gold and silver sparkled like stars, and her face—

Chaol couldn't breathe as he beheld the wild joy on Yrene's face, the unchecked exhilaration.

Farasha marked the mare gaining on them, meeting them beat for beat, and made to charge ahead. To leave them in the dust.

He checked her with the reins and his feet, marveling that he could even do so. That the woman now closing in, now riding beside him, now beaming at him as if he were the only thing in this barren, burning sea . . . She had done this. Given him this.

Yrene was smiling, and then she was laughing, as if she could not contain it inside her.

Chaol thought it was the most beautiful sound he'd ever heard.

And that this moment, flying together over the sands, devouring the desert wind, her hair a golden-brown banner behind her . . .

Chaol felt, perhaps for the first time, as if he was awake.

And he was grateful, right down to his very bones, for it.

⇥ 44 ⇤

Yrene was soaked in sweat, though it dried so quickly that she only *felt* its essence clinging.

Thankfully, the oasis was shaded and cool, a large, shallow pool in its center. Horses were led into the heaviest shade to be watered and brushed down, and servants and guards claimed a hidden spot for their own washing and enjoyment.

No sign of any sort of cave that Nousha had mentioned, or the city of the dead that Hasar claimed lurked in the jungle beyond. But the site was sprawling, and in the large pool . . . The royals were already soaking in the cool waters.

Renia, Yrene saw immediately, was only wearing a thin silk shift—that did little to hide her considerable assets as she emerged from the water, laughing at something Hasar said.

"Well, then," Chaol said, coughing beside Yrene.

"I told you about the parties," she muttered, heading to the tents spread through the towering palms and brush. They were white and gilded, each marked with the prince or princess's banner. But with Sartaq and Duva not with them, Chaol and Yrene had been assigned them, respectively.

Mercifully, the two were near each other, but Yrene took in the open tent flaps, the entire space as large as the cottage she'd shared with her mother, then turned toward Chaol's retreating back. His limp, even with the cane, was deeper than it'd been that morning. And she'd seen how stiffly he'd gotten off that infernal horse.

"I know you want to wash up," Yrene said. "But I need to take a look at you. At your back and legs, I mean. After all that riding."

Perhaps she shouldn't have raced him. She hadn't even remembered who'd reached the oasis border anyway. She'd been too busy laughing, feeling as if she were coming out of her body and would likely never feel that way again. Too busy looking at his face, filled with such light.

Chaol paused at his tent flaps, cane wobbling, as if he'd put far more weight on it than he let on. But it was the relief in his face as he asked, "Your tent or mine?" that made her worry—just a tad.

"Mine," she said, aware of the servants and nobility who likely had no idea she was even the cause of this excursion, but who would happily report her comings and goings. He nodded, and she monitored each rise and placement of his legs, the shifting of his torso, the way he leaned on that cane.

As Chaol edged past her and into the tent, he murmured in her ear, "I won, by the way."

Yrene glanced toward the sun now making its descent and felt her core tighten in answer.

⌒

He was sore but could thankfully still walk by the time Yrene finished her thorough examination. And set of soothing stretches for his legs and back. And massage.

Chaol had the distinct feeling she was toying with him, even as her hands remained chaste. Uninterested.

She even had the nerve to call for a servant to ask for a jug of water.

The tent was fit for the princess who usually occupied it. A large bed lay in the center upon a raised platform, the floors covered with ornate rugs. Sitting areas were scattered throughout, along with a curtained-off washing-up and privy, and there was gold *everywhere*.

Either the servants had brought it with them yesterday, or the people of this land so feared the wrath of the khaganate that they didn't dare rob this place. Or were so well-cared for they didn't need to.

The others were all in the oasis pool by the time he shrugged on his now-dry clothes and they emerged to seek out their quarry.

They'd whispered in the tent—neither of them had spotted anything of interest upon arrival. And in the oasis pool, definitely no indication of a cave or ruins near the bathing royals and their friends. Comfortable, relaxed. Free, in ways that Adarlan had never been, to its detriment. He wasn't naive enough to think that no scheming or intrigue was now playing out in the cool waters, but he'd never heard of Adarlanian nobles going to a swimming hole and enjoying themselves.

Though he certainly wondered what the hell Hasar was thinking in throwing such a party for Yrene, manipulated into it or no, considering the princess was well aware Yrene barely knew most of those gathered.

Yrene hesitated at the edge of the clearing and glanced at him beneath lowered lashes—a look anyone might interpret as shy. A woman perhaps hesitant to strip down to the light clothes they wore in the waters. Letting any onlookers forget that she was a healer and wholly used to far more skin showing. "I find I'm not up to bathing," Yrene murmured over the laughter and splashing of those within the oasis waters. "Care for a walk?"

Pleasant, polite words as she inclined her head through the few acres of untamed jungle sprawling to the left. She didn't think herself a courtier, but she could certainly lie well enough. He supposed that as a healer, it was a skill that proved useful.

"It would be my pleasure," Chaol said, offering his arm.

Yrene hesitated again, the portrait of modesty—peering over her shoulder at those in the pool. The royals watching. Kashin included.

He would let her choose when and how to make it clear to the prince—*again*—that she was not interested. Though he couldn't avoid a faint tinge of guilt as she looped her arm through his and they stepped into the murkiness of the oasis jungle.

Kashin was a good man. Chaol doubted his words about being willing to go to war were lies. And to risk antagonizing the prince by perhaps flaunting what he had with Yrene . . . Chaol glanced sidelong at her, his cane digging into the roots and soft soil. She offered him a faint smile, cheeks still flushed with the sun.

To hell with worrying over antagonizing Kashin.

The oasis spring's gurgling blended with the sighing palms overhead as they headed deeper between the fauna, picking their own way—no direction in mind. "In Anielle," he said, "there are dozens of hot springs along the valley floor, near the Silver Lake. Kept warm by the vents in the earth. When I was a boy, we'd often soak in them after a day of training."

She asked carefully, as if realizing that he'd indeed offered up this piece of him, "Was it that training that inspired you to join the guard?"

His voice was thick as he finally said, "Part of it. I was just . . . good at it. Fighting and fencing and archery and all of it. I received the training that was befitting for the heir of a lord to a mountain people who had long fended off wild men from the Fangs. But my real training began when I arrived in Rifthold and joined the royal guard."

She slowed while he navigated around a tricky nest of roots, letting him focus on where to place his feet and the cane.

"I suppose being stubborn and bullheaded made you a good pupil for the discipline aspect."

Chaol chuckled, nudging her with his elbow. "It did. I was the first one on the training pitch and the last one off. Even though I was walloped every single day." His chest tightened as he remembered their faces, those men who had trained him, who had pushed and pushed him, left

493

him limping and bleeding, and then made sure he got patched up in the barracks that night. Usually with a hearty meal and a clap on the back.

And it was in honor of those men, his brothers, that he said hoarsely, "They weren't all bad men, Yrene. The ones I . . . I grew up with, whom I commanded . . . They were good men."

He saw Ress's laughing face, the blush the young guard could never hide around Aelin. His eyes burned.

Yrene stopped, the oasis humming around them, and his back and legs were more than grateful for the reprieve as she removed her arm from his. Touched his cheek. "If they are partially responsible for you being . . . you," she said, rising up to brush her mouth against his, "then I believe that they are."

"Were," he breathed.

And there it was. That one word, swallowed by the loam and shade of the oasis, that he could barely stand. *Were.*

He could still retreat—retreat from this invisible precipice now before them. Yrene remained standing close, a hand resting over his heart, waiting for him to decide whether to speak.

And maybe it was only because she held her hand over his heart that he whispered, "They were tortured for weeks this spring. Then butchered and left to hang from the castle gates."

Grief and horror guttered in her eyes. He could hardly stomach it as he managed to go on, "Not one of them broke. When the king and—others . . ." He could not bring himself to finish. Not yet. Perhaps not ever, to face that suspicion and likely truth. "When they questioned the guards about me. Not a single one of them broke."

He didn't have the words for it—that courage, that sacrifice.

Yrene's throat bobbed, and she cupped his cheek.

And Chaol finally breathed, "It was my fault. The king—he did it to punish me. For running, for helping the rebels in Rifthold. He . . . it was all because of me."

"You can't blame yourself." Simple, honest words.

And utterly untrue.

They snapped him back into himself, more effectively than a thrown bucket of cold water.

Chaol pushed out of her touch.

He shouldn't have told her, shouldn't have brought it up. On her birthday, gods above. While they were supposed to focus on finding any sort of scrap of information that might help them.

He'd brought his sword and dagger, and as he limped into the palms and ferns, leaving Yrene to follow, he checked to ensure they were both still buckled at his waist. Checked them because he had to do *something* with his shaking hands, his raw insides.

He folded the words, the memories back into himself. Deeper. Sealed them away as he counted his weapons, one after another.

Yrene only trailed him, saying nothing while they picked their way deeper into the jungle. The entire site was larger than many villages, and yet little of the green had been tamed—certainly no path to be found, or indication of a city of the dead beneath them.

Until fallen pale pillars began to appear between the roots and bushes. A good sign, he supposed. If there were a cave, it might be nearby—perhaps as some ancient dwelling.

But the level of architecture they climbed over and walked around, forcing him to select his steps carefully . . . "These weren't some cave-dwelling people who buried their dead in holes," he observed, cane scraping over the ancient stone.

"Hasar said it was a *city* of the dead." Yrene frowned at the ornate columns and slabs of carved stone, crusted with forest life. "A sprawling necropolis, right beneath our feet."

He studied the jungle floor. "But I thought the khagan's people left their dead under the open sky in the heart of their home territory."

"They do." Yrene ran her hands over a pillar carved with animals and strange creatures. "But . . . this site predates the khaganate. The Torre

495

and Antica, too. To whoever was here before." A set of crumbling steps led to a platform where the trees had grown through the stone itself, knocking over carved columns in their wake. "Hasar claimed the tunnels are all clever traps. Either designed to keep looters out—or keep the dead inside."

Despite the heat, the hair on his arms rose. "You're telling me this now?"

"I assumed Nousha meant something different. That it would be a *cave*, and if it was connected to these ruins, she'd have mentioned it." Yrene stepped onto the platform, and his legs protested as he followed her up. "But I don't see any sort of rock formations here—none large enough for a cave. The only stone . . . it's from this." The sprawling gateway into the necropolis beneath, Hasar had claimed.

They surveyed the mangled complex, the enormous pillars now broken or covered in roots and vines. Silence lay as heavy as the shaded heat. As if none of the singing birds or humming insects from the oasis dared venture here.

"It's unsettling," she murmured.

They had twenty guards within shouting distance, and yet he found his free hand drifting toward his sword. If a city of the dead slumbered beneath their feet, perhaps Hasar was right. They should be left to sleep.

Yrene turned in place, surveying the pillars, the carvings. No caves—none at all. "Nousha knew the location, though," she mused. "It must have been important—the site. To the Torre."

"But its importance was forgotten over time, or warped. So that only the name, the sense of its importance remained."

"Healers were always drawn to this realm, you know," Yrene said distantly, running a hand over a column. "The land just . . . blessed them with the magic. More than any other kind. As if this were some breeding ground for healing."

"Why?"

She traced a carving on a column longer than most ships. "Why does anything thrive? Plants grow best in certain conditions—those most advantageous to them."

"And the southern continent is a place for healers to thrive?"

Something had snagged her interest, making her words mumbled as she said, "Maybe it was a sanctuary."

He approached, wincing at the slicing pain down his spine. It was forgotten as he examined the carving beneath her palm.

Two opposing forces had been etched into the column's broad face. On the left: tall, broad-shouldered warriors, armed with swords and shields, with rippling flame and bursting water, animals of all kinds in the air or at their knees. Pointed ears—those were pointed ears on the figures' heads.

And facing them . . .

"You said nothing is coincidence." Yrene pointed to the army facing the Fae one.

Smaller than the Fae, their bodies bulkier. Claws and fangs and wicked-looking blades.

She mouthed a word.

Valg.

Holy gods.

Yrene rushed to the other pillars, ripping away vines and dirt. More Fae faces. Figures.

Some were depicted in one-on-one battles against Valg commanders. Some felled by them. Some triumphing.

Chaol moved with her as much as he could manage. Looking, looking—

There, tucked into the dense shadows of squatting, thick palms. A square, crumbling structure. A mausoleum.

"A cave," Yrene whispered. Or what might have been interpreted as one, as knowledge turned muddled.

Chaol ripped away the vines for her with his free hand, his back protesting.

Ripped and tore them down to survey what had been carved into the gates of the necropolis.

"Nousha said legend claimed some of those scrolls came from here," Chaol said. "From a place full of Wyrdmarks, of carvings of the

Fae and Valg. But this was no living city. So they had to have been removed from tombs or archives below our feet." From the doorway just beyond them.

"They did not bury humans here," Yrene whispered.

For the markings on the sealed, stone gates . . . "The Old Language."

He'd seen it inked on Rowan's face and arm.

This was a Fae burial site. *Fae*—not human.

Chaol said, "I thought only one group of Fae ever left Doranelle—to establish Terrasen with Brannon."

"Maybe another settled here during whatever this war was."

The first war. The first demon war, before Elena and Gavin were born, before Terrasen.

Chaol studied Yrene. Her bloodless face. "Or maybe they wanted to hide something."

Yrene frowned at the ground as if she could see to the tombs beneath. "A treasure?"

"Of a different sort."

She met his eyes at his tone—his stillness. And fear, cool and sharp, slid into his heart.

Yrene said softly, "I don't understand."

"Fae magic is passed down through their bloodlines. It doesn't appear at random. Perhaps these people came here. And then were forgotten by the world, forces good and evil. Perhaps they knew this place was far away enough to remain untouched. That wars would be waged elsewhere. By them." He jerked his chin to a carving of a Valg soldier. "While the southern continent remained mostly mortal-held. While the seeds planted here by the Fae were bred into the human bloodlines and grew into a people gifted and prone to healing magic."

"An interesting theory," she said hoarsely, "but you don't know if it could stand to reason."

"If you wanted to hide something precious, wouldn't you conceal it in plain sight? In a place where you were willing to bet a powerful force

498

would spring up to defend it? Like an empire. Several of them. Whose walls had not been breached by outside conquerors for the entirety of its history. Who would see the value of its healers and think their gift was for one thing, but never know that it might be a treasure waiting to be used at another time. A weapon."

"We do not kill."

"No," Chaol said, his blood going cold. "But you and all the healers here . . . There is only one other such place in the world. Guarded as heavily, protected by a power just as mighty."

"Doranelle—the Fae healers in Doranelle."

Guarded by Maeve. Fiercely.

Who had fought in that first war. Who had fought against the Valg.

"What does it mean?" she breathed.

Chaol had the sense of the ground slipping from beneath him. "I was sent here to retrieve an army. But I wonder . . . I wonder if some other force brought me to retrieve something else."

She slid her hand into his, a silent promise. One he'd think of later.

"Perhaps that is why whoever it is that's been stalking the Torre, was hunting me," Yrene whispered. "If they are indeed sent from Morath . . . They don't want us realizing any of this. Through healing you."

He squeezed her fingers. "And those scrolls in the library . . . either they were taken or brought from here, forgotten save for legend about where they came from. Where the healers of this land might have originated from."

Not the necropolis—but the Fae people who had built it.

"The scrolls," she blurted. "If we return and find someone to—to translate them . . ."

"They might explain this. What the healers could do against the Valg."

She swallowed. "Hafiza. I wonder if she knows what those scrolls are, somehow. The Healer on High is not just a position of power, but of learning. She's a walking library herself, taught things by her

499

predecessor that no one else at the Torre knows." She twisted a curl around a finger. "It's worth showing her some of the texts. To see if she might know what they are."

A gamble to share the information with anyone else, but one worth taking. Chaol nodded.

Someone's laughter pierced through even the heavy silence of the oasis.

Yrene released his hand. "We'll need to smile, enjoy ourselves amongst them. And then leave at first light."

"I'll send word to Nesryn to return. As soon as we're back. I'm not sure we can afford any longer to wait for the khagan's aid."

"We'll try to convince him again anyway," she promised. He angled his head. "You will still have to win this war, Chaol," she said quietly. "Regardless of what role we might play."

He brushed a thumb over her cheek. "I have no intention of losing it."

⌇

It was no easy task to pretend they had not stumbled across something enormous. That something had not rattled them down to their bones.

Hasar grew bored of bathing and called for music and dancing and lunch. Which turned into hours of lounging in the shade, listening to the musicians, eating an array of delicacies that Yrene had no idea how they'd managed to bring all the way out here.

But as the sun set, they all dispersed into their tents to change for dinner. After what she'd learned with Chaol, even being alone for a moment had her jumpy, but Yrene washed and changed into the purple gauzy gown Hasar had provided.

Chaol was waiting outside the tent.

Hasar had brought him clothes, too. Beautiful deep blue that brought out the gold in his brown eyes, the summer-kissed tan of his skin.

Yrene blushed as his gaze slid along her neckline, to the swaths of skin the flowing folds of the dress revealed along her waist. Her thighs. Silver and clear beads had been sewn onto the entire thing, making the gown shimmer like the stars now flickering to life in the night sky above them.

Torches and lanterns had been lit around the oasis pool, tables and couches and cushions brought out. Music was playing, people were already loosing themselves upon the feast laid across the various tables, with Hasar holding court, regal as any queen from her spot at the centermost table alongside the fire-gilded pool.

She spotted Yrene and signaled her over. Chaol, too.

Two seats had been left open to the princess's right. Yrene could have sworn Chaol sized them up with each step, as if scanning the chairs, those around them, the oasis itself for any pitfalls or threats. His hand brushed the sliver of skin exposed down the column of her spine—as if in confirmation that all was clear.

"You did not think I forgot my honored guest, did you?" Hasar said, kissing her cheeks. Chaol bowed to the princess as much as he could manage, and claimed his seat on Yrene's other side, leaning his cane against the table.

"Today has been wonderful," Yrene said, and wasn't lying. "Thank you."

Hasar was quiet for a beat, looking Yrene over with unusual softness. "I know I am not an easy person to care for, or an easy friend to have," she said, her dark eyes meeting Yrene's at last. "But you have never once made me feel that way."

Yrene's throat tightened at the bald words. Hasar inclined her head, waving to the party around them. "This is the least I can do to honor my friend." Renia gently patted Hasar's arm, as if in approval and understanding.

So Yrene bowed her head and said to the princess, "I have no interest in easy friends—easy people. I think I trust them less than the difficult ones, and find them far less compelling, too."

That brought a grin to Hasar's face. She leaned down the table to survey Chaol and drawl, "You look quite handsome, Lord Westfall."

"And you are looking beautiful, Princess."

Hasar, while well dressed, would never be called such. But she accepted the compliment with that cat's smile that somehow reminded Yrene of that stranger in Innish—that knowledge that beauty was fleeting, yet power . . . power was a far more valuable currency.

The feast unfolded, and Yrene suffered through a not-so-unguarded toast from Hasar to her *dear, loyal, clever friend*. But she drank with them. Chaol, too. Wine and honey ale, their glasses refilled before Yrene could even notice the near-silent reach of the servants pouring.

It took all of thirty minutes before talk of the war started.

Arghun began it first. A mocking toast, to safety and serenity in such tumultuous times.

Yrene drank but tried to hide her surprise as she found Chaol doing so as well, a vague smile plastered on his face.

Then Hasar began musing on whether the Western Wastes, with everyone so focused upon the eastern half of the continent, was fair game to interested parties.

Chaol only shrugged. As if he'd reached some conclusion this afternoon. Some realization about this war, and the role of these royals in it.

Hasar seemed to notice, too. And for all that this was meant to be a birthday party, the princess pondered aloud to no one in particular, "Perhaps Aelin Galathynius should drag her esteemed self down here and select one of my brothers to marry. Perhaps then we would consider assisting her. If such influence remained in the family."

Meaning all that flame, all that brute power . . . tied to this continent, bred into the bloodline, never to be a threat.

"My brothers would have to stomach being with someone like that, of course," Hasar went on, "but they are not such weak-blooded men as you might believe." A glance at Kashin, who seemed to pretend not to hear, even as Arghun snorted. Yrene wondered if the others knew how adept Kashin was at drowning out their taunting—that he never fell for their baiting simply because he couldn't be bothered to care.

Chaol answered Hasar with equal mildness, "As interesting as it would be to see Aelin Galathynius deal with all of you . . ." A secret, knowing smile, as if Chaol might very well enjoy seeing that sight. As if Aelin might very well make blood sport out of them all. "Marriage is not an option for her."

Hasar's brows lifted. "To a man?"

Renia gave her a sharp look that Hasar ignored.

Chaol chuckled. "To anyone. Beyond her beloved."

"King Dorian," Arghun said, swirling his wine. "I'm surprised she can stomach *him*."

Chaol stiffened, but shook his head. "No. Another prince—foreign-born and powerful."

All the royals stilled. Even Kashin looked their way.

"Who, pray tell, is that?" Hasar sipped her wine, those keen eyes darkening.

"Prince Rowan Whitethorn, of Doranelle. Former commander to Queen Maeve, and a member of her royal household."

Yrene could have sworn the blood drained wholly from Arghun's face. "Aelin Galathynius is to wed Rowan Whitethorn?"

From the way the prince said the name . . . he'd indeed heard of this Rowan.

Chaol had mentioned Rowan more than once in passing—Rowan, who had managed to heal much of the damage in his spine. A Fae Prince. And Aelin's beloved.

Chaol shrugged. "They are *carranam*, and he swore the blood oath to her."

"He swore that oath to Maeve," Arghun countered.

Chaol leaned back in his seat. "He did. And Aelin got Maeve to free him from it so he could swear it to her. Right in Maeve's face."

Arghun and Hasar swapped glances. "How," the former demanded.

Chaol's mouth turned up at the corner. "Through the same way Aelin achieves all her ends." He flicked his brows up. "She encircled Maeve's city in fire. And when Maeve told her that Doranelle was made of stone, Aelin simply replied that her people were not."

A chill snaked down Yrene's spine.

"So she is a brute and a madwoman," Hasar sniffed.

"Is she? Who else has taken on Maeve and walked away, let alone gotten what they want out of it?"

"She would have destroyed an entire city for one man," Hasar snapped.

"The most powerful pure-blooded Fae male in the world," Chaol said simply. "A worthy asset for any court. Especially when they had fallen in love with each other."

Though his eyes danced as he spoke, a tremor of tension ran beneath the last words.

But Arghun seized on the words. "If it is a love match, then they risk knowing their enemies will go after him to punish her." Arghun smiled as if to say he was already thinking of doing so.

Chaol snorted, and the prince straightened. "Good luck to anyone who tries to go after Rowan Whitethorn."

"Because Aelin will burn them to ash?" Hasar asked with poisoned sweetness.

But it was Kashin who answered softly, "Because Rowan Whitethorn will always be the person who walks away from that encounter. Not the assailant."

A pause of silence.

Then Hasar said, "Well, if Aelin cannot represent her continent, perhaps we shall look elsewhere." She smirked at Kashin. "Perhaps Yrene Towers might be offered in the queen's stead."

"I am not noble-born," Yrene blurted. "Or royal." Hasar had lost her mind.

Hasar shrugged. "I'm sure Lord Westfall, as Hand, can find you a title. Make you a countess or duchess or whatever terms you call them. Of course, we'd know you were little more than a milkmaid dressed in

504

jewels, but if it stayed amongst us . . . I'm sure there are some here who would not mind your humble beginnings." She'd done as much with Renia—for Renia.

The amusement faded from Chaol's face. "You sound as if you now want to be a part of this war, Princess."

Hasar waved a hand. "I am merely musing on the possibilities." She surveyed Yrene and Kashin, and the food in Yrene's stomach turned leaden. "I've always said you would make such beautiful children."

"If they were allowed to live by your future khagan."

"A small consideration—to be later dealt with."

Kashin leaned forward, his jaw tight. "The wine goes to your head, sister."

Hasar rolled her eyes. "Why not? Yrene is the unspoken heir of the Torre. It is a position of power—and if Lord Westfall were to bestow upon her a royal title . . . say, spin a little story that her royal lineage was newly discovered, she might very well wed you, Ka—"

"She will not."

Chaol's words were flat. Hard.

Color stained Kashin's face as he asked softly, "And why is that, Lord Westfall?"

Chaol held the man's gaze. "She will not marry you."

Hasar smiled. "I think the lady may speak for herself."

Yrene wanted to flip her chair back into the pool and sink to the bottom. And live there, under the surface, forever. Rather than face the prince waiting for an answer, the princess who was smirking like a demon, and the lord whose face was hard with rage.

But if it was a serious offer, if doing something like that could lead to the full might of the southern continent's armies coming to help them, save them . . .

"Don't you even consider it," Chaol said too quietly. "She's full of shit."

People gasped. Hasar barked a laugh.

Arghun snapped, "You will speak with respect to my sister, or you will find yourself with legs that don't work again."

Chaol ignored them. Yrene's hands shook badly enough that she slid them beneath the table.

Had the princess brought her out here to corner her into agreeing to this preposterous idea, or had it merely been a whim, an idle thought to taunt and gnaw at Lord Westfall?

Chaol seemed to be on the verge of opening his mouth to say more, to push this ridiculous idea out of her head, but he hesitated.

Not because he agreed, Yrene realized, but because he wanted to give her the space to choose for herself. A man used to giving orders, to being obeyed. And yet Yrene had the sense that this, too, was new to him. The patience; the trust.

And she trusted him. To do what he had to. To find a way to survive this war, whether with this army or another one. If it did not happen here, with these people, he'd sail elsewhere.

Yrene looked to Hasar, to Kashin and the others, some smirking, some swapping disgusted glances. Arghun most of all. Revolted at the thought of sullying his family's bloodline.

She trusted Chaol.

She did not trust these royals.

Yrene smiled at Hasar, then Kashin. "This is very grave talk for my birthday. Why should I choose one man tonight when I have so many handsome ones in my company right now?"

She could have sworn a shudder of relief went through Chaol.

"Indeed," Hasar crooned, her smile sharpening. Yrene tried not to balk at the invisible fangs revealed in that smile. "Betrothals are rather odious things. Look at poor Duva, stuck with that brooding, sad-eyed princeling."

And so the conversation moved on. Yrene did not glance to Kashin or the others. She looked only at her constantly refilled goblet—and drank it. Or at Chaol, who appeared half inclined to lean across Yrene and flip Hasar's chair right back into the pool.

But the meal passed, and Yrene kept drinking—enough so that when she stood after dessert, she had not realized precisely how much she'd imbibed. The world tipped and swayed, and Chaol steadied her with a hand on her elbow, even as he was none too steady on his feet.

"Seems like they can't hold their liquor up north," Arghun said with a snort.

Chaol chuckled. "I'd advise never to say that to someone from Terrasen."

"I suppose there's nothing else to do while living amongst all the snow and sheep beyond drink," Arghun drawled, lounging in his chair.

"That may be," Chaol said, putting an arm on Yrene's back to guide her to the trees and tents, "but it won't stop Aelin Galathynius or Aedion Ashryver from drinking you under the table."

"Or under a chair?" Hasar crooned to Chaol.

Maybe it was the wine. Maybe it was the heat, or the hand on her back, or the fact that this man beside her had fought and fought and never once complained about it.

Yrene lunged for the princess.

And though Chaol might have decided against pushing Hasar into the pool behind her, Yrene had no such qualms about doing it herself. One heartbeat, Hasar was smirking up at her.

The next, her legs and skirts and jewels went sky-up, her shriek piercing across the dunes as Yrene shoved the princess, chair and all, into the water.

❦ 45 ❧

Yrene knew she was a dead woman.

Knew it the moment Hasar hit the dark water and everyone leaped to their feet, shouting and drawing blades.

Chaol had Yrene behind him in an instant, a sword half out—a blade she hadn't even seen him reach for before it was in his hand.

The pool was not deep, and Hasar swiftly stood, soaked and seething, teeth bared and hair utterly limp as she pointed at Yrene.

No one spoke.

She pointed and pointed, and Yrene braced for the death order.

They'd kill her, and then kill Chaol for trying to save her.

She felt him sizing up all the guards, the princes, the viziers. Every person who would get in the way to the horses, every person who might put up a fight.

But a low, fizzing sounded behind Yrene.

She looked to see Renia clutching her stomach, another hand over her mouth, as she looked at her lover and *howled*.

Hasar whirled on Renia, who just stuck out a finger, pointing and roaring with laughter. Tears leaked from the woman's eyes.

Then Kashin tipped his head back and bellowed with amusement.

Yrene and Chaol did not dare move.

Not until Hasar shoved away a servant who'd flung himself into the pool to help her, crawled back onto the paved lip, and looked Yrene dead in the eye with the full wrath of all the mighty khagans before her.

Silence again.

But then the princess snorted. "I was wondering when you'd grow a backbone."

She walked away, trailing water behind her, Renia howling again.

Yrene caught Chaol's stare—watched him slowly release the hand on his sword. Watched his pupils shrink again. Watched him realize . . .

They were not going to die.

"With that," Yrene said quietly, "I think it's time for bed."

Renia paused her laughing long enough to say, "I'd be gone before she returns."

Yrene nodded, and led Chaol by the wrist back toward the trees and dark and torches.

She couldn't help but wonder if Renia and Kashin's laughter had in part been true amusement, but also a gift. A birthday gift, to keep them from the gallows. From the two people who understood best just how deadly Hasar's moods could be.

Keeping her head, Yrene decided, was a very good birthday gift indeed.

It would have been easy for Chaol to roar at Yrene. To demand how she could even *think* to risk her life like that. Months ago, he would have. Hell, he was still debating it.

Even as they slipped into her spacious tent, he continued soothing the instincts that had come bellowing to the surface the moment those guards had pressed in and reached for their swords.

509

Some small part of him was profoundly, knee-wobblingly grateful none of those guards were ones he'd trained with these weeks—that he hadn't been forced to make that choice, cross that line between them.

But he'd seen the terror in Yrene's eyes. The moment she'd realized what was about to happen, what would have happened if the princess's lover and Kashin had not stepped in to defuse the situation.

Chaol knew Yrene had done it for him.

For the mocking, hateful insult.

And from the way she paced inside the tent, wending between the couches and tables and cushions . . . Chaol also knew she was well aware of the rest.

He took up a seat on the rolled arm of a chair, leaning the cane beside it, and waited.

Yrene whirled toward him, stunning in that purple gown, which had nearly knocked his knees from beneath him when she'd first emerged from the tent. Not just for how well it suited her, but the swaths of supple skin. The curves. The light and color of her.

"Before you begin shouting," Yrene declared, "I should say that what just happened is proof that I should *not* be marrying a prince."

Chaol crossed his arms. "Having lived with a prince for most of my life, I'd say quite the opposite."

She waved a hand, pacing more. "I know it was stupid."

"Incredibly."

Yrene hissed—not at him. The memory. The temper. "I don't regret doing it."

A smile tugged on his mouth. "It's an image I'll likely remember for the rest of my life."

He would. The way Hasar's feet had gone over her head, her shrieking face right before she hit the water—

"How can you be so amused?"

"Oh, I'm not." His lips indeed curved. "But it's certainly entertaining to see that temper of yours turned on someone other than me."

"I don't have a temper."

He raised a brow. "I have known a fair number of people with tempers, and yours, Yrene Towers, ranks among the finest of them."

"Like Aelin Galathynius."

A shadow passed over him. "She would have greatly enjoyed the sight of Hasar flipping into the pool."

"Is she really marrying that Fae Prince?"

"Maybe. Likely."

"Are you—upset about it?"

And though she asked it casually, that healer's mask a portrait of calm curiosity, he selected his words carefully.

"Aelin was very important to me. She still is—though in a different way. And for a while . . . it was not easy, to change the dreams I'd planned for my future. Especially the dreams with her."

Yrene angled her head, the lantern light dancing in her soft curls. "Why?"

"Because when I met Aelin, when I fell in love with her, she was not . . . She went by another name. Another title and identity. And things between us fell apart before I knew the truth, but . . . I think I knew. When I learned she was truly Aelin. I knew that between her and Dorian, I . . ."

"You would never leave Adarlan. Or him."

He fiddled with the cane beside him, running his hands over the smooth wood. "She knew it, too, I think. Long before I did. But she still . . . She left, at one point. It's a long story, but she went off to Wendlyn alone. And that was where she met Prince Rowan. And out of respect to me, because we had not truly ended it, she waited. For him. They both did. And when she came back to Rifthold, it ended. Between us, I mean. Officially. Badly. I handled it badly, and she did, too, and it just . . . We made our peace, before we parted ways months ago. And they left together. As it should be. They are . . . If you ever meet them, you'll get it. Like Hasar, she isn't an easy person to be with, to understand. Aelin frightens *everyone*." He snorted. "But not him. I think that's why she fell

511

in love with him, against her best intentions. Rowan beheld all Aelin was and is, and he was not afraid."

Yrene was quiet for a moment. "But you were?"

"It was a . . . rough period for me. Everything I knew was trampled. Everything. And she . . . I think I placed the blame for a great deal of it upon her. Began to see her as a monster."

"Is she?"

"It depends on who's telling the story, I suppose." Chaol studied the intricate pattern of the red-and-green rug beneath his boots. "But I don't think so. There is no one else that I would trust to handle this war. No one else I would trust to take on all of Morath but Aelin. Even Dorian. If there's some way to win, she'll find it. The costs might be high, but she'll do it." He shook his head. "And it's your birthday. We should probably talk of nicer things."

Yrene didn't smile. "You waited for her while she was gone. Didn't you? Even knowing what—who—she really was."

He hadn't admitted it, even to himself.

His throat tightened. "Yes."

She now studied that woven carpet beneath them. "But you—you don't still love her?"

"No," he said, and had never meant anything more. He added softly, "Or Nesryn."

Her brows rose at that, but he wrapped a hand around the cane, groaning softly as he pushed to his feet and made his way toward her. She tracked each movement, unable to set aside the healing, her eyes darting over his legs, his middle, the way he gripped the cane.

Chaol halted a step away, pulling a small bundle out of his pocket. Silently, he extended it to her, the black velvet like the rippling dunes beyond them.

"What's that?"

He only held out the folded piece of fabric. "They didn't have a box I liked, so I just used the cloth—"

512

Yrene took it from his hand, her fingers shaking slightly as she folded back the edges of the bundle that he'd been carrying all day.

In the lantern light, the silver locket shimmered and danced as she lifted it up between her fingers, eyes wide. "I can't take this."

"You'd better," he said as she lowered the oval locket into her palm to examine it. "I had your initials carved onto it."

Indeed, she was already tracing the swirling letters he'd asked the jeweler in Antica to engrave on the front. She turned it over to the back—

Yrene put a hand to her throat, right over that scar.

"Mountains. And seas," she whispered.

"So you never forget that you climbed them and crossed them. That you—only you—got yourself here."

She let out a small, soft laugh—a sound of pure joy. He couldn't let himself identify the other sound within it.

"I bought it," Chaol clarified instead, "so you could keep whatever it is you always carry in your pocket inside. So you don't have to keep moving it from dress to dress. Whatever it is."

Surprise lighted her eyes. "You know?"

"I don't know *what* it is, but I see you holding something in there all the time."

He'd calculated that it was small, and based the locket's size upon it. He'd never seen an indentation or weight in her pockets to suggest its bulk, and had studied other objects she'd placed within there while working on him—papers, vials—against the utter flatness of it. Perhaps it was a lock of hair, some small stone—

"It's nothing as fine as a party in the desert—"

"No one has given me a gift since I was eleven."

Since her mother.

"A birthday gift, I mean," she clarified. "I . . ."

She slid the locket's fine silver chain over her head, the links catching in the stray, luscious curls. He watched her lift the mass of her hair over the chain, setting it dangling down to the edge of her breasts. Against the

513

honey-brown of her skin, the locket was like quicksilver. She traced her slim fingers over the engraved surface.

Chaol's chest tightened as she lifted her head, and he found silver lining her eyes.

"Thank you," she said softly.

He shrugged, unable to come up with a response.

Yrene only walked over, and he braced himself, readied himself, as her hands cupped his face. As she stared into his eyes.

"I am glad," she whispered, "that you do not love that queen. Or Nesryn."

His heart thundered through every inch of him.

Yrene rose onto her toes and pressed a kiss, light as a caress, to his mouth. Never breaking his stare.

He read the unspoken words there. He wondered if she read the ones not voiced by him, either.

"I will cherish it always," Yrene said, and he knew she wasn't talking about the locket. Not as she lowered a hand from his face to his chest. Atop his raging heart. "No matter what may befall the world." Another featherlight kiss. "No matter the oceans, or mountains, or forests in the way."

Any leash on himself snapped. Letting his cane thump to the floor, Chaol drifted a hand around her waist, his thumb stroking along the sliver of bare skin the dress revealed. The other he plunged into that luxurious, heavy hair, cupping the back of her head as he tilted her face upward. As he studied those brown-gold eyes, the emotion simmering in them.

"I am glad that I do not love them, either, Yrene Towers," he whispered onto her lips.

Then his mouth was on hers, and she opened for him, the heat and silk of her driving a groan from deep in his throat.

Her hands speared into his hair, onto his shoulders, across his chest and up his neck. As if she could not touch enough of him.

Chaol reveled in the fingers she dug into his clothes, as if they were claws seeking purchase. He slid his tongue against hers, and her moan as she pushed herself against him—

Chaol backed them toward the bed, its white sheets near-glowing in the lantern light, not caring that his steps were uneven, staggering. Not with that dress little more than cobwebs and mist, not when he never took his mouth from hers, remained *unable* to take his mouth from hers.

Yrene's knees hit the mattress behind them, and she drew her lips away enough to protest, "Your back—"

"I'll manage." He slanted his mouth over hers again, her kiss searing him to his very soul.

His. She was his, and he had never had anything he could call such. Wanted to call such.

Chaol couldn't bring himself to rip his mouth away from Yrene's long enough to ask if she considered him hers. To explain that he already knew his own answer. Had perhaps known from the moment she'd walked into that sitting room and did not look at him with an ounce of pity or sadness.

He nudged her with a press of his hips, and she let him lay her upon the bed gently—reverently.

Her reach for him, hauling him atop her, was anything but.

Chaol huffed a laugh against her warm neck, the skin softer than silk, as she scrabbled with his buttons, his buckles. She writhed against him, and as he settled his weight over her, every hard part of him lining up with so many soft parts of her . . .

He was going to fly out of his skin.

Yrene's breath was sharp and ragged against his ear, her hands tugging desperately at his shirt, trying to slide to his back beneath.

"I'd think you were sick of touching my back."

She shut him up with a plundering kiss that made him forget language for a while.

Forget about his name and his title and everything but her.

Yrene.

Yrene.

Yrene.

She moaned when he slid a hand up her thigh, baring her skin beneath the folds of that gown. When he did it to the other leg. When he nipped at her mouth and traced idle circles with his fingers over those beautiful thighs, starting along their outer edge and arcing over—

Yrene did not appreciate being toyed with.

Not as she wrapped a hand around him, and his entire body bowed into the touch, the sensation of it. Not just a hand stroking over him, but *Yrene* doing it—

He couldn't think, couldn't do anything but taste and touch and yield.

And yet—

He found words. Found language again. Long enough to ask, "Have you ever—"

"Yes." The word was a rough pant. "Once."

Chaol shoved against the ripple of darkness, the line on that throat. He only kissed it instead. Licked it. Then asked against her skin, his mouth skirting up her jaw, "Do you want to—"

"Keep going."

But he made himself pause. Made himself rise to look at her face, his hands on her sleek thighs and her hand still gripping him, stroking him. "Yes, then?"

Yrene's eyes were gold flame. "Yes," she breathed. She leaned up, kissed him gently. Not lightly, but sweetly. Openly. "Yes."

A shudder wracked through him at the words, and he gripped her thigh right where it met her hip. Yrene released him to lift her hips, dragging herself over him. Feeling him, with only the thin gossamer panel of her gown between them. Nothing beneath.

Chaol slid it to the side, bunching the material at her waist. He dipped his head, eager to look his fill, then to touch and taste and learn what made Yrene Towers lose control entirely—

"Later," Yrene begged hoarsely. "Later."

He couldn't bring himself to deny her anything. This woman who held everything he was, all he had left, in her beautiful hands.

So Chaol removed his shirt, his pants following with a few, trickier maneuvers. Then he removed that dress of hers, leaving it in scraps on the floor beside the bed.

Until Yrene only wore that locket. Until Chaol surveyed every inch of her and found himself unable to breathe.

"I will cherish it always," Chaol whispered as he slid into her, slow and deep. Pleasure rippled down his spine. "No matter what may befall the world." Yrene kissed his neck, his shoulder, his jaw. "No matter the oceans, or mountains, or forests in the way."

Chaol held Yrene's stare as he stilled, letting her adjust. Letting *himself* adjust to the sensation that the entire axis of the world had shifted. Looking into those eyes of hers, swimming with brightness, he wondered if she felt it, too.

But Yrene kissed him again, in answer and silent demand. And as Chaol began to move in her, he realized that here, amongst the dunes and stars . . . Here, in the heart of a foreign land . . . Here, with her, he was home.

⊰ 46 ⊱

It broke her, and unmade her, and rebirthed her.

Sprawled over Chaol's chest hours later, listening to the thump of his heartbeat, Yrene still did not have words for what had passed between them. Not the physical joining, not the repeated bouts of it, but simply the sense of *him*. Of belonging.

She'd never known it could *be* like that. Her quick, unimpressive, and only brush with sex had been just last autumn, and had left her in no hurry to seek it out again. But this . . .

He'd made sure she found her pleasure. Repeatedly. Before he ever found his own.

And beyond that, the *things* he made her feel—

Not just as a result of his body, but who he was . . .

Yrene pressed an idle kiss to the sculpted muscle of his chest, savoring the fingers he still trained down her spine, over and over.

It was safety, and joy, and comfort, and knowing that no matter what befell them . . . He would not balk. He would not break. Yrene nuzzled her face against him.

It was dangerous, she knew, to feel such things. She'd known what lay in her eyes when he'd looked at her. The heart she'd offered up without saying as much. But seeing that locket that he'd somehow found and had been so thoughtful about . . . Her initials were beautifully done, but the mountains and waves . . . It was stunning work, done by a master jeweler in Antica.

"I didn't do it on my own," Yrene murmured against his skin.

"Hmm?"

She ran her fingers over the grooves of Chaol's stomach before rising onto an elbow to study his face in the dimness. The lanterns had long since burned out, and silence had settled over the camp, replaced by the buzz and hum of beetles in the palm trees. "Getting here. The mountains yes, but the seas . . . Someone helped me."

Alertness filled those sated eyes. "Oh?"

Yrene plucked up the locket. Between bouts of lovemaking, when she'd gone to move his cane within easy reach of the bed, she'd slid the small note inside. The fit had been perfect.

"I was stuck in Innish, with no way of leaving. And one night, this stranger appeared at the inn. She was . . . everything I was not. Everything I'd forgotten. She was waiting for a boat, and during the three nights she was there, I think she *wanted* the lowlifes to try to rob her—she was spoiling for a fight. But she kept her distance. I was left with cleaning up alone that night . . ."

Chaol's hand tensed on her back, but he said nothing.

"And mercenaries who had given me a hard time earlier that evening found me in the alley."

He went utterly still.

"I think—I *know* they wanted to . . ." She shook off the icy grip of horror, even all these years later. "The woman, girl, whatever she was, she interrupted before they could so much as try. She . . . dealt with them. And when she finished, she taught me how to defend myself."

His hand began stroking again. "So that's how you learned."

She ran a hand over the scar on her neck. "But other mercenaries, friends of the earlier ones, returned. One held a knife to my throat to get her to drop her weapons. She refused to do so. So I used what she'd taught me to disarm and disable the man."

He blew out an impressed breath that ruffled her hair.

"To her, it was a test. She'd been aware of the second group circling, and told me she wanted me to have some *controlled* experience. I'd never heard of anything more ridiculous." The woman had been either brilliant or insane. Likely both. "But she told me . . . told me it was better to be suffering in the streets of Antica than in Innish. And that if I wanted to come here, I should go. That if I wanted something, I should *take* it. She told me to fight for my miserable life."

Yrene brushed the sweat-damp hair from his eyes. "I patched her up and she went on her way. And when I got back to my room . . . She had left me a bag of gold. And a golden brooch with a ruby the size of a robin's egg. To pay for my passage here, and any tuition at the Torre."

He blinked in surprise. Yrene whispered, voice breaking, "I think she was a god. I—I don't know who would *do* that. I have a little gold left, but the brooch . . . I never sold it. I still have it."

He frowned at the necklace, as if he'd misjudged its size.

Yrene added, "That's not what I keep in my pocket." His brows rose. "I left Innish that morning. I took the gold and the brooch and got on a ship here. So I crossed mountains alone, yes—but the Narrow Sea . . ." Yrene traced the waves on the locket. "I crossed because of her. I teach the women at the Torre because she told me to share the knowledge with any women who would listen. I teach it because it makes me feel like I'm paying her back, in some small way."

Yrene ran her thumb over the initials on the front. "I never learned her name. She only left a note with two lines. *For wherever you need to go—and then some. The world needs more healers.* That's what I keep in my pocket—that little scrap of paper. What's now in here." Yrene tapped the locket. "I know it's silly, but it gave me courage. When things were hard, it gave me courage. It still does."

Chaol swept the hair from her brow and kissed it. "There is nothing silly about it. And whoever she is . . . I will be forever grateful."

"Me too," Yrene whispered as he slid his mouth over her jaw and her toes curled. "Me too."

⊰ 47 ⊱

The pass between the twin peaks of Dagul was larger than it looked.

It went on and on, a maze of jagged, towering rock.

Nesryn and Sartaq did not dare stop.

Webs sometimes blocked their way, or hovered above, but still they charged onward, seeking any sort of path upward. To where Kadara might pluck them into the sky.

For down here, with the cramped, narrow walls of the pass, the ruk could not reach them. If they were to stand a chance of being rescued, they'd have to find a way up.

Nesryn didn't dare let Falkan out—not yet. Not when so many things could still go so wrong, and letting the spiders know what sort of card they had up their sleeve . . . No, not yet would she risk using him.

But the temptation gnawed on her. The walls were smooth, ill-fitted for climbing, and as they hurried through the pass, hour after hour, Sartaq's wet, labored breaths echoed off the rock.

He was in no state to climb. He was barely able to stay upright, or grip his sword.

Nesryn kept an arrow nocked, ready to fly as they rounded corner after corner, glancing up every now and then.

The pass was so tight in spots that they had to squeeze through, the sky a watery trickle high above. They did not speak, did not dare do more than breathe as they kept their steps light.

It made no difference. Nesryn knew it made little difference.

A trap had been laid for them, and they had fallen into it. The *kharankui* knew where they were. Were likely following at their leisure, herding them along.

It had been hours since they'd last heard the boom of Kadara's wings.

And the light . . . it was beginning to fade.

Once darkness fell, once the way became too dark to manage . . . Nesryn pressed a hand to Falkan, still in her pocket. When the night settled upon the pass, she decided, then she'd use him.

They pushed through a particularly tight passage between two near-kissing boulders, Sartaq grunting behind her. "We have to be nearing the end," he breathed.

She didn't tell him that she doubted the spiders were stupid enough to allow them to walk right out of the other side of the pass and into Kadara's awaiting talons. If the injured ruk could even manage their weight.

Nesryn just pushed onward, the pass becoming a fraction wider, counting her breaths. They were likely some of her last—

Thinking that way helped no one and nothing. She'd stared down death this summer, when that wave of glass had come crashing toward her. Had stared it down, and been saved.

Perhaps she would be lucky again, too.

Sartaq stumbled out behind her, breathing hard. Water. They desperately needed water—and bandages for his wounds. If the spiders did not

523

find them, then the lack of water in the arid pass might very well kill them first. Long before any help arrived from the Eridun rukhin.

Nesryn forced one step in front of another, the path narrowing again, the rock as tight as a vise. She twisted sideways, edging through, her swords scraping.

Sartaq grunted, then let out a pained curse. "I'm stuck."

She found him indeed wedged behind her, the bulk of his broad chest and shoulders pinned. He shoved himself forward, blood leaking from his wounds as he pushed and pulled.

"Stop," she ordered. "Stop—wriggle back out if you can." There was no other way through and nothing to climb over, but if they removed his weapons—

His dark eyes met hers. She saw the words forming.

You keep going.

"Sartaq," she breathed.

They heard it then.

Claws clicking on stone. Skittering along.

Many of them. Too many. Coming from behind, closing in.

Nesryn grabbed the prince's hand, tugging. "Push," she panted. *"Push."*

He grunted in pain, the veins in his neck bulging as he tried to squeeze through, his boots scraping on the loose rock—

Nesryn dug her own feet in, gritting her teeth as she hauled him forward.

Click, click, click—

"Harder," she gasped.

Sartaq angled his head, shoving against the rock that held him.

"What a fine morsel, our guest," hissed a soft female voice. "So large he cannot even fit through the passage. How we shall feast."

Nesryn heaved and heaved, her grip treacherously slippery with sweat and blood from both of them, but she clamped onto his wrist hard enough that she felt bones shift beneath—

"Go," he whispered, straining to push through. "You run."

524

Falkan was shifting in her pocket, trying to emerge. But with the rock pressing on her chest, the passage was too tight for even him to poke out his head—

"A pretty pair," that female continued. "How her hair shines like a moonless night. We shall take you both back to our home, our honored guests."

A sob clawed its way up Nesryn's throat. "Please," she begged, scanning the rock high above them, the lip into the upper reaches of the narrow pass, the curving horns of the peaks, tugging and tugging on Sartaq's arm. *"Please,"* she begged them, begged *anyone.*

But Sartaq's face went calm. So calm.

He stopped pushing, stopped trying to haul himself forward.

Nesryn shook her head, *pulling* on his arm.

He did not move. Not an inch.

His dark eyes met hers. There was no fear in them.

Sartaq said to her, clear and steady, "I heard the spies' stories of you. The fearless Balruhni woman in Adarlan's empire. Neith's Arrow. And I knew . . ."

Nesryn sobbed, tugging and tugging.

Sartaq smiled at her—gently. Sweetly. In a way she had not yet seen.

"I loved you before I ever set eyes on you," he said.

"Please," Nesryn wept.

Sartaq's hand tightened on hers. "I wish we'd had time."

A hiss behind him, a rising bulk of shining black—

Then the prince was gone. Ripped from her hands.

As if he had never been.

Nesryn could barely see through her tears as she edged and squeezed along the pass. As she hurtled over rocks, arms straining, feet unfaltering.

Keep going. The words were a song in her blood, her bones as she plunged onward.

Keep going and get out; find *help*—

But the passage at last opened into a wider chamber. Nesryn staggered from the vise that had held her, panting, Sartaq's blood still coating her palms, his face still swimming before her—

The path curved ahead, and she stumbled for it, hand flying to where Falkan now poked his head out. She sobbed at the sight of him, sobbed as the clicking and hissing again began to sound behind her, closing in once more.

It was over. It was done, and she had as good as killed him. She should have never left, should have never done *any* of it—

She sprinted toward the curve in the pass, chips of shale scattering from beneath her boots.

Take you both back to our home . . .

Alive. The spider had talked as if they would be taken *alive* to their lair. For a brief window before the *feasting* began. And if she had spoken true . . .

Nesryn slapped a hand over a wriggling Falkan, earning a squeak of outrage.

But she said, soft as the wind through the grass, "Not yet. Not yet, my friend."

And as Nesryn slowed her steps, as she stopped entirely, she whispered her plan to him.

～

The *kharankui* did not try to hide their arrival.

Hissing and laughing, they skittered around the corner of the pass.

And halted when they beheld Nesryn panting on her knees, blood from slices in her arms, her collarbone, filling the tight air with her scent. She saw them note the sprayed shale around her, flecks of her blood on it.

As if she had taken a bad fall. As if she could no longer go on.

Clicking, chattering to one another, they surrounded her. A wall of

526

ancient, reeking limbs and fangs and swollen, bulbous abdomens. And eyes. More eyes than she could count, her reflection in all of them.

Her trembling was not faked.

"Pity it did not give much sport," one pouted.

"We shall have it later," another replied.

Nesryn shook harder.

One sighed. "How fresh her blood smells. How clean."

"P-please," she begged.

The *kharankui* just laughed.

Then the one behind her pounced.

Pinning her to the shale, rock slicing her face, her hands, Nesryn screamed against the claws that dug into her back. Screamed as she managed to look over her shoulder to see those spinnerets hovering above her legs.

To see the silk that shot from them, ready to be woven. To wrap her tightly.

❧ 48 ❧

Nesryn awoke to sharp biting.

She jerked upright, a scream on her lips—

It died when she felt the little teeth biting at her neck, her ear. Nipping her awake.

Falkan. She winced, her head throbbing. Bile surged up her throat.

Not biting at her head. But the silk that bound her body, the thick strands reeking. And the cave she was in . . .

No, not cave. But a covered section of the pass. Dimly illuminated by the moon.

She scanned the dark to either side, the arch of stone above them no more than thirty feet wide, keeping her breathing steady—

There. Sprawled on the ground nearby, covered foot to neck with silk. His face crusted with blood, eyes closed—

Sartaq's chest rose and fell.

Nesryn shuddered with the force of keeping her sob contained as Falkan slithered down her body, chewing at the strands with his vicious teeth.

She didn't need to tell the shifter to hurry. She scanned the empty passage, scanned the dim stars beyond.

Wherever they were . . . It was different here.

The rock smooth. Polished. And carved. Countless carvings had been etched in the space, ancient and primitive.

Falkan chewed and chewed, the silk snapping strand by strand.

"Sartaq," Nesryn dared to whisper. "Sartaq." The prince did not stir.

Clicking sounded from beyond the archway. "Stop," she murmured to Falkan. "*Stop*."

The shifter halted his path down her back. Clung to her leathers as a shadow darker than the night emerged from around the corner behind them. Or ahead—she had no idea where true north lay. If they were still within the pass itself, or atop another peak.

The spider was slightly larger than the others. Her blackness deeper. As if the starlight itself was loath to touch her.

The *kharankui* halted as she noted Nesryn staring at her.

Nesryn controlled her breathing, rallying her mind to come up with *something* to buy them time, buy Sartaq and Falkan time . . .

"You are the ones who have been poking about in forgotten places," the spider said in Halha, her voice beautiful, lyrical.

Nesryn swallowed once, twice, trying and failing to moisten her paper-dry tongue. She managed to rasp, "Yes."

"What is it that you seek?"

Falkan pinched her back in warning—and order. Keep her distracted. While he chewed.

Nesryn blurted, "We were paid by a merchant, who traded with your sisters to the north, the stygian spiders—"

"Sisters!" The spider hissed. "Our blood kin they may be, but no true sisters of the soul. Gentlehearted fools, trading with mortals—*trading*, when we were born to *devour* you."

Nesryn's hands shook behind her back. "T-that is why he sent us. He was unimpressed by them. S-said they did not live up to the legend . . ."

529

She had no idea what was spewing from her mouth. "So he wished to see you, see if you might t-t-trade."

Falkan brushed against her arm in quiet comfort.

"Trade? We have nothing to trade, beyond the bones of your kin."

"There is no Spidersilk here?"

"No. Though we delight in tasting your dreams, your years. Before we finish with you."

Had they already done so for Sartaq? Was that why he did not stir? Nesryn forced herself to ask as the threads behind her snapped free so slowly, "Then—then what is it you do here?"

The spider took a step forward, and Nesryn braced herself. But the spider lifted a thin, clawed leg and pointed to one of the polished, carved walls. "We wait."

And as her eyes at last adjusted to the dimness, Nesryn saw what the spider pointed to.

A carving of an archway—a gate.

And a cloaked figure standing within it.

She squinted, straining to make out who stood there. "W-who do you wait for?"

Houlun had said the Valg had once passed through here—

The spider brushed aside the dirt crusted over the figure. Revealing long, flowing hair etched there. And what she'd thought to be a cloak . . . It was a dress.

"Our queen," the spider said. "We wait for Her Dark Majesty to return at last."

"Not—not Erawan?" Servants to a dark crown, Houlun had said . . .

The spider spat, the venom landing near Sartaq's covered feet. "Not him. Never *him*."

"Then who—"

"We wait for the Queen of the Valg," the spider purred, rubbing against the carving. "Who in this world calls herself Maeve."

☙ 49 ❧

Queen of the Valg.

"Maeve is Queen of the *Fae*," Nesryn countered carefully.

The spider chuckled, low and wicked. "So she has made them believe."

Think, think, think. "What—what a mighty and powerful queen she must be," Nesryn stammered. "To rule both." Falkan furiously chewed, each strand slowly, so slowly, yielding. "Will you—will you tell me the tale?"

The spider studied her, those depthless eyes like pits of hell. "It will not buy you your life, mortal."

"I—I know." She shook further, the words tumbling out. "But stories . . . I have always loved stories—of these lands especially. *Wind-seeker*, my mother called me, because I was always drifting where the wind tugged me, always dreaming of those stories. And here . . . here the wind has taken me. So I would hear one last tale, if you allow it. Before I meet my end."

The spider remained quiet for a heartbeat. Another. Then she settled herself beneath the carving of the archway—the Wyrdgate. "Consider it a gift—for your boldness in even asking."

Nesryn said nothing, heart thundering through every part of her body.

"Long ago," the spider said softly in that beautiful voice, "in another world, another lifetime, there existed a land of dark, and cold, and wind. Ruled by three kings, masters of shadow and pain. Brothers. The world had not always been that way, had not been born that way. But they waged a mighty war. A war to end all wars. And those three kings conquered it. Turned it into a wasteland, a paradise for those who had dwelled in darkness. For a thousand years, they ruled, equal in power, their sons and daughters spread throughout the land to ensure their continued dominion. Until a queen appeared—her power a new, dark song in the world. Such wondrous things she could do with her power, such horrible, wondrous things . . ."

The spider sighed. "They each desired her, those kings. Pursued her, wooed her. But she only deigned to ally with one, the strongest of them."

"Erawan," Nesryn murmured.

"No. Orcus, eldest of the Valg kings. They wed, but Maeve was not content. Restless, our queen spent long hours pondering the riddles of the world—of other worlds. And with her gifts, she found a way to look. To pierce the veil between worlds. To see realms of green, of light and song." The spider spat, as if such a thing were abhorrent. "And one day, when Orcus was gone to see his brothers, she took a path between realms. Stepped beyond her world, and into the next."

Nesryn's blood went cold. "H-how?"

"She had watched. Had learned of such rips between worlds. A door that could open and close at random, or if one knew the right words." The spider's dark eyes gleamed. "We came with her—her beloved handmaidens. We stepped with her into this . . . place. To this very spot."

Nesryn glanced at the polished stone. Even Falkan seemed to pause to do the same.

"She bade us stay—to guard the gate. Lest anyone should pursue her. For she had decided she did not wish to go back. To her husband, her world. So she went, and we only heard whisperings through our sisters and smaller kin, carried on the wind." The spider fell silent.

Nesryn pushed, "What did you hear?"

"That Orcus arrived, his brothers in tow. That Orcus had learned of his wife's leaving and discovered how she'd done it. Went beyond what she'd done, and found a way to *control* the gate between worlds. Made keys to do so, shared with his brothers. Three keys, for the three kings.

"They went from world to world, opening gates as they willed it, sweeping in their armies and laying waste to those realms as they hunted for her. Until they reached this world."

Nesryn could barely draw breath to ask, "And they found her?"

"No," the spider said, something like a smile in its voice. "For Her Dark Majesty had left these mountains, had found another land, and prepared herself well. She knew that one day she would be found. And planned to hide within plain sight. So she did. She came across a lovely, long-lived people—near-immortals themselves—ruled over by two sister-queens."

Mab and Mora. Holy gods—

"And using her powers, she ripped into their minds. Made them believe they had a sister, an eldest sister to rule with them. Three queens—for the three kings that might one day come. When they returned to their palace, she tore into the minds of all those who dwelled there, too. And any who came. Planting the thought that a third queen had always existed, always ruled. If they somehow resisted her power, she found ways to end them." A wicked chuckle.

Nesryn had heard the legends. Of Maeve's dark, unnamed power—a darkness that could devour the stars. That Maeve had never revealed a Fae form, only that deadly darkness. And she had lived far beyond the lifespan of any known Fae. Lived so long that the only comparable lifespan . . . Erawan.

A Valg life span. For a Valg queen.

The spider again paused. Falkan had nearly reached her hands—but still not enough to free them.

Nesryn asked, "So the Valg kings arrived, but did not know who faced them in the war?"

"Precisely." A delighted purr. "Disguised in a Fae body, they did not recognize her, the fools. But she used it against them. Knew how to defeat them, how their armies worked. And when she realized what they had done to arrive here, the keys they possessed . . . she wanted them. To banish them, kill them, and to use the keys as she saw fit within this world. And others.

"So she took them. Snuck in and took them, surrounding herself with Fae warriors so others might not ask just *how* she knew so many things. Oh, the clever queen claimed it was from communing with the spirit world, but . . . she knew. She had run those war camps. Knew how the kings worked. So she stole the keys. Managed to send two of those kings back, Orcus one of them. And before she could go after the final king, the youngest one who loved his brothers so very deeply, the keys were taken from her." A hiss.

"By Brannon," Nesryn breathed.

"Yes, the fire-king. He saw the darkness in her but did not recognize it. He wondered, suspected, but all he'd known of the Valg, our people, were their *male* soldiers. Their grunts and princes and kings. He did not know that a female . . . How different, how extraordinary a female Valg is. Even *he* was tricked by her; she found paths into his mind to keep him from truly realizing it." Another soft, lovely laugh. "Even now, when all should be clear to his meddlesome spirit . . . Even now, he does not know. To his oncoming doom—yes, to his doom, and the other's."

Nausea roiled through her. *Aelin.* Aelin's doom.

"But while he did not guess correctly about our queen's origins, he still knew that his fire . . . She greatly feared his fire. As all true Valg do."

Nesryn tucked away that kernel. "He left, building his kingdom far away, and she built her defenses, too. So many clever defenses, should Erawan rise again and realize that the queen he'd sought for his brother, conquered worlds to find, was here all along. That she had built armies of Fae, and would let them battle each other."

A spider in a web. That's what Maeve was.

Falkan reached Nesryn's hands, chewing through the silk there. Sartaq remained unconscious, so perilously close to the spider.

"So you have waited these thousands of years—for her to return to these mountains?"

"She ordered us to hold the pass, to guard the rip in the world. So we have. And so we will, until she summons us to her side once more."

Nesryn's head spun. Maeve—she'd think on it later. If they lived through this.

She flicked her fingers at Falkan, signaling him.

Silently, keeping to the shadows, the shifter scuttled into the dark.

"And now you know—how the Black Watch came to dwell here." The spider rose with a mighty heave. "I hope it was a fitting final tale for you, Wind-seeker."

Nesryn opened her mouth as the spider advanced, rotating her wrists behind her back—

"Sister," a female voice hissed from the darkness beyond. "Sister, a word."

The spider halted, pivoting her bulbous body toward the archway entrance. "*What.*"

A beat of fear. "There is a problem, sister. A threat."

The spider scuttled toward her kin, snapping, "Tell me."

"Ruks on the northern horizon. Twenty at least—"

The spider hissed. "Guard the mortals. I shall deal with the birds."

Clicking legs, shale shifting all around her. Nesryn's heart hammered as she flexed her aching fingers. "Sartaq," she breathed.

His eyes flicked open across the way. Alert. Calm.

The other spider crawled in, smaller than her leader. Sartaq tensed, shoulders straining as if he'd try to burst from the silk that held him.

But the spider only whispered, "*Hurry.*"

⊰ 50 ⊱

Sartaq sagged at Falkan's voice as it came from the *kharankui*'s hideous mouth.

Nesryn hauled her hands free from the webbing, swallowing her grunt of pain as the fibers tore at her skin. Falkan's mouth and tongue had to be aching—

She glanced at the spider hovering over Sartaq, slicing through the silk binding the prince with slashes of the claws. Indeed, where those pincers waved, blood leaked out.

"Quickly," the shifter whispered. "Your weapons are in the corner there."

She could just make out the faint gleam of starlight on the curve of her bow, along the naked silver of her Asterion short-sword.

Falkan cut through Sartaq's bindings, and the prince sprang free, shoving off the webbing. He swayed as he stood, bracing a hand on the stone. Blood, there was so much blood all over him—

But he rushed to her, ripping at the threads still covering her feet. "Are you hurt?"

"Faster," Falkan said, glancing to the archway entrance behind. "It won't take her long to realize no one's coming."

Nesryn's feet came free, and Sartaq hauled her up. "Did you hear what she said about Maeve—"

"Oh, I heard," Sartaq breathed as they rushed to their weapons. He handed her the bow and quiver, the Fae blade. Grabbed his own Asterion daggers as he hissed to Falkan, "Which way?"

The shifter scuttled forward, past the carving of Maeve. "Here—there is a slope upward. We're just on the other side of the pass. If we can get up high—"

"Have you seen Kadara?"

"No," the shifter said. "But—"

They didn't wait to hear the rest as they crept on silent feet from the archway, entering the starlight-filled pass beyond. Sure enough, a rough slope of loose stone rose from the ground, as if it were a path into the stars themselves.

They'd made it halfway up the treacherous slope, Falkan a dark shadow at their backs, when a shriek rose from the mountain beyond. But the skies were empty, no sign of Kadara—

"Fire," Nesryn breathed as they hurtled toward the apex of the peak. "She said all Valg hate fire. *They* hate fire." For the spiders, devouring life, devouring souls . . . They were as Valg as Erawan. Hailed from the same dark hell. "Get the flint from your pocket," she ordered the prince.

"And light *what*?" His eyes drifted to the arrows at her back as they halted atop the narrow apex of the peak—the curved horn. "We're trapped up here." He scanned the sky. "It might not buy us anything."

Nesryn withdrew an arrow, shouldering her bow as she tugged a strip of her shirt from beneath the jacket of her flying leathers. She ripped off the bottom, sliced the piece in two, and wrapped one around the shaft of the arrow. "We need kindling," she said as Sartaq withdrew the flint stone from his breast pocket.

A knife flashed, and then a section of Sartaq's braid was in his outstretched hand.

She didn't hesitate. Just wrapped the braid around the fabric, holding the arrow out for him as he struck the flint over and over. Sparks flew, drifting—

One caught. Fire flared. Just as darkness spilled into the pass below. Shoulder to shoulder, the spiders surged for them. Two dozen at least.

Nesryn nocked the arrow, drawing back the string—and aimed up.

Not directly to them. But a shot into the sky, high enough to pierce the frosty stars.

The spiders paused, watching the arrow reach its zenith and then plunge down, down—

"Another," Nesryn said, taking that second strip of fabric and wrapping it again around the head of her next arrow. Only three remained in her quiver. Sartaq sliced off a second piece of his braid, looping it over the tip. Flint struck, sparks glowed, and as that first arrow plummeted toward the spiders scattering from its path, she loosed her second arrow.

The spiders were so distracted looking up they did not stare ahead.

The largest of them, the one who had spoken to her for so long, least of all.

And as Nesryn's burning arrow slammed into her abdomen, sticking deep, the spider's scream shook the very stones beneath them.

"Another," Nesryn breathed, fumbling for her next arrow as Sartaq ripped the fabric from his shirt. "Hurry."

Nowhere to go, no way to keep them at bay.

"Shift," she told Falkan, who monitored the panicking spiders, who balked at their leader's screaming orders to put out the fire atop her abdomen. "If you are going to shift into something, do it *now*."

The shifter turned that hideous spider's face toward them. Sartaq sliced off another piece of his braid and slid it over the head of her third arrow. "I will hold them," Falkan said.

Sparks showered, flame kindled on that third flaming arrow.

"A favor, Captain," the shifter said to her.

Time. They did not have *time*—

"When I was seven, my older brother sired a bastard daughter off a poor woman in Rifthold. Abandoned them both. It has been twenty years since then, and from when I was old enough to go to the city, to begin my trade, I looked for her. Found the mother after some years—on her deathbed. She could barely talk long enough to say she'd kicked the girl out. She did not know where my niece was. Didn't care. She died before she could give me a name."

Nesryn's hands shook as she aimed the arrow toward the spider trying to edge past her burning sister. Sartaq warned, "Hurry."

Falkan said, "If she survived, if she is grown, she might have the shifter gift, too. But it doesn't matter if she does or does not. What matters . . . She is my family. All I have left. And I have looked for her for a very long time."

Nesryn fired the third arrow. A spider screamed as it found its mark. The others fell back.

"Find her," Falkan said, taking a step toward the horrors churning below. "My fortune—all of it is for her. And I may have failed her in this life. But not in my death."

Nesryn opened her mouth, not believing it, the words surging up—

But Falkan sprinted down the path. Leaped right in front of that burning line of spiders.

Sartaq grabbed her elbow, pointing toward the steep slope downward from the tiny peak. "This—"

One moment, she was standing upright. The next, Sartaq had thrown her back, his sword whining.

She stumbled, arms flailing to keep her upright as she realized what

540

had crept up the other side of the peak. The spider now hissing at them, enormous fangs dripping venom to the stone.

It lunged for Sartaq with its front two legs.

He dodged one and swung down, striking true.

Black blood sprayed, the spider shrieking—but not before it slashed that claw deep into the prince's thigh.

Nesryn moved, her fourth arrow flying, right into one of those eyes. The fifth and final arrow flew a moment later, shooting for the spider's open mouth as it screamed.

It bit down on the arrow, slicing it in half.

Nesryn dropped her bow and drew her Fae blade.

The spider hissed at it.

Nesryn stepped between Sartaq and the spider. Down below, the *kharankui* screamed and shrieked. She did not dare to look to see what Falkan was doing. If he still fought.

The blade was a sliver of moonlight between her and the spider.

The *kharankui* advanced a step. Nesryn yielded one, Sartaq struggling to rise beside her.

"*I will make you beg for death,*" the spider seethed, advancing again.

It recoiled, preparing to spring.

Make it count; make the swing count—

The spider leaped.

And went tumbling off the cliff as a dark ruk slammed into it, roaring her fury.

Not Kadara. But Arcas.

Borte.

⇥ 51 ⇤

A whirlwind of fury, Arcas reared up, then dove again, Borte's battle cry ringing off the stones as she and her ruk aimed for the *kharankui* in the pass below. To the spider holding them off, blood—red blood—leaking from him.

Another cry split the night, one she'd learned as well as her own voice.

And there was Kadara, sailing hard for them, two other ruks in her wake.

Sartaq let out what might have been a sob as one of the other ruks broke away, diving to where Borte swept and lunged and shattered through the *kharankui* ranks.

A ruk of darkest brown feathers . . . and a young man atop it.

Yeran.

Nesryn did not recognize the other rider who sailed in behind Kadara. Blood stained Kadara's golden feathers, but she flew steady, hovering overhead as the other ruk closed in.

"Hold still, and don't fear the drop," Sartaq breathed, brushing a hand over Nesryn's cheek. In the moonlight, his face was caked in dirt and blood, his eyes full of pain, and yet—

Then there was a wall of wings, and mighty talons spread wide.

They wrapped around her waist and beneath her upper thighs, hauling her sitting upright into the air, Sartaq clutched in the other, and then the great bird shot into the night.

The wind roared, but the ruk lifted them higher. Kadara fell into rank behind—guarding their rear. Through her whipping hair, Nesryn looked back toward the fire-limned pass.

To where Borte and Yeran now soared upward, a dark form clutched in the claws of Yeran's ruk. Utterly limp.

Borte was not done.

A light sparked atop her ruk. A flaming arrow.

Borte fired it high into the sky.

A signal, Nesryn realized as countless wings filled the air around them. And as Borte's arrow landed atop a web, flame erupting, hundreds of lights kindled in the sky.

Ruk riders. Each bearing a flaming arrow. Each now pointing downward.

Like a rain of shooting stars, the arrows fell upon the darkness of Dagul. Landed on web and tree. And caught fire. One after another after another.

Until the night was lit up, until smoke streamed, mingling with the rising screams from the peaks and wood.

The ruks veered northward, Nesryn shaking as she clung to the talons holding her. Across the way, Sartaq met her gaze, his now-shoulder-length hair rippling in the wind.

With the flames below, it made the wounds to his face, his hands, his neck all the more gruesome. His skin was wan, his lips pale, his eyes heavy with exhaustion and relief. And yet . . .

Sartaq smiled, barely a curve of his mouth. The words the prince had confessed drifted on the wind between them.

She could not take her eyes from him. Could not look away.

So Nesryn smiled back.

And below and behind them, long into the night, the Dagul Fells burned.

⊰ 52 ⊱

Chaol and Yrene galloped back to Antica at dawn.

They left a note for Hasar, claiming that Yrene had a gravely ill patient who needed to be checked on, and raced across the dunes under the rising sun.

Neither of them had slept much, but if what they'd guessed about the healers was true, they did not risk lingering.

Chaol's back ached thanks to yesterday's ride and last night's . . . other ride. Multiple rides. And by the time the minarets and white walls of Antica appeared, he was hissing through his teeth.

Yrene frowned at him the entire painful trek through the packed streets to the palace. They hadn't discussed sleeping arrangements, but he didn't care if he had to walk up every single one of the stairs of the Torre. Either her bed or his. The thought of leaving her, even for a heartbeat—

Chaol winced as he climbed off Farasha, the black mare suspiciously well behaved, and accepted the cane the nearest stable hand had retrieved from Yrene's mare.

He managed a few steps toward her, his limp deep and splintering, but Yrene held out a warning hand. "Do *not* think about attempting to lift me off this horse, or carry me, or *anything*."

He gave her a wry look, but obeyed. "*Anything*?"

She turned a beautiful shade of scarlet as she slid off the mare, passing the reins to the waiting stable hand. The man sagged with relief, utterly grateful to not have the task of handling the impetuous Farasha, who was currently sizing up the poor man attempting to drag her toward the stables as if she'd have him for lunch. Hellas's horse indeed.

"Yes, *anything*," Yrene said, fluffing out her wrinkled clothes. "It's likely because of *anything* that you're limping worse than before."

Chaol let her fall into step beside him, and balanced on his cane long enough to press a kiss to her temple. He didn't care who saw. Who reported on it. They could all go to hell. But behind them, he could have sworn Shen and the other guards were grinning from ear to ear.

Chaol winked at her. "Then you'd better heal me, Yrene Towers, because I plan to do a great deal of *anything* with you tonight."

She flushed even deeper, but angled her chin upward, prim and proper. "Let's focus on these scrolls first, you rogue."

Chaol grinned, broad and unrestrained, and felt it in every inch of his aching body as they strode back inside the palace.

⌒

Any joy was short-lived.

Chaol picked up on the humming threads of something amiss the moment they entered their quiet wing. The moment he saw the guards murmuring, the servants scurrying about. Yrene only shared a glance with him, and they hurried along as fast as he could manage. Strands of fire shot along his back, down his thighs, but if something had happened—

The doors to his suite were ajar, with two guards posted outside, who gave him looks full of pity and dread. His stomach turned.

Nesryn. If she had come back, if something had happened with that Valg hunting them—

He stormed into the suite, his protesting body going distant, his head full of roaring silence.

Nesryn's door was open.

But no body lay sprawled on the bed. No blood stained the carpet, or splattered the walls.

His room was the same. But both bedrooms . . . Trashed.

Shredded, as if some great wind had shattered the windows and torn through the space.

The sitting room was worse. Their usual gold couch—gutted. The pictures, the art overturned or cracked or slashed.

The desk had been looted, the carpets flipped over—

Kadja was kneeling in the corner, gathering pieces of a broken vase.

"Be careful," Yrene hissed, striding to the girl as she plucked up pieces with her bare hands. "Get a broom and dustpan rather than use your own hands."

"Who did this," Chaol asked quietly.

Fear glimmered in Kadja's eyes as she rose. "It was like this when I came in this morning."

Yrene demanded, "You didn't hear anything at all?"

The sharp doubt in those words made him tense. Yrene hadn't trusted the servant girl for an instant, making up tasks that would keep her away, but for Kadja to *do* this—

"With you gone, my lord, I . . . I took the night to visit my parents."

He tried not to cringe. A family. She had family here, and he'd never bothered to ask—

"And can your parents swear to the fact that you were with them all night?"

Chaol whirled. "Yrene."

Yrene didn't so much as glance at him as she studied Kadja. The

547

servant girl withered under that fierce stare. "But I suppose leaving the door unlocked for someone would have been smarter."

Kadja cringed, shoulders curving inward.

"Yrene—this could have been from anything. Anyone."

"Yes, anyone. Especially someone who was looking for something."

The words clicked at the same moment the disarray of the room did.

Chaol faced the servant girl. "Don't clean any more of the mess. Everything in here might offer some proof of who did this." He frowned. "How much did you manage to clean already?"

From the state of the room, not much.

"I only just started. I thought you wouldn't return until tonight, so I didn't—"

"It's fine." At her cringe, he added, "Go to your parents. Take the day off, Kadja. I'm glad you weren't here when this happened."

Yrene gave him a frown that said the girl might very well have been the cause of this, but kept her mouth shut. Within a minute, Kadja had left, closing the hall doors with a quiet click.

Yrene ran her hands over her face. "They took everything. *Everything.*"

"Did they?" He limped to the desk, peering into the drawers as he braced a hand on the surface. His back ached and writhed—

Yrene stormed to the gold couch, lifting the ruined cushions. "All those books, the scrolls . . ."

"It was common knowledge that we'd be gone." He leaned fully against the desk, nearly sighing at the weight it took off his back.

Yrene carved a path through the room, inspecting all the places she'd ferreted away those books and scrolls. "They took it all. Even *The Song of Beginning.*"

"What about the bedroom?"

She vanished instantly. Chaol rubbed at his back, hissing softly. More rustling, then, "Ha!"

She emerged again, waving one of his boots in the air. "At least they didn't find this."

That first scroll. He rallied a smile to his mouth. "At least there's that."

Yrene held his boot to her chest as if it were a babe. "They're getting desperate. That makes people dangerous. We shouldn't stay here."

He surveyed the damage. "You're right."

"Then we'll go directly to the Torre."

He glanced through the open doors to the foyer. To Nesryn's bedroom. She was due back soon. And when she did return, to find him gone, with Yrene . . . He'd treated her abominably. He'd let himself forget what he'd promised, what he'd implied, in Rifthold. On the ship here. And Nesryn might not hold him to any promises, but he'd broken too many of them.

"What is it?" Yrene's question was barely more than a whisper.

Chaol closed his eyes. He was a bastard. He'd dragged Nesryn here, and this was how he'd treated her. While she was off hunting for answers, risking her life, while she sought some shred of hope for raising an army . . . He'd send that message—immediately. To return as fast as she could.

"It's nothing," Chaol said at last. "Perhaps you should stay at the Torre tonight. There are enough guards there to make anyone think twice." He added when hurt flickered in her eyes, "I can't appear to be running away. Especially with the royals now starting to think I might be someone of interest. That Aelin continues to be such a source of worry and intrigue . . . perhaps I should use that to my advantage." He fiddled with the cane, tossing it from one hand to another. "But I should stay here. And you, Yrene, you should go."

She opened her mouth to object, but paused, straightening. A steely glint entered her eyes. "I'll take Hafiza the scroll myself, then."

He hated the edge to her voice as he nodded, the dimming of those eyes. He'd done wrong by her, too. In not first ending things with Nesryn, to make it clear. He'd made a mess of it.

A fool. He'd been a fool to think he could rise above this. Move beyond the person he'd been, the mistakes he'd made.

A fool.

⊰ 53 ⊱

Yrene stormed up the Torre steps, careful not to crush the scroll in her fist.

The trashing of his room had rattled him. Rattled her, too, but . . .

It wasn't fear of harm or death. Something else had shaken him.

In her other hand, she clutched the locket, the metal warm against her skin.

Someone knew they were close to discovering whatever it was they wanted to keep secret. Or at the very least *suspected* they might learn something and had destroyed any possible sources. And after what they'd started to piece together in the ruins amid Aksara . . .

Yrene checked her temper as she reached the top landing of the Torre, the heat smothering.

Hafiza was in her private workshop, tutting to herself over a tonic that rippled with thick smoke. "Ah, Yrene," she said without looking up while she measured in a drop of some liquid. Vials and basins and bowls covered the desk, scattered between the open books and a set of bronze hourglasses of various time measurements. "How was your party?"

Revelatory. "Lovely."

"I assume the young lord finally handed over his heart."

Yrene coughed.

Hafiza smiled as she lifted her head at last. "Oh, I knew."

"We are not—that is to say, there is nothing official—"

"That locket suggests otherwise."

Yrene clapped a hand over it, cheeks heating. "He is not—he is a *lord.*"

At Hafiza's raised brows, Yrene's temper whetted itself. Who else knew? Who else had seen and commented and betted?

"He is a Lord of Adarlan," she clarified.

"So?"

"Adarlan."

"I thought you had moved past that."

Perhaps she had. Perhaps she hadn't. "It is nothing to be concerned about."

A knowing smile. "Good."

Yrene took a long breath through her nose.

"But, unfortunately, you are not here to give me all the juicy details."

"Och." Yrene grimaced. "No."

Hafiza measured another few drops into her tonic, the substance within roiling. She plucked up her ten-minute hourglass and turned it over, bone-white sand trickling into the ancient base. A proclamation of a meeting begun even before Hafiza said, "I assume it has something to do with that scroll in your hand?"

Yrene looked to the open hall, then rushed to shut the door. Then the open windows.

By the time she'd finished, Hafiza had set down the tonic, her face unusually grave.

Yrene explained the ransacking of their room. The books and scrolls taken. The ruins at the oasis and their wild theory that perhaps the healers had not just arisen here, but had been *planted* here, in secret. Against the Valg and their kings.

551

And for the first time since Yrene had known her, the ancient woman's brown face seemed to go a bit colorless. Her clear dark eyes turned wide.

"You are certain—that these are the forces amassing on your continent?" Hafiza settled herself into the small chair behind the worktable.

"Yes. Lord Westfall has seen them himself. Battled them. It is why he came. Not to raise an army against mere men loyal to Adarlan's empire, but an army to fight demons who wear the bodies of men, demons who breed monsters. So vast and terrible that even the full might of Aelin Galathynius and Dorian Havilliard is not enough."

Hafiza shook her head, her nimbus of white hair flowing. "And now you two believe that the healers have some role to play?"

Yrene paced. "Perhaps. We were relentlessly hunted down on our own continent, and I know it doesn't sound like anything to go on, but if a settlement of healing-inclined Fae did start a civilization here long ago . . . *Why?* Why leave Doranelle, why come so far, and leave so few traces, yet ensure that the healing legacy survived?"

"That is why you have come—and brought this scroll."

Yrene placed the scroll before the Healer on High. "Since Nousha only knew vague legends and didn't know how to read the language written here, I thought you might actually have the truth. Or tell me what this scroll might be about."

Hafiza carefully unfurled the scroll, weighing its corners with various vials. Dark, strange letters had been inked there. The Healer on High traced a wrinkled finger over a few of them. "I do not know how to read such a language." She ran her hand over the parchment again.

Yrene's shoulders sagged.

"But it reminds me . . ." Hafiza scanned the bookshelves in her workshop, some of them sealed behind glass. She rose, hobbling to a locked case in the shadowy corner of the room. The doors there were not glass at all—but metal. Iron.

She withdrew a key from around her neck and opened it. Beckoned Yrene over.

Half stumbling through the room in her haste, Yrene reached Hafiza's side. On a few of the spines of the tomes, near-rotting with age . . ."Wyrdmarks," Yrene murmured.

"I was told these were not books for human eyes—that it was knowledge best kept locked away and forgotten, lest it find its way into the world."

"Why?"

Hafiza shrugged, studying but not touching the ancient texts shelved before them. "That was all my predecessor told me: *They are not meant for human eyes.* Oh, once or twice, I've been drunk enough to debate opening up the books, but every time I take out this key . . ." She toyed with the long necklace, the key of blackest iron hanging from it. A match to the cabinet. "I reconsider."

Hafiza weighed the key in her palm. "I do not know how to read these books, nor what this language is, but if those scrolls and books were in the library itself, then the fact that *these* have been locked up here . . . Perhaps this is the sort of information worth killing for."

Ice skittered down her spine. "Chaol—Lord Westfall knows someone who can read these markings." Aelin Galathynius, he'd told her. "Perhaps we should bring them to her. The scroll, and these few books."

Hafiza's mouth tightened as she closed the iron doors to the cabinet and locked it with a heavy click. "I shall have to think on it, Yrene. The risks. Whether these books should leave."

Yrene nodded. "Yes, of course. But I fear we may not have much time."

Hafiza slid the iron key back under her robes and returned to the worktable, Yrene trailing her. "I do know a little of the history," Hafiza admitted. "I thought it myth, but . . . my predecessor told me, when I first came. During the Winter Moon festival. She was drunk, because I'd plied her with alcohol to get her to reveal her secrets. But instead, she gave me a rambling history lesson." Hafiza snorted, shaking her head. "I never forgot it, mostly because I was so disappointed that three bottles of expensive wine—purchased with all the money I had—got me so little."

Yrene leaned against the ancient worktable as Hafiza sat and interlaced her fingers in her lap. "She told me that long ago, before man stumbled here, before the horse-lords and the ruks above the steppes, this land indeed belonged to Fae. A small, pretty little kingdom, its capital here. Antica was built atop its ruins. But they erected temples to their gods beyond the city walls—out in the mountains, in the river-lands, in the dunes."

"Like the necropolis at Aksara."

"Yes. And she told me that they did not burn their bodies, but entombed them within sarcophagi so thick no hammer or device could open them. Sealed with spells and clever locks. Never to be opened."

"Why?"

"The drunk goat told me that it was because they lived in fear of someone getting *in*. To take their bodies."

Yrene was glad she was leaning on the table. "The way the Valg now use humans for possession."

A nod. "She rambled about how they had left their knowledge of healing for us to find. That they had stolen it from elsewhere, and that their teachings formed the basis of the Torre. That Kamala herself had been trained in their arts, their records discovered in tombs and catacombs long since lost to us. She founded the Torre based off what she and her small order learned. Worshipped Silba because she was their healing god, too." Hafiza gestured to the owls carved throughout her workroom, the Torre itself, and rubbed at her temple. "So your theory could hold water. I never learned how the Fae came here, where they went and why they faded away. But they were here, and according to my predecessor, they left some sort of knowledge or power behind." A frown toward that locked bookcase.

"That someone is now trying to erase." Yrene swallowed. "Nousha will kill me when she hears those books and scrolls were taken."

"Oh, she might very well. But she'll likely go on the hunt for whoever did it first."

"What does any of it *mean*, though? Why go to so much trouble?"

Hafiza strode back to her tonic, the hourglass nearly empty. "Perhaps that is for you to learn." She added a few more drops of liquid to her tonic, grabbed the one-minute glass, and flipped it over. "I shall consider the books, Yrene."

Yrene returned to her room, flung open the window to let in the breeze to the stifling chamber, and sat on her bed for all of a minute before she was walking again.

She'd left the scroll with Hafiza, figuring the locked bookcase was safer than anywhere else, but it was not scrolls or ancient books that filled her head as she turned left and headed downstairs.

Progress. They had made progress on Chaol's injury, significantly so, and returned to find their room trashed.

His room—not theirs. He'd made that clear enough earlier.

Yrene's steps were unfaltering, even as her legs ached from nearly two days' worth of riding. There had to be some connection—his progress, these attacks.

She'd never get any thinking done up in her quiet, stuffy room. Or in the library, not when she'd be jumping at every footstep or meow from a curious Baast Cat.

But there was one place, quiet and safe. One place where she might work through the tangled threads that had brought them here.

The Womb was empty.

After Yrene had washed and changed into the pale, thin lavender robe, she'd padded into the steam-filled chamber, unable to help looking toward that tub by the far wall. Toward where that healer had cried mere hours before her death.

Yrene scrubbed her hands over her face, taking a steadying breath.

The tubs on either side beckoned, the bubbling waters inviting, promising to soothe her aching limbs. But Yrene remained in the center of the chamber, amid all those faintly ringing bells, and stared up into the darkness high above.

From a stalactite too far in the gloom to see, a droplet of water fell—landing on her brow. Yrene closed her eyes at the cool, hard splash, but made no move to wipe away the water.

The bells sang and murmured, the voices of their long-dead sisters. She wondered if that healer who had died . . . If her voice was now singing here.

Yrene peered up at the nearest string of bells hung across the chamber, various sizes and makes. Her own bell . . .

On bare, silent feet, Yrene padded to the little stalagmite jutting from the floor near the wall, to the chain sagging between it and another pillar a few feet away. Seven other bells hung from it, but Yrene needed no reminder of which was hers.

Yrene smiled at the small silver bell, purchased with that stranger's gold. There was her name, etched into the side—maybe by the same jeweler Chaol had found for the amulet hanging from her neck. Even in here, she had not wanted to part with it.

Gently, she brushed her finger over the bell, over her name and the date she'd entered the Torre.

A faint, sweet ringing leaped away in the wake of her touch. It echoed off the rock walls, off the other bells. Setting some of them ringing, as if in answer.

Around and around the sound of her bell danced, and Yrene turned in place, as if she could follow it. And when it faded . . .

Yrene flicked her bell again. A louder, clearer sound.

The ringing flitted through the room, and she watched it, tracked it.

It faded once more. But not before her power flickered in answer.

With hands that did not entirely belong to her, Yrene rang her bell a third time.

And as its singing filled the room, Yrene began to walk.

Everywhere its ringing went, Yrene followed.

Her bare feet slapping against the damp stone, she tracked the sound's path through the Womb, as if it were a rabbit racing ahead of her.

Around the stalagmites rising from the floor. Ducking under the stalactites drooping from above. Crossing the room; slithering down the walls; setting the candles guttering. On and on, she tracked that sound.

Past the bells of generations of healers, all singing in its wake.

Yrene streamed her fingers along them, too.

A wave of sound answered.

You must enter where you fear to tread.

Yrene walked on, the bells ringing, ringing, ringing. Still she followed the sound of her own bell, that sweet, clear song beckoning onward. Pulling her.

That darkness still dwelled in him; in his wound. They had beaten it so far back, yet it remained. Yesterday, he'd told her things that broke her heart, but not the entire story.

But if the key to defeating that shred of Valg blackness did not lie in facing the memories alone, if blind blasts of her magic did nothing . . .

Yrene followed the silver bell's ringing to where it halted:

An ancient corner of the room, the chains rusted with age, some of the bells green from oxidation.

Here, the sound of her bell went silent.

No, not silent. But waiting. Humming against the corner of stone.

There was a small bell, hanging just by the end of the chain. So oxidized that the writing was nearly impossible to read.

But Yrene read the name there.

Yafa Towers

She did not feel the hard bite of stone as she fell to her knees. As she read that name, the date—the date from two hundred years ago.

A Towers woman. A Towers healer. Here—with her. A Towers woman had been singing in this room during the years Yrene had dwelled here. Even now, even so far from home, she had never once been alone.

Yafa. Yrene mouthed the name, a hand on her heart.

Enter where you fear to tread . . .

Yrene peered up into the darkness of the Womb overhead.

Feeding. The Valg's power had been feeding off him . . .

Yes, the darkness above seemed to say. Not a drip sounded; not a bell chimed.

Yrene gazed down at her hands, lying limp at her sides. Summoned forth the faint white glow of her power. Let it fill the room, echo off the rock in silent song. Echo off those bells, the voices of thousands of her sisters, the Towers voice before her.

Enter where you fear to tread . . .

Not the void lurking within him. But the void within herself.

The one that had started the day those soldiers had gathered around her cottage, had hauled her out by her hair into the bright grasses.

Had Yafa known, here in this chamber so far beneath the earth, what happened that day across the sea? Had she watched the past two months and sent up her ancient, rusted song in silent urging?

They weren't bad men, Yrene.

No, they were not. The men he'd commanded, trained with, who had worn the same uniform, bowed to the same king as the soldiers who had come that day . . .

They were not bad men. People existed in Adarlan worth saving—worth fighting for. They were not her enemy, had never been. Perhaps she'd known that long before he'd revealed it in the oasis yesterday. Perhaps she had not wanted to.

But the thing that remained inside him, that shred of the demon who had ordered it all . . .

I know what you are, Yrene said silently.

For it was the same thing that had dwelled inside her these years, taking from her, even as it sustained her. A different creature, but still one and the same.

Yrene spooled her magic back inside herself, the glow fading. She smiled up at the sweet darkness above. *I understand now.*

Another drop of water kissed her brow in answer.

Smiling, Yrene reached out a hand to her ancestor's bell. And rang it.

⊰ 54 ⊱

Chaol awoke the next morning and could barely move.

They'd repaired his room, added extra guards, and by the time the royals at last returned from the dunes at sundown, all was in order.

He didn't see Yrene for the rest of that day, and wondered if she and the Healer on High had indeed found something of worth in that scroll. But when dinner came and she still hadn't appeared, he sent Kadja to ask Shen for a report.

Shen himself had returned—blushing a bit, no doubt thanks to the beauty of the servant girl who'd led him here—and revealed that he'd made sure word was received from the Torre that Yrene had returned safely and had not left the tower since.

Still, Chaol had debated calling for Yrene when his back began to ache to the point of being unbearable, when even the cane couldn't help him hobble across the room. But the suite was not safe. And if she began to stay here, and Nesryn returned before he could explain—

He couldn't get the thought out of his mind. What he'd done, the trust he'd broken.

So he'd managed to take a bath, hoping to ease his sore muscles, and had nearly crawled into bed.

Chaol awoke at dawn, tried to reach for his cane beside the bed, and bit down his bark of pain.

Panic crashed into him, wild and sharp. He gritted his teeth, trying to fight through it.

Toes. He could move his toes. And his ankles. And his knees—

His neck arched at the rippling agony as he shifted his knees, his thighs, his hips.

Oh, gods. He'd pushed it too far, he'd—

The door flung open, and there she was, in that purple gown.

Yrene's eyes widened, then settled—as if she'd been about to tell him something.

Instead, that mask of steady calm slid over her face while she tied her hair back in her usual half-up fashion and approached on unfaltering feet. "Can you move?"

"Yes, but the pain—" He could barely speak.

Dropping her satchel to the carpet, Yrene rolled up her sleeves. "Can you turn over?"

No. He'd tried, and—

She didn't wait for his answer. "Describe exactly what you did yesterday, from the moment I left until now."

Chaol did. All of it, right until the bath—

Yrene swore viciously. "Ice. *Ice* to help strained muscles, *not* heat." She blew out a breath. "I need you to roll over. It will hurt like hell, but it's best if you do it in one go—"

He didn't wait. He gritted his teeth and did it.

A scream shattered from his throat, but Yrene was instantly there, hands on his cheek, his hair, mouth against his temple. "Good," she breathed onto his skin. "Brave man."

561

He hadn't bothered with more than undershorts while sleeping, so she had little to do to prepare him as she hovered her hands over his back, tracing the air above his skin.

"It . . . it crept back," she breathed.

"I'm not surprised," he said through his teeth. Not at all.

She lowered her hands to her sides. "Why?"

He traced a finger over the embroidered coverlet. "Just—do what you have to."

Yrene paused at his deflection—then riffled through her bag for something. The bit. She held it in her hands, however, instead of sliding it into his mouth. "I'm going in," she said quietly.

"All right."

"No—I'm going in, and I'm ending this. Today. Right now."

It took a moment for the words to sink in. All that it'd entail. He dared ask, "And what if I can't?" *Face it, endure it?*

There was no fear in Yrene's eyes, no hesitation. "That's not my question to answer."

No, it never had been. Chaol watched the sunlight dance on her locket, over those mountains and seas. What she might now witness within him, how badly he'd failed, over and over—

But they had walked this far down the road. Together. She had not turned away. From any of it.

And neither would he.

His throat thick, Chaol managed to say, "You could hurt yourself if you stay too long."

Again, no ripple of doubt or terror. "I have a theory. I want to test it." Yrene slid the bit between his lips, and he clamped down lightly. "And you—you're the only person I can try it on."

It occurred to Chaol, right as she laid her hands on his bare spine, why he was the only one she could try it on. But there was nothing he could do as pain and blackness slammed into him.

No way to stop Yrene as she plunged into his body, her magic a white swarming light around them, inside them.

The Valg. His body had been tainted by their power, and Yrene—

⁓

Yrene did not hesitate.

She soared through him, down the ladder of his spine, down the corridors of his bones and blood.

She was a spear of light, fired straight into the dark, aiming for that hovering shadow that had stretched out once more. That had tried to reclaim him.

Yrene slammed into the darkness and screamed.

It roared back, and they tangled, grappling.

It was foreign and cold and hollow; it was rife with rot and wind and hate.

Yrene threw herself into it. Every last drop.

And above, as if the surface of a night-dark sea separated them, Chaol bellowed with agony.

Today. It ended today.

I know what you are.

So Yrene fought, and so the darkness raged back.

⊰ 55 ⊱

The agony tore through him, unending and depthless.

He blacked out within a minute. Leaving him to free-fall into this place. This pit.

The bottom of the descent.

The hollow hell beneath the roots of a mountain.

Here, where all was locked and buried. Here, where all had come to take root.

The empty foundation, mined and hacked apart, crumbled away into nothing but this pit.

Nothing.

Nothing.

Nothing.

Worthless and nothing.

He saw his father first. His mother and brother and that cold mountain keep. Saw the stairs crusted with the ice and snow, stained with blood. Saw the man he'd gladly sold himself out to, thinking it would get Aelin to safety. *Celaena* to safety.

He'd sent the woman he'd loved to the safety of another assassination. Had sent her to Wendlyn, thinking it better than Adarlan. To *kill* its royal family.

His father emerged from the dark, the mirror of the man he might have become, might one day be. Distaste and disappointment etched his father's features as he beheld him, the son that might have been.

His father's asking price . . . he'd thought it a prison sentence.

But perhaps it had been a shot at freedom—at saving his useless, wayward son from the evil he likely suspected was about to be unleashed.

He had broken that promise to his father.

He hated him, and yet his father—that horrible, miserable bastard—had upheld his end of the bargain.

He . . . he had not.

Oath-breaker. Traitor.

Everything he had done, Aelin had come to rip it apart. Starting with his honor.

She, with her fluidity, that murky area in which she dwelled . . . He'd broken his vows for her. Broken everything he was for her.

He could see her, in the dark.

The gold hair, those turquoise eyes that had been the last clue, the final piece of the puzzle.

Liar. Murderer. Thief.

She basked in the sun atop a chaise longue on the balcony of that suite she'd occupied in the palace, a book in her lap. Tilting her head to the side, she looked him over with that lazy half smile. A cat being stirred from its repose.

He hated her.

He hated that face, the amusement and sharpness. The temper and viciousness that could reduce someone to shreds without so much as a word—only a look. Only a beat of silence.

She *enjoyed* such things. Savored them.

And he had been so bewitched by it, this woman who had been a living flame. He'd been willing to leave it all behind. The honor. The vows he'd made.

For this haughty, swaggering, self-righteous woman, he had shattered parts of himself.

And afterward, she had walked away, as if he were a broken toy.

Right into the arms of that Fae Prince, who emerged from the dark. Who approached that lounge chair on the balcony and sat on its end.

Her half smile turned different. Her eyes sparked.

The lethal, predatory interest honed in on the prince. She seemed to glow brighter. Become more aware. More centered. More . . . alive.

Fire and ice. An end and a beginning.

They did not touch each other.

They only sat on that chaise, some unspoken conversation passing between them. As if they had finally found some reflection of themselves in the world.

He hated them.

He *hated* them for that ease, that intensity, that sense of completion.

She had wrecked him, wrecked his life, and had then strolled right to this prince, as if she were going from one room to another.

And when it had all gone to hell, when he'd turned his back on everything he knew, when he had lied to the one who mattered most to keep her secrets, she had not been there to fight. To help.

She had only returned, months later, and thrown it in his face.

His uselessness. His nothingness.

You remind me of how the world ought to be. What the world can be.

Lies. The words of a girl who had been grateful to him for offering her freedom, for pushing and pushing her until she was roaring at the world again.

A girl who had stopped existing the night they'd found that body on the bed.

When she had ripped his face open.

When she had tried to plunge that dagger into his heart.

The predator he'd seen in those eyes . . . it had been unleashed.

There were no leashes that could ever keep her restrained. And words like *honor* and *duty* and *trust*, they were gone.

She had gutted that courtesan in the tunnels. She'd let the man's body drop, closed her eyes, and had looked precisely as she had during those throes of passion. And when she had opened her eyes again . . .

Killer. Liar. Thief.

She was still sitting on the chaise, the Fae Prince beside her, both of them watching that scene in the tunnel, as if they were spectators in a sport.

Watching Archer Finn slump to the stones, his blood leaking from him, face taut with shock and pain. Watching Chaol stand there, unable to move or speak, as she breathed in the death before her, the vengeance.

As Celaena Sardothien ended, shattering completely.

He had still tried to protect her. To get her out. To atone.

You will always be my enemy.

She had roared those words with ten years' worth of rage.

And she had meant it. Meant it as any child who had lost and suffered at Adarlan's hand would mean it.

As Yrene meant it.

The garden appeared in another pocket of the darkness. The garden and the cottage and the mother and laughing child.

Yrene.

The thing he had not seen coming. The person he had not expected to find.

Here in the darkness . . . here she was.

And yet he had still failed. Hadn't done right by her, or by Nesryn.

He should have waited, should have respected them both enough

567

to end one and begin with another, but he supposed he had failed in that, too.

Aelin and Rowan remained on that chaise in the sunshine.

He saw the Fae Prince gently, reverently, take Aelin's hand, turning it over. Exposing her wrist to the sun. Exposing the faint marks of shackles.

He saw Rowan rub a thumb over those scars. Saw the fire in Aelin's eyes bank.

Over and over, Rowan brushed those scars with his thumb. And Aelin's mask slid off.

There was fire in that face. And rage. And cunning.

But also sorrow. Fear. Despair. Guilt.

Shame.

Pride and hope and love. The weight of a burden she had run from, but now . . .

I love you.

I'm sorry.

She had tried to explain. Had said it as clearly as she could. Had given him the truth so he might piece it together when she had left and understand. She meant those words. *I'm sorry.*

Sorry for the lies. For what she had done to him, his life. For swearing that she would pick him, choose him, no matter what. *Always.*

He wanted to hate her for that lie. That false promise, which she had discarded in the misty forests of Wendlyn.

And yet.

There, with that prince, without the mask . . . That was the bottom of her pit.

She had come to Rowan, soul limping. She had come to him as she was, as she had never been with anyone. And she had returned whole.

Still she had waited—waited to be with him.

Chaol had been lusting for Yrene, had taken her into his bed without so much as thinking of Nesryn, and yet Aelin . . .

She and Rowan looked to him now. Still as an animal in the woods, both of them. But their eyes full of understanding. Knowing.

She had fallen in love with someone else, had wanted someone else—as badly as he wanted Yrene.

And yet it was Aelin, godless and irreverent, who had honored him. More than he'd honored Nesryn.

Aelin's chin dipped as if to say *yes*.

And Rowan . . . The prince had let her return to Adarlan. To make right by her kingdom, but to also decide for herself what she wanted. Who she wanted. And if Aelin had chosen Chaol instead . . . He knew, deep down, Rowan would have backed off. If it had made Aelin happy, Rowan would have walked away without ever telling her what he felt.

Shame pressed on him, sickening and oily.

He had called her a monster. For her power, her actions, and yet . . .

He did not blame her.

He understood.

That perhaps she had promised things, but . . . she had changed. The path had changed.

He understood.

He'd promised Nesryn—or had implied it. And when he had changed, when the path had altered; when Yrene appeared down it . . .

He understood.

Aelin smiled softly at him as she and Rowan rippled into a sunbeam and vanished.

Leaving a red marble floor, blood pooling across it.

A head bumping vulgarly over smooth tile.

A prince screaming in agony, in rage and despair.

I love you.

Go.

That—if there had been a cleaving, it was that moment.

When he turned and ran. And he left his friend, his brother, in that chamber.

When he ran from that fight, that death.

Dorian had forgiven him. Did not hold it against him.

Yet he had still run. Still left.

Everything he had planned, worked to save, all came crumbling down.

Dorian stood before him, hands in his pockets, a faint smile on his face.

He did not deserve to serve such a man. Such a king.

The darkness pushed in further. Revealing that bloody council room. Revealing the prince and king he'd served. Revealing what they had done. To his men.

In that chamber beneath the castle.

How Dorian had smiled. Smiled while Ress had screamed, while Brullo had spat in his face.

His fault—all of it. Every moment of pain, those deaths . . .

It showed him Dorian's hands as they wielded those instruments beneath the castle. As blood spurted and bone sundered. Unfaltering, clean hands. And that smile.

He knew. He had known, had guessed. Nothing would ever make it right. For his men; for Dorian, left to live with it.

For Dorian, whom he'd abandoned in that castle.

That moment, over and over, the darkness showed him.

As Dorian held his ground. As he revealed his magic, as good as a death sentence, and bought him time to run.

He had been so afraid—so afraid of magic, of loss, of *everything*. And that fear . . . it had driven him to it anyway. It had hurried him down this path. He had clung so hard, had fought against it, and it had cost him everything. Too late. He'd been too late to see clearly.

And when the worst had happened; when he saw that collar; when he saw his men swinging from the gates, their broken bodies picked over by crows . . .

It had cracked him through to his foundation. To this hollow pit beneath the mountain he'd been.

He had fallen apart. Had let himself lose sight of it.

And he had found some glimmer of peace in Rifthold, even after the injury, and yet . . .

It was like applying a patch over a knife wound to the gut.

He had not healed. Unmoored and raging, he had not *wanted* to heal. Not really. His body, yes, but even that . . .

Some part of him had whispered it was deserved.

And the soul-wound . . . He had been content to let it fester.

Failure and liar and oath-breaker.

The darkness swarmed, a wind stirring it.

He could stay here forever. In the ageless dark.

Yes, the darkness whispered.

He could remain, and rage and hate and curl into nothing but shadow.

But Dorian remained before him, still smiling faintly. Waiting.

Waiting.

For—him.

He had made one promise. He had not broken it yet.

To save them.

His friend, his kingdom.

He still had that.

Even here at the bottom of this dark hell, he still had that.

And the road that he had traveled so far . . . No, he would not look back.

What if we go on, only to more pain and despair?

Aelin had smiled at his question, posed on that rooftop in Rifthold. As if she had understood, long before he did, that he would find this pit. And learn the answer for himself.

Then it is not the end.

This . . .

This was not the end. This crack in him, this bottom, was not the end.

He had one promise left.

571

To that he would still hold.

It is not the end.

He smiled at Dorian, whose sapphire eyes shone with joy—with love.

"I'm coming home," he whispered to his brother, his king.

Dorian only bowed his head and vanished into the darkness.

Leaving Yrene standing behind him.

She was glowing with white light, bright as a newborn star.

Yrene said quietly, "The darkness belongs to you. To shape as you will. To give it power or render it harmless."

"Was it ever the Valg's to begin with?" His words echoed into nothing.

"Yes. But it is yours to keep now. This place, this final kernel of it."

It would remain in him, a scar and a reminder. "Will it grow again?"

"Only if you let it. Only if you do not fill it with better things. Only if you do not forgive." He knew she didn't just mean others. "But if you are kind to yourself, if you—if you love yourself . . ." Yrene's mouth trembled. "If you love yourself as much as I love you . . ."

Something began to pound in his chest. A drumbeat that had gone silent down here.

Yrene held a hand toward him, her iridescence rippling into the darkness.

It is not the end.

"Will it hurt?" he asked hoarsely. "The way back—the way out?"

The path back to life, to himself.

"Yes," Yrene whispered. "But just this one last time. The darkness does not want to lose you."

"I'm afraid I can't say the same."

Yrene's smile was brighter than the glow rippling off her body. A star. She was a fallen star.

She extended her hand again. A silent promise—of what waited on the other side of the dark.

He still had much to do. Oaths to keep.

And looking at her, at that smile . . .

Life. He had *life* to savor, to fight for.

And the breaking that had started and ended here . . . Yes, it belonged to him. He was *allowed* to break, so that this forging might begin.

So that *he* might begin again.

He owed it to his king, his country.

And he owed it to himself.

Yrene nodded as if to say yes.

So Chaol stood.

He surveyed the darkness, this piece of him. He did not balk at it.

And smiling at Yrene, he took her hand.

⊰ 56 ⊱

It was agony and despair and fear. It was joy and laughter and rest.

It was life, all of it, and as that darkness lunged for Chaol and Yrene, he did not fear it.

He only looked toward the dark and smiled.

Not broken.

Made anew.

And when the darkness beheld him . . .

Chaol slid a hand against its cheek. Kissed its brow.

It loosened its grip and tumbled back into that pit. Curled up on that rocky floor and quietly, carefully, watched him.

He had the sense of rising up, of being sucked through a too-thin door. Yrene grasped him, hauling him along with her.

She did not let go. Did not falter. She speared them upward, a star racing into the night.

White light slammed into them—

No. Daylight.

He squeezed his eyes shut against the brightness.

The first thing he felt was nothing.

No pain. No numbness. No ache or exhaustion.

Gone.

His legs were . . . He moved one. It flowed and shifted without a flicker of pain or tension.

Smooth as butter.

He looked to the right, to where Yrene always sat.

She was simply smiling down at him.

"How," he rasped.

Joy lit her stunning eyes. "My theory . . . I'll explain later."

"Is the mark—"

Her mouth tightened. "It is smaller, but . . . still there." She poked a point on his spine. "Though I do not feel anything when I touch it. Nothing at all."

A reminder. As if some god wanted him to remember this, remember what had occurred.

He sat up, marveling at the ease, the lack of stiffness. "You healed me."

"I think we both get considerable credit this time." Her lips were too pale, skin wan.

Chaol brushed her cheek with his knuckles. "Are you feeling well?"

"I'm—tired. But fine. Are *you* feeling well?"

He scooped Yrene into his lap and buried his head in her neck. "Yes," he breathed. "A thousand times, yes."

His chest . . . there was a lightness to it. To his shoulders.

She batted him away. "You still need to be careful. This newly healed, you could still injure yourself. Give your body time to rest—to let the healing set."

He lifted a brow. "What, exactly, does resting entail?"

Yrene's smile turned wicked. "Some things that only special patients get to learn."

His skin tightened over his bones, but Yrene slid off his lap. "You might want to bathe."

He blinked, looking at himself. At the bed. And cringed.

That was vomit. On the sheets, on his left arm.

"When—"

"I'm not sure."

The setting sun was indeed gilding the garden, cramming the room with long shadows.

Hours. All day, they'd been in here.

Chaol moved off the bed, marveling at how he slid through the world like a blade through silk.

He felt her watching him as he strode for the bathing room. "Hot water is safe now?" he called over his shoulder, stripping off his undershorts and stepping into the deliciously warm bath.

"Yes," she called back. "You're not full of strained muscles."

He dunked under the water, scrubbing himself off. Every movement . . . holy gods.

When he broke from the surface, wiping the water from his face, she was standing in the arched doorway.

He went still at the smokiness in her eyes.

Slowly, Yrene undid the laces down the front of that pale purple gown. Let it ripple to the floor, along with her undergarments.

His mouth turned dry as she kept her eyes upon him, hips swishing with every step she took to the pool. To the stairs.

Yrene stepped into the water, and his blood roared in his ears.

Chaol was upon her before she'd hit the last step.

They missed dinner. And dessert.

And midnight *kahve*.

Kadja snuck in during the bath to change the sheets. Yrene couldn't bring herself to be mortified at what the servant had likely heard. They certainly hadn't been quiet in the water.

And certainly weren't quiet during the hours following.

Yrene was limp with exhaustion when they peeled apart, sweaty enough that another trip to the bath was imminent. Chaol's chest rose and fell in mighty gulps.

In the desert, he'd been unbelievable. But now, healed—beyond the spine, the legs; healed in that dark, rotting place within his soul . . .

He pressed a kiss to her sweat-sticky brow, his lips catching in the stray curls that had appeared thanks to the bath. His other hand drew circles on her lower back.

"You said something—down in that pit," he murmured.

Yrene was too tired to form words beyond a low "Mmm."

"You said that you love me."

Well, that woke her up.

Her stomach clenched. "Don't feel obligated to—"

Chaol silenced her with that steady, unruffled look. "Is it true?"

She traced the scar down his cheek. She had not seen much of the beginning, had only broken into his memories in time to see that beautiful, dark-haired man—*Dorian*—smiling at him. But she had sensed it, known who had given him that recent scar.

"Yes." And though her voice was soft, she meant it with every inch of her soul.

The corners of his mouth tugged upward. "Then it is a good thing, Yrene Towers, that I love you as well."

Her chest tightened; she became too full for her body, for what coursed through her.

"From the moment you walked into the sitting room that first day," Chaol said. "I think I knew, even then."

"I was a stranger."

"You looked at me without an ounce of pity. You saw *me*. Not the chair or the injury. You saw me. It was the first time I'd felt . . . seen. Felt *awake*, in a long time."

She kissed his chest, right over his heart. "How could I resist these muscles?"

His laugh rumbled into her mouth, her bones. "The consummate professional."

Yrene smiled onto his skin. "The healers will never let me hear the end of this. Hafiza is already beside herself with glee."

But she stiffened, considering the road ahead. The choices.

Chaol said after a moment, "When Nesryn returns, I plan to make it clear. Though I think she knew before I did."

Yrene nodded, trying to fight off the shakiness that crept over her.

"And beyond that . . . The choice is yours, Yrene. When you leave. How you leave. If you truly want to leave at all."

She braced herself.

"But if you'll have me . . . there will be a place for you on my ship. At my side."

She let out a dainty hum and traced a circle around his nipple. "What sort of place?"

Chaol stretched out like a cat, tucking his arms behind his head as he drawled, "The usual options: scullery maid, cook, dishwasher—"

She poked his ribs, and he laughed. It was a beautiful sound, rich and deep.

But his brown eyes softened as he cupped her face. "What place would you like, Yrene?"

Her heart thundered at the question, the timbre of his voice. But she smirked and said, "Whichever one gives me the right to yell at you if you push yourself too hard." She drew her hand along his legs, his back. Careful—he'd have to be so, so careful for a while.

A corner of Chaol's mouth kicked up, and he hauled her over him. "I think I know of just the position."

⊰ 57 ⊱

The Eridun aerie was madness when they returned.

Falkan was alive—barely—and had caused such panic upon the ruks' arrival at Altun that Houlun had to leap in front of the limp spider to keep the other ruks from shredding him apart.

Sartaq had managed to stand long enough to embrace Kadara, order a healer to come for her immediately, then wrap his arms around Borte, who was spattered in black blood and grinning from ear to ear. Then Sartaq clasped arms with Yeran, whom Borte pointedly ignored, which Nesryn supposed was an improvement from outright hostility.

"How?" Sartaq asked Borte while Nesryn hovered near the unconscious form of Falkan, still not trusting the ruks to control themselves.

Yeran, his company of Berlad ruks having returned to their own aerie, stepped away from his awaiting mount and answered instead, "Borte came to get me. Said she was going on a stupidly dangerous mission and I could either let her die alone or come along."

Sartaq rasped a laugh. "You were forbidden," he told Borte, glancing toward where Houlun knelt at Falkan's side, the hearth-mother indeed looking torn between relief and outright rage.

Borte sniffed. "By my hearth-mother *here*. As I am currently betrothed to a captain of the Berlad"—emphasis on *currently*, to Yeran's chagrin, it seemed—"I also can claim partial loyalty to the hearth-mother *there*. Who had no qualms about letting me spend some *quality time* with my betrothed."

"We will have words, she and I," Houlun seethed as she rose to her feet and strode past, ordering several people to bring Falkan farther into the hall. Wincing at the spider's weight, they gingerly obeyed.

Borte shrugged, turning to follow Houlun to where the shifter would be patched up as best they could manage in that spider's body. "At least his hearth-mother's sense of quality time is in line with my own," she said, and walked off.

Yet as she left, Nesryn could have sworn Borte gave Yeran a secret, small smile.

Yeran stared after her for a long moment, then turned to them. Gave them a crooked grin. "She promised to set a date. That's how she got my hearth-mother to approve." He winked at Sartaq. "Too bad I didn't tell her that I don't approve of the date at all."

And with that, he strode after Borte, jogging a few steps to catch up. She whirled on him, sharp words already snapping from her lips, but allowed him to follow her into the hall.

When Nesryn faced Sartaq, it was in time to see him sway.

She lunged, her aching body protesting as she caught the prince around the middle. Someone shouted for a healer, but Sartaq got his legs beneath him, even as he kept his arms about her.

Nesryn found herself disinclined to remove her own arms from his waist.

Sartaq stared down at her, that soft, sweet smile on his mouth again. "You saved me."

"It seemed a sorry end for the tales of the Winged Prince," she replied, frowning at the gash in his leg. "You should be sitting—"

Across the hall, light flashed, people cried out . . . and then the spider was gone. Replaced by a man, covered in slashing cuts and blood.

When Nesryn looked back, Sartaq's gaze was on her face.

Her throat closed up, her mouth pressing into a trembling line as she realized that they were here. They were here, and alive, and she had never known such true terror and despair as she had in those moments when he had been hauled away.

"Don't cry," he murmured, leaning down to brush his mouth over the tears that escaped. He said against her skin, "Whatever would they say about Neith's Arrow then?"

Nesryn laughed despite herself, despite what had happened, and wrapped her arms around him as tightly as she dared, resting her head against his chest.

Sartaq just wordlessly stroked her hair and held her right back.

The Council of Clans met two days later at dawn.

Hearth-mothers and their captains from every aerie gathered in the hall, so many that the space was filled.

Nesryn had slept the entirety of the day before.

Not in her room, but curled in bed beside the prince now standing with her before the assembled group.

They had both been patched up and bathed, and though Sartaq had not so much as kissed her . . . Nesryn had not objected when he led her by the hand and limped into his bedroom.

So they had slept. And when they had awoken, when their wounds had been rebandaged, they'd emerged to find the hall full of riders.

Falkan sat against the far wall, his arm in a sling, but eyes clear. Nesryn had smiled at him as she'd entered, but now was not the time for that reunion. Or the possible truths she bore.

When Houlun had finished welcoming everyone, when silence fell on the hall, Nesryn stood shoulder to shoulder with Sartaq. It was strange to see him with the shorter hair—strange, but not awful. It would grow back, he said when she had frowned that morning.

All eyes shifted between them, some warm and welcoming, some worried, some hard.

Sartaq said to the group gathered, "The *kharankui* have stirred again." Murmurs and shifting rustled through the hall. "And though the threat was dealt with bravely and fiercely by the Berlad clan, the spiders will likely return again. They have heard a dark call through the world. And they are poised to answer it."

Nesryn stepped forward. Lifted her chin. And though the words filled her with dread, speaking them here felt as natural as breathing. "We learned many things in the Pass of Dagul," Nesryn said, voice ringing out across the pillars and stones of the hall. "Things that will change the war in the north. And change this world."

Every eye was on her now. Houlun nodded from her spot near Borte, who smiled in encouragement. Yeran sat nearby, half watching his betrothed.

Sartaq's fingers brushed hers. Once—in urging. And promise.

"We do not face an army of men in the northern continent," Nesryn went on. "But of demons. And if we do not rise to meet this threat, if we do not rise to meet it as one people, of *all* lands . . . Then we will find our doom instead."

So she told them. The full history. Of Erawan. And Maeve.

She did not mention the quest for the keys, but by the time she was done, the hall was astir as clans whispered to one another.

"I leave this choice to you," Sartaq said, voice unfaltering. "The horrors in the Dagul Fells are only the start. I will pass no judgment, should you choose to remain. But all who fly with me, we soar under the khagan's banner. We shall leave you to debate amongst yourselves."

And with that, taking Nesryn by the hand, Sartaq led her from the hall, Falkan falling into step behind them. Borte and Houlun remained, as heads of the Eridun clan. Nesryn knew how they would side, that they would fly north, but the others . . .

Whispers had turned into full-on debate by the time they reached one of the private gathering spaces for the family. But Sartaq was only in the small room for a moment before he headed to the kitchens, leaving Nesryn and Falkan with a wink and a promise to bring back food.

Alone with the shifter, Nesryn strode to the fire and warmed her hands. "How are you feeling?" she asked, glancing over her shoulder to where Falkan eased into a low-backed wooden chair.

"Everything hurts." Falkan grimaced, rubbing at his leg. "Remind me never to do anything heroic again."

She chuckled over the crackle of the fire. "Thank you—for doing that."

"I have no one in my life who would miss me anyway."

Her throat tightened. But she asked, "If we fly north—to Antica, and finally to the northern continent . . ." She could no longer bring herself to say the word. *Home.* "Will you come?"

The shifter was silent for a long moment. "Would you want me there? Any of you?"

Nesryn turned from the fire at last, eyes burning. "I have something to tell you."

⁓

Falkan wept.

Put his head in his hands and wept when Nesryn told him what she suspected. She did not know much of Lysandra's personal history, but the ages, the location matched. Only the description did not. The mother had described a plain, brown-haired girl. Not a black-haired, green-eyed beauty.

But yes—yes, he would come. To war, and to find her. His niece. His last shred of family in the world, for whom he had never stopped looking.

Sartaq returned with food, and thirty minutes later, word came from the hall.

The clans had decided.

Hands shaking, Nesryn strode to the door, to where Sartaq held out a hand.

Their fingers interlaced, and he led her toward the now-silent hall. Falkan rose painfully from his chair, groaning as he brushed away his tears, and limped after them.

They made it a handful of steps before a messenger came barreling down the hall.

Nesryn pulled away from Sartaq to let him deal with the panting, wild-eyed girl. But it was to Nesryn the messenger extended the letter.

Nesryn's hands shook as she recognized the handwriting on it.

She felt Sartaq stiffen as he, too, realized that the writing was Chaol's. He stepped back, eyes shuttered, to let her read it.

She read the message twice. Had to take a steady breath to keep from vomiting.

"He—he requests my presence in Antica. *Needs* it," she said, the note fluttering in her shaking hand. "He begs us to return immediately. As fast as the winds can carry us."

Sartaq took the letter to read for himself. Falkan remained quiet and watchful as the prince read it. Swore.

"Something is wrong," Sartaq said, and Nesryn nodded.

If Chaol, who never asked for help, never *wanted* help, had told them to hurry . . . She glanced toward the council, still waiting to announce their decision.

But Nesryn only asked the prince, "How soon can we be airborne?"

⤙ 58 ⤚

Morning came and went, and Yrene was in no rush to rise from bed. Neither was Chaol. They ate a leisurely lunch in the sitting room, not bothering with proper clothes.

Hafiza would decide in her own time whether to give them those books. So they'd just have to wait. And then wait to encounter Aelin Galathynius again, or anyone else who might be able to decipher them. Chaol said as much, after Yrene told him what Hafiza had confirmed.

"There must be considerable information inside those books," Chaol mused as he chewed on pomegranate seeds, the fruit like small rubies he popped into his mouth.

"If they date back as far as we think," Yrene said, "if many of those texts came from the necropolis or similar sites, it could be a trove. About the Valg. Our connection to them."

"Aelin lucked out in Rifthold, when she stumbled across those few books."

He'd told her last night—of the assassin named Celaena, who had turned out to be a queen named Aelin. The entire history of it, laid bare. A long one, and a sad one. His voice had grown hoarse when he'd talked of Dorian. Of the collar and the Valg prince. Of those they had lost. Of his own role, the sacrifices he'd made, the promises he'd broken. All of it.

And if Yrene had not loved him already, she would have loved him then, learning that truth. Seeing the man he was becoming, turning into, after all of it.

"The king somehow missed them during his initial research and purging."

"Or perhaps some god made sure he did," Yrene mused. She lifted a brow. "I don't suppose there are any Baast Cats at that library."

Chaol shook his head and set down the looted corpse of the pome-granate. "Aelin has always had a god or two perched on her shoulder. Nothing would surprise me at this point."

Yrene considered. "Whatever did happen with the king? If he had that Valg demon."

Chaol's face darkened as he leaned back on the not-nearly-as-comfortable replacement for the shredded gold sofa. "Aelin healed him."

Yrene sat up straighter. "How?"

"She burned it out of him. Well, she and Dorian did."

"And the man—the true king—survived it?"

"No. Initially, yes. But neither Aelin nor Dorian wanted to talk much about what happened on that bridge. He survived long enough to explain what had been done, but I think he was fading fast. Then Aelin destroyed the castle. And him with it."

"But fire rid the Valg demon within him?"

"Yes. And I think it helped save Dorian, too. Or at least bought him enough freedom to fight back on his own." He angled his head. "Why do you ask?"

"Because that theory I had . . ." Yrene's knee bounced. She scanned

586

the room, the doors. No one nearby. "I think . . ." She leaned closer, gripping his knee. "I think the Valg are parasites. Infections."

He opened his mouth, but Yrene plowed ahead. "Hafiza and I pulled a tapeworm from Hasar when I first came here. They feed off their host, much in the same way the Valg do. Take over basic needs—like hunger. And eventually kill their hosts, when all those resources have been used up."

Chaol went utterly still. "But these are no mindless grubs."

"Yes, and that was what I wanted to see with you yesterday. How much awareness that darkness had. The extent of their power. If it had left some sort of parasite in your bloodstream. It didn't, but . . . There was the other parasite—feeding off you, giving it control."

He was silent.

Yrene cleared her throat, caressing her thumb over his wrist. "I realized the night before. That I had one of my own. My hatred, my anger and fear and pain." She brushed away a stray curl. "They were all parasites, feeding on me these years. Sustaining me, but also feeding on me."

And once she had understood that—that the place she most feared to tread was *inside* herself, where she might have to acknowledge what, exactly, dwelled within *her* . . .

"When I realized what *I* was doing, I understood that's what the Valg truly is, deep down. What your own shadows are. *Parasites.* And enduring it these weeks was not the same as *facing* it. So I attacked it as I would any other parasite; swarmed around it. Made it come to you—attack *you* as hard as it could to get away from *me*. So that *you* might face it, defeat it. So you might go where you feared most to tread, and decide whether, at last, you were ready to fight back."

His eyes were clear, bright. "That's a big realization."

"It certainly was." She considered what he'd related—about Aelin and the demon inside the dead king. "Fire is cleansing. Purifying. But amongst the healing arts, it's not often used. Too unwieldy. Water is better-tuned to the healing. But then there are raw healing gifts. Like mine."

"Light," Chaol said. "It looked like swarming lights, against their darkness."

She nodded. "Aelin managed to get Dorian and his father free. Roughly, crudely, and one did not survive. But what if a *healer* with my sort of gifts was to treat someone possessed—*infected* by the Valg? The ring, the collar, they're implantation devices. Like a bad bit of water, or tainted food. Merely a carrier for something small, the kernel of those demons, who then grow within their hosts. Removing it is the first step, but you said the demon can remain even afterward."

His chest began to heave in an uneven rhythm as he nodded.

Yrene whispered, "I think I can heal them. I think the Valg . . . I think they are parasites, and I can *treat* the people they infect."

"Then everyone Erawan has captured, held with those rings and collars—"

"We could potentially free them."

He squeezed her hand. "But you'd have to get close to them. And their power, Yrene—"

"I would assume that is where Aelin and Dorian would come in. To hold them down."

"There's no way to test this, though. Without considerable risk." His jaw tightened. "It has to be why Erawan's agent is hunting you. To erase the knowledge of that. To keep you from realizing it by healing me. And relaying it to other healers."

"If that is the case, though . . . Why now? Why wait this long?"

"Perhaps Erawan did not even consider it. Until Aelin purged the Valg from Dorian and the king." He rubbed at his chest. "But there is a ring. It belonged to Athril, friend to King Brannon and Maeve. It granted Athril immunity from the Valg. It was lost to history—the only one of its kind. Aelin found it. And Maeve wanted it badly enough that she traded Rowan for it. Legend said Mala herself forged it for Athril, but . . . Mala loved Brannon, not Athril."

Chaol shot up from the couch, and Yrene watched him pace. "There was a tapestry. In Aelin's old room. A tapestry that showed a stag, and hid the entrance that led down to the tomb where the Wyrdkey had been hidden by Brannon. It was Aelin's first clue that set her down this path."

"And?" The word was a push of air.

"And there was an owl on it amongst the forest animals. It was Athril's form. Not Brannon's. All of that was coded—the tapestry, the tomb. Symbols upon symbols. But the owl . . . We never thought. Never considered."

"Considered what?"

Chaol halted in the middle of the room. "That the owl might not just be Athril's animal form, but his sigil because of his loyalty to someone else."

And despite the warm day, Yrene's blood chilled as she said, "Silba."

Chaol nodded slowly. "Goddess of Healing."

Yrene whispered, "Mala did not make that ring of immunity."

"No. She didn't."

Silba did.

"We need to go to Hafiza," Yrene said softly. "Even if she won't let us take the books, we should ask her to look at them—see for ourselves what might have survived all this time. What those Fae healers might have learned in that war."

He motioned her to rise. "We'll go now."

But the suite doors opened, and Hasar breezed in, her gold-and-green dress flowing.

"Well," she said, smirking at their lack of clothes, their disheveled hair. "At least you two are comfortable."

Yrene had the sense the world was about to be knocked from beneath her as the princess smiled at Chaol. "We've had some news. From your lands."

"What is it." The words were ground out.

Hasar picked at her nails. "Oh, just that Queen Maeve's armada managed to find the host Aelin Galathynius has been so sneakily patching together. There was *quite* the battle."

⊰ 59 ⊱

Chaol debated strangling the smirking princess. But he managed to keep his hands at his sides, managed to keep his chin high despite the fact that he was only wearing his pants, and said, "What. Happened."

A naval battle. Aelin against *Maeve*. He waited for the dangling sword to drop. If he had been too late—

Hasar looked up from her nails. "It was a spectacle, apparently. A Fae armada versus a cobbled-together human force—"

"Hasar, please," Yrene murmured.

The princess sighed at the ceiling. "Fine. Maeve was trounced."

Chaol sank onto the sofa.

Aelin—thank the gods Aelin had managed to find a way—

"Though there were some interesting details." Then the princess rattled off the facts. The numbers. A third of Maeve's armada, bearing Whitethorn flags, had turned on their own and joined Terrasen's fleet. Dorian had fought—held the front lines with Rowan. Then a pack of wyverns had soared in from nowhere—to fight for Aelin.

Manon Blackbeak. Chaol would be willing to bet his life that somehow, either through Aelin or Dorian, that witch had done them a favor, and possibly altered the course of this war.

"The magic, they say, was impressive," Hasar went on. "Ice and wind and water." Dorian and Rowan. "Even rumor of a shape-shifter." Lysandra. "But no darkness. Or whatever Maeve fights with. And no flame."

Chaol braced his forearms on his knees.

"Though some reports claim they spotted flame and shadow on shore—far away. Flickers of both. There and gone. And no one spotted Aelin or the Dark Queen in the fleet."

It would have been like Aelin, to shift the battle between her and Maeve to the shore. To minimize casualties, so she could unleash her full power without hesitation.

"As I said," Hasar continued, fluffing the skirts of her dress, "They were victorious. Aelin was spotted returning to her armada hours later. They've set sail—north, apparently."

He muttered a prayer of thanks to Mala. And a prayer of thanks to whatever god watched over Dorian, too. "Any major casualties?"

"To their men, yes, but not to any of the interesting players," Hasar said, and Chaol hated her. "But Maeve . . . there and gone, not a whisper of her left." She frowned at the windows. "Maybe she'll sail here to lick her wounds."

Chaol prayed that wouldn't be the case. Yet if Maeve's armada still sat in the Narrow Sea when they took the crossing . . . "But the others sail north now—to where?" *Where can I find my king, my brother?*

"I'd assume Terrasen, now that Aelin has her armada. Oh, and another one."

Hasar smiled at him. Waiting for the question—the plea.

"What other armada," Chaol forced himself to ask.

Hasar shrugged, walking from the room. "Turns out, Aelin called in a debt. To the Silent Assassins of the Red Desert."

Chaol's eyes burned.

"And to Wendlyn."

His hands began shaking.

"How many ships," he breathed.

"All of them," Hasar said, hand on the door. "All of Wendlyn's armada came, commanded by Crown Prince Galan himself."

Aelin . . . Chaol's blood sparked, and he looked to Yrene. Her eyes were wide, bright. Bright with hope—burning, precious hope.

"Turns out," Hasar mused, as if it were a passing thought, "there are quite a few people who think highly of her. And who believe in what she's selling."

"Which is what?" Yrene whispered.

Hasar shrugged. "I assume it's what she tried to sell to me, when she wrote me a message weeks ago, asking for my aid. From one princess to another."

Chaol took a shuddering breath. "What did Aelin promise you?"

Hasar smiled to herself. "A better world."

⇥ 60 ⇤

Chaol was bristling beside Yrene as they hurried through Antica's narrow streets, crammed with people going home for the night. Not with rage, she realized, but purpose.

Aelin had mustered an army, and if they could join with them, bring some force from the khaganate . . . Yrene beheld the hope in his eyes. The focus.

A fool's shot at this war. But only if they could convince the royals.

One last push, he declared to her as they entered the cool interior of the Torre and hurried up the stairs. He didn't care if he had to crawl in front of the khagan. He would make one last attempt at convincing him.

But first: Hafiza. And the books that might contain a far more valuable weapon than swords or arrows: knowledge.

His steps did not falter as they wound up the endless interior of the Torre. Even with all that weighed on them, Chaol still murmured in her ear, "No wonder those legs of yours are so pretty."

Yrene batted him off, her face heating. "Cad."

At this hour, most of the acolytes were already heading down to dinner. Several beamed at Chaol as they passed him on the stairs, some younger ones giggling. He gave them all warm, indulgent smiles that sent them into further fits.

Hers. He was hers, Yrene wanted to crow at them. This beautiful, brave, selfless man—he was hers.

And she was going home with him.

It was that thought that sobered her slightly. The sense that these endless hikes up the interior of the Torre might now be limited. That she might not smell the lavender and baked bread for a long time. Not hear those giggles.

Chaol's hand brushed hers as if to say he understood. Yrene only gripped his fingers tightly. Yes, she would leave a part of herself here. But what she took with her upon leaving . . . Yrene was smiling when they at last reached the top of the Torre.

Chaol panted, bracing a hand on the wall of the landing. Hafiza's office door was cracked open, letting in the last of the sunset. "Whoever built this thing was a sadist."

Yrene laughed, knocking on Hafiza's office door and pushing it open. "That would be Kamala. And rumor says she—" Yrene halted, finding the Healer on High's office empty.

She edged around him on the landing, striding for the workroom—the door ajar. "Hafiza?"

No answer, but she pushed open the door anyway.

Empty. That bookcase, mercifully, still locked.

Likely making rounds, or at dinner, then. Though they'd seen everyone coming down after the dinner bell's summons, and Hafiza hadn't been among them.

"Wait here," Yrene said, and bounded down the stairs to the next landing, a level above Yrene's own room.

"Eretia," she said, stepping into the small room.

The healer grunted in answer. "Saw a nice backside walk past here a moment ago."

Chaol's cough sounded from above.

Yrene snorted, but said, "Do you know where Hafiza is?"

"In her workroom." The woman didn't so much as turn. "She's been in there all day."

"You're . . . certain?"

"Yes. Saw her go in, shut the door, and she hasn't come out."

"The door was open just now."

"Then she likely slipped past me."

Without saying a word? That wasn't Hafiza's nature.

Yrene scratched her head, scanning the landing behind her. The few doors on it. She didn't bother saying good-bye to Eretia before knocking on them. One was empty; the other healer told her the same: Hafiza was in her workroom.

Chaol was waiting atop the stairs when Yrene climbed back up. "No luck?"

Yrene tapped her foot on the ground. Perhaps she was paranoid, but . . .

"Let's check the mess hall," was all she said.

She caught the gleam in Chaol's eyes. The worry—and warning.

They went down two levels until Yrene halted on her own landing.

Her door was shut—but there was something wedged beneath it. As if a passing foot had kicked it under. "What is that?"

Chaol drew his sword so fast she didn't even see him move, every movement of his body, his blade, a dance. She bent and pulled the object out. Metal scraped on stone.

And there, dangling from its chain . . . Hafiza's iron key.

Chaol studied the door, the stairs, as Yrene pulled the necklace over her head with shaking fingers. "She didn't slide it there by accident," he said.

And if she had thought to hide the key here . . . "She knew something was coming for her."

"There was no sign of forced entry or attack upstairs," he countered.

"She could have just been spooked, but . . . Hafiza does nothing without thought."

Chaol put a hand on the small of her back, ushering her toward the stairs. "We need to notify the guard—start a search party."

She was going to be ill. She was going to vomit right down the steps.

If she had brought this upon Hafiza—

Panic helped no one. Nothing.

She forced herself to take a breath. Another one. "We need to be quick. Can your back—"

"I can manage. It feels fine."

Yrene assessed his stance, his balance. "Then hurry."

⸻

Around and around, they flew down the steps of the Torre. Asking anyone who passed if they'd seen Hafiza. *In her workroom*, they all said.

As if she had simply vanished into nothing. Into shadow.

Chaol had seen enough, endured enough, to listen to his gut.

And his gut told him that something either had happened or was unfurling.

Yrene's face was bone white with dread, that iron key bouncing against her chest with each of their steps. They reached the bottom of the Torre, and Yrene had the guard on alert in a matter of words, calmly explaining that the Healer on High was missing.

But search parties took too long to organize. Anything could happen in the span of minutes. Seconds.

In the busy hallway of the Torre's main level, Yrene called out to a few healers about Hafiza's location. No, she was not in the mess hall. No, she was not in the herb gardens. They had just been that way and had not seen her.

It was an enormous complex. "We'd cover more ground if we split up," Yrene panted, scanning the hall.

"No. They might be expecting that. We stick together."

Yrene scrubbed her hands over her face. "Widespread hysteria might make the—person act quicker. Rasher. We keep it quiet." She lowered her hands. "Where do we start? She could be in the city, she could be *d*—"

"How many exits lead from the Torre into the streets?"

"Just the main gate, and a small side one for the deliveries. Both heavily guarded."

They visited both within a span of minutes. Nothing. The guards were well trained and had kept a record of everyone who went in and out. Hafiza had not been seen. And no wagons had come in or left since early morning. Before Eretia had last seen her.

"She has to be somewhere on the premises," Chaol said, surveying the tower looming above, the physicians' complex. "Unless you can think of another way in or out. Perhaps something that might have been forgotten."

Yrene went wholly still, her eyes bright as flame in the sinking twilight.

"The library," she breathed, and launched into a sprint.

Swift—she was swift, and it was all he could do to keep up with her. To *run*. Holy gods, he was *running*, and—

"There are rumors of tunnels in the library," Yrene panted, leading him down a familiar hallway. "Deep below. That connect outside. To where, we don't know. Rumor claims they were sealed up, but—"

His heart thundered. "It would explain how they were able to come and go unnoticed."

And if the old woman had been brought down there . . .

"How did they even get her to go? Without anyone noticing?"

He didn't want to answer. The Valg could summon shadows if they wished. And hide within them. And those shadows could turn deadly in an instant.

Yrene slid to a stop in front of the main library desk, Nousha's head snapping up. The marble was so smooth Yrene had to grapple at the edges of the desk to keep from falling.

"Have you seen Hafiza?" she blurted.

Nousha looked between them. Noted the sword he still had out.

"What is wrong."

"Where are the tunnels?" Yrene demanded. "The ones they boarded up—where *are* they?"

Behind her, a storm-gray Baast Cat leaped up from its vigil by the hearth and sprinted into the library proper.

Nousha gazed at an ancient bell the size of a melon atop the desk. A hammer lay beside it.

Yrene slapped her hand on the hammer. "Don't. It will alert them that—that we know."

The woman's brown skin seemed to go wan. "Head down to the bottom level. Walk straight to the wall. Cut left. Take that to the farthest wall—the very end. Where the stone is rough and unpolished. Cut right. You'll see them."

Yrene's chest heaved, but she nodded, muttering the directions to herself. Chaol memorized them, planted them in his mind.

Nousha rose to her feet. "Shall I summon the guard?"

"Yes," Chaol said. "But quietly. Send them after us. As fast as you can."

Nousha's hands shook as she folded them in front of her middle. "Those tunnels have been left untouched for a very long time. Be on your guard. Even we do not know what lies down there."

Chaol debated mentioning the usefulness of cryptic warnings before plunging into battle, but simply entwined his fingers through Yrene's and launched them down the hall.

❄ 61 ❄

Yrene counted every step. Not that it helped, but her brain just produced the numbers in an endless tally.

One, two, three . . . Forty.

Three hundred.

Four twenty-four.

Seven hundred twenty-one.

Down and down they went, scanning every shadow and aisle, every alcove and reading room and nook. Nothing.

Only acolytes quietly working, many packing up for the night. No Baast Cats—not one.

Eight hundred thirty.

One thousand three.

They hit the bottom of the library, the lights dimmer. Sleepier.

The shadows more alert. Yrene saw faces in all of them.

Chaol plunged ahead, sword like quicksilver as they followed Nousha's directions.

The temperature dropped. The lights became fewer and farther between.

Leather books were replaced with crumbling scrolls. Scrolls replaced by carved tablets. Wooden shelves gave way to stone alcoves. The marble floor turned uncut. So did the walls.

"Here," Chaol breathed, and drew her into a stop, his sword lifting.

The hall before them was lit by a sole candle. Left to burn on the ground.

And down it: four doors.

Three sealed with heavy stone, but the fourth . . . Open. The stone rolled aside. Another lone candle before it, illumining the darkness beyond.

A tunnel. Deeper than the Womb—deeper than any level of the Torre.

Chaol pointed to the rough dirt of the passage ahead. "Tracks. Two sets, side by side."

Sure enough, the ground had been disturbed.

He whirled to her. "You stay here, I'll—"

"No." He weighed the word, her stance, as she added, "Together. We do this together."

Chaol took another moment to consider, then nodded. Carefully, he led her along, showing her where to step to avoid any loud noises on loose bits of stone.

The candle beckoned by the open tunnel doorway. A beacon. An invitation.

The light danced along his blade as he angled it before the tunnel entrance.

Nothing but fallen blocks of stone and an endless dark passage greeted them.

Yrene breathed in through her nose, out through her mouth. Hafiza. Hafiza was in there. Either hurt or worse, and—

Chaol linked his hand with hers and led her into the dark.

They inched along in silence for untold minutes. Until the light from the sole candle faded behind them—and another appeared. Faintly, far off. As if around a distant corner.

As if someone was waiting.

⁓

Chaol knew it was a trap.

Knew the Healer on High had not been the target, but the bait. But if they arrived too late . . .

He would not let that happen.

They inched toward that second candle, the light as good as ringing the dinner bell.

But he moved forward nonetheless, Yrene keeping pace beside him.

The sole candle grew brighter.

Not a candle. A golden light from the passage beyond. Gilding the stone wall behind it.

Yrene tried to hurry, but he kept their pace slow. Quiet as death.

Though he had no doubt whoever it was already knew they were coming.

They reached the turn in the tunnel, and he studied the light on the far wall, trying to read for any shadows or disruptions. Only light.

He peered around the corner. Yrene did so, too.

Her breath snagged. He had seen some sights in the past year, but this . . .

It was a chamber, as enormous as the entire throne room in Rifthold's palace, perhaps larger. The ceiling held aloft on carved pillars receding into the gloom, a set of stairs leading down from the tunnel onto the main floor. He knew why the light had been golden upon the walls.

For illuminated by the torches that burned throughout . . . *Gold*.

The wealth of an ancient empire filled the chamber. Chests and statues and trinkets of pure gold. Suits of armor. Swords.

And scattered amongst it all were sarcophagi. Built not from gold, but impenetrable stone.

601

A tomb—and a trove. And at the very back, rising up on a towering dais . . .

Yrene let out a small sound at the sight of the gagged and bound Healer on High seated on a golden throne. But it was the woman standing beside the healer, a knife resting on her round belly, that made Chaol's blood go cold.

Duva. The khagan's now-youngest daughter.

She smiled at them as they approached—and the expression was not human.

It was Valg.

⇥ 62 ⇤

"Well," said the thing inside the princess, "it certainly took you long enough."

The words echoed down the massive chamber, bouncing off stone and gold.

Chaol assessed every shadow, every object they passed. All possible weapons. All possible escape routes.

Hafiza did not move as they neared, walking down the broad avenue between the endless, glittering gold and sarcophagi. A necropolis.

Perhaps one enormous, subterranean city, stretching from the desert to here.

When they'd visited Aksara, Duva had remained behind. Claiming that her pregnancy—

Yrene's hiss told him she realized the same.

Duva was pregnant—and the Valg had a hold on her.

Chaol sized up the odds. A Valg-infested princess, armed with a knife and whatever dark magic, the Healer on High tied to the throne . . .

And Yrene.

"Because I see you calculating, Lord Westfall, I'll spare you the trouble and lay out your options for you." Duva traced gentle, idle lines over her full womb with that knife, barely disturbing the fabric of her gown. "See, you'll have to pick. Me, the Healer on High, or Yrene Towers." The princess smiled and whispered again, "*Yrene*."

And that voice . . .

Yrene shook beside him. The voice from that night.

But Yrene lifted her chin as they halted at the base of those steep dais steps, and said to the princess, unfaltering as any queen, "What is it that you want?"

Duva angled her head, her eyes wholly black. The ebony of the Valg. "Don't you want to know *how*?"

"I'm sure you'll tell us, anyway," Chaol said.

Duva's eyes narrowed with annoyance, but she let out a small laugh. "These tunnels run right between the palace and the Torre. Those immortal Fae brats buried their royals here. Renegades of Mora's noble line." She swept an arm to encompass the room. "I'm sure the khagan would be beside himself to learn of how much gold sits beneath his feet. Another hand to play when the time calls for it."

Yrene stared and stared at Hafiza, who was watching them calmly.

A woman ready for her end. Who now only wanted to make sure Yrene did not think her frightened.

"I was waiting for you to figure out it was me," Duva said. "When I destroyed all those precious books and scrolls, I thought you'd certainly realize I was the only one who hadn't gone to the party. But then I realized—how *could* you suspect me?" She laid a hand on her full womb. "It was why he chose her to begin with. Lovely, gentle Duva. Too kind to ever be a contender for the throne." A snake's smile. "Do you know Hasar tried to take the ring first? She spied it in the wedding trove sent by *Perrington* and wanted it. But Duva snatched it before she could." She

604

held up her finger, revealing the broad silver band. Not a glimmer of Wyrdstone.

"It's beneath," she whispered. "A clever little trick to hide it. And the moment she spoke her vows to that sweet, lovesick human prince, this went on her hand." Duva smirked. "And no one even noticed." A flash of her white teeth. "Except for keen-eyed little sister." She clicked her tongue. "Tumelun suspected something was wrong. Caught me poking about in forgotten places. So I caught her, too." Duva chuckled. "Or didn't, I suppose. Since I shoved her right off that balcony."

Yrene sucked in a breath.

"Such a wild, impetuous princess," Duva drawled. "Prone to such *moods*. I couldn't very well have her going to her beloved parents and whining about me, could I?"

"You *bitch*," Yrene snapped.

"That's what she called me," Duva replied. "Said I didn't seem *right*." She rubbed a hand over her belly, then tapped a finger to the side of her head. "You should have heard how she screamed. Duva—how Duva *screamed* when I pushed the brat off the balcony. But I shut her up fast enough, didn't I?" She again brought that knife up to her belly and scraped over the silk fabric.

"Why are you *here*," Yrene breathed. "What do you *want*?"

"You."

Chaol's heart stumbled at the word.

Duva straightened. "The Dark King heard whispers. Whispers that a healer blessed with Silba's gifts had entered the Torre. And it made him so very, very wary."

"Because I can wipe you all out like the parasites you are?"

Chaol shot Yrene a warning glance.

But Duva plucked the dagger off her womb and studied the blade. "Why do you think Maeve has hoarded her healers, never allowing them to leave her patrolled borders? She knew we would return. She wanted to be ready—to protect herself. Her prized favorites, those Doranelle healers. Her secret army." Duva hummed, motioning with the dagger to the necropolis. "How clever those Fae were, who escaped her clutches after the last war. They ran all the way here—the healers who knew their queen would keep them penned up like animals. And then they bred the magic into the land, into its people. Encouraged the right powers to rise up, to ensure this land would always be strong, defended. And then they vanished, taking their treasures and histories beneath the earth. Ensuring they were forgotten below, while their little *garden* was planted above."

"Why," was all Chaol said.

"To give those Maeve did not consider important a fighting chance should Erawan return." Duva clicked her tongue. "So noble, those renegade Fae. And thus the Torre grew—and His Dark Majesty indeed rose again, and then fell, and then slept. And even he forgot what someone with the right gifts might do. But then he awoke once more. And he remembered the healers. So he made sure to purge the gifted ones from the northern lands." A smile at Yrene, hateful and cold. "But it seems a little healer slipped the butcher's block. And made it all the way to this city, with an empire to guard her."

Yrene's breathing was ragged. He saw the guilt and dread settle in. That in coming here, she had brought this upon them. Tumelun, Duva, the Torre, the khaganate.

But what Yrene did not realize, Chaol instead saw it for her. Saw it with the weight of a continent, a world, upon him. Saw what had terrified Erawan enough to dispatch one of his agents.

Because Yrene, ripe with power and facing down that preening Valg demon . . . Hope.

It was hope that stood beside him, hidden and protected these years in this city, and in the years before it, spirited across the earth by the gods themselves, concealed from the forces poised to destroy her.

A kernel of hope.

The most dangerous of all weapons against Erawan, against the Valg's ancient darkness.

What he had been brought here to retrieve for his homeland, his people. What he had been brought here to *protect*. More precious than soldiers, than any weapon. Their only shot at salvation.

Hope.

"Why not kill me, then," Yrene demanded. "Why not just kill me?"

Chaol hadn't dared ask or think the question.

Duva rested her dagger upon her belly again. "Because you are so much more useful to Erawan alive, Yrene Towers."

⁓

Yrene was shaking. In her bones, she was trembling.

"I am no one," Yrene breathed.

That blade—that blade sat atop that womb. And Hafiza remained still and watchful, ever calm, beside Duva.

"Are you?" the princess crooned. "Two years is an *unnaturally* swift pace to climb so high in the Torre. Is it not, Healer?"

Yrene wanted to vomit as the demon inside Duva looked upon Hafiza.

Hafiza met her stare unflinchingly.

Duva laughed quietly. "She knew. She said as much to me when I spirited her out of her room earlier. That I was coming for you. Silba's Heir."

Yrene's hand slid to her locket. The note within.

The world needs more healers.

Had it been Silba herself who had come that night in Innish, who had sent her here, with a message she would later understand?

The world needed more healers—to fight Erawan.

"That was why Erawan sent me," Duva drawled. "To be his spy. To see if a healer with those gifts—*the* gifts—might indeed emerge from the Torre. And to keep you from learning too much." A little shrug. "Of course, killing that brat-princess and the other healer were . . . mistakes,

607

but I'm sure His Dark Majesty will forgive me for it when I return with you in tow."

Roaring filled her head, so loud Yrene could barely hear herself as she snapped, "If you mean to bring me to him, why kill the healer you mistook for me? And why not kill every healer in this city and spare yourselves the trouble?"

Duva snorted, waving that dagger. "Because *that* would raise too many questions. *Why* was Erawan targeting your kind? Certain key players might have started pondering. So the Torre was to be left alone—in ignorance. Dwelling here, removed from the north, never leaving these shores. Until it's time for my liege to deal with *this* empire." A smile that made Yrene's blood ice over. "As for that healer . . . It had nothing to do with how she resembled you. She was in the wrong place at the wrong time. Well, the right time for *me*, since I was frightfully hungry and I couldn't exactly feed without being noticed. But to drum up some fear in you, to make you realize the danger and stop working on that Adarlanian fool, stop prying too far into such ancient matters. But you did not listen, did you?"

Yrene's hands curled into claws at her sides.

Duva went on, "Too bad, Yrene Towers. Too bad. For every day you worked on him, healed him, it became clear that you, indeed, were the one. The one my Dark King covets. And after Duva's own palace spies told her that you had healed him fully, once he was walking again and you proved beyond doubt that you were the one I'd been sent to find . . ." She sneered at Hafiza, and Yrene wanted to rip that expression right off her face. "I knew outright attack would be complicated. But luring you down here . . . Too easy. I'm rather disappointed. So," she declared, flipping the knife in her hand, "you will be coming with me, Yrene Towers. To Morath."

Chaol stepped in front of Yrene. "You are forgetting one thing."

Duva lifted a groomed eyebrow. "Oh?"

"You have not won yet."

Go, Yrene wanted to tell him. *Go*.

For that was dark power starting to curl around Duva's fingers, around the hilt of her dagger.

"What's amusing, Lord Westfall," Duva said, peering down at them from atop the dais, "is that you think you can buy yourself time until the guards come. But by then, you will be dead, and no one would *dare* question my word when I tell them you tried to kill us down here. To take this gold back to your poor little kingdom after you wasted your own upon ordering those weapons from my father's vizier. Why, you could buy yourself a thousand armies with this."

Yrene hissed, "You still have *us* to contend with."

"I suppose." Duva pulled something from her pocket. Another ring, crafted from stone so dark it swallowed the light. No doubt sent directly from Morath. "But once you put this on . . . you'll do whatever I say."

"And why should I *ever*—"

Duva rested the knife against Hafiza's throat. "That's why."

Yrene looked to Chaol, but he was sizing up the room, the stairs and exits.

The dark power twining around Duva's fingers.

"So," Duva said, taking one step down the dais. "Let's begin."

She made it a second step before it happened.

Chaol did not move. But Hafiza did.

She hurled her body, chair and all, the entire weight of that golden throne, down the stairs.

Right atop Duva.

Yrene screamed, running for them, Chaol launching into motion.

Hafiza and the baby, the baby and Hafiza—

Crone and princess tumbled down those steep stairs, wood snapping. Wood, not metal. The throne had been painted, and now it shattered as they rolled, Duva shrieking and Hafiza so silent, even as her gag came free—

They hit the stone floor with a crack that Yrene felt in her heart.

Chaol was instantly there, not going for Duva, sprawled on the ground, but for Hafiza, limp and unmoving. He hauled her back, splinters and ropes clinging to her, her mouth gaping—

Eyes cracking open—

Yrene sobbed, grabbing Hafiza by the other arm and helping him heave her out of the way, toward a towering statue of a Fae soldier.

Just as Duva rose up on her elbows, hair loose around her face, and seethed, "You rotting pile of *shit*—"

Chaol shot upright, sword angled before them while Yrene fumbled for her magic to heal the ancient, frail body.

The old woman managed to raise her arm long enough to grip Yrene's wrist. *Go*, she seemed to say.

Duva climbed to her feet, long splinters embedded in her neck, blood dripping from her mouth. Black blood.

Chaol gave Yrene all of one look over his shoulder. *Run.*

And take Hafiza with her.

Yrene opened her mouth to tell him *no*, but he had already faced ahead again. Toward the princess who advanced one step.

Her dress was torn, revealing the firm, round belly beneath. A fall like that with a baby—

A baby.

Yrene gripped Hafiza under her thin shoulders, hauling her slight weight across the floor.

Chaol wouldn't kill her. Duva.

Yrene sobbed through her clenched teeth as she dragged Hafiza back and back through that gold-lined avenue, the statues looking on unfeelingly.

He wouldn't so much as harm Duva, not with that baby in her womb.

Yrene's chest caved in at the low hum of power that filled the room.

He would not fight back. He would buy Yrene time.

To get Hafiza out and to run.

Duva purred, "This will likely hurt a great deal."

Yrene whirled back just as shadows lashed from the princess, aimed right at Chaol.

He rolled to the side, the blast going wide and striking the statue he ducked behind.

"Such theatrics," Duva tutted, and Yrene hurried, sliding Hafiza toward those distant stairs. Leaving him—leaving him behind.

But movement caught her eye, and then—

A statue crashed into the princess's path.

Duva blasted it aside with her power. Gold showered the room in chunks that thundered atop the sarcophagi, the cracking echoing through the chamber.

"You will make this boring," Duva tsked, and hurled a handful of darkness toward where he'd been. Yrene stumbled as the room shuddered, but she kept upright.

Another blow.

Another.

Duva hissed, rounding the sarcophagus where she'd guessed Chaol was hiding. She fired her power blindly.

Chaol appeared, shield in hand.

Not a shield—an ancient mirror.

The power bounced off the metal, shattering glass, even as it rebounded into the princess.

Yrene saw the blood first. On both of them.

Then saw the dread in his face as Duva was blasted back, slamming into a stone sarcophagus so hard her bones cracked.

Duva hit the ground and did not move.

Yrene waited one breath. Two.

She lowered Hafiza to the floor and ran. Ran right for Chaol, where he panted, gaping at the woman's fallen body.

"What have I done," he breathed, refusing to take his eyes off the too-still princess. Blood slid down his face from the shards of that mirror, but nothing major—nothing lethal.

Duva, however . . .

Yrene shoved past him, past his sword, to the princess on the ground. If she was down, she could potentially get the Valg demon out, potentially try to fix her body—

She turned Duva over.

And found the princess smiling at her.

It happened so fast. Too fast.

Duva lunged for her face, her throat, black bands of power leaping from her palms.

Then Yrene was not there. Then she was on the stones, thrown to the side as Chaol hurled himself between her and the princess.

No shield, no weapon.

Only his back, utterly exposed, as he shoved Yrene away and took the full brunt of the Valg attack.

⊰ 63 ⊱

Agony roared through his spine. Down his legs. His arms. Into his very fingertips.

Worse than it had been in the glass castle.

Worse than in those healing sessions.

But all he could see, all he'd seen, was Yrene, that power spearing for her heart—

Chaol hit the ground, and Yrene's scream shattered through the pain.

Get up get up get up

"Such a pity all that hard work amounted to nothing," Duva trilled, and pointed a finger at his spine. "Your poor, poor back."

That dark power slammed into his spine again.

Something cracked.

Again. Again.

The feeling in his legs vanished first.

"*Stop,*" Yrene sobbed, on her knees. "*Stop!*"

"Run," he breathed, forcing his palms flat onto the stones, forcing his arms to push, to lift him—

Duva only reached into her pocket and pulled out that black ring. "You know how this stops."

"*No*," he snarled, and his back bellowed as he tried and tried to get his legs beneath him—

Yrene crawled away a step. Another. Eyes darting between them.

Not again. He would not endure seeing this, endure *living* this one more time.

But then he beheld what Yrene grabbed in her right hand.

What she had been crawling toward.

His sword.

Duva snickered, stepping over his sprawled, unmoving legs as she advanced on Yrene. As Yrene rose to her feet and lifted his sword between them.

The blade trembled, and Yrene's shoulders shook as she sobbed through her teeth.

"What do you think that could possibly do," Duva crooned, "against this?"

Whips of dark power unfurled from the princess's palms.

No. He groaned the word, screamed it at his body, at the wounds pushing in, the agony dragging him under. Duva lifted her arm to strike—

And Yrene threw the sword. A straight throw, unskilled and wild.

But Duva ducked—

Yrene ran.

Swift as a doe, she turned and ran, sprinting into the labyrinth of corpses and treasure.

And like a hound on a scent, Duva snarled and gave chase.

⁓

She had no plan. She had nothing.

No options. Nothing whatsoever.

Chaol's spine—

Gone. All that work . . . shattered.

Yrene ran through the piles of gold, searching, searching—

Duva's shadows blasted around her, sending shards of gold flying into the air. Gilding every breath Yrene took.

She snatched a short-sword off a chest overflowing with treasure as she ran, the blade whirring through the air.

If she could trap her, get Duva down for long enough—

A lash of power shattered the stone sarcophagus before her. Chunks of rock soared.

Yrene heard the thud before she felt the impact.

Then her head bleated with pain, and the world tilted.

She fought to stay upright with every heartbeat, every bit of focus she'd ever mastered.

Yrene did not let her feet falter. She kept moving, buying them any sort of time. Rounding a statue, she—

Duva stood before her.

Yrene careened into her, that short-sword so close to the princess's gut, to that womb—

She splayed her hands, dropping the weapon. Duva held firm, arms snatching around Yrene's neck and middle. Pinning her.

The princess hissed, hauling her back toward that avenue, "This body does not like so much running."

Yrene thrashed, but Duva held firm. Too strong—for someone her size, she was too strong.

"I want you to see this. Want you both to see this," Duva jeered in her ear.

Chaol had crawled halfway across the path. Crawled, trailing blood, his legs unresponsive. To help her.

He stilled, blood sliding from his mouth as Duva stepped onto the walkway, pressing Yrene against her.

"Shall I make you watch me kill him, or make him watch me put that ring on you?"

And even with that arm shoved against her throat, Yrene snarled, "*Don't you touch him.*"

Blood on his gritted teeth, Chaol's arms strained and buckled as he tried to rise.

"It's too bad I don't have two rings," Duva mused to Chaol. "I'm sure your friends would pay handsomely for you." A grunt. "But I suppose your death will be equally devastating."

Duva loosened her arm from Yrene's middle to point at him—

Yrene moved.

She stomped down on the princess's foot. Right on the instep.

And as the princess lurched, Yrene slammed her palm into the woman's elbow, freeing the arm across her throat.

So Yrene could whirl and drive her elbow straight into Duva's face.

Duva dropped like a stone, blood spurting.

Yrene lunged for the dagger at Chaol's side. The blade whined as she whipped it free of its sheath and threw herself atop the stunned princess, straddling her.

Aimed that blade high, to plunge into the woman's neck, to sever that head. Bit by bit.

"*Don't,*" Chaol rasped, the word full of blood.

Duva had destroyed it—destroyed *everything*.

From the blood coming out of his mouth, up his throat . . .

Yrene wept, the dagger poised over the princess's neck.

He was dying. Duva had ripped open something within him.

Duva's brows began to twitch and furrow as she stirred.

Now.

She had to do it now. Drive this blade in. End it.

End it, and perhaps she could save him. Stop that lethal internal bleeding. But his spine, his *spine*—

A life. She had sworn an oath never to take a life.

And with this woman before her, the second life in her womb . . .

The dagger lowered. She'd do it. She'd *do* it, and—

"Yrene," Chaol breathed, and the word was so full of pain, so quiet . . .

It was too late.

Her magic could feel it, his death. She had never told him of that terrible gift—that healers *knew* when death sat near. Silba, lady of gentle deaths.

The death she would give Duva and her child would not be that sort of death.

Chaol's death would not be that sort of death.

But she . . .

But she . . .

The princess looked so young, even as she stirred. And the life in her womb . . .

The life before her . . .

Yrene dropped the knife to the floor.

Its clattering echoed over gold and stone and bones.

Chaol closed his eyes in what she could have sworn was relief.

A light hand touched her shoulder.

She knew that touch. Hafiza.

But as Yrene looked, as she turned and sobbed—

Two others stood behind the Healer on High, holding her upright. Letting Hafiza lean down beside Duva and blow a breath onto the princess's face, sending her into undisturbed slumber.

Nesryn. Her hair was windblown, her cheeks rosy and chapped—

And Sartaq, his own hair far shorter. The prince's face was taut, his eyes wide as he beheld his unconscious, bloody sister. As Nesryn breathed, "We were too late—"

Yrene lunged across the stones to Chaol. Her knees tore on the rock, but she barely felt it, barely felt the blood sliding down her temple as she took his head in her lap and closed her eyes, rallying her power.

White flared, but there was red and black everywhere.

Too much. Too many broken and torn and ravaged things—

His chest was barely rising. He did not open his eyes.

617

"*Wake up*," she ordered him, her voice breaking. She plunged into her power, but the damage . . . It was like trying to patch up holes in a sinking ship.

Too much. Too much and—

Shouting and steps all around them.

His life began to thin and turn to mist around her magic. Death circled, an eagle with an eye upon them.

"*Fight it*," Yrene sobbed, shaking him. "You stubborn bastard, *fight it*."

What was the point of it, the point of any of it, if now, when it mattered—

"Please," she whispered.

Chaol's chest rose, a high note before the last plunge—

She could not endure it. Would not endure it—

A light flickered. Inside that failing mass of red and black.

A candle ignited. A bloom of white.

Then another.

Another.

Blooming lights, along that broken interior. And where they shone . . .

Flesh knitted. Bone smoothed.

Light after light after light.

His chest continued to rise and fall. Rise and fall.

But in the hurt and the dark and the light . . .

A woman's voice that was both familiar and foreign. A voice that was both Hafiza's and . . . another. Someone who was not human, never had been. Speaking through Hafiza herself, their voices blending into the blackness.

The damage is too great. There must be a cost if it is to be repaired.

All those lights seemed to hesitate at that otherworldly voice.

Yrene brushed herself along them, waded through them like a field of white flowers, the lights bobbing and swaying in this quiet place of pain.

Not lights . . . but healers.

She knew their lights, their essences. Eretia—that was Eretia closest to her.

The voice that was both Hafiza and Other said again, *There must be a cost.*

For what the princess had done to him . . . There was no returning from it.

I will pay it. Yrene said into the pain and dark and light.

A daughter of Fenharrow will pay the debt of a son of Adarlan?

Yes.

She could have sworn a gentle, warm hand brushed her face.

And Yrene knew it did not belong to Hafiza or the Other. Did not belong to any healer alive.

But to one who had never left her, even when she had been turned into ash on the wind.

The Other said, *You offer this of your own free will?*

Yes. With my entire heart.

It had been his from the start, anyway.

Those loving, phantom hands brushed her cheek again and faded away.

The Other said, *I chose well. You shall pay the debt, Yrene Towers. And I hope you shall see it for what it truly is.*

Yrene tried to speak. But light flared, soft and soothing.

It blinded her, within and without. Left her cringing over Chaol's head, her fingers grappled into his shirt. Feeling his heartbeats thunder into her palms. The scrape of his breath against her ear.

There were hands on her shoulders. Two sets. They tightened, a silent command to lift her head. Yrene did.

Hafiza stood behind her, Eretia at her side. Each with a hand on her shoulder.

Behind them stood two healers each. Hands on their shoulders.

Behind them, two more. And more. And more.

A living chain of power.

All the healers in the Torre, young and old, stood in that room of gold and bone.

All connected. All channeling to Yrene, to the grip she still held on Chaol.

Nesryn and Sartaq stood a few feet away, the former with a hand over her mouth. Because Chaol—

The healers of the Torre lowered their hands, severing that bridge of contact, as Chaol's feet moved. Then his knees.

And then his eyes cracked open, and he was staring up at Yrene, her tears plopping onto his blood-crusted face. He lifted a hand to brush her lips. "Dead?"

"Alive," she breathed, and lowered her face to his. "Very much alive."

Chaol smiled against her mouth, sighing deep as he said, "Good."

Yrene raised her head, and he smiled up at her again, cracked blood sliding away from his face with the motion.

And where that scar had once sliced down his cheek . . . only unmarred skin remained.

⇥ 64 ⇤

Chaol's body ached, but it was the ache of newness. Of sore muscles, not broken ones.

And the air in his lungs . . . it did not burn to breathe.

Yrene helped him sit up, his head spinning.

He blinked, finding Nesryn and Sartaq before them as the healers began to file away, their faces grim. The prince's long braid had been cut in favor of loose, shoulder-length hair, and Nesryn . . . it was ruk leathers she wore, her dark eyes brighter than he'd ever seen—even with the graveness of her expression.

Chaol rasped, "What—"

"You sent a note to come back," Nesryn said, her face deathly pale. "We flew as fast as we could. We were told you'd come to the Torre earlier this evening. The guards were right behind us, until we outran them. We got a bit lost down here, but then . . . cats led the way."

A bemused, puzzled glance over her shoulder, to where half a dozen beryl-eyed cats sat on the tunnel steps, cleaning themselves. They noticed the human attention and scattered, tails high.

Sartaq added, smiling faintly, "We also thought healers might be necessary, and asked some to follow. But apparently, a great number more wanted to come."

Considering the number of women filing out after the vanished cats . . . All of them. All of them had come.

Behind Chaol and Yrene, Eretia was tending to Hafiza. Alive, clear-eyed, but . . . frail.

Eretia clucked over the elderly woman, chiding her for such heroics. But even as she did, the woman's eyes were bright with tears. Perhaps more, as Hafiza brushed a thumb over Eretia's cheek.

"Is she—" Sartaq began, jerking his chin toward Duva, sprawled on the floor.

"Unconscious," Hafiza rasped. "She will sleep until roused."

"Even with a Valg ring on her?" Nesryn asked as Sartaq made to pick up his sister from the stone floor. She blocked him with an arm across his middle, earning an incredulous look from the prince. There were cuts and scabs on both of them, Chaol realized. And the way the prince had moved—with a limp. Something had happened—

"Even with the ring, she will remain asleep," Hafiza said.

Yrene was just staring at the princess, the dagger on the floor nearby.

Sartaq saw it, too. And said quietly to Yrene, "Thank you—for sparing her."

Yrene just pressed her face against Chaol's chest. He stroked a hand down her hair, finding it wet—

"You're bleeding—"

"I'm fine," she said onto his shirt.

Chaol pulled back, scanning her face. The bloody temple. "That is anything but fine," he said, whipping his head toward Eretia. "She's hurt—"

Eretia rolled her eyes. "Good to see none of this put you out of your usual spirits."

Chaol gave the woman a flat stare.

Hafiza peered over Eretia's shoulder and wryly asked Yrene, "Are you certain this pushy man was worth the cost?"

Before Yrene could answer, Chaol demanded, "What cost?"

A stillness crept over them, and even Yrene looked to Hafiza as the woman extracted herself from Eretia's care. The Healer on High said quietly, "The damage was too great. Even with all of us . . . Death held you by the hand."

He turned to Yrene, dread curling in his stomach. "What did you do," he breathed. She didn't meet his stare.

"She likely made a fool's bargain, that's what," Eretia snapped. "Offered to pay the price without even being told what it was. To save your neck. We all heard."

Eretia was close to not having a functioning neck herself, but Chaol said as calmly as he could, "Pay the price to *whom?*"

"Not a payment," Hafiza corrected, setting a hand on Eretia's shoulder to quiet her, "but a restoration of balance. To the one who likes to see it intact. Who spoke through me as we all gathered within you."

"What was the cost," Chaol rasped. If she'd given up anything, he'd find a way to retrieve it. He didn't care what he had to pay, he'd—

"To keep your life tethered in this world, we had to bind it to another. To hers. Two lives," Hafiza clarified, "now sharing one thread. But even with that . . ." She gestured to his legs, the foot he slid up to brace on the floor. "The demon broke many, many parts of you. Too many. And in order to save most of you, there was a cost, too."

Yrene went still. "What do you mean?"

Hafiza again looked between them. "There remains some damage to the spine—impacting the lower portions of the legs. That even we could not repair."

Chaol glanced between the Healer on High and his legs, currently moving. He went so far as to put some weight on them. They held.

Hafiza went on, "With the life-bond between you, Yrene's power

623

flowing into you . . . It will act as a brace. Stabilizing the area, granting you ability to use your legs whenever Yrene's magic is at its fullest." He steeled himself for the *but*. Hafiza smiled grimly. "But when Yrene's power flags, when she is drained or tired, your injury will regain control, and your ability to walk will again be impaired. It will require you to use a cane at the very least—on hard days, perhaps many days, the chair. But the injury to your spine will remain."

The words settled in him. Floated through and settled.

Yrene was wholly silent. So still that he faced her.

"Can't I just heal him again?" She leaned toward him, as if she'd do just that.

Hafiza shook her head. "It is part of the balance—the cost. Do not tempt the compassion of the force that granted this to you."

But Chaol touched Yrene's hand. "It is no burden, Yrene," he said softly. "To be given this. It is no burden at all."

Yet agony filled her face. "But I—"

"Using the chair is not a punishment. It is not a prison," he said. "It never was. And I am as much of a man in that chair, or with that cane, as I am standing on my feet." He brushed away the tear that slipped down her cheek.

"I wanted to heal you," she breathed.

"You did," he said, smiling. "Yrene, in every way that truly matters . . . You did."

Chaol wiped away the other tears that fell, brushing a kiss to her hot cheek.

"There is another piece to the life-bond, to this bargain," Hafiza added gently. They turned to her. "When it is time, whether the death is kind or cruel . . . It will claim you both."

Yrene's golden eyes were still lined with silver. But there was no fear in her face, no lingering sorrow—none.

"Together," Chaol said quietly, and interlaced their hands.

Her strength would be his strength. And when Yrene went, he would go. But if he went before her—

Dread curled in his gut.

"The true price of all this," Hafiza said, reading the panic. "Not fear for your own life, but what losing your life will do to the other."

"I suggest you not go to war," Eretia grumbled.

But Yrene shook her head, shoulders straightening as she declared, "We shall go to war." Pointing to Duva, she looked at Sartaq. As if she had not just offered up her very *life* to save his—"*That* is what Erawan will do. To all of you. If we do not go."

"I know," Sartaq said quietly. The prince turned to Nesryn, and as she held his stare . . . Chaol saw it. The glimmer between them. A bond, new and trembling. But there it was, right along with the cuts and wounds they both bore. "I know," Sartaq said again, his fingers brushing Nesryn's.

Nesryn met Chaol's eyes then.

She smiled softly at him, glancing to where Yrene now asked Hafiza about whether she could stand. He'd never seen Nesryn appear so . . . settled. So quietly happy.

Chaol swallowed. *I'm sorry*, he said silently.

Nesryn shook her head as Sartaq scooped his sister into his arms with a grunt, the prince balancing his weight on his good leg. *I think I did just fine.*

Chaol smiled. *Then I am happy for you.*

Nesryn's eyes widened as Chaol at last got to his feet, taking Yrene with him. His movements were as smooth as any maneuver he might have made without the invisible brace of Yrene's magic flowing between them.

Nesryn wiped away her tears as Chaol closed the distance between them and embraced her tightly. "Thank you," he said in Nesryn's ear.

She squeezed him back. "Thank *you*—for bringing me here. To all of this."

To the prince who now looked at Nesryn with a quiet, burning sort of emotion.

She added, "We have many things to tell you."

Chaol nodded. "And we you."

They pulled apart, and Yrene approached—throwing her arms around Nesryn as well.

"What are we going to do with all this gold?" Eretia demanded, leading Hafiza away as the guards formed a living path for them out of the tomb. "Such tacky junk," she spat, frowning at a towering statue of a Fae soldier.

Chaol laughed, and Yrene joined him, sliding her arm around his middle as they trailed behind the healers.

Alive, Yrene had said to him. As they walked out of the dark, Chaol at last felt it was true.

Sartaq took Duva to the khagan. Called in his brothers and sister.

Because Yrene insisted they be there. Chaol and Hafiza insisted they be there.

The khagan, in the first hint of emotion Yrene had ever seen from the man, lunged for the unconscious, bloody Duva as Sartaq limped into the hall where they'd been waiting. Viziers pressed in. Hasar let out a gasp of what Yrene could have sworn was true pain.

Sartaq did not let his father touch her. Did not let anyone but Nesryn come close as he laid Duva on a low couch.

Yrene kept a few steps back, silent and watching, Chaol at her side.

This bond between them . . . She could feel it, almost. Like a living band of cool, silken light flowing from her—into him.

And he truly did not seem to mind that a piece of his spine, his nerves, would retain permanent damage for as long as they lived.

Yes, he'd now be able to move his legs with limited motion, even when her magic was drained. But standing—never a possibility during those times. She supposed they'd soon learn how and when the level of her power correlated with whether he required cane or chair or neither.

But Chaol was right. Whether he stood or limped or sat . . . it did not change him. Who he was. She had fallen in love with him well before he'd ever stood. She would love him no matter how he moved through the world.

What if we fight? Yrene had asked him on the trek over here. *What then?*

Chaol had only kissed her temple. *We fight all the time already. It'll be nothing new.* He'd added, *Do you think I'd want to be with anyone who didn't hand my ass to me on a regular basis?*

But she'd frowned. He'd continued, *And this bond between us, Yrene . . . it changes nothing. With you and me. You'll need your own space; I'll need mine. So if you think for one moment that you're going to get away with flimsy excuses for never leaving my side—*

She'd poked him in the ribs. *As if I'll want to hang around you all day like some lovesick girl!*

Chaol had laughed, tucking her in tighter. But Yrene had only patted his arm and said, *And I think you can take care of yourself just fine.*

He'd just kissed her brow again. And that had been that.

Yrene now brushed her fingers against his, Chaol's hand curling around her own, as Sartaq cleared his throat and held up Duva's limp hand. To display the wedding band there. "Our sister has been enslaved by a demon sent by Perrington in the form of this ring."

Murmurs and shifting about. Arghun spat, "Nonsense."

"Perrington is no man. He is Erawan," Sartaq declared, ignoring his elder brother, and Yrene realized Nesryn must have told him everything. "The Valg king."

Still holding Yrene's hand, Chaol added for all to hear, "Erawan sent this ring as a wedding gift, knowing Duva would put it on—knowing the demon would entrap her. On her wedding day." They'd left the second ring at the Torre, locked within one of the ancient chests, to be disposed of later.

"The babe," the khagan demanded, eyes on that torn-up belly, the scratches marring her neck where Hafiza had already removed the worst of the splinters.

"These are lies," Arghun seethed. "From desperate, scheming people."

"They are not lies," Hafiza cut in, chin high. "And we have witnesses who will tell you otherwise. Guards, healers, and your own brother, Prince, if you will not believe us."

To challenge the word of the Healer on High . . . Arghun shut his mouth.

Kashin shoved to the front of the crowd, earning a glare from Hasar as he shouldered past her. "That explains . . ." He peered at his sleeping sister. "She has not been the same."

"She was the same," Arghun snapped.

Kashin leveled a glare on his eldest brother. "If you ever deigned to spend any time with her, you would have known the differences." He shook his head. "I thought her morose from the arranged marriage, then the pregnancy." Grief flooded his eyes as he faced Chaol. "She did it, didn't she? She killed Tumelun."

A ripple of shock went through the room as all eyes fixed upon him. But Chaol instead turned to the khagan, whose face was bloodless and devastated in a way that Yrene had not yet known, and could not imagine. To lose a child, to endure this . . . "Yes," Chaol said, bowing his head to the khagan. "The demon confessed to it, but it was not Duva. The demon made it sound as if Duva fought every second—raged against your daughter's death."

The khagan closed his eyes for a long moment.

Kashin lifted his palms to Yrene in the heavy silence. "Can you fix her? If she still somehow remains inside?" A broken plea. Not from a prince to a healer, but one friend to another. As they had once been—as she hoped they might again be.

The gathering focused upon Yrene now. She didn't let an ounce of doubt curve her spine as she said, "I shall try."

Chaol added, "There are things you should know, Great Khagan. About Erawan. The threat he poses. What you and this land might offer against him. And stand to gain in the process."

"You think to scheme at a time like this?" Arghun snapped.

"No," Chaol said clearly, unhesitatingly. "But consider that Morath has already reached these shores. Has already killed and harmed those you care for. And if we do not rise to face this threat . . ." His fingers tightened on Yrene's. "Princess Duva will only be the first. And Princess Tumelun will not be the last victim of Erawan and the Valg."

Nesryn stepped forward. "We come with grave tidings from the south, Great Khagan. The *kharankui* are stirring again, called by their dark . . . master." Many stirred at the term she'd used. But some glanced to each other, confusion in their eyes, and Nesryn explained, "Creatures of darkness from the Valg realm. This war has already leaked into these lands."

Murmuring silence and rustling robes.

But the khagan didn't tear his eyes away from his unconscious daughter. "Save her," he said—the words directed to Yrene.

Hafiza nodded subtly to Yrene, motioning her forward.

The message was clear enough: a test. The final one. Not between Yrene and the Healer on High. But something far greater.

Perhaps what had indeed called Yrene to these shores. Guided her across two empires, over mountains and seas.

An infection. A parasite. Yrene had faced them before.

But this demon inside . . . Yrene approached the sleeping princess.

And began.

⊰ 65 ⊱

Yrene's hands did not tremble as she held them before her.

White light glowed around her fingers, encasing them, shielding them as she picked up the sleeping princess's hand. It was so slight—so delicate, compared to the horrors she'd done with it.

Yrene's magic rippled and bent as she reached for the false wedding ring. As if it were some sort of lodestone, warping the world around it.

Chaol's hand settled on her back in silent support.

She steeled herself, sucking in a breath as her fingers closed around the ring.

It was worse.

So much worse than what had been within Chaol.

Where his had been a mere shadow, this was an inky pool of blackness. Corruption. The opposite of everything in this world.

Yrene panted through her teeth, her magic flaring around her hand, the light a barrier, a glove between her and that ring, and *pulled*.

The ring slid off.

And Duva began screaming.

Her body arched off the couch, Sartaq and Kashin lunging for her legs and shoulders, respectively.

Teeth gritted, the princes pinned their sister as she thrashed against them, shrieking wordlessly as Hafiza's sleeping spell kept her unconscious.

"*You're hurting her*," the khagan snapped. Yrene did not bother to look toward him as she studied Duva. The body the princess slammed up and down, over and over.

"*Hush*," Hasar hissed at her father. "Let her work. Someone fetch a blacksmith to crack open that damned ring."

The world beyond them faded into blur and sound. Yrene was distantly aware of a young man—Duva's husband—sprinting up to them. Covering his mouth with a cry; being held at bay by Nesryn.

Chaol just continued to kneel beside Yrene, removing his hand from her back with a final, soothing rub, while she stared and stared at Duva as she writhed.

"She will hurt *herself*," Arghun seethed. "Stop this—"

A true parasite. A living shadow within the princess. Filling her blood, planted in her mind.

She could feel the Valg demon within, raging and screeching.

Yrene lifted her hands before her. The white light filled her skin. She *became* that light, held within the now-faint borders of her body.

Someone gasped as Yrene reached her glowing, blinding hands toward the princess's chest, as if guided by some invisible tug.

The demon began to panic, sensing her approach.

Distantly, she heard Sartaq swear. Heard the crack of wood as Duva drove her foot into the arm of the couch.

There was only the thrashing Valg, scrabbling at power. Only her incandescent hands, reaching for the princess.

Yrene laid her glowing hands on Duva's chest.

631

Light flared, bright as a sun. People cried out.

But as quickly as it had appeared, the light vanished, sucked into Yrene—into where her hands met Duva's chest. Sucked into the princess herself.

Along with Yrene.

It was a dark storm within.

Cold, and raging, and ancient.

Yrene felt it squatting there. Squatting *everywhere*. A tapeworm indeed.

"*You will all die*—" the Valg demon began to hiss.

Yrene unleashed her power.

A torrent of white light flooded every vein and bone and nerve.

Not a river, but a band of light made up of the countless kernels of her power—so many they were legion, all hunting out each dark, festering corner, each screaming crevice of malice.

Far away, beyond, a blacksmith arrived. A hammer struck metal.

Hasar snarled—the sound echoed by Chaol, right at Yrene's ear.

Half aware, she saw the black, glittering stone held within the metal as they carefully passed it around on a vizier's kerchief.

The Valg demon roared as her magic smothered it, drowned it. Yrene panted against the onslaught as it pushed back. Shoved at her.

Chaol's hand again began to rub down her back in soothing lines.

More of the world faded away.

I am not afraid of you, Yrene said into the dark. *And you have nowhere to run.*

Duva thrashed, trying to unseat Yrene's grip. Yrene pressed down harder on her chest.

Time slowed and bent. She was dimly aware of the ache in her knees, the cramp in her back. Dimly aware of Sartaq and Kashin refusing to offer their position to someone else.

Still Yrene sent her magic flowing into Duva. Filling her with that devouring light.

The demon screamed the entire time.

But bit by bit, she blasted it back, blasted it deeper.

Until she saw it, curled within the core of her.

Its true form . . . It was as horrific as she'd imagined.

Smoke swirled and coiled about it, revealing glimpses of gangly limbs and talons, mostly hairless gray, slick skin, and unnaturally large dark eyes that raged as she looked upon it.

Truly *looked* upon it.

It hissed, revealing pointed, fish-sharp teeth. *Your world shall fall. As the others have done. As all others will.*

The demon dug claws deep into the darkness. Duva screamed.

"Pathetic," Yrene told it.

Perhaps she spoke the word aloud, for silence fell.

Distantly, that bond flowing away . . . it thinned. The hand on her back drifted away.

"Utterly pathetic," Yrene repeated, her magic rallying behind her in a mighty, cresting white wave. "For a prince to prey on a helpless woman."

The demon scrambled back against the wave, clawing at the dark as if it would tunnel *through* Duva.

Yrene pushed forward. Let her wave fall.

And as her power slammed into that last remnant of the demon, it laughed. *No prince am I, girl. But a* princess. *And my sisters shall soon find you.*

Yrene's light erupted, shredding and cleaving, devouring any last scrap of darkness—

Yrene snapped back into her body, collapsing against the floor. Chaol shouted her name.

But Hasar was there, hauling her upright as Yrene lunged for Duva, hands flaring—

But Duva coughed, choking, trying to twist onto her side.

"Turn her," Yrene rasped to the princes, who obeyed. Just as Duva heaved, and vomited over the edge of the couch. It splattered Yrene's knees, reeking to deepest hell. But she scanned the mess. Food—mostly food, and speckles of blood.

Duva retched again, a deep, choking noise.

Only black smoke broke from her lips. She retched again, and again.

Until a tendril dribbled onto the emerald floors.

And as the shadows slithered out of Duva's lips . . . Yrene felt it. Even as her magic strained and buckled, she felt the last of that Valg demon vanish into nothing.

A bit of dew dissolved by the sun.

Her body became cold and aching. Empty. Her magic drained to the dregs.

She blinked up at the wall of people standing around the couch.

The khagan's sons now flanked their father, hands on their swords, faces grim.

Lethal—with rage. Not at Yrene, not at Duva, but the man who had sent this to their house. Their family.

Duva's face relaxed on an exhaled breath, color blooming on her cheeks.

Duva's husband tried to surge for her again, but Yrene stopped him with an upheld hand.

Heavy—her hand was so heavy. But she held the young man's panicked stare. Which had not been on his wife's face, but the belly. Yrene nodded to him as if to say, *I will look*.

Then she laid her hands on that round, high womb.

Sent her magic probing, dancing along it—the life within.

Something new and joyous answered back.

Loudly.

Its kick roused Duva with an *ooph*, her eyelids fluttering open.

Duva blinked at them all. Blinked at Yrene, the hand she still laid on her belly. "Is it—" The words were a broken rasp.

Yrene smiled, panting softly, relief a crushing weight in her chest. "Healthy and human."

Duva just stared at Yrene until tears filled and flowed from those dark eyes.

Her husband sank into a chair and covered his face, shoulders shaking.

There was a flurry of motion, and then the khagan was there.

And the most powerful man on the earth fell to his knees before that couch and reached for his daughter. Crushed her against him.

"Is it true, Duva?" Arghun demanded from the head of the couch, and Yrene resisted the urge to snap at him about giving the woman some space to sort through all she'd endured.

Sartaq had no reservations. He snarled at his elder brother, "*Shut your mouth.*"

But before Arghun could hiss a retort, Duva lifted her head from the khagan's shoulder.

Tears leaked down her cheeks as she surveyed Sartaq and Arghun. Then Hasar. Then Kashin. And lastly the husband who lifted his head from his hands.

Shadows still lined that lovely face, but—human ones.

"It is true," Duva whispered, her voice breaking as she looked back to her brothers and sister. "All of it."

And as everything that confession implied sank in, the khagan gathered her to him again, rocking her gently while she wept.

Hasar lingered by the foot of the couch as her brothers pressed in to embrace their sister, something like longing on her face.

Hasar noticed Yrene's stare and mouthed the words: *Thank you.*

Yrene only bowed her head and backed toward where Chaol was waiting. Not at her side, but sitting in his chair next to a nearby pillar. He must have asked a servant to bring it from his suite when the tether between them had grown thin as she battled within Duva.

Chaol wheeled over to her, scanning her features. But his own face held no grief, no frustration.

Only awe—awe and such adoration it snatched her breath away. Yrene settled in his lap, and he looped his arms around her as she kissed his cheek.

A door slammed open across the hall, and rushing feet and skirts filled the air. And sobbing. The Grand Empress was sobbing as she threw herself toward her daughter.

She made it within a foot before Kashin leaped in, grabbing his mother by the waist, her white gown swaying with the force of her halted sprint. She spoke in Halha, too fast for Yrene to understand, her skin ashen against the jet black of her long, straight hair. She did not seem to notice anyone but the daughter before her as Kashin murmured an explanation, his hand stroking down his mother's thin back in soothing lines.

The Grand Empress just fell to her knees and folded Duva into her arms.

An old ache stirred in Yrene at the sight of that mother and daughter, at the sight of both of them, weeping with grief and joy.

Chaol squeezed her shoulder in quiet understanding as Yrene slid off his lap and they turned to leave.

"Anything," the khagan said over his shoulder to Yrene, the man still kneeling by Duva and his wife as Hasar at last swept in to embrace her sister. Their mother just enfolded both princesses, kissing the sisters on their cheeks and brows and hair as they held together tightly. "Anything you desire," the khagan said. "Ask it, and it is yours."

Yrene did not hesitate. The words tumbled from her lips.

"A favor, Great Khagan. I would ask you a favor."

The palace was in uproar, but Chaol and Yrene still found themselves alone with Nesryn and Sartaq, sitting, of all places, in their suite.

The prince and Nesryn had joined them on the long walk back to the room, Chaol wheeling his chair close to Yrene's side. She'd been swaying on her feet, and was too damned stubborn to mention it. Even went so far as to assess *him* with those sharp healer's eyes, inquiring after his back, his legs. As if *he* was the one who'd drained his power to the dregs.

He'd felt it, the shifting within his body as mighty waves of her power flowed into Duva. The growing strain along parts of his back and legs. Only then had he left her side during the healing, his steps uneven as he'd gone to lean against the wooden arm of a nearby couch and quietly asked the nearest servant to bring his chair. By the time they'd returned, he'd needed it—his legs still capable of some motion, but not standing.

But it did not frustrate him, did not embarrass him. If this was to be his body's natural state for the rest of his life . . . it was not a punishment, not at all.

He was still thinking that when they reached his suite, mulling over how they might work out a schedule of him fighting in battle with her healing.

For he would fight. And if her power was drained, he'd fight then, too. Whether on horseback or in the chair itself.

And when Yrene needed to heal, when the magic in her veins summoned her to those killing fields and their bond grew thin . . . he'd manage with a cane, or the chair. He would not shrink from it.

If he survived the battle. The war. If *they* survived.

He and Yrene found spots on the sorry replacement for the gold couch—which he was honestly debating bringing back to Adarlan with him, broken bits and all—while Nesryn and the prince sat, carefully, in separate chairs. Chaol tried not to look too aware or amused by it.

"How did you know we were in such trouble?" Yrene asked at last. "Before you linked up with the guards, I mean."

Sartaq blinked, stumbling out of his thoughts. A corner of his mouth lifted. "Kadja," he said, jerking his chin toward the servant currently setting a tea service before them. "She was the one who saw Duva leave—down to those tunnels. She's in my . . . employ."

Chaol studied the servant, who made no sign that she'd heard. "Thank you," he rasped.

But Yrene went one step further, taking the woman's hand and squeezing it. "We owe you a life debt," she said. "How can we repay you?"

Kadja only shook her head and backed out of the room. They stared after her for a moment.

"Arghun is no doubt debating whether to punish her for it," Sartaq mused. "On the one hand, it saved Duva. On the other hand . . . she didn't tell him at all."

Nesryn frowned. "We need to find a way to shield her, then. If he's that ungrateful."

"Oh, he is," Sartaq said, and Chaol tried not to blink at the casualness between them, or her use of *we*. "But I'll think on it."

Chaol refrained from revealing that one word to Shen, and Kadja would have a faithful protector for the rest of her life.

Yrene only asked, "What now?"

Nesryn ran a hand through her dark hair. Different. Yes, there was something wholly different about her. She glanced to Sartaq—not for permission, but . . . as if reassuring herself that he was there. Then she said the words that made Chaol glad he was already sitting.

"Maeve is a Valg queen."

It all came out then. What she and Sartaq had learned these past weeks: stygian spiders, who were really Valg foot soldiers. A shape-shifter who might be Lysandra's uncle. And a Valg queen who had been masquerading as Fae for thousands of years, hiding from the demon kings she'd drawn to this world in her attempt to escape them.

"That explains why the Fae healers might have fled, too," Yrene murmured when Nesryn fell silent. "Why Maeve's own healer compound lies on the border with the mortal world. Perhaps not so they can have access to humans who need care . . . but as a border patrol against the Valg, should they ever try to encroach her territory."

How close the Valg had unwittingly come when Aelin had fought those princes in Wendlyn.

"It also explains why Aelin reported an owl at Maeve's side when they first met," Nesryn said, gesturing to Yrene, whose brows bunched.

Then Yrene blurted, "The owl must be the Fae form of a healer. Some healer of hers that she keeps close—as a bodyguard. Has let everyone believe to be some pet . . ."

Chaol's head spun. Sartaq gave him a look as if to say he understood the feeling well.

"What happened before we arrived?" Nesryn asked. "When we found you . . ."

Yrene's hand clenched his. And it was his turn to tell them what they had learned, what they had endured. That regardless of what Maeve might plan to do . . . There remained Erawan to face.

Until Yrene murmured, "When I was healing Duva, the demon . . ." She rubbed at her chest. He'd never seen anything so remarkable as that healing: the blinding glow of her hands, the near-holy expression on her face. As if she were Silba herself. "The demon told me it was not a Valg prince . . . but a princess."

Silence. Until Nesryn said, "The spider. It claimed the Valg kings had sons *and* daughters. Princes and princesses."

Chaol swore. No, his legs would not be able to function anytime soon, with or without Yrene's slowly refilling well of power. "We're going to need a Fire-Bringer, it seems," he said. And to translate the books Hafiza said she would gladly hand over to their cause.

Nesryn chewed on her lip. "Aelin now sails north to Terrasen, an armada with her. The witches as well."

"Or just the Thirteen," Chaol countered. "The reports were murky. It might not even be Manon Blackbeak's coven, actually."

"It is," Nesryn said. "I'd bet everything on it." She slid her attention to Sartaq, who nodded—silent permission. Nesryn braced her forearms on her knees. "We did not return alone when we raced back here."

Chaol glanced between them. "How many?"

Sartaq's face tightened. "The rukhin are vital enough internally that I can only risk bringing half." Chaol waited. "So I brought a thousand."

He was indeed glad he was sitting down. A thousand ruk riders . . . Chaol scratched his jaw. "If we can join Aelin's host, along with the Thirteen and any other Ironteeth Manon Blackbeak can sway to our side . . ."

"We will have an aerial legion to combat Morath's," Nesryn finished, eyes bright. With hope, yes, but something like dread, too. As if she perhaps realized what combating would ensue. The lives at stake. Yet she turned to Yrene. "And if you can heal those infected by the Valg . . ."

"We still need to find a way to get their hosts down," Sartaq said. "Long enough for Yrene and any others to heal them." Yes, there was that to account for, too.

Yrene cut in, "Well, as you said, we have Aelin Fire-Bringer fighting for us, don't we? If she can produce flame, surely she can produce smoke." Her mouth quirked to the side. "I might have some ideas."

Yrene opened her mouth as if she'd say more, but the suite doors blew open and Hasar breezed in.

Hasar seemed to check herself at the sight of Sartaq. "It seems I'm late for the war council."

Sartaq crossed an ankle over a knee. "Who says that's what we're discussing?"

Hasar claimed a seat for herself and adjusted the fall of her hair over a shoulder. "You mean to tell me the ruks shitting up the roofs are just here to make you look important?"

Sartaq huffed a quiet laugh. "Yes, sister?"

The princess only looked to Yrene, then Chaol. "I will come with you."

Chaol didn't dare move. Yrene said, "Alone?"

"Not alone." The mocking amusement was gone from her face. "You saved Duva's life. And ours, if she had grown more bold." A glance to Sartaq, who watched with mild surprise. "Duva is the best of us. The best of me." Hasar's throat bobbed. "So I will go with you, with whatever ships I can bring, so that my sister will never again look over her shoulder in fear."

Except in fear of one another, Chaol refrained from saying.

But Hasar caught the words in his eyes. "Not her," she said quietly. "All the others," she added with a stark look at Sartaq, who nodded grimly. "But never Duva."

An unspoken promise, Chaol realized, among the other siblings.

"So you will have to suffer my company for a while yet, Lord Westfall," Hasar said, but that edged smile was not as sharp. "Because for my sisters, both living and dead, I will march with my *sulde* to the gates of Morath and make that demon bastard pay." She met Yrene's stare. "And for you, Yrene Towers. For what you did for Duva, I will help you save your land."

Yrene rose, her hands shaking. And none of them spoke a word as Yrene reached Hasar's seat and threw her arms around her neck to hold the princess tightly.

⊰ 66 ⊱

Nesryn was utterly drained. Wanted to sleep for a week. A month.

But she somehow found herself walking the halls, aiming for Kadara's minaret. Alone.

Sartaq had gone to see his father, Hasar joining him. And though it certainly was not awkward with Chaol and Yrene . . . Nesryn gave them their privacy. He had been upon Death's threshold after all. She had few illusions about what was likely about to take place in that suite.

And that she'd have to find quarters of her own.

Nesryn supposed she'd have to find quarters for a few people tonight anyway—starting with Borte, who'd marveled at Antica and the sea, even as they'd swept in as fast as the winds could carry them. And Falkan, who'd indeed come with them, riding as a field mouse in Borte's pocket, Yeran none too pleased about it. Or so he'd seemed the last time she'd seen him at the Eridun aerie, Sartaq charging the various hearth-mothers and the captains to rally their rukhin and fly for Antica.

Nesryn reached the stairwell leading up to the minaret when the page found her. The boy was out of breath but managed a graceful bow as he handed her a letter.

It was dated two weeks ago. In her uncle's handwriting.

Her fingers trembled as she broke the seal.

A minute later, she was racing up the minaret stairs.

~

People cried out in awe and surprise when the reddish-brown ruk sailed over the buildings and homes of Antica.

Nesryn murmured to the bird, guiding him toward the Runni Quarter while they flew on a salt-kissed breeze as fast as his wings could carry them.

She had claimed him upon leaving the Eridun aerie.

Had gone right to the nests, where he had still waited for a rider who would never return, and looked deep into his golden eyes. Had told him that her name was Nesryn Faliq, and she was daughter of Sayed and Cybele Faliq, and that she would be his rider, if he would have her.

She wondered if the ruk, whose late rider had called him Salkhi, had known the burning in her eyes had not been from the roaring wind as he'd bowed his head to her.

Then she'd flown him, Salkhi keeping pace with Kadara at the head of the host as the rukhin sailed northward. Raced to Antica.

And now, as Salkhi landed in the street outside her uncle's home, some vendors abandoning their carts in outright terror, some children dropping their games to gawk, then grin—Nesryn patted her ruk on his broad neck and dismounted.

The front gates to her uncle's house banged open.

And as she saw her father standing there, as her sister shoved past, her children pouring out in a shrieking gaggle . . .

Nesryn fell to her knees and wept.

~

643

How Sartaq found her two hours later, Nesryn didn't know. Though she supposed a ruk sitting in the street of a fancy quarter of Antica was sure to cause a stir. And be easy to spot.

She had wept and laughed and held her family for untold minutes, right in the middle of the street, Salkhi looking on.

And when her uncle and aunt had called them in to *at least cry over a good cup of tea*, her family had told her of their adventures. The wild seas they had sailed, the enemies their ship had dodged on their voyage here. But they had made it—and here they would stay while the war raged, her father said, to the nods of her uncle and aunt.

When she emerged from the house gates at last, her father claiming the honor of escorting Nesryn to Salkhi—after he'd shooed off her sister to go *manage that circus of children*—Nesryn had halted so quickly her father had nearly slammed into her.

Because standing beside Salkhi was Sartaq, a half smile on his face. And on the other side of Salkhi . . . Kadara patiently waited, the two ruks a proud pair indeed.

Her father's eyes widened, as if recognizing the ruk before the prince.

But then her father bowed. Deeply.

Nesryn had told her family—in moderate detail—what had befallen her amongst the rukhin. Her sister and aunt had glared at her when the various children began to declare that they, too, would be ruk riders. And then took off through the house, shrieking and flapping their arms, leaping off furniture with wild abandon.

She expected Sartaq to wait to be approached, but the prince spotted her father and strode forward. Then reached out and clasped his hand. "I heard Captain Faliq's family had at last arrived safely," Sartaq said by way of greeting. "I thought I'd come to welcome you myself."

Something swelled in her chest to the point of pain as Sartaq inclined his head to her father.

Sayed Faliq looked like he might very well keel over dead, either from the gesture of respect or Kadara's mere presence behind them. Indeed, several small heads now popped behind his legs, scanning the prince, then the ruks, and then—

"*KADARA!*"

Her aunt and uncle's youngest child—no more than four—screamed the ruk's name loud enough that anyone in the city who didn't know the bird was on this street was now well aware.

Sartaq laughed as the children shoved past Nesryn's father, racing for the golden bird.

Her sister was on their heels, warning springing from her lips—

Until Kadara lowered herself to the ground, Salkhi following suit. The children halted, reverence stealing over them as they reached out tentative hands toward the two ruks and stroked them gently.

Nesryn's sister sighed with relief. Then realized who stood before Nesryn and their father.

Delara went red. She patted her dress, as if it would somehow cover the fresh food stains courtesy of her youngest. Then she slowly backed into the house, bowing as she went.

Sartaq laughed as she vanished—but not before Delara gave Nesryn a sharp look that said, *Oh, you are so smitten it's not even a laughing matter.*

Nesryn gave her sister a vulgar gesture behind her back that their father chose not to see.

Her father was saying to Sartaq, "I apologize if my grandchildren, nieces, and nephews take some liberties with your ruk, Prince."

But Sartaq smiled broadly—a brighter grin than any she'd seen him give before. "Kadara pretends to be a noble mount, but she's more of a mother hen than anything."

Kadara puffed her feathers, earning squeals of delight from the children.

Nesryn's father squeezed her shoulder before he said to the prince, "I think I'll go keep them from trying to fly off on her."

And then they were alone. In the street. Outside her uncle's house. All of Antica now gawking at them.

Sartaq did not seem to notice. Certainly not as he said, "Walk with me?"

Swallowing, with a backward glance toward where her father was now overseeing the gaggle of children attempting to climb onto Salkhi and Kadara, Nesryn nodded.

They headed toward the quiet, clean alley behind her uncle's house, walking in silence for a few steps. Until Sartaq said, "I spoke to my father."

And she wondered, then, if this meeting was not to be a good one. If the army they had brought was to be ordered back to its aeries. Or if the prince, the life she saw for herself in those beautiful mountains . . . if perhaps the reality of that, too, had found them.

For he was a prince. And for all that she loved her family, for all that they made her so proud, there was not one noble drop of blood in their lineage. Her father shaking Sartaq's hand was the closest any Faliq had ever come to royalty.

Nesryn managed to say, "Oh?"

"We . . . discussed things."

Her chest sank at the careful words. "I see."

Sartaq stopped, the sandy alley humming with the buzzing bees in the jasmine that climbed the walls of the bordering courtyards. The one behind them: the back, private courtyard belonging to her family. She wished she could slither over the wall and hide within. Rather than hear this.

But Nesryn made herself meet the prince's eyes. Saw him scanning her face.

"I told him," Sartaq said at last, "that I planned to lead the rukhin against Erawan, with or without his consent."

Worse. This was getting worse and worse. She wished his face weren't so damn unreadable.

Sartaq took a breath. "He asked me why."

"I hope you told him that the fate of the world might depend upon it."

Sartaq chuckled. "I did. But I also told him that the woman I love now plans to head into war. And I intend to follow her."

She didn't let the words sink in. Didn't let herself believe any of it, until he'd finished.

"He told me that you are common-born. That a would-be Heir of the khagan needs to wed a princess, or a lady, or someone with lands and alliances to offer."

Her throat closed up. She tried to shut out the sound, the words. Didn't want to hear the rest.

But Sartaq took her hand. "I told him if that was what it took to be chosen as Heir, I didn't want it. And I walked out."

Nesryn sucked in a breath. "Are you *insane*?"

Sartaq smiled faintly. "I certainly hope not, for the sake of this empire." He tugged her closer, until their bodies were nearly touching. "Because my father appointed me Heir before I could walk out of the room."

Nesryn left her body. Could only manage to breathe.

And when she tried to bow, Sartaq gripped her shoulders tightly. Stopped her before her head could even lower.

"Never from you," he said quietly.

Heir—he'd been made *Heir*. To all this. This land she loved, this land she still wished to explore so much it ached.

Sartaq lifted a hand to cup her cheek, his calluses scraping against her skin. "We fly to war. Much is uncertain ahead. Save for this." He brushed his mouth against hers. "Save for what I feel for you. No demon army, no dark queen or king, will change that."

Nesryn shook, letting the words sink in. "I—Sartaq, you are *Heir*—"

He pulled back to study her again. "We will go to war, Nesryn Faliq. And when we shatter Erawan and his armies, when the darkness is at last banished from this world . . . Then you and I will fly back here. Together." He kissed her again—a bare caress of his mouth. "And so we shall remain for the rest of our days."

She heard the offer, the promise.

The world he laid at her feet.

She trembled at it. What he so freely gave. Not the empire and crown, but . . . the life. His heart.

Nesryn wondered if he knew her heart had been his from that very first ride atop Kadara.

Sartaq smiled as if to say yes, he had.

So she wrapped her arms around his neck and kissed him.

It was tentative, and soft, and full of wonder, that kiss. He tasted like the wind, like a mountain spring. He tasted like home.

Nesryn clasped his face in her hands as she pulled back. "To war, Sartaq," she breathed, memorizing every line of his face. "And then we'll see what comes after."

Sartaq gave her a knowing, cocky grin. As if he'd fully decided what would come after and nothing she could say would ever convince him otherwise.

And from the courtyard just a wall away, her sister shouted, loud enough for the entire neighborhood to hear, "*I told you, Father!*"

⚜ 67 ⚜

Two weeks later, it was barely dawn when Yrene found herself on the deck of a fine, massive ship and watched the sun rise over Antica for the last time.

The ship was abuzz with activity, but she stood at the rail, and counted the minarets of the palace. Ran an eye over every shining quarter, the city stirring in the new light.

Autumn winds were already whipping the seas, the ship bobbing and lurching beneath her.

Home. They were to sail home today.

She hadn't made many good-byes, had not needed to. But Kashin had still found her, right as she'd ridden to the docks. Chaol had given the prince a nod before leading her mare onto the ship.

For a long moment, Kashin had stared at the ship—the others gathered in the harbor. Then he'd said quietly, "I wish I had never said a word to you on the steppes that night."

Yrene began to shake her head, unsure of what to even say.

"I have missed having you—as my friend," Kashin went on. "I do not have many of them."

"I know," she managed to get out. And then added, "I missed having you as my friend, too."

For she had. And what he was now willing to do for her, her people . . .

She took Kashin's hand. Squeezed it. There was still pain in his eyes, limning his handsome face, but . . . understanding. And a clear, undaunted gleam as he beheld the northern horizon.

The prince squeezed her hand in return. "Thank you again—for Duva." A small smile toward that northern sky. "We shall meet again, Yrene Towers. I am certain of it."

She smiled back at him, beyond words. But Kashin winked, pulling his hand from hers. "My *sulde* still blows northward. Who knows what I may find on the road ahead? Especially now that Sartaq has the burden of being Heir, and I'm free to do as I please."

The city had been in an uproar about it. Celebrating, debating—it still raged on. What the other royal siblings thought, Yrene did not know, but . . . there was peace in Kashin's eyes. And in the eyes of the others, when Yrene had seen them. And part of her indeed wondered if Sartaq had struck some unspoken agreement that went beyond *Never Duva*. To perhaps even *Never Us*.

Yrene had smiled again at the prince—at her friend. "Thank you, for all your kindness."

Kashin had only bowed to her and strode off into the gray light.

And in the hour since then, Yrene had stood on the deck of this ship, silently watching the awakening city behind it, while the others readied things around and below.

For long minutes, she breathed in the sea and the spices and the sounds of Antica under the rising sun. Took them deep into her lungs, letting them settle. Let her eyes drink their fill of the cream-colored stones of the Torre Cesme rising above it all.

Even in the early morning, the tower was a beacon, a jutting lance of hope and calm.

She wondered if she would ever see it again. For what lay ahead of them . . .

Yrene braced her hands on the rail as another gust of wind rocked the ship. A wind from inland, as if all thirty-six gods of Antica blew a collective breath to send them skittering home.

Across the Narrow Sea—and to war.

The ship began to move at last, the world a riot of action and color and sound, but Yrene remained at the rail. Watching the city grow smaller and smaller.

And even when the coast was little more than a shadow, Yrene could have sworn she still saw the Torre standing above it, glinting white in the sun, as if it were an arm upraised in farewell.

⊰ 68 ⊱

Chaol Westfall took none of his steps for granted. Even the ones that had sent him rushing to a bucket to hurl up the contents of his stomach for the first few days at sea.

But one of the advantages of traveling with a healer was that Yrene easily soothed his stomach. And after two weeks at sea, dodging fierce storms that the captain only called Ship-Wreckers . . . his stomach had finally forgiven him.

He found Yrene at the prow railing, gazing toward land. Or where the land would be, if they dared sail close enough. They were keeping far out as they skirted up the coast of their continent, and from his meeting with the captain moments before, they were somewhere near northern Eyllwe. Close to the Fenharrow border.

No sign of Aelin or her armada, but that was to be expected, considering how long they'd been delayed in Antica before leaving.

But Chaol pushed that from his mind as he slid his arms around Yrene's waist and pressed a kiss to the crook of her neck.

She didn't so much as freeze at the touch from behind. As if she'd learned the cadence of his steps. As if she took none of them for granted, either.

Yrene leaned back into him, her body loosening with a sigh as she laid her hands atop where his rested over her stomach.

It had taken a full day after Duva's healing before he'd been able to walk with the cane—albeit stiffly and unevenly. As it had been in those early days of recovery: his back strained to the point of aching, every step requiring his full attention. But he'd gritted his teeth, Yrene murmuring encouragement when he had to figure out various movements. A day after that, most of the limp had eased, though he'd kept the cane; and a day later, he'd walked with minimal discomfort.

But even now, after these two weeks at sea with little for Yrene to heal beyond queasy stomachs and sunburns, Chaol kept the cane in their stateroom, the chair stored belowdecks, for when they were next needed.

He peered over Yrene's shoulder, down to their interlaced fingers. To the twin rings now gracing both of their hands.

"Watching the horizon won't get us there any faster," he murmured onto her neck.

"Neither will teasing your wife about it."

Chaol smiled against her skin. "How else am I to amuse myself during the long hours than by teasing you, Lady Westfall?"

Yrene snorted, as she always did at the title. But Chaol had never heard anything finer—other than the vows they'd spoken in Silba's temple at the Torre two and a half weeks ago. The ceremony had been small, but Hasar had insisted on a feast afterward that put to shame all the others they'd had in the palace. The princess might have been many things, but she certainly knew how to throw a party.

And how to lead an armada.

Gods help him when Hasar and Aedion met.

"For someone who hates being called Lord Westfall," Yrene mused, "you certainly seem to enjoy using the title for me."

"You're suited to it," he said, kissing her neck again.

"Yes, so suited to it that Eretia won't stop mocking me with her curtsying and bowing."

"Eretia is someone whom I could have gladly left behind in Antica."

Yrene chuckled, but pinched his wrist, stepping out of his embrace. "You'll be glad for her when we get to land."

"I certainly hope so."

Yrene pinched him again, but Chaol caught her hand and pressed a kiss to her fingers.

Wife—his wife. He'd never seen the path ahead so clearly as he had that afternoon three weeks ago, when he'd spied her sitting in the garden and just . . . knew. He'd known what he wanted, and so he'd gone to her chair, knelt down before it, and simply asked.

Will you marry me, Yrene? Will you be my wife?

She'd flung her arms around his neck, knocking them both right into the fountain. Where they had remained, to the annoyance of the fish, kissing until a servant had pointedly coughed on their way past.

And looking at her now, the sea air curling tendrils of her hair, bringing out those freckles on her nose and cheeks . . . Chaol smiled.

Yrene's answering smile was brighter than the sun on the sea around them.

He'd brought that damned gold couch with them, shredded cushions and all. It had earned him no shortage of comments from Hasar when it was hauled into the cargo hold, but he didn't care. If they survived this war, he'd build a house for Yrene around the damn thing. Along with a stable for Farasha, currently terrorizing the poor soldiers tasked with mucking out her stall aboard the ship.

A wedding gift from Hasar, along with Yrene's own Muniqi horse.

He'd almost told the princess that she could keep Hellas's Horse, but there was something to be said about the prospect of charging down Morath foot soldiers atop a horse named Butterfly.

Still leaning against him, Yrene wrapped a hand around the locket she never took off, save to bathe. He wondered if he could have it changed to reflect her new initials.

No longer Yrene Towers—but Yrene Westfall.

She smiled down at the locket, the silver near-blinding in the midday sun. "I suppose I don't need my little note any longer."

"Why?"

"Because I am not alone," she said, running her fingers over the metal. "And because I found my courage."

He kissed her cheek, but said nothing as she opened the locket and carefully removed the browned scrap. The wind tried to rip it from her fingers, but Yrene held tight, unfolding the slender fragment.

She scanned the text she'd read a thousand times. "I wonder if she'll return for this war. Whoever she was. She spoke of the empire like . . ." Yrene shook her head, more to herself, and folded it shut again. "Perhaps she will come home to fight, from wherever she sailed off to." She offered him the piece of paper and turned away to the sea ahead.

Chaol took the scrap from Yrene, the paper velvet-soft from its countless readings and foldings and how she'd held it in her pocket, clutched it, all these years.

He unfolded the note and read the words he already knew were within:

For wherever you need to go—and then some. The world needs more healers.

The waves quieted. The ship itself seemed to pause.

Chaol glanced to Yrene, smiling serenely at the sea, then to the note.

To the handwriting he knew as well as his own.

Yrene went still at the tears he could not stop from sliding down his face. "What's wrong?"

She would have been sixteen, nearly seventeen then. And if she had been in Innish . . .

It would have been on her way to the Red Desert, to train with the Silent Assassins. The bruises Yrene had described . . . The beating Arobynn Hamel had given her as punishment for freeing Rolfe's slaves and wrecking Skull's Bay.

"Chaol?"

For wherever you need to go—and then some. The world needs more healers.

There, in her handwriting . . .

Chaol looked up at last, blinking away tears as he scanned his wife's face. Every beautiful line, those golden eyes.

A gift.

A gift from a queen who had seen another woman in hell and thought to reach back a hand. With no thought of it ever being returned. A moment of kindness, a tug on a thread . . .

And even Aelin could not have known that in saving a barmaid from those mercenaries, in teaching her to defend herself, in giving her that gold and this note . . .

Even Aelin could not have known or dreamed or guessed how that moment of kindness would be answered.

Not just by a healer blessed by Silba herself, capable of wiping the Valg away.

But by the three hundred healers who had come with her.

The three hundred healers from the Torre, now spread across the one thousand ships of the khagan himself.

A favor, Yrene had asked of the man in return for saving his most beloved daughter.

Anything, the khagan had promised.

Yrene had knelt before the khagan. *Save my people.*

That was all she asked. All she had begged.

Save my people.

So the khagan had answered.

With one thousand ships from Hasar's armada, and his own. Filled with Kashin's foot soldiers and Darghan cavalry.

And above them, spanning the horizon far behind the flagship on which Chaol and Yrene now sailed . . . Above them flew one thousand rukhin led by Sartaq and Nesryn, from every aerie and hearth.

An army to challenge Morath, with more to come, still rallying in

656

Antica under Kashin's command. Two weeks, Chaol had given the khagan and Kashin, but with the autumn storms, he had not wanted to risk waiting longer. So this initial host . . . Only half. Only half, and yet the scope of what sailed and flew behind him . . .

Chaol folded the note along its well-worn lines and carefully set it back within Yrene's locket.

"Keep it a while longer," he said softly. "I think there's someone who will want to see that."

Yrene's eyes filled with surprise and curiosity, but she asked nothing as Chaol again slid his arms around her and held her tightly.

Every step, all of it, had led here.

From that keep in the snow-blasted mountains where a man with a face as hard as the rock around them had thrown him into the cold; to that salt mine in Endovier, where an assassin with eyes like wildfire had smirked at him, unbroken despite a year in hell.

An assassin who had found his wife, or they had found each other, two gods-blessed women wandering the shadowed ruins of the world. And who now held the fate of it between them.

Every step. Every curve into darkness. Every moment of despair and rage and pain.

It had led him to precisely where he needed to be.

Where he *wanted* to be.

A moment of kindness. From a young woman who ended lives to a young woman who saved them.

That shriveled scrap of darkness within him shrank further. Shrank and fractured into nothing but dust that was swept away by the sea wind. Past the one thousand ships sailing proud and unyielding behind him. Past the healers scattered amongst the soldiers and horses, Hafiza leading them, who had all come when Yrene had also asked them to save her people. Past the ruks soaring through the clouds, scanning for any threats ahead.

Yrene was watching him warily. He kissed her once—twice.

He did not regret. He did not look back.

657

Not with Yrene in his arms, at his side. Not with the note she carried, that bit of proof . . . that bit of proof that he was exactly where he was meant to be. That he had always been headed there. *Here.*

"Will I ever hear an explanation for this dramatic reaction," Yrene said at last, clicking her tongue, "or are you just going to kiss me for the rest of the day?"

Chaol rumbled a laugh. "It's a long story." He slung an arm around her waist and stared out toward the horizon with her. "And you might want to sit down first."

"Those are my favorite kinds," she said, winking.

Chaol laughed again, feeling the sound in every part of him, letting it ring clear and bright as a bell. A final, joyous pealing before the storm of war swept in.

"Come on," he said to Yrene, nodding to the soldiers working alongside Hasar's men to keep the ships sailing swiftly for the north—to battle and bloodshed. "I'll tell you over lunch."

Yrene rose onto her toes to kiss him before he led them toward their spacious stateroom. "This story of yours had better be worth it," she said with a wry grin.

Chaol smiled back at his wife, at the light he'd unknowingly walked toward his entire life, even when he had not been able to see it.

"It is," he said quietly to Yrene. "It is."

FIREHEART

They had entombed her in darkness and iron.

She slept, for they had forced her to—had wafted curling, sweet smoke through the cleverly hidden airholes in the slab of iron above. Around. Beneath.

A coffin built by an ancient queen to trap the sun inside.

Draped with iron, encased in it, she slept. Dreamed.

Drifted through seas, through darkness, through fire. A princess of nothing. Nameless.

The princess sang to the darkness, to the flame. And they sang back.

There was no beginning or end or middle. Only the song, and the sea, and the iron sarcophagus that had become her bower.

Until they were gone.

Until blinding light flooded the slumbering, warm dark. Until the wind swept in, crisp and scented with rain.

She could not feel it on her face. Not with the death-mask still chained to it.

Her eyes cracked open. The light burned away all shape and color after so long in the dim depths.

But a face appeared before her—above her. Peering over the lid that had been hauled aside.

Dark, flowing hair. Moon-pale skin. Lips as red as blood.

The ancient queen's mouth parted in a smile.

Teeth as white as bone.

"You're awake. Good."

Lovely and cold, it was a voice that could devour the stars.

From somewhere, from the blinding light, rough and scar-flecked hands reached into the coffin. Grasped the chains binding her. The queen's huntsman; the queen's blade.

He hauled the princess upright, her body a distant, aching thing. She did not want to slide back into this body. Struggled against it, clawing for the flame and the darkness that now ebbed away from her like a morning tide.

But the huntsman yanked her closer to that cruel, beautiful face watching with a spider's smile.

And he held her still as that ancient queen purred, "Let's begin."

THE SERIES CONTINUES
IN 2018

ACKNOWLEDGMENTS

Yet again, I'm faced with the daunting prospect of conveying my gratitude for the many wonderful people in my life who made this book a reality. But my endless love and thanks go out to:

My husband, Josh: You are my light, my rock, my best friend, my safe harbor—basically, my *everything*. Thank you for taking such good care of me, for loving me, for joining me on this incredible journey. Your laugh is my favorite sound in the entire world.

To Annie: You sat with me for the months it took to write and edit this book, so part of me feels like your name should be on the cover, too, but until they start giving canine companions writing credits, this will have to suffice. I love you, baby pup. Your curly tail, your bat-like ears, your general sass, and the unfailing pep in your step . . . All of it. Here's to writing many more books together—and many more cuddles.

To my agent, Tamar: Ten books in, and I'm still unable to convey how grateful I am for all that you do. Thank you, thank you, thank you for being in my corner, for working so damn hard, and for being an all-around badass.

To Laura Bernier: Your guidance, wisdom, and excitement for this book made working on it such a delight. Thank you *so much* for all of your hard work and edits—and for helping me to transform this book.

To the global team at Bloomsbury, for being the best goddamn publishing team on the planet: Bethany Buck, Cindy Loh, Cristina Gilbert, Kathleen Farrar, Nigel Newton, Rebecca McNally, Sonia Palmisano, Emma Hopkin, Ian Lamb, Emma Bradshaw, Lizzy Mason, Courtney Griffin, Erica Barmash, Emily Ritter, Grace Whooley, Eshani Agrawal, Alice Grigg, Elise Burns, Jenny Collins, Beth Eller, Kerry Johnson, Kelly de Groot, Ashley Poston, Lucy Mackay-Sim, Hali Baumstein, Melissa Kavonic, Oona Patrick, Diane Aronson, Donna Mark, John Candell, Nicholas Church, Anna Bernard, Charlotte Davis, and the entire foreign rights team. Thank you, as always, for all that you do for me and my books. I'm honored to work with every single one of you.

To Jon Cassir, Kira Snyder, Anna Foerster, and the team at Mark Gordon: You guys are the best. I'm so ecstatic these books are in your hands.

To Cassie Homer: Thank you x infinity for everything you do. You are absolutely fantastic. To David Arntzen: You've had our back since the very beginning. Thank you for all of your hard work and kindness. And a massive thank-you to the incomparable Maura Wogan and Victoria Cook, aka the best legal team around.

To Lynette Noni: I am so, so happy that we've gotten to know each other since that Supanova a few years ago! Thank you to the moon and back for all of your help with this book, for being a genius brainstorming partner, and for just being *you*.

To Roshani Chokshi: To begin with: You're right up my wall. Thank you for the laughter, the solid advice, and for being an actual ray of sunshine. I'm honored to call you my friend.

To Steph Brown: You are my partner in fangirling. Thank you for all of your support—and for your friendship. It means more to me than I can possibly say. Can't wait for our next LotR marathon (#FellowshipoftheDrink).

To Jennifer Armentrout for being one of the most welcoming, warm, and generous people I've ever met, to Renée Ahdieh for the dinners that never fail to make me smile and laugh, to Alice Fanchiang for being a fellow fangirl and an all-around joy to know, and to Christina Hobbs and Lauren Billings for being two of my favorite people.

To Charlie Bowater: Where do I even start? Thank you for the spectacular map(s), thank you for the art that continues to blow my mind and inspire me, thank you for *everything*. I can't even tell you what an honor it is to work with you, and how much your art means to me.

To Kati Gardner and Avery Olmstead: Thank you from the bottom of my heart for your thoughtful feedback and insight—I can't begin to tell you how invaluable it was, and how much it shaped this book. And beyond that, it was such a delight to get to know you both.

To Jack Weatherford, whose *Genghis Khan and the Making of the Modern World* forever changed my view of history and provided such inspiration for the realm of the khaganate. And thank you to Paul Kahn, for his brilliant adaptation of the *Secret History of the Mongols*, and to Caroline Humphrey, for her article, "Rituals of Death in Mongolia."

To my parents and my family: thank you for all the joy, love, and support you bring into my world. To the newest addition to my family, my niece: You have already made my life brighter by being in it. May you grow up to be one fierce lady.

A massive thank-you to my amazing friends: Jennifer Kelly, Alexa Santiago, Kelly Grabowski, Vilma Gonzalez, Rachel Domingo, Jessica Reigle, Laura Ashforth, Sasha Alsberg, and Diyana Wan. To Louisse Ang: At this point, I feel like a broken record when it comes to thanking you for all that you do, but *thank you so much* for being so supportive and marvelous.

And to *you*, dear reader: thank you for making every bit of hard work worth it, and for being the loveliest group of people I've ever met. I adore you all.